In PURSUIT
of LIFE

In Pursuit of Life

ALLAN BARRIE

To order additional copies of this book, contact:
Xlibris Corporation
1-888-795-4274
www.Xlibris.com
Orders@Xlibris.com
110049

6/1/2012

To:
Calvin

On behalf of my son Norman
Marks I sincerely hope you
enjoy this book as much as I
enjoyed writing it

allen Barrie

PROLOGUE

Friday, February 12, 2010

The doorbell rang at the home of Alexander Miller in suburban Chatsworth, California—a sprawling ranch-style home nestled away in a cul-de-sac on an acre of land.

"I'll get it," Alex said and proceeded to answer the front door.

"Alexander Miller, please," the FedEx man said. "Parcel for you. Please sign here," he said as he handed a box over to Alex and left.

Alex looked at the box as he carried it into the house. It was quite heavy, and it aroused his curiosity.

"I wasn't expecting anything. I wonder what it is," he said. "Honey, were you expecting a parcel from anyone? There isn't any return address. I wonder what it is?" he said to his wife Louise.

"No, dear, I'm not expecting anything. Maybe one of your patients has sent you a gift for saving their life, who knows and neither will we if you don't open it now. Let's find out. This is exciting," she said.

Alex placed the package on the counter in their kitchen and proceeded to open the package. He went at it slowly, not knowing what to expect; his anticipation was clearly visible.

Finally, the package was opened. It contained what appeared at first glance to be a set of books. There were no markings on the covers of the books, but attached to the top of the package was an envelope with a notation on it.

"Please read before opening the box."

He carefully removed the envelope from the package and opened it and began to read the enclosed letter.

"Sweetheart, what does it say? Please, honey, I want to know as much as you do," she said.

He began to read the letter out loud in a quivering voice as he sat down at the kitchen table. It was quite obvious that he was very shaken by the letter he now held in his hand. He looked pale and very apprehensive as he began.

February 5, 2010

Dear Son,

I do hope I have the right to address you as "son." It is not easy to explain to one's son why his father didn't contact him for over forty years. I am sorry I did not turn out to be the ideal father you must have always wanted. I am sure you are wondering why I'm contacting you after all this time. Why didn't I contact you sooner? What possessed me to hide away from you and miss out the most wonderful experience a father and son could ever share in growing up together? Perhaps after reading the journals I have enclosed, you may understand what drove me to remain outside your life. I am your biological father. Even though you may not believe me, the fact is that I love you and always have. It was this deep love for you that influenced my decision. Before making any final judgments as to my real character and my value as a man and as your father, please keep an open mind as my reasons for my decisions will become quite clear.

It is extremely important to me that your opinion of me is based on facts and not on some hatred or misinformed details you may have heard. I am trying to explain how my life was and what kind of world I lived in all the years we have been apart. I have never stopped missing and loving you. It has been a very lonely existence for me, as you will see by reading these journals that I have carefully kept. I could not easily speak to anyone about my troubles and what decisions I should make regarding my son's life or mine. These journals were my only companions for years and have helped me remain sane and close to you. Though through my travels I did meet many people, I was still very much alone. What happened is chronicled in these volumes. I hope, once you have read these journals, you will understand me a lot better and open your heart and let me, as your father, share a little of your life.

My first and only desire was to protect you from harm, and to that end that I could not allow you to become a part of my life even though I very much wanted to be with you on a day-to-day basis. My love for you was far stronger than my selfish desires, so I placed you in the very capable hands of your uncle Johnny and aunt Sophie. I knew you would be brought up with love that would be true and from the heart. I knew my brother would carry out my wishes and give you every opportunity to achieve whatever goals you wanted. Your education was guaranteed and, with your aunt and uncle, your safety as well. When your mother tragically died, you were only two years old, and I could not jeopardize your welfare in any way at all. You were all I was left with, and I loved you so much. Your mother loved you with all her heart. You were her pride and joy; she could not have been more proud of you. Today, she is watching over you from her special place in heaven, and I know she would be so proud of her son, the doctor. She would have loved her grandchildren with all of her heart and would have made both you and Louise always her best friends. You would have loved her as well, as she was very beautiful and kind and so very understanding. She always laughed at things and believed in the best for everyone. Life was precious to her, and when you were born, everything changed in her life. She gave up her career as an actress and model and dedicated her life to her son Alexander. She walked on air because of you. She loved you with all of her heart. I have missed her every day for the last fifty years, and I have never been able nor have I wanted to replace her. No, Alex, there was never another woman, and there could never be one.

What happened? Why did we part as a family? Why did all this happen? Why? These words sound so empty on a piece of paper, yet they are very important in solving the motivational factors that led up to our separation. What drove me to make this decision? To understand the core reasons, it is essential that you read the journals I have sent to you, as they contain a day-to-day record of our lives back then. The journals were written at the end of each day or as close to that schedule as possible. Later, as the years progressed, I stopped writing them on a daily basis because of a multitude of events that made it, at times, impossible to write. I wrote as often as I could so that I could keep a record of so many years with the hope that one day I will be able to sit down and read them with you. When she died and other things took place, I could not write every day because of circumstances. I spent time being incarcerated, and lost hope that I would ever have a chance to read these notes with anyone. I longed to be a part of the family and to share the life that I led with those I loved.

I tried to repeat conversations as I remembered them. I felt it would be best for the reader when trying to understand what was going on by doing that. I used an unconventional method to relate the scenes as they took place.

Most journals recount the days' past events and do not contain any dialogue. I wrote these journals as if the reader was there each day and saw and heard what took place. How else could I recount what happened on a daily basis? You must understand that I made decisions which I thought were very sound at the time. Like most people, our minds help us make decisions that lead us into or away from trouble. No matter how hard you try to make the right decision, you cannot always do so. Hindsight is a great way to see what you did wrong, but it doesn't change what has already happened. I tried to think clearly and made mistakes, lots of mistakes—mistakes that led me into danger. Even though I was, as I thought, very intelligent, I still made terrible errors and miscalculations. I am human, and I admit that I could have done things differently at times. Once again, hindsight can be a cruel judge. That was not the case. I had to live with what was and not what should have been. Who could I trust with my most precious secrets? Secrets that I had to guard religiously and yet, at times, I let my guard down allowed others to know what they were. There were some who were my true friends and helped me along the way, but very few. My writings were special to me. Without them, I could not have survived. The days and nights that passed were lonely and hard, but the journals helped fill the emptiness. If they seem to be a little slow in action at times, it was the way life was then. The journals were my only outlet, my only way I could unload the stress of each day even when that day did not seem to contain any overt stress at all. I wrote it in the best way I knew how, even though I did not take journalism in university.

Your mother was a force that kept me alive. When I fell, she picked me up. When I felt like calling it all quits, she pushed me onward. After she passed away, she remained with me in my heart and mind and I spent many nights talking to her. I have not filled the pages of the journals with enough accolades about Natalia; if I did, I would need so many more volumes, as she was my life and my inspiration. I have done things that I am not proud of. I have done what was necessary to survive, at a great cost to those I loved and to myself. Now I have reached the final road in my life and would like to be a part of your family and share what life I have left with you and your family. I know it is a lot to ask after all these years, but it is all I have left. I want to get to know my son and daughter. I want to share what time I have left with my grandchildren before they grow up and have no time for an old man. I want you all to get to know me, and I want to get to know all of you.

Please give me a chance to be a part of the family and to love you all with all of my heart. Please, Alex, please open your heart and let me in. Read the journals with an open mind and try to place yourself in my shoes.

You are a doctor, and you must make decisions on a daily basis that affect other people's lives and often impact your own life and those you hold so dear. I had to do that, and I know in my heart, with you, I made the right decision. I just don't want to leave this planet without me being able to hold and love you once again. I want to come home now, please!

Your loving father
Harry

Alex was severely shaken and quite speechless as he put the letter down and looked at Louise. "This is mind boggling. It's something I never expected. Honey, I never thought I'd ever hear from him, honestly. I'm shaking. This is unbelievable. I just can't imagine what's in those journals. I really don't know if I can open my heart enough and let him into my life at this point. I don't think it's fair to put you through this, after all, you don't even know him, and neither do I," he said.

"Don't be so judgmental, Alex. After all, he is your father, and there's a story here. You must listen to the story and let your mind and heart tell you what is right. The mystery of why he left you might be answered after all these years. Ever since we've known each other, you have wondered about your mother and father. Now you have the opportunity to satisfy all those unanswered questions. Take the plunge and start finding out what it's all about. My life has been affected by this person who calls himself your father through you. If not for him, I would not be married to you. If you don't get answers, all the doubts you have will go unanswered. I've never known him and neither have our kids. What happens here will affect all our lives for a long time. There has to be some serious circumstances attached to his decision to have you brought up by his brother. We have to listen, and we have to be strong. Please, trust me on this," Louise said.

"I know you're right. I'm just afraid of what I'll find. I want to know who he is and talk to him. I want to know why I was cast aside. And I hope we are strong enough to understand and forgive. What surprises me most of all is why Uncle Johnny and Aunt Sophie never told us anything about him except that he was a very kind and gentle man who loved me dearly. That was all they would ever say. Nothing was ever said about where he was or what happened to him or whether he was alive or dead. I hope these journals will open the doors which have been closed for so long and let him in, to our lives. I'll need your help with this, Louise. So let's get to it," he said as he opened the first volume and began to read aloud.

January, 1957

I stood there in disbelief, looking at the two guys lying in the vestibule of the apartment building. They were dead. That was certain. How did all this happen? I'm not a killer, and I know I wouldn't do anything that would cause anyone to die. I was shaking like a leaf at the very thought that I might have just killed two people. It didn't matter who they were or that it was in self-defense or they were Mafia goons. I never saw anyone die before. It was so unreal that I could hardly speak. What was happening to my life?

My only experience I ever had with the Mafia was a few years ago. I had just walked out of the front door of my parent's home to go back to NYU. I noticed two very big guys get out of a large dark car and walk toward the house.

"Harry Miller?" one of the guys said to me.

"Yes, what is it?" I asked.

"Please come with us," he said.

"I'm on my way to school, and I don't have the time right now. Tell me what this is about, and, maybe, we can settle this now or arrange a time for us to meet," I said.

"You are coming with us, now!" they said in unison as they grabbed my arms and lifted me off the ground and carried me to the car.

"Hey, what the hell is going on?" I yelled but got no response.

"I'd keep my mouth shut until we get to where we are going. You know what you did, and you'll have a chance to straighten it all out. Stay quiet or you will get a smack in your face," one of the big goons said.

We drove in silence as they would not speak to me, for about thirty minutes, until we finally came to a warehouse in Tribeca in lower Manhattan.

"Get out. And no funny stuff if you don't want to get hurt," one guy said as they both flanked me and made sure I was cooperative.

I entered the warehouse and could hardly see anything until my eyes adjusted to the dim light. We walked a little way and then turned right as they opened a door, which opened into a large open area. In the middle of the room, there was a table and four chairs and nothing else. The windows were way up high—at least fourteen feet high and barred. At the other end, I saw another door, which appeared to be closed at that time.

"Sit down at the table. The boss will be here very soon," they said.

A minute later, the door opened, and a guy walked through. He was about six feet two and was well-built with slicked back black hair. He was well dressed in a suit and was wearing a shirt and tie. He walked slowly toward the table where I was sitting. I waited as I had no other choice while he spoke to one of his goons.

When he got real close to me, one of the guys said, "Hey, boss, we didn't rough him up yet, what do you want us to do with him?"

"Who the hell is this guy?" the boss asked.

"Harry Miller, boss. He was at the address you gave us," the goon said.

"This is not Harry Miller! I don't know who you are, but something is wrong here!" he said, looking very annoyed.

"What the hell is going on?" I asked in a very controlled and relaxed tone. "I am Harry Miller, and I don't know who you are. I've never ever seen you before. What the hell is happening here?" I asked once again.

"Let me explain, Harry. I am Arnie Zambola, and I run a small but honest poker game after hours. You know what I mean? Harry Miller came in here about six months ago and started playing poker. After a while, he became a regular. A few weeks ago, he lost all his bread. Naturally, when he asked for credit, there was no hesitation, and we staked him for $10K. He lost that as well, and we have not seen him since. And guess what, Harry? He gave us your address. Naturally, I sent the boys out to get you so that we could straighten out this mess before someone gets hurt. That's where we are, and I'm sorry about the confusion. I wonder why the bastard used your name and address. I guess he was setting us up to fuck us real good. You could have been badly hurt, and it all was because of this son of a bitch. Would you have any idea who this prick might be?" he said.

"I really have no idea whatsoever. I'd like to find this prick as well and hit him once on the face. What does he look like?" I asked.

"He is about six feet tall with blond hair and must weigh about 190 lbs. Does this description fit anyone you know?" Arnie said.

"Offhand no, but I will keep my eyes open in case I do see this asshole. Give me your phone number, and I'll let you know if I do run into him," I said.

"Don't you worry. We'll find this guy, and he'll get his ass kicked. All I can say is we are sorry about all this. Can I drop you off somewhere?" he asked in a very nice way.

"No harm done, Mr. Zambola. I'm just glad you recognized that I was not the guy. I hope you get the bastard and get him to stop using my name," I said.

"No need, Harry. We'll find him as all these guys can't help themselves when they have the gambling bug. They usually screw themselves because they can't stop gambling. I'll get my money and a piece of flesh as well. Sorry again. Please let me have my guys drop you off at school. It's the least I can do," he said.

I left with the guys who picked me up. The ride was much more pleasant this time. They dropped me off at NYU. That was my only experience with the Mob and it left me with the impression that they are not really bad guys; they only hurt those that directly hurt them. I never thought about it again, until now.

Back to the two dead guys on the floor, I did not know what these guys wanted with me! I then put two and two together. Three days ago Larry and I had a terrible argument. I was upset over Larry's attitude when I told him that Rachel and I wanted to buy a new house and move on with our lives. I told him I wanted to find another job and maybe move out to New Jersey. I tried to explain that I did appreciate everything he did for me but it was time to move on. He started to get very angry, telling me in no uncertain terms that my first loyalty was to him and the Mafia and there was no quitting in my job resume.

"Where else in the world can a young guy earn three grand a week? Where else do you get the easy life, filled with great food and plenty of cash? Do you think it was because of your looks?" he said very loudly.

"Listen, Larry, I appreciate everything you have done for me, but it's your daughter I love, and we have to move on," I shouted at him. "I want to quit working for you and find another job even if I don't make the same kind of bucks. I didn't want to be involved in this kind of business. When I started, I didn't know you did anything illegal, and now I'm sucked in. There is no future in it, and I will only wind up being sent to jail or being killed. I discussed it with Rachel, and we agreed that if we do have children, we cannot afford to be involved in this kind of business," I said in a gentle but firm tone.

Larry got very insulted, so he warned me once again that there is no quitting in this business, "If you persist in this line of thought, your life would not be worth shit. You little bastard, do you think you can take my bread and then tell me you'll quit. The money is better than good. You have done far better than anyone of your friends and your fancy college graduates, and this is how you want to repay me? No way, Harry, you stay and you behave, or else . . . ," he said in a very menacing tone.

I got very angry and started to yell at Larry and threatened him and the Mafia that if I had to, I would bury them all. I was hot and really didn't mean what I said.

Later that day, I apologized to Larry and told him that I just said that for effect and didn't mean it at all and I would never turn against my own family and that I would be faithful at all times. Larry told me to forget it as he understands and knows I didn't mean it. I left it at that and didn't think about it again until today when I saw these guys. These guys were here to kill me, not to protect Ron, our mark; he was nothing to them.

Peter didn't know what was happening either, but he was street savvy and ready for action at all times. I was out here to collect or enforce the rules for Larry, but I didn't realize that when Larry and I were arguing, Giuseppe "Big Bull" Conti overheard us and reported this to someone in the Gambino family. From that point on, I was a marked man, as they considered me as a threat to their operations. After all, Larry was only one of their minions that ran a very lucrative loan-sharking business in Manhattan under the guise of a legitimate loan company. To anyone who may have inquired, Larry's loan company competed with Beneficial Finance and Household Finance—two leaders in the legitimate loan business. The bosses from the Gambino family must have contacted Larry and read the riot act to him, and now I have Larry conspiring with the Mob bosses to have me iced. With Larry's cooperation, it was easy to monitor my movements. Larry sent me on this collection along with Peter Gambizi and didn't think twice about mentioning it to Giuseppe Conti. The wheels were now set in motion, and there was no turning back.

We had just arrived at the building on Ninety-Sixth Street and Broadway. I didn't think it was important to look around, as I was not expecting any problems. I came here to see a client who borrowed some money from my father-in-law, Larry Casparizzi. He was past due, and an example had to be made.

We could not allow our reputation to be questioned, we collect no matter what. The rules of this business are fear and reprisals if you fail to pay your debt on time. There were no reprieves from a debt, not even death as they would hunt out assets one may have, including life insurance from his wife and children. Failure to enforce these rules would send a very bad message to all of their clients.

We arrived along with my assistant Peter Gambizi. Peter was a big guy; he stood over 6"5' and had to weigh three hundred pounds or more. He was one tough dude and could handle himself real well. As we looked at the directory, we noticed two guys standing in the lobby.

Peter took one look and said, "This is trouble, Harry. I know the guy on the left. He's a hit man and must be here to hit our client. I don't know why they would do that if Larry sent us out here. It doesn't make any sense at all. Stay alert and be ready for anything. Be ready for a fight, Harry. Do you have a weapon?"

"No, I don't carry a gun," I said as Peter slipped one into my jacket pocket.

We located our guy's name and turned to walk toward the elevator when one of the goons said, "Peter, we're not here for you. I know you a long time, man. So turn around and leave. You"—he pointed at me—"Yes, you, stay," he said as he pulled out his gun and pointed it at me.

"I can't leave, man. I must stay with Harry. What the hell is this about?" Peter said with a very determined look.

"Hey, Peter, take the door, and you won't be involved. It's not your fight."

The extra large size goon said, "Look, man, we don't want any trouble either, but we've got a job to do, just like you. We have got to talk to a rat, and then we'll leave. You can come along as well. But we still got to talk to him, you understand?" he said in a very serious tone.

"Look, asshole, no one talks to anyone. Now fuck off, Peter, or I will fuck you over," he said.

I turned around and in one motion said to Peter, "You leave. I'll handle these guys. They won't hurt me. I'm Larry's son-in-law. They wouldn't hurt me." All at once I whirled around and had a gun in my hand. "Move out of the way, asshole, unless you want to die."

Everything happened so fast. Peter had his gun out, and before I knew it, he had fired a shot toward the Mob guy who was reaching for his gun. Peter then whirled around and shot the second Mob guy right in the eye. And all the problems were over for now. I was still holding my gun. I never had time to pull the trigger, and I was in a shock.

I never killed anyone before, let alone seeing someone dying in front of me. I was shaking and could hardly remain standing. This was terrible. I felt like throwing up. I was queasy, and my ears hurt. I couldn't hear anything and was in pain. My ears were ringing, and my heart was pounding. This was a rush that I never experienced before. Calmly, Peter moved the two guys out of vestibule into the stairwell leading to the basement and piled one on top of another and gently closed the door. I was still standing there as if frozen in time.

"Hey, Harry, wake up. Get hold of yourself. We had to do what we did or we would both be lying there instead of them. Now let's get on with our job," Peter said.

I woke up and realized what had just happened, Peter was right, we had to move on!

We proceeded to Ron's apartment and found him shivering in his boots. He took one look at the size of Peter and the mean look on his face and nearly fainted when he tried to speak.

He stuttered and shook violently as he said, "What happened out there? I heard gun shots and lots of noise."

"Nothing. We didn't see anything at all. Now, Ron, where is $14K you owe us? We are in a hurry. So let's get the money, and this will be over with, now!" I said.

"Listen, I don't have the full amount. I can give you $5K now, and I'll pay the rest tomorrow," he said as he handed me a bundle of crumpled up bills.

"Listen, you piece of shit, this is what you said yesterday and didn't show up. I'll give you one more chance. You have the $10K tomorrow, or it will be your last day on this earth. I hope that's crystal clear to you," I said.

"Hey, man, it's only $9K. What's with the extra grand?" he said.

"That is the vig for the extra day. And by the way, I'd get the hell out of here because this place will be crawling with cops very soon. You stop by the office tomorrow and drop off the bread. If you don't show, I promise you there will be no place you can go where we won't find you, and there will be no reprieve. I'm being nice, Ron. This is not my nature, so keep your word." I turned, and we left.

I said to Peter as we started moving in traffic, "I really don't understand why anyone would want to kill me? I hope it was a mistake. But you better be careful, Peter, because they may send others, and now you could be dragged in. I'll tell Larry that you were not there when these guys tried to whack me. That should take care of your involvement."

"No way, Harry. Just tell Larry that I waited in the car while you saw Ron and didn't know anything of what happened. Don't say anything unless Larry asks. If he doesn't, then let it go. Never tell anyone more than they need to know, always remember that. Good luck, Harry. Be very careful and trust no one," he said. I thanked him for saving my life.

I walked into the office and immediately understood things, as I saw the look of surprise on Larry's face. "Hey, Harry, how did it go?" Larry asked.

"Here," I said as I threw the envelope down with five grand in it, "Ron will stop by the office tomorrow and leave another ten grand to pay off the debt. I thought it was better to take the five and scare the shit out of him. I'm pretty sure he will show up tomorrow," I said.

"Where is Peter?" Larry said.

"He could not stay with me as he had a personal problem to take care of. I went to Ron's on my own. There was no danger. Ron is scared shitless of us all, so I knew there wouldn't be any trouble," I said.

"Great job, Harry. You see how easy this job is," he said. "I hope you have forgotten our little argument we had. I know things will be fine," he added.

"Yes, sir, I have forgotten it all and am heading home to spend the night with Rachel. See you tomorrow. Have a great night," I said to Larry as I turned toward the door and headed out.

Thursday, January 31, 1957

I spent the last two hours with Rachel explaining the reality of life and the problems I know we have.

"Let me tell you, Rachel. Larry can't be trusted even if he is your father. He will stick a knife in your back without hesitation. I don't know what we can do, but we must be careful and be watchful as there are killers out there ready to kill me for sure and perhaps you as well," I said with conviction as I held her hands in mine. "I love you very much, and I want to make sure your life would not be in danger. But how can I do that?"

"I love you, too, Harry. But how can I separate my own father from all this? Please tell me how, and I will do, it but I don't think I can," she said as tears swelled in her eyes.

"I don't know, but you realize that Larry is involved with the Mafia and his first loyalty is to them. There is no getting out for anyone, especially Larry. He can't even think of protecting me even if he wants to. There is a code that these people follow, and once you are in, you are in for life. I certainly don't want anything to happen to Larry. He has been so good to me and has made our lives better and better all the time. He's never pressurized me into anything and has always been a mench. But, Rachel, sweetheart, when it comes to my life or his, I'm afraid I have to choose me and if you are thrown into the mix, I have to put you first. Let's work on getting all this worked out so that we can move on. That is all I want," I said as I kissed her on the lips softly and held her close.

Friday, February 1, 1957

I stood there in disbelief, looking out the upstairs window. How could this happen to me? Harry Miller, in the prime of life, twenty-four years old and full of piss and vinegar, well educated, smart in the ways of life, and making big money. I wore great two hundred and fifty dollars suits and top-of-the-line-Italian shoes, and I always had a grand in my pocket. I had my hair styled and nails manicured every week and always drove the best cars. At six feet and one hundred and eighty pounds, I was healthy. And I always looked great with that dark Italian look, even though I was Jewish. And I never—yes, never—had a shortage of women. Of course, I gave all that up when I married Rachel. I was planning to buy a new car—a 57 Caddy. I always wanted a red one, a convertible with leather seats and a great radio. Buying a new car was very exciting. Now I guess I'll have to put that on hold until I find out what this crap was all about. I was still in a state of shock when I looked out the window at the two plainclothes cops. You can tell a cop a mile away. From them coming to my door, I knew something was screwed up heavily. I couldn't put it all together; my mind was a jumble of thoughts! Wow! Tonight of all nights, what do they want with me? How the hell did they know I was home tonight? It was as if they expected me to be here. It seemed to be well planned to catch me at a time when access to lawyers, bail, or a judge would be far more difficult then a weeknight. Usually on Friday nights, I am far away. I always go out of town for the weekend to my retreat in the Pocono Mountains, just eighty-five miles away from Manhattan. This Friday, I felt a cold coming on and called Rachel and said, "Let's not go out of town this weekend. I feel a little under the weather." What a coincidence—two cops at my front door and nowhere to go. I let Rachel answer the door and listened from my spot on the second floor of the house: "Is Harry Miller here?"

"Who are you?"

"Inspector Johnson and Detective Martin. Could you please call him, as we must see him?"

"What is the problem," Rachel said, "what is wrong?"

"Are you Mrs. Miller?"

"Yes, what is this about? What has Harry done?"

"Sorry, Mrs. Miller, we have to see Harry. We have some very important questions to ask him. Is he here?"

My mind was blown apart as I could not, in those few minutes, understand what would they want with me.

"Harry is not here. He went to our house in the Pocono Mountains. I usually go with him, but I didn't feel well, so I stayed home."

Rachel was great—fast thinking as she said it loud enough for me to hear, but not too loud to create any suspicion.

"If you would like to look around the house, you are more than welcome. Would you like me to call Harry at the Pocono house?" she said.

"No, thanks, Mrs. Miller. Please tell Harry to call me when he gets back. Here is my card," he said.

What was going on? Why didn't she ask for more information? Why was she so cooperative and calm? Any wife would demand more information or freak out, I thought. How often do two cops walk up to your door at seven thirty at night and ask for you? I would think your wife should freak out. It would only be normal. Wow! My mind was blown, and I was getting pissed off. I was so paranoid, especially after the events of yesterday and now this. I knew if I was a witness to something, they would have called me during the day to ask me to meet with them. When they come at seven thirty on a Friday night, it sucks and smells rotten.

I waited until these two guys left and came down and said, "Thanks, honey. That was fast thinking. What the hell do these guys really want? It just seems so strange that I was nearly killed a couple of days ago and now two cops want me. Maybe they are not real cops and this is just to get hold of me and rub me out."

"Honey, I think they are real cops. Please call Larry and tell him what happened, no matter what he still wants to protect his own ass. I know he will help us. Harry, please, for me," she said.

"Let me call this inspector. I'll tell him I am in Poconos and want to know what is going on. Then I'll call Larry," I said.

I waited until ten thirty to place the call. I figured it would give him time to get back to his office and add a little more legitimacy to my call.

"Hi, I'm Harry Miller. What can I do for you?"

Inspector Johnson immediately gave me his badge number and said, "Thanks for calling back so quickly. We have a warrant for your arrest as a material witness."

"A warrant for my arrest, what kind of bullshit is this? What does the warrant say," I demanded!

He said, "Sure thing" and started to read that I was wanted for questioning in a case against Larry Spinelli for fraud, conspiracy to commit fraud, and for extortion. It listed a bunch of names that I never heard of as well as the words "does." I could not believe my ears and, although I wanted to run away, I just stood there, speechless.

Finally, I said, "Can I meet you tomorrow? I'm in the Poconos and will drive back in the morning?"

"Sure thing. We will be here waiting for you, let's say, about 11:00 a.m."

Evidently, they weren't afraid of my running away, or that I was any danger to them or anyone else. My mind raced as I kept thinking where did I go wrong? What did I do to get into this mess? Then I got hold of myself as I thought about the argument Larry and I had, and now this. I was sure the entire Mafia organization would now think I was a stoolie and would do anything to get rid of me. All I could think of was to take it easy and go with the flow and get in touch with an attorney now and be nice, and you might get to the bottom of this. I would have Larry call our attorney, Arnold Vignola. He was the best criminal attorney in town. No need to worry. It would get straight by tomorrow and I would be back in control of my life once again.

I called Larry, and after explaining what is going on, he told me to stay put and wait for his call. He called back a few minutes later and told me that he spoke with Arnold Vignola and he will meet me tomorrow morning at seven in Danny's bar. He also said that I should be there on time and I should not worry about anything.

"Please stay off the phone, Harry, at least for the time being," Larry said.

All the costs for Arnold would be picked up by Larry, and he would stand beside me.

"Larry, were you aware that some guys were sent out to put a hit on me when I went to Ron's? Why didn't you warn me? Now you say you will help me. How can I trust you? Tell me, Larry, how can I?" I said.

"Harry, I didn't know anyone was out to get you. But don't worry, I will straighten this out. You will not be harmed, I promise," he said and hung up.

Not a word was said for at least five minutes. Finally, I said to Rachel, "Here I am, Harry Miller, reasonably successful in the finance business. We are eating at the best places in town and living a very quiet life. What will people say about me? Will this get into the newspapers? What happened? Where did I go wrong?"

"Honey, you didn't go wrong, it's just a mistake. Everything will be okay. Please don't worry. I love you and will be with you always. Let's go to bed," she said.

"I'll be up soon. I just want to sit here and think a little," I said as Rachel went upstairs to our bedroom.

We were married last year, a small wedding by Mob standards—about four hundred people and lots of cash gifts. But what did I really know about her? Prom queen at Central High, everyone's pinup girl, tall—about five feet five inches, a blonde with great tits and a smile that could melt steel, blue eyes, and with an innocence that made you want to jump her bones. The rumor was that her father was a big time Mafia guy. He was filthy rich and made sure his daughter always had everything she wanted. I met her father, Larry Casparizzi, twice—the first time was when she invited me to Ciros' for dinner. I arrived at about seven fifteen. Rachel was already there, and I was escorted to the table and met six other guys—all quite big and wearing suits. She introduced me, but I could not remember their names. Larry had not arrived yet. A few minutes later, Larry arrived with a gorgeous blonde at his side. Rachel got up and kissed her dad on each cheek and then said, "Dad, I want you to meet Harry Miller."

"Nice to meet you, sir," I said.

"Cut the sir, will you?" Larry said. "Let me introduce you to Glenda and Angelo, Pasquali, Gino, Lou, Vincente, and Oscar."

I found out that Rachel's Mom died a few years ago, and although Larry lived in Atlantic Beach, he also had a couple of penthouses in Manhattan, and Rachel lived in one of them—the Seventy-Second and Third Avenue building. I was never in Ciros before. That place was class and very expensive. Larry ordered champagne and caviar. I was treated like a family member and spent the rest of the evening eating and listening to small talk.

Larry asked me, "What do you do for a living, Harry?"

"I just graduated from NYU in business administration, and I am just starting to look for real work. I interned at Household Finance on Fifty-Seventh and Madison while I was at NYU. I guess my specialty is finance and business. I just want to make a lot of money and settle down."

Larry looked at me and said, "Why don't you come and see me? I own several finance companies and could always use a smart guy like you. Lou, give him a card."

Lou was a giant of guy, must have been 6'6" and at least two hundred and fifty pounds. He spoke with a very recognizable Brooklyn accent. He stood up and handed me a card. "Here you are, Harry. Just give me a call when you want to come by."

Boy what a night that was! I drank too much, ate too much, and fell in love with Rachel and her father, Larry, that night. She invited me to her penthouse, and I declined, as I was a little wary of Larry and his gang and also wanted to make the best impression I could.

I wanted to sleep with her, but then I just put it out of my mind. I kissed her and said, "Tomorrow, Rachel, we will get together. I promise. I really want to, but not tonight."

Our next meeting with Larry was at his penthouse in Dakota on the west side, just across from Central Park. We met to discuss our wedding plans and get his approval.

He was great and, within five minutes, said, "If you two love each other, then go ahead. I am with you. Welcome to the family."

He hugged and kissed me on both the cheeks. I told him that we discussed it and we did not want a large wedding, just the immediate family. I wanted to set up a meeting between Larry and my mom and dad, but he said, "I'll meet them at the wedding."

Of course, I had taken Rachel to meet my folks a few days earlier, and they loved her even though she wasn't Jewish. My brother Billy and his wife also met Rachel when we went for Chinese food on Sunday, and they also liked her a lot. She married me after just a few weeks of dating! Maybe it was because she had just broken up with this geek Brad, who ran off and married her best friend. Who knows? Certainly I loved her and thought she loved me. She didn't work, but she sure knew how to shop and dream of fancy cars, big houses, and a life of fun, always. Did she screw around? Did she had a lover? I worked for Larry Casparizzi, Rachel's dad, a well connected guy in the Italian community. If his daughter was fooling around, he would find out, and things would be very nasty. He was a great guy and owned many different companies from the garment district to finance companies, including the one I worked for—Capitol Investment Corp., one of his many companies—and I had it pretty good.

I took in the applications and filed them with the loan papers. No credit checks were ever made on these people, as it was not a traditional loan company or operated like a bank. People came in and sold us a series of checks, post-dated a week apart. Let's say for one hundred dollars, each gave me thirty-six of them, and for every thirty-six hundred, we gave them fifteen hundred. "Take it or leave it" was our motto. "If you want more, go to a bank" is what we told them. This was a discounting method we used, which did not come under any lending act as it was our right to buy those checks at any price the seller was willing to sell them. I could not see anything illegal here! It wasn't like loan sharking as we only bought notes and post-dated checks. Most of the clients were gamblers or characters with dubious reputations that just seem to get by. There was no need to worry about collection, as Larry's crew handled the collection department; very rarely did a check bounce. If a check bounced, usually the customer would be in our office before we knew and would pay cash for the face value of the check and also an additional one hundred dollar as fine. There never was an argument; no questions were asked. Usually, the guy says he was sorry and would tell a story of how he could not get to the bank on time or some crap like that. We didn't care what was the reason as long as we were getting paid. Larry collected from everyone, and if the borrower met with an accident or die, he would collect it from their widows. No, this finance company had never lost a loan. Although I had nothing to do with collections, I met the collectors. They were very big and dangerous-looking guys.

None of them smoked. They were all over 6' tall, and all of them weighed at least two hundred and fifty pounds of muscle. They worked out in a special gym, which Larry owned and lifted weights regularly. They always wore dark suits with white shirts and ties. They were creatures of habit and always ate at the same restaurants and always followed a schedule. They drove their cars with the doors locked and never got into their car before checking it out to make sure there weren't any booby traps. Lou was the head guy and was very nice to me whenever we met, and he always talked sports, mostly horse racing. I learned from him what a tout was and how this kind of guy took money from everyone for tips, which were often not real. The race track was the biggest source of customers for Capitol Investment, as there always were guys who lost all their money on the last race and needed more for the next race. They were also connected with every illegal gambling place where losers always needed more money. Big Al was the main guy at the track. His real name was Albert Capuzzi, but everyone knew him and called him "Big Al." He was 6'4" of all muscle with his hair slicked back with some kind of cream that smelled like perfume and made his black hair look darker. He was always dressed to the nines, in his dark suit, white shirt, and tie. No one would every think he was an enforcer. And he looked like a retired football player who took up banking. Big Al had a seat in the clubhouse section of Yonkers as well as Aqueduct when the horses were running there, and every loser knew where to find him. If you borrowed a "C" note from him, you had to give back one hundred and twenty in a week. If you borrowed more, you were required to come into the office on Forty-Second Street and Eighth Avenue, just above Kitty's strip joint and complete your check transaction. You should sign a series of checks made payable to another individual and then that guy would sell those checks to Capitol Investments at a discounted rate. The checks were properly endorsed, and a note was signed between the second guy and Capitol for the transaction to become legal. This was an ingenious method, as it removed any liability for usury the company may have been exposed to. I thought up the idea for Larry. Of course, I thought I was doing everyone a favor. Larry rewarded me with a ten grand—bonus for my method. I thought life was good.

Now here I am, two years later, in this stinking mess. Did I go blind? Did I let things get out of hand just to take care of her? Did my greed for lots of money and the taste of the good life blind me to all the other shit that was taking place around me? I let my emotions get the better of me and said things to Larry I wish I could take back, but once it was said, then it was too late. There is no question in my mind that I screwed up. I am part of them now like it or not, and there is a little chance of ever getting out by any other way than death.

I could not sleep as I lay there in my bed wondering just what the hell was going on. I thought back on my life and could not understand why a guy like me was in this jam. I was brought up on the right side of the tracks. I had great parents who always gave me everything I ever wanted and taught me the difference between right and wrong. I was always taught to be kind and tolerant of others and not to envy anyone. I graduated from NYU and certainly didn't need to work for a Mafia company. Greed and the lure for big money took me down the road of bad decisions and a lot of risks that I certainly didn't need. It would be my undoing. My desire to be the guy who made it and show everyone that I was very successful and had it all would lead me to doom. New cars, great clothes, eat at any restaurant you want, and never ever have to stand in line. Every place in New York always opened their doors to Rachel and me. I tipped big and was always polite and nice to everyone. No matter though, Harry was still Larry Casparrizzi's son-in-law. And just who was Larry? He wasn't one of the five family leaders. So why did he rate such a lofty position? Larry was a leader who ran numbers years ago and was a loyal soldier in the Castallano family. He is now second or third in command. No one fucked with Larry. When I joined the family, I didn't know all that. I thought he owned a legitimate finance business, but I didn't quit when I learned more. I stayed. Greed and the love of what we call the "good life" melted my brain and that was why I was here now—a part of an organization I never wanted. I started to understand why you can never get out once you are in.

My brothers, Billy, Morton, Bernie, and Johnny were great guys and were always there for me. What will they say when they hear that I am in trouble and that I am accused of being involved with the Mafia? You hear about this all the time and wonder how this could ever happen to you! Now I must call Billy as soon as Vignola gets me out of this mess. I know he will understand as he has been around a lot longer than I. Thank God Morton is living somewhere in Pennsylvania with his wife and kids, so he won't know anything about this. I will call him as soon as the dust clears and explain everything to him. I really don't know what I will explain, as I do not understand everything myself. Bernie is at West Point, so he won't know anything for a while. I just hope this doesn't cause him any problems with his career in the army. It has always been his pride and joy. Johnny is far too young, and it would take a lot of explaining. He just started at NYU and really does not know what he wants. I really don't want to screw him up with problems of mine that he may not understand. What about Mom, my pride and joy? She has always been there for me, and now she will be hurt. But she will be at my side no matter what. I just wish this did not happen as it will hurt them a great deal. My dad, Louis, will never understand and will think I am guilty, even before he heard what it was all about. He was a tough, straight guy, who worked all his life, finally reaching the level of chief mechanic for General Motors. There was no better auto mechanic in the world. Whenever a problem persisted, they called Louis Miller. He was flown to Detroit hundreds of times to help solve mechanical problems. He was a rock, with no room for error. He was my dad, and I was proud of him.

I loved him a lot, although we didn't talk about that. After all, he was a man, and men talked about baseball, football, and horse racing. How will he react to all this? I can just see him now, ranting and raving, calling my mom some uncomplimentary names about her son. I am sure he will not talk to me and will not accept any explanation from me or my brothers. What the hell! There is little I can do now. It's out of my hands now, and I have to deal with it and so will my family.

Saturday, February 2, 1957

I couldn't sleep, so getting up very early was easy. I sat at the edge of my bed wondering if I should take Rachel with me when I meet with Vignola. What would happen today? I just could not believe I was sitting here, helpless. I, Harry Miller, who always took charge of things, was helpless.

I decided to leave Rachel at home and went off to meet Vignola. I walked into Danny's Bar and sat down at a table. There were no other customers in the place, and Vignola hadn't arrived yet. I waited about five more minutes, when the door opened and in walked this tall good-looking man. He was about six feet three and must have weighed easily 200 lbs—all muscle. He had jet black hair and wore a very expensive pinstripe suit.

He extended his hand and said, "Arnold Vignola. You must be Harry Miller?"

"A pleasure to meet you. Now let's get to work," I said.

"Now let's get down to what is real and what is not. I have already spoken with Inspector Sam Johnson," he said as he cut me off. "Let me speak and then you can ask me anything you want, okay? They claim you are aware of some serious crimes. They believe that you are part of the Mafia, my friend, and have helped these guys pull off some serious shit. There is murder, extortion, fraud, and so many other offenses that I could spend all day going over them, but I won't. They really don't want you. They want those behind the scenes—the big guys—and they believe you can help them. You work with them or you take a fall. They claim they have plenty of evidence that it will make it easy to convict you as a very willing coconspirator. They will try taking away all your money, your cars, your houses, and make you eat shit and then throw away the key. I hope I am making myself clear?"

I was shocked and could not believe what bullshit was being thrown at me. It was time for me to ask a few questions. "I really don't know what they are talking about. I was never involved in any murder or any of the things they want to accuse me of," I said very anxiously.

"They claim they know what you do, who you work for, and what goes on," Vignola said.

"I work for Capitol Investments Corp. I help process loans and make sure the paperwork is in order. That is all I do."

"Listen, Harry," Vignola said, "they claim they have it all on film. The feds are involved, the city cops, they even have the Canadian Mounted Police and Interpol in this group—quite an impressive array of agencies that seem to want your ass. Of course, they all don't have jurisdiction and not all can go after you. But you need not worry about that, it is my job to handle it."

Vignola said he would take an approach that I want to cooperate. He would make some calls and maybe he could get things to go a little smoother. "Sure thing. I'll make all the calls I need to, and in the meantime, you stay away from everyone. I don't want any conversations without clearing it with me. One more thing, Harry, your life won't be worth a plug nickel if it gets known that you are cooperating with them without my participation. It doesn't matter that Larry Casparizzi is your father-in-law. He will off you quicker than you can, say like Jackie Robinson."

That didn't sound so good. I was in the middle of it and had to think what was best for me. It smelled like a royal set up, and I was the bait. Abe and I were going to see a lot of each other and I'd better be very cautious what I say to anyone including Vignola.

"Take my advice, Harry. Don't trust anyone." He turned and walked away, leaving me hanging. As he reached the door, he called back to me, "Sit where you are, I'll be back in one minute, and we will start to strategize this."

I sat there wondering what the hell is going on and how will I ever get out of this mess. Vignola came back with a lot of papers in his hands and sat down again. "Now listen to me, Harry. We can't do much until Monday, until then I'll have my assistant, Jack Beauregard, watch over you. If you need anything, he will take care of it. I want you to go home and stay there until Monday morning and then I want you at my office bright and early. You can trust Jack with your life. He is real good. I'll be meeting with Sam Johnson on Monday at ten thirty. So stay calm until then. We will meet at my office at 7:45 a.m., Monday morning. Now go home and relax. Nothing will happen until Monday." He shook my hand and asked me to sign a retainer form and left.

I returned home and sat down with Rachel and told her to call Larry. She asked, "Is it really necessary to call him, Harry?"

"Really necessary?" I yelled. "What do you think this is? A simple traffic ticket? Come on, Rachel, get your shit together and call him. I'm sure he can pull some strings and get me out of this."

"Okay, I'll call him," she said.

"You don't sound too enthusiastic about it. Am I missing something? What the hell is going on?"

I could not believe my ears, to hear my wife, my lover, and partner sound as if she didn't give a shit if I ever got out of this mess. Maybe it was me feeling sorry for myself or my fear of what is yet to come. Either way I expected a lot from her and probably was just being an asshole. Her father, Larry, was a very strong guy around town. He was my boss, and he could make a single phone call, and I'd be in less trouble. So what the hell was the problem?

Of course, according to Vignola, the feds were after Larry and wanted to nail him very badly.

"I will do what I can, Harry," Rachel said unconvincingly. "I'll call my dad and see if we can get something going today, if not, it will have to wait until Monday. I will come with you on Monday when you see Vignola."

I didn't have much choice but to wait and think about what the hell they wanted from me and why Rachel seemed so distant. If the tables were reversed, I would turn the town upside down to get her out of the trouble. I guess the set up for Harry Miller was on the way, and she was a part of it. I regretted thinking that way. I loved her, and I knew she loved me as well. I'd better get that thought out of my head. Why would she compromise? Larry was her father. Why bring heat on him? Rachel called Larry and left a message for him. I could understand his reluctance to speak on the phone.

About ten thirty, Jack Beauregard arrived and tried to assure me to remain calm and said things will work out.

"Arnold is a great lawyer. He will get it all straight very soon. Don't fuck it up. Please have faith," he said.

"I hope you can let me in on the deal. It sucks, man. It really sucks," I said.

"I spoke with Arnold, and he instructed me to see you and do whatever I can," said Beauregard. "All I do know is that they claim to have a lot of shit against you. It's all circumstantial, but what they really want is you to be their informant against your father-in-law and the Mob. I can't give you any specifics at this time, as they are not confiding in me, but I will guarantee you that they will want to arrest you and oppose bail unless we give them something to hang their hat on. Of course, I don't know what charge they can use to arrest you on, but they will find one even if it is bullshit. We can't do anything until Monday. So let's just relax."

I looked at Beauregard and said, "Well, it's easy for you to say, but it's my life, and I don't like it at all."

I'll do my best," he said. "Let me do what I do best and that is to keep you calm and not worry. Let's get drunk and have a little fun. We can't do anything else until Monday."

I was surprised that Vignola, who was without doubt a Mob lawyer, had one of his men sit with me for all the weekend. I guess they didn't trust me at all and probably were told to make sure they keep an eye on me.

I was bushed and probably didn't realize how tired I really was. I fell asleep while still talking to Jack. It seemed like forever, but was only twelve noon when I woke up, and Jack was still there waiting for me. It seemed to me that Jack was assigned to stay with me all the time until I settled down. He was really protecting the big boys and stroking me.

All he wanted was to make sure I would not speak to anyone especially the cops.

"I'm sorry, Jack, I guess I was so tired I fell asleep on you. So what do we do until Monday about this shit? Is it all right with the cops that I do not call them today as I promised?" I said.

"No problem, Arnold has spoken with the inspector, and he expects us in court on Monday at ten thirty. Arnold is trying to get the warrant squashed and offer your fullest cooperation. Of course, we will not allow any questions unless we are present. We are only trying to buy time, Harry, which will allow Arnold time to straighten this all out. There is no question that you were not involved in any of those things they claim. Perhaps, we could plead to a loan sharking charge and get probation. No matter what, Arnold will make a deal to get this thing straightened out. We have to play it close to the vest because you can easily find yourself having both sides after you. If this happens, your life will be worthless. The cops don't have any proof against you. They are just fishing, and it's up to you not to take the bait. Relax, Harry, it's easier to think when you are at ease. Stress and worry will not change what happened yesterday and won't help with tomorrow, so cool it, and we'll come out on top," Jack said.

I spent another hour with Jack and agreed with him to take it easy. I finally convinced him that it isn't necessary to babysit me. He finally left and gave me every number I'd need if something should happen. If not, I must be at Arnold's office at seven forty-five Monday morning. As soon as Jack left, I called a friend of mine from college. I explained the deal to him and asked if we could meet to review my options. He suggested we meet later that afternoon at Barney's for a drink and we can sit and discuss the whole affair.

I made my way to Barney's on Second Avenue and Sixty-Second Street to meet with Moe. I sat at the bar, while waiting for Moe, and ordered vodka on the rocks with a twist of lemon. No sooner my drink was placed in front of me, Moe walked in. He was a short guy. He only stood five feet six. He weighed no more than 150 lbs. He was wearing a dark suit that looked like he had slept in it. His white shirt looked a little soiled and was open at the collar. His wavy blond hair was extra long and looked a little unkempt, but it suited him quite well.

"How are you, Harry?" he asked as he extended his hand.

We took a table in the far corner, and I proceeded to relate the events of the last few weeks.

"Harry, what can I say? This is some story, and I'm glad I'm not in your shoes. I don't like the fact that the cops would be easily satisfied by a phone call from Arnold Vignola. It smells like you are being set up by both, the cops and the Mob. The usual procedure would be to have you come in at once and either get a bail hearing or keep you over the weekend. To just to let you walk away because your lawyer called is beyond belief. Be very careful, my friend, things are not as they seem," Moe said.

"This sounds great, Moe. So what do you think I should do?" I said.

"First, I'd be very careful what I tell to Vignola and Jack, as they are obviously working for the Mob. I'll try to get in touch with the inspector. I know Sam Johnson quite well and can vouch for him. He is one of the most honest cops I ever knew. The problem here is that he is doing his job that is being orchestrated by his superiors. He probably doesn't know that you are innocent and is hell-bent on getting you in court. Let me talk to him, and I'll see what I can do, and then I'll call you. I think we should set up a phone station where I can call you. Most likely your phone at home is tapped, so let's not take any chances. Let's find a telephone booth and use it as our drop," Moe said.

We left the restaurant and found a telephone booth on Third Avenue and made arrangements to speak at four this afternoon. Moe said he'd call me with news after reaching the inspector.

At four, I was waiting at the telephone booth. I was very anxious, as I wanted to hear from Moe because I felt he was the only honest person I could trust. The phone rang, and I picked it up after two rings. "Hello, is that you?" I said into the phone.

"Yes, Harry, it's me. I spoke with Sam Johnson, and he opened my eyes a great deal. Here is the story how he knows it. They have no proof at all about any crimes except for the loan sharking charge, and that one is very weak and it was only a very circumstantial case. The other charges are all bullshit to frighten you into being an informant for the feds. He is on your side and does not like what he is being forced to do. But it's his job, and he has to do what he is told. If you go in to see him, he would put you under protective custody immediately and work with the feds to get you a new identity and start a new life once you have finished testifying. It's not the most wonderful position to be in, but that is all he can offer. He also knows that there are informers working for the cops and will report your actions to the Mob as fast as possible. You are between a rock and a hard place and really have nowhere to go. At least not yet," Moe said.

"That is a heavy load you have just placed on my back, my friend," I said.

"I want you to place all your assets in my hands. I'll keep them for you so that you will always be liquid, and funds will be there for you. I'll protect your assets so that no one can go after any of them at any time. We must keep this private between us, not even your wife should know about this. No one, Harry, absolutely no one," Moe said.

"Okay, I'll do that at once and give you all my cash tomorrow or as soon as I can. Larry has promised me a bundle of money. Once I get it, I'll bring that as well to you. In the meantime, I guess I'll continue with Arnold and Jack as if nothing has changed," I said.

"Listen, Harry, I suggest you call the inspector. He can pick you up and make it all look like he didn't keep his promise. He will use some excuse to get Arnold Vignola off his back for going back on his promise. If you do this, he will not oppose letting you out on your own recognizance, thus allowing you free movement. Two can play the game as well, and Inspector Johnson wants the upper hand. This way he gets his wish. This doesn't mean the danger has passed, Harry. Anything can go wrong, especially because the Mob has many insiders on their payroll," Moe said.

"I'm being used no matter which side I'm on. The Mob is using me to take the fall and close the investigation, and the cops are using me to get the Mob. I'm screwed no matter what I do. Thanks, Moe, I'll follow your advice. I probably will not be able to get the money over to you until sometime during the week."

I called Inspector Johnson as soon as I hung up on Moe. He got on the phone and said, "Inspector Johnson here. How can I help you?"

"This is Harry Miller, and I'd like to discuss this situation with you. I spoke with a very good friend, Moe Arnold, and he suggested I call you," I said.

"I'm glad you called, Harry. I think it would be best if you came in and I'll take care of the rest. You have to trust me. Things will be okay. When can you come in?" he said.

"I can be at the station in thirty minutes. Just give me the address," I said.

"No, Harry, I don't want you coming to the station. There are far too many eyes and ears here. Tell me where are you, and I'll pick you up and take you where you will be safe," he said.

I gave him directions and waited for him to arrive. I was standing on the corner of Forty-Second Street and Broadway, when I saw a black sedan driving very slowly close to the curb.

The window opened and someone yelled out, "Harry Miller? Get in."

I approached the car slowly as the rear door opened, and I jumped in.

"I'm Inspector Johnson. Pleased to meet you, Harry," he said.

"I'm glad it's you. I was nervous about jumping into a slow moving vehicle. I could not see who was in the car," I said.

"Well, it is all good, Harry. This is Detective Raoul Martin, another guy you can trust. What I plan on doing, Harry, is taking you down to one of our holding areas where there are no other prisoners. I'll call Arnold Vignola and tell him I picked you up because I got a tip that you were about to leave town and we could not take that chance. It's good enough to save face for the time being. I want you to call your wife and tell her to get in touch with your lawyer fast. You must act as if you are scared and you are angry so that we can eliminate suspicion that you are cooperating. The Mob will burn your ass if they thought we worked this out together. Let's get the show on the road, Harry," he said.

I called Rachel and acted as upset as best I could. "Get me out of here, please, sweetheart. This place sucks. Call Arnold and tell him to get down here fast please," I told her. I gave her the number for Inspector Johnson and asked her to call me with news. I also told her to get in touch with her dad. So far the plan seemed to be working, and I was safe for the time being. I was placed in a cell with the door left unlocked. There were no other people in this building—no guards, no prisoners at all. We were all alone.

The inspector came to my cell and sat down. "How are you getting along, Harry?" he asked.

"I'm fine, Inspector. But can you tell me what we are doing here and what is the plan?" I asked.

"Let me explain the facts to you, Harry. I was given a phony arrest warrant for you. The real job was to get you to agree to cooperate with us in our prosecution against organized crime. You have been under surveillance for a long time, and we know you have not committed any murders or any other crimes. We know you did your job and didn't get involved with the other stuff. We also know that you can help us put away the big boys because you know just what is going on. You know the names of those on the take. You know who gives the orders to have someone killed, and you know how the number racket works as well as the bookie joints and the protection racket. You see, Harry, like it or not, you got yourself in the middle of this fiasco, and now you've got to take a stand. If you don't work with us, we will find a way to force you to cooperate. Let me make this very clear to you, Harry. If we leak it that you are working with us and let you go free, the Mob will come after you with guns blazing. If you work with us, we will get you a new identity and place you in the witness protection program. The problem with that program is that we don't know who the paid informers are. So your life and those you love will always be in jeopardy unless we clean up our act. I suggest the following scenario, which will allow you time to get things straightened out and help both of us," the inspector said.

"That sounds great. I wonder what that could be," I said half joking.

"You cannot tell your attorney anything about this conversation we have just had. It is very important you remember this, because Vignola works for those we are trying to catch. He is a Mob lawyer, so his interest is with those who pay him the big money. Once in the Mob, you really can't get out. They don't have a retirement program, and Vignola is in deep and wouldn't dare cross them. You are not one of those who want to be the first to test the Mob's retirement plan, so you have to be very careful at all times. I can arrange it with the judge when you come before him to agree to drop the arrest warrant and to instruct you to make yourself available as a witness. This will keep you out of jail, and you will not require a lawyer any longer. We will have to go through the motions that you are a very uncooperative witness and stipulate some severe conditions. Your passport will have to be surrendered, and you will have to report to me whenever you wish to leave the city. Of course, Harry, this will all be a show between us. I think you may have to stay here overnight if a judge is not available right now. Your lawyer will try to round up a judge to get you out of here today, so I'll try to find one we can work with and make him available. Why don't you relax in your cell? I'll let you know what is going a little later. Harry, do we have a deal?" he said.

"Look, Inspector, I really don't know as much as you think, but I am willing to help as long as you play straight with me. A mutual friend has stood good for you, and I trust him a lot. So I'm going to work with you. Please remember, Inspector, I will work with you and only you. If I smell a rat, I run and hide. I want a new life, not the end of life," I replied.

I returned to my cell and lay down while the wheels of justice went into motion. All of a sudden, I was woken up and grabbed by two big cops and dragged into a room that was no bigger than my bedroom and could barely handle fifteen people. I looked around, and there was my lawyer Jack Beauregard, Inspector Johnson, and a couple of other people I didn't know. No Rachel anywhere!

"Please remove the cuffs, Officer," Jack said.

Once they removed the cuffs, Jack took me to one corner and said, "I called Larry. He is standing by to arrange bail if you should need it, although the inspector indicated he may agree to a conditional release without bail. I also promised the inspector and agreed that you will present yourself at his office on Monday morning and surrender your passport. I also agreed that you will meet him on Tuesday at 10:00 a.m. at his office, together with Arnold or myself and discuss the case."

"Okay, if that is what I must do to get out of here, I'll do it," I said.

At that moment, a side door opened and a judge in a black robe rushed hurriedly to his bench.

"Court will come to order, Judge Oscar Cohen presiding. Case no. 43874692NY the people of New York State vs. Harry Miller," he continued to read the charges as the rear door of the little courtroom opened, and Rachel walked in. I made eye contact, but had to stay focused on the judge.

The Judge then said to me, "Mr. Miller, I sentence you to life in prison. Take him away."

At that moment, I woke up screaming, "No, I didn't do anything, please."

"Harry, wake up."

I looked straight ahead as Rachel was shaking me. "Harry you are dreaming. What is it all about?" she said.

I cleared my head and looked around and realized I was still in my cell.

"Wow! I had a nightmare and lost my memory and forgot where I was. I really am fucked up. Sorry, guys, I'll try to be a lot stronger and clear my mind of this shit. No more drinking for me," I said.

Rachel looked at me as if I was nuts and said, "Look, Harry, Jack Beauregard has arranged your release on your own recognizance. You will have to meet Inspector Johnson on Monday to surrender your passport. First, you will keep your early appointment with Mr. Vignola, and then you and your lawyer will see the inspector. Now let's get out of here and relax a little until Monday," she said.

Sunday, February 3, 1957

I had a very busy day ahead of me, as I had to meet with Larry and discuss the entire situation. I needed answers to what is going on and what should be done. Rachel and I spent last night at home talking about the events. She explained to me that she was in shock and didn't know how to react. She said she was sorry and would be a rock at my side until this was cleared up. Of course, I still did not understand just what was up, but I understood that I did know a lot of people and, of course, knew how the loan sharking business worked and could possibly help the authorities. But I knew that my life might not be worth a plug nickel if I agreed to work with them. We were going to Larry's for breakfast, and I was hoping I would be able to get a few things straight.

Rachel and I left early, as the drive to Long Island was not always an easy one. Today, it should be a breeze, being Sunday and early morning. We arrived about an hour later in Atlantic beach, where Larry lived. I loved the place—right on the Atlantic Ocean. It always felt safe here; who could get at you from here? The back of the property was on the ocean, and the sides were surrounded with a stone fence that was about ten feet high. The front of the estate was set back about a thousand feet from the street with giant steel gates at the entrance with stone walls that were also ten feet high. At the gate was a small guard shack, manned by one of Larry's guys, who called ahead to announce who was at the gate and get permission to let them in. There were also a couple of cameras along with people patrolling the grounds.

This was the first time I saw all this security. I could not believe why so much security, especially out here, where there is virtually no crime at all. Of course, I understood, because I now knew who my father-in-law was.

"Hi, Larry, how are you doing?"

I didn't know what else to say. We hugged for a minute. He embraced Rachel and then he looked at me and said, "What kind of a mess did you get into?" I started to speak, but Larry's look said not now, so I didn't say anything.

He called, "Sal, get your ass in here, and I want to speak with you."

"Yes, boss," Sal said as he came into the large sitting room. "What do you need, boss?"

"Rachel, are you hungry?" Larry asked.

"I could eat a little breakfast as long as you join me," Rachel said as she took my arm and started walking toward the dinning room.

"Sal, get the cook to rustle up some breakfast. I'm hungry too."

"Okay, boss, on the double."

After eating a breakfast fit for a king, Larry motioned to me and said, "Let's go outside and talk a little. Just follow me. Rachel, stay here and find something that will amuse you."

We went outside and walked, in silence, close to the ocean. And then Larry said, "Okay, what do they want and how did they get to you?"

"Larry," I said, "I don't know how they got to me. It was certainly strange that the only time they came for me was Friday night. It was a good thing Rachel thought real fast and said I was gone to the mountains. They came to the house with a phony warrant. I think they wanted to get me alone and see what they could get out of me before I get to an attorney. It's really strange to me,"

"I know the charges are all bullshit," Larry said. "I had Jack read them to me. But why you, and what do they think you know?"

"Here's is what they told Rachel, Larry. This cop, Inspector Johnson, was very clear. He wants me to help them nail you and others. He claims you are organized crime and they got plenty of proof," I said.

"If they got plenty of proof, why do they need you?" Larry said.

"How the fuck do I know, Larry? This is what they said. They claimed they have films of what is going on and that the FBI and Interpol along with the Mounties are involved. If I don't help them, they will put me away for twenty-five years or more," I said.

"Fuck them," Larry yelled. "Who the fuck do they think they are?"

"Larry, please tell me what to do, and I will do it. If it means doing time, I will do it. But how do I get them off my back?"

Larry looked at me and finally said, "Listen to me, you don't know anything. All you have to do is say that—you know nothing. And there is nothing they can do to you. If they want to arrest you, we'll handle all the legal. Just don't say anything without your lawyer present."

I just stared at Larry as he carried on, "If you tell them anything, you are dead. Do you understand me? Dead."

I could not believe what I just heard. I'm being threatened from both the sides, and this is too much to handle.

"Larry, how can you say that? We are family, and I would never say anything that would hurt you. Never," I said.

"I just wanted to see how you would react. But remember, kid, we are not dealing with amateurs here, no fucking way," Larry said.

"Larry, I have to protect Rachel as well. Shit, I'm in the middle of the lake with no boat, what the fuck should I do? Larry, you got to help me, what do I do now?"

"Just relax. I will speak to Vignola tomorrow and find out just where we stand. I will talk to you through him only from now on. Do not try to contact me, and no telephone conversations with anyone. You got me? I will talk to Rachel now, and she will understand and do what I tell her. You do not come to the office anymore. Just stay away and don't make any contact with the boys. I will make sure you get plenty of money each week so that you don't have to worry on that count. You will follow Vignola's direction, as he will be speaking for me. I know you have been at the office a long time and saw a lot of shit go down. Forget whatever you saw and speak to no one. It is so fucking dangerous. If the big boys should think for one minute that you are a liability, they'll kill you in a heartbeat. Just stay quiet and wait. No talking to anyone. Disappear and stay hidden until I get this straightened out. Now get the fuck of here, and we will get this shit straightened out. Just listen to me, and do not speak to anyone. Your life may depend on it, and I only want to protect you and Rachel. Stay calm, and we'll do it right."

"One thing, Larry, you never answered me why the big boys want me dead. I asked you the other day when I told you about the two hit men that came after me in the Bronx. You just ignored it, but it is very important," I said.

"I think, when we had our little argument, someone overheard you threatening to screw me and reported that to the big boys. I straightened all that out with them, and I don't think you need to worry about it any longer. You apologized to me, and I knew deep in my heart that you didn't mean what you said. But let that be a lesson to you, Harry. Be very careful about what you say and to whom. Remember that the walls have ears and there are ass kissers everywhere. Keep your mouth shut and never let anyone know what you are thinking. Now get the hell out of here and follow the rules," Larry said.

I thought that was the last time I would ever see Larry Casparizzi or speak with him again. He was known as a man of his word and a mean one at that. He then talked to Rachel so that she would understand everything. No other mention of this meeting was ever to be discussed. Larry didn't exist, and neither did I.

I also did not have a job any longer and had my instructions. "Shut up," or else I'd be out of this world. We drove home almost in silence, as Rachel didn't want to talk too much, although I tried to get a conversation started. I parked the car and went into the house.

I was very fucked up and angry as I slammed the door and said, "Rachel, get your ass over here. Let's talk."

She came into the living room and sat down and said, "What the hell do you want me to say?"

"Just talk to me, baby. Just a little conversation will do," I said.

"Harry," she said, "what can I say? My father wants me to choose between you and him. And no matter what I choose, I lose."

"Baby," I said, "we are one. We will see this through together. There is no use in us fighting. We have each other, and we must try to do the right thing."

"That's pretty easy for you to say," Rachel said half crying. "How will I pay the rent, buy clothes, eat, do anything? Larry pays for everything. If I go against him, I will have nothing, not even him as he will disown me and throw me out to rot."

"What horseshit this is!" I yelled. "I am your husband for fuck sake, or do you think it will be that easy to throw me out as well?"

"Stop this shit, Harry," she yelled at me. "You took the easy way out when you went to work for him. For you, it was a breeze—take two grand a week—and what the hell do you care?"

"You piece of shit, you spent the money pretty well and you never once told me your father was Mafia. You never once felt bad or asked me to find another job, and you knew I could get into trouble. You didn't ask me to find another job. No sirree, you never once gave a shit as long as you got yours. This was turning into an all-out war with no solution. If we don't stop this argument, we are going to hurt each other. The question is who would do it first. I can't take your shit any longer. You are nothing more than a slut. I'll solve this on my own, bitch."

With that, I walked out of the room and went to our bedroom and slammed the door. I was pissed, and now I was alone and understood the position Rachel took very well—it was me against the Mob and the feds; a choice I will have to make soon, if I live that long.

Monday, February 4, 1957

I left the house early, as I did not want to get into it again with Rachel and went to Horn and Hardart's for some coffee and a doughnut. I wanted to spend a little time alone and think about what options are left open to me. I grabbed a corner table where I could be alone for a little while. It was 7:00 a.m., and in another few minutes, hundreds of people will stop in for their early morning coffee fix, and being alone may not be viable.

I had my passport with me, in case I decided to leave the country fast. What a way to think! But I didn't know what lay ahead of me. Even though Larry said he would pay this tremendous legal bill, who knows if he is really going to? Who is going to be on my side and who will be on the other side of the fence? I cannot answer these things at present, as my mind was still racing with the realization that Larry and his crew can easily kill me and solve their problems. Larry probably isn't thinking along those lines because of Rachel. But what if she tells him that we have had a big blowup? He might change his mind. Once he feels Rachel is out of the way, he'll stop at nothing to get rid of me. He certainly doesn't need excess baggage, especially one that is a threat to him. I'd better play it very carefully and hold my temper until I know where I stand and who is on my team and who isn't. I finished my coffee and went outside to the pay phone. I wanted to call Billy and talk with him. I dialed his number at his office and waited. Usually, Billy was an early bird, as he liked to miss the traffic in Manhattan from his place in Queens. Billy owned a leather factory just off Seventh Avenue and Thirty-Sixth Street and did quite well. I supposed he was paying his dues, as the Mob controlled the shmata business, and he was no different. I never spoke to Billy about this, because I really wanted to keep my nose out of it.

"Trident Leather, can I help you?" I heard and recognized Billy's voice.

"I sure hope so, Bro. How are you?" I said.

"Great," Billy replied. "What's going on so early in the morning?"

"I have some serious problems and need your help. When can we get together and talk?" I said.

"What's the problem, Harry?" Billy said.

"I can't talk over the phone and have to meet someone at nine, and then I have a meeting with my lawyer at ten. So can I come to you any time after twelve?"

"What kind of shit have you gotten into now? Harry, it's has to be serious, when you mention a lawyer," Billy said.

"You bet your ass it is," I said as calmly as possible. "I surely hope you can help me, Billy. I surely hope so!"

"Okay, I'll meet you at one at Oscar's on Seventh. You know where it is, Harry," Billy said.

"Sure. Okay, I'll see you then, and by the way, Billy, don't tell anyone that I am in any kind of trouble. You are the only one I have spoken with. Mom and Dad know nothing. Please!" I said.

"Okay, Harry, don't you worry, it's between us. See you at one."

I called Arnold Vignola, even though it was early in the morning and confirmed my appointment with him at eleven.

He then told me, "Harry, I spoke with Inspector Johnson and agreed with him that you would stop first thing in the morning and drop off your passport. By doing this, we are showing good faith. And he has agreed not to take you into to custody. We will work some deal in the future, but in the meantime, we should get the heat off you. It also shows Larry and the others that you are okay and things seem to be working out. I will then have time to take the proper steps to get this all quashed. Before you know it, it will be a thing of the past and, eventually, it will all go away." He gave me the address where to drop off the passport and see the inspector.

I went over to the address Arnold gave me, and although I was early, I found the inspector in. He came down a flight of stairs and asked me to follow him back up to his office.

"Sit down, Harry. Did you bring the passport?" he asked.

"Sure thing," I replied as I handed it over to him. "Can I get a receipt for it? I just like to have one in case I should ever need it," I said.

"No problem," he said and wrote me out a receipt. "Have you decided what you are going to do, Harry?" he said.

"Not yet. You guys don't leave me with too many options, do you?" I said.

"Life is a bitch, Harry," the inspector said. "You play with matches you might get burnt, so now you know what this is all about."

"I'll get back in touch with you later," I said as I got up to leave.

"No rush, Harry. Take a minute and let me show you something that might help convince you what kind of people we are dealing with." He got up and left the room, returning a minute later with a file in his hand.

"Let me show this, Harry," he said as he opened the file and took out a photo of male I recognized from the finance office. The guy's face was a mess; it looked like someone ran their car over it a few times. It was really gruesome.

"He's dead, Harry, beaten to pulp by a bunch of goons, to set an example. I guess the message is if you borrow money, you got to pay it back."

I stared at the picture and couldn't believe that just a few weeks ago, this guy came in and borrowed five grand. Wow! This was something! My reaction was one of calm as I didn't want the inspector to know that I recognized the victim. I'm sure the inspector knew I was shaken up by this. But he didn't say a word, and neither did I.

I had to get out of there. It was lot more than I bargained for. I got up and started to leave, when he said, "By the way, Harry, he was married with two kids."

I wanted to throw up. The photo was horrible, and I thought that could be me. And what about his wife? My head was spinning. What to do, where to go, I really didn't know and couldn't think straight. I had to get out of there. It was nearly ten, so I decided to walk to Forty-Third and Lexington to see Vignola. I was early and needed to clear my head. I reached Vignola's office with five minutes to spare. I took the elevator up to the twenty-second floor and entered his office. A very sexy-looking blonde was sitting behind a desk, looking a lot like a movie star instead of a legal secretary.

"May I help you?" she purred.

"You sure can. Harry Miller to see Mr. Vignola," I said.

"Did you have an appointment, Mr. Miller?" she said.

"Yes. Please let him know I am here."

She picked up the phone and said, "Mr. Miller to see Mr. Vignola." She listened for a moment and said, "Please take a seat. He will be right with you Mr. Miller."

"Thanks," I said and sat down in a very comfortable leather chair and waited. Five minutes passed, as I kept on looking at my watch as if I had somewhere else to go.

"Excuse me, Mr. Miller, if you would follow me, Mr. Vignola will see you now."

I walked down a forty-feet hallway with doors on both the sides all the way along. There must be a lot of lawyers in this office, I thought. At the far end, a little to the right, I saw an open door with a large desk and surrounded by glass with a view of the west side of the city. Wow, what a view! I thought, expensive! She motioned me to a very good-looking leather chair positioned in front of the desk and turned and walked out.

"Harry, how are you?"

I stood up and extended my hand to a six feet three inch giant of a man. He looked like he was the king of the world with slicked back black hair, great eyes, and a smile that would melt butter.

"I really can't say it is a pleasure to see you again, Mr. Vignola," I said.

"Let's not stand on ceremony here. Please call me Arnold. I am here to help if I can, so let's get to it!" he said.

"I am not sure where to begin, but I guess Jack filled you in on the details up to now," I said.

"He sure did, and I also spoke with Larry Casparizzi and Inspector Johnson to see if we can put a lid on all this," he said.

"Boy, what a mess!" I said. "What do we do from here?"

"First thing, Harry, let me caution you that you speak to no one without me being present, no matter what they promise and/or threaten you with. I hope that is clear!" Vignola said.

"I understand completely," I responded. "But what the hell is going on and how am I going to get this shit straightened out?"

"Calm down, Harry. I am here to help you and to do the worrying for you, so just keep yourself relaxed and understand that there are good people looking after your best interests," Vignola said.

Once again, I nodded my understanding as Arnold went on.

"In the first instance, we have to understand that the district attorney's offices along with the FBI are looking to use you so that they can go after Larry and Larry's other associates," he said. "You must follow my advice at all times, or things will not go well for you, Harry, always remember that I'm too strong and too well connected to be screwed with."

I just sat there in awe, not believing what I am hearing. I stared right through Arnold Vignola and shivered as I felt weak.

Finally, I spoke, "Arnold, what am I going to do? Where will I get the money to pay you? Where will they strike at me next? I just can't help it. I have never been arrested before and have never faced such circumstances."

"Harry, let me put you at ease. Please listen to me carefully. It is just you and I in here, so I will lay it on the line. Please listen until I am done."

I nodded once again and just sat there. What else could I do? Except sit back and listen! Like it or not, I am now a part of organized crime and must cooperate, or I will be toast. "I'm all ears, Arnold," I said.

"Okay, Harry, as far as the cost, you don't have to worry. Your legal bills have been taken care of. As far as you are concerned, Larry has assured me that an envelope will be left here at this office each week as long as you work with us and do as you're told. Two and a half grand should take good care of you each week. So relax and let us do the work. The cops think they have an easy mark with you. All they are trying to do is nail Larry and his organization. It seems that they have had you and the office under surveillance for the last three months. It seems that they have tapped the phone lines at the office, at your home, and at other locations. It seems that they feel they have enough evidence against you to make you fold and become an informer against Larry and some others. Of course, they are going to ask you to lie and make up stories that will fuck Larry, and they will make up bullshit and try to connect you and many of the boys at your office to a scheme of murder and other crimes. This type of crap has gone on for years. We can only defeat them if we do not fall into their trap of bullshit. You remain strong and leave everything to me, and you will come out of this smelling like a rose."

"Are you sure you can straighten this out?" I said.

"Sure. I can," Arnold responded.

"So during this time, do I stay away from Larry?"

"Yes, you do, simply because they are tailing you and tapping your phone, there is no need to give them any additional ammunition to work with," Vignola said.

"What about Rachel? She is my wife and also Larry's daughter. How does this impact our lives?" I said.

"I can't answer for Rachel, but can assure you that Larry wants her protected at all times and will not let any harm come to her. She understands the situation and will not create any problems. She is a trooper. You and Rachel just go about your lives as normal as possible, continue to go out of town on weekends and spend a lot of time together. Over the next few months, you are going to be a busy guy between meeting with me and with the DA. Just take it easy and don't worry. That's my job," Arnold said.

"So what do I do from here?" I said once again.

"Harry, please, relax. I have everything under control. I sent word that I am your lawyer of record and that no interview, arrests, or any attempt to contact you should be made without me. I am sure the DA, will make sure this procedure is followed. I have given my word that if they need to speak with you, I will bring you in. In a few days, we will find out what the DA's office has in mind and how they have planned to proceed. In the meantime, just relax. Have a drink and enjoy life and do not worry. If you get a call from anyone, call me at once. Here is my card with my home number on it. I don't care what time of night. If something goes down, call me. Do not speak on the phone about anything other than simple normal things. Your phones are tapped."

"Okay, Arnold, I'm in your hands, and you will have my complete cooperation. Just don't let me down, please!" I said.

"For the last time, Harry, stop worrying. I am on your team. By the way, Harry, Larry wants you to be safe always, so he is putting Vinnie Garlotti on the watch over you and Rachel. Vinnie will stay out of sight and will just be watching your back. He'll make sure that no one fucks with you at any time," Vignola said with a smile.

"Do I really need a bodyguard, Arnold?" I said.

"Sure, Harry, we don't know what the DA is up to. This way Vinnie is always watching. And by the way, Harry, don't forget to stop by every Friday morning and pick up your envelope. It will be waiting for you at the front desk. If you are busy, have Rachel stop by. As a matter of expediency, I will organize one drop every month so that you don't have to come by every Friday. I just want to be very clear with you, Harry. I am your lawyer and everything we say to each other is confidential and is covered by law, so, Harry, there is never a need to bullshit me. I'm here for you. One other thing, Harry, let's be honest with each other. You have worked for Larry for two years and you are fully aware of the people who came by the office as well as those who worked there. You know that Larry is one of the upper echelons in the Gambino family. You may not know much, but the feds think you know a lot. The family doesn't know how much you know, so don't fuck up, because you can easily get it from either side. Trust me, and we will get out of this mess without too much trouble. I am your friend and am always on your side, but I also get my orders from others. I will report back that you are solid and that you will not talk under any circumstances. Time will take care of everything else, so just relax and enjoy life. You got money, you got Rachel, and you got your health. Let's keep it all together, and the end will come quicker than you think."

I got up from the chair, shaken by the words I just heard, as it was obvious I was being dismissed, and headed for the door. Just as I entered the reception, a voice called out, "Mr. Miller, excuse me. This envelope is for you."

It was the beautiful blonde holding an envelope in her super-looking hand.

"Thanks," I said and continued out of the office. As I waited for the elevator, I opened the envelope, and there was a lot of money in it. I didn't bother to count it and just stuffed into my pocket as the elevator arrived. I was the only one on the elevator on the twenty-second floor. I wondered where Vinnie was. By the time I reached the ground floor, the elevator was full, and three guys could have been Vinnie. I decided not to worry about it and went out on to Lexington Avenue and hailed a cab; time to go and meet Billy at Oscars.

I entered Oscars and looked around to find Billy. The place was packed. The noise was deafening. Finally, I saw Billy sitting at a table in the rear of this massive luncheonette. It was obvious that Oscars catered to the garment industry. You could easily see it on the faces of all those who were eating and talking—all at the same time. I made my way to Billy's table. "Hey, Bro, how the hell are you?" I said as I hugged my brother.

Billy is taller than I. He stood 6'2" and wore his hair slicked back, leaving his handsome face to attract every broad around.

"Great to see you, Harry. You look well," he said as he motioned to me to sit right down. "Do you want to order something, Harry?" Billy said with a big grin. "It's on me."

"Sure. What's good in this joint?" I asked.

"Everything is great. Try some chicken soup. It's almost as good as Mom's. Hey, Sybil, I want you to meet my brother, Harry," he said, as this old lady—she must have been sixty years if a day—came over with a big smile.

"He looks a lot like you, Billy," she said.

"Bring Harry a nice bowl of chicken soup. Would you please, sweetheart?" Billy said. "So, Harry, tell me what's going on and how can I help?"

"I just don't know where to begin, Billy. I feel like a piece of shit, as I don't visit you often enough and don't call as much as I should and now I am here for help, or at least advice," I said.

"What the hell do you think brothers are for? We are family and are always there for each other in good times or in troubled ones. The Millers stand together no matter what. Staying in touch doesn't change that ever. So tell me what is going on," Billy said with conviction.

"As you know, I was working for Rachel's dad, Larry. Well, it turns out that he is Mob connected. It also turned out that I was working for a shylock and not a real finance company. The money was great, and I felt that I wasn't doing anything wrong. After all, Billy, lending money regardless of rates is as old as time itself. They needed a shmuck like me to be the front person, and I fell in nicely. The clients came into the office—people that you only read about in newspapers and others you don't want to read about. I stayed and made big bucks and minded my own business.

"I did my job well and even gave Larry tips on how to do business better. I was never involved in the collection of bad debts, but I did meet some of the muscle boys every now and then. Last week, the cops came by the apartment looking for me. They wanted to make a deal with me about the operation. Rachel acted as if I wasn't home and told them she would call me in the Poconos to let me know the cops were here. I then called and spoke with Inspector Johnson. And he told me that they had the office under surveillance for a long time and knew just what was going on. All they want from me is to be a witness in their investigation. They want to go after the Mob, and I am a key witness." I went on to tell Billy everything that has gone on since, including the blowup with Rachel. "Help them, and I'm fucked by the feds. Fuck them, and I'm fucked by them. What the hell do I do?" I said as I had to stop while the soup was being served.

"Harry, I know what you are going through. I know who these bastards are, and I can't begin to tell you how much fucking money they take from me. I pay them to stay in business. They are my partners, like it or not. If I don't cooperate, they will put me out of business, if I'm lucky, or kill me. So I know what you are up against, and I wish I could make it all go away, but I can't," Billy said with tears in his eyes.

"I'm sorry, Billy, I didn't know these bastards had their fingers in your pocket. I really didn't know," I said.

"Wake up, Harry, they run the garment industry. Nothing goes on without their okay. They run the trucks. You don't cooperate, then you don't ship any merchandise. If you don't hire the people they say, you don't have workers. They put people on the payroll who never ever show up. This is life in this business. How I wish I could just pack up and leave. No such luck, Harry. I have a family, and my kids don't know a damn thing about this. Maggie thinks the leather business is the greatest and her only complaint is that I work too hard and eat too little. Boy, what a nightmare this is!"

"What can I say, Billy? I just never knew because you never told me, and I was not that interested, I guess. Boy, here I am asking you for advice and you've got bigger problems than me. What a barrel of shit we're in, brothers to the end. Boy, what an end! I know Billy. I went in with my eyes open, and the longer I stayed with Larry, the more I knew I should get out. I didn't, because the money was great. I was greedy, and now it's time to pay the piper," I said.

"Listen to me, Harry," Billy said looking very serious. "These people can't be trusted, worse, they can't tell the truth if their lives were depending on it. They are extremely dangerous and can kill you for no reason, let alone because some fucker wakes up tomorrow morning and had a dream that you were a rat. No, Harry, these bastards will kill you in the end. First of all, Harry, you are Jew. You don't fit in their family, especially in the upper echelon. They owe you nothing and will send you money as long as it is in their interest, all the while they are counting the days when they can send some hit man to cut your balls off and stuff them in your mouth. Get the fuck away as soon as you can. Change your name, your face, and your life. This is your only chance, Harry. Please believe me. I will handle Mom and Dad and the rest of the family. I will make sure they all understand and remember this. Harry, they will always love you. In a year or two, after all is settled, you can call me, and I will arrange to get the folks to visit, and we can become a family again. Do you need money? Please, Harry, don't be shy. I don't have a lot, but I can get ten grand if it helps," Billy said with sweetness on his face and love in his voice.

"No, thanks, Billy, money is not one of my problems. I think you are right, but I have to do this carefully as I have a tail with me all the time. This one is supposed to protect Rachel and me in case anyone wants to go after us. Thanks, Billy. Just don't worry about me, I'll get by. You probably won't hear from me for a while," I said as I got up from the table and puts my arms around him. "I love you, Bro, and always will. Thanks for everything. I'll get in touch as soon as I can." And with that said and tears running down my face, I turned and left Oscars and my brother Billy. I was scared, but I was getting a lot more determined to win this war, I just needed to understand the playing field.

I arrived home and no one was there. I found a note on the kitchen counter from Rachel.

"Went shopping at Bloomies, be back about six. See you then. I love you."

It was a little after three, so I decided to look into the envelope I stuffed into my pocket when leaving the lawyer's office. Much to my surprise, there was ten grand in there in crisp C-notes. This was making me more nervous, but money was money, so I shoved it into my pocket and went to check up on my bodyguard. So far I have not detected Vinnie anywhere. I could not believe that he was that good to evade me. Or was I really that lousy at picking up a tail? When Rachel came home, she was carrying a few bags. So I assumed her shopping spree was successful.

"Hi, sweetheart," I said as I kissed her gently on the lips.

"How was your meeting with Arnold?" she asked.

"Let's change and go out for dinner," I said. "We can talk about it over a drink and some good food."

"Okay, give me thirty minutes to get out of these things and put something on," she said as she rushed upstairs to put away her stuff.

I waited downstairs and mixed myself a vodka martini, very dry. Finally, Rachel came down and looked like we were going to a ball. She was stunning; a queen as always.

"Where do you want go, honey?" she said.

"Let's just go and decide when we get outside," I said, while making a gesture that our house could be bugged.

Once we were on Third Avenue and Seventieth, we began walking uptown, and I spotted Vinnie in a black Cadillac, cruising, because we were going in the opposite way of traffic. I spotted the car door opening and some very big and ugly dude getting out and starting to walk uptown, following us, without worrying if we knew it or not.

As we walked, I said to Rachel, "We are being followed by one of your father's goons. No matter where we go until this shit blows over, we are being protected, or at least that is the excuse they are using. I also want you to know that our phone is tapped and, probably, there are bugs all over the house. That is why I didn't want to talk about it at home."

"Are you sure, Harry?" Rachel said in a tone that sounded very concerned. You mean to say someone heard us argue last night. And, Harry, people have been listening to me whenever I spoke on the phone or to anyone?"

"Yes, I'm sure and so is Arnold. I have been instructed not to contact Larry and to be very careful what we say over the phone or in the apartment. It seems that the FBI and the DA are going to try to get me to testify against Larry and his crew. They are going to try and use threats and phony charges to get me to turn in. I need your support and hope that I can handle this."

Rachel looked at me for a moment and said, "Listen to me, Harry. I don't like shit like this, and I have no intentions of getting in the middle. Larry is my father, and you are my husband. Do you know how dangerous Larry is?"

I could not believe what I just heard, like what new revelation did she pass on to me.

"Of course, I know how dangerous he is, and I don't think he would give a fucking shit if he had to off me, or you for that matter, to save his ass. No, I don't kid myself Rachel, not for one second," I said.

"Okay, Harry, smart ass, what are we going to do?"

"How the fuck do I know what we are going to do. I don't even know if you are with me or against me!"

"Harry, how could you even question where I stand? I am right here with you and will be to the bitter end." She smiled and kissed me; her eyes were moist. And I believed her.

"Let's go in here and eat," I said as we were in front of Angelo's restaurant. We turned and went in and were escorted to a table in the far back—one fit for lovers who want to be alone. I looked at Rachel and said, "I love you, but still don't know what to do. On one side, we got your father's goons, and on the other side, we got the cops. We can't run away, we can't trust anyone, what a barrel of shit we are in!"

"Okay, Harry, let's order, have a couple of drinks, go home, and make love. Maybe tomorrow we will see a way out, maybe, sweetheart, but we will survive."

Tuesday, February 5, 1957

We woke up arm in arm; it was about six thirty in the morning. I jumped into the shower, while Rachel decided to get some more shut eye. I went downstairs to the kitchen and flipped on the TV, turned on the fire for the coffee, went to the front door picked up the paper, and went back to the kitchen, when I heard on the TV. "Breaking news. The pictures you are seeing is the scene across from Angelo's restaurant on Third Avenue, where a gun battle took place and two people were killed. The dead have been identified as reputed mobsters Vinnie Garlotti and Giuseppe "Big Bull" Conti. The gun battle took place about 10:00 p.m. last night and has all the earmarks of a gangland war." The newscast went on to let us know that, while details are still sketchy. It seems that rival families are at war over disputed territories. I could not hold still, I yelled, "Rachel, wake up. There is trouble, big trouble." I ran upstairs and shook her. "Get up, Rachel, get up now."

"What's the problem, Harry? What the fuck? You look like you've seen a ghost. What the hell?" she asked as she jumped out of bed.

"Our bodyguards were shot to death last night. We've got to get out of here, now."

Rachel turned white and could hardly speak. "Where shall we go?"

"Let's get out of here. Grab some clothes, and let's move, now!"

We packed a few things and made sure we took all our money and ran out to Third Avenue and headed downtown. We didn't know where we were going but we just had to get away from the apartment. I stopped at a pay phone and called Arnold Vignola at home. I didn't think he would be at the office; it was only seven fifteen in the morning, way too early for him. A woman answered, and I asked her to please put Arnold Vignola on the phone.

"Who is this?" she said, as she called out, "Arnold, there is someone on the phone for you."

I heard a click, and Arnold spoke, "Who is this? It better be important."

"It's me, Harry Miller. It's urgent. Our bodyguards were shot to death last night. I must see you. Shall I meet you at your office?"

"I'll be there in forty-five minutes," Vignola said and slammed down the phone.

Rachel and I jumped into a cab and made our way to Arnold's office. I was watching to see if anyone was following us, but could not detect anyone. I knew we would be at Arnold's early, but did not know where else to go. I wasn't going to involve anyone from my family as it was too dangerous. And until I had some answers, I'd better lay low. We took the elevator to the twenty-second floor and waited for Arnold to arrive.

Rachel was very agitated. I could not blame her in the least. Our guardian angels were smitten and were very nearer to our home. They must have felt we were safely away for the night before they went to get something to eat. I guess they were being followed, but why? These were Larry's guys, and he doesn't have a beef with anyone, so why? She couldn't call her father as we were instructed not to do so. What a bunch of crap! We waited what seemed like forever until Arnold arrived.

"This is my wife, Rachel," I said as we followed him into his office.

He motioned for us to sit down and said, "I saw the news and I spoke with the powers that be and discovered that this thing is getting out of hand."

I sat there dumbfounded as I listened to him carry on. "No one knows for sure exactly why your bodyguards were killed. The assumption is that they were out to get you, Harry, and your bodyguards were in the way. They seem to think you are a threat to the organization and know way too much."

"That is so fucked up. I know nothing and can't hurt a soul," I said.

"Listen, Harry, it could be that the DA'S office let a word slip out that you were going to cooperate. It could be that some mole gave them news that you are ready to crack, I can't say for sure. But we've got to take steps to guarantee your safety, both of you. If the hit was to get you two, then you are in grave danger. They won't quit, and there is little I can do," Arnold said.

"Whatever we decide, we will have to do it alone," I said.

Rachel jumped up from her chair and said, "Harry, let's get out of here. This is all bullshit, and no one cares about us. Let's go!"

"Wait a minute, Harry," Arnold stood and said. "I don't like it when you want to walk out of here with that attitude. I am on your team, and it is my job to protect you and help wherever I can. Now let's sit down for a few more minutes and pay attention to me. I think you should find a hotel, pay cash, and check in under different names. Tell no one where you are until I can get some more news. I will nose around and find out what is going on. In the meantime, Rachel, you call Larry and tell him you got to see him. I know he said not to call, but you are his daughter and it's quite natural for you to call. Make sure your call is from a pay phone and don't tell him where you are and where you are holed up. Never say a word on the phone about Harry. Do not mention his name. His line could be bugged, and if it is we don't want to lead them to you. Set up a time to meet, because you miss him and you are afraid and you need money and want to see him alone. Harry you lay low and do not go to meet Larry. The less people you see, the better it is." I looked at him as if he was crazy. What the hell are we into? Who the hell are these people? It seems like a war, and we are in the middle of it. Organized crime—boy, this sounds pretty unorganized.

"Arnold, do you think all this is really necessary, maybe you are wrong about the hit?" I said.

"And maybe I was right. Do you really want to find out?" he said looking very annoyed. "Just follow my instructions. It's for your own good. Now get the hell out of here. And, Harry, just trust me!"

We left the office and carefully made our way over to Third Avenue and then hailed a cab to the Westside and walked from Broadway and Forty-Fourth, to the Galaxy Hotel on Eighth and Fifty-First. Rachel went in and got a room. Then she came out and got me, and I went with her to the room—my new home for the next few days; here we shall make our war plans. I decided if they want war, they'll get war. I'm not going down without a fight. I may not know much about this stuff, but I will certainly learn very quickly how to defend myself against these bastards. What the hell makes them so damn smart. I am far more intelligent then ten of them put together. I will have Rachel get me a gun and shall start to use if I have to. I will not be fucked around with and live like an animal.

"Rachel, when you see Larry, you tell him I want a gun. I'm not going to allow us to get screwed over like this. You tell Larry I need a gun now. It must be unregistered and clean and tell him I also need ammunition for it."

Rachel looked at me and said, "Are you crazy? You don't know how to shoot or handle a gun. How will you protect us when you know shit about those things?"

"Hey, I'll learn, and I'll learn real fast. Do you think those wop bastards can handle guns better than me? No fucking way. And once they see me shooting back, they'll have a little more respect for me! You leave that to me, just get me a gun," I said.

"Okay, Harry, we are not Bonnic and Clyde here, but I do agree we've got to do something or we will be killed very soon," she said.

"Okay, babe, please go and call Larry and be very careful when you leave the hotel. Look around and make sure you are not followed. Make sure when you use a phone, it is not one directly outside this hotel, just in case they can trace it," I said.

"Don't be so paranoid, Harry." Rachel smiled. "And trust me, I'm not that stupid. I'm sorry. I'm just so damned edgy. I want us to come out of this alive, and I love you. Yes, I really love you. I told you, Harry,

I'm in it all the way to the end with you at my side," she said as she came closer and then kissed me hard. "Let's fuck, Harry, this shit makes me horny."

"Yes, baby, it does the same to me."

I took her in my arms and pushed her gently onto the bed, while I was pulling up her skirt. She grabbed my belt and flipped it open and pulled it out from my pants. The next thing I knew was I licking her neck and then her beautiful round nipples and slowly making my way down to her vagina.

"Fuck me, bitch, fuck me hard," I yelled.

"Oh yes, give it to me. Give it to me everywhere. Oh, Harry, I love you so much. Nobody fucks as good as you do, nobody."

We must have made love for an hour or two. All I know was I was spent and Rachel was fast asleep. I guess we won't call Larry today; we'll get a fresh start tomorrow.

Wednesday, February 6, 1957

"What time is it?" Rachel said in a sleepy, sexy voice.

"I think it's about eight in the morning."

"Shit, we have a lot to do. Let's get the fuck out of bed, now, Harry, now!"

Rachel jumped into the shower, and I flipped on the TV as I sat there on the edge of the bed, waiting for Rachel to get done. She just didn't like two in the shower, it fucked up her hair.

"Okay, all done, it's yours now, Harry!"

"Thanks, you look great. Don't forget that you want to look like 'one of the crowd,' so dress very low-key."

"What about breakfast, Harry?" Rachel said as she started picking out her wardrobe for the day.

"Check to see if they have room service and order up some shit."

As I headed to bathroom, I saw Rachel pick the phone. She was really getting better and better every day. After enjoying a breakfast of eggs, bacon, and coffee, we planned our day.

"I will stay here in the room so that no one will see me by accident or design," I said to Rachel. "I'll watch some TV and read a little and wait for you to get back. Please, Rachel, don't take any unnecessary risks.

Watch to see that you are not being followed and do not call here unless you are sure you are at a secure phone and alone," I said.

"I got it. Please don't worry. I'll take care of things. I'm a big girl and will make you proud. By the way, Harry, I love you so much, especially when you worry about me."

With that said, she hugged me and left to take care of the things we need to stay alive. I spent the rest of the day just sitting around the room and watching TV, my highlight being when the maid came in to do the room. I went out of the room, but did not go downstairs. I went up to the roof, where no one would see me, or so I thought. There I was on the Thirtieth floor and walking up the staircase to the roof, when I saw someone who looked very suspicious. At the top of the stairs, I saw a dark suit—about two hundred and twenty pounds, no taller than 5 10 , with greased back hair. His back was to me, so he didn't see me start up the stairs. I backed down the two steps I had taken, my heart beating so fast that I thought he'd hear it. I thought he turned to look down just as I turned the corner, but I couldn't be sure. How did they find me so soon? I took the stairs down—two at a time—and headed to my room. The maid had just finished and was on the way out as I entered. I poured myself a shot of Crown Royal and sat down on the edge of the bed to think. A shot of whisky makes you feel stronger when you are in a state of shock, as I was.

I could not reach Rachel and I really couldn't leave the hotel. Trouble was outside my room, and I was certain they were watching the elevators and the front and back entrances. "This was going to be very tricky as I was at a terrible disadvantage. I couldn't alert Rachel, and calling anyone might make a lot more trouble or get me killed. Fuck what do I do about this? Rachel would be a sitting duck when she returned or did they grab her already? They didn't know what room I was in. If they did, I wouldn't be sitting here right now. Could they have grabbed Rachel? I didn't think so and she would never rat me out. I told myself to remember Arnold Vignola's words. "Trust no one, Harry, no one." "Harry, stop thinking and remember you are smarter than they are. They won't stick around all day and eventually they will leave, especially when they don't see any activity." I figured they must be checking out a lot of hotels once they discovered we did not go home last night. There was nothing to do other than to wait for Rachel; this was going to be a long day.

At 4:00 p.m., Rachel called, "Darling, it's me," she said.

"I can't tell you how glad I am to hear your voice."

"Is everything all right?"

"Listen to me, Rachel, don't say a word until I finish. I went out of the room for few minutes and saw one of their goons on the roof area," I said in a very perplexed voice.

"What the hell? You were not supposed to leave the room. Can't you follow your own advice?" she screamed at me.

"I know, I know, but the maid was here, so I thought it best that I leave for a few minutes. Don't worry, he didn't see me. But I don't know if they are still here or what. We have to be very careful from here on. Please tell me what happened today."

She started to speak in a much calmer voice, "Listen to me carefully. I spoke with the man, and he assured me he had nothing to do with the hit. He set up a meeting with me for seven tonight. He will bring me the item you asked for, even though he thinks you are really fucked up if you think you can handle it that way. Here's what we got to do. I can't come back there until I know the coast is clear. I got to meet the man at seven, so I will hang out where I am until then. I will call you after my meeting, and you may have to leave the hotel and change places or I will be able to get back in. I am watching every step I take and making sure no one recognizes me. I am not sure you will recognize me either. Just hang in there. Do nothing until you hear from me. Don't order any food and don't answer the door, just hang tight until we formulate a plan to get out of there."

With that, she hung up, and I was no nearer to a solution then I was before. I still knew nothing but couldn't do a thing about it, for now! Time passed very slowly or it seemed that way to me—sitting there in the room, not knowing if there is somebody outside my door waiting to gun me down. Finally, Rachel called. It was ten thirty, pretty late, but I was happy just to hear her voice.

"How are you doing? I'm sorry I'm so late, but it took time as I had to be sure I wasn't followed and that Larry wasn't followed," she said.

"I am just happy to hear your voice. Please tell me what happened and what do we do from here?"

I was really on edge, and I knew that my voice let her know that, but there was very little I could do, I was scared.

"First you have to get out of there. I can't come to you. Larry says the place is being watched as well as every other hotel in the area, so get the hell out and get out without anyone seeing you."

I panicked. "How the hell am I going to do that?" I cried.

"Shit. I don't know, but that's what you got to do tonight," she said.

"Listen, Rachel, how will I know who to look for? How will I know where the fucking Mob guy is waiting? How will I get out of here?" I was getting real scared.

"Okay, listen to me. Relax, you're no good if you panic," Rachel said calmly. "If you are frightened, you will make mistakes. So just relax, have a drink, and let's take this step by step, okay?"

"Okay, what do you want me to do?" I said into the phone.

Rachel spoke up, trying to put some authority into her voice, "Go to the closet, you'll find some of my clothes hanging there. Put something on that will make you look like a woman. Try to look and act feminine. They're looking for a couple or a guy not for a chick. Seeing that it's this late, the hotel will have less people hanging around, so you will be able to spot these assholes easily. Act like a hooker if you can and forget everything else. Leave everything behind. We'll get new clothes tomorrow! I picked up a lot of money from the man, so we don't have to worry about that! Once you get out the front door, start walking toward Forty-Second Street and mix with the crowd. This is the hour hookers do well. Just be careful, you don't overdo it, you might get picked up by the cops." She was cool as a cucumber. I couldn't believe it, but she was there and solid as a rock.

"Okay, where do I go from there?" I said.

"Walk along Forty-Second until you get to Third. You will see a black Caddie driving slowly to your left. Be sure you are walking on the right side of the street and you are going toward Third Avenue When the car slows down, to almost no speed, the rear door will open, jump in, and shut up. These are Larry's guys, and they will bring you to me. Now you must leave in the next fifteen minutes and walk at a normal pace and act like you are looking for a john. Now get to it, Harry. Get your ass into something, hurry. I need you, so don't let anything happen. I love you!"

I hung up and quickly went to the closet to choose some appropriate hooker outfit. It wasn't easy. It took me nine minutes to get into a dress, shave my legs, and build a pair of tits. I then put on lipstick, eye shadow, and other crap that hookers do. And I must admit I looked pretty good. I found a hat so that I could hide my hair or lack of it. The only problem was the shoes.

She only had pumps in the closet, and they were two sizes too small. But I made do, I had no other choice. I grabbed her coat and threw it over my shoulders. I couldn't wear it—the sleeves would be short, and it would be a dead giveaway. I went to the door and opened it just enough to see if anyone was in the hall or not. I stepped into the hallway and so far I couldn't see anyone, as I closed the door and began the walk to the elevator. What a break! I thought, no one on the elevator, maybe this will work, when the bell rang. The car stopped and the door opened, and a guy and a hooker were in the car. She gave me dirty look, like I was on her turf. But her guy was so fucked up that he didn't know what was happening. He kept on putting his head on her tits and mumbling. This was a stroke of luck. If I could use her, I could easily fool the goons! I was planning alternative routes of escape, in case there was trouble—get rid of the shoes and run barefoot, and throw away the coat and run like hell. I looked at the hooker as a plan came into my mind. I had to work fast, as the elevator will be in the lobby any second. I must take a chance. What can I lose? It can't get any worse, and this is my only chance.

I said to the hooker, "Want to make a fast C-note?"

"Hey, you're not a broad. What do want me to do? You gay, a tranny, who the fuck are you?" the hooker said.

"Shh, just listen, my wife has some guys looking for me, and I don't want to get into any shit with her. If I can just walk out with you guys—like arm in arm so that anyone looking will see two hookers and one john—then, once we hit the street, I will go my way and you go on yours. Please, she's really been a bitch about all this, and I can't afford to get caught!"

She looked at me and said, "Two hundred, and you got a deal."

I quickly pulled out two one hundred dollar bills and gave it to her just as the door opened, and there we were in the lobby—the real hooker and her guy and I. I went out hugging real tight. She did me a solid by acting like we were two bitches working together and had a real sucker with us. I saw out of the corner of my eye—one goon standing near the front door and picked up another standing just left of the elevator bank. They were there all right, but they were looking for a man not a hooker. One of the goons looked our way and then went back to his newspaper.

We went outside and the hooker said, "Just keep going, we'll let up after this block. Thanks for the two hundred. It was the easiest bread I have made in weeks."

We reached the corner of Fifty-Seven and Broadway, and she went straight and I went east on Fifty-Seventh, breathing a little easier. I reached Madison Avenue and turned right toward Forty-Second Street, trying to walk as normally as possible in lady's shoes. I kept walking constantly looking back, sideways, and in every direction possible to see if anyone suspicious was near. So far so good. I finally reached Forty-Second Street and turned left toward Lexington and stayed on the right-hand side as instructed. I walked at a very normal pace, constantly looking behind me. Finally, I saw this big black car coming along real slow and very close to the curb. As it approached me, the rear door opened, and a voice yelled out, "Get the fuck in here. Come on, hurry up."

I reached out with my left hand and grabbed a piece of the open door and then just jumped into the back of the car. The door closed, and the car picked up speed as we moved on. I saw a big Italian with shoulders the size of an airplane wing and hands to boot sitting besides me and looking at me as if I was a piece of shit.

"Nice to have you on board. I'm Luigi Bolla, and I'm going to take good care of you. Larry said to make sure you were safe, always. So you listen to me and everything will be okay. Don't be a hero," he said.

"Hey Luigi," I said half out of breath, "I'll do what you say, man, whatever you say.

Let's just get out of here, quick!"

"Harry, you look great. If I didn't have a wife I'd be chasing you." He laughed so hard that I thought he'd have a heart attack.

"Hey, I'm Frank, and you do look sweet. What you'd charge for a blow job?"

I looked up and said, "Cut the shit. This was the only way I could get out of the hotel without being killed."

Frank just smiled and said, "I was just fucking with your head, soon you'll be out of those things, and you can get some rest."

I looked out the window, and it seemed like we were headed toward the Holland Tunnel. So we were either going to Jersey or some place in that general direction. We drove for hours or at least it seemed like it. I looked out the window, and we were now on route Eighty West, going toward the Delaware Water Gap.

"Hey, guys, how far is this place?"

"Relax," Luigi said, "we'll soon be there."

Thursday, February 7, 1957

It was still dark, and we have been travelling for at least four hours. It must have been near four in the morning; I lost track of time. Finally we pulled off the main road and turned on to a narrow winding road that was very dark. If anyone was following us, we would easily see their headlights, and on this road, there is no way one could drive without the lights on. I looked out the window and could see for miles; the sky was crystal clear, and there was no sign of life, nothing was moving but us. It seemed like this road had stretched on and on without an end. Soon we arrived at a steel gate that was closed. Frank pulled the car into the drive, stopped, and got out. He punched some numbers into a keypad, and as the gate opened, he slowly returned to the car. We moved forward slowly, as I watched Frank look back to make sure the gate was closing as it should. We drove at least a mile or two on a one-lane road and finally came to a bridge that crossed a partially frozen river.

On the other side of the bridge was a circular driveway that seemed to go on forever, and at the center was a house that was one of the biggest I have ever seen. It could have easily been a hotel, but the absence of cars led me to believe we were probably the only occupants. We crossed the bridge, and as we did, every light in the area went on and illuminated the area as if it was midday. I also saw people walking along the driveway as we approached the house. There were—I counted—six guys aiming their guns directly at the car. I spied additional troops perched on the roof of the building with their guns aimed at the surrounding area, in case there were others behind. I heard the barking of dogs but could not see any. We pulled up to the front door, and Frank quickly got out and ran to my side to open the door. I stepped out with Luigi right behind me.

"Just walk directly to the house, we'll be fine," Frank said in a hoarse voice.

We entered the house, and two guys greeted us at the door. "Welcome home, Luigi, how are things going?" a tall guy with long wavy blond hair said.

"Just tired. Driving all fucking night doesn't make me happy," replied Luigi.

"Hey," a thick shouldered, fat neck guy, with arms that looked like cannons with hands protruding and looked like a killing machine, said, "Just go right in and make yourself at home. Kitchen ain't open yet, but I'll get one of the boys to rustle you up some java."

I looked at Luigi and said, "Where is Rachel?"

He looked at me as if I was nuts and said with a smile, "She'll be here after lunch, so relax, take a shower, and get some sleep. Make yourself look and smell great for her. You don't want to look all worn out."

"Okay," I said. "Where is my room? I am really tired and want to get out of these fucking ladies' clothes. What a day to remember, or should I say forget!"

The big-shouldered guy came back into the room and looked at me. "I'm Mario. I run da joint here. If you need anything, just call me. Got dat?" he said.

"Sure thing. Just show me where my room is, I need sleep real bad," I said.

"Sure," he said, "follow me and make sure you always tell me where you're going, capish? Do not leave the house, even for a walk. It's my job to take care of you, and I ain't gonna let anythin' happen to ya."

We walked up a winding staircase to the second floor. All I could see is door after door on one side of the hallway. The place was big with plenty of rooms, an army must sleep here, I thought. We walked down the hallway until Mario stopped in front of the third door and opened it. I looked in and couldn't believe my eyes; the place was unreal. The room was the size of three rooms with its own bathroom, shower, steam/sauna room, a sitting room, and a bedroom to boot. The windows overlooked the grounds, as it was just getting light outside, and I could see a big mountain in the background with tall evergreen trees. What a sight! What a place! Everything looked so clean and peaceful.

"Here you are," Mario said. "Take it easy. Have a little sleep, and we will call you later. If you need anything, just call on the intercom over here"—he showed me a small box that I thought was a cosmetic container—"Just push the top down and then speak, your request will be taken care of at once, or I'll kill the fucker who doesn't do it, capish?"

"Sure thing, Mario," I replied. I just wanted to sleep. "I need to sleep, please let me sleep."

I took off the ladies' clothes and was out like a light the second my head hit the pillow. When I woke up, I was a little disorientated as it was still light and it was a little difficult to put everything in order. I drove all night and was taken to a place somewhere in Pennsylvania in a house that belonged to I really don't know who. Things started to come back to me as I jumped into the shower and felt human again. What time was it? Where was Rachel? I jumped out of the shower and hit my intercom.

"Yeah, what do you want?" a voice grunted back.

"What time is it?"

"It's four thirty. Are you hungry?"

"No, I will wait. Where is Rachel?" I said.

"She will be here in fifteen minutes. Keep your shirt on, Harry," the voice said.

"Okay, okay, I'll be down in a few minutes, if it's okay with you!" I said.

"Just call me when you're ready, and Mario will come up and get you. We don't want you walking around by yourself."

The voice clicked off, and I was in my room alone again. I checked out the closet and found plenty of clothes that would fit me. I put on a pair of jeans and a sweater, combed my hair, and put some Brylcreem on it to keep it back and called down, "Hey, guys, I'm ready."

Mario came to the room within five minutes and motioned to me to follow him. We went downstairs and into a kitchen area, where they had a few guys playing poker, and grabbed a pot of coffee and poured in a cup.

"Mario, when does Rachel arrive?" I asked easily, trying not to be a pain in the ass.

"I spoke with her driver, and she should be here in a few minutes. We are taking a very different route to get her here undetected. We had to be very careful that we are not being followed by anyone. Also remember, we got to be careful that no one finds out about this location or that you are out of New York. You are not supposed to leave the state, so we've got to lie low, capish?"

I never gave it much thought, but Mario was right.

"What happens if they do find out?" I asked.

"It depends who finds out. If it is the feds, they'll lock you up and throw away the key. They'd say you were ready to run, and even if you tell them you were just trying to save your own life, no one would believe it. If it's the Mob, you would be dead and dat would be dat," Mario said in a very deadpan manner.

I guess I'd better just relax and do what I can to stay alive for now.

Finally, Rachel arrived. She looked like shit, but what can you expect after hours in a car. And who knows where she spent last night.

"Great to see you, honey," I said as I went over and kissed her.

"Oh, Harry, I've spent the last twenty-four hours running around in circles getting here. Let's sit down and talk. We've got a lot to go over," she said in a tired voice. I took her arm and led her to the staircase.

Mario looked on and said, "Don't forget to check in with me whenever you want to go anywhere."

We went up the stairs to our room, and once the door was shut behind us, I grabbed Rachel and hugged her and kissed her very passionately.

"Do you want to shower? Do you want to change clothes? Tell me what you want to do before we talk, you must be tired!" I said sincerely.

"No, Harry, we got to talk and decide what we're going to do, and we got to do it now. Larry is on his way here, and he will not take any shit from us or anyone else. We got to make some very serious and dangerous decisions, now!"

Her voice was tense, and her emotions showed on her face. She was drawn like I have never seen before. She was afraid, no doubt about it.

"Okay, honey," I said, "try to relax and take it slow and real easy and talk to me. We can work it out together."

She moved closer to me and sat me down on the edge of the bed and looked into my eyes. "All right, Harry, here it is. You worked for Larry and you know just what went on in that office. You knew the guys who collected, you knew the vigorish that was collected, and you know the penalties. Larry didn't worry about you after all you are family and he thought a college graduate would help make the business more legitimate. You brought class to a loan shark. While you were working there, the feds were sitting outside in cars, vans, and who knows what else, taking pictures, taping conversations, and tapping the phones. They saw every soldier from every family come and go out of your office. They saw every racetrack tout come in and could only imagine what they wanted, as they watched and watched and watched some more. They finally decided that you were the weakest link, the best one to grab and that you will tell them everything they need to know to back up their films and tapes. The tapes of the telephone conversations are no good unless they can put a face and a name to them. They figured you knew every transaction and could identify each family member and place them with a crime. You could help them fuck up the Mob where it hurts the most, right in their operations. J. Edgar Hoover has gone wild with this development, as he wants to bust organized crime and needs an informer to confirm that the Mafia actually exists. You are it, Harry. They have never had inside information before, and now they think they have the guy who will help them confirm everything. They need you, Harry. They need to know how the Mob really works. You know what I mean, Harry? Once they decided to pick you up, they also let a few things slip out—stuff like Larry Casparizzi's son-in-law, Harry Miller, is cooperating with them. It looks like a deal was made, and Hoover decided that it was a calculated risk but one well worth it to find some jerk to help them, as they start to build their cases against the big boys. Once the Mob guys heard these rumors, they reported back to the big boss. The families called a meeting, and it was decided that a hit be ordered on you now, even if you are not the leak. They did not want to take any chances. The Gambino family was given the job, and the Bonanno family were to back him up. Not so bad so far, eh? Well, it gets worse, Harry. They didn't call Larry to this meeting and decided that they would whack him as well. This is war, Harry. They have gone to the mattresses and will only be happy when they rub us all out. That includes Larry, you, and me. I hope you do understand that!"

I saw the anguish on her face and could hear it in her voice. There was no place to run, and we just had to work this out. I started to speak, "Rachel, please, listen to me. We will handle this. We will, I promise! I won't let anything happen to you, I swear it."

"Great, Harry, now you are the protector. You can't even fire a gun and you're soft-hearted. So how are you going to protect me, let alone yourself?" she said.

"I don't know just yet, but, Rachel, you know I am smart, smarter than these fucking assholes. I'll figure it out. I promise you, I will."

She started to take off her clothes and throw them all over the room. She was crying badly now as she kept muttering, "I don't want to die. I don't want to die! I'm too young. I didn't do anything, and I know even less. Why me? Why pick on us? Fuck, all my life I had to hide, lie, and never really be me because Larry was my father. What are we going to do, Harry, what?"

"Go take a shower, you will feel better, and I can think. By the way, did you bring me the gun I asked for?" I said sternly.

"Yes," she said as she took it out of her handbag and handed it to me. "He said it is clean, whatever that means."

"Thanks, Rachel, now go take your shower. We'll discuss this later," I said.

It was seven thirty and dark when Larry arrived. Another army came along with him, and guards were doubled. Rachel and I were sitting in the main room with the fireplace, burning up a storm. We got up immediately upon hearing Larry's voice.

"Hi, Dad," Rachel shouted, "it's great to see you. Are you all right?"

"I'm fine, we got to talk, now!" he said as he motioned to Mario. "Where can we have a little privacy?" Larry said.

"Just follow me, boss," Mario said. "I'll make sure no one disturbs you."

We followed Mario down the hall to a large room that had another fireplace, a couple of sofas, and a few posh arm chairs and a big pool table at one end and a bar at the other.

"Make yourselves comfortable. Just call me if you need anything, boss, I'll just be outside the door to make sure you are not disturbed."

Mario left the room, and Rachel sat down on one of the sofas and motioned me to sit besides her. Larry didn't sit; he just paced around and mumbled to himself.

Finally he said, "Harry, you know we're in deep shit! I told Rachel yesterday that an all-out war has begun. I didn't ask for it, believe me, things are getting out of hand. We got to make some decisions and take some steps now or someone's going to get killed."

"Larry," I said, "whatever you want me to do I'll do, but fuck, how do we fight these animals?"

"I sent word to the commission that I want a meeting. The Bonanno, Gambino, Colombo, Genovese, and Lucchesse families must attend this meeting so that we can get this shit worked out. I answer to Vito, but it is hard for him to intervene unless I can show some kind of proof that I am with him and always has been. I spoke to Anthony Provenzano, and he said, he would talk to Vito and try to get this hit taken off, but we can't trust anyone."

"Okay, Larry, where do we go from here?" I said. "I was told I could be arrested and placed in protective custody. By being out of the state it seems I have violated some agreement. I can assure you I don't know of any agreement as none exists. It seems I'm the one getting fucked no matter what I do. No shit, guys, we are all getting fucked because the cops set all this up to get a war started. They wanted us to fight among ourselves and maybe they will find a jerk like you Harry to tell them things they don't know. This asshole Hoover has a hard on for the family and believes there is organized crime, he will stop at nothing to prove his theory," Larry said. "I just don't see what this talk is doing to help us?"

Rachel stood up and said, "Come on guys let's plan something that will make this all go away or at least a plan to protect our lives."

"Okay, here is what I think we should do. I called for a commission meeting on Saturday, until then you guys stay right here," Larry said. "Don't call anyone, don't leave the house, and don't lose hope. Harry, you call the inspector and tell him you are hiding and will call him on Monday in case he needs you. This way we eliminate any concerns he may have, and he will not expect you to stay in touch until Monday. Remember, Harry, you wouldn't last half as long in the slammer. So going in is not an option. Mario," Larry shouted, "get in here."

It took Mario a second to respond, and as fast as a lightning, he was standing next to Larry. "What's up, boss?" Mario said.

"I am leaving these kids with you. Protect them with your life. They go nowhere without you. Have their food tasted and make sure their wine is the best. I want you to teach Harry how to shoot and keep them busy and happy. Can you handle all that, Mario?"

"Easy, boss. They are taken care of. Don't you worry about a thing!"

"Oh by the way, Mario, trust no one. I mean, no one," Larry said. "Kids, I got to get going. I'll talk to you soon, just listen to Mario, and things will be okay."

"I sure as hell hope so, Larry," I said. "I'll hear from you on Sunday, by that time I'll be a crack shot." I smiled, and so did Larry as he kissed Rachel on both the cheeks and left the room.

Friday, February 8, 1957

I woke up at eight thirty. I must have been very tired to sleep that long. Rachel was lying besides me, still asleep. I jumped out of bed and took a quick shower and tried to leave the room, but the door was locked. I knocked on the door, and Mario opened it and let me out.

"Where are you going?" Mario said.

"I have to call the inspector so that there won't be any heat. Where can I use a safe phone, Mario?"

He locked the door and said, "Just follow me. Stay close and say nothing to anyone. We'll call from the other room."

"Is this phone safe? Can anyone listen in? Can it be traced to here? If it is not safe, then we have to use a pay phone," I told Mario.

"No worries, no one can listen, and the line is not traceable. When I say something is safe, I mean it is safe. Do what you have to do," Mario said with a smile.

I placed the call to Inspector Johnson and informed him that I am presently incognito and will call him on Monday to see if he should need me. He told me that he heard here and there that things were not so comfortable for me and anytime I chose to come to see him, he could and would arrange protection around the clock. I thanked him and hung up.

Rachel woke up at noon and wanted to spend the day relaxing by walking through the grounds and just taking in all the nature that surrounded this magnificent retreat. I spent the day learning how to shoot the gun that Larry left for me. Shooting a gun was easy; aiming a gun was very hard. Mario was very patient with me as he showed me how to compensate for height and distance and my own unsteady hand. By the end of the day, I was tired, and my arm hurt, but I felt more confident with a gun in my hand now. I felt I was ready for anyone who decided to shoot at me. I told Rachel how good I felt with a gun on my person and that it made me feel strong, almost invincible. Having the gun made me more relaxed and confident and gave me the feeling that we would survive.

Saturday, February 9, 1957

A new day, and hopefully some answers. I could not understand how these guys could live here day after day doing nothing more than eating, playing cards, and sleeping. Boring—that's how I saw it. This was not a vacation for me, but I was thankful they were here taking care of Rachel and me.

I spent half my day practicing with my new handgun and then just relaxing with Rachel. About 6:00 p.m., I got a phone call from Larry, "The hit is off, you can go outside, and you can go home. I gave assurances to the commission that you would not ever cooperate with the feds and that you were being set up. Be very careful, Harry. I'm sure that someone in the DA's office is a snitch and is telling them what goes on or is a double agent and gives the Mob the information the DA's office wants. Say nothing, trust no one, and be careful. I don't trust the commission, and I don't trust the DA. So my advice is to be careful and watch what you say and to whom. I need time to take steps to protect myself and my boys, so don't fuck anything up. My reputation is on the line, Harry, if you let me down, my life isn't worth a shit. Don't fuck me up and don't cooperate with them. I hope it is clear to you, because if you do decide to work with those ratbags, I will kill you myself. Respect is what we need, Harry, and remember "omertà" always. Let me speak to Rachel, and I will instruct Mario to take you home. Just be careful and make sure you know how to use your gun."

I gave Rachel the phone and let her have her moment alone with Larry. I called Mario over and said, "It looks like we straightened out things for the moment, but I don't give a shit. I will use that gun if someone starts with me again. Hey, I just wanted to say thanks for caring and being there for me. You're a very good man, Mario. If you ever need anything, just give me a call, and I'll be there for you."

Mario drove the car to the front door, and Rachel and I jumped into be driven home. Mario didn't want anyone to know where we're going, so he drove the car and didn't take any of the guys with him. I was still very nervous and wary of everything. This was a nightmare, and it was just beginning and I would not like it to end with my demise. During the ride back, I cautioned Rachel that our place is still bugged, so we must be very careful on what we say when we are at home. We will go out for dinner and plan our future when we are alone and can talk safely. When we decide where to go we will not discuss it at home. We arrived at our place late in the day and said our good-byes to Mario.

Upon leaving, he said to me, "Be very careful and trust no one. Most of these guys are liars and would just as soon kill you for a dime."

He gave me a phone number and told me to guard it with my life and if I ever needed him, just call. We decided to just kick back and relax and order in some Chinese. Tomorrow would be a day of getting our shit together and preparing for an all-out war. This situation would not go away as easily as Larry wanted me to believe. I must be ready to face this head-on.

Sunday, February 10, 1957

Rachel and I just laid back and talked a lot about us and nothing relevant to the situation. We decided to go out for brunch at the Mayflower Hotel, where they had a real super brunch, and most importantly, we would have the opportunity to be alone.

We discussed what we were going to do as we both knew this was not going to go away as easily as Larry had said. These Mafia families have just postponed things and would find a time when I am not on my guard and would try to whack me. There was no need to have my body found because the message was clear to all, "Talk and you are dead." To disappear was a sufficient signal that no one escapes the Mob's justice if you cross them. And even though we assured them I would not assist the feds, neither of us believed that they bought that shit. So what do we do? Who do we trust in this situation? Larry was not to be trusted even if he was Rachel's father; he wasn't mine. Once they get rid of me, Rachel would be safe, and Larry would take care of her. I was disposable, and they were going to continue chasing until they get rid of me. No question in my mind, but how do I protect myself? Rachel suggested we call Inspector Sam Johnson and level with him, if he didn't already know about the situation. If we worked something out, maybe we could buy a new identity, move to a new town or country. There had to be one person we could trust, and we've got to find that person before it is too late. At least I knew Rachel was with me and she was willing to die for me or with me. How many guys could have a woman like this? I was a lucky guy to have Rachel, even if her father was a mobster.

We spent the day just hanging out and trying to resolve what we should do. One thing we decided was that we would leave our apartment tomorrow and find something else. We would not tell Larry or anyone else where it was and would hope that no one finds out. I put all my money together, including the money Rachel gave me, which she got from Larry. That brought my little fortune to a little over $700K. I then told Rachel that I needed a little air and would take a walk. I told her I will be back soon and left the apartment. I called Moe and agreed to meet at his office on Fifty-Seventh and Seventh in an hour.

I met Moe and gave him the money and told him that there would be additional funds coming in and I would make sure it was dropped off at his place. No one must know about our friendship, not even Rachel. I don't want you to be compromised ever and I don't want to ruin the trust the Mob has in you.

I told Moe what happened in the last few days and he said, "Harry, get the hell out of town. You will have to get rid of Rachel and travel alone. Change your identity now and start anew. This is the only way you can save Rachel and yourself. I'll get in touch with Johnson and explain. I'll tell him that you will be available when he needs you. I'll be your middleman,

Harry, but please don't waste any time and do it now! These guys are not going to stop looking for you. Rachel's life isn't worth a plug nickel if you stay with her. This is the sacrifice you both have to make if you are to keep her alive and keep yourself mobile and undercover," he said.

I left Moe's office feeling a little better, but knowing that I must set a plan in motion real fast. I thought I would go see Arnold Vignola tomorrow to discuss matters and see what could be done. I did not trust Arnold as I know he worked for Larry and got big bucks from him. His only loyalty was to money, and I was nothing more than a disposable asshole whose value was set only in how much Larry paid him.

Monday, February 11, 1957

I woke up very early and looked out to see snow flurries falling. I spent an hour or so writing instructions for Rachel. I didn't want to speak because of the bugging of our place. It was safer for both of us to leave her a note.

I woke Rachel. "Honey, I was thinking it over all night. Maybe it would be best if you stay here while I see Arnold," I said. I then pointed to the paper I had written and had her look it over.

> When you wake up, I want you to go to the bank, close our account, and withdraw all our money. If they don't have enough cash, get a certified check for the balance made payable to yourself. Stop in at the supermarket and act like you are shopping for our dinner. Buy a few things and put them in a shopping bag and return home. I will call you and let it ring twice and hang up. Once you hear two rings, know it's time to leave. Do not take anything with you. We can always buy new things. Please don't even think of taking any essentials. Make sure no one sees you, act as if you are going out shopping, in case you should miss being watched or followed. Meet me in front of the Pierre Hotel. Go into the lobby and go to the ladies room and then carefully look out to make sure there is no one following you. Then walk around the lobby further and check to see that no one is following you and then leave by the front door. I will be in one of the buggies on the Park side on Fifty-Seventh

Street. You will see me. Walk over and get in unless you feel you're being watched. If you think someone is watching you, just pass the buggy and keep walking, I will see who is following you and will take care of them. You just keep on walking no matter what you hear. Keep going, and I will catch up to you as fast as I can. No matter what, keep walking and don't turn around. Just trust me, honey, it has to be this way. They will never leave us alone. We have to stand up and fight back.

Rachel just stared at me and nodded her head. I kissed her on the lips and then held her tight. I went to our small safe I had installed in the floor, under the rug, and emptied it. There was about $50K in there and I left. I had on my heavy coat on over my jeans, but most importantly, I had my gun and plenty of rounds with me and fifty grand in cash for an emergency.

I made my way to Vignola's office and sat in the waiting room, while the receptionist announced that I was here without an appointment.

"Please follow me, Mr. Miller. Mr. Vignola will see you. Please be aware that he has an appointment in fifteen minutes," she said.

"Thanks, I'll keep that in mind," I said as I walked into Arnold's ornate office.

"What emergency do you have, Harry?"

"Nothing very serious except that people are trying to kill me," I stated in a concerned voice.

"Sit down, Harry, and tell me what's it all about? I thought Larry took care of everything, so now you can relax," he said as he motioned me to a chair.

"I don't want to take up too much of your time. I just have to be clear on where we stand and just how much I can tell you."

Vignola stood up with an indignant look and stared at me as he began shouting at me, "What kind of shit are you pulling with me? Who the fuck do you think you are, you little piece of shit, accusing me of being a whore?"

"Hold on a minute," I shouted louder. "I didn't come here to fight with you. I just wanted to establish a few things between us. I am not accusing you of sharing information with anyone or being disloyal or unethical to me or any of your clients, but I have been fucked over, and things just don't look that good. Now just relax, and I'll pretend I didn't hear those insults. I only want to know where I stand with you and what will you do for me."

He looked at me, eyes bulging and his face red with anger. He must have thought it best to cool off and talk about it. "Okay, Harry," he said in a civil voice and sat down behind his desk. "What is the problem and why do you think I would betray you?"

"Look, Mr. Vignola," I used his last name only to diffuse the situation. I thought a little sign of respect would salve the most chaffed attitude. "I have been followed everywhere I have gone. Two goons watched the hotel where I stayed, and only because Larry intervened with the commission, did a hit on my life get removed, or so they say. Now I am here and can't trust anyone, as my life is on the fucking line."

He fidgeted in his chair and said, "So why do you accuse me?"

"I am not accusing you. I am just asking where you stand! Larry pays you to take care of me. Do you report to Larry?"

He stared at me, and once again his veins began to stand out. "Look, Harry, even if Larry pays me, I keep all our information confidential. I don't talk to anyone about you except you, you got that?" he said through clenched teeth.

"I got it and thanks for confirming that you are my attorney no matter what," I said as nicely as I could. "What I am going to say better remain between us, or your life as well as mine won't be worth a shit."

"Wait a minute, Harry," he jumped up and said. "You can fire me as your attorney if you feel I am not on your team, but don't threaten me."

I paid no attention to his last tirade and continued on, "All I'm saying is if word got out, they'd kill you as easily as me. Here is what I want to do as I feel it is the only way out for me. I can't get a fair shake with the Mob, whatever they say today will not hold true tomorrow. The bullshit that the hit has been removed is nothing more than a stall. They will ease off and then when everything is quiet, they will find me, and I will disappear. Of course, they will all deny that they had anything to do with it. Larry won't give a shit either way, because they won't touch Rachel, and he doesn't care if his son-in-law got whacked. He'll probably say I ran away and left his poor daughter stranded. Regardless of all this, I have to protect myself, if I don't, I'm dead. I think our best bet is to arrange an arrest with the inspector. Take me in and place me somewhere in protective custody in exchange for my fullest cooperation. They have to agree to give me a new identity and arrange for me to leave the country and start a new life elsewhere. Simple as that and, perhaps, I can remain alive. Maybe, I can beat these mother fuckers once and for all? If I don't do this, I am dead. It's just a matter of what day."

His look was one of total disbelief. I thought he'd shit himself as he said, "Are you crazy? Are you a complete nut case? Do you know who you're fucking with? These people will never rest until you die, they'll turn the world upside down to get your ass. And what will they do to me if I am part of this? Why did you have to even tell me about this, why did you?" he said.

"Tell me, Arnold," I said very quietly, "what would you do if you are faced with the same deal? Tell me what the fuck would you do?"

He looked at me and finally sat down, as if he was resigned to this and said, "Harry, I am fucked either way. So what do you want me to do? I think you are insane to even think about cooperating with the feds. In the end, you will get whacked by the Mob or them. Now tell me what you want me to do?"

"Nothing at all, just for the moment, I need to think a little more clearly as to what I am going to do. You have answered my question about your loyalty by showing me very simply how you feel about my cooperation. I will make all the arrangements, and if I cut a deal myself, I will do it on my time and only I will know what the conditions are. This way you will never know when, where, and what is coming down. You can act as surprised as everyone once the news gets out," I said very coolly and without emotion. "All I need from you is to be certain I can count on you when I need you, either in court or in the feds' offices or wherever you will be there to defend me?"

"That's all, that's all," he screamed at me. "Boy, you really want to get me killed, don't you?"

"Listen, Arnold," I screamed back. "If you don't want to be involved then find a way to get out now! I know you won't because you like the bread too much and don't want to fuck up your life style. Be ready to help me or I will kill you myself. I will blow your fucking head off and not think twice about it." I took out my gun and pointed at him.

"Are you crazy?" he nervously said. "Put that away. I'll work with you, I promise. Now put that thing away."

At that moment, his intercom buzzed and a voice said, "Your nine fifteen appointment is here, should I have them wait?"

He spoke into the intercom, "Have them wait, I'll only be a few more minutes."

He looked at me and said, "Harry, I'll be here for you. Please don't ever threaten me again. I love money not violence. But let me tell you one thing, Harry, something you may not know, but need to know now. They have someone inside who is telling them everything. So even if you changed your name and your address, the inside contact will tell them. You see, Harry, money buys lots of different kinds of loyalties, not just lawyers. They have judges, cops, bailiffs, and every other type of person who loves money on their payroll. So agreeing to cooperate would only buy you a better coffin quicker."

I looked at him and bent over his desk, my face no more than a foot away and said, "Thanks for the information, Arnold, just stay cool, and you will survive, fuck me, and I'll kill you. If this is the case, I cannot win by cooperating. You can tell anyone who may ask that I was here today and told you that I am going to disappear. You can tell your Mob bosses that I promised you I will not be helping the feds and I will not hang around. Give them that message, and that should make things easier for you. I hope I never have to use your services. One last word, Arnold, I will return and kill you if I find out you have betrayed me. Let them know that I am not a snitch and I will not help the feds. Make sure you deliver that message." I moved back from his desk, picked up my overcoat and said, "So long, Arnold, be well, you may be hearing from me, I certainly hope that won't be necessary."

With that said, I walked out of his office and went through the waiting room area and noticed that the two guys waiting to go in were guineas that I was pretty certain I had seen before. This did not look good, and now I thought I had told Arnold too much. I kept on walking, as the receptionist called out, "Gentlemen, please follow me. Mr. Vignola will see you now."

I went down the elevator and out on to Lexington looking around in every direction to try and see if was being followed. So far no tail, but who knew what they were talking about upstairs or who Arnold might have called? I walked toward Forty-Second Street and checked out the street in every direction, trying to pick out if I was being followed. It's like being at a baseball game with thirty thousand fans and everyone is leaving at the same time, go figure which one was the assassin? I couldn't see anyone, so I stopped in at a donut shop and went directly to the pay phone; from here I could see the street and could see if someone was coming after me.

I called Inspector Johnson. "Hi, it's me, Harry Miller," I said in a very relaxed tone, "I need to see you, it's very important. We got to meet somewhere private. We got to be certain that no one is following either of us and no one sees me talking with you."

"Well, Harry, what is the problem?" he said.

"I can't speak over the phone. Where can we meet?" I said.

"Okay, let's meet on the corner of Thirteenth and Eighth Avenue. You'll see me standing on the corner. Walk by me without any sign of recognition, and I will follow you. Walk up to Seventh Avenue and turn right, you'll see a little bar halfway down the block on your right side, it's called Clancy's. Go in and sit down at the bar and order a drink. I'll be along in a minute or two. I just want to make sure no one is following us."

"I'll see you in one hour. Is that okay with you?" he said.

"Sure, see you in one hour." I hung up and decided it will take an hour to walk to the meeting place. This way, I can continue to watch for any suspicious characters. I arrived at the meeting place and saw the inspector standing on the corner. I walked by and continued to Seventh Avenue and turned right and walked another sixty feet, and there was Clancy's Bar & Grill. I walked by, just to make sure no one was waiting for me and then turned back and went in and was immediately hit by the darkness of the place; it was a sleazy looking dive with the smell of stale cigarette, tobacco, and beer. I sat down at the bar and couldn't believe that at this hour, someone else would be sitting there. But at the end of the bar, there was a guy that looked drunk already.

"What will it be?" the tall heavyset bartender said.

"A Heineken, please," I said.

"One beer coming up," he said. "By the way, I'm Lou. I own the joint and mix the drinks. What's your moniker?"

"Harry," I replied and tried to act as if I didn't want to talk. I could tell that wasn't going to work. He was going to get a conversation started no matter what! I decided to direct the small talk my way. "I am just on my way to a job interview and decided to have a cold one before I go any further, you know, how it is when you got to impress some jerk just so that he'll give you work. The funny thing is that I probably could get any job I wanted, so why this?" I said.

"Yeah, I know how it is, that's why I started this bar. It ain't much, but it keeps bread on the table, and I ain't going to answer to anyone, except my missus," he said with a laugh.

Just then the inspector walked in and sat down next to me. "Harry, what the hell are you doing here?" he said, "I haven't seen you in years. Let's grab a table and catch up on old times! Are you married? What do you do for a living?"

Of course, this was done for the bartender's benefit so as not to create any suspicion. "Hey, Lou, another beer over here for my buddy," I yelled out.

"Coming right up," Lou yelled back.

We made our way to a back table where we could talk without anyone overhearing us.

After Lou brought the beer, I began to speak in a low but a very relaxed tone. "Sam, I hope you don't mind if I call you Sam. I have a problem, and I'm sure you know it. I want to get out of this mess with my life. I want to be safe and not worry that every day someone is out there looking to kill me. I don't know what I can tell you, because I don't know that much. If I agree to help you, will you help me?"

He looked at me and said, "Look, Harry, I can't promise anything, but I think there is a way we can work together. First, I have to pass this along to my bosses and get their okay. I think they will want some assurances from you about the information and how far are you willing to go. You know this crap, Harry. It is all about the recognition of busting the Mob and who can get credit for grabbing the big guy. I will do what I can, but no promises," the inspector said.

"That is bullshit, and you know it. I will not be set up by you and your group. It makes no sense to me simply because you won't or can't guarantee my safety and allow me a chance at a future. No way, Sam, get real and set down some promises in writing that can be carried out if I am to be your pigeon. Listen, I have been shot at, followed, and kept prisoner by very terrible people. My wife is safe because she's Larry's daughter, and Larry doesn't give a shit if I live or die. I got into this dilemma because of you, and now I am offering my help, but I need some serious assurances," I said.

"I will talk to my bosses and get back to you, Harry," Sam said.

"Just remember, Sam," I said, "I trust you, but you don't know who is on the take in your group so be very careful to whom you talk to and what information you give anyone. You know they have their hands in everyone's pockets. Just be careful."

"How will I get in touch with you, Harry?" he said.

"I'll get in touch with you. Give me a number that is private and safe. I will call you tomorrow at ten in the morning."

He wrote down a number on a napkin and swigged down his beer and left. I followed him a few minutes later and went to the pay phone just outside the bar. I made two phone calls: first I called Mario and asked him to get me an old car and place it behind the Museum of Modern Art in Central Park, and then I called Rachel and let it ring twice and hung up. Now I must get over to the Pierre to meet her and get us on the way to our new life.

I arrived at the Pierre Hotel and immediately hired a buggy. I paid the driver for four hours and promised him a big tip if he just did what I say and see nothing. I sat in the buggy, looking like a tourist, waiting for Rachel to appear. Finally, I saw her come out of the hotel and look around. She saw me but did not walk to the buggy as we planned. She started walking toward Eighth Avenue on Fifty-Seventh Street. I could see a heavy set guy—no mistaking him as a goon—hair greased back and his suit and coat was standard gangster gear. They must all shop at Gangsters Beau Brummell specialty shop. I told the buggy driver to take the buggy along Fifty-Seventh Street, and just walk the horse slowly. I told I would get out shortly and then get back in again, and to just look straight ahead. A few feet down the street, I got out of buggy and began walking behind the goon who was about seventy feet behind Rachel. I walked closer and closer to him and, finally, was only two feet behind him when I pulled out my gun with the silencer attached and fired two shots in his back. He fell at once, as I kept walking. I caught up to Rachel and took her by the arm.

"Let's go this way. Get into the buggy and just act as if we are tourists," I said.

She looked pale but determined to see this through as we got into the buggy.

"Let's take a ride through Central Park, driver," I said and off we went as I looked back and noticed a crowd around someone lying on the sidewalk. I didn't let that bother me, even though it was my first kill, but a very necessary one. Maybe, now the message will be crystal clear. Don't fuck with Harry Miller, he will fuck you up. I was on a high. I never thought killing someone could produce this feeling. I think it was the relief that I could fight back. And most importantly, the message to these guys was that I was not going to be intimidated. Of course, I was not a fool and knew that I had very little chance against these guys. There were too many of them and who knows when they would strike next. But for now, I felt I had the upper hand and felt good about it. For now, no one was following us. I asked the driver to let us off at the end of the Park, just behind the Museum of Modern Art. Mario proved to be the most loyal of all people, and there was the proof—an old car just as requested. Mario placed it there as requested and left the keys under the mat and a tank full of gas.

Thanks to Mario, we were able to get a head start on anyone who might be looking for us. Best of all, no one knew what kind of car Rachel and I drove away toward upstate New York, where we would take a motel for the night and catch our breaths.

Tuesday, February 12, 1957

I woke up and left the motel to find a pay phone I could use to call the inspector. I found his number and made the call.

"Johnson here."

"Hi, it's me," I said. "Can you speak freely?"

"Yes, not a problem. I am alone, and the line has been checked for bugs, we can say whatever we want," he said.

"Well, what news do you have for me?" I said.

"Did you hear about Tony 'the Mouse' Garcia?" he said.

"No, I never heard of him. Who is this Tony?" I said.

"He was shot yesterday on Fifty-Seventh Street near the Pierre hotel. He died this morning they are saying this was a hit by a rival family trying to take over Midtown numbers," the inspector said.

"Sorry, I didn't hear about it," I said. "I was too busy making sure I didn't get killed."

"Well, Harry," he said, "we are willing to give you a new identity and move you out of the state to any place in America you would like. We will give you twenty-five grand to help you get started, and a new passport and some references so that you can get a job. We will give you this in writing and have it ratified by a judge so that you will be assured of our sincerity in this deal." He hesitated then continued, "It all boils down to you. Will you give us everything you know and, if need be, testify in open court? Will you, Harry? That is the key to it all. And by the way, Harry, you will receive immunity from prosecution for any crime you may have committed up to the date of the signed agreement. If you go out and do another crime after that date, you will be prosecuted like anyone else and all help will end."

I thought for a moment and said, "This includes Rachel as well, doesn't it?"

"Of course, it is for both of you," he said.

"I will talk it over with Rachel and call you tomorrow at the same number, same time." I hung up and went back to the motel to talk to Rachel.

Wednesday, February 13, 1957

Rachel and I had agreed that this was the only way out. We couldn't think of any other way and now it all boiled down to trusting the feds. Wow, what a choice!

I called the inspector. "We are ready to accept your terms. We'll cooperate with you, but there are a few things we have to get straight," I said.

"What are they?" Johnson asked.

"Will Rachel be protected while all this is going on?"

"Of course, we understand what we have to do, and we'll do it right," Johnson said.

"When do we get started on this trip?" I said.

"We can start today, but you want something in writing and signed by a judge," Johnson said.

"You bet your ass," I said.

"I need a few days to put all this together. In the meantime, you can stay where you are if you feel safe enough," Johnson said. "Harry, if you want to come in now, you are welcome, but I think it would be best if you stay away from here until we can get all the papers ready and make sure that all those involved are clean," he added.

"I appreciate that, Sam, I really do. Having a snitch in your camp would make this exercise useless and our lives will be like chopped liver," I said.

We agreed that I would call him on Friday and see where we stand. It looked like we would be hiding out for at least four or five days before we could finalize the deal.

"Rachel, let's take a vacation," I ran into our motel room and announced.

"Harry, are you crazy?" she said.

"No, I'm not nuts, but look we have to sit around for at least four or five days until we get some answers from the feds. So why not enjoy ourselves? Who knows this could be the last vacation we take in a long while."

"Okay, Harry," Rachel said, "Where shall we go? Here we are, in upstate New York. It's winter. Atlantic City sucks in winter with nothing really to do. We are close to Canada. Maybe we could go to Montreal. Who would recognize us there? I always wanted to see that city in the winter and I heard they have great restaurants. Okay, Harry, let's do it!"

I looked at her with love in my eyes and with a warm heart and held her close to me. "Okay, let's get packed. If we leave now, we can be there by seven tonight." I started to help Rachel pack our few things, and then I wiped down the room and made sure it was clean and off we went. I checked the paperwork for the car Mario left us to be certain we had some registration if we were stopped. I found the papers that were made out to Ronald Weatherly in Philadelphia. I memorized the address just in case I would have to repeat it to some cop. Our story would be very cut and dried.

I told Rachel, "My friend Ronald lent me his car, if we are ever asked. I don't think we need to worry about it, but just in case. Okay, honey, let's get moving."

We left the motel and headed north along the New York State Thruway. We arrived at the border, crossing at about six thirty.

"Hi," I said as I rolled down my window.

"Name, please, and where were you born," I was asked.

"Harry Miller and my wife, Rachel. We were born in USA," I said.

"What is the purpose of your trip to Canada?"

I responded, "Just a few days to see Montreal in the winter. We have only been here in summer."

He looked into the car and then said, "Have a good time."

"That was easy," I said to Rachel.

She responded, "You know, Harry, I feel free, funny, but I feel we can just keep going, and no one will ever bother us again. It feels great."

"Well, for the next few days, let's forget everything and just have a great time. I'll call Sam on Friday as I promised, and we'll see what plans we might have for the next week, in the meantime, let's party."

Thursday, February 14, 1957

We had taken a room in the Mount Royal hotel—a huge place in the heart of downtown, Montreal on Peel Street, just near St. Catherine Street. We decided to ask the concierge what was going on there and how best to see it all. We wanted to take in some of the local color and have a good time while we still had the chance to do so.

"What is there to do in this beautiful city of yours?" Rachel asked.

"Every kind of store is to be found along St. Catherine Street and some very exclusive shops on Peel Street. If you get tired, then there are so many very good restaurants to stop in and have some great food. Just make a left turn when you exit the hotel, and walk about half a block, that will be St. Catherine Street, and then just turn left and walk and enjoy," the concierge said with an accent that was definitely French.

Across the hotel, we noticed a nightclub called "The Downbeat," and next to it, we saw a great-looking building that seemed like it was there since the early settlers found this city. The facade of this great-looking building was all stone and looked like a medieval castle with a coat of arms that read, "The House of Seagram's." I remembered the name because of the whisky we drank, and also on the way into Montreal, we saw a great big distillery with the Seagram's name on it. We were going to have a great time here. This was a good decision to come here and forget our problems for a few days.

After a full day of exploring, shopping, and just walking a lot, we returned to our hotel room and relaxed. We decided to eat in the hotel's special dining room. It was called The Kon Tiki and was decorated in Polynesian style and looked like a Polynesian hut and served, as we were told, great Polynesian food. It was great to be in this atmosphere, where we could forget the troubles we had. The food was great, and the drinks were even better. And we had our fill of both. After dinner, we decided to just take it easy and get a good night's rest. Tomorrow I would call Sam, and then we could party undisturbed all weekend.

Friday, February 15, 1957

I called Sam, and he told me that it would be at least a week before everything was in place. He assured me that there wasn't going to be any problems, except that he had to make certain everyone involved had 100 percent security clearance. The FBI was working with him, and they were responsible for very tight security. The papers will be signed by Judge Samuel Smyth of the Superior Court of New York and countersigned by Federal Judge, James Cohen. In this way, we will be covered as long as we cooperate and tell the truth. It sounded good to me as I hung up and went back to our room and told Rachel the news and that we had at least a week to kill.

That night we dined at the Polynesian restaurant again and enjoyed it once again. Around 10:00 p.m., we went to the Downbeat nightclub and, after a $20 tip to the doorman and another twenty to the maître d', we got a table near the front and relaxed as we ordered drinks and took in the floor show. I was getting a little hammered when I thought I noticed some guy looking at us in a funny way. After a little while, I was sure we were being watched.

I leaned over to Rachel. "See the guy in the suit, greased hair. Look just over there near the bar."

"Yeah, I see him, Harry. Do you know him?" she asked.

"Hell, no, but why is he looking at us?"

"Let's leave, Harry, let's leave now," she said in a very concerned voice.

"Okay, but don't stare at him. I don't want to let him know we are on to him," I said.

I signaled for the check and got up to leave.

"Don't act as if we are in any rush. Let's get our coats and make as if we're going to another club, Okay, honey?" I said.

We got our coats and went down the stairs to the street and waited a minute to see if the guy was following us. A few doors to the left of the nightclub was a small dress shop that had its doors recessed. We chose to stand back in the doorway so that he could not see us right away. We waited less than a minute and sure enough he came out and looked in both the directions and then panicked when he did not see us. There was no question we were being followed. No one knows we are here. How did this happen? Was the hit sent to Canada as well? I knew that the Mob operated here in Montreal, but didn't know they would send out a hit notice. Carmine Galante was sent to solidify the Mob's interests here in Montreal. I guess the word went out that we were to be eliminated if we ever showed our faces in this part of the world, and no one bothered to inform anyone that the hit had been removed, and you know why, because it was never really cancelled. I didn't carry my gun with me, as

I didn't feel I needed it here. This cannot happen again. I must be well prepared for anything from now on, no matter where I am.

My first concern was to get rid of this guy. I sure as hell didn't want him to know that we were staying at the hotel across the road. We waited in the vestibule of the dress shop to see what direction he took. If he decided to walk in our direction, he would see us within a second or two, and then we would have to try to outrun him or something like that. We waited another minute as people walked by and glanced at us but continued on their way. I guess they thought two lovers in an embrace only deserved a passing glance. Much to our relief, the guy turned right on Peel Street and walked toward St. Catherine Street carefully looking back every few seconds. Finally, he turned left on St. Catherine's Street, now was our chance to get back to the hotel unnoticed. We waited at least five minutes and ran across the street to the hotel and up to our room. Thank goodness, I did not register as Harry Miller; I used the name Ronald Weatherly. "Rachel," I said in a very relaxed voice, "how do you think they knew were here?"

"I just don't know, Harry," she said.

"Did you call anyone when we stopped for gas?" I said.

"Only Larry. Oh my goodness, I never thought they'd tap his phone, he's one of them," she said very worried.

"Well, I guess that's how they got the news. It's a good thing. I didn't tell you which hotel we were staying at, and they don't know what car I am driving," I said.

"Okay, there is no use in worrying how they found out any longer. Let's get our heads together and make some plans. I think we have to get out of Montreal now, the sooner the better. No more phone calls to Larry or anyone. If you do call Larry, please, don't ever tell him where we are or what we are doing, okay?" I said.

"It never ends, never. Who would think my father would have anything to do with our deaths? I'm certain he does not know his phone is tapped," Rachel muttered.

I knew that the Bonanno family was here in Montreal and Carmine Galante was their man here. He was a mean son of a bitch and would love to blow my head off. It would earn him some very valuable points with the big bosses. What to do and where to go? That was the big question, and I felt we had to act fast. It was only a matter of time before they find us here. I told Rachel that we have to be ready to get out of here at a moment's notice.

"I think we better get out of here tonight, Rachel. There is no use in hanging around until we are in bigger trouble."

"Where are we going to go?" she said a little hysterically. "Where, Harry, when will it stop? I'm tired, scared, and I just want to hide away somewhere, please, Harry, please!"

I took her in my arms and held her tight. I stroked her hair, tried to make her relax. What could I say to her?

"Rachel, maybe it would be best if you went home to Larry and wait there. You will be safe. They are only after me, and you can say you left me because I was a rat and you just couldn't live with me any longer. Tell him that you want a divorce and never want to hear from me again. Whatever you want is okay with me. But this is the only way you can stay alive."

"Harry, are you crazy?" Rachel said with tears running down her face. "I love you, and I am staying. If I die with you, then its fine with me, but I couldn't live with myself wondering where you are and what might happen to you. You know what I mean."

"Sure, I know what you mean," I said. "But, Rachel, we will survive better apart. They want me, not you. We can hook up later when I get my new identity. You can take a trip to Europe or somewhere and we can hook up. Sweetheart, I love you, and I don't want you to get killed or even hurt. Please, believe me, life without you is no life for me, but now, I have to think of you and only you. I also will need you on the outside when I go into custody. Be smart, make the sacrifice today so that we can be together tomorrow. I love you, sweetheart."

Rachel looked at me, her eyes filled with tears. She looked so sad, so hurt, and so beautiful.

"Kiss me, sweetheart. Hold me, please," she said as I took her in my arms again and held tight.

It was 2:00 a.m., and I thought it was best that we get a little sleep.

"Let's get some sleep and set a wake-up call for four thirty and then let's roll on out of here," I said.

Saturday, February 16, 1957

Four thirty in the morning, the phone rang, and I jumped out of bed with my gun in my hand, ready for action until I realized it was our wake up call.

"Okay, thanks," I said and put the phone back.

I shook Rachel and said, "Let's get going. We've got to get on the road as fast as possible."

We packed our few things, and were ready in fifteen minutes. I walked over to the door and opened it a crack in case they were watching the hallway. There was no one that I could see.

"Okay, sweetheart, let's get moving," I said as I opened the door wider and started to walk out into the hallway. I took two steps into the hallway and caught sight of one big dude at the very end of the hall near the elevators. I tried to retreat back to the room, but he saw me and yelled, "Harry."

I could see his hand reach into his coat to pull out a gun. I ran as fast as I could toward this guy, because I didn't trust my ability to shoot and hit him at this distance. The closer I got, the better chance I had of hitting him. I was about ten feet when I started to shoot. The first bullet missed him completely, but my next shot caught him right between the eyes, and down he went his gun still in hand. I turned the corner to see if he was alone and saw no one. I turned around, and there was Rachel behind me.

"Let's get out of here, now," I said as we quickly took the stairs down to the lobby. We were only five floors up, so we made good time.

In the lobby, everything seemed very quiet. There were two people in the lobby—one was sitting on a sofa, and another was reading a newspaper while sitting in chair with a perfect view of the front entrance. My gun had a silencer on it, and he never used his, so maybe no one heard anything. What about the shot I missed? Where did it go? Who cares about that? We've got a lot more important things to worry about. We proceeded down the stairs into the garage to get our car. The attendant was sleeping in his little booth, but he woke up on my first knock on his window. I gave him the ticket, and he disappeared; it seemed like forever until he finally brought the car to us. It felt like time was at a standstill. I gave him a ten and told him to go back to sleep. We jumped in the car and took off. I tried not to drive too fast, as I didn't want to appear to be in a hurry. We drove over the Mercier Bridge and continued toward Plattsburg, New York. It was only fifty miles away. I thought once we get into US, we would get another car in case they were aware of this one. I had now killed two people, and it was getting easier and easier to do. The fact that I could hit these guys where it hurts was giving me confidence and courage beyond my wildest imagination. I never knew I could do this, but now I was convinced I could beat the Mob.

It was 6:00 a.m. when we reached the border and drove through without any problems. A few minutes later, we were in Plattsburg. I decided to drive south and hope that Lake George would be awake soon enough to get rid of the car. About seven, it started to snow. In a few minutes, it was coming down so hard that you couldn't see ten feet ahead. We slowed our speed to 30 mph, as we didn't need anymore screw ups now.

"Rachel, I want you to call Larry when we reach Lake George and tell him you are in Albany and left me in Montreal. You tell him you ran away from me and you want to come home. Ask him to meet you at LaGuardia Airport. You will call him back with flight details. When he asks what happened to me, tell him you left me in Montreal and you don't know where I went from there. You tell him that you can't continue being with me while all this is happening. It is only a matter of time until you get whacked and that is not the way you want to leave this planet. If this situation does not go away, I want to divorce him. Tell him you need him and plead him to help you!" I went over the story again and again so that she would not make any errors. Deception was the key here.

"Now here is what we are going to do, Rachel," I said. "I am going to buy a cheap car, maybe two hundred bucks or so. You will drive this one, and we will find a spot to dump it. We will drive to Albany, and you can catch a flight to New York. You call Larry and give him your flight number and time of arrival. Once you and Larry are alone and you are sure no one can be listening, you can tell Larry what happened and let him know his phone is tapped. Most importantly, do not tell Larry anything about us or that I am not really in Montreal. The less Larry knows about me, the better it will be for us, we can always explain later. I love you. We are going to make it just fine, trust me."

We arrived in Lake George about ten in the morning, and the streets were empty. The snow was still coming down pretty hard, and moving along the streets was still quite difficult.

Nevertheless, I felt it best to move on and try to find a used car lot that was open. In the meantime, we stopped at a Howard Johnson to eat something and freshen up a bit. It was Saturday, and the place should be alive with people. I guess the weather screwed that up. We entered the dinning area and took a table and ordered two coffees.

"Go get change and make your call," I said. "Keep it brief as we do not want to leave any clues that you are not in Albany."

Rachel got up and went to the cashier and got change and made her call. "Daddy, it's me Rachel. Listen, I'm in Albany."

"Are you all right?" Larry said.

"Yes, I'm fine, Daddy. I ran away from Harry. I couldn't take it anymore. I left him in Montreal. I just want to come home."

"Do you want me to send someone to pick you up in Albany?" Larry said.

"No, Daddy, I will fly to New York. You pick me up at La Guardia. I'll call you back with flight information as there is a snow storm and all flights are late. Daddy, I miss you very much. I love you." Rachel hung up and returned to the table. It took less than three minutes. "Okay, it's all done, now we got to get me to Albany," she said.

"No shit. Let's eat and get on our way. If I can't get a car here, I'll get one in Glen Falls. I don't think we will have any trouble there," I said.

We ate and left the diner. The snow had stopped falling, and the street cleaners were out in force plowing the streets. No one wanted to lose a weekend of business. Who could afford it? Just as we were about to scrap buying a car in Lake George, we saw a small car lot. A guy with a broom was sweeping off the snow from the windshields of the cars on the lot. He looked pretty sleazy, my kind of guy, let's see what we can do here.

"Rachel, pull up over here and stay in the car. I'm going to see if I can make a deal for another car," I said.

I jumped out and walked over, "Hey, how are you doing? Hell of a lot of snow sure sucks for business. I'm looking for a second car to get me to the ski hills and back to Manhattan on weekends only. Nothing fancy, just a clunker that will make it with no problems. What have you got?" I said as cheerfully as possible.

"You came on the right day. Business sucks, and today will be really slow and I can make you a deal you can't turn down," he said with a big smile. "Let's take a look at this Chevy Impala—a great car, 55, low mileage, only got forty-seven thousand miles, and the tires are almost new. Here, sit down in it," he said as he opened the door.

"How much is it?" I asked.

"This baby is going for a grand, which is a steal, but I'll cut that down for you because of the snow and the day is half gone. How you gonna pay for this?" he said.

"Cash," I said. "If you want to make a deal now, you'd better sharpen your pencil," I said and half turned to leave.

"Wait a minute, partner," he said with a smile from ear to ear, "I can let this baby go for seven hundred and fifty. Now that's a deal. It's a good thing no one else showed up for work today or I'd get my ass reamed for giving this baby away for such a ridiculous price. What the hell! I'm committed, and I'll stick to it," he said.

"Still too high. I'll give you five hundred as long a she checks out. Let's start her up and we will take it for ride around the block," I said. I figured if the car was in good shape and if he took the test drive, then the sale will be easy at five hundred. We left the lot, and I drove the car around the block. The radio played, the brakes worked, and the engine sounded okay. The seats were a little dirty, and the wipers didn't run so well; they needed new blades.

"Well, what do you think, partner?" he said with eyes wide.

"Well," I said, "If you put on new wiper blades and change the oil, I'll take it. I didn't want to spend this much time and money, but I need to get home before my wife finds out I fucked up her car."

"I need at least six hundred for this baby. Come on, pal, let's close the deal," he said.

"I'll give you five hundred and fifty, not a penny more," I said as I started to count out the C-notes.

"You got a deal, give me half an hour, and the car will be ready. Let's fill out the paperwork so that I can register the car to you," he said happily.

I gave him the name of Ronald Weatherly, just like the car Mario gave us. Rachel and I went to another diner and had a soft drink while the car was being prepared. The plan was to drive to Albany and somewhere along the way remove the license plates and abandon the car. I would take Rachel to the airport and then I would continue on my way, not to Manhattan but to some safe place. I didn't want Rachel to know where my final destination would be so that she couldn't tell anyone where I went. We left Lake George in two cars until I noticed a two lane auxiliary road that was recently plowed. It looked like this road would never end and was going nowhere near civilization. We ditched the old car on this lonely side road. We removed the plates and went through the car to make sure we removed everything that could cause us any problems in the future.

We wiped down the car to remove any fingerprints, but left the keys. I figured if somebody comes along and the car starts, maybe they will take it home with them. It would be best if someone just took it home and used it.

I dropped Rachel off at the airport and left her with five hundred bucks; she wouldn't need money once Larry picked her up. He'd give her all she needed. We arranged a code system so that we could stay in touch. I would call her at Larry's place and let it ring twice, which would let her know it's me calling. After two rings, I would hang up and call back and let it ring two times again and hang up. I would call back and ask for Sam Jones. If the phone is tapped, she would tell me I have the wrong number, and I would try tomorrow at the same time. If the phones were clean, she would say, "This is Sam." We will follow that routine for a little while and see how that works; at no time, will I give her an address where to find me.

Sunday, February 17, 1957

I spent last night in Newark at a cheesy motel and rested. I needed to get myself together and be alert in case I run into any trouble. I woke real early and checked out and spent the day driving south. I got as far as Georgia and stayed the night at a no name motel under the name of Robert Smith from Connecticut.

Monday, February 18, 1957

I left early in the morning on a beautiful day. I wanted to reach Florida today. I was getting tired of driving and running. The drive was quite uneventful; as a matter of fact, it was boring. Nevertheless, I drove into Florida and stopped a little after Jacksonville to have something to eat and to feel the wonderful heat of the sun. I called Moe to let him know that I am all right and on the way to a permanent place. I was searching for a place where I can be safe and perhaps live in relative peace. I told him that, with a little luck, maybe after some time, this will all go away and I could resume my life as I once knew it. Moe advised me to be very careful because the Mob loves to vacation in sunny Florida and I could easily be recognized. He said I should make sure I change my appearance as a precaution as there are Mob guys everywhere. Moe wished me luck and promised me that he would stay on top of the situation at all times and I should check in at least twice a week. I promised him I would and hung up.

I continued on my way toward southern Florida and felt quite good about things. I was starting to relax and believed I had made the right decision in regard to Rachel. I had plenty of time to think about the entire situation while making this long drive. The more I broke down the logic of my decision, the more I was convinced I did right. The Mob was after me, and if any harm came to Rachel, it would actually be collateral damage. Now that I had separated myself from Rachel, I was sure the Mob will not bother her nor would they go after Larry.

After all, Larry was an important cog in the wheel of their loan sharking business and made them a lot of money. He was also a stand-up guy in Mob terms, so leaving him and Rachel alone was a plus for the bosses. I was sure they would watch Rachel closely for a while just to make sure she was not in touch with me. I would be very careful on how often I contacted her and how I do it. Most importantly for me was not to take any unnecessary risks. I wasn't out of the woods just yet. I decided to stop in Orlando for the night and pick up various things I would need when arriving in Miami. I also wanted to check out Orlando and see if it was a good place for me to get lost in. I stayed in my motel room for the night as I didn't want to go to any clubs until I altered my appearance. Caution was far more important than an evening out in some smoky bar.

Tuesday, February 19, 1957

I spent most of the morning driving around Orlando, checking out the city. After a few hours of driving, I decided I did not like Orlando and would not really want to stay there. I finally left a little after three and drove, at the posted speed limit, further south.

I arrived in West Palm Beach at 7:00 p.m., and I was exhausted and needed a good shower and a good sleep. I found the Palm Motel off Okeechobee Boulevard and checked in. I was very tired after spending the last few days in my car. I showered and found a diner and had something to eat and then went back to the motel and crashed.

Wednesday, February 20, 1957

I woke refreshed and ready to meet the day head-on and decide what to do with the rest of my life. I had to get out of this mess before it got too ugly and someone got seriously hurt, namely me! I placed a call to Inspector Johnson on his secure line.

"Johnson here," he said.

"Harry here, any news at this time?" I said.

"No news yet, Harry. We placed the entire deal in the hands of the attorney general and are waiting for his response. We are sure he will run with it, but we must follow procedure. In the meantime, how are you doing?" the inspector said.

"I'm hanging in there, doing the best I can at this time. I wanted to let you know that Rachel and I have split up. We just couldn't handle life like this, and she was not certain that she could go through with the deal. We decided to split, and I wanted you to know where it all stands. She has gone back to live with her dad, and we will get a divorce in time. You can advise the powers that Rachel is no longer part of the deal. It just might work out better this way, who really knows. I just want to know how long this will take as I have to watch my ass. I'm sure you know the entire Mob is after me! They'd love to know where I am and whack me!" I said trying to sound nonchalant.

"I heard there were one hundred big ones out there for the guy who gets you. The talk on the street is that everyone wants to collect that reward. It sure is a lot of money, so you know you are hot. Be very careful and keep out of sight as much as you can," he said in a matter-of-fact tone.

"Boy, you are really a nice guy," I replied. "All you can say is 'Harry, I have great news for you, there are guys out there ready to whack you.' You are a great morale booster."

"I didn't mean to piss on your parade, Harry," he said. "I was just trying to keep you informed so that you know what's going on and you realize the gravity of the situation. Do you have gun, Harry?"

"You bet your sweet ass, I do. Do you think I'm going to let myself walk into some trap without some kind of protection? I can't get any help from you and your lousy feds, and I am being chased by every Mob guy in the world," I said angrily.

"Harry, don't get carried away," the inspector said.

"What the fuck is the matter with you? Don't get carried away! You crack me up, my life is upside down and could be snuffed out at anytime and you tell me 'don't get carried away,' boy, you are a real joy."

"I only meant that if you kill anyone of those bastards, you will get immunity. Remember, Harry, immunity is up to the day you come in and the papers are signed, anything after that, you will be prosecuted."

"You really make feel warm and fuzzy inside, you son of a bitch. I'm not a killer and don't want to become one, but I'm not going to be butchered by a bunch of guinea assholes."

I hung up and went back to my room. I was fuming and forgot about being scared for a few minutes. Maybe that was his goal—to frighten me into an offense that would help me forget the real gravity of the situation I was in. Who knows, I certainly didn't, as I just wished I could be somewhere else and just relax with Rachel. That reminded me that I had to call her and see what was going on at her end.

I went off to a different pay phone. I saw that in the movies and seemed the right thing to do under these circumstances. I went through the ritual we had arranged, and finally let it ring through. "Is Sam Jones there?" I said.

"You can speak. This is a clean line, Larry checked it out. How are you? Where are you? Is everything all right?" she asked.

"Things are fine. No one knows where I am, and I want to keep it that way. So far the feds haven't come through with anything. I am alive and missing you a lot. It's lonely without you, and I want you near," I said.

"I know, I feel the same way, but right now we gotta lay low. Word is out that I left you. Larry made sure everyone who is connected knows that I kissed you off," Rachel said.

"That's the plan, baby, but it makes me feel like shit. I'm not real happy about it, but it is best all the way around. Never mind this now, we need to keep our heads clear. Tell me what Larry said."

"Well," she said, "he told me to tell you to stay hidden. If you need money, tell me where you want me to send it, and I will. There is a contract out on you, and every mother fucker is looking for you. You're worth a hundred grand alive, preferably dead. Every two-bit prick is looking for Harry Miller, so change your looks and act very cool, please, I love you and need you."

"Today is my day for great news," I said. "The inspector just about told me that half the world wants me dead and the other half doesn't give a shit. You come along and confirm what the inspector said. It doesn't help keep my spirits up. It seems I am fucked no matter what I do."

The operator cut in and said, "Please deposit an additional $3.75 to continue this call."

"Okay, hold on a second," I said as I dropped quarter after quarter into the phone. After a few clicks, I said, "Are you there?"

"I'm still here, and I still love you, and even though I am not there, I am with you all the way. Please believe me, Harry I love you with all my heart," she said.

"Okay, I'm going to change my looks and I'm going to find a better place to stay. I have enough money for now. But it won't last forever, and neither will I if we don't resolve this situation very soon," I said.

"Larry can't do a thing. If he tries to help you, he will get whacked. He has to act as if he hates your guts. You know he doesn't, and he will do whatever I ask. But only you and I and Larry will know the real truth. Keep your head high and don't get down, we will solve this or kill every one of those Mob bastards. Just trust me and love me. It will all turn out great someday. I love you, honey. I love you so much."

"I love you, too, Rachel. I love you lots and lots. I'll call tomorrow and follow the same routine. It would be great if you could arrange to leave $10K or $15K with Moe so that when I do need the money, it will be waiting for me."

I hung up and felt empty as if the world had just fallen in on me and I was sinking fast. I took hold of myself and gave myself a pep talk that went like this, "I must get myself together and use the brain I have always been so proud of. I can beat these assholes through intelligence and preparedness. I had to believe in myself or all would be lost. Whatever it takes to survive I will do, no matter what is thrown at me." This I promised myself as I prepared to leave West Palm Beach and move on further south!

I was going to leave West Palm Beach for places farther south when I decided I should take all the steps necessary to change my appearance, while I was still there. In this way, I would arrive wherever I decide to stay and would look like the guy I wanted to be. Anyone who meets me would only remember me as the new guy. No, I would stay here for another night and get myself together so that I could meet and greet the new day tomorrow.

Thursday, February 21, 1957

I spent most of the morning coloring my hair from dark to light. I was now a dirty blond with lighter eyebrows. I didn't like the way it looked, so I spent another four hours undoing what I did and now had a head of hair that was pitch black, a mustache to match, and darkened eyebrows and lashes. I also bought glasses and now looked very professional. No one would ever recognize me as I added a mole on my left side of my neck. I bought a new pair of shoes that added another three inches to my height. I figured no one would ever recognize me as Harry Miller in this disguise. My biggest concern was keeping this disguise up daily.

I had spoken with Rachel earlier this morning, and things were still the same. I told her I would call her on Saturday again. I was now ready to move out of this flea bag and upgrade. If I had to be someone else, I might as well start living like someone else . . . I knew who I was, the guys looking for me didn't. I felt very satisfied, and now felt I had the upper hand. I checked out and drove toward Miami. I wasn't sure if I should take a hotel room or rent an apartment. This was the winter season, and it was not unusual for people from the east to rent an apartment for one month or two. I stopped at Ft. Lauderdale and stopped at a liquor store to pick up a bottle of vodka. While there, I noticed a book "Take one! Free, Apartment rentals" I picked one up and threw it into the bag and left. Once in the car, I opened the book, and there it was—listings for all types of apartments in Pompano Beach, Ft. Lauderdale, Lauderdale by the sea, and so on. I found one that sounded very good for a snowbird and called. I spoke with a woman who said she had a furnished one bedroom available in a doorman building off A1A in Pompano. She asked four hundred and fifty a week or fifteen hundred for a month, payable in advance plus a deposit of five hundred for furniture damage. If I wanted maid service, it was an additional fifty-five a week and that included linen changes three times a week with no service on Sunday. Parking was included using the outdoor lot; if I wanted to park my car inside, then it was an additional thirty-five per month.

I set up an appointment to meet the lady in one hour. The front of the building was facing the street A1A, and the rear was on the ocean side. You walked out the back door, and you were on the beach. The apartment was completely furnished, very clean, and bright. The balcony faced the ocean. It all looked too good to be true. I took the deal once I saw the place. The apartment was on the twentieth floor and had a view of the Atlantic Ocean. This was a doorman building with plenty of people coming and going, nothing unusual for vacationers like me.

If someone asked the doorman for Harry Miller or gave a description of him, they would be told, "No one in this building fits that description." If they had a picture, the doorman would not recognize it at all. This was a great place to relax and just hideaway. I really felt I hit the jackpot, at least for now! I met with the agent and paid for one month and decided not to have a phone installed in the apartment, after all I did not know how long I would be here and I didn't need another thread to connect to Harry Miller now that I have assumed my new identity as Harold Robinson of Parsippany, New Jersey. I spent the rest of the day sun bathing on the beach and just plain relaxing. I picked up a sandwich at a local deli and took it home to eat and relax. The sun made me tired along with the stress of the situation. Getting a good night's sleep was in the cards.

Friday, February 22, 1957

It was six thirty in the morning, and the sun was not up just yet, but the air was warm, and I felt great. The sound of the waves on the beach made me feel a real calmness. I didn't think about hit men or cops or anything other than how warm it was and how nice it was to watch the waves coming onto shore one after another. Peace—it was so nice and so welcome. I decided to vegetate by the beach today, get some more color and just relax. I stayed on beach until three, when I felt I had enough sun and best go in.

At about five, I decided to get started on scoping out the night life here and also finding a place to eat. I decided to go to a bar I noticed earlier when driving along A1A. The Beachcomber looked like a nice hangout right by the ocean in Lauderdale by the sea. I went in and sat at the bar and ordered vodka on the rocks with a twist. Soon I was on a second drink and building a relationship with the bartender, a real nice guy sort of hippy looking with long strangled hair and a beard to match. He was here for the winter from Minnesota, where he bartended in the summer.

"There's no money here in summertime, dead as a fuckin' door nail," he said.

We exchanged names; his was Ron, and we made small talk.

"What's the night life like around here?" I asked.

"It's great. Lots of chicks here for the winter looking to hook a rich guy. They usually move on after the season. This place gets crazy about ten when the party people start coming in. Then there's the Baldacci Barn on Oakland Boulevard, a wild place, plenty of bimbos and action all the time. I love the place because it's loaded with broads, but I don't like the owners. It's owned by the bent-nose boys, and everyone knows these guys aren't nice. A guy named Tony Anthony runs the place. I can hook you up if you want."

"Well, it's my first night here, so I think I will just take it easy. Maybe, tomorrow I will get serious about some action. I'll see you tomorrow, man. You take it easy."

I left him a ten-dollar tip on a twenty-three dollar bill. I just wanted him on my side if I needed him.

Saturday, February 23, 1957

What a great day!—plenty of sunshine, waves, and miles and miles of beach. I went out on the balcony with a cup of coffee and just sat there. I couldn't believe this was my life after all the shit I'd been through.

I went out to a pay phone and called Rachel and spoke with her for a few minutes as nothing had changed. The news was pretty sparse. Larry seemed to think that everyone thought the situation would settle down as long as nothing was made news worthy. Rachel let me know that the Mob thought that we have broken up and she was getting a divorce. This part of the plan seemed to be working as she claimed the pressure was off Larry and her. I hung up and decided to spend the rest of the day at the beach and get a good tan, although I have been doing this for the past two days and my tan was just starting to look great.

It was 6:00 p.m. when I quit the beach and dressed into a pair of very casual slacks and headed off to The Beachcomber, my new home away from home.

"Hey, Ron, how's tricks?" I asked in a very upbeat tone.

"Great, man, just terrific. How did your day go?"

"I just took in a little sun and relaxed. Now I'm ready for a night of fun and some action," I said with a big smile on my face.

"I hear you, man, I hear you. What are you drinking?" Ron said with a smile from ear to ear,

"I'll have my usual vodka, on the rocks with a twist."

I watched him pour a double and knew he was on my team. I sat there sipping my drink and watching the bar fill up. I knew what I was doing was risky as I should be laying low until this situation got straightened out. But I felt lonely, and I wanted to test my new appearance. I knew there were a lot of Mob guys here. They too liked to spend time in warm climates during the winter. I felt being hidden away is not for me, I need company, and I need to be with someone. Sure I love Rachel, but she is not here for me to hold so I must find another, even if it's for a night. Trouble was lurking around the corner, I could feel it, but what the hell I wasn't a prisoner and wasn't going to live like one. I also felt that with my new appearance no one would recognize me. Go for it, man, go have a good time, I told myself.

After a little while, Ron came over to me and suggested, "I know if you go to Baldacci's Barn, there is plenty of action, and you will be very happy. I will call ahead and speak to Antonio and arrange everything. You'll be treated like royalty, and you will have a great night. What do you think, Harold, are you game?"

"Of course, I am, Ron," I said as I slipped him a twenty. "I'll grab something to eat, let me have a hamburger—medium, all dressed, and then, I'll go over there and scope out the joint."

I arrived at Baldacci about nine, and Ron was right on, the place was jumping. There was a line at the door, and it seemed that not too many were being let in. I asked for Antonio and was told to go inside and someone will join me and get Antonio.

I went into the lobby area, where a beautiful young woman asked me my name.

"Harold Robinson, and I'd like to see Antonio," I said.

"Please wait here, Harold, I'll get Sal. It won't be long," she said as she disappeared behind a solid purple door. I couldn't see a thing standing in this small and closed in area.

A minute later, a big guy with a smile that was wide and warm came into the room and said, "Hi I'm Sal. You're here to see Antonio?"

"Yes, I am Harold Robinson, and I would like to see Antonio. I was recommended by Ron from the Beachcomber. He said he would call ahead and set it all up."

"Great, Harold, it's a pleasure to meet you. Please follow me, and I will give you the rundown of the club," Sal said.

I followed Sal through a regular nightclub, where the bar was crowded and people were talking loudly as some background music played. I was a little sorry about coming here, as this type of place was not my scene at all. This is where you get into trouble when some jerk gets a little too drunk and thinks you are looking at his girl. I was about to apologize to Sal, when he just kept walking through another door and led me into a beautiful club—one that I have never seen before and was removed from the noise and chaos of the Baldacci's Club we just passed through. The lights were low, but not dark, and I could see that the main area was filled with people wearing bathrobes sitting at tables, talking and drinking. I was not allowed into the club proper as that was against the rules as explained to me by Sal. I looked through the display window and could see that the waitresses were beautiful and dressed in miniskirts and all were topless. A huge bar stretched the entire length of the room, with televisions at every corner mounted high up. This area was also filled with people who were drinking and talking to some very pretty ladies who sat at their tables. The atmosphere looked very relaxing and euphoric. I was being carried into another world, very clearly separated from the one I just left.

While standing there, a big burly guy, with some locks of blond hair mixed into his auburn head came by.

"Hi, I'm Antonio. I am sorry I could not greet you, I was tied up. I do hope Sal has taken good care of you? Just follow me. Nice place, eh? It is different, and when you see it all, you will understand why the ambiance is so perfect. It's a great place to escape and forget the world outside. I'm sure you will enjoy yourself. If there is anything you may need, just ask for me or Sal," he said as he opened a purple padded door, which revealed another purple door. "No one can enter until the door behind you is firmly locked in place. It's just a security precaution."

We continued along a long hallway past three other doors that led nowhere. The music was soft, the lighting was very subdued and serene; it was all very relaxing. He knocked on the door, and it opened it to a huge area that smelled like a swimming pool or steam room. I looked ahead of me, and sitting at a table in swim shorts was a guy that looked like God's gift to women. He was just beautiful—blond hair, muscular with features that seemed to be chiseled out of granite.

He stood up and introduced himself, "I am Renaldo. Ron spoke highly of you, Harold. Welcome to Baldacci's, a great place to relax and unwind. Please join me for a drink and let me introduce you. This is Tanya, and this is Roberta, they are here to serve you and make you very happy."

I stood there in awe. I couldn't believe that this place existed, but here I was, in heaven.

"Hi, I'm glad to meet you. I feel a little overdressed for this place."

"Don't worry, honey," Tanya said, "we'll get you into some very casual clothing soon. First let's take a tour of the place so that you can choose your pleasure."

I looked at Antonio and motioned him over to a corner of the area. "Is this for real, man?" I asked.

"Of course, Harold, this is for real. I'm not kidding you, it's the best ever! Let Renaldo take care of you. He'll explain everything, and you can take it from there. For five big ones, there are no questions asked. Just have a good time. Everything is included. If you want to tip the girls, it's up to you. No money is allowed inside the club at anytime. If you want to leave a tip for the girls, you can pick up an envelope when you leave and just deposit it at the desk. Make sure you write the girl's name on the envelope. All drinks in the club are yours to enjoy at no charge. We do not tolerate any abuse of alcohol, and drug use is prohibited."

Renaldo looked pleased and proud as he explained this to me. I gave him five C-notes and was immediately given a robe to change into and a locker to place my clothing. Tanya came with me and explained a little to me before we began the tour.

"Harold, you must never enter the main club called The Barn unless you place all your clothes and belongings in your locker. The proper attire here is a robe and slippers, and these are provided. No money is ever permitted in The Barn, and you may not ever propose to any of the hostesses. This is a club of love, and if you fall in love that is your affair. Who are we to interfere with that natural and quite normal practice? Try to keep your falling in love inside the club, as we frown upon liaisons with our staff. You are here to unwind, to relax, and forget the outside world. Let's get started on your tour," she said with a smile.

I was amazed and excited as she showed me around the club. First stop was a large lounge area that had many sofas and tables nearby and very beautiful waitresses walking around topless in very short miniskirts, bringing you any drink of your choice. Next to that room was a few television sets and tables set up for cards or backgammon. The scene was just so serene; one could live here all the time. There were plants everywhere, and the music played softly in the background. The entire scene just relaxed me and put me into a mood of total freedom. Any stress I might have had just went out the window.

Tanya looked at me and said, "So far, do you like what you see?"

"Of course, I love it. I just can't believe this exists," I said.

"Let's continue with the tour as the best is yet to come. What you are about to see will blow your mind, this is guaranteed," Tanya said with a big smile. "This is the Arabian room, a room that appears exactly as a sheik's tent would look in Arabia complete with the colorful curtains adorning the walls and ceiling. To add to the flavor, we have Arabian rugs on the floor, a hookah, and pillows of all sizes, even down to grains of sand on the floor and bowls of fruits, dates, and nuts. The lighting is sultry and very erotic and easily makes one want to just lay down on one of those huge pillows and be caressed and stay here forever," she said with pride.

Belly dancing music was heard softly through this room. If you shut your eyes, you could easily imagine a beautiful belly dancer doing her thing especially for you. Tanya then pulled a hanging rope. A beautiful maiden appeared, wearing a veil and a mesh dress covering her breasts leaving her beautiful, tanned skin bare in her midriff. She wore mesh bottoms with pointed pink shoes and looked ravishing. I was smitten, never wanting to leave this place.

Tanya moved along and said, "This is just the beginning, please, come along with me, and I'll show you much more than you can imagine."

I followed her anxious as ever to see what else there was in store for me.

We entered another room that was lit with a blue light. Everything in that room looked different. Tanya's teeth were the whitest I have ever seen. Everything in this room was surreal, especially the music. The music that was playing was serene and exotic at this time, and the carpet on the floor was as white as snow. That was a sexy room, as aromas filled the air of sweet incense and roses of every kind. Rose petals were on the floor, and a polar bear's skin lay on the floor, ready to cuddle into. A beautiful looking native woman, who wore nothing more than a pair of Eskimo boots and a body to die for, was there. I wanted just to cuddle up and make love to her forever.

Tanya asked me, "What do you think so far?"

"It's absolutely mind boggling. I've never thought anything like this existed. What is the story? How does it work?" I said.

"Well, Harold, all you have to do is to choose where you want to be. It's like choosing the environment you want to be in and then choose the hostess of your choice to spend some time with you in that special environment. Easy, isn't it? And the best part is if you are a member, your dues are paid and you can take advantage of The Barn at anytime when it's open. There is a small environmental charge of a hundred dollars every time you use an area as you have just seen. That reserves the area for one hour for you and your hostess of choice to spend together. Unfortunately, we cannot allow anymore than one hour as there are other members with reservations. Whatever you and the hostess discuss is your own private business. One small caution, at no time can you solicit or offer money to any hostess for sexual favors. If you should attempt to offer any hostess money or entice them by a promise of some sort, your membership will be cancelled and you will not be permitted into The Barn again. If you want to tip a hostess, you may, the amount is entirely at your discretion, and this can be done simply by placing whatever you want into an envelope and writing her name on it and placing it in a box located outside as you leave. Remember, Harold, you never have any money in this club, it is forbidden. I know I have repeated this again and again, Harold, it is so important as we do not want a reputation that we are a brothel or offer sexual favors at any time. Let's walk this way, as I have more environments to show you," she said.

As we walked down another hallway, she turned to me and said, "There are a few other rules that you should be made aware of. You cannot enter the 'Barn' section of the club wearing any clothes. You will be provided a locker and a robe. You do not need money as drinks and foods are free at all times. In this way, you cannot be tempted to solicit anyone and cannot bring any illegal substances into the club. I'm sorry, Harold, if I am repeating myself, but I cannot emphasize how important the rules are. There is no smoking of any kind except in the main lounge. Cigarettes and cigars will be provided when requested. Let's go in here. You will love the Roman spa."

She opened a door, and I thought I was in Rome back in the days of Caesar. In front of my wide open eyes was one marble sculptor after another surrounding the marble stairs that took one up to the Roman baths. On the wall was a mural depicting life in Rome. The room smelled of perfume, and the lights were candle types and were giving off the appearance of a night in the court of the Romans. Large towels were strewn on the floor, and a table, low to the floor and fashioned out of marble, held bowls of fruit and other foods. A large decanter of wine stood in the middle of the table and bowls, most likely to be used as dishes, which were stacked on the end of the table. The most exciting part of this room was the flow of the water as it cascaded from the upper bath to the middle one and then to the lower bath with gentle sprays bouncing in the air. It was exotic and erotic beyond description.

"This is one of our most popular environments and often is booked for more than one hour. We have several Roman-spa settings in order to accommodate all those who request this type of environment."

I was in a state of excitement filled with peace and euphoria like I had never felt before. I just wanted to remain here for days as time just stood still in this heavenly place. I could not believe what I had been shown, the beauty and peace of it all. It was so wonderful.

Tanya spoke and woke me out of my dream like state, "We also have an environment that simulates—an oasis, completely with palm trees, desert sand, and green grass. If you come this way, I'll see if that area is free at this time."

As we walked along the hallway, she continued with her tour. "All in all there are twenty-one different areas to choose from, and they all can be booked in advance. I highly recommend making reservations well in advance in order to avoid any disappointments," she concluded.

I liked what I have just seen. This was my kind of place I was so glad Ron sent me here. Could there be a better place to hang out than this? I didn't think so, I was stoked!

"Okay, Tanya, where is the catch?" I asked.

"There is no catch at all. This is your private club to enjoy, and its open seven days a week from 11:00 a.m. to 2:00 a.m. All we ask is that you obey the rules and enjoy yourself. Do not tell people that this club is a whorehouse as it's not. If you like these environments, then enjoy them and keep it private. We don't need the law breathing down our necks because they heard that things are going on here that are illegal. I hope you get my drift, Harold."

"I sure do, and I will respect this place always," I said.

"I want you to meet Lionel. He will arrange everything for you and then feel free to enjoy the 'Barn.' See you around, Harold," she said and took off.

I stood alone in the very posh lounge that could be described as a super great room. Chairs were plush, and there were sofas scattered in different parts. There was four television sets strategically placed so one could watch a different program without interfering with another. I also noticed that each plush chair had a set of head phones so one could listen to their own program, choose their own music or listen to news and/or stock market results. At one end, there was a bar filled with every type of liquor available. There wasn't any bar stools as this bar was to serve the private members of the Barn. All drinks were on the house; this was a perk that came with the membership. Adjacent to the great room was another room, where I spied three billiard tables and five card tables. Each table and chair was of the highest quality craftsmanship and all staffed by very attractive and very shapely hostesses, who were ready to serve your every need. Very pleasing to the eye and very calming, this place was a heaven and a far cry from the nightmare I was trying to forget.

As I stood there, a tall, handsome man about thirty years old with great blond hair and beautiful blue eyes came into the room. He was wearing a very casual pair of white slacks and a white T-shirt that displayed his muscular body.

"Hi, you must be Harold? I'm Lionel and will be your liaison here at The Barn."

I shook hands with him and felt a strong, firm grip. "It's a pleasure to meet you. This place is something else. I sure hope I can use it often enough while I am visiting Florida?"

"I hope so as well, Harold. It will be a pleasure to help you achieve that," he said. "Now let sit down here, and I'll explain the rules and exactly how this club works. The owners are people who wanted to provide a very enclosed and safe environment for you to indulge your favorite fantasies. Of course, to do that, there is a cost, and we feel we have kept it very reasonable. I'm sure Tanya has explained to you many of the rules of the club."

I answered at once, "Yes, she has, and I understand that discretion is very important."

"Good," he said, "now let's get on with it. You understand that you will be given a locker to place your clothing and any other belongings.

You are only permitted the robe we provide, no other clothing and no money in the club proper. I have some forms that you must sign to complete this. The form repeats the rules, especially that no solicitations can take place. If you are discovered propositioning anyone in this place, you will be forbidden from coming to the club again and no refund of any money will be given. It is very important you understand that and sign the document that states that very clearly. No guns are permitted in the club. If you should have a gun with you, you must declare it when entering the club. A special envelope will be provided, and the gun will be placed in a safe and will be returned to you when you leave the building. No drugs of any kind can be brought in. We have a zero-tolerance policy. No gambling in the club. If you want to play cards that is fine with us, and we will provide chips for your use. If you place a value on those chips, it is not our concern, cash it in elsewhere. Once again, you will be required to sign a document agreeing to these policies. The club is here for your enjoyment. Please enjoy and be discreet. The charges are as Tanya has explained. One hundred dollars per hour when you choose an environment and no charge when you use the remaining areas of the club, including the swimming pool and sauna, weight room, steam room, and any other amenities. Membership is twenty-five hundred per year, and it can be increased only when your year renews. A lifetime membership can be purchased for ten thousand dollars, and it is as stated, a lifetime membership, and there cannot ever be any increases. Any tips you wish to leave for anyone must be left at the front desk. An envelope will be provided and all you have to do is write the persons' name on it and drop in the tip box as indicated on your way out. Also, do not sign your name. Tips are not required, but certainly not discouraged. If you have a wife or a girlfriend please keep them away from this club, as we do not want any disputes here and will not tolerate any. Your shit is your shit. Keep it outside always."

He then took out a bunch of papers handed them to me and indicated where I was to sign.

I signed them all and said, "Lionel, I did not bring twenty-five hundred in cash with me, can I pay this tomorrow?"

"Of course, Harold, there is no need to fret about it, we'll still be here tomorrow and the day after and so on. I will instruct the front desk that you will be paying your membership on your next visit. In the meantime, you can spend as much time as you like in the club tonight, but you cannot use any of the environments as they are all booked in advance. If you want to book for tomorrow, I suggest you do so now in order to avoid being disappointed. If you want to spend more time here tonight, you are most welcome."

"Thanks, Lionel, but I'll skip that for tonight. I will make a reservation for tomorrow and shall be fully paid up by then and will feel a lot better. This place is great, and I am sure I will enjoy every second I'm here. Thanks, Lionel."

"No problem, Harold, love to have you. See you tomorrow."

I left the club very excited and headed directly to my apartment. I needed something new in my life, and this was it.

Sunday, February 24, 1957

I woke up feeling great and not thinking about my predicament at all. I called Rachel, even though I didn't want to, but I had to find out what was going on. Of course, I was starting to doubt anything she may tell me as I detected a very different attitude. I spent very little time on the phone with her. The call was a downer as it brought me back to reality. Rachel told me that the hunt was on and that the contract had been doubled to two hundred K and every two-bit punk had my description.

"Please lay low, sweetheart. I don't know for sure, but I'll bet they must have contacted every one of their hit men in the Mob network. Please be careful and always be on the lookout for trouble. Trust no one, Harry. Be careful. I love you and need you, please! I also want to let you know that I will be dropping off an envelope with fifteen K tomorrow at Moe's," she said.

"I am keeping out of sight most of the time as I don't go out anywhere. I don't look the same as I did in the past, I doubt if anyone would recognize me including you. I think I could pass you by in the street and you wouldn't know it's me. I try to blend in with everyone else. I don't want to bring any attention to myself, so I stay mostly indoors. It's almost like being in the slammer. Forget about me, sweetheart, how are you doing, are you okay?" I said.

"Come on, what's not to be okay about. I live with Larry. I get everything I want and need, and it's easy. I am fine, except that I miss you a lot. You don't worry about me, just you be careful. I love you!" Rachel said.

"Me, too," I responded. "I got to go now. I'm running out of quarters. I'll call you on Tuesday, same time. I love you."

I couldn't wait to get the day over with as I wanted to get back to The Barn. I wanted to hide from the dangers and forget who I was, even if it was for only a night. I needed to be with people or I would go out of my mind. I spent the day on the beach and finally had enough sunshine and sea water. I went home, showered, and shaved and put on a little cologne. I took plenty of money and, of course, my gun. I planned on leaving it in the car, but in no way could I leave home without it. No matter what I was thinking, I still was a hunted man, and vigilance was the most important part of the equation. If you ever read detective magazines, you see how the crooks are so stupid, and in many cases actually lead the cops to them.

I thought I would not be stupid and would not leave any trail. Harry Miller would not exist any longer but Harold Robinson would. I know I would have to make up some cover story as to my previous life. In order to succeed, I would have to make sure any story I do tell was consistent and comes easily to me. I certainly do not want to arouse any suspicion. I was just a guy looking for fun while on vacation. I left around four in the afternoon and headed along Oakland Park Boulevard toward The Barn. I drove slowly as I did not want to get a ticket. The last thing I needed was a cop who might be connected or they should find the gun. No, sir, not me, I was going to be very careful.

I parked in the rear of the club and used the back entrance thus avoiding the nightclub and went in. Sitting at the front desk was a beautiful looking redhead with a smile that would melt your heart very quickly.

"Hi, I'm Harold Robinson," I said cheerfully.

"I'm Betsy. Welcome to The Barn," she said.

"I was here last night—"

She interrupted me, "I know Harold, I have been expecting you. Did you get fully briefed about the rules?"

"Yes, I did," I responded eagerly.

"Okay, then let's get started. If you have any valuables you do not wish to leave in your locker, you may leave them in our safe. They will be returned when you leave," she said.

"Great, I do have a few things I want to leave in the safe, if I may. By the way Betsy, I want to pay my membership. Here is twenty-five hundred as promised."

I peeled off crisp new C-notes, and Betsy gave me a receipt. She then gave me a large envelope and asked me to put whatever I wanted to place in safekeeping in to that envelope and write my name across it.

Once the envelope was sealed, I was to write my name across the flap to prevent any tampering. As soon as Betsy returned, she handed me a key.

"This is your locker number. Please place all your clothing and footwear in your locker. You cannot take anything into the club. You will find a robe in your locker and a pair of disposable slippers. That's your wardrobe for the night. Enjoy yourself Harold and meet the hostesses. I see you have an appointment for the Arabian environment at seven and that will be one hundred Harold. Because it is your first time visiting us, please ask any hostess who is free to show you around. Also, Harold, tonight you get a hostess of our choice. If you wish to choose a special person, you may do so, but that must be done in advance. Until you get to know all the hostesses, you will be assigned one at random. I hope you understand and realize that we want to please you, always. If something is not to your liking, please let us know. And if it's something special you wish, just let me know, and I will make sure it is taken care of. Now go have a good time. I'll see you later."

I entered through the door into a small area, no bigger than three feet by four feet with a door at the other end. I could not open the exit door until the door I used to enter was shut completely. I noticed a camera above my head in the left corner and some sort of beam that seemed to shine across the area. In less than a few seconds, a green light appeared and I opened the second door and entered into an area that had a small desk with a beautiful maiden sitting behind it. She was dark skinned, obviously a great sun tan, with great blonde hair.

"Hi, I'm Shari, your locker room hostess," she said with a great big smile.

"Nice to meet you. I'm Harold Ro—"

I stopped as she had her finger by her mouth with the "don't speak signal" and spoke up at once.

"We don't need last names in here, Harold. So please respect that courtesy," she said again with a smile that was radiant.

"I'm sorry. I guess I goofed. It won't happen again, Shari," I said.

"Well, Harold," she said, "you will find the locker room to the left. Please place everything you are wearing in your locker. There are slippers provided as well. Take a shower if you wish or just go right into the main area of the club. Your appointment is at seven, so you have some time to do a little weight lifting, play cards, and watch TV or whatever you would like. If you would like some food, please tell them at the bar. Drinks are on the house, so please feel free to enjoy the drink of your choice. Our very sweet and great looking hostesses will gladly take your drink and food order and serve you like a sultan or king. This is your home away from home, Harold, and here you will always be treated like royalty. Enjoy!"

I walked away in a dream-like state and found my locker. Sure enough, as Shari said, the place was immaculate and everything I would need was in my locker waiting for me. Once I had my robe on, I attached the key to the inside pocket via a little hook that was sewn in especially for this purpose. The objective is to forget the outside world—this is the new world for the next few hours—and get lost in the paradise.

I hung around the club and met several other members—Jack, Len, Sam, and a few other names I have already forgotten. I saw a couple of the Mob guys; they were so easy to spot even wearing bathrobes. I made sure to stay clear of them, although my appearance would not connect Harry to Harold. Nevertheless, I felt a pound of caution would be optimum here. Any mistakes regardless of how trivial would be my undoing. I couldn't tell what time it was or how fast time had passed, except that it seemed like I just got here, and now a beautiful young lady came by and sweetly said, "Harold, my name is Tina, and I'm your hostess for the Arabian environment," she said softly.

"Is it seven already?" I said. I don't know why I said that, but I was so awe struck by this beautiful woman that I didn't know what to say. I stared at a pair of blue eyes that sparkled on a face of a soft reddish brown skin with a mix of dark blonde and auburn hair, about five feet four wearing a white shawl type dress that just screamed sex. She was hot, and so was I.

"Yes, it is, and we must go to the Arabian environment now. Let's not lose any time as we only have an hour to spend together and to get to know each other. Would you like a drink? I will have it sent to our location."

I replied, "Yes, I'll have vodka on the rocks with a piece of lemon, thanks." As we walked along the hallway toward the Arabian room, she stopped at an intercom on the wall and pressed a button.

In a moment, a voice asked "How may I help you?"

Tina responded, "One vodka on the rocks with a twist, for the Arabian room, please, thanks."

"On the way," the intercom voice responded.

"Now that's done, let's relax," she said with a smile.

We entered the room that made me feel like I had just entered a real Arabian tent in the middle of the desert. The walls were covered from the floor to ceiling with very shear curtains of many colors. The environment was as if we were on the desert, with sand on the floor and rugs of great colors and thick wool. Pillows of every size and shape adorned the floor, and lanterns gave us very erotic lighting. In the center was a table, very low to the floor with a large dish of grapes and another dish of dates, figs, and oranges. We just started to settle down on a pillow when there was a knock on the door. "Must be the drink," Tina said and got up to answer the door.

Standing in the doorway was a small doll—perhaps five feet tall with dark hair, wearing a maid's apron, high heeled shoes, and a little white maid's hat. She was beautiful and looked like a doll out of a magazine.

"Vodka, on the rocks with a twist. Enjoy." And off she went.

"Wow! She looks great. Who is that?" I asked Tina as I sat down and sipped my drink.

"That was Pumpkin, isn't she great? She is full of personality. You'll get to know her as she serves the lounge as well. We all love her. She is just the greatest," Tina said.

We sat there on the pillows, talking a bit, and I said to Tina, "I like you, and I am sure you know that you turn me on. What can we do about it? I'd like to get to know you better, and maybe we can see each other off premises?" I said.

"That is impossible, Harold. I work here, and the rules are clear—no fraternization with members. I just can't, and I do understand that you are turned on, after all everything we do here is to make you feel warm and fuzzy and treat you like a king. I am glad to know I'm doing the job so well," she said.

"I'm glad you are so honest with me," I said as I took her hand and brought her close to me. I kissed her gently and held her in my arms for a moment and then looked into her beautiful blue eyes and said, "You are so beautiful and nice."

"Thank you, Harold, it's so sweet of you to say. Would you like a great Arabian massage?" she said.

"You bet your life I would."

She took out a large bath towel and placed it on top of the largest pillow and said, "Take off your robe and lie down on your stomach. Let me rub sweet smelling oils all over you and make you feel like royalty. Relax, let me do all the work. Just enjoy and whatever your cares are, they will disappear, I promise you that."

I lay there and felt the softest and smoothest pair of hands I have ever felt touch my skin, and I began to feel warm and full of desire. I wanted this woman and I wanted her real bad. I was sure she knew that as well, and soon she said, "Okay, Harold, turn over and lie on your back."

I was being pampered and made to feel as if I entered a different world—one I have never ever experienced before. In less than a minute, I was as hard as a rock and wanted to jump her bones. I started to speak and couldn't say a word. I just lay there and dreamt about her.

"Sweetie, you seem to be very horny, let me help you with that," she said and took my cock in her hand and gently rubbed it. She then took off her Arabian dress to reveal a body that made me hornier than ever, if that was possible. Her breasts were firm, and she didn't have an ounce of fat on her bronze-colored skin. She was a goddess, and I was her slave and ready for action. We made love for a long time, and she was everything I expected. If I had to seclude myself for the rest of my life with one person, she was the one. This was heaven, and I just couldn't stop loving every second of it. All at once, I was awoken from my trance by a bell, a faint one at that, but nonetheless a bell.

Tina looked at me and said, "That's our signal that our time is up. I'm sorry as I enjoyed that so much. I want to see you again, so please ask for me. You are special to me, Harold," she said in her soft voice.

"Sure thing, Tina. I enjoyed this a lot and will ask for you again, this is certain," I said as we left the Arabian room. Tina said good-bye, and I went into the lounge and just relaxed a little. Pumpkin came by and asked me if I wanted another drink, which I promptly ordered. As I sat there sipping my drink, I noticed a few guys playing cards and one of them looked familiar to me. I walked around toward the card table to get a better look and see if anyone would recognize me. It was stupid of me, but I had to know if I was truly different or not. I didn't think for a moment that I was not wearing my special shoes while here in the club so my height was no longer part of my disguise. I kept watching these Mob guys as they played cards when one the guys moved from one side to the other thus allowing me a complete view of him. I was shaken when I saw him. There was Mario asking the guys if he could join them and play cards with his buddies. Mario, the guy who helped me with the car and who was, obviously, on my side. He didn't recognize me, and I wasn't about to introduce myself. I was still shaking when I got up and went to the locker room. I decided to get the hell out of there as fast as I could. I showered and changed into street clothes and went up front to pick up my stuff in the safe. I left Tina a two hundred-dollar tip in an envelope and dropped it into a box called "suggestions" and left. Before leaving, I made an appointment for tomorrow at eight and asked if I could have Tina again. I was told that Monday was her day off but they would be happy to assign another hostess of equal or better than Tina. I could not imagine someone better than Tina, but it was a thought that I am sure would stay with me until tomorrow. I left and drove home. My mind was filled with trepidation because I saw Mario and the fact that the Mob was so close. It was mind boggling to say the least.

I arrived home and spent a few hours just thinking about the presence of the Mob. Of course, I did realize that Florida was the number one stomping ground for Mob guys to relax and get the cold out of their system. I was told by Ron the bartender at The Beachcomber that the Barn was owned by the Mob. It should not have been a surprise to me at all, but it did not change the fact that it was disturbing.

Monday, February 25, 1957

I called the inspector to ask where I stood on the deal we had discussed and to keep him happy as well. I didn't want any suspicion on his part about me being out of his jurisdiction. The longer he felt I was on his side the better off I would be.

"Hi, Sam, have you anything new to report?" I said.

"Nothing yet, although it seems we should wrap this up by the end of this week. How are you doing?" he said.

"I'm fine and lying low. I hear half the world is looking to off me and collect the hit money."

"Yeah, that's what I hear as well, and because of that I told my bosses that we'd better get you in here soon or there will be no deal," the inspector said.

"You mean I'll be dead soon if this shit isn't taken care of!" I said.

"Call me on Wednesday, and I hope to have some news by then. In the meantime, take care and take no chances," he said.

"Listen to me, Sam. I can't understand why this is taking so long. If you really want my help and your real goal is to prosecute those fuckers, who seem to be hurting people, then what stands in your way to move forward and close the deal? I think there are a few snitches in the woodpile, my friend, and I think you're just jerking me off. Maybe and I say this without any proof. Are you working for the Mob or protecting law-abiding folks? To me, it seems the feds would jump at the chance to get a real witness and yet you can't get a deal put down on paper fast especially when there are lives in jeopardy? There is something wrong here, and I think I'd best keep on hiding if I want to stay alive. I think if they don't get me, you guys will, and right now it is best to keep out of sight and not let myself be a target. I'll bet someone is making some real bucks on all of this," I said with a lot of anger in my voice.

"Who the hell are you to talk like that to me? I have never been on the take, and I never would be. I agree with you that something smells with this whole thing, but you just remember, Harry, I'm the only ally you have and I have no power to do more than I am doing at this time. There are higher ups that make the decisions and I am supposed to follow them. If I tried to find out who the turncoats are, I'd probably wind up in the trunk of a fucking car. I hope you get my drift, Harry, I can't do much except promise you this, I'm your friend and will always protect you the best I can, but trust no one, and believe me I don't. I do not want any harm to come to you and will always be truthful to you, this I guarantee. I am not on their team and never would be."

He hung up so quickly that I could not say another word, but I was sure now that Sam was on my side but was powerless and I was in trouble.

I immediately called Rachel, "Hi, honey, what's new at your end?" I said.

"Things are the same. I can't do much as I'm stuck out here in Long Island. I miss you a lot and wish we could be together."

"So do I, so do I," I said with a longing inside of me.

"I heard that they have upped the ante to get you and soon you will disappear. I am so worried I can't even trust my own father. Larry is so secretive on what he does and where he goes that I am getting worried. He said that they all believe we have parted and are getting divorced he wants it kept that way. We can't count on him for help. I found out that the story that the commission held off was all bullshit to get Larry back in the good graces of the families and to get you to trust him. Friday, Albert Anastasia, Frank Costello, Gaetano Luchese, Joe Profaci, and Joe Bonanno held a meeting with their top lieutenants and Larry and his guys to patch things up and get things back as they should be. It was confirmed that we are not a team any longer, so now they will leave me be. Larry is back operating the numbers and loan business. Its business as usual and they will handle the job of finding you. While you are hiding, you cannot help the feds and they intend to make sure you stay in hiding until they find you. I know they are looking everywhere. I love you, please believe me, I do. I get my information from the one friend you have, Mario. He has left for Florida to organize some stuff there for Larry, but in his heart he cares about you. Please take care of yourself and don't take any foolish chances. The last I heard, while listening to Larry and some Mob boss talk yesterday, was that they think you are either in Florida or the Bahamas. They are going full blast to get you. They say they must before the feds get you into protective custody. Even though they have some juice with the feds and some judges, it will be hard to get at you if you go inside, so they want it taken care of now."

I was stunned that they could pin point my location—Florida or the Bahamas. That is pretty close. I said to Rachel, "I got to go now. I will call you in a couple of days. Please don't worry at all. If you should not hear from me, don't get bent out of shape. I just may be on the move. I'm not in Florida or the Bahamas. So don't worry. I love you."

I hung up and went back to my apartment, more concerned now than ever before. Why didn't the feds take action quickly? Why was I being jerked off by them? I thought the fix was on and it was a matter of time, very little time. I made up my mind once, and for all that I must play the inspector as well to save myself. I felt he was sincere and I could trust him, but the people around him must be on the Mob's payroll. My instincts told me that they were using him to find me even though he didn't know it. I knew in my heart of hearts that they would not agree to my terms now or ever. If they acted as if they might work with me, it would only be to get me to drop my guard and allow the Mob to get me first. It would be very easy for them to claim that they did all they could to protect me and the Mob must have infiltrated their confidential files. They would announce that an investigation was being conducted to find out what went wrong. The problem with that scenario was that I would be history no matter what their investigation reveals this was certain. I must get out of town and head for parts unknown and start a new life, alone! I thought I had to end all contact with Rachel and anyone else who could lead them to me. It wouldn't be easy, but I could do it and I'd best start right now!

I did not leave the apartment until after five as I did not want to hang out on the beach. I felt very much alone as I spent the day thinking about my next move. I could have gone to The Barn and spend the afternoon in the lounge, but I wanted to be alone to gather my thoughts so that I could think more clearly and plan my next course of action. I entered the club a little after five and checked in as I usually do. I left everything in my locker and had left my gun and money in the safe up front. I sat in the lounge and saw Pumpkin. She recognized me at once.

She came running over and said, "Hi, Harold, do you want a drink? Vodka on the rocks with a twist, isn't that right?

"You have a great memory to go along with a great body," I said in a very happy tone.

"Thanks, Harold, you're sweet. Just relax and I'll bring your drink in a few minutes. Do you want any snacks as well?" she said.

"Sure thing, Pumpkin, bring me whatever you've got."

In a few minutes, she was back with a tray of shrimp, chicken wings, and some sort of dumplings as well as my drink. She put the tray down beside me on a little side table and said, "Enjoy, Harold, and by the way one of the hostesses Ellie would love to chat with you. Can I send her over?"

"Of course, Pumpkin. I want to meet everyone here, it will make me feel more comfortable and at home," I said.

She went off, and a moment later, a tall, dark-haired beauty with legs that seemed to be endless arrived. Her face was a dead ringer for Ava Gardner as she came over to my table.

"Hi, I'm Ellie, and I just wanted to meet you, Harold."

I looked at her and saw a beautiful looking woman with class. She carried herself as if she was royalty.

"I am so glad to meet you, Ellie. You are a beautiful woman," I said.

"Why thanks, Harold, we are going to get along real well with wonderful compliments like these," she sexily said.

"Would you like a drink?" I asked.

"I'll have a champagne cocktail, let me ring for Pumpkin."

She went over to the intercom on the wall nearby and spoke. A moment later another hostess arrived carrying her champagne cocktail.

"This is Candy. Candy, this is Harold," she said.

"It's a pleasure to meet you, Harold. Can I refresh your drink?" she said.

"Sure, you can, vodka on the rocks with a twist," I said.

"I know what you are drinking. I'll be right back."

I watched her leave with her beautiful natural red hair and an ass to die for, which was just beckoning to me. I was wrapped up in this place, who wouldn't be?

"So, Harold, how do you like the club?" Ellie asked.

"I think it's great, and I will frequent it as often as I can while I am here," I said.

"And how long will that be?" Ellie asked innocently.

"I have to be back at work in a week or so, but I will try to come back soon to visit with you all," I said.

"You're nice, Harold, and word is getting around the club that you are generous as well. It is good to meet nice and generous people. Most people just want to have sex all the time and forget about meeting people and discovering what makes them tick. You seem different, Harold. I sure hope I am not disappointed with my opinion of you." She kissed me on the cheek and squeezed my arm gently.

"I am a decent guy who wants to meet nice people and share some of my time with them, Ellie. So far everyone here has been so very nice, and they all seem to be so genuine. This makes me happy, and the club seems to have a diverse group of members. It looks like, from all appearances, that you have guys from all walks of life. This is great and can only help make this place a resounding success," I said.

It was now getting closer to seven, and I was starting to feel sorry I didn't make my appointment earlier. Ellie had left as she had to meet with some of her members, and I had run out of conversation. I was watching a group of guys get together to play cards, and there was Mario once again. He showed no signs of recognition as he went right by me to take a seat at the card table. Another guy I recognized as one of the Mob guys was Tony Guido. I met him once at Larry's office and didn't forget his face. He was tall, skinny with greased black as coal hair. He looked like a tough and hard Frank Sinatra. He owned all the adult theaters in Florida as well as a very large money lending business. There were two other big guys near him, they didn't play card. They just watched. It was obvious to me that they were his bodyguards, and either Tony owned this club or was a very important part of the operation. The situation was getting very difficult for me fireworks could erupt at any time. I had to be very careful and watch what I say. I knew I should not drink too much; I must keep control at all times and make sure I don't say something that would cause me some very serious trouble. I stood by the table, listening to the guys as they played cards; what I heard blew my mind.

"Did you hear about this asshole in New York, Harry Miller? There's two hundred Gs out for his head," Tony said as he began shuffling the cards.

"Yeah, I heard he might head for Florida. What the fuck! He certainly ain't here, so let's play cards," one of the guys said.

I was laughing to myself and trying to be as casual as I could be. I moved away from the table and went over to the lounge again and ordered another drink. I'll just sip on it for a while and wait until my time comes up. I was back in the locker room getting dressed and felt great. I had just finished an hour of great sex with someone even better than Tina. This could easily become a habit. The people and place made me feel so damn good and let me get rid of some of the stress that was thrust upon me since some people decided to kill me. I told myself not to get sucked into this life no matter how wonderful it seemed. Trouble is around the corner, and it isn't going away. I picked up my stuff, including my gun and left the club.

As I drove along Oakland Park Boulevard, I noticed a black sedan behind me. I could not be sure if it was following me or not so I decided to make some turns and see if they stayed with me. I turned right on a residential street, and the black sedan followed. I turned right again on to another small and very quiet street and pulled into a parking space. The black sedan kept on going, and about five hundred feet ahead pulled over and stopped. I waited about fifteen minutes, and so did the sedan. I started the car again and pulled into a driveway without using my headlights. I backed out of the driveway and started up the street. I had just come down with my lights still out. I looked in the rear view mirror and saw that the sedan was turning around. I gunned it and turned back onto Federal Highway and drove a couple of blocks and turned on to Sunset toward the water. I was driving as carefully as I could without speeding as I used evasive action by taking side streets. Whether the sedan lost me or I could not find it, I wasn't sure, so I drove around for another hour just to see if I was being followed. Once I was certain I had lost them, I headed for home.

I guess the club was a focal point and they must be following me because my car had New York plates. I was very upset with myself because I screwed up. I should have rented a car with local plates, as most tourists do. Using my own car was a stupid mistake and could easily have cost me my life. It also didn't make sense to throw around money if I was too cheap to fly from New York. I left a very generous tip for Tina the first night, and I was certain by the actions of the other girls that they all knew about it. When Ellie told me that word had gotten around about my generosity, I should have been suspicious at once. I was blinded by my need for company and the atmosphere of the club. My dick got hard and my brain got soft. I was a fool, and it could have been game over. If they knew who I was, they would have taken me down immediately. There was no doubt about it. I think they wanted to be sure, and although I didn't match up with the description, they had to make certain. A $200K reward for my life was a lot of money, and there were a lot of guys who would like to have that kind of money and would do anything for it. I thought my club days were over. I didn't know what to think, but I felt just by losing them, I might have confirmed that I am the guy they were looking for. What a dilemma this was! And I certainly didn't help thing by being careless. All I knew was that I was making things a lot worse for myself by not being careful. I vowed to take things a lot slower and make sure I had covered all angles.

I went back to my apartment and decided to get a good night's sleep. I screwed up, but I didn't use the address of the condo as my place. I gave them an address in New Jersey and told them I was at the Sheraton in Lauderdale. They now had my license number, and if they ran the plates, they would find a hole in my story. My plates were from New York, and I said I was from New Jersey. My car was parked indoors so if they were driving around they would not see it parked anywhere. Of course, I didn't know how strong their connections were but two hundred K was a big incentive.

If they called every building doorman and gave my description as well as the make and license number of the car, it would only be a matter of a few minutes until they got here. I decided to pack up my suitcase and take it down to the garage and leave it in my car. I then returned to the apartment and began the job of wiping everything down. I washed the place as best I could and left it neat and clean. I didn't have much, but whatever I wanted was in my suitcase. I threw out all the garbage in the incinerator including anything that may lead anyone to me.

Tuesday, February 26, 1957

It was a little after midnight when I finished cleaning the place from top to bottom. I finally gave the apartment another check up before leaving just to make sure I didn't leave anything behind. Maybe I was being too careful, but after the screw-ups I had made I'd better make certain I had left nothing to chance.

I went down to the car and removed my license plate and placed another in its place. At this hour, it was easy to remove a plate from another car parked in the garage and put mine in its place. Odds are that the owner of this car wouldn't realize that the plate had been changed for a few days, and by that time, I would have gotten rid of this car. I pulled out of the garage onto A1A and started on my journey, when I noticed a big black Cadillac exiting the driveway from the next door building. I felt that Lady Luck was on my side as I watched the car turn into the driveway of my building. I left Lauderdale by the sea and drove north in the nick of time. I wanted to get as far away from here and get rid of this car, the sooner the better. I was getting tired of running. All I wanted was to end this nightmare and stay in one place. If I went back east, my risk would increase an awful lot and easily improve their chances of finding me. If I moved out west, my chances were a lot better, perhaps I could lose them.

As I drove along, I blamed the inspector and his people because they did not do anything to protect me and acted as if there was no rush. If they told me tomorrow that they will meet all my conditions, how in hell would I get to them? Most importantly how could I trust them after the way they have acted on my behalf? I was very screwed up and really did not know what avenue to take. One mistake, and I was dead, but my first step was to get the hell out of here as fast as I can. The more miles I can put between them and myself would be make me feel a lot more comfortable.

I drove without stopping until first light, when I reached Tampa and had to fill up. I stopped in at a Howard Johnson for breakfast and picked up a map that would help me navigate my way out west. It was around eight thirty, and I wanted to get rid of the car now. I found a used car lot and parked my car two blocks away and walked back to it.

I found a very tired looking guy, who was just opening the small office. I asked him about a Chevy he had in the lot, and he perked up right away. I negotiated a price, and for five hundred dollars, I made a deal with him, and forty-five minutes later drove out of his lot in my new car with temporary Florida plates. I drove around the corner to my old car and removed my luggage and anything else that was in the car. I removed the plates and left the car where I parked it and wiped it down thoroughly. One more thing off my back, and now I can move on and maybe get them off my trail.

I drove about one hundred miles and stopped at a service area and called Moe at his office, "Hey, Moe, how are you and things in the big city?" I said.

"Harry, it's so nice to hear your voice. I was worried if you were all right. Where are you?" he said.

"I'm just outside of Tampa and moving west. I have to get as far away from here as possible. The two hundred K offered for my head is a very high incentive for every cowboy to try and find me. I don't relish being dead so I must move on. I had a close call because I was lazy and didn't take enough precautions. This will not happen again I can assure you. I had to call you to let you know what I'm doing and stay in touch. I also wanted to know if the situation has changed and perhaps you may have heard some news, anything at all," I said.

"Please be very careful when you call me. If I speak in a cool tone, wait until I let you know the coast is clear. When I address you as 'Harry' you will know all is okay, and you can speak freely. Here is what I have heard from the folks that are chasing you. They pin pointed your whereabouts as Florida and have sent a lot of Mob enforcers there to find you. It seems you didn't have an ironclad cover story and somehow they pieced it together that you could be in Florida. You must do things a little slower, Harry, and make certain you don't leave any trails or clues that will lead them to you. Thank goodness you changed your looks, but that will not always work when you leave other clues. Please be careful and take your time, consider every option and make sure whatever you have left behind cannot be traced back to you. You are top priority on their hit list, you can count on that. If you decide to give yourself up to the inspector, they will find a way to eliminate you when you do. The inspector means well, but he is a pawn in this chess game they are playing. He really is powerless and is being manipulated by the Mob even though he doesn't know it. The Mob has too many people on their team, and these people are very well connected. So please be careful. If you need funds, let me know, and I'll make arrangements to get it to you. Just trust yourself and no one else, please, Harry, be very careful," he said.

I told him I didn't need any money and I'll get back in touch when I get settled. I decided that California was the best place to begin again. I could always go to Mexico if I had to, but most of all I can get lost in San Francisco or Los Angeles. I made a decision that I would not go easily. I would start fighting as of now! I would be smart, and I would confuse the shit out of them and kill as many as I have to until they stop looking and let me go on with my life or kill me. I knew this was a bunch of crap as these animals would not stop until I was eliminated. I just needed to establish my own witness protection plan and start a new life as a new person.

I now had a 55 Chevrolet Bel Air with very low mileage and Florida plates. I felt good because I now had a different car that they didn't know about, and they wouldn't really know what direction I was taking. They weren't sure if I was Harry, but I was a suspect, especially after my actions of moving out. Of course, if they only tried to piece together, who I was they could never match me up. I looked different and could not believe they would go so far as to try to find my New Jersey address. I would stop very shortly for the day and change my appearance again so I would be a different person on the road.

I figured it would take me five or six days to get to California, but most importantly, I would be out of harm's way, for a while at least. I was on the way to Chicago and hoped to arrive there sometimes tomorrow night. I pulled into a dumpy looking motel and took a room for the night and began my transformation. I was lucky I had taken my make-up kit with me. I really needed it now. Where could I find the material I needed to change my looks out here? Maybe, my luck was changing I sure as hell hoped so. I also picked up a map so that I could better plan the route to California. I really would prefer to bypass Chicago if I can.

Wednesday, February 27, 1957

I got on the road and stuck to the speed limit as I drove toward Tallahassee. I did not want to draw any attention to myself especially by a cop. I finally left the State of Florida and entered Alabama. As I drove along, I decided I'd best call Rachel. I didn't really want to, as I felt our marriage was rapidly coming to an end. Even though she was on my side, she really could not continue to live like this. No matter what she may say to me on the phone I must make sure that her only concern was Rachel. It's not like I blame her. I probably would do the same if the roles were reversed. I pulled into another Howard Johnson and called.

"Hi, sweetheart, how are you feeling?" I said.

"I'm fine, except I miss you a lot and can't stand not knowing if you are alive or not," Rachel said.

"Stop that stuff. What do you mean if I am alive or not? If I was dead, you would have the news very quickly," I said quite sharply.

"I overheard Larry yesterday when he was told that they thought they had found you in Florida. Are you really in Florida?" she asked.

"No, I'm not, and I won't tell you where I am. It is best that you don't know so that no mistakes can be made," I replied. "Listen to me, Rachel," I continued, "I'll let you know just where I am as soon as I get there. Right now I don't know where that will be. If things don't go the way I think they should, I will disappear, and this nightmare will be over for us all. If things go the way I want, I will then let you know where I am, and you can join me. There will be no coming back once you join me. So please be careful, be patient, and just love me and have faith," I said.

"I do love you, and I will be careful. I can't guarantee patience, but I'll try," she said.

"Listen to me, Rachel. I want you to think about this very carefully and be responsible once in your life. You can quit all this by divorcing me. I won't try to contest it in anyway, as I understand the stress and danger you are under because of me. Think about it, it may be better if you choose this path as it will remove you from a direct hit from the Mob. Please don't think I want you to leave me because that isn't true, but I do want what is best for you. You don't have to answer me this second, but please promise me you will think about it and evaluate your situation, please!" I said.

"Harry, why are you talking this way?" she said. "Yes, I'll think about it, but I really don't want to be without you.

"I've got to go now. I will call you on Friday. Don't worry, I can take care of myself, and I will be careful. I love you a lot," I said as I hung up and got back into the car and got on my way. I decided not to call the inspector today; let him wait.

Thursday, February 28, 1957

I could not continue driving like this, so I finally decided to rest in Mississippi. I was very tired and very worn out mentally as I drove and thought. This was really taking a lot out of me and sort of making me a little crazy. I got a good night's sleep and continued on my way.

I drove through the rest of Mississippi and on to Louisiana, where I finally reached Baton Rouge and decided to take a motel for the night and get on the road early.

Friday, March 1, 1957

I left real early and drove into the State of Texas. I stopped and called the inspector, "Hi, Sam, it's me," I said.

"Well, it's about time. Where are you?" he said.

"It's none of your business for the moment. Just tell me the deal is settled so that I can arrange things and get out of harm's way," I said quite loudly.

"Well, we are still waiting for the attorney general to agree with your requests," he said very sheepishly.

"What a bunch of bullshit this is! You are amazing, Sam. You threaten me with an arrest on trumped up charges only to get me to be an informer against the Mob and now you just abandon me. You must think I am some real asshole who doesn't realize he is being fucked over. You think I am going to come back to your jail just to be your sucker? Better think twice, Sam. I wanted to be on your side, and you are just making a fool out of me. How can I trust you? You are worse than the guys you want me to go up against. Listen to me, and listen well, my good man. I will call you on Tuesday, and you either have news for me that guarantees my safety and agrees to all of my terms or you can forget my help in anyway. There is no way you can come after me after I agreed to help and asked for very simple safeguards. I know it's not in your hands and that you would do all you could to help me, but, Sam, you are in a cesspool of corrupt officials. A word of advice, Sam. Trust no one, not even your boss. They will fuck you somewhere down the line. And by the way, Sam, you will have a hard time finding me, I can promise you that," I said and hung up.

I was scared and very angry. How could these motherfuckers think that I would just cooperate with them without guarantees? Who is worse, the law or the lawbreakers? Who the fuck knows, certainly not I.

I knew one thing. When cops want help, they make deals fast, so someone on the Mob's payroll is derailing the deal. They were buying time so that they could find me and get me out of the way before the feds could get their hands on me. I was sure the attorney general had never heard of me and knew nothing of this deal. Let's get on with the war. It's my only option at this time.

Saturday, March 2, 1957

I drove through Texas. It was one of the most boring trip I have ever taken. It seemed to take forever and only made me anxious to get the hell out of there and get on my way to New Mexico. I took a little detour when I entered into Arizona because I wanted to see the Grand Canyon. I drove through Flagstaff in Northern Arizona and saw the Grand Canyon, even though it was freezing.

It was an awesome sight to see—so majestic and peaceful. The Colorado River looked like a little stream from my vantage point. It was a relief from the freezing cold to come down to Boulder City and move on to Las Vegas, where the temperature was a little warmer. I needed rest and a little relaxing, so I pulled into the Dunes and decided to spend the night there. I thought maybe, I would play a little blackjack, eat some good food, and in the morning move on. Next to New York, this place was Mafia city, although these goons didn't recognize me at all. If they knew who I was, they would have a special place for me—far out in the desert where no one would ever find me. I checked in under the name Ralph Meeker as I had some fake papers and some kind of identification under this name that I found in the Chevy Bel Air. I carried my one suitcase to my room and put the "Do Not Disturb sign" on the doorknob. I grabbed a quick shower and then decided to take a walk around the casino. I just needed to stretch my legs a little. The place was busy with people playing, craps, blackjack, slots, keno; you name it, and it was there.

This was the first time I have ever been in a casino, it was quite exciting. I didn't realize that everything everyone does is watched closely on cameras and spotters. People walk above our heads and look through peep holes so that they can watch us, as we give our money to them. Every mirror must be a two-way so that they can watch from there as well. I found out about all these security measures at the bar when I met this woman who had just lost a bundle and was a little upset. She sat down beside me, as I was nursing a drink, and she began to spout off about the spotters and the mirrors. She was upset after losing over ten K. Bouncers were everywhere; you can just tell exactly who they are. I made sure my gun was close, as this place scared the shit out of me. Once again, I realized that I had made another error by stopping in at this place. After making my run through the casino, I decided to get back to my room and get some sleep and get the hell out of this place. I was tired and I could use a good sleep after the long drive. As I entered the hallway leading to my room, I saw two guys at my door with guns in their hands. Obviously, they thought I was in the room because the "Do Not Disturb sign" was still hanging on the knob. It was a good thing that the surveillance cameras did not go into the room areas and only the casino.

I hung back and waited in a doorway to see what they were up to, when one of them knocked on the door. "Room service," he said and waited. No response, he repeated his knock and said, "Room service." Still no response, he finally took out a key and inserted it into the lock. The door opened, and they went in. I decided it would be best if I blew their heads off in the room rather than make a run for it. I started heading toward the room when a voice in my head said, "Don't go in there," so I changed my mind. Leaving Vegas right now was one of my thoughts, but if I did that wouldn't it be a confirmation that I was Harry Miller? Of course, it would, but what to do? I continued to stand in the hallway watching the door to my room and waiting. I decided to wait until they left the room and then I would call the front desk and report a theft. If I act as any other legitimate guest, then the proper course of action was to call the front desk and report it and get indignant about it. I thought it's a chance I have to take. Maybe it would work, or would they blow me away? No, I must make a stand, and it might as well be here. They know my car. They were probably watching the car as well to see if I'd run. No I would take my chances now. I turned back to the casino and walked over to the hotel front desk.

"Hi, I'm Ralph Meeker, room 302. I'd like to report a break-in in my room. I was going to my room a minute ago and when I noticed two guys fiddling with the lock on my door and then they opened the door and went in. I am sure your hotel does not like this type of activity. I suggest you send someone to investigate. I just hope they don't steal all my clothes," I said,

"What is your room number again, sir," he said.

"302, and hurry, I want those bastards caught in the act," I said.

"If I may suggest, sir, would you like to have drink in our VIP lounge while we sort this out?" he said.

"Sure thing, and let's get this straightened out quick."

I called over a bellboy and asked him to show me where the VIP lounge was. I didn't have time to try a drink when a very well dressed man came in and introduced himself.

"Mr. Meeker, I am Steve Gallo, General Manager of the Dunes. Let me apologize for the inconvenience and rest assured that we will get to the bottom of this. In the meantime, it's our pleasure to have you as our guest of the Dunes Hotel & Casino, so please enjoy."

"Thank you, Mr. Gallo. I do appreciate your concern, but I would like to get into my room as soon as possible. Did you catch the intruders?" I asked.

"Yes, as a matter-of-fact they were arrested a few minutes ago. Your things will be brought to your new suite in a few minutes. We do apologize. This is not the way our guests are treated. Rest assured we are handling the situation and have it under control. This will not happen again, Mr. Meeker."

I don't know what happened or what came down, but I did spend the night in a wonderful suite and ate to my heart's content. Of course, no charge, not for anything. I was Mr. Gallo's guest. Perhaps, my stand removed their suspicions of me, perhaps not, in any case, I didn't care. I only knew I had to be very careful in what my actions would be while I was around this place.

Sunday, March 3, 1957

I was up very early because I wanted to get the hell out of Vegas. I left Las Vegas around seven in the morning and kept an eye out that I wasn't followed. I was nervous as hell as I drove out of the city and took route 15 to Los Angeles. I started to relax when I reached Barstow; so far nothing happened, and I drove on to Los Angeles I arrived a little after one in the afternoon and found a hotel on Pico Boulevard near Twentieth Street, in Santa Monica. I left the car six blocks away just in case anyone might be looking for it. After the Dunes, I cannot trust anything or anyone.

I walked the six blocks to the hotel. I checked in using the name Allen Foster and got some shut eye. I woke up at around 4:00 p.m. and went out to see what was going on in this area. I had met a guy from Los Angeles while I was going to school and I still had his name and address, who was the only person I knew. Should I call him? I decided not to. The less people who knew me as Harry Miller would be a safer bet for my survival. If I was to have a new start, I could not look up anyone who would know me.

I decided to find a bar and have a few drinks and meet some people. You could always meet someone in a bar that was shady and guaranteed someone who knows someone to get things rolling when one wants to establish a new identity. It's a risk, but I have no other choice, I've got to get established, and it's got to be done fast. It was possible that the Vegas crowd might have put it all together and have advised the Mob that I was headed for Los Angeles. Even if they were wrong, they would still alert their contacts here. My description using my old disguise was certainly out there, so first things first, change my appearance. The second step is to change cars once again and that will need a new identity to get the car registered properly. I went to a thrifty drug and bought hair dye and a few other make-up items I would need. I also found a Salvation Army outlet where I picked up some used clothes to help change my appearance. When in thrifty, I bought a pair of glasses that would change my face as well as mascara, eye shadow and rouge as I needed a new look. I wanted to add fifteen years and ten pounds to myself. This would change the way people would look at me. I wanted to go to the bar tonight to get something started, but before I do, I had to make the changes.

I worked on my new appearance until about eight it took so long because I just wasn't happy about the results and had to do it over and over again. I now looked at least ten years older as I added lines and a mustache. My hair was now black as was my eyebrows, mustache and eyelashes. I knew this was going to be an ongoing job as I had to look the same each day. The coloring would last at least a month before I would have to redo it again. The rest I could maintain on a daily basis. Along with the new appearance I needed a new set of papers that would give me a fighting chance to dig in here. I decided to remove the temporary Florida license plates I had on the car. I would drive it somewhere on the other side of town and just abandon it there. It would not be difficult to get a new car here in Los Angeles. Everywhere I went, there were car lots. I would get a new car for a few hundred dollars, a clunker just to get me around. I wasn't going to let these motherfuckers find me so easily.

It was dark, and it was Sunday, so the bars would not be crowded, but I had to make the move. Time was not on my side, so I decided to take a walk on Pico until I found an interesting-looking bar with the right kind of people in it. I finally stopped in at Johnny's Bar because it was dark and looked like a place that would be a little raunchy. Once inside, there was a long bar to my left with mostly empty stools. On my right was an open area that was probably used as a dance floor and then booths lined the wall. In the very rear of the place there were two large pool tables with action as I walked in.

This was the kind of place that you could find a sleazebag with anything you might need. The only thing I need now was time and a good cover story for the bartender.

I sat down at the bar and ordered a draft beer and just sipped slowly, minding my own business.

"Hey, pal, I haven't seen you in here before. Are you new to the neighborhood? By the way, I'm Johnny!" he said as he extended his hand to me.

"Nice to know you, Johnny. I'm Allen, Allen Foster. I used to live in Venice, but my wife and I just split up. I'm staying at a hotel nearby until I find a permanent place. What a bummer! I didn't see it coming. She dumped me and threw me out of the house. The bitch changed the locks, went and got a court order that I can't come within five hundred feet of her. She said I threatened her. That's crap. I never threatened anyone in my life," I said.

"Sorry about that," Johnny said. "Women can be real bitches, especially when they want something. Let me buy you a drink, Allen, you sure look like you can use it."

"Thanks, Johnny, I appreciate it. I don't have any friends here in this part of town. Thanks," I said.

Johnny walked down to the other end of the bar and poured a drink for a guy sitting there and walked back to my end and said, "Where are you from, Allen?"

"I moved here from Pennsylvania, a small town called Tannersville. I came here because my wife said she was bored living in such a small place and she hated the winters. Got a rented place in Venice on Nineteenth Street near the Pacific Coast Highway and settled in. I started looking for a job, and she was supposed to do the same. I found a job, working for a marketing company, making phone calls all day and setting up appointments for aluminum windows and sidings. I got paid five bucks for every appointment I made and twenty bucks for every one sold. It wasn't much of a job, but it put bread on the table, and I could make a couple of hundred a week. In the meantime, she went out looking for a job as a secretary, or at least that's what she told me. She was really walking around the boardwalk and meeting guys. I think she was turning tricks because she always seemed to have plenty of money. She was acting pretty shitty with me, always telling me that I didn't make enough money, and I really don't want to take her out to nice places. I was getting very discouraged," I said to Johnny as he went to greet two new customers.

"Sorry, Allen, I'll be right back," he said.

I felt my story was going well, and I guessed I would have to frequent this place a few more times before I get the confidence of Johnny and get what I need. I decided that another drink was in order and if would allow me to complete my story. Caution was my credo, "Don't drink too much." So I decided on this drink being my last for tonight.

"Okay, Allen, I'm all ears, another beer?"

"Sure," I said.

"Here you are. Enjoy and remember, Allen, I am always here, ready to listen. If you feel like shit, or you have to unload, stop by Johnny's."

"Thanks," I said, "What got me was that she was just a country girl, never been out of a small town. She certainly used me to get here and now she doesn't need me. Worst of all, she won't let me into even get my wallet. I have no ID, no license, no anything. I have to write to DMV in Pennsylvania, and that could take weeks. What a bitch!"

"That's pretty low, "Johnny said. "If there is anything I can do, just let me know."

"Hey, Johnny, thanks for your offer. You're a stand-up guy, I appreciate it. What I will do is probably buy a phony ID so I can get by until I get my stuff back from Pennsylvania. I don't even know where to get that. Not to worry, I'll ask some guys at work who might know," I said.

"Hey, you be careful who you talk to about shit like that. You can get into trouble, even lose your job, so just take it easy," Johnny said.

"Good advice, Johnny, thanks," I said.

I finished my last beer and said goodnight and left. I went back to my hotel room to get some sleep. Tomorrow would be soon enough to put the move on Johnny.

Monday, March 4, 1957

I woke up early and immediately called Rachel to find out what was new and if she heard any updates. She told me nothing new other than she missed me and that from all she had heard, they were close to finding me.

"I heard you were in Florida, and they missed you by minutes," she said in a matter-of fact way. "You lied to me and told you were not in Florida. I don't like that. If you love me, you have to trust me and can't lie at anytime. In any case, I am so happy to hear your voice and to know that you are safe. I love you with all my heart. Please believe that," she said.

"I could not tell you that, Rachel, because I wasn't in Florida. If I did tell you where I was and you slipped up, what would happen to me? What if you, not on purpose, let it slip after a couple of drinks? I just can't take any chances, sweetie I love you with all of my heart, too, and never want to lie to you or put you in harm's way. Please understand that, please. If you don't know where I am, you can't make any mistakes," I said as gently as I could.

"I do love you. Really I do. It's just frustrating being away from you," she said. "I need to be with you and to hold you, to feel your body next to mine. It's not easy for me and I'm sure it's pretty lonely and dangerous for you. I love you always, you just remember that."

"Did you give what I told you any thought? Please don't brush it under the rug. It's too important for both of us."

On that note, I said good-bye and promised to call in a few days again. I wanted her to know that the information she was getting from Larry was wrong. Who knows if she was telling Larry everything I tell her? Blood is thicker than water, and her father was paying all her bills. He was the most important person in her life at this time.

I then placed a call to the inspector. "Sam, it's me. What the hell is going on?" I said very sternly. "Do you think this can go on forever? Either I will be dead or someone else will be, but something has to be done and done now!"

"Be calm. I think we will have all the papers signed by tomorrow and all the conditions agreed to," he said. "Once that is done, we will arrange to bring you in and protect you. Hold on one more day, and I'm pretty certain it will be resolved. I am sorry it took so long, but we had to get signatures and approvals. It wasn't easy, Harry, it sure wasn't easy," he pleaded his case.

"I just don't understand, Sam. Every story I have ever read about the cops was that they were always thrilled to get an informer on their side. You guys have put me through shit beyond belief, That sort of makes me believe you've got someone there that doesn't have my best interest at heart. It all seems like bullshit to me. Okay, Sam, I will call Wednesday morning same time, and this better be legit or someone is going to get their ass shot off."

I hung up and went back to my room. I was very uneasy and did not trust anyone. I didn't trust Sam Johnson, the great inspector. Even though deep in my heart, I believed he was a decent and honest cop. During this last call why did he use my name? He never, in all the weeks we have spoken, used my name. He had always been so careful or at least he tried to make me feel that way. No way does it take this long for a deal to be made, especially when they instigated it in the first place. Why was I picked up? Why threaten me if he didn't want a deal? Did he bite off more than he could chew? Was he part of their organization? Was someone in his group working for the Mob? Was I fucked? It all didn't make sense because I had read and heard that guys get arrested and in a day or two they make a deal that was ratified by a judge and that was it. This case was big and was exactly what they all wanted. To bring down the Mob was their goal so why was my deal taking so long? Something smelled pretty bad with the whole thing. And who was getting screwed here, me and only me. I knew I was being paranoid, but who wouldn't be in these circumstances? How do I know where to turn and who can

I trust? The world was spinning, and the doorway to hell was opening wider and wider. This nightmare was getting more and more complicated and with all these hit men on my ass, I think my chances were getting slimmer and slimmer. I decided I desperately need some sleep if I am to clear my head and think rationally about all this. Later when my mind was a little more settled, I would be able to clearly make some decisions. I had to make the right move, or I'm history. There was no room for error; my life depended upon it.

I woke up at about five thirty in the afternoon, took a shower, made sure my appearance was the same, dressed, and left for Johnny's Bar. I needed to get a driver's license and other documents as well as a car. I need to be mobile, in case I have to run without warning. I walked in and saw Johnny behind the bar.

"Hey, Johnny, how's it going?" I said as I sat down at the bar.

"Pretty shitty today. Business is always slow on Mondays, but today it has been quieter than usual. What can I get you, Allen?" he said.

"A Stoli on the rocks with a twist," I said. I sat there sipping my drink when Johnny said,

"Listen, Allen, you were talking about the ID you need, are you serious about that?" he said in a much lower voice than usual even though the place was empty. I was floored by this as I did not expect to be able to cut through the trust factor so quickly, I thought very quickly and told myself, "Harry take advantage of this, it may never happen again."

"Sure thing, Johnny. I really need to open a bank account, get a car, and start to live again. I don't go back to court with the bitch until April. Yes, sirree, I need it now," I sounded a little desperate, but it was what I had to do to make Johnny feel comfortable.

"Well, Allen, there is a guy who comes in here every once in awhile I think he may be able help you. It won't be cheap but he is the best and very reliable," Johnny said very sincerely.

"Really, that would be great. When can I meet the guy?" I said with a lot of enthusiasm.

"Let me make a phone call. I think I can get him to see you very soon." Johnny left and went to the other end of the bar and made a phone call. He came back a minute later and said that the guy will come over here in a few minutes.

"Great Johnny, I sure do appreciate this. Thanks," I said very sincerely. I continued to sip my drink when a short guy, no more than 5'4" tall, wearing a leatherjacket and a pair of jeans walks in. His face was covered with pockmarks on both cheeks. His hair was greased back and flat. He didn't look trustworthy, but a guy who deals in this type of stuff shouldn't be trusted. I also didn't have much of choice, so I went on gut feelings.

"Allen, I want you to meet Gus," Johnny said.

"Hey, Gus, a pleasure to meet you. Can I buy you a drink?" I said as friendly as possible.

"Sure, Johnny, my usual," Gus said.

Johnny went to the other end of the bar, and Gus sat down next to me and said, "So you need some papers! What do you need? The whole works or just a piece or two?" he said that in a deep baritone voice, which was far stronger than his size.

"My wife threw me out and refused to let me back into get my stuff. I need it all until my license gets here from Pennsylvania. That could take months. In the meantime, I got to live," I said.

"It will cost you three hundred bucks for a Social Security card and driver's license. If you want a passport, it will cost an extra four hundred. I'll need a couple of passport size photos. If this is okay, then bring me five hundred in cash and the photos tomorrow and leave them with Johnny in a sealed envelope. I will leave your papers and passport here at Johnny's on Friday. Write down your name and address, date of birth, hair and eye colors so that I can get started. Is that clear?" he said quite emphatically.

"Clear as clear can be. Let me give you five hundred now, and I will leave the balance as instructed," I said as I took out a roll of bills from my pocket and counted off five clean one hundred dollar bills. Gus picked up the money and walked out. It took all of five minutes. I stayed at the bar for another two hours so that Johnny wouldn't feel that the only thing I needed from him were the papers. I left and went back to my room and had a good night's sleep.

Tuesday, March 5, 1957

I decided that today would be good day to just see Los Angeles and stay away from Johnny's Bar. I dressed and made sure my disguise was in order and went downtown to Hollywood and Vine. I had to go shopping for a wig, as I wanted to be able to maintain the same hair style easily. I walked along the famous Hollywood Boulevard and found a shop that sells and rents costumes, wigs, beards etc. I spent two hours finding the right wig I needed. I bought two of them.

The story I concocted for the costume shop was that I was auditioning for some parts and needed this look. I spent nearly three hundred on both wigs. I then checked out the sidewalk of the stars in front of Grumman's Chinese Theater on Hollywood Boulevard. I decided to take a guided tour and kill a few hours. Later that afternoon, I bought a newspaper and picked up some Chinese food and went back to my room to relax and get some rest.

Wednesday, March 6, 1957

I called the inspector first thing as I wanted to get this resolved. "Hi, Sam, what news do you have?" I asked at once not wanting to waste time.

"Everything is set, Harry. The judge has signed all the papers, and we are ready for you. Where are you? We'd like to arrange to pick you up as soon as possible and get started on this project," he said.

I felt ill at ease once again, as he used my name, something we never do. "Okay, Sam, I will have my wife call you and get things organized. Give her copies of the signed papers, and I will then call you back so that we can arrange a safe pick up," I said.

"It is highly unusual to do it this way. We can give your attorney the copies of the agreements and work through him if that's okay with you, but giving them to your wife, who lives with the enemy, is a little dicey," the inspector said.

"You may be right, Sam" I said. "Let me arrange it with my attorney, and once I do that I will call you back. It shouldn't take more than a day at most and we can organize from there," I said.

"Okay, Harry, call me back soon. We are anxious to get started," he said.

I hung up and felt very nervous and extremely suspicious. Why all this cloak and dagger? I felt Sam was being compromised. They got to him and he was being manipulated. Caution was the key word here. "Be very careful, Harry Miller, no good will come of all this."

I called Rachel and explained what the inspector and I talked about and how the deal will work. "Darling, be very careful. I think they have some people in the NYPD as well as the feds and probably the judge, who are reporting everything," she said and continued, "these papers are just a bunch of bullshit. I don't think the judge knows anything about it and has never signed them. Something stinks in this deal, so please be careful. I heard my dad talking to Mario yesterday and it seems that the council has increased the number to two hundred K, That's big bucks and will make a lot of honest people turn bad. Why not call Moe Arnold? He is a good lawyer, a friend, and he can get those papers for you. Do you want me to call him? I will gladly do it. I think you need someone who will watch out for you," she said very lovingly.

"You are right. I will call Moe right after I get off with you and let him in on the deal. I'll give him your number so that he can call you with an update. If things go right, I will see you in a few days. The agreement includes your disappearance and establishing a new identity together. I will call you back soon. I love you very much."

I hung up and placed a call to Moe Arnold. Moe was our attorney and friend when we had a serious car crash two years ago. He represented Rachel and I and spent a lot of time with us. He was a great guy, who had graduated from NYU a few years ago, and although he was only thirty, he was a feisty lawyer. He was no more than five foot-six inches and weighed in at one hundred and forty pounds. In court, he was like a heavyweight and fought hard to get the most he could in a settlement. He took twenty-five percent of the settlement and never once asked for any up front money to cover out of pocket expenses. We got to know each other real well and played cards a few times together. We spoke to each other at least once a week. We had developed a friendship.

"Hi, Moe, how the hell are you?" I said very sincerely.

"Is everything good?" he said, "What's going on? Please bring me up to date."

I told him everything that has taken place. I reminded him that I spoke with him a week ago and would always stay in touch. It was a good thing I had so many quarters for the phone.

"Now you are aware of everything, and I need someone to go see Inspector Sam Johnson—his number is 212-333-9875—and pick up the documents. I need these documents to be put away in a very safe place and copies made and kept in another place. My concern is your safety and nothing else. I feel that there are those in the police, feds, and DA's office that have access to all this information and then passes it along to the Mob. These guys play for keeps. There is a lot at stake here," I said.

"I understand, Harry, and I will be glad to take care of this," Moe said. "You are my friend, and that is what friends are for, how do you want to proceed?"

"You know the inspector very well, so I think you guys should arrange to use a made up name. This way if anyone is reporting to the Mob, your identity will be protected. How about Aaron Zoltan? I think that will do!" I said.

"Okay, Harry, I'll use Aaron Zoltan. What else would you like me to do?" he said.

"I think you should call him from a pay phone and set up a meeting at a very public place, like Penn Station, Grand Central. Pick a spot and set up a password with him. If the password is not used, then there is danger close by and you should get the hell out of there. Also tell him to bring three copies of the agreement. I will also request that he bring three copies. Once he gives you the password, you give him the prearranged response, take the papers, and get the hell out of there. Bring with two self-addressed envelopes and mail the papers to yourself and to another address at once and keep one copy with you. Make sure you are not followed. If you think someone is watching you, try to lose them on your way out. If you feel you can't lose them, then abort. I'm sorry, Moe, if this all sounds very melodramatic, like a movie, but reality can be frightening, and this stuff is real. Please be careful, please. I will call you tomorrow at this same time to confirm that all went according to plan and, of course, that the agreement is real and binding. My life is at stake. I can't afford any crap from the DA's office or the cops, and you're my only hope for a fair deal. Of course, Moe, if you prefer not to do this, I will understand completely. Of course, Moe, you will bill me for your time. No arguments about that," I said.

"Harry, you can count on me, this is exciting, and I want to do this. Please don't worry. I have a gun and a permit, and I love the excitement. Do you know how boring a civil attorney's work gets? Leases, agreements, divorce, auto accidents. It's a no action job, the only thing that changes daily is the weather and sometimes that doesn't even change," he said laughing.

"Okay, Moe, let me call the inspector, and I will call you back as quickly as possible. And Moe, thanks for being there, you're a real friend." I hung up and proceeded to go get more change so that I can spend more time on another phone.

I called the inspector, "Hi again, it's me. My friend will call you once we get off the phone. His name is Aaron Zoltan. That is Z-o-l-t-a-n. He will set up, directly with you, a place and time to get these papers. Please bring with three copies of the agreement and be very careful that you are not followed. Once he has confirmed the receipt of the agreement and the papers are in order, I will call you and make arrangements for my coming in. It's pretty simple, Sam. So let's get the show on the road."

I hung up and proceeded to call Moe back and gave him the okay to proceed and that the inspector was expecting his call. I also reminded Moe that he should not call Rachel and tell her anything. It would not look good if the Mob found out that she was involved in anything that has to do with me.

I then proceeded to a photo shop I noticed on Pico, near Westwood, and had passport photos taken. From there, I went to Johnny's Bar and saw Johnny as he was just coming on shift.

"Hey, pal, how you doing? I just wanted to leave these with you for Gus and have a drink with you. You have been a great pal, Johnny. I really appreciate everything you have done for me. If you ever need anything that I can do for you, just say the word, it's yours." I picked up my vodka and started to sip it slowly.

"It was nothing, Allen, nothing at all. You are a good guy, I could tell. I've been in this bartending business for years, and I can tell an asshole and a real guy apart. You are a good guy, and I hope we stay friends for a long time," Johnny said with a smile from ear to ear. I sat there for another couple of hours shooting the shit with Johnny and drinking one too many. I left and went home and crashed without getting undressed.

Thursday, March 7, 1957

I woke up with my head spinning. I jumped into the shower swallowed a couple of aspirins I started to feel alive again after the shower and a couple of coffees and decided it was time to check in with Moe to see if all went as planned. I filled my pockets with change and made my call.

"Hey, Moe, how are you? Did everything go all right?" I said.

"Yes and no. I called the inspector, and he was very nervous about all this secret code stuff. I finally had to tell him to stop worrying and get the show on the road. I finally said to him it's a go or let's forget the deal. Well, he got real uppity and finally agreed to meet at Grand Central at 3:00 p.m. We settled on our password and so on. I thought everything was a go until he asked me for my number so that he could get in touch if things should change. I lost it at this point and told him to get fucked. I told him that I knew him well so there's no need to bullshit each another. I asked him either there is an agreement or not so why all this cloak and dagger? I told him to get with it or I am hanging up."

"This doesn't sound like a done deal when he acts this way, Moe," I said.

"Hold on a second. It got better. He asked me not to hang up and told we would meet as arranged. He said, 'I have everything properly signed, but I need to know who you are and how to get in touch with Harry?' Boy, the balls of this guy. Something doesn't seem kosher here. So I said to him let's get this shit done *now!* Harry will get in touch with you after he knows everything went smoothly and all is in order," Moe said.

"So did you meet and get the papers?" I asked anxiously.

"No, I didn't. Because I don't believe he had any papers. I think he was setting you up and is out to fuck you. I told him I'd call tomorrow and set a new meeting at a place I choose, and if it is yes, I will be there, or no, I won't. No more horseshit. No more stalling, and then I hung up. I feel, Harry, he wants to get you to come in, and there is no doubt in my mind that someone is working with the Mob. Maybe it's not him, but his bosses sure as hell are. Call me again tomorrow, and I will let you know if it came down or not. In the meantime, take the advice of a friend. Trust no one and be very careful. I'll speak to you tomorrow. By the way, Harry, don't get your hopes up too high, I don't think there will be a deal."

He hung up. I was shocked after listening to Moe. Should I call the inspector or should I just leave it alone? I didn't know what to do and could not discuss it with anyone. Finally, I decided to call the piece of garbage, inspector.

"Sam, it's me. Tell me what the hell is going on? I will only speak for a very short time, so don't bother tracing this call. Now what's up, shithead?" I said loudly.

"Harry, you can't speak to me like that," he said.

"Shut your face and tell me in ten seconds just what is going on?" I said. I then hung up and waited another ten minutes and called back, "Sam, you have less than a minute to tell me," I said quickly.

"I just wasn't sure who this guy was. I'll take care of everything tomorrow, guaranteed," he said.

"Fuck you." I hung up and went to Johnny's Bar. I was hot and very screwed up.

Friday, March 8, 1957

I called Rachel early. as the events of yesterday blew my mind and I wanted to get her call out of the way so that I'd be mentally prepared for what may transpire today.

"Hi, honey, how are you? Hope you are doing okay and have some news for me?" I said as cheerfully as possible.

"No, I don't have any real news. Things seem to be really fucked up over here. There are lots of rumors and I heard Larry telling someone on the phone that he does not know where you are and hasn't heard from you in a long time and hopes he never hears from you. I'm not sure someone won't come and grab me just because they are such assholes and want you very badly," Rachel said.

"I know, sweetheart, it seems they are setting me up, and I can't really trust anyone. So far the inspector has bullshitted me and has not produced a fucking piece of paper. I think they are working together with the Mob to eliminate me. Once out of the way, they can blame me for anything they want and resume normal business. I guess the attorney general will be satisfied if he gets a fall guy just to show the public that he is doing a great job in eradicating organized crime," I said with a little hate in my voice.

"Look, I don't want you to start feeling this way, Harry. We will get it all worked out. I just don't know who to turn to and what more I can do," she said quite upset.

"Rachel, I want you to send a message, please," I said.

"But how if I'm not supposed to hear from you?" she protested. "People would find it strange that we are separated and then I am speaking for you!" she shrieked again.

I could tell she was losing it. The pressure was more than she could bear "Listen to me. You can tell Larry that I called today to threaten you. Tell him I said if it's war, they want, then war they'll get. Tell him I said I won't be fucked over any longer. If you say it that way, he will pass the message along to the right people, and you will be out of the picture. Larry will protect you from me and anyone else who would try to come and get you," I said.

"Larry has full time bodyguards watching me 24/7, so I guess I'll be safe," she said.

"Look, Rachel, there is something going on, and I am the patsy. I have to take steps now and try to get this situation stabilized. Please pass this along and find out all you can. I will call you tomorrow. Remember, I love you, and if we are going to have a future, we have to get rid of this problem now! I love you, call you tomorrow." I hung up over her tears and decided to calm down a little before I called Moe.

I must get a couple more guns that would help me cut the bastards down to size. If they wanted war, I would give them war. It was them or me, and only one could win. As far as I was concerned, it would be me. There was no other option, none whatsoever. I went back to my apartment and looked at my disguise in the mirror. I had to be perfect at all times if I was to continue being someone else. This battle required all of my expertise. I took off my hat and examined my thick hair with a little shock of gray and my mustache and short beard colored to look the same as my hair. I also wore tinted glasses to help with the final look. The beard, mustache, and hair were all false, but were essential in my desire to carry out this deception.

I was sure that not even Rachel would recognize me, I felt good on how I looked and now all I had to do was to be very careful of what I said and to whom. It was just after noon when I decided to go to Johnny's Bar and see if my new ID had arrived. I walked in and saw Johnny wiping down the bar. The place was pretty full, and Johnny was busy running from one end to the other and being friends with everyone.

"Hi, Allen, have a seat. I'll be right with you," Johnny yelled from the other end of the bar.

"Thanks, don't mind if I do," I said.

After a few minutes, Johnny came over with my drink in his hand. "I have something for you," he said as he slid an envelope over to me. I opened it, and there was a perfect driver's license, a Social Security card along with a passport that looked just like any other. Allen Foster was born and was real from this day on. I felt great! I handed an envelope to Johnny and our deal was done. I sat at the bar for another thirty minutes, chewing the fat with some dude and enjoying another drink. If he was a Mob guy, he certainly didn't recognize me, and now with my new identification, I was on my way to starting a new life. I told Johnny that I had to get back to work as I paid for the drink with a crisp new C-note.

"That's for you, Johnny. You were great. I appreciate everything. I got to get back to work. I'll see you later. Enjoy your day and, Johnny, thanks again."

I left the bar feeling like I was reborn, I hadn't felt this good in months. I almost forgot that my life was in peril and that I had to be vigilant at all times. I was getting tired of changing my appearance so often, but if I wanted to stay alive I had to do it as often as it was necessary. Nevertheless, a new beginning was at hand. If the Mob wanted to fuck with me, they were going to get a fight and a pretty good one at that. I went to Arnie's Pawn Brokers, located just a few blocks from the bar.

"I was wondering if you have any rifles I may buy. I have decided to take up shooting and figured this was the best place to get started."

"Sure thing. My name is Oscar Molino. I own this shop. I'll take good care of you just tell me what kind of rifle you are looking for?" he said.

"Oscar, I'm Allen Foster. Great to meet you. To be honest with you, I really don't know anything about guns. I just thought it would be great to start going to a rifle range and shoot at some targets. Maybe, I'll become good enough to enter a contest? I have always wanted to do something like that. I need an expert's help in selection and stuff like that," I said quite innocently.

"Well, first I need to see some form of identification, and then let's get you outfitted. I need the identification because when I sell a firearm, I must register it in my book. The cops check my book every week. Rifles are not the same as handguns so you can take the gun with you right now and there is nothing more we have to do. With a handgun we are supposed to wait a day or two," he said.

"That's okay with me, Oscar. here is my driver's license, is that okay?" I said.

"Sure that's fine, Allen. now let me see what we can do for you. I have a Winchester 22. This rifle takes up to twenty bullets and can reload automatically. It's not a very special rifle but great as a learner model. It will let you shoot a target from at least hundred feet away.

It won't kill anything unless you strike them between the eyes or a lot closer. I also have a Remington 12 gauge shotgun, a good gun to learn on with some kick. I can let you have both for seventy dollars, and that's a steal. I also have this 38 Colt handgun that you can use on the shooting range. It will help you focus on aim and being steady. I'll throw in the 38 for an even hundred bucks for all three. What do you think? he said.

"Well, Oscar, I really don't know what to say. If I don't like anyone of these, can I come in and exchange it for another?" I asked.

"Of course, Allen, anytime. You realize that I have to make a profit, so I may not buy the guns back at the same price, but I will buy them back," he said. He dated the sale two days ago so that taking the handgun would not be a problem. I left with the three guns and a pocketful of ammunition. I knew these were not great guns, but they would do for my purpose. I was happy and filled with confidence, most importantly, I felt ready to handle anything at all. I went directly to my small but great apartment and placed my guns in the closet. I thought I would deal with them later as it was getting late and I had to call Moe.

I went out to the payphone and called Moe, "What's up, buddy, did things go the right way?" I said.

"No, sorry, Harry, it was a complete fiasco. I set up a meet at the corner of Forty-Second, and Lexington. There is a newsstand on the corner, so I instructed him to pick up a paper and start reading it. I asked him to hold the paper real high, over the shoulder and look up at it. That would give me the clue that everything is in order. I told him to stay at newsstand until I approach him and tell him to follow me. In this way, I get a terrific view of the four corners and can see if anyone is following or watching. I went there at four, as I instructed him to be there at four fifteen. I watched from the other side of the street to see if he was alone or not. I couldn't tell, because there were so many people coming and going. I brought a bum with me and gave him a twenty to go across the street and say to the guy with the newspaper the word, "OX" and instruct him to follow him. I instructed the bum to walk on Lexington toward Forty-First Street and leave the guy standing on the corner and take off. I told him if he does this right, I'll give him another twenty.

"The bum went over to the inspector and said something, and he started walking, when I noticed another guy following them. Once they crossed Forty-Second Street, the guy following started to walk a lot faster and another guy came from across the street. I saw the gun come out of the guy's pocket, as he walked over to the bum. I left the corner at once and moved to the opposite side of the street to observe what was going on. They realized they screwed up when they realized this guy was a street person and made the bum take them to the corner where I was standing. I saw them hit the bum across the side of the head and move away toward the curb, where a dark Cadillac stopped for a second where they jumped in and off they went. This was supposed to be hit, and I would have been the target if I had made the meet as agreed. This is heavy stuff, Harry, what have you gotten me into?" Moe said.

"Moe, I didn't think it was this bad, but I know what I must do. Sorry for putting you in harm's way. That was not my intention and I will not do it again. Thanks, Moe, for your help," I said.

"Listen, Harry, I went into this with my eyes wide open. I wanted to help and I am still willing to do whatever I can. It seems to me that I am your only friend and the only one you can trust. Don't shut me out, please," he said very sincerely.

"Moe, I don't know what to say. Thanks for being such a good friend. I will be in touch." I hung up and went out to buy a car. I need one so I can be mobile. I stopped in at used car dealer on Sepulveda Boulevard in Culver City and found a beat up 55 Ford. It was 6:30 p.m., and I now had a car, guns, and a new name. I thought if this was the beginning of a new life, I'd better get started on living it now.

Saturday, March 9, 1957

I called the inspector on the private number I had.

"Well, what is the story now, Sam?" I said.

"Listen to me, and try to understand. I did what I was told to do, and I had no idea that there were people following me. I am glad you did not show up and sent that bum. Otherwise, you would be a goner by now. I want you to know that I was on your side and still am. Don't try to come in, Harry. They want you dead, and no matter what deal I make with you, it will not be kept. Please call me every once in a while, but stay away and keep out of sight. Always call me on this private number, it's always secure and I'm the only one who will answer it. Please believe me, Harry I am sorry for the runaround and the dangers you are in. At first, I thought the actions they brought to me were justified and my bosses were on the up and up, but I have since learned that the whole department is corrupt. It goes as far and as deep as you can imagine and then some and it affects every agency. I honestly thought that with you, we would be able to bring down a lot of people in the Mob and put a dent into organized crime here in New York. It was all bullshit, and I was used and lied to all along the way. I have been on this job for a long time, and I can't afford to lose all the years I have put in. But I promise you, Harry, I'll never lie to you. Please be careful and trust me I won't sell you down the river. I'm sorry for what has happened, really I am," he said.

"Thanks, Sam, thanks for being honest with me. I'll stay in touch with you from time to time," I said and disconnected the line.

There was not much I could do about resolving my dilemma, especially now that it was the weekend. I took a drive out to the Valley where the country air would feel good, and I would be able to relax and think about my next move. A lazy weekend at that, probably the last lazy time I will have. The Valley was great as there was very little traffic and less people. I just drove around and explored the place and took in the peaceful environment. I needed to clear my head and get myself back on track to establish my new life.

I drove back to Los Angeles and went to Johnny's Bar and had a drink. I asked Johnny where to go to have a good time, and he said, "Just relax and enjoy your drink. I will make a few calls and see what is happening around town tonight. I don't always stand behind the bar, Allen. I do go out and get laid every now and then."

I laughed and gave him a thumb's up. "Sorry, Johnny, I never gave it a thought. You see how people screw up. It's so easy. I never asked you what you do after you leave here. Sorry, I just thought you always tended bar and slept," I sarcastically said. "Hey, Johnny, I appreciate your friendship and hope we will always be friends, let's enjoy. Make your call, and let's see if we can get fucked up tonight," I said.

"You got it," Johnny replied and went off to the other end of the bar and made a phone call or two. In a few minutes, he returned with a drink in his hand. He put it down in front of me and said.

"Allen, we are going to a party. I just spoke to Lisa. She's a good friend I've known for years, and she invited both of us to Venice Beach. There is a great party going on tonight, and there will be plenty of chicks. We should be there by 9:30 tonight, so let me get things under control here and we can get out of here. I live in Santa Monica, not far from Venice.

Do you want me to pick you up, or do you prefer to take your own car?"
Johnny said.

"Let's take our own cars, just in case we get lucky," I said.

Sunday, March 10, 1957

I woke up at around ten and tried to remember what happened to
me last night. I know I had a good time and I met this great-looking
gal, but why can't I remember how I got home? My head hurt like hell.
It felt like a bomb went off inside, I must have had plenty of drinks and
one too many for sure. I decided to just hang out and not drink today.
I would just get myself together for tomorrow. I knew it's going to be a
week of stress and action. I couldn't go on living like this and must get
things resolved. I knew everyone was afraid of the Mob and with good
reason. They were nasty and vicious killers, but if someone stands up
to these bastards, I think they would run faster than a jack rabbit. I got
nothing to lose; they were hunting for me, I thought I'll turn the tables
on them and hunt them. I would bet no one ever took that road! One
thing for sure they would not expect this.

I felt better after coming to grips with an overall strategy and now to
plan the war. Even if I did nothing at all, I felt a lot better when I made
up war plans because they gave me a light at the end of the tunnel.

First thing, I would now put everything I know about the Mob and
Larry's connections down on paper and deposit it in a very safe place.
Perhaps it could be my insurance policy if something happens, in either
case I had nothing to lose by doing this. I would record all that I know,
on tape as well, and would place the tape and copies in very secure
places. These would be my insurance policies. I could send a copy to
Larry with instructions to pass it along to the heads of the families. I
would offer him a deal that while I was untouched. No one would ever
hear these tapes or read the notes. But if anything should happen to me,
then copies would be sent to the proper people as well as newspapers and
television stations. I would add that all I want was to be left alone and
if that could be then no one need be hurt. If not I would kill each and
every one of them one by one and make sure the feds prosecute those of
you that are left alive. That would be the essence of my note. The tapes
would speak for themselves. I spent the rest of the day recording and

running to stores to pick up more tapes and more tapes. It took nine and a half hours to complete my transcripts and notes of things I knew and things I thought I knew when I worked for Larry. Even if some of the things I wrote down and recorded were complete fabrication, the Mob would never really know it. They would only panic and get more paranoid and try in some way to resolve this without these records ever becoming public. Of course, I didn't think for a moment that any of this would ever be used, but it was good exercise for my mind and helped me feel that I did accomplish something. All of this exhausted me to the point of allowing me to get a good night's sleep, something I have needed for a long while.

Monday, March 11, 1957

I woke up early, showered and felt like a new man. I decided to call the inspector first. "Hi, Sam, hope you enjoyed your weekend. Let me tell you something between us. I hope I am not making a mistake placing my trust in you. After Friday's conversation, I have found a new and honest respect for you. Thanks for telling me the truth. I have taken steps in the event that something happens to me that will reveal everything I know. I have recorded everything I know about the Mob as well as the involvement of your department as you explained to me last Friday. I have carefully hidden the information so that no one can get to it unless something terrible happens to me. I just wanted you to know that it would be best if you ran interference for me by making sure there will not be any heat from your people. As long as this is done, then you have nothing to concern yourself about and it will remain as our little secret. Sam, I had to do this to protect my ass and at least have a chance at starting a new life without fear. I hope you can guarantee me that you will respect my wishes."

"Harry, you have my word that I will make as certain as I can to make sure your name gets lost in the paperwork jungle and things are forgotten. Thanks for confiding in me, and Harry, I think you did the right thing," he said.

I hung up as I did not want to talk any further. I called back at once.

"Hello, Harry, don't hang up. I'm not tracing the call, I swear," he said.

"I'm so frightened about everything, Sam, I'm scared to death," I said and I hung up again. I waited ten minutes and called back.

"Let me finish my call and get on with what I have to do. I will not call you back again. I will not talk to you about this ever again. Leave me alone, and I will not hassle you. Try to create any shit for me, and you're going down. Got me?" I said.

"Harry, listen please. I am sorry for the crap that came down. They have some shit on me and are holding that over my head. I have very little choice," he said.

"Well, now you have even less choices as I am holding this over your head. Have a good life, asshole," I said.

"Harry, listen to me and then you can hang up. I was very sincere and wanted to help you. I want to put these bastards away, but it seems they have more juice than I do. I will make sure no one here tries to cause you any problems. I will always be your friend and I will not try to find you. Please believe me I have always had your best interest in mind. I'm sorry, Harry. If there is anything I can do, please let me know. In regard to anything we talk about, it is private, and no one will ever know our plans. Take good care of yourself and remember I am on your team," he said.

I hung up and called Rachel, "Hi, honey, how's life over there?" I asked.

"I miss you so much. There is lots of heat over something that happened on Friday. It seems that someone was supposed to meet with the cops, and the boys were there, and all kinds of shit came down. I heard Larry being yelled at that if he hears from you or I hear from you, he'd better get in touch, or his ass is a toast," she said.

"Things must be heating up over there, I guess," I said.

"I really don't know what to say other than you are someone who everyone wants to find, dead or alive. What are we going to do, Harry?" she said.

"We are not going to do anything. It's far too dangerous for you. I know you are lonely, but it has to be this way for a little while longer. I am taking steps that will keep the Mob bosses guessing for a while. I don't want you to get into any trouble, so I will not tell you anything about it, the less you know the better off you will be. You can't tell them what you don't know. I am going on the warpath, and if I'm going to die I will take as many of these bastards as possible with me. If they agree to let it all go away, we can start a new life somewhere together and put this all behind us. It's not easy when the fucking cops are as bad as the Mob. I just can't take this kind of life anymore."

I took a breath, and she said, "Honey, please let me help. Let me be a part of it. I can handle myself, and I won't be in the way, I promise."

With that said, I hesitated for a moment and then came back to her, "I can't let you get involved. Please understand that! If something happened to you, I could never live with myself. Besides it will be easier to find two of us. I can move easier as one. Trust me, sweetheart, this won't last too long. They will know I mean business. Believe me, they will regret the day they started with me. Just remember I love you so very much and we will be together real soon, I promise. Also remember this, if you should be compromised, and I call, just say 'Is that you, Harry?' and I will know that you are in trouble. I want you to act upset at my calling you and act as if it isn't acceptable. Yell at me if you have to, but always act as if I had no right to call you, understand!"

"Okay," she said, "I'll be on your side here and keep you posted. I am with you always. I love you. I love you, always." She was gone, and now it was up to me to get things started.

It was just after eleven, and I had the whole day ahead of me to think about what I should do and how. I thought about involving Johnny. He was a bar owner and knew everybody. I figured I would tell him that I heard that there was a reward out for some guy from New York and if this guy comes into the bar, we could both take him and collect the money and that from what I heard it was more than we could make in a few years. In this way, I could easily get the ball rolling, and soon these assholes would stop by the bar to see if this guy Harry had ever shown his face here. This would give me a clue as to who these guys were. And it would be a lot easier for me to whack a few of them and the message would be delivered loud and clear. It's not like the opposing side wear uniforms so identifying them was impossible unless you make a plan like this one. If I searched for them, it would bring attention to myself. And where would I look? I think I would let them reveal themselves and knock a few off when they do.

I drove over to the bar. "Hey, Allan, how the hell are you doing?" Johnny said.

"Just fine, keeping my head above the water, the usual, Johnny."

"Coming right up," Johnny said.

I sat there sipping my vodka and waiting for things to quiet down. There were two other guys at the bar so I didn't want to start any serious conversation until the coast was clear. I waited and sipped and waited until the bar was finally empty.

"Johnny, let me ask you a question," I said.

"Go ahead, what can I do for you?" Johnny said.

"I hate to ask you, but I am looking for some Mob guys. I know they are here, and if I want to get some kind of work that will pay better, they are the people I need to know."

Johnny looked at me like I was crazy. Finally, he said, "Are you sick, Allen? You don't fuck around with these guys. Once you get involved, you stay involved. I like you and don't want to see you hurt. If you need a few bucks, I'll lend it to you, but please don't get involved," he said.

"Listen to me, Johnny," I said, "I heard that the Mob is looking for some guy from back east and there are a lot of bucks on his head. I can certainly use the money, and I'm sure you can too. I can't tell you everything because I don't want you to get hurt in anyway. But if we should point them in the right direction to find the guy they are looking for, how do I alert them and how do we get our share of the money?"

"Look, Allen," Johnny said, "I'm not afraid of anyone or anything. Once I am friends with someone, I'd go to the end of the earth for them. I'm loyal, but I'm not nuts. If you want to level with me, we can discuss this, but please stop bullshitting me. Now if you want my help, you will have to trust me and tell me the problem, maybe, we can settle it without them. Who knows what we can do, but it can't be "we" if you don't level with me. I hope you understand where I'm coming from?" I was lost for words and had to just lie back for a few minutes and think about what I should do.

"Give me another drink, and let me think a while, I need a little time, Johnny, just a little time," I said.

I called Johnny over and asked him, "When will you be off?"

"It's Monday and pretty quiet. My relief comes in at six. I'm all yours after that," he said.

It was four thirty, no use leaving and coming back. I said to Johnny, "I'll just hang around here until you are done and then we can go get something to eat. You pick a place where we can be private and talk about things," I said.

"I thought we'd go over to Angelo's. The food is great, and we can talk privately. I'll get a table in a corner so that we can be alone, no listeners," Johnny said as he wiped the bar.

"Okay with me, we can drive over in my car or I'll follow you, either way is fine with me.

We drove over to Angelo's, a small neighborhood type of Italian restaurant. No more than twenty tables and a very cozy atmosphere. No bar was visible, but drinks were being served. We went in, and at once a guy in a white apron came running to greet us.

"Johnny, how are you? It's been a while since you last come to see me. Nice to see you. Welcome!" he said.

"Allen, this is Angelo, the best chef in America," Johnny said with a big smile, "If you haven't eaten here before, you haven't tasted the very best Italian cooking anywhere."

"Nice to meet you, Angelo," I said.

Angelo took us to a table in front of the restaurant and Johnny said, "Angelo, we need to talk business. Give us a table in the back where things will be a little more private, capish?"

We followed Angelo to a table at the very rear of the restaurant and sat down. In less than a minute, Angelo reappeared with a bottle of wine in his hand and two glasses. "This is for you, on the house, enjoy."

He opened the wine and poured a little in Johnny's glass and waited. Johnny swirled the wine around the glass, and finally, after smelling it for a moment tasted it and said, "It's very good, Angelo, thanks for this nice wine." Angelo smiled and left us to ourselves.

"So, Allan, what's the deal. I'm really very curious," Johnny said.

"Let me start," I said. "I want you to understand that everything I tell you is in strict confidence. I believe in your friendship and loyalty. I trust you implicitly or else I wouldn't be here. It is a matter of life and death, and I wouldn't want to be the one to cause anyone's death. The story goes back a way. A friend of mine, a real nice guy fell in love with this great looking girl while attending university. Little did he know that his girlfriend's father was a big shot in the Mafia. Everything seemed very legitimate on the surface. She was a gorgeous-looking broad from a very rich family. She had new cars— the latest in fashion—and never seemed to lack anything. My friend was in love, and so was she. They went everywhere together and planned to be married upon graduation. After graduation, they decided they want to get married as soon as possible and announced this to both his and her parents, and everything seemed to be great. Her father was a great guy and wanted a real nice wedding at the Ritz Carlton. No problem he was paying and that was his wish. She was on cloud nine, and my friend's parents were just as happy."

"Can I take your order?" Angelo was at our table asking, "How about a little calamari appetizer? For the main course, let me make you something special—an Osso Buco to die for."

"Okay, Angelo, I leave it in your hands," Johnny said.

Angelo left us and Johnny continued,

"Okay, Allen, this sounds very interesting, and I got time, so give it all to me," Johnny said.

"Where was I? Oh yes, they were getting married, right? The wedding went off without a problem, and both sides of the families were very happy for the young couple. Her father insisted that my friend come to work for him because he wanted his son-in-law to have a good job and his college degree would fit right in. He owned a finance company and was looking for a general manager at the time, so this opportunity seemed to fit everyone's needs. Seeing that he was a university graduate with a BA, he could use him and why not keep it in the family? It seemed to have worked out very nicely for everyone at the time. They moved into her apartment on Seventy-Second Street on the Upper East Side of Manhattan, and their life was great. There was no shortage of money. Lots of love making and partying. They had a life everyone dreamed about, and they thought it would never end. A couple of years went by, and then one day two cops came and took my friend away. They said they had some charges against him, but that was bullshit. The truth was they wanted him to be a key witness against the Mob.

"All five families came and went through the office where my friend worked, and the cops including the feds thought he knew plenty and wanted him to tell it all. In the course of the two years, he saw a lot of these Mob assholes come and go as they did business with the guy's father-in-law. They ran the biggest loan shark operation in New York. It didn't take my friend long to figure out what they did and who each one of these people were. He understood how the loan shark business worked, but he didn't give a shit because he didn't do anything other than make sure the books were kosher. His job was to make sure the company would not get fucked over by the IRS. He made sure that the books that were inspected were right and always matched the records with the bank accounts. He made sure that the payroll was kept properly, just in case anyone who would like to look into the company. He made that all the taxes were paid on time, and the figures were correct. He was a solid guy and never agreed to help the feds and locals in anyway. They threatened my friend with fake charges and threats of a long prison term if he did not agree to cooperate with them. My friend was naive and thought because he refused to agree to help, all would be over and he would resume his life. He didn't know that some of the cops were on the payroll of the Mob, as well as some of the judges, prosecutors, and lawyers. He was being set up, and he didn't know it. The feds were watching this operation for a long while and because there were informers, who worked for the feds they let the Mob know. Once the Mob knew all about the sting operation, they decided they needed a fall guy and that would close the investigation. It would appear to the press and the upper echelon at the FBI that they got their man, and the case would be closed. They told him that his father-in-law was a big part of the Mob and various other shit. My friend was shocked and could not believe what he heard. Cutting the story short, they arranged a release through his lawyer, who was also on the Mob's payroll. Once he was released, he went to see another lawyer who was also on the Mob payroll because his father-in-law insisted on it for his protection. All legal fees would be paid by the Mob and his father-In-Law. My friend finally agreed, through this lawyer, that he would cooperate with the cops if he received certain guarantees that would allow him a new start elsewhere, under a new name, with protection and money to start a new life. Giving up one's family and past history was not a simple matter. But death was also not an option. He refused to tell them anything unless this agreement was signed by a federal judge.

"Of course, they told him they would need time to get the paperwork set up and in the meantime he could remain free on his own recognizance and stay out of sight until they are ready. It didn't take more than a few hours after he moved out of his place and took a hotel under a phony name that a hit team arrived to take him out. This also included his new bride, as she was considered no different than him even though. She was the daughter of one of their own. Now understand this. He didn't want to agree to anything, but the attorney who is paid by the Mob insisted that he cooperate. He was set up because the Mob wanted to see if their internal system was in place. At no time did my friend want to cooperate or could have cooperated as he knew very little about the Mob's operations.

"What they wanted was to eliminate my friend, and then the case would be closed. My friend was pretty dumb, but not that dumb and started to understand that he was being set-up. My friend went into hiding from the cops and the Mob. Of course, he took his wife with him, and the two of them tried to hide and plan some sort of action that might extricate them from this mess. My friend and his wife checked into a hotel under a false name. They felt pretty secure. It didn't take long for the Mob to find them. It seems that they were checking out every hotel in midtown, Manhattan and really didn't know exactly where they were, but by accident they found them. The irony with the situation regarding the paperwork with the feds was simply set-up to trap my friend. He had no experience with this type of stuff and thought this was normal, but began to realize that they were setting him up to take the fall and that there was no judge to sign anything. Now here is a guy, who never has had a fight in his life and is now faced with death. He doesn't know anything about this kind of shit and is scared out of his mind.

That is why my friend decided that he must outsmart these guys and set out a plan and he was in a hotel hiding. After some careful and scary maneuvers, he was able to leave the hotel dressed as a woman and miss being whacked. He got a gun, although he didn't know how to use it and decided to learn how and to save his own life. To keep his wife around meant problems, and because her father was a big shot Mob guy, they would be placed in danger. My friend and his wife decided that she should go live with her father and tell him she ran away from my friend. She was going to divorce this low life piece of shit and wanted nothing to do with him. They felt the pressure would be off her, and he could act alone. With the help of some people, they managed to elude the hotel hit men and set their plan to work. She went home, and he disappeared."

I stopped to let Angelo put some food on our table and take another drink of this great wine.

"Thanks, Angelo, everything is great," Johnny said, and Angelo left "I can't believe what I am hearing, Allen," Johnny said, as I continued my story.

"This friend of mine went out of town to a remote place and practiced day after day for two solid weeks with his gun. He became an expert marksman and now decided to take the war far away from family and see if things could be settled. Maybe, he would never have to use his gun and life can return to normal. He stayed in touch with his wife through codes they set up before parting. He went across the country and changed his appearance, his name, his cars, as well as locations often. Yet they were still out there and wanted him dead. A reward was set up of two hundred K for anyone who killed my friend. With that kind of money, his life was in deep shit anywhere he went. I spoke with him a few times through the special codes we arranged, and he has related to me what has happened.

"The cops are bought and paid for by the Mob. There are honest cops around, but who they are no one knows. You have no way of telling the difference between the good and the bad ones. One day—I tell this to give you an example how deep their informers are in the police department—my friend got a very close friend to meet the cops and get a copy of the signed documents that the judge supposedly signed. It was a setup as the Mob had the entire meeting staked out and nearly killed his friend. Only through quick thinking and taking some evasive actions, did he avert being killed.

"Finally, he decided that he cannot go on this way and his only way out is to go after them. If he turns the tables and becomes the hunter, they will get fucked up and might quit this vendetta. My friend is an innocent bystander in this and has never run afoul of the law. Now he has to become as bad as the Mob and the corrupt cops just to save his own life, why? I figured if you can get me into the Mob, maybe I can get to the right people and save my friend's life. I can explain that he knows nothing and does not want to speak to anyone."

Johnny looked at me, "I am stunned at your story and your willingness to get involved. Remember this, Allen, once you become a member of their organization, you cannot get out. Are you willing to risk all that?"

"You bet your life, Johnny, he is my best friend, and I would give my life for him as I know he would for me," I said with as much conviction as I could muster.

Angelo arrived with the main dish, and we settled down to eating. I didn't say another word, and Johnny ate without a sound.

Finally, we looked up at each other, and Johnny said, "Allen, tell me the truth, are we talking about you? I can't think of it any other way. I got you the new identification, I became your friend, and I know nothing about you, except what you tell me. So please level with me. We're in too deep to lie to one another."

I looked at Johnny and saw a very sincere guy and a very nervous one at that. "Johnny, I don't want to involve you more than I have to, can't you understand that?" I said.

"Boy, you are something else man, you have already involved me beyond belief. I could easily make my own conclusions and make a phone call, and you're a dead man in less than an hour, so don't give me the bullshit of involvement. You have already trusted me by telling me this story, so why are you talking about trust any longer? Be straight, and if I can help, I will, but I will not hurt you. If I can't help, I'll walk away, and this conversation will be gone forever. I will not be tempted by the big money being offered for this guy's life. Now be straight with me, and let's move on."

I was shocked at his directness, but respected him as I knew he was right.

"Okay, Johnny, okay, I'm the guy, and it's my life I want to save. I need your help, Johnny. Can you help me, can you?" I said with sincerity.

I looked at Johnny and could honestly feel his friendship. I haven't been around too many people to be able to read everyone, but this guy was an open book. I think he was feeling good that finally he could help someone, no matter what the risks were.

No doubt, Johnny was hooked and I'd better take advantage while I can. I've got to get out of this mess and get on with my life. I must have spaced out for a minute as I was brought back in focus when Johnny said, "We have a lot of work to do, Allen, a lot of work. It's getting late, so let's set some time for tomorrow and make a game plan. I will organize my schedule for you."

So what time is best?" I said.

"Anytime tomorrow, how about nine thirty? I'll pick you up wherever you want me to, and we can take an hour or two to make some plans."

"That sounds good to me," Johnny said. "Pick me up in front of the bar at ten tomorrow morning."

We shook hands to close the deal. I took Johnny back to the bar so that he could pick up his car and went home.

Tuesday, March 12,1957

I didn't sleep well as I wondered if I had made a mistake telling Johnny the whole story. What if I get there in the morning, and he had some guys waiting for me? Maybe the lure of all that money was a lot stronger than loyalty. I was getting myself into a real bad state of mind. If anyone was paranoid, it was me. And thinking about Johnny and what I told him, made me more obsessed. I thought and thought and finally decided that I have gone too far. There is no turning back now, so I must trust Johnny. It's too late to change things around. Deep in my heart, I did have faith in Johnny and felt my trust would not be in vain.

I made sure my gun was loaded as I dressed to pick Johnny up at the bar. I was very careful when I approached the bar, as I studied the area for a few minutes to make sure everything was right. I couldn't see anything suspicious, so I continued on to the bar.

"Good morning, Allen. I see you are right on time, how are you doing this beautiful day?" Johnny said.

"I'm fine to tell you the truth but a little concerned. I keep wondering if I was too open with you last night," I said. "So where to, Johnny?"

"We'll go out to Malibu and stop at the beach. It's noisy enough, so if anyone is listening they can't overhear our conversation. We can sit around and plan our next move. It is obvious to me that we have to take the initiative if we are to succeed. I'm pretty sure that they have their guys looking for you everywhere. It will only be a matter of time until they find you. With two hundred K on your head, yes, you heard me right, I heard that at the bar a week ago but never thought it was you. They showed me a picture of a guy, but he sure didn't look like you and gave me a number to call if I see him. They are paying two hundred K for you, and if we aren't careful, someone will find you out. So let's make a plan as to where you want to go, where you want to live, and how we get that going? Also let's put aside this bullshit about mistrust. I wouldn't be here if I was turning you in. It would be over by now," Johnny said.

I was flabbergasted with his hard and cold assessment of the situation. It's like making a proper business plan, except this was real life. We drove along the ten freeway until we reached the end and turned on to the PCH and drove toward Malibu. Neither of us spoke. I guessed the ball was in my court and Johnny could only wait until I was ready to lay out some kind of plan. We finally reached Gladstones and decided to just continue a little farther and park on the beach as most lookers did. Let's watch the ocean make waves and noise. It was a beautiful day, as the sun glistened off the water. The world seemed peaceful. Who could imagine the turmoil I was going through?

"Well, Johnny, let's look at it all from my point of view and how I see things," I said. "I love my wife, but she is a liability and could help them find me, inadvertently perhaps, but still a problem. I need money, and she is the only source of getting large amounts from her father. So we have to keep her for a while and still make sure that I stay alive. Once I have a plan set, I will take her out of the picture and start a new life."

"Okay," Johnny said, "column one is 'wife' and we'll put that on the plus side for now! What's next?"

"The cops are corrupt and work for the Mob. They will not bother to look for me as long as I stay out of their hair. That means keep out of New York, so I think we can eliminate them for now," I said. "Next we have to consider the Mob itself. They are all across the country, but their brain power is very limited. There is no way we can set up a meeting and straighten this out as they would kill me on sight. It's so easy. I would be glad to disappear, and I am out of their hair and no one gets hurt, but that won't work for these assholes. So what do we do in order to disappear once and for all?"

I sat there thinking, as I looked out at the Pacific Ocean and wondered, "Is there really a solution, or am I just a dreamer?" Finally I spoke up and said, "Okay, Johnny, I think I need to establish where and when I am going to disappear. Then I need to equip myself to shoot it out with these fuckers, if I kill a few of them they may stop and leave me alone. Of course, I think that is bullshit, they will not rest until they eliminate me. What a fucked up situation and all for no reason," I said,

"Well, what can I do if you don't have plan?" Johnny said. "I will help, I will work with you, but first you need a direction and a plan. Give me a plan, and I will tell you what I think about it. I will be as objective as I can, and we can clean it up and make it work. I know we can. So let's get to work. Enough of this crap of how it could have been or if I do this, they will do that. No way can we ever do anything if we dwell on ifs and buts etc."

"Johnny, you are a friend, and I'm sorry for doubting your sincerity," I said. "I will take the rest of day to formulate a plan, and we can meet tomorrow, and you can tell me what you think. Is that all right with you?" I said.

"Okay with me, but tomorrow I work all day. I'll meet you at eight, right here. I'll bring my own car, and we can go to Gladstones for something to eat and review. I'll see you then." I drove him back to the bar and went home.

Wednesday, March 13, 1957

I spent the day thinking of what was the best approach to meet this situation head-on. I wanted to bring Rachel out to California and together we could start a new life.

I had a new name and with that we could easily blend in somewhere. We could be another young couple in suburbia, same as everyone else. That sounded great, and all we had to do was to keep our noses clean. No traffic tickets and no stupid things and never get into any trouble. The cops were not looking for me at least that was what Sam had led me to believe even if it wasn't true. It's not priority with them. If I was ever arrested, they didn't have my prints, so I didn't think they would connect me to my new identification. It sounded easy, but it made my heart skip a beat as I thought it through. What about Rachel? Would she be able to live like this? Would she be able to cut Larry out of her life and move on as a new person? What a life! What a risk! Yet I could not think of anything else other than taking steps that would give us that chance. I also had another very serious dilemma. I told Johnny far too much, and he could prove to be my undoing. What the hell was I thinking when I emptied my heart to Johnny? Why did I always create such problems? I just didn't understand myself, really I didn't. I decided to call Rachel and bounce some of it off her. Let's see what she had to say and what side of the fence she was on? Better now than later. So I called, "Hi, Rachel, how are you doing?" I said.

"Honey, how are you? I am so happy to hear from you, where are you?" she said.

"I wanted to talk to you and hear your voice, I miss you so much. I decided that we have to make a decision as to what we are going to do and get our lives back on track." I hesitated and continued, "I was hoping that you could come and meet me, and we can start a new life together under another name. With a little luck, everyone will get very tired of looking for us, and we can just raise a family and move on. We will get jobs, and with us both working, we can really start a new life," I said with a great deal of enthusiasm.

"Let me get it straight in my head," she said. "I would have to leave here and never return, and I'd have to leave Larry and never let him know where I am. All family ties would be over, and we would have to start all over. If we make one mistake, we get caught by the Mob or the cops. Correct me if I'm wrong, sweetheart. I just want to know how we are going to pull this off and live like human beings. Am I asking too much?" she said with a lot of sarcasm.

I knew she was upset, and I tried to calm her down. "I know it's a tough decision, but I can't think of another way. I love you so much and don't want to lose you. I miss the hell out of you and need you close. I know you feel the same way, so what alternative do we have?" I said as softly as I could.

"I don't know, maybe I can talk to Larry and see what he can do. Maybe he can speak with someone to get the wolves off your back. I know that they understand now that you are not going to talk and that the cops have nothing on you. I'm sure Larry will have some ideas. Let me talk with him before we make any decision. Please wait and let me see what I can do from this end. Let me go now and call me back in two hours and let's see what we can come up with, please."

She hung up. I felt alone and lost. Am I losing her or what? I decided to relax as best I could and wait out the two hours. I thought maybe she would have a very good solution to our problems. I also prepared myself for the eventuality if she told me to shove it. What do I do? Should I just tell her to forget about me and I would start again or do I take some other course? What other course could I take other than to have an all-out war with the Mob! How could I win against the sheer numbers they have? Yet, if I am going to die, I might as well take as many of these bastards with me. It's not an easy decision to make, but what choices have I really got?

I made the call, and Rachel answered as usual, "Hi, sweetheart, I know you are sitting there worried about me and about us, so let's get right to the meat of it." I waited, not saying a word.

"Okay, I spoke with Larry," she said, "and he feels it would be useless for me to join you under the circumstances you have presented. He cannot do anything for you, because he has already told the Mob that you are out of our lives, and he doesn't want anything to do with you. I also feel it is useless for us because our lives will never be the same. I love you, but love alone isn't enough, we need more than that. I can't live wondering who is watching me or will someone discover that I am not who I am? They know who I am, and finding me will be easy and will lead them directly to you. Even if it takes a year or two or more, they will not stop looking. Life will be very difficult for us, and at any time you could be killed. No, I just can't do that and I won't. The irony of it all is that I just learned I am pregnant. I'm three months in and never knew it, sure I didn't get my period, but I thought that was due to stress because of the situation and all that I was under. I found out yesterday that I am pregnant. Congratulations, Harry, you are going to be a father, and I want you alive and near me. I am a realist and know this can't be so, I think we have to part just to maintain our sanity and increase your chances of staying alive. I also need to be able to have this baby without too much distraction. I'll always love you, and I'll always love our baby, but it is unwise and unhealthy for us to be together.

If you need money, you know we have plenty here for you. Just tell me where to send it. I'll be waiting for you if you can get this shit cleared up, if not I will have to divorce you. When that will be is entirely up to you, because only you can clear up this mess. I know how you must feel, sweetheart, but I have no other choice!"

I was speechless, she was giving me my walking papers and at the same time told me I was a father and "get out and make a life." Wow!

"Listen to me," I said as calmly as I could, "I didn't create this mess. I went to work for Larry at your insistence; you never told me he was in the Mob. You threw me to the wolves, and now you tell me to go fuck myself! Boy, that's really love isn't it? I can't believe my ears, but there is little I can do about it. Screwed again because I loved you so much, and now I am discarded like a piece of old meat. Great, just fucking great." I was starting to lose it, so I just shut up for a minute and waited.

Finally she said, "I am sorry you feel that way, but staying alive is the most important thing to me, especially now that I am carrying your baby. And it should be the most important thing to you as well."

I started to speak, but my voice just cracked and could not say a word. I hung up so that I could compose myself for a few minutes. I decided that I'd better think it all through before I make any decisions, especially now that I am upset I could easily make the wrong move.

I called Rachel back, "Hi, I'm sorry about my reaction. I was hurt, and it's really tough to be alone. I love you and want you to be with me always. I'll fight this war until they yell enough and decide I'm not worth it any longer. My first obligation is to protect you and the baby, so I'll not let you know where I am. I'll take care of business, and then we'll get back together. If this takes longer than a few months, then please go ahead and divorce me. I'll not stand in your way ever. I love you and always will. Maybe one day, I'll be able to see our baby. In the meantime, I won't make your life difficult, I promise. I will need money, and I don't want you to think I am trying to be greedy in anyway, but I'll need about five hundred K. Please give Moe five hundred K for me as soon as you can. I don't want to put you in jeopardy at any time, so please deal through Moe. It will keep you safe. Can you do this quickly?" I said.

"I'll call him now and make sure he gets the money tomorrow. I love you, Harry. I love you very much. Please be careful, we need you," she said.

"I love you, too, and I'll be careful. Take care and be healthy. I love you." And she hung up.

I called Johnny and confirmed our meeting for tomorrow at the same place at eight. I spent the rest of the day planning Harry's war against the Mob. I was pumped. I was going to be a father before the year was out. I have until December to change my destiny. "Bring it on," I said and went to bed.

Thursday, March 14, 1957

I had formulated a plan and called Rachel first thing.

"It's me," I said. "I want you to do the following for me and listen to me very carefully. Did you call Moe yet about the money?"

"No, not yet, I was just getting ready to organize that. I have to be very careful that no one is watching me. I'll call him right now," she said.

"I think I have about three hundred K in the stash," I said. "If we are short, Larry will put in the difference," she said.

"Do you have enough to live on?" I said.

"Harry, don't worry about us. I have whatever I need. Larry gives me money everyday, please, we'll be fine," she assured me.

"Get in touch with Moe and arrange the transfer. I will call him and tell him to expect your call. Give me fifteen minutes. I will not call you for a while, as I must take care of things the best way I can. If I can get things cleared up, I will return to you if you will still be there waiting. If you can't wait, I'll understand and hope that the child you carry will keep us bonded, if not as lovers, at least as friends that have a common thread. I want you to promise me you will put my name on our child's birth certificate. I want to share the joy of a child with you, and I am determined to do it," I said.

"I will, Harry, I promise," she said.

I continued, "I will contact you periodically to find out how you and the baby are doing. I will not discuss what I am doing or where I am as that could only compromise you. I feel like shit. But I understand how you feel and the circumstances. Just try and wait for me, please try. I love you. I love you very, very much." And I hung up. I just could not continue to speak to her any longer. I felt like I was falling apart, ready to lose it all.

My resolve to come out of this victorious was fortified by the ass kicking I just got from my wife. I knew she was right, but it still didn't ease the pain. I could not call anyone in my family as I did not want them to inherit any trouble from me. I loved them all too much for this, and I am sure I have hurt them more than I could imagine just by disappearing and staying out of touch. One day, I'll be able to set things right again, one day for sure.

I called Moe Arnold and told him the situation. I asked him to please call my mother and explain that I am fine and love them all and will be in touch soon. I told him about the money and what Rachel and I have discussed and the baby too. I knew I could count on my real and very true friend to help me. He cautioned me about these people that they were rough assholes. But he said he supported me one hundred percent, and if there is anything he could do, just name it.

I was sitting at a table in Gladstones, looking out at the Pacific Ocean when Johnny walked in. The ocean looked so inviting. I sat there, imagining sailing away forever.

"Hi, Allen," Johnny said as he approached the table, "how are doing today?"

"Pretty good. I have a lot to tell you, and I want to run my plan by you. Do you want a drink?"

"Yes, get me a Coors, with a glass," he said.

I told him what Rachel and I discussed about the baby and then I started in on my plan. I left out Moe and the money, as I didn't think it was relevant.

"If I keep using the name Allen and maintain wearing this disguise, they will not find me easily and that is not what I want. I need them to find me so that I can kill a few of those bastards. This will deliver a real message to them. I already delivered a message to the cops that I am not their pawn and they don't have any real case against me, so they have to drop it."

Johnny looked at me with a wry smile and said, "Are you crazy? Do you know who these guys are? Of course not, you think you kill a few, and they are gone out of your life forever. No way, Allen, it doesn't work that way at all, and I don't want you to look like an asshole, especially a dead one." He stopped for a moment to catch his breath and went on, "I know what you are thinking. But that is the wrong plan. Let me give you a plan I think will work and may get you on the road to a new life with no one looking for you ever."

"That sounds great. I'm all ears. That may be the best news I have gotten in a long time, Carry on, Johnny," I said.

"I believe the ultimate objective is to get out from under and start fresh. Now that the wife problem is resolved, we only have one to worry about—you!"

I nodded and said, "Well, Johnny, that is not as easy as I do have family, people I know and love. What do I do with them all? Just throw them all in the garbage! Or do I start again, raise my own family, and tell them that I have no past. It just isn't so cut and dry?"

I looked at Johnny to see his reaction as I felt I knew where he was coming from, but he just sat there without any expression and said to me, "I really don't give a shit about things like that. I have to think objectively and can only worry about you all other people cannot be part of the equation. Of course, you will find a way to get your family involved, in time, but first you must establish your own identity. Begin being someone new. Allen Foster has to begin somewhere, why not right here, why not?"

I stared at Johnny. He believed what he was saying. It was written all over him that he was one hundred percent into this!

"What will I do? I can't just apply for a job because I haven't got any papers. My college degree is worthless under my old name, and Allen Foster doesn't have any. Also let's accept the fact that we can easily make up some papers, what if the company checks it out? What if they make a call to the university to verify the diploma and get a little more information? I'm fucked at that point. Of course, what the hell can they do other than fire me! Maybe it would work, just maybe!"

Johnny smiled and said, "I see you are starting to think my way. I don't know what kind of papers I can get, but what the hell, Allen? Let's give it a try. In the meantime, I suggest you get this shit out of your head, you cannot shoot your way back into your old life, and the Mob isn't just going to lie down and die. You can kill a few, but eventually they will kill you and anyone who is associated with you. So let's build a new life and move on."

"Okay," I said, "You find out what the costs are for a proper graduation certificate together with a list of grades. I will give you a copy of actual papers and we can fashion a set that will be similar. I will maintain my disguise and keep a low profile until we can get all the stuff together. I'm still going to carry my gun, and with this added time, I'm going to become the best shot in the world. Yes, sir, I'm going on a training course, survival, my friend, is the name of the game, only it will be those guys who better learn how to survive. I'm just getting started, and I am sure no one will want to fuck with me, I'm sure of it!" With that said, Johnny and I ordered something to eat.

I promised to drop by the bar tomorrow and leave the information that should appear on the diploma so that he could make sure there was some legitimacy to the document. We agreed on tomorrow's schedule, as I dropped him off by his car and drove home. It was time to relax and stop running even if it was for only a few hours. Tomorrow would come soon enough and the running would begin again!

Friday, March 15, 1957

I must have been tired. It was 8:00 a.m., and I was still in bed. I jumped out of bed, shaved, and took a shower. I ate some cereal and had a cup of coffee. No rush, I thought. It's Friday, and the weekend is upon us, so let's get ready to enjoy it the best I could. I left the apartment to drop off the diploma information at Johnny's Bar and then drove to the Valley to Jim's Shooting Gallery on Reseda and Parthenia Boulevard. I wanted to practice in an out of the way place. Usually, the only people that used this shooting range were local Valley folks. No one would drive all this way when there are so many shooting ranges in Los Angeles. No one would recognize me out here in the Valley. This was farmland, and no one other than locals would be here. I could then drive back to Los Angeles after I finish and have a hell of a weekend. I could hone my skills as a shooter out here in the Valley and no one would take note of my frequent visits. As much as I was concerned of the days that lie ahead, I was exhilarated with the prospect of killing a few of these mobsters, I could hardly wait. I knew Johnny had told me many times that I could not win by killing a few of them, and I most certainly could not kill all of them.

I had spent over an hour shooting. My aim was getting better as I hit the target more and more with each reload. It was just a little after noon when I finally left the shooting gallery.

I drove back to Los Angeles on the 405 and got off at the Sunset Street exit. I decided to stop in at the Holiday Inn, the only circular hotel I have ever seen. I knew they had a bar on the top floor, so I went there to pass some time and to see if there was any action. I didn't expect much at this hour of the day, but this was Friday and anything could happen. The bar was pretty empty except for two girls sitting at the bar. I sat down and ordered vodka on the rocks and just sat back.

"How you doing?" I asked one of the girls a couple of stools away from me.

"Great, having a nice time," she answered.

She was a pretty good-looking gal, blonde hair, with great big blue eyes. She looked pretty trim and wore a black dress with a very low cut front; great tits from my vantage point.

"I'm Allen, pleasure to meet you. What's you're name?" I said.

"I'm Rachael, and this is my friend Barbara."

I picked up my drink and moved closer to the girls. Barbara had black hair with brown eyes, a great looking body, and the biggest pair of tits I have ever seen.

"It's real nice to meet you. What brings you to this place so early in the day?" I asked.

Rachael looked at me with a great big smile and the whitest teeth I have ever seen and said, "We are staying here in the hotel. We arrived yesterday from Chicago. This is our first trip to Los Angeles, and we are just getting started. I'm from Atlanta, and Barbara is from Chicago. Are you from here?"

"No, not really. I was living in New York, but moved out here last year and am still learning where everything is located," I said as I looked at my glass and decided I needed another drink. "Would you girls like a drink?" I said.

"We can use it. We have nowhere to go and seeing that it's the beginning of a weekend, why not get the celebration started early?"

I motioned to the bartender. "Another round, please."

"Let's go sit at a table. It will be more comfortable and we can talk a lot easier," I said to the girls.

We moved to a table, got a menu so we could snack on some food and drink ourselves into a great mood for the weekend festivities.

"Listen, girls, I am free for the weekend so why not hook up together and see Los Angeles and party a little? I know a few places that might be interesting and we can have some great fun," I said with a smile.

"Well," Barbara said, "it might just work out. Can you handle the two of us or do we need to find another partner?"

I smiled and said, "I think I can. It'll be fun trying. Now what do you want to do about getting the weekend going? I can call a friend and see if he can join us or we can just wing it and see the town! It's up to you. I'll do whatever you want."

We were getting pretty friendly, especially after a few drinks.

"Let's plan on an evening in downtown Los Angeles. We can go out, have dinner, and later stop in at a club and see what is happening. It's Friday, and things happen. What do you think?"

Rachael looked me in the eye with her big blue eyes and super smile and said, "Where do you live, Allen?"

"I live in Venice. It's not too far from here would you like to come over to my place for a while? It's not a palace, but if you decide to ditch this place, you are welcome to stay with me, and it's a lot cheaper." I looked at them both, as they looked at each other. I knew by their expressions what the answer would be.

"Okay, Allen, let's check out of here and move to your place. But let me warn you," Rachel said, "if we don't get along, we move. Is that clear enough?"

"Sure thing," I said, "I like you girls and really want some company. You have nothing to lose. I hope this leads to a lot of good times together. Let's get started!"

They gathered their suitcases and checked out of the hotel and piled into my car. Of course, my place was a little small and having only one bedroom, but there was a living room with a sofa, and it was cozy for us all. When young people feel they are good together, the size of the place is not important. They took over the apartment and made themselves at home, walking around just about naked and being as comfortable they would be at home. It was great to see some action in my dull and very quiet place. I called Johnny at the bar and explained that I picked up two gorgeous girls and if he wanted to join us for dinner tonight, he was very welcome. I also asked him to suggest some good night spots for the girls. He suggested we stop by the bar for a drink on him and make sure I brought the girls. He said he would decide then if it's worth joining us or not. I guess he wasn't sure if my taste in women was up to his standard. I told the girls about the plan, and we all agreed to relax a little a get ready for some partying. I was pretty horny, and so were my guests. It didn't take long until Barbara came real close and started to rub my penis and kissed me.

Rachael moved closer and said, "Let's take a little nap before we go out. I know we will have a lot of fun."

We moved into the bedroom, and everyone jumped on to the bed. We had sex every way possible. It was great, I didn't want it to ever end. Rachael was hot and told me that she really cares about me and wanted to be with me the entire weekend. She hoped Barbara would find someone that made her feel as good as she felt.

At seven, we arrived at Johnny's Bar. I looked at Johnny's face as we walked in and knew he was hooked.

"Hey, Allen," he shouted, "Come over here, come sit."

I walked over and said, "I want you girls to meet a good friend of mine, Johnny, who also owns this bar. Johnny, this is Barbara."

She said, "Hi, Johnny, nice to meet you, are you going to join us tonight?"

"Sure thing," Johnny said with a smile as wide as an eight lane freeway. "This is Rachael, Johnny."

She smiled and said, "Nice to meet you. Allen has said a lot of nice things about you."

"What are you drinking?" Johnny said. "How about some good champagne?" he added.

"That would be great, but we don't want you to think we are taking advantage," Barbara said with a big smile.

"Of course not," Johnny said.

Getting plastered at Johnny's bar was easy, as he kept on bringing out bottle after bottle of champagne.

I finally said to Johnny, "Hey, let's get out of here and get something to eat. If we keep on drinking and no eating, we will be shit faced."

"What would you girls like to eat?" Johnny said.

Of course, we were a little fucked up, so food was not a priority. But we had to eat, or else we wouldn't last the rest of the night.

"We are new here, Johnny," Barbara said. "So why don't you guys show us the real Los Angeles and let's get fucked up."

"I've got some real good clubs in mind. Let me get this place organized, and I'll be ready to blow this joint and get the party started. Have another drink and give me five minutes, and we'll go," he said.

We left the bar and went to Trader Vics for some great Polynesian food, and then Johnny suggested a private club that he knew. "We can just get fucked up and stay there for the night. The guys who own this club are great, and we can party all night."

"You say the word, and we'll do it," Rachael said. "Let's see what the new place has to offer, and we'll decide. As long as I am with Allen, I don't care where we go."

Saturday, March 16, 1957

I woke up with Rachael besides me, and in some room, definitely not my apartment.

"What time is it?" I asked and then looked at my watch. It's six thirty in the morning, what the hell! It's Saturday, I thought, why worry? I was in Johnny's place and had a large size headache. A couple of aspirins and a glass of juice, and I was ready to face another day.

"Hey, what do you guys want to do today?" I said at the top of my voice.

It seemed that no one really wanted to get up. I guess we celebrated a little too much, and heavy heads were the norm for today.

"I don't know, can't I just sleep a little longer?" Rachael said.

"Sure, it's Saturday. So who really gives shit, except Johnny who might have to open his bar. Never mind, it's our day to enjoy. Let me check the weather and then we can decide," I said as I went to the window to see what the day looked like. "It seems to be sunny, so why don't we plan a day in Venice. We can walk on the boardwalk and eat some crap at the pier."

"Sounds like a plan to me," Rachael said. As I kept looking outside, I noticed a black Cadillac parked across the street with two guys in it. They looked large with slicked back hair and suits. The car was a Mob car, and these guys looked Mob all the way. Where did we go last night that would have aroused suspicions? I'll ask Johnny in a few minutes. I continued to watch their actions, as they were looking at the front entrance of the building and waiting.

We were in an apartment building, and they probably were not certain which apartment was the right one they were looking for. It didn't look good, and I didn't know what to do at this point. I didn't look the same. I haven't spoken to anyone about this except Johnny so what's the score? There was a price on my head, and two hundred and fifty K would certainly turn one's loyalty around. I felt like a fool for trusting Johnny and letting him know just what it's all about. I felt like a real asshole and could not contain my anger at myself and with Johnny. I grabbed my gun and checked it to make sure it was loaded and placed in my waist. Rachael was still half asleep, so she didn't see anything. I decided that the easiest way to solve this immediate problem was to take these two guys out and then to deal with Johnny. I went down the stairs and left the building through a service door at the rear into a small lane that separated the buildings. The lane couldn't be more than three feet wide and was used as an emergency exit and to store a lot of metal trash cans. I slowly made my way toward the front of the building, keeping myself flat against the wall. I knew these guys would be looking at the front entrance and, with a little bit of luck, would never see me. They were so engrossed in their vigil watching the front door as I turned left away from the building and walked slowly toward the next street.

I then crossed the intersection and was now on the same side as these two Mob guys in the Cadillac. I turned right and began walking toward the parked car. My guess was that they didn't know what I looked like and that Johnny was going to finger me when I left the building. I was right as I walked by the parked Cadillac, and they didn't show any signs of recognition. As I reached the back of the Cadillac, I swiftly turned right and pulled open the back door and jumped in.

"Don't either of you move, or your brains will be all over this fucking car. What the hell are you doing here?" I demanded in a very strong tone. "Tell me now, or I'll blow your fucking heads off, now, assholes."

The heavier set guy sitting in the driver's seat said, "Hey, buddy, what's wrong with you? We're just waiting for a friend who lives in that building. We're not cops, and we're not here to make trouble. Now put down that piece before someone gets hurt."

"Just keep your hands where I can see them. Put them on the dash and keep them there. I know you are carrying, so first you shithead."

I pointed the gun to the guy in the passenger's seat. "One hand only, and if you value your life, don't fuck around. Just take your gun out and throw it in the back."

He slowly placed his hand in the inside of his jacket and removed a thirty-eight revolver and threw that in the back.

"Good boy. Now you do the same and very, very slowly."

All at once, the guy on my right made a fast move toward my arm, while the other guy was getting his gun out. I pulled the trigger on my gun, and his face splattered all over the windshield. I whirled around, and the driver was taking his gun out from his inside jacket pocket.

"Don't you move a thing, or I'll blow your head off."

He stopped moving his arm, and just sat there waiting for my next command.

"Now slowly take your hand out and throw your gun onto the back seat," I said. He took the gun out slowly and tossed it over his shoulder onto the back seat.

"Now answer a few questions for me, and I'll let you go. If you lie to me, you are toast. There is no use in playing games. Who told you where I was?" I said.

"No one, man. Like I told you, we were just waiting for a friend," he said.

I placed one shot through his right shoulder and said. "As long as you want to continue lying to me, I will continue to shoot you full of lead. Now tell me the truth."

"Johnny said he could deliver this guy we wanted, if we came by his place at seven this morning. He wanted us to split the reward three ways," he said.

I was incensed by this and the thought that I was so stupid as to trust him. I shot this goon through the left eye. There was a thud, and he fell limp. Blood was everywhere. The smell of cordite was all over the car along with the stench of blood. I calmly got out of the car and looked around. It seemed that no one was disturbed by all this gunfire the neighborhood seemed to still be asleep. I opened the back door and went around to the driver's door, opened it, and with all my strength, pushed this guy over to the other asshole. I got in, and started the Cadillac, put her into gear, and off I went. I drove a few blocks until Olympic and

Twenty-Eighth Street and found a perfect parking spot under a large oak tree and left the car there with the keys in the ignition. I wiped down the steering wheel and every where else I may have touched and left the two dead mobsters.

It took me twenty minutes to walk back to the apartment. I went back in the same way I went out. My clothes smelled of cordite and were covered in blood. I needed a shower and had to get rid of these clothes. I found a garbage bag and placed the clothes in it. I took a shower and cleaned myself up until I felt clean again. All this time, Barbara and Johnny were asleep in the other room and Rachael didn't stir. I went into Johnny's room and gently woke him up, "Hey, Johnny, it's almost nine in the morning. Do you have to open?"

"Thanks, Allen, not until eleven on a Saturday," he said.

"I must have been pretty fucked up last night, Johnny. I really tore up some of my clothes. Would you mind if I borrow a shirt and a pair of pants just until I get home," I asked him.

"No problem, help yourself to whatever you may need and wake me at nine thirty, please," Johnny said as he turned over and went back to sleep. I found a pair of jeans that fit pretty good and also a sweater.

I grabbed a pair of rubber thongs I noticed on the floor of the closet, and I was ready to go. I woke Rachael and said, "Hey, sweetheart, let's get out of here and go over to my place. I need to get some new clothes, and we can see what the day has in store for us. I know it's still early, but if you get out of bed now, I'll make the rest of your day very worthwhile. You can shower at my place, and then we'll get breakfast."

"Hey, what about Barbara?" she said.

"I think she is still asleep. We'll call later and wake them up, If they want to join us great, if not, we'll be on our own. Let's go, chop, chop, I need to get moving," I said very decisively.

She jumped out of bed and into her dress and was ready, even though she was a mess. I took down Johnny's number from the phone on the wall in the kitchen and grabbed my garbage bag and off we went. My gun was tucked into my back waistband, and I was pumped for more action. I don't know why, but killing the goons gave me a rush. My adrenalin kicked in, and all I wanted was to get out of here before I exploded. My justification was that I was doing society a favor, and I wasn't even getting paid for it. I had decided not to mention anything to Johnny at this time. I now know without any doubt that he was a turncoat, and I would deal with that later. I will watch him very closely from now on.

We arrived at my apartment at nine forty, and I immediately called Johnny to wake him. I was sure that Barbara would never remember where I lived, and Johnny sure as hell didn't. I felt safe for a little while, but knew that this was temporary I had to get my shit together and plan a better way of life. I didn't have to find out if in fact it was Johnny who set me up, I knew that for a fact now. I didn't know how yet, but I will figure out a way and then have it out with Johnny. In the meantime, I felt it was best to play dumb, as I didn't want Johnny to know that I had any suspicion at all. I still have to find out what happened last night, I must do it at once.

I looked at Rachael as she came out of the shower and asked her, "Was I a big idiot last night?"

She looked at me wondering what was the matter and said, "You were pretty shit faced, but you didn't do anything crazy. You met some guy at the party and you were talking to him a lot. I didn't hear what you said, but the guy looked very sleazy. If you ask me, he looked like a gangster. He asked me where you were from. I told him New York, I hope that was okay? He also wanted to know if you knew a guy named Harry Miller. He kept on asking you about that, but I didn't hear what your answer was because I went over to the bar. I didn't like him at all. I was glad to get out of there."

I realized that Johnny was the problem, and so was I. I'd better get hold of myself and watch my actions. From now on no more drinking to excess. I couldn't afford to lose control ever. I couldn't blame Rachael, as she had no idea and only said what I told her. I should have never told her I was from New York. Stupid mistakes, that's what I keep on making. If I don't watch myself better, I'll lead them to me and that will be the end.

Once they find out that their two guys are dead, they'll know that the identification was real. What a stupid mistake! I'm lucky I'm still breathing.

At the same time, I am grateful that I had Rachael as she was great company and good looking to boot. I just need to be careful so that she doesn't know more than she needs to. I needed a little diversion, and she was perfect. Johnny called to tell me that Barbara was going to spend some time with him at the bar and we should plan to meet there later for dinner. I let Rachael speak with her, and they made arrangements to speak at about five. In the meantime, Johnny was going to take Barbara over to some store he knew and buy her a new wardrobe. We were free for the day, and I loved it. We spent the rest of the day just walking on the boardwalk and buying little trinkets and things that Rachael loved. It was great and took my mind off the double killing.

At five, I called Johnny at the bar. "Hey, Johnny, what is going on, anything on tap for tonight?"

"Hi, Allen, how's your head? Did you guys have a good day?" he asked.

I detected something wrong in his voice. It was not the usual Johnny, and once again, I jumped to a conclusion that he must have been disappointed that I was still alive and perhaps the Mob called him to ask what happened. I didn't hear anything on the news, so perhaps no one looked into the black Cadillac yet. I hated myself for thinking this way, especially after all the things he did for me.

"We had a great time and are ready for another night on the town. Did you have anything in mind, Johnny, or do you just want to play it by ear?" I said as relaxed as I could be.

"Let me see what is happening, and I'll call you back in a few minutes," he said.

"I'm not at home, Johnny, I'm on the boardwalk with Rachael, so let me call you back in thirty minutes, okay?" I said and hung up.

"So what are we doing tonight, Allen?" Rachael said with a big smile.

"I don't know I just spoke with Johnny, and he is making some calls to see what's going on in town, I'll call him back in thirty minutes. I wouldn't mind if we just went out—the two of us—had a nice dinner, and went home and made love. But whatever you want, Rachael is okay with me. I love being with you, you're the greatest," I said and kissed her softly.

"I don't mind us taking it easy as well. Maybe we can go to a club and dance a little after we eat and then go home and make love. Tomorrow is Sunday, and we can sleep all day, what do you think?" she said with a big smile and those shining baby blues.

I called Johnny back, "Hey, Johnny, what's up?" I said.

"Barbara and I want to spend tonight together. I hope you don't mind, Allen?" he said.

"Of course not, we will find our own way around and speak with you tomorrow, have fun." I hung up and felt relieved, but wary of Johnny. After what one of the Mob guys told me, I could never trust him again.

Rachel and I went out for dinner at a great steak house on Santa Monica Boulevard and then went to the upside down club and danced until midnight. We left the club at midnight and went home to spend the night together.

Sunday, March 17, 1957

St. Patrick's Day was upon us, and going out would be stupid. Every bar was celebrating, and it would be chaos for us. We decided to stay home and eat Chinese food, while we watch some basketball and relax. I spent a good part of the day asking myself just what was wrong with me. It seemed that I just couldn't make the right decision no matter how hard I try. One thing for sure was that this was a new experience for me. I had never been schooled in the art of evasion and never in my life did I ever imagine that I would have to understand the workings of the criminal mind. My university education never touched on organized crime or how to face the odds if one should find themselves suddenly thrust into an unavoidable situation. I learned how to keep a set of books and to balance the fine line of profit and loss, but I never had one lesson, not one at all on the realism of life. Of course, this was not an excuse for stupidity, and I certainly displayed an abundance of it. I kept crossing the line by not keeping the past secret and exposing the very thing I was trying to keep hidden. I promised myself that I would think before I act and then once again I act without thinking. Here I am the guy who bragged how simple it would be to defeat the Mob because of the brain power. The only power I have displayed so far was one of stupidity and this must stop once and for all.

I was glad we didn't go out, as I was down, and all the crowds out there would have bummed me out. The irony of it all was that I met a great girl, and her name was Rachael. That was something, and I felt a little weird about it, but life must go on.

Monday, March 18, 1957

It was five thirty in the morning when I woke up and put on the news. There it was, top news story of the weekend.

POLICE DISCOVER GANGLAND KILLINGS IN SANTA MONICA

The announcer went on to say Although all the details are not in yet, we have it from the Santa Monica Police Chief, Louis Reed that it appears that we are witnessing a Mob feud. A passerby noticed a discolored and shattered windshield on a parked car on a side street in Santa Monica.

Upon a closer look, the passerby noticed a body on the floor of the car and called the police. Our reporter on the scene has informed us that the Santa Monica Police have found two victims, who were shot and killed. It is alleged that the victims are well known members of a local crime family. At this time, we are not able to release further information as this is an ongoing investigation and details are still sketchy.

We have a report from an anonymous tipster that a gang war is going on between the Italian Mob and the Mexican Mob. This scene has the look of a gang related hit. We'll bring you further details, as we receive them live from our Channel 4 newsroom.

According to the news report, it appeared as a gangland hit. I guessed my little evasive action worked. Needless to say, I still must be very careful as they will be sending out more hit squads. I decided it would be best to find another place to live and to change my appearance once again. I could not waste a moment in getting a new place. I don't know what I'll do with the girls. I could let them stay here and keep my new place to myself, but it could prove dangerous for them and result in another major error. I told myself that I must think slowly and properly and try my very best to make the right decision.

I left Rachael a note that I'll be back by twelve as I had to go and take care of some business. I drove to Sherman Oaks in the Valley and found a fully furnished apartment hotel. The Strathmore was located on Moorpark near Van Nuys Boulevard and was just perfect for me. The apartment building was designed for the traveler and those who needed a place for short period of times. I registered as Alan Poe and gave them two months rent in advance as well as a five hundred dollar furniture deposit. I didn't care as long as I had a place to stay and I was not known to anyone. I had to disappear once again, and I needed to it now. I needed to prepare a plan of attack or a proper defense and had to make sure I'm living in a secured environment. I made a decision to keep this place private. No one would know that I would be way out in the Valley. This would remain my very own private place.

It was twelve thirty when I got back to my apartment and found that Rachael had taken a shower, got dressed, and cleaned the place up a bit.

"Hi, honey," she said, "did you take care of business?"

"Yes, I did, thanks, what do you want to do today?" I asked.

"I just spoke to Barbara, and she wants to come back here. I think she has had enough of Johnny and his bar. I didn't know the address here, so I said we will come and get her as soon as you get back. I hope you don't mind, I only thought it would be best this way," she said.

"Okay, let's go and get her and then we can get some lunch, are you ready? I said.

"Let me call her and let her know we are on the way," she said.

"No, don't bother, we'll just go there and surprise them. I don't want any ill feelings between Johnny and Barbara. If we arrive and take Barbara for lunch, Johnny can't think any negative thoughts. Once we are away from the bar, we really don't care what Johnny thinks, but this way we avoid confrontations."

We arrived at Johnny's bar around one. It was crowded with lunch time trade. We saw Barbara sitting at the end of the bar, where some guy was hitting on her. She looked over and saw us and a big smile appeared.

"Hey, you guys, nice to see you. How you all doing?" she said as she waved to us.

Rachael ran over and gave her a hug and a kiss on the cheek and said, "We were in the area and decided to stop in and see you and Johnny," she said loud enough so that Johnny could hear her clearly.

"Hi, Johnny," she shouted. "Boy, you look busy. I guess we better get out of your hair and catch up with you later," she said.

"Hey, you guys are welcome to stay," Johnny said.

"No need to take up paying seats, Johnny," I said. "Call me later, and we'll hook up something for tonight. Okay, see you later, pal," I said.

We left and went back to the apartment. During the entire drive back, Barbara did not stop talking about her time with Johnny. She paid no attention to the streets or anything that would give her a clue where I live.

"Hey, Allen, I just don't think Johnny is for me. He is a nice guy, but a little strange as he wanted to do weird things to me in bed. It was fun, I guess, but I want to meet some other dudes," she said. I didn't respond and just kept on driving until we got home.

Rachael sat down beside me and said, "Allen, I think something funny is happening. I care about you and want you to know that I am ready for anything that might come down." She kissed me real hard and looked at me with a look of inquiry.

"What do you think is going down?" I said.

"Well," she said, "Barb was telling me that while we were at the club the other night and you and I were dancing, Johnny kept going to the payphone to make a call. He did this three times and then came back to the table and suggested we all should stay at his place for the night. Later while we were dancing, she thought she saw him slip something into your drink. She wasn't sure if that is what she actually saw, so she didn't say anything. Maybe it was her imagination or something else, but she was convinced that he did slip something in. About twenty minutes later, you started to fade, and Johnny said let's all go home. I was ten sheets to the wind, and you were not much better and just kept on babbling. I don't remember another thing until morning. Something is fishy with that guy, Barb says not to trust him and he's bad."

"You might be right, honey," I said. "I trusted Johnny, and I was mistaken. Please stay with me, and I'll try to explain everything to you, but not right now. We have to be very careful and stay away from Johnny. Let's get our shit together and plan our next step."

Here I was, once again ready to trust someone I hardly knew. I trusted Johnny and thought I couldn't be wrong. I read him as being sincere and someone who professed an honest friendship. I should have known that two hundred and fifty K was too big a temptation to put honesty and friendship aside. It's a stretch to think friendship would be that strong especially since we have only known one another such a short time. Now I was with this woman and was considering confiding in her. I realized how hard it was to be alone all the time. Everyone needs someone to talk to and at times to lean on. You just can't keep on running forever. But you don't have to spill your guts every time you meet someone.

Tuesday, March 19, 1957

Rachael and I went to my new place in the Valley. So much for my keeping this place private. What an idiot I was. I needed someone to talk to, someone to bounce things off. If I was wrong again so be it, but I can't live alone and just wait until they find and kill me.

I felt this was different as Rachel was a woman that cared about me although she was young and that I only knew her for a few short days. I still felt I could trust her with my life. I liked her a lot and knew deep inside that she would stand tall for me no matter what. She was wild and ready for action and most importantly honest. There was no bullshit as to who she was and what she wanted, and she was too young to have formulated any type of mean streak. No she was good for me, and I believed in her even if an alarm keeps going off inside me.

We left Barbara at the old place while we went to look at the new one. I told Rachael everything including the fact that I was married to a girl whose name was also Rachel. I told her that survival was what I try to do each day. I also told her about my change of appearance and how I had to make it so that I could maintain it. She loved that part as it was exciting for her. She promised me there and then that she would never ever reveal anything I have told her, even if we do split up for any reason at all. I believed her and felt that she would be loyal. It made me feel good.

I had to change my appearance once again as Johnny knew what I looked like, and now more than ever the Mob was going to come after me. Rachael took it as if it was a game, but wanted in and swore loyalty to me no matter what.

She decided to speak with Barbara and try to get her to go back to Chicago now as she was only a liability. It would also be for her own safety, as it would be best if she returned to Chicago. It was our plan to change our appearance as well as our names and move on. It was most important that Barbara did not know what our new appearance will be or our new names. As long as she didn't know she could never be compromised. Once again, I will have to change my name and get new papers. What a way to live, I thought, but I had no other choice. Money was not the problem, as I still had plenty andcould call Moe if I needed anymore. A new beginning was at hand, and I was getting ready to face it with my new partner. I still had to remain with my present appearance in case I see Johnny or anyone who may know me.

I called Johnny just to see where his head was at this time. I wanted him to think that things were still the same. It was best to keep Johnny guessing at all times. If he was suspicious about me having anything to do with the Mob guys being rubbed out, he didn't say anything. A little doubt in his mind would go a long way.

"Hey, Johnny, how are you?" I said.

"Allen, where have you been? I expected you to stop in for a drink. What's up?" he said.

"Nothing special. I was very busy with the two broads and now that they are leaving, I'll have some free time. Barbara is going back to Chicago tonight, and Rachael is going to Atlanta on Wednesday. We had a good time, and now it's time to get back to reality," I said.

"By the way, Allen, I have those University papers. You can pick them up anytime," Johnny said.

"Thanks, Johnny, I'll pass by some time today or tomorrow. See you later, pal." I hung up and went back to getting things in order.

Wednesday, March 20, 1957

As it turned out, Barbara was scheduled to return to Chicago on Friday anyway, so that problem was solved. Rachael agreed to stay with me, as she put it, "Through thick and thin I'm with you." We agreed to act as if nothing is wrong and just enjoy the next few days until Barbara leaves. She had an early flight on Pan Am, and we were going to take her to the airport. I left the girls at the apartment and drove to Johnny's Bar to pick up the certificates. I walked in and saw Johnny wiping down the bar, the place was empty as it was only ten thirty.

"Hi, Johnny, how about that drink?" I said.

"Nice to see you, Allen, I thought you forgot about your old pal Johnny. A little pussy, and friends don't count." Johnny laughed.

"Give me the usual. I know it's a little early, but what the hell! We might as well live dangerously," I said.

Johnny brought me the drink and said, "Excuse me a minute, Allen, I have to get your stuff out of the office. I'll be right back."

I watched him go into his little office and close the door. I got off the bar stool and walked over to the office door and listened. I could hear Johnny talking on the phone and could make out some of the words. I heard, "He's here having a drink. I'll stall him, but hurry he won't be here forever. I'll do my best, just get over here."

This was enough for me and confirmed beyond any doubt that Johnny was a dirty rat. I turned the handle and opened the door; Johnny looked up and had an expression of shock on his face.

"I'm just looking for that damn certificate. It's got be around here somewhere," he said.

"I'm sorry, Johnny, but I never thought you of all people would do this to me, never ever."

I stood there with my gun pointing straight at him. No time for bullshit here, those guys were on the way.

"Good-bye, Johnny, this is the reward a traitor gets," I said.

"No! Please, Allen, I was pressured. They said they would kill me if I didn't help them get to you. Please, Allen, I'll give you money, but don't do this to me. They are on the way here. Please, Allen, I'll tell them I couldn't keep you and you left. Please don't do it" Johnny pleaded. "Please, Allen, please I beg you don't kill me," he cried.

I pulled the trigger and watched the blood squirt out from where his right eye used to be. I closed the office door and went back to bar and wiped the glass clean and placed it in the wet sink behind the bar. I opened the cash drawer and took all the money that was in there and left it open. I then slowly walked out of the bar never to return again. I drove home and spent the rest of the day in bed with Rachael and Barbara. We went out for dinner and drank a few at the Colossal Club in Hawthorne. I made sure I limited my drinks and kept my wits about me at all times. We got in around midnight and had a threesome once again and crashed.

Thursday, March 21, 1957

I read the *Los Angeles Times* and saw a report on page seven that Johnny's Bar was robbed yesterday morning and the bar owner was shot to death. Sgt. William Morrison of the LAPD homicide Wilshire Division stated that it was an apparent robbery.

It appeared that when the manager refused to open the safe, they shot him. I felt good to have eliminated one more threat and to know they will not be able to connect me with that crime. I had to get rid of the gun as that could be the only link to Johnny's death. My next move was to get rid of the gun that morning. So I left the girls alone for a while and went over to Woodley and Balboa where the city had plenty of parks and lots of lakes.

I stopped at a supermarket and picked up old bread, so anyone who would see me walking along the water's edge would see a guy feeding the ducks. I spent an hour walking and feeding the ducks. I also tied a small rock on to the trigger of the gun, as I slipped it into the water. I had plenty of guns at home so staying well armed didn't worry me. In the case of Johnny and, if they compare notes, they will find that the same gun killed the two Mob guys. This might be good because they might make the three killings a Mob killing. I really didn't give a shit. I just wanted get on with my life. My war with the Mob was well on its way and to date. I was way ahead, but I knew deep down that this could not last. They had far more resources than I. I went back to the apartment and gathered up all the papers I had on Allen Foster. It was time these were destroyed in case there were any papers left over at Johnny's. I never did get the diploma from Johnny, so perhaps they could connect that to me. It was time for Allen Foster to disappear once for all.

Friday, March, 22, 1957

We took Barbara to the airport and saw her off. What a relief for us, we now felt that a weight was removed from our shoulders. We can now get to work on changing our identity, moving and getting things in order. Rachael was anxious to get into her new role. This was all an act to her, and she loved it. She always wanted to be in show business, so this role was right up her alley. I knew she would be loyal, but she was young and didn't always think before acting and sometimes neither did I. Nevertheless, we are on the way to a new start. We are now an army of two. We moved out of the apartment at once and cleaned the place completely. We took everything we needed and packed everything else into a couple of garbage bags. We removed the phone and threw it into the garbage along with some clothes. We stopped at a dumpster in the back of a shopping center and disposed of the bags.

Rachael went in to Hollywood and found a make-up store that works with the movie studios. She let them know that she was auditioning for a part and needed to arrive all made up. She spent six-hundred and fifty dollars on all kinds of make-up, dyes, etc. She was really into this big time. She returned to our Sherman Oaks apartment and spent the day working with me on the change of our appearance. I now had very black hair, with thick eyebrows and eyelashes and a pencil sized mustache. My height had changed because of the elevator shoes we bought earlier. I looked a lot older and a lot sleazier. She said I looked like a Puerto Rican, but I certainly didn't look like Harry or Allen. I was now Bill Darby of Santa Monica, California. Rachael really had a talent with make-up. She was good, which was obvious when I looked in the mirror, even I didn't recognize myself.

Rachael was now a dirty blonde, and it was hard to change her great body that moved like a cat. Her eyebrows and lashes were all dyed to match, and her eye color was brown. Her hair was long and flowing, and now dirty blonde in color. She looked great and would make heads spin, and she was no longer Rachael.

She walked into the living room and announced, "Meet Tina Wilks from Orlando, Florida—actress, singer, and model."

Tina was in heaven with her new identity and, of course, her new look. If anyone was born to play a part, she certainly was.

Saturday, March 23, 1957

We spent Saturday driving around the Valley and getting a feel of the area. We also wanted to put our new looks to the test and see the reaction of people, even though no one in the Valley knew us by any description. Although I didn't want us to stand out, it was impossible not to when walking along with Tina. Men stopped what they were doing to gawk and stare at her; she was a stunner. I felt that it might be very good for me as no one usually remembers the guy with the gorgeous woman; they only remember her!

We needed a driver's license and other identification forms to establish our new identities. We decided to let Tina go out and find the proper papers. It was best that no one see me. The Mob wouldn't be looking for a woman, and one as beautiful as Tina would easily have guys breaking their necks for her. If she made contact, the source would be very cooperative just to impress her.

Tina dropped me off at the apartment and went out bar hopping. We had agreed that a bar was the best place to find someone who could supply what we needed. I stayed home and watched television and waited for Tina to return. Around 6:00 p.m., she returned home and told me she had made the contact.

"It will cost about a thousand bucks, but it is well worth it," she said.

"Are you sure this person is reliable?" I asked.

"No, I'm not one hundred percent certain, but what the hell! We have to take a chance, don't we?" Tina said.

"Sure, honey, we sure do. Great job, thanks for taking care of things. I mean it, yes, I do," I said and gave her a big kiss and held her close.

"I'll meet the guy tomorrow at the corner of Ventura and Corbin, and we'll go have a sit down and take care of things. My good looks and sexy voice got me directed to the right person first off. As far as the bartender knows is that I am an above average hooker who just moved in from Atlanta. I promised to cut him in on any action I get out of his bar. He was all over me. What more could I do? I had to confide in him that I needed a little help. Once I told him what I needed, he was Mr. Service. He couldn't do enough for me. I asked him to get me in touch with someone who could get me a driver's license and Social Security card. I told him I need two sets, one for my brother, and one for me. I gave him a description of you and, of course, he knows what I look like. I told him my name as well as the one you want to go by, and he said it would be taken care of," she proudly told me of her escapades.

It felt funny. I think I was jealous of her, yet I asked myself why? You just met her a week ago, and she means nothing to you. I guessed the decency in me was coming out, even though I certainly have not been very decent lately when I was forced to kill another human being. And deep down, I liked her. I liked her a lot.

Sunday, March 24, 1957

Tina slept until ten thirty, and when she finally got herself together, it was almost noon. She had to meet the contact at three thirty, so we decided to go to the Sagebrush Cantina for brunch. We found ourselves in this terrific bar filled with lots of people from every walk of life—bikers, doctors, actors, and so many women who were looking for guys, and, of course, guys looking for women as well. They had a brunch that was bigger than I had ever seen, table after table filled with all kinds of food. There was a shooter section, where you had oysters dropped into your glass of vodka and shot it down. All this was yours for only nine dollars and ninety-five cents. What a deal! And you could eat and eat until you were ready to bust. A Mexican Mariachi band played great music and sang as well as they walked from table to table. For a few bucks, these guys would sing just about any song you requested. On a sunny day like today, it was a great place to spend a Sunday afternoon. As far as I was concerned, every guy and many women looked at Tina. She wore a black dress, very low cut for all to see that she has great tits. Her shiny white teeth made her smile even more radiant than ever. She was sexy, and she knew it. We had a wonderful time, and during the few hours we were there, Tina made a lot of new friends. There is no question that Bill and Tina were on the scene now. We were an item and ready for action. Our story was well rehearsed. We were two actors who have been friends for years, and we came to Hollywood together to become full time actors.

We stopped in at a Sears store and took passport photos and made up an address for our driver's license. We used a vacant lot on Van Nuys Boulevard near Moorpark Avenue, in Sherman Oaks. Tina dropped me off at the apartment and went off to the meeting and to hopefully finalize the transaction. I gave her a thousand dollars and waited for her return.

It was close to six when she returned and said as she ran over and put her arms around me, "We will have the stuff on Tuesday. I only gave him half the money and told him will pay the rest when I see the finished products. I'm sure they will be super, after all he wants to get into my pants, and I'm letting him believe he can," she said, her voice filled with excitement.

"Great job, sweetheart, you're making me jealous. I just can't help it knowing how beautiful you are, and I care about you a lot. Every guy in the world wants to get into your pants, especially me. Thanks for your help and your faith in me, it means a lot to me," I said.

"And remember, Bill, you are the only one that does get into my pants," she said as she kissed me gently on the lips.

"Would you like something to eat, my queen," I said.

We went off to eat, another experience filled with gawking men and jealous women. We returned home and decided to relax for the rest of the night. We enjoyed watching the *Ed Sullivan Show, He Had Senior Wenches and His Little Guy in the Box on the Show*. It was very funny. We watched the beginning of a movie, but I could not keep my eyes open and fell asleep in Tina's arms.

Monday, March 25, 1957

We spent the day looking at new cars. We had decided that we should get rid of my old car as it is in the name of Allen Foster. We went to a number of used car lots and finally settled on selling the car to one lot, even though he was not going to give us the best price and buy another car at a different dealer under our new identity. We decided to wait until tomorrow when we get our new identifications. We spent the rest of the day at a bar on Van Nuys Boulevard and then walked home. I stopped on the way home at a pay phone with a pocket full of quarters and made a call to Rachel.

"Hi, honey, how are you?" I said.

"I'm so glad you called. I've missed you terribly. I heard about a shooting in Los Angeles and must know one thing. Are you behind the shooting of the Mob guys in Los Angeles?" she asked.

"I don't know what you are talking about. What guys and what shootings?" I said.

"Let me set you straight, Harry. I heard Larry and some of the boys speaking last night. They believe that you have declared war on the Mob and it was you who killed the guys in Los Angeles the other day. It seems that the families want to set up a meet with you and call off this vendetta."

"Bullshit, do you think I'm stupid enough to fall for that crap? And let me repeat myself, I don't know of any shootings and don't want to know," I said.

"You can always tell me the truth, Harry; I'm on your team," she said.

"I don't have time now. I will call back later," I said and hung up because I was getting angry, even though my anger was an act to placate

Rachel. I guess I was getting carried away with my own bullshit, so ending the call was best. I was happy to know that the news travelled so far, yet I was pleased that the message has been delivered. "Fuck with Harry Miller, and you're dead," I said to myself as Tina and I headed home.

Tuesday, March 26, 1957

Tina was scheduled to meet her contact at noon and pick up our new papers. I went out and found a pay phone and called Rachel, "Hi, it's me. What's cooking?" I said.

"I thought you were calling me back?" she said.

"What do you call this, of course I'm calling you back, but I can't stay on the phone too long, and sometimes, I can't find another phone so easily," I said.

"You know, Harry, you haven't said you love me for a long time now. Is there something wrong?" she said.

"Of course, not, I do love you. But my mind is reeling with this situation, and I can't always feel romantic. Please understand, Rachel, it's not easy looking over your shoulder every minute and moving from place to place. No, it isn't easy at all," I said.

"I'm sorry, Harry, I know you love me, and I don't want to add to your problems.

I spoke with Larry last night, and he agrees with you. Once they know where you are, they will kill you. The fact that they give you their word means nothing. Be careful, please, he also said if you are the one who's knocking these guys off more power to you. You're getting them angry, and they are frustrated why they can't find you, but they are not quitting. So be careful. Harry, they are pissed and will stop at nothing to get you. You have made assholes out of them, and the Mob is not used to this kind of reputation. They will fuck you over, Harry, so please, Harry, please be very careful. I need you and love you," she said.

"I will, I promise you. I love you, take care of yourself. I'll call you soon. I have to go now." I hung up and went back to the apartment to wait for Tina. It was around six when she walked into the apartment.

"Hi, Bill, I'm home," she said.

"Hi, how did it all go? You look tired but as usual great," I said.

"Well, I'm glad you missed me, and yes I have it. Here take a look at these, I think they are great," she said with a big smile on her face.

I looked at the driver's licenses and passports, and at first glance, I found them to be great. I then took out my old passport and began an inch by inch check. They were very close to perfect. I was sure no one would pick up on them, as they were very genuine looking. We had requested that the passports should be dated July 1956 and that a visa stamp should be in the passport, perhaps two or three to add to the authenticity. Ours had a stamp from Denmark and another from The United Kingdom. The stamps coincided with a trip in January 1957, so everything looked great. We each had a passport in our new names as well as a driver's license from the State of California. We also had a new Social Security numbers and cards if we should ever need them. We planned on adding a library card as well as a few other cards that people normally carry. I felt we were on the road to a new life without hassles. It was too late for us to go out and get our new car, we decided to stay in and make love.

Wednesday, March 27, 1957

We awoke to a cloudy, misty kind of day. It looked like it might rain, but who cared. We were having a great time and starting to enjoy our new lives.

"Rise and shine," I said. "It's a lousy day, but what the hell! Let's get out of here and get some breakfast and go get ourselves a car. No cares or worries today and maybe every day!" I said.

We went to a deli on Ventura Boulevard and had a great breakfast. We then took a walk along Van Nuys where there were several car dealers. We stopped at each one and checked out the cars they had. Finally, we made a decision and bought a very simple Plymouth that would not attract any attention and drove out of the lot happier than ever. The car was brand new and set me back sixteen hundred bucks. We spent the rest of the day riding around the Valley and ending up in the Santa Susana Mountains, where a western town was built just to shoot cowboy movies. It looked just like the real deal as it had a saloon, a sheriff's office, a general store, a main street and so on. It was a real western looking town in the middle of nowhere where Randolph Scott, Tom Mix, Gene Autry, and Roy Rogers and so many others all starred in western movies. The day was shot when we finally called it quits and headed back to our apartment. We stopped at Maria's restaurant for some spaghetti and meat balls and headed home.

Thursday, March 28, 1957

Last night, Tina and I talked about her career. Although she was young, she was very talented as she played piano and guitar and sang. She sang a couple of songs, especially for me, and I thought she was very good. Of course, it did not hurt in the least that she was so beautiful, it made it easy to look at, and every song sounded better and better the more you looked.

"I saw an ad in the paper for this club called "The Basement," where they are holding auditions for singers and I really want to start my singing once again," she said.

"Sounds great. Would you like me to come with you or would that make you nervous?" I said as softly as possible.

"No, you stay here and relax. I'll take the car and should be back by dinner time. I'll call you later," she said as she put on a very revealing pink dress with most of her tits showing. She was a knockout, and anyone who looked at her would be smitten by her beauty. I felt lucky to be the guy she chose to be with.

Around seven, Tina came home. She looked tired and little drunk. "Did you get the job?" I asked. "Sure did, I start tomorrow at eight.

I do two shows a night—eight and ten—and three on Saturday. The extra one is at midnight. It's so exciting to be on stage in front of so many people, I just love it so much," she said.

"You look like you are tired. I think you'd better lie down and rest a while," I said.

In ten minutes, she was asleep. I read the paper and watched a little TV and went to sleep.

Friday, March 29, 1957

Tina wanted me to see her first show at "The Basement," a club located on the Marina. It seemed like a nice place with a piano bar and a small stage at the end of a dance floor. The bar ran the entire length of the club with stools all along, except for an area, where I noticed all the waitresses gathered to place and pick up their drink orders. The club was a happening place and filling up pretty fast. The people that were there seemed pretty well to do and about the twenty-five to thirty-five-year-old bracket. Waitresses were on a first name basis with many of the customers. It added to a relaxed atmosphere, making drinking easy. Tina's picture was hanging on the wall at the entrance, she looked great. After waiting what seemed to be forever, the announcer picked up the mike and introduced Tina Wilks, who has just finished an engagement in Atlanta at the Boat Club. When she came out on stage, my heart skipped a beat, she was gorgeous. What was happening to me? Was I falling in love? Wow! This is unreal, but I have to go with the flow, and that's what is going on in my heart and mind. She wowed them with one song after another, and each time, they gave her a standing ovation and made her come back for two more encores. Of course, most of the audience was male, and they were mesmerized with her. She was super and was going to be a real success if she kept her head about her. I didn't want to be a downer, especially on this her first night, but I did notice that she always had a drink in her hand.

By the time ten thirty rolled around, she was feeling no pain at all. I let it slide as I chalked it up to first night jitters. What a night for us both, but especially for her. I imagined everyone envied me for being her guy or whatever they thought I was to her. It was a great feeling for both of us. We went home and drank champagne until sleep took us over.

Saturday, March 30, 1957

We spent the day hanging around the house and Tina putting her sheet music together. Tonight was the big night—three shows and maybe some real agents would be there. Word must have gotten out as guys love to brag, and those who were there Friday night were no different. We just played it by ear, but she started drinking early and a little too much for my liking.

"Tina baby," I said in a soft tone, "Please don't drink anymore, you've got three shows to do tonight, and you want to be at your best, just like last night. You were great, just great."

"I know you're right Bill, but I'm a little nervous. I don't know why, I wasn't last night. I'll be okay. All I need is a little rest, and I'll knock them dead, I promise," she said in a sweet innocent tone and a smile to boot.

We arrived at the club, and I was more nervous than her. I tried my best not show it as I didn't want to dampen this night for her. She went into the back to check notes with the band and get ready for the first show. The place was packed; they actually had to turn people away. Word had gotten out that a new star was born, and Tina Wilks was it. She started her performance with an Elvis song, "Don't be Cruel," as she said, "To get the place hopping." She hit them with some great songs and finished her performance with "Love Me Tender." The house came down. They stood and clapped and begged for more. At this rate, she wouldn't make three shows due to exhaustion. I went back stage to see how she was doing and saw a Mob scene at her dressing room door.

"Get back, please. Miss Wilks must rest until her next performance. If you want an autographed picture, please wait in line in an orderly fashion."

I couldn't believe my eyes as there were at least fifty people in this small hallway. I noticed this very big guy standing outside Tina's door. He looked very dangerous and was not letting anyone in. I guessed she now had a bodyguard.

I approached the door and said, "I'm Bill Darby, Miss Wilks's manager, may I go in?"

"Wait right here, and I'll check with Miss Wilks," he said and opened the door and went into her dressing room.

He came out almost at once and said, "Okay, Mr. Darby, you can go in."

"Tina, what a show! You were great. Everyone loves you. Wow, what a performance! I love watching and listening, and guess that I love being with you. I love you," I said with excitement in my voice.

"Thanks, Bill, it was great, and I'm just so whacked. This is more than I ever thought. They love me. I never thought it would be like this. It's so exciting and guess what, and they really, really love me," she said with pride.

"I know isn't it great, you are terrific. Everyone wants your autograph, and everyone wants you to sing and never stop. What a deal, what a day! It'll always be in my memory," I said.

"Thanks, Bill, thanks for being with me. I couldn't have done it without you. I need you stay close and help me. Please don't leave me," she said.

"I won't," I answered. What a night it was for her. I was exhausted as well and felt the excitement, it was exhilarating. I couldn't understand how she was able to do three shows, but she did it, and when she closed with her final song "Walking In the Rain," the house erupted with a loud cheer and applause that lasted over ten minutes. It made goose pimples run up and down my spine.

As we prepared to leave, the manager of the club came into the dressing room and said, "You were great, Tina, we want to extend your contract an additional four weeks at double what you are getting. What do you say to that?"

He stood there waiting for an answer when I said, "I'm sorry, but Tina can't give you an answer tonight, she's too exhausted. We'll get back to you tomorrow." Before he could say another word, we exited the dressing room and headed home.

Sunday, March 31, 1957

We didn't get to bed until four in the morning, so getting up early was not in the cards. It was around noon when I awoke, and Tina was still asleep. I showered and dressed as quietly as I could. I went to the deli and brought back some bagels and lox to help celebrate this day with her when she wakes up. I returned with a bag full of goodies and found Tina getting out of the shower, looking real good and smiling from ear to ear.

"Well, how do you feel?" I asked.

"I'm not sure if this is for real or what! I am still so excited. I can't think straight, but I will, yes, I will," she said.

"Let's relax and eat something. I went out and got some bagels and lots of Jewish stuff that you will like. Just relax and I'll make it all ready," I said.

I was happy for her and excited for myself. Something to do, to keep busy with and forget the bullshit that I have been going through. I decided to maintain my vigilance as I knew from stories I had read that most people get caught because they start to believe that they are safe and beyond detection. I wouldn't let that happen to me. I couldn't let it happen if I want to stay alive. Of course, I am the idiot that had made blunder after blunder, so stay on top of it, I kept telling myself.

We ate and drank champagne and then made love for a little while.

"Hey, what time is it?" Tina shouted.

"It's four thirty, why do we have to worry about time? You aren't scheduled for tonight, are you?" I asked.

"No, I'm not, but Luigi wants me to meet him at the club around seven thirty. He wants to introduce me to some other people who want to talk about my career. I didn't tell you last night because I was too exhausted and the excitement of it all was too much. I want you to come along with me. I won't make any moves without you. I need you at my side," she said.

"Who the hell is Luigi?" I asked. "I'm sorry, honey, I forgot to introduce you. Things were so hectic back there at the club that it was the last thing on my mind.

Remember the big guy outside my dressing room, that's Luigi's bodyguard, Armando, his boss is Luigi Conti, a big shot in Los Angeles and Las Vegas. He takes care of acts like mine and told me he can promote me to the top. He can get me gigs in Vegas at top dollar and also arrange a recording deal. I want you to meet him and see what you think. I think this might be my big chance," she stated very sincerely.

"Just remember my situation. If this guy is Mob, and I'll bet he is, then I'm taking a real chance. What if he recognizes me? What if things get crazy? Are you ready to split at a moment's notice if we have to?" I asked.

"I never thought of it, but let me tell you, Bill. The best place to hide from them is to be among them. They would never believe that you would have the balls to stand there face-to-face with them. No I don't think we have anything to worry about, we just have to stay cool and make sure we don't make any mistakes," she said.

Well, I could hardly believe my ears, what wisdom from an eighteen year-old from the South. She may not have the education, but sure as hell had street smarts.

"Okay, fuck it, let's move forward, and let's get the ball rolling. I love you and would like to see you succeed so I'll go along with it. Just remember, I'm your manager, and you have to listen to me. The last thing we need is for us to fight," I said as I kissed on the top of her head.

We arrived at the "Basement" at seven twenty-five and went inside and sat down at the bar. Tina was not scheduled to sing until Tuesday. Sunday was a quiet night anyway, and the place had only a few people listening to a piano player sing and play requests. We ordered a couple of drinks and waited for Luigi to arrive. It was little after seven thirty when Armando came in and walked up to the bar.

"Nice to see you. Luigi wants to meet in the back booth on the left, just follow me."

We got up and followed Armando. When we got near the booth, I easily recognized a greased back Mob guy. You can spot them a mile away with the gold chains, the pinky rings, and the dark suits. Manicured nails and shiny shoes and fat fingers make it easy to spot a Mob looking guy, guaranteed he didn't carry a gun, his bodyguard did.

He got up from the booth and said, "I'm Luigi Conti, and you are?"

"Bill Darby, Tina's manager, a pleasure to meet you," I said with a big smile.

"Tina, I didn't know you have a manager, why didn't you tell me?" he said pleasantly.

"I'm sorry. I didn't think it was important when we talked last night and things were so hectic. We only talked for a minute. Is it a problem?" she said.

"Let's hope not," Luigi replied. "Would you like a drink? Champagne, wine, whatever you like?" Luigi asked very congenially.

"Champagne would be great," Tina responded.

Luigi motioned to Armando and told him to get a couple bottles of Dom Perignon and make sure it was very cold.

"Okay, let's get down to real things. In this entertainment business, it is who you know I'm sure you understand that. Tina you are a great singer. You look fabulous, and everyone goes crazy when they see you. To play clubs, you need someone who knows the score or else they will take advantage of you and your career may not go very far. To make records, you need a manager as well as PR. It don't matter how pretty you are, all that does is make guys want to fuck you. Records sell because they want to listen to you. You can fuck your way to the top, and sometimes it works, and sometimes it is nothing more than a fuck. I tell you this because you are new and you need to know the truth about show business. I am well connected and have clout in all the right places. No one fucks around with Luigi Conti, nobody! What I say goes in a lot of places, and if I say Tina starts tomorrow in your club, then she starts. If I say no Tina in any club, then you don't work. Get the picture?" he said softly.

"Of course, she gets it. We aren't stupid. You are the man, we understand," I said quietly. I had dealt with scumbags like this back in New York all the time at Larry's office and knew how their brains worked. They just needed ego massaging and their heads got bigger and bigger.

"Okay, here's the deal. I like what I see and will make Tina a super star on the following terms. I will be her new manager and shall make all the decisions as to where she performs and how much she gets. I own her—lock, stock, and barrel. If you two are together, then that's fine with me, but you, Bill, stay out of the entertainment business. She does what I say, and no fucking interference from you. Up to now are we clear and is it okay with you?" he said directing his question to Tina.

"Sure thing, Luigi, as long as you don't interfere with Bill and I in our private lives, I am sure we can live with this," she said. I looked at her like she was mad, but could not say a word.

"Good, from now on, you will receive two thousand dollars a week and play wherever I tell you. Soon that will go up to five times, but first we have to get you known. Bill, you have to stay in the background. If you want to travel with Tina, that is fine, but no jealousy, no mixing in, no noise out of you. All expenses will be taken care of, and you will both always travel first class. No guns, no drugs, no gambling, no turning tricks. If I say jump, you jump, if I say I want you to meet someone very important, I'll tell you what you have to do with him. Never do more or less, and always keep your mouth shut about us. That is all today. Let's get out of here and go home and get some rest. Give Armando your home address and phone number in case I need you. In the meantime, relax and enjoy your days off. You are performing on Tuesday, and there will some very important people here to watch you. Look sexy like you always do and sing the shit out of every song."

"Bill, you relax and have a drink or two and enjoy the show and then go home. Tina will come home later in a limo and will always ride in a limo from now on," he said and got up putting his hand in his pocket and taking out a wad of bills. He counted off ten crisp C notes and gave it to Tina. This was a message to me that I was no longer any part of the equation.

"This is for odds and ends, enjoy, it's yours, see you on Tuesday. Oh by the way, you were offered a new contract here at the club, just tell him to see me." He bent over and kissed her on the cheek and turned and went out the door. Our business was over, and a new world was about to begin. I could not ever have thought that I would be here, doing this, but neither did I ever think that the entire Mob would be after me. The one thing that made me laugh was the fact that they were working with me and giving me money to boot. If the big boys back in New York had any idea where I was, they would have Luigi whack me double quick. I would have to call Moe tomorrow and find out how strong Luigi really is.

Monday, April 1, 1957

We spent the day just fooling around and talking about the deal. I called Rachel and found out that the Mob feels I was in Los Angeles and have alerted everyone to lookout for me. She also told me that some FBI guy came by Larry's office looking for me, even though he knew I wasn't there. He just wanted to leave a message that they are looking for me and left a message that I should call him. He left his card with Larry. The visit was a crock of shit, as I felt it was just another nail in my coffin being put there by the feds to keep the heat on. Perhaps, they thought they could force my hand and get me come in for protection. Who knows, who cares, right now the Mob is protecting me, and I feel very safe this way.

I called Moe and asked him to please find out all he could about a guy named Luigi Conti out of Los Angeles and Las Vegas. I promised to call back tomorrow and hung up.

I then called the inspector and asked him, "Sam, do you know why the FBI came by Larry's office looking for me? I'm pretty sure they are up to date and know I wouldn't be there?"

"I swear I don't know anything about this, but I will inquire and let you know. It just doesn't make any sense, Harry, no sense at all," he said. I told him I'd call him back tomorrow and hung up.

Tuesday, April 2, 1957

We hung around the apartment for most of the day. I went out earlier to call Moe and see what he found out about Luigi Conti. Moe told me that he was a heavy hitter and was well connected in most of the casinos. He had his hand in all entertainment that was scheduled in Las Vegas and the West Coast.

He certainly could pull strings and put someone on the road to stardom. Once he has his hands on you, he owns you, and getting out is usually impossible. It was rumored that he was involved with Sinatra back in the days when he was down on his luck. Of course, they are only rumors, and no one knows for sure. He certainly let me know that this guy was scary and very dangerous.

I then called the inspector and found out that it was an end play orchestrated by the feds to see if a message would be delivered to me.

"They are fully aware of everything that is going on and knew you wouldn't be at Larry's office. Just ignore them and things will be fine. This I promise you," he said.

I guess I had no other choice but to believe in what he said. I had planned on driving Tina to the club tonight until I heard the knock on the door. "I'll get it," I yelled out as I went to the door. I opened the door and there was a monster of guy, he stood at least 7' tall. He was big and had to weigh in at three hundred pounds or more. He wore a regulation Mob issue suit of black with a white shirt and dark tie. He had black, slicked back hair and looked scary.

"Hi, I'm here to drive Tina to work. I'm Tony Dee," he said very gently, but with a Brooklyn accent.

"A pleasure to meet you. I'm Bill Darby, her manager," I said as we shook hands. "Come on in, would you like a drink?" I asked.

"No, thanks, I don't drink when I'm on the job. Mr. Conti doesn't like anyone drinking when they are working. We always have to be on our toes, and drinking could make us a little sloppy. You know the saying, 'Loose lips sink ships' I never forget it," he said.

I called out to Tina to let her know that her driver was here and to get herself ready. "Have a seat, Tony. I'll check on Tina. When do you want to leave for the club?" I asked.

"Mr. Conti likes his people to be a little early, so I think we should get started now, if it's all right with Tina," he said with a wink.

I went into the bedroom and Tina was just putting on her makeup.

"How you doing, honey? Tony is here and wants to leave now. Do you think you will be ready in a few minutes?" I asked.

"Sure thing, all I have left is to just put on a dress," she said as she pulled this red dress up over her thighs and on to her breasts. "Here, zip me up."

"Do you think this dress will stay up? There's nothing to hold it other than your beautiful tits. You look great, and I know you will be super tonight as always," I said as I zipped her up.

Off we went with Tony in a limousine with a bar in the back. "Just make yourself comfortable, enjoy the bar if you like," Tony said into a small microphone that seemed to hang from the visor.

"Thanks, Tony, we will make ourselves a drink. I'll check out the supply and see what the star wants. This is the life, Tony. Are you going to be our regular driver?" I asked as I found a bottle of Moet champagne in the fridge. I opened the bottle and poured ourselves two glasses to celebrate the first night of a super star.

Wednesday, April 3, 1957

After a full house and a great show, we went to an after hour's club with Luigi. Tina sang for a bunch of Mob guys until four in the morning and wowed them. Tony finally took us home arriving after 5:00 a.m. We slept until one, or should I say I slept until one and Tina stayed in bed until three.

"Hey there, how are you feeling after a night of singing and partying?" I said as I gently kissed her on the forehead.

"I'm tired, but I'll be okay once I shower and eat something. What have we got to eat?" she said groggily.

"I'll whip you up some eggs. I think we have some bread. Do you want coffee?" I asked.

"Sure, I could use a bloody Mary much better, but coffee will get me started," she yelled to me as she jumped out of bed and walked to the bathroom. I fixed breakfast as well as her bloody Mary.

"Let's talk a little, Tina, "I said.

"Okay, what do you want to talk about?" she said.

"Well, you know the situation. I just feel it's a matter of time before these guys start to put two and two together. Maybe they won't figure out who I am, but we got to look at it from the bad side. It's the only way to be safe. It won't take them long to get rid of me. They are only putting up with me because of you, but soon you will be the star, and they won't need me," I said.

She looked at me with a smile on her face and said, "Listen, Bill, we went into this deal together, and I don't want you to leave me. I am in love with you and need you at my side. I know I'm going to make a lot of money with these guys and I'm going to have to do a lot of things to get to the top, but I'm ready to do it, no matter what it takes. But I need you. You are my rock. You keep me straight, and when I'm not with you, I am not the same person."

I looked at her with a smile on my face and took her hand in mine and said, "I am glad you feel that way, but remember, you can't give your life to these guys. They are Mafia, mobsters, and gangsters. They only know one thing, *money* and nothing else. They will own you, and once you are in, you are in for life. Remember they give nothing for nothing. Every dollar you make comes from them. You are a talented person. You sing great and look beautiful. Every guy that watches you sing gets a boner and dreams of fucking you. You are a very sexy woman, and you know it, but most of all they know it. I'm the guy they don't really want around, and they will find ways to get rid of me. How do you think I'm going to feel when one of these guys wants to sleep with you? How am I going to handle that when Luigi wants you sleep with a pal of his? I can go on and on, but there is no use. Just tell me what we are going to do?"

"I love you, and if I sleep with someone, it is business, not love. I want to get to the top, and if this is the road I have to take then so be it, but always understand that it is you I love and no one else. Bill, I'll try my best to always be discreet and not embarrass you, but please never take anything that happens or is said outside of our private lives to heart. Look at it like it was a movie. I'm just acting and when the shooting is over, I'm back at home, with you. Please accept it and love me for me. Now kiss me and let's go make love," she said very sincerely.

Deep down I knew this would not work out, but who am I to disappoint her in her quest to be famous. I will be prepared to lose her even though it may break my heart.

Tony arrived precisely at seven to pick up Tina for her performance at the club. I decided I would miss it tonight and just stay home and relax.

Thursday, April 4, 1957

It was six thirty in the morning when I woke up. I didn't even hear Tina come in because she never did come home last night. I was concerned a little but not overly worried, as I jumped into the shower and got ready to face a new day. I dressed and decided to call Rachel. I went to pay phone a few blocks from the apartment and called her.

"Hi, how are you? I just wanted to hear your voice and find out if there is any news at your end?" I said.

"Harry, it's great to hear from you," she said with a little sarcasm in her voice.

"I was busy trying to formulate a plan to end this ordeal once and for all, but so far I haven't been able to come up with one," I said.

"I'm sorry, Harry, but I thought you would call me more often. Did you find another woman?" she said, but didn't give me any time to answer as she continued. "If Larry knew I was talking to you, he would have a fit. He's under a lot of pressure to find you. They are now accusing him of helping you get away, and he's hot now. You know how he is, Harry. If he knew where you were, he would come and kill you himself. He doesn't want his business and his life threatened, and it's coming to that. I live in a fortress with armed guards. I can't even go out of the house without an entourage. Whatever I need is here, and if it isn't, they will get it for me. It's not easy, Harry, not easy at all. Even if I wanted to meet you somewhere, I can't get away. I'm sorry, Harry, I'm really very depressed and don't know what to do," she cried.

I could imagine the tears running down her cheeks.

"Listen to me. I don't know what to do either. I wish I could help you, but I have my hands full just staying alive. These bastards are out to kill me and will stop at nothing. Maybe it's best if we just get the divorce as we discussed. Maybe that will show them that you and I are not together once and for all," I said in as mellow a tone as I could.

"I think that I have to do that," she said. "And if you survive and we still want each other, we can always remarry. I do love you, but this is no life for either of us. The fucking cops are looking for you because they don't want you talking to anyone about them. The mobsters want to kill you, and now Larry wants you dead. I think this is good-bye, Harry. Even though my heart is breaking, this is best. I will never hurt you, and I will help you whenever I can, but for now I must have you out of my life. I'm sorry, Harry. I love you and probably always will. I'll arrange all the legal paperwork for the divorce. Our child will always be our child, and if you should ever get out of this mess, you can call me and if I am still single you can come and see your baby. No matter what, Harry, our baby will always be ours. This I promise you with all my heart. Call me whenever you can, but be very careful. I love you. Good-bye, Harry."

There was a click and the phone was dead. She was gone and most likely out of my life. In one way, I felt relieved but abandoned in another. I went back to the apartment to see if Tina had returned home. She hadn't arrived, so I made myself some toast and coffee and read the paper.

It was around noon when the phone rang. It was Tina.

"I'm sorry I didn't call you earlier, Bill, but I was asleep. I'm in Vegas, we are at the Dunes. Luigi asked me to fly here right after the show. I didn't have time to call and didn't want to wake you in the middle of the night. I've never been here before. It's great. Guess what, Bill, I sang here at the Dunes in the lounge last night, and they loved it. I'm flying back at three thirty, and Tony will take me home. I'll see you about four, I love you, Bill," she said and then she was gone.

Twice in one day I had women end their conversations with me by hanging up. What a day this has been! I wondered what more the day had in store for me. I went to the shooting range and fired a few rounds to keep my gun-handling talents sharp. I got home around four and just kicked back. Finally, Tina arrived, she rushed over and hugged me and gave me a big kiss.

"How do I look?" she asked.

"You look great, super great. These new clothes look so good on you. You would think they were made for you. You are the most beautiful woman I have ever seen. Welcome home!" I said as I hugged her. I was glad to see her, and she looked fabulous.

I'm on a roll I said to myself, just enjoy it. We relaxed for a while until Tony arrived to pick her up for tonight's show.

I decided to stay home once again as I felt I would only be in her way. I had made up my mind earlier in the day that no matter I will stay friends with Tina and not let my emotions take over. Our affair is great and should last as long as she was in Los Angeles but once she had agreed with Luigi to move her career forward, I would be a thing of the past. The best I could hope for would be to get Tina to help me survive and that could best be done by me staying in the background.

Friday, April 5, 1957

I spent the day hanging around the apartment with Tina. She was scheduled to be picked up a little earlier by Tony, as Luigi wanted her at "The Basement" early because he had scheduled a meeting with some recording guru. It meant a lot to Tina, so I felt it best if I stayed at home again and not get in the way.

Tony arrived at four, and off they went. I wished Tina good luck and told her that I loved her and to be very careful. I hung around the apartment until six and then went out for a drive and stopped in at a bar for drink before heading home. While at the bar, I met Sally Goober, a really nice looking girl with great red hair and a body that was petite and great looking. I remained at the bar for a couple of hours drinking with Sally and just having a great time. I took her number and promised to call her real soon. I left the bar at nine thirty and went home.

Saturday, April 6, 1957

I spent the day riding around the Valley. I spent two hours at the gun range and then went up the mountain on the other side of Topanga Canyon Boulevard. in the Santa Susana Mountains. I did all this on my own as Tina was fast asleep for most of the day. She didn't get home until four thirty in the morning after doing three shows and then entertaining Luigi and the record guy. I didn't have the heart to disturb her, so doing stuff on my own was in the cards. I arrived home at six and found a note from Tina, "I love you, sweetheart. I'm off to work. Will see you later tonight."

I watched TV and went to bed.

Sunday, April 7, 1957

Nothing unusual as Tina slept most of the day and left around seven with Tony to perform. I was beginning to find this type of life very boring, and I didn't really care for it.

I needed this down time to relax and let time pass between myself and the Mob, so it really served my purpose. No matter I was still not too happy with our relationship and decided to talk to Tina about it whenever she would stay at home long enough. I went to bed early.

Monday, April 8, 1957

I woke Tina up at eleven and tried to get her to go with me to Santa Monica and walk on the beach for a few hours. She was not working tonight, and I figured we would grab a bite to eat while at the pier and just have a great day. I also wanted to talk with her and I thought this was a perfect chance to do so.

"Hey, lazy bones, get up," I said. "Let's get out of here and go the beach and have a little fun, how about it?"

"Please let me sleep. I'm really tired, and I have so much to do later, please, pretty please," she said.

"What things do you have to do later? I asked.

She sat up and reached for a smoke and looked at me with half open eyes. "Luigi wants me to meet some very big producers tonight. This could be a big opportunity for me. Of course, you are also welcome to come along. I wouldn't think of going without you," she said.

I looked at her and said, "What the hell is going on? I know I said I wouldn't get upset by any of this, but I don't know if we should trust Luigi and his gang. These guys are hardcore Mafia. We better be very careful."

"Don't be so paranoid, Bill. They are nice, and all Luigi wants is that I make a lot of money so that he can get his piece of the action. He wants me to sign a contract agreeing to his 20 percent commission. What do you think?"

"I think it stinks, and I also think that the shit will hit the fan real soon. The contract is just bullshit. They don't need paperwork to control you and take your money, it's just in case something happens and they have to work with the law," I said.

"Listen, Bill, I am making over three thousand a week. No one is putting any pressure on me at all, and this is just the beginning. I know we are going to hit it big. I just know it. I see the crowds every night, and they are getting bigger and bigger all the time. I know I'm just about to break into the big time. It's you and I, please believe me, and that is for always. I really don't care about rest of them. Whatever I do is for us. Just you remember that," she said with tears in her eyes.

She actually believed in this fairy tale and that these guys were going to be straight with her. I really could not burst her bubble; she looked so innocent and beautiful.

"Okay, let's give it a shot, but when I say no, it has to be no, capish?" I said and hugged her.

Tony arrived about six thirty and picked us up and took us to a restaurant in Los Angeles called the Reef Club, on the corner of La Cienega and Wilshire. The place was posh, with a great big bandstand, a very large bar on the left as you enter. The place was filled with people dressed to the nines. The men wore dark suits, and their women were in gowns or long dresses. It seemed every table had champagne buckets filled with bottle of the bubbly stuff. We were taken to a large table where six people were sitting. I recognized Armando, as he stood a little bit back from the table and watched everyone in the room. He was here to do his job—protect Luigi. There were four empty places that I gathered were for us.

Luigi rose from the table and extended his hand to Tina and introduced her to everyone.

"Tina, I want you to meet, Sylvano Pressi, Arturo Gambino, Maria Capresse, Horatio Zamby, and Carmine Hernandez. I don't expect you to remember everyone at once, but you will in time." Pointing to me he said, "This is Bill Darby, Tina's manager." I shook hands with everyone and sat down. All the attention was focused on Tina; of course, as she was the hit of the party, and she loved it. They had ordered caviar and champagne and asked us to order whatever we wanted.

Maria spoke to Tina, "You are a beautiful woman and, as I was told, with a voice like an angel. Do you think you could sing a song for us tonight? I'll ask the orchestra to accommodate us. What about it, Tina?" she smiled and gave Tina a look that said she would be better off not refusing!

"I'd be happy to, but I didn't come prepared, so don't judge me too seriously. Do you want to eat first or would you like me to sing?" Tina said.

"Why don't you sing a song or two, and then we can forget singing and eat and drink the night away," Horatio said as he got up and went to the maître d' and whispered something in his ear. "Whenever you are ready my dear," Horatio said.

Tina left the table and spoke to the orchestra leader and then proceeded to the bandstand area. "Ladies and gentlemen, we are honored here tonight to have a very special guest, Miss Tina Wilks. Although Miss Wilks is here to enjoy a night of fun, she has gracefully agreed to sing a song or two from her latest show. Please welcome Tina Wilks."

Most people did not know who the hell Tina Wilks was, but no one wanted to admit it, so they stood and applauded.

"Thank you very much for the warm welcome. I came for dinner tonight and not to entertain, but I have been asked if I would sing for you, and I have said yes. So here goes nothing, as I'll do my best for you, because I love singing even if I'm not prepared," Tina said as she stood there with the microphone in her hand. Once she had stated her disclaimer and felt a lot better about singing, I knew she had the audience hooked so no matter how poorly she may sing, they will go wild over it. The men were insane with desire, and the women wanted to hear this beautiful goddess perform even though they were extremely jealous. She chose "Walking in the Rain" and closed with "Somewhere Over the Rainbow." The crowd gave her a standing ovation and just kept cheering "Bravo, bravo." It seemed it lasted forever. She finally returned to the table, and everyone began to speak at once, congratulating her and giving her the highest of compliments.

Finally Luigi stood up, "A toast to Tina, one of the greatest performances I have ever seen." With that, he raised his glass of champagne and smiled at Tina. I was proud of her, but very nervous as I felt a serious life change coming on.

The party began to break up at eleven thirty and I said, "Tony, will you please drive Tina and I home? We are tired and have a big day ahead of us tomorrow."

"Why so early, Bill? I'm sure Tina would rather spend some time with us at Ray's Cantina. Of course, you are welcome to come along. There will be some big time agents there tonight, and I'd like her to meet them. It's important, Bill, very important for Tina," Luigi said.

"Come on, Bill, let's go to Ray's. It'll be fun," Tina said with a big smile.

Tuesday, April 9, 1957

We slept most of the day, as we didn't get home until six thirty in the morning. Tina was going to be on stage again tonight, so she only had time to take a shower and get ready for Tony.

"I'm staying home tonight, honey, I hope you don't mind?" I said.

"No, not at all if that's what you want to do. I'll try to get home right after the show. Luigi wanted to talk to me about doing a month in Las Vegas. I told him he'd have to speak with you. He didn't like that, but didn't make a scene. He said he would in the next few days. Maybe it would be better if you would be there tonight," she said.

"When did he tell you about Vegas?" I said.

"Last night. He just mentioned it in an offhand way. He said I'd probably make ten K a week. That's pretty big money, don't you think so?" Tina said.

"Maybe you're right, it might be better for me to be there tonight. I'll get dressed," I said.

Tony arrived promptly at seven, and off we went. Tina's first show went off as usual, and Luigi didn't show up. Around ten, he arrived with Armando and another guy I didn't recognize. He came over to my table and sat down.

"How you doing, Bill," Luigi said.

"I'm fine, Luigi, how are you?" I said.

The waiter came over to the table and took my glass away. I didn't pay too much attention, but did notice that he handled my glass from the bottom and stopped near the bar and gave something to the stranger who came in with Luigi. It was my glass and the stranger had wrapped it in a cloth and put in his pocket. My heart started to pound as this was not good. The guy was probably a cop on the take and would run my prints. This was going to be trouble. I didn't think I had much to worry about as the cops never did take my fingerprints or that was what I thought.

"Bill, I wanted to talk to you about Tina," Luigi said with a sly smile. "She is a beautiful woman, and she sings great. People love looking at her and get mesmerized when she gets up on the stage. I want her in Vegas. She can make an easy ten grand a week. What do you say, Bill? Are you in?" he said.

I could hardly hear what Luigi was saying, as I could not take my eyes off the stranger with my glass in his pocket.

"Sure, Luigi, I'm with you. Let's do it," I said. "Excuse me a minute, I have to use the bathroom," I stood up and began walking toward the bar. I didn't know what my game plan was until I was a few feet away. As I passed the corner of the bar, I slipped and fell into the stranger, and in an effort to stop my fall grabbed his suit pocket. The pocket tore open, and the glass fell on the floor shattering in pieces.

"I'm so sorry. I slipped and just grabbed on to the first thing I saw. Please let me know, I'll pay for the repairs. My name is Bill Darby, and I'm the manager of Tina Wilks. If you need my address and telephone number, I'll jot it down for you, really I'm sorry," I insisted.

"Forget it, accidents happen. My girlfriend will sew the pocket up. It'll be as good as new. Great singer you have there, Bill. She is wonderful and easy to look at." He smiled and walked away.

I continued on to the bathroom, but knew the jig was up. There was another glass on the table where I sat with Luigi but I didn't touch that one yet. It was a matter of time until they found something on me and got the results. I knew now that I must find a way to alter my fingerprints very quickly. That was another loophole I didn't count on. I was sloppy once again and nervous. Regardless, it was time to start packing; both my clothes and my gun and resume my running. It seemed I would be running forever.

Wednesday, April 10, 1957

I did not get much sleep as the events of last night rattled me a lot. I had to get things in motion before I get shot, and time is short. It wouldn't be long before they figured out the broken-glass trick.

I left Tina asleep and drove to Santa Monica where I picked up a free apartment rental magazine and found a place for rent on Stewart (Twenty-Eighth Street) just off Pico. I called the number and spoke with a man and found out it was only a room. I asked him if I could come over within the next ten to fifteen minutes, as I was in the neighborhood. He told to come ahead.

I rang the bell, and a man in his late seventies answered the door. "I called about the room for rent, "I said.

"Come right in, let me show you the room, and the rest of the house," he said.

"I'm Tom Ferris," I said as I extended my hand. I'm so glad to be able to find a place so quickly. Your house seems quite nice, do you live alone?" I asked as we walked down a narrow short hallway.

"I'm Victor Johnson. My friends call me Vic. My wife died two years ago, and I've lived here alone since then. It's so lonely and would be nice to have someone share the house with me. It would be nice to have someone to talk to as it does get lonely every now and then." He seemed to be suspended in space while walking along until he opened a door to a small but neat and clean room. There was window looking out over the backyard. The place seemed to be well kept, and the yard was neatly mowed and well groomed.

"What do you think, Tom? I'm only asking fifty dollars a week, and you can use the kitchen. We only have one bathroom, but I'm sure we can share that easily," he said.

"Well, I have to think about it, Vic," I said. "I was looking for something a little more private, but maybe this will do. I don't know anyone from around here, and if I met a woman, I would be intruding upon your privacy. You know what I mean, Vic?" I said.

"Tom, I was young once as well, and I understand. No need to worry about me. As long as you don't cause a ruckus, I'd be happy to spend a little time in my rocking chair with my pipe and leave you alone," he said with a sly smile.

"Seeing that you put it that way, Vic, I'll take it. I can move in right now as I don't have much stuff. Here's two hundred dollars to cover the first four weeks. Is that all right, Vic?" I said.

"It's okay with me, Tom, you seem like a nice young man, and I think it would be okay to take a chance on you," he said. I went to my car and brought in one suitcase and placed it in the room. There was nothing in the suitcase that would reveal my old or new name in case old Vic decided to become nosy.

He gave me a key and said, "You just come and go as you please. You can join me for dinner anytime you are around. It's nice to have you, Tom, real nice."

I left and went back to the apartment, where Tina was still asleep. It was a little after two, so I decided it would be best if I wake her. We had a lot to talk about. I told her what happened at the club last night and that I have taken another place in case something does come down.

"Trust me," I said, "Just trust me. It is for your own good. If something happens, all you have to say is that I moved out a few days ago, and you don't know where I am. Simple as that. If you don't, they will do things to you that will be very unpleasant, and your singing career will be over. You knew the score from the very beginning, and now you must play the game. Please, Tina, please. I love you and don't want to see you hurt," I said as I kissed her.

She was crying and holding me tight. It was nice to know she really cared. We agreed that we would continue as normal, but would be careful. She could not know my new name or address. This she understood.

We made love and laughed with each other until six, and then she had to get ready for her show and for Tony to pick her up. I told her to keep her eyes and ears open just in case there was any news. Tony picked her up on schedule, and I left shortly thereafter to spend the night with Vic.

Thursday, April 11, 1957

I went back to our apartment at about ten that morning. I was very careful to make sure no one was watching the place. I drove around the block for at least a half hour and then parked two blocks away and walked very carefully back. So far it seemed that things were very quiet and life was normal. I went into the apartment and found Tina fast asleep, her clothes all over the place. She must have been tired and drunk when she got in. I let her sleep for a while, and then I made enough noise to wake her. She saw me and smiled, then held her head in her hands.

"I'm sorry, Bill, I've got a really bad headache. What the hell did I do last night? I just can't remember coming home," she said.

"Please be careful, you don't want to get into trouble and say something you shouldn't. I'll bet you took a few pills last night?" I said.

"I don't know what I took. I remember Luigi offering me something to smoke and then he opened some champagne, and that is all I remember," she said.

"Tina, please, be on your toes, you can't afford to get mixed up in this. They will hurt you, badly," I said.

"I know, Bill, let's quit and get out of here. Fuck them with the big money. I'd rather be with you. Please, Bill, let's just blow out of here, now," she said quite hysterically.

"No, I think that's a bad idea. I think it would be better if you follow your dream. You are a great singer and a great actress, so let's do it my way. I don't want to be the one who stood in your way to stardom. Our relationship will be shit in no time if we let this happen, so let's not think that way at all. Please, I love you and care about you and want to see your career take you to the stars just like you always wanted. Okay, Tina, listen closely, please," I said. "I'm out of here and will disappear. You tell Luigi that you had a big argument with your manager and didn't know if he would continue being your manager. Yesterday when you got home, you caught me with another woman. You tell him that you threw him out as that was all he deserved and hope you finally got rid of that bastard. Then go through the usual stuff of what a bastard I was to act like that and so on. You can explain that you and your manager did not have a romantic relationship but it was agreed that neither of us would ever bring anyone home. He violated that rule and was standing in your way to a future in show business. I will disappear and get in touch with you in a few days. If you should move out of here, and it is most likely you will, we will need a common place to get in touch. Leave me a note to Bill Darby c/o the General Post Office of Los Angeles. I will go get it and then get back to you. Any number you give me must be one that only you can answer, we can't afford anyone else ever picking it up. Can you do that?" I asked.

"Of course, I can do that, but what good will it do for us if we can't get together?" she asked.

"I just feel we have to stay close. I don't want to think about anything bad, but if things get very hairy for you, you will need my help. So stay in touch, and we will be able to get things straight eventually. Just be careful. Above all, don't drink too much and be very careful of drugs. It will be your undoing if you should get too smashed and say something you shouldn't. If you really love me, then you will pull this off. Eventually you will be a big enough star that they would have to leave you alone. Or maybe, you will meet someone new and forget about me, either way, we must stick together for now," she agreed, and I left before Tony got there, so her story would prove to be true.

Friday, April 12, 1957

It was one in the afternoon when I visited Tina once again. I made sure no one was watching the apartment as I walked around the block twice and then went into the building when I was certain there wasn't any danger. Tina had nothing new to report as things couldn't change much in one night. That was what we thought, but caution was the most important step we had to always take. It was bothering me a lot that things were so quiet perhaps my paranoia was to blame. I told Tina that I'd rather be wrong about my feelings then be dead, because I didn't want to take my intuition seriously. She said she would be very observant and report back to me if there was any news at all. I gave her a phone number of a telephone booth located at the corner of Pico & Stewart in Santa Monica. I would be at the phone booth every day at six in the evening and also at nine in the morning. If there is something urgent, she can get me at those times.

If I didn't answer the phone, she should wait a few minutes and call back, and if that failed she should try the next prearranged call time. We were doing our best to make sense of the situation and to stay in touch. I knew I could not keep on coming by during the day to see her forever. I left her at about five and went back to my room at Victor's place and decided to spend the night with Victor and get to know him a little better.

Saturday, April 13, 1957

I spent my time at my new digs and walked the neighborhood for a few hours to get acquainted with the area. I watched TV with Vic and got to know the guy real well. He really was a very nice guy, who was very lonely. He missed his wife, who passed away two years ago and welcomed my company. It was nice to just relax and enjoy the peace of the moment. I didn't try to reach Tina or go over to the apartment I thought it was too dangerous especially on a Saturday. I did stop in at the telephone booth at six as per our arrangement to see if perhaps she would be calling me. There was no call this evening, as I waited fifteen minutes and then went back home to relax once again with Victor. He had made a great dinner of roast chicken that was really very delicious.

Sunday, April 14, 1957

I went to the telephone booth at nine in case Tina wanted to call. I waited a few minutes, when the phone rang, and it was Tina. I was thrilled to finally receive a call from her and that our system was working.

"Hi, Bill, how are you?" Tina said.

"I am fine, a little lonely. I missed you a lot," I said.

"How about coming over to see me? I would love to see you today and spend a little time together. I don't have to work until eight tonight, and Tony won't pick me up until seven so we have a little time to be with each other," she said.

"Okay, sweetheart, I'll be over in about an hour. Go back to sleep, and I'll see you very soon. Love you," I said as I hung up and returned home.

An hour later, I was at Tina's place and crawled into her bed. She was fast asleep until I started to rub my hands all over her beautiful body. We made love for a couple of hours and then sat around and talked. She told me that she did hear Luigi talking with someone about me and what an asshole I was. She said that Luigi was very pleased that I got rid of you and hoped that was the last he would hear about this guy.

"I didn't hear anything else, but will keep my eyes and ears open at all times. I really miss you, Bill, I miss you a lot," she said.

I left at four thirty and went back to Victor's house. I picked up some Chinese food for both of us. Luckily, I called Victor in advance to warn him that he should not cook as I will bring home some food. We ate and watched the *Ed Sullivan Show* on the TV, and then I went to bed.

Monday, April 15, 1957

I met with Tina at around noon. I had spoken with her on the phone, and she said she had some very important news for me. Again I used extreme caution to make sure I was not under any surveillance and asked Tina to make sure no one was watching the apartment. We hugged and kissed like long lost lovers.

"I missed you, my darling," I said.

"So have I, very much," she said. "Well, I told Luigi that you are gone and I don't know where the hell you went," she said. "He seemed happy about it and asked me why, if we had a fight, and I said no. I told him that I could not understand why you had to screw around with another woman in our apartment, especially when we had an agreement that neither of us would ever do that. We fought, and you left. I know you are not coming back because you took your clothes. I acted upset and cried a little so that he wouldn't feel I was taking this too lightly," she said.

"Good, now we have to just wait and see what happens, but, please, be careful. We can't continue to meet like this because they will catch us one day, and then we both are toast. I need your contact information as soon as possible," I said.

"I know, Bill, but Luigi is talking about moving to Las Vegas within the next week. I'll have to get a spot in Vegas for you to contact me. Oh I love you, Bill, I love you very much," she said.

I told her to continue using the phone booth number until she is settled in Las Vegas and we can set-up a proper contact system.

Tuesday, April 16, 1957

I called Tina at two in the afternoon. She sounded very nervous. "Hello, who is this?" she said.

I immediately knew there was something wrong and hung up at once. I called back an hour later, and this time she said, "I'm so sorry I could not speak. Armando was here with Tony, and they were looking around the apartment for any sign of you. Luigi told me last night that your name isn't Bill Darby, you are wanted by the police, and your real name is Harry Miller. You are a murderer, and they are looking everywhere for you. I'm so lucky that you left and did not kill me. I think they believe I knew nothing about you. I had to act scared and told Luigi that I must get out of the apartment in case you should return.

He sent over his guys today to check it out, and they will move everything out tomorrow. I won't be coming back here tonight so this is our last connection until I give you a contact number. Be careful. They are dangerous, I love you," she said and hung up.

I made it just in time and now to organize a plan that will be effective. Even though I used a disguise and another name, they still made me, I wonder how?

Wednesday, April 17, 1957

I did not think that anyone would find me so soon. Living at Vic's place should keep me pretty well out of sight. It seemed that destiny had me pegged for failure. Each time I made a move, I was eventually found out or something happened to screw up my plan. I just didn't have any luck, or was it that I was not making luck work for me? I would have to be more diligent and very careful from now on.

It was a little after two when I finally left the house and drove along Pico. I was going downtown along the city streets rather than the freeway when I stopped at a light on Pico and Westwood. Before I knew it, this bozo jumped into the car on the passenger's side and yelled, "Just keep driving, Harry, I'll tell you where to turn, one fucking wrong move, and I'll plug you right here. I get the same reward if you're dead, asshole, so don't try anything." I looked over at him and as he shouted, "Keep your fucking eyes on the road, asshole."

My heart beat so fast that I could hardly breathe. My hands started to sweat and my mind was racing a million miles an hour, how can I get rid of this guy? How did this guy know my name? How did he find me? These thoughts ran through my mind. "Be calm," I told myself, "think clearly and let's get out of this situation first. We'll find out how and what later, now is the important time." As we drove along at a safe and comfortable speed, we approached the intersection of Pico and Robertson. The light had just turned yellow when I gunned the accelerator and made a sharp left turn onto Robertson. We just missed being hit, but it was enough of a distraction to throw this guy off balance for a split second. I lunged forward and grabbed his gun hand with my right hand and tried to keep the car straight with my left. I jammed the brakes and let go of the wheel, and with all my might, I pushed as hard as I could against his shoulder and grabbed the door handle with my left hand. As it opened, he started to fall out as the car careened to the right and hit a lamp post head-on. He went flying into the window of a furniture store, while I was pinned by the steering wheel on my left leg. My head hit the top of the dash and I tasted warm blood in my mouth. I pulled as hard as I could to get my left leg out from under, but it wouldn't budge. By this time, there was a large crowd of people around the car, shouting and saying things.

"Are you all right?"

"The police are on the way"

"Don't move, we'll get help!"

The next thing I remember was waking up in a hospital with bandages on my head and aches and pains everywhere.

"Where am I? What happened? Am I alive?" I tried to move but my head felt like a thousand pound weight was on it. It hurt, and I couldn't move.

"Take it easy, you're in UCLA hospital. My name is Joanne, and I'm one of the nurses here. You were in a very serious car accident and are very lucky to be alive. Just relax, the doctor will be here to see you shortly and explain what things need mending. Just rest. That is all you can do," she said as she left the room. I don't know how long I waited, when I looked up, there was a guy in white jacket with a stethoscope hanging from his neck.

"Well, I see you are awake, Bill," he said. "That was a nasty accident you had. You need rest, and you'll be fine. You banged your head pretty severely, and it looks like you have broken your nose and suffered a concussion. Your left leg is badly lacerated, but no broken bones. You are lucky to be alive. I wish I could say the same for the other guy. He was thrown from the car and died instantly when he hit the store window. The police will be along later, as they need a statement from you, until then rest. I'll check on you again tomorrow."

Thursday, April 18, 1957

I must have slept through the night, as it was six thirty in the morning and a nurse was waking me to give me a pill. "Good morning, how are you feeling? You look a lot better today," she said.

"What day is it?" I asked.

"Thursday, and it's going to be a beautiful day. Are you hungry?" she asked.

"My head still hurts, but my stomach seems empty. Sure thing, what's for breakfast?" I asked.

"The usual, it'll be along in a few minutes. In the meantime, do you feel up to getting out of bed?" she asked as she handed me my robe.

I managed to get out of bed and walk, with a limp, over to the bathroom. I felt okay, my leg hurt, but not that bad. All I could think about was getting out of here. What if the Mob knew I was here? If he knew who I was and where I was, what makes you think they don't

know? What if the cops want to hold me and take my prints? There
were so many things going through my mind at once, I felt dizzy. I
finally sat down at the edge of the bed and decided to ride it out for
at least another day, what choice did I have. I was in no condition to
run, the war would be over very fast. I'll take my chances with the
cops, maybe they want to ask some routine questions and that will be
that? I thought if they felt I was a criminal or I was a dangerous guy
or had a suspicion I was involved in something, I would have been
strapped to the bed, and a cop would have been stationed at the door
of my hospital room. Since none of these things happened I felt the
best place for me right now is to stay put. I was here under Bill Darby,
with a proper license and a good address. So I best see it through to
avoid any suspicion.

Around two in the afternoon, I received a visitor.

"I'm Lieutenant Koransky, LAPD," he said as he flashed his badge
and handed me his card. "I would like to ask a few questions about the
accident. Just what the hell happened? Did you lose control of car? As
you know your passenger was killed instantly when his head struck the
plate glass of the furniture store." He stated with authority but not in a
threatening manner.

"First of all, let me set the record straight. I didn't know that guy at
all. When I was stopped at a light on Pico and Westwood, he opened
the passenger door and jumped in. I was shocked, but before I could say
anything, he pointed a gun at me and told me drive properly and not
to try to get help. I shit in my pants. I've never seen a gun and to have
one pointed at me by a crazed maniac made me crazy. All I could think
of was how to get this guy out of the car, I knew he was going to hurt
me bad if not kill me. He said he was taking the car and wants all my
money, and as long as I do as he says, he'll let me go. Of course, I didn't
believe he would let me go, but I had very little choice in the matter. I
waited until a chance came and hit the gas at the corner and turned left
just as the light changed. He fell off balance and was just getting back
to normal when the car hit the pole. I don't remember another thing.
That's it!" I said in a slow and very controlled manner.

"Well, Bill, let me tell you how lucky you are. This guy, whose real
name is Ronald Switzer, was wanted by us and the feds. He is wanted for
murder in Alabama and attempted murder here in California. He has a
record as long as your arm. He was a very bad guy. He would have killed

you in a flash. You are lucky, young man, real lucky," he said. "I'll need you to come down to the station, when you are feeling better, and sign a statement. It won't take very long, but has to be done for the records. You don't have to worry about anything; we are not going to charge you with anything. The DA is grateful that you saved the taxpayers a lot of money by helping us rid society of this guy. He was mean and rotten to the core. If anything, you are a hero, but your car is totaled. By the way, there was a reward of ten thousand dollars for his capture. I really don't know if you are eligible, but I would think, you sure should get it. I'll check into it for you and let you know when you call me. It will help you get a new car and have some change left over. I have your address, Bill. You still are there, aren't you?" he asked.

"Sure thing, still in Sherman Oaks. I will report this to my insurance company and hope they will help me out as well?" I said.

"Get well, nice to meet you, and I'm glad you are okay." With that said, he turned around and walked out of the room.

"Wow! A reward, isn't that the irony of the century? I need some sleep now!"

Friday, April 19, 1957

I couldn't get the reward part out of my head. What trouble could I get into by claiming it? I don't think any, so why not get it? I'll need a new car anyways as this one was a toast. I just hoped that no one had taken my picture for a story in the papers that would be the last straw. I wondered if they found my gun in the car. Of course, if they did, I would only claim it was the other guy's gun. There was no way they could trace this gun, so I thought I was in the clear. Nothing I could do about it now!

Saturday, April 20, 1957

The doctor just left and said I could go home on Sunday. They wanted to observe me for another day to make sure my head injury did not cause me any problems. All my other aches and pains would heal day by day. I was told I had to take things easy, and in a couple of weeks, I should be almost as good as new.

Sunday, April 21, 1957

I left the hospital at about ten thirty and went to my new address in Santa Monica. I had the cab driver leave me a few blocks away from my location just in case. When I arrived at the house, Vic was sitting on the front porch, "Hi, Vic, I'm sorry I haven't been home, I had a car accident," I said.

"Are you all right, Tom?" he said with concern.

"I'm fine now, a little banged up, but I'll be okay," I said as I showed him my leg and he saw the bruise on the top of my head. "I think I'll just relax today and take care of things tomorrow," I said as I started walking down the hall to my room.

"Listen, Tom, do you need anything? I'll get it for you, how about some food, I can rustle something up right now if you want!" he said.

"Thanks a lot, Vic, but right now all I want is to sleep a little more. How about you and I having dinner together tonight? Maybe some Chinese or something!" I said.

"That sounds great, Tom, great," he said with a big smile. "It's so nice to have you back home again."

Monday, April 22, 1957

I got up real early and called the garage that had my car. I also called the insurance company to report the accident and give them the police report and number. They said they would send an appraiser to the garage and settle it there. I gave them Vic's telephone number for them to call me back. I went to the garage that was located on Olympic Boulevard. near Centinela. My car was a total loss; it's a miracle I survived. I told the guy that I had to get my personal things out of the car. I searched the car for the gun and found it exactly where I put it, under the driver's seat. It must have jammed in there when the seat moved with the impact. It was hard to get it out, but, I finally did. I took my papers that were in the glove compartment and left.

I returned home to spend the rest of the day resting and getting myself together for the days to come.

Tuesday, April 23, 1957

I called Lieutenant Koransky to set up an appointment.

"Guess what, kid," he said, "You are entitled to the reward. I need you to fill out a form when you come in, and in a few weeks you will receive ten grand, not bad!" he said.

"Gee that's great. What time do you want me to come by, I'm free most of the day," I said.

"About three, is that okay with you?" he said.

"Great, I'll see you then," I said and hung up. I was concerned about the meeting with the cop, what did they know that I didn't? Did they want my picture? I was really very nervous about it all, but had very little choice now. If I didn't show up, the cop will get suspicious and who knows what investigation it would trigger. My decision was made, I had to continue and play it through, let the chips fall where they may.

I arrived at the station a little before three and asked for Lieutenant Koransky and was directed to a set of double doors.

"Just follow the hallway to the very end and turn right, that's his office. He's waiting for you now, and by the way, congratulation., for taking out that scumbag Switzer, what a creep," he said with a big, friendly smile.

I went down the hall and turned right into Koransky's office.

"Nice to see you, Bill, take seat and relax. I have your statement right here, why don't you read it and then sign it on the bottom where the x is," he said with a big smile on his face.

"Sure thing Lieutenant, let's see what you got here!" I said as I sat down and started to read this three page report. All it said in the report that I was accosted by Switzer and forced to drive at gun point. The accident was a direct cause of Switzer's threats and insistence that Bill Darby drive to a location unknown at this point. The report stated it almost word for word as I told him in the hospital. I signed it and returned it to him and got up ready to go when he said, "Not so fast, Bill, it's not everyday when someone does something heroic as you did. The City of Los Angeles and the LAPD want you to know that we do appreciate your deeds and will award you the Medal of Bravery. These awards take place in September as we honor those who have done more than asked of them without regard to their safety. Congratulations are in order, Bill, thanks on behalf of us all. By the way, here are the forms for you to complete for the reward. You can complete them at home and drop them off here so that I can attach my report and recommendation to it.

Within four to six weeks you will receive the reward. Isn't that great?" He motioned to a uniformed officer to call someone to come into his office. Before I knew it, I was being introduced to the district attorney, the chief of police, and at least six or seven other policemen. My head was spinning, and my cheeks hurt from smiling so much.

"Let's get a few photos. One with the chief and district attorney. Just stand in the middle of the two, Bill, relax and smile. Okay, let's get one with you shaking hands with the chief. And now one with you shaking hands with the DA. Great shots, these will look good in the paper. You're going to be a celebrity, Bill. I hope you can handle it?" They all laughed and slapped me on the back.

"Hey, guys, please don't put the photos in the paper, until I tell my girlfriend and my face is healed a little better. Can't we take some more photos when the black eyes are gone?" I said very humbly.

"You're right, Bill, let's wait a few weeks and have another photo session, and we can show both the "before and after" photos." the DA said.

"I like that idea. It looks much better, and we can call a press conference as well. Why not award the medal when we have the press conference. We can get the Mayor to set a date and do some great PR for Los Angeles I love it. Let's get the show on the road," the chief said, beaming as if he had just invented public relations.

At least I put off the pictures for at least a month, but I would have to pay the price sooner or later. I'm sure they were going to want to hand me the reward at that ceremony. I'd better have formulated a real good plan before then, or I would be screwed by both the sides. I went home very depressed, but safe for a little while. I still was able to control the situation, at least until now!

Wednesday, April 24, 1957

I woke up and spent the rest of the day just vegetating at home. Vic was great to me. He waited on me all day long. Anything I wanted, he got for me. He was great and started to come alive. All he ever wanted was to be needed. I loved this old guy; he was true in his feelings, and his actions proved it. He was a kind man, who cared about me. It's so funny how one person's problems can be another's life saving thing. Vic was a new man, and so was I.

Thursday. April 25, 1957

I didn't realize just how banged up I was until I sat down and just rested. I spent the day doing nothing. Vic insisted I just rest the entire day, and once again, he waited on me hand and foot. I lived like a king for another day, thanks to Victor.

Friday, April 25, 1957

More rest. And being taken care of by Vic. He was in heaven being my nurse, doctor, and friend. He set up the TV, so that I could watch and still lie down. He loved the "I Love Lucy Show" and made sure not to miss a single episode. He was a very nice and kind man in every way possible.

Saturday and Sunday, April 26 and 27, 1957

Rest and more rest. I was getting stronger and stronger each day, especially with Vic's help and kind treatment. He kept saying to me, "There is no rush. Soon you'll be back to normal again." We walked along the street and watched a local baseball game just down from the house. It was a warm and sunny day, and Victor made the time go by faster.

On Sunday morning, I took Victor out to Norm's Diner on Lincoln Boulevard near Olympic for breakfast. He was so thrilled to be out and having someone to talk to. He ate and ate and then agreed to take a nice drive along the Pacific Coast Highway and just take in the sights and enjoy the beauty that surrounded us. We had a great time and didn't get home until a little after three. It was a great day, once again thanks to Victor.

Monday, April 28, 1957

I felt like a new man. My leg still hurt, but nowhere near what it did. In real life, you don't heal in a day. Only in the movies or detective novels. I inquired about getting a set of weights and set up a daily workout. I asked Vic if he knew where I could get a set of weights and if it would be okay if I put them in the backyard. I got the green light from Vic, who volunteered to be my personal trainer. We planned to go weight shopping the next day together. For Vic, it was very exciting that he felt alive again and could hardly wait for tomorrow to come! I felt good that I was doing something real good for a great guy. Victor was lost when I first moved in, and now he was a productive and very happy man. It was nice to see, and I believe had added years to his life.

Tuesday, April 29, 1957

Vic took me on Olympic Boulevard to a place called Weider. He said they make all sorts of weights and he knows someone who works there. He thought we could get a discount and get a hell of a deal. We sure did, as we carried these heavy weights into the house and placed them on the back porch. "I think the porch will cave in, Vic," I said as we placed the last of the weights on the floor.

"Don't you worry about that, Tom. I built this porch, and it can handle this weight easily. Let's get it unpacked and see how many we can set up today so that you can start your routine tomorrow," he said as he moved off to open a box containing some equipment. We spent a grand, and I think we got enough to open a gymnasium. It was worth every penny just to watch Vic set the weights up. He was thrilled at being needed and took his job very seriously. It was nice to see as we worked well into the night to get the weights set up. I was now ready to begin getting my body into the best shape ever, and I had Victor to thank for this.

Wednesday, April 30, 1957

I exercised for one hour as Vic would not let me leave the house unless I went through the routine. He carefully wrote out for me first. He said that I could not start the day without first doing my routine.

One day on one set of muscles, and the next day on another set, and then I must repeat the routine again the following day. He carefully drew a chart that covered a full week and advised me the next chart would be more difficult as I get better at it. After I showered, I took a bus to the central post office to see if there was any word from Tina. I still didn't have a new car. I wanted to wait until I receive a check from the insurance company. I did miss her, although in the last few days, I was too preoccupied to think about her. There was indeed a message with a phone number. I was to call her at four in the afternoon. She made sure I understood that this was a safe phone, and I should be on time.

At exactly four o'clock, I was at the telephone booth and called Tina. After two rings, she answered. "Hi, how are you? I've missed you so much," she said.

"I'm fine, and I miss you a lot. Is everything going okay with you? I asked.

"I'm singing, and I'm making lots of money. Luigi has big plans for me, so I'm going along. But I miss you a lot, really I do. I have been listening if there is any talk about you or anyone who may look like you, but so far, it has been quiet. I miss you so much," she said.

"It isn't easy for me either, but we have to do it this way until things settle down," I said. "I'll call you next Wednesday at this time and, of course, at this number. If something changes, please send me the letter again, and I will follow it. Love you very much, be good and break a leg," I said and hung up before she could start crying or carrying on about things.

I went home and spent the night with Vic. I wanted to exercise again, but Vic cautioned me against it.

He said, "You have to allow the muscles to heal for at least twenty-four hours before using them again under stress. Relax, and we'll do more weights tomorrow with different muscles."

Thursday, May 1, 1957

I went car shopping right after I finished exercising. Yesterday, I was content in using the buses and didn't feel I needed a car and today I was thinking differently. I don't think I could really answer to anyone why the change of heart, but that was how my mind seemed to work. I always had excuse number one. I need wheels and fast, just in case I have to get out of here on the double. I finally found a good used 1956 Oldsmobile 98 convertible with only twenty-two thousand miles out. It was red with white leather seats and a great radio with an electric antenna. Heads turned when I drove down to the beach with the top down; the girls just migrated to the car and, of course, the driver. I put the car under Tom Ferris and used Vic's address. As far as I was concerned, no one would know anything about me except that I am another young guy who likes to party and must have money. The car was inspected as indicated by the sticker on the windshield and was dated December. So I didn't have to renew until the end of the year.

I drove my new car down the street and pulled into Vic's driveway. He ran off the porch when he saw it was me and could not help smiling from ear to ear. "Wow! What a beauty Tom, how much did it set you back?" Vic said.

"A pretty penny, Vic, but it's worth every cent, isn't it a great-looking car?" I said.

"I wish I was twenty years younger, Tom, I would have loved a car like this," Vic said.

"Anytime you want to drive this baby, please feel free to do so. I really mean it Vic I would love you to enjoy it," I said.

Friday, May 2, 1957

I spent the day with Vic polishing the car. Vic and I worked very hard giving the car a new coat of wax. The car shined as if it was just out of the showroom, and Vic and I were very proud of our handy work. We decided to take an afternoon drive along the Pacific Coast Highway and check out the great beaches. We drove north and finally reached Pepperdine University and turned around and drove back toward Santa Monica. We parked, and we walked on the Santa Monica Pier for a little while and then went home to relax. We had run out of daylight, as we fully used the day having a great time. I can't believe how happy Vic looked this day. He was so thrilled at this outing. It made my heart feel good. We decided to pick up some Chinese food and take it home, where Vic and I could eat and talk about how much fun we had today. Vic and I were getting to be very good friends. He was really a very nice person, and I was so glad I met him. In my topsy turvy world, I needed someone down to earth like Vic; he was an honest and true friend.

Saturday, May 3, 1957

I did my weight program that Vic had laid out for me and then took Vic out for the day. We went to Tijuana to experience the Mexican way of life. We had a great time and returned home well after midnight. Vic had a rip roaring time, and so did I.

Sunday, May 4, 1957

I just rested to get my strength back. I was starting to feel like my old self once again. I called Rachel in New York and got the update as to what is going on. So far it all seemed very quiet, too quiet for my liking. She was still on her "we-go-our-separate-ways" kick. I called Moe Arnold at home and asked him to arrange a certified bank check payable to Tom Ferris for ten grand. I instructed him to mail the check to Tom Ferris c/o Los Angeles General Post office and I will pick it up there. Moe was a great friend and was always there for me, always! He never questioned my motives or compromised my location. He never asked why I needed this or that he just helped and gave advice from the heart. He was just a great friend, who was willing to put his life on the line for me. I felt much better after these calls, because no news was good for me. I believed that perhaps the pressure has eased a little and maybe the Mob has finally seen the light that I am not a stoolie and I really don't want to be involved in any of their actions. Of course, I didn't think it was that simple, but I needed a little reinforcement of will to continue, and this little respite was it. I understood real well, when I slowed down that I was grasping at straws but everyone needs a straw now and then even if it is short lived.

I called Vic and asked him if he wanted to join me for a drive on PCH as it was a glorious day. He said he would, so I passed by the house and off we went with the top down and fun and sun in our hearts. Vic seemed so happy, and so was I as well! We drove along the PCH and before we knew it, we were almost at Santa Barbara.

"Hey, Vic did we forget the time of day. We certainly took a long drive, today, didn't we?" I said.

"Tom, I must tell you I have never been so content and happy since Martha died. Thanks for the eye opening look at life. You are a good friend," he said with a tear in his eye.

We turned around and started back toward our place, it would be at least one hour before we would get near the house, but the day was beautiful, and we were both very happy.

We drove along the PCH until we reached Malibu and decided it would nice to finish the day off by having a drink and something to eat. It was nearly six, and the sun still shone as it started to recede and reflect off the Pacific. It was a magnificent sight that made you feel good and give thanks for being alive. We stopped at the Reef Restaurant that was just before Sunset and PCH and had a great seafood dinner. Vic and I had a couple of drinks and finally left and drove home.

This was a great day for us both even though I still had concerns in the back of my mind of the dangers that awaited me. It was nice to have some time off from those worries, and Vic was the one who helped me escape for a day. I loved the guy.

Monday, May 5, 1957

I completed my exercise program for the day and decided to go to the gun range and practice my shooting. I didn't want to get rusty or complacent. No matter how great a day was, I could never forget that these guys were still looking for me and would not quit. I felt I always must be on my guard and be prepared for any contingency, even though yesterday I let my guard down for a day and loved it. I thought about it a lot this day because of the activities I was doing. Shooting your guns at a range reminds you that you are fighting a battle every day. This was a far cry from the peace and tranquility of yesterday.

I arrived home at five thirty and found Vic in the kitchen, cooking up a storm. He had prepared a meal fit for a king, and I guessed I was the king.

"You are just in time, Tom," Vic said. "I decided to cook a special dinner for us to celebrate our friendship and show you my feelings. I am so grateful you came along and found my little room for rent. You do know, Tom, this whole house is yours and always will be. Tonight we are eating a special dish that I made from scratch. A rack of lamb covered with special herbs and spices that will make your mouth water. I also went out and found a very special Chateau Lafitte 1950 for us to drink with our meal tonight. Please relax and let me serve you the meal of a lifetime," he said.

I could only tell you this about the meal—it was the best I have ever tasted, and the wine was unbelievable. Vic was in heaven as he watched me enjoy the meal. Vic wasn't a big drinker any longer, but after a couple of glasses of this superb wine, Vic became very talkative and told me his life story.

He was a policeman all his life. That was all he ever wanted be and straight from high school, he applied to the Detroit Police Department. He went to the police academy and became a full time cop way back 1908 and stayed in Detroit until 1939. He met his wife, Martha, in Detroit and married there. They had two kids, both girls, who were now married and had children of their own. One of his daughters lived in upstate New York, in a small town called Poughkeepsie. She had three children, who were all grown and married as well and were scattered across the country. His other daughter died last year from breast cancer and left two children who have moved somewhere in the U.S. The sad part was relationship between him and his daughters was not very good. They had not called or visited him in at least five years and didn't even send condolences when Martha died. Martha and Vic moved to Los Angeles in 1939, where he became a LAPD police officer. He stayed with the force until 1951 when he retired to this house with Martha. In 1955, for some reason, Martha was sitting in her favorite chair and had a massive heart attack and died within five minutes. He explained how devastated he was and how lonely the house and life itself became.

When one is sick you have time to prepare for death but when death comes at you in an instant no one is prepared. Since that time he existed and actually wished he would die as life all alone was not a very enjoyable trip. He longed for Martha as he said and only learned in the last little while when I came along how wonderful life could be. He now feels guilty because he doesn't think about Martha as he did before.

Martha was a wonderful time in his life, and now he had found a new path filled with love and caring. It was a great feeling to know that I was instrumental in helping someone turn around their life. How I wished I could turn my own life around as well.

After helping Vic do the dishes and just relaxing a little bit more, we turned in for the night. This was a great day, and I found another dear friend in Vic.

Tuesday, May 6, 1957

I woke early and did my weight program as per Vic's chart and then decided to take a drive to the Valley and take in some more shooting. I took Sepulveda to get to the Valley when I noticed a big, black Cadillac in my rear view mirror. It seemed to stay a few car lengths behind, but kept on following my movements. I decided to slow down and pull over just past Sunset and make as if I was reading something. I parked there for a few moments while the Cadillac continued on. I saw three guys in the car—two up front and one in the back and although I could not make out their faces. They appeared to be big. I pulled back into traffic and continued north on Sepulveda, looking everywhere for the black car. I didn't see it, perhaps I was wrong? A strong feeling came over me that told me to be careful. "Watch out," I told myself. All of a sudden, I saw in the rear view mirror the same black Cadillac following me once again. My heart began to race and sweat started to form on my forehead. "Relax, be calm," I told myself. I started to formulate a plan that would work to get rid of these guys. I didn't relish the thought of facing three. One against three is not very good odds, so I needed a plan that would get rid of them. I turned on to Ventura Boulevard. and decided to take one of the side streets to see if I can lose them. The worst part was the fact they now had my license number and description of the car. How did they get that so fast? I was at a loss to figure out how they knew? I made a swift right turn to Reseda and gunned the car so that I'd be way ahead of them. They came right after me as fast as they could, no longer were they concerned about being spotted. They wanted to hurt me that was my only thought at this time. I turned sharply left on to Sherman Way and continued to Corbin and turned right and once again hit the accelerator. I was up to eighty on a city street and they were still with me. All of a sudden, I heard the pop of a gun and another and another. I was weaving, making it harder for the shooter to get a clear shot. In the meantime I was reaching under my seat to get my gun and trying to keep the car on the road. Finally, I felt the cold steel of the gun and pulled it up to me. I felt a little better to know I can fight back. I know I can't really get a good shot while I am moving at this speed.

I can see the Cadillac pulling out and trying to get even with me, they are pulling up to my side of the car. I can see through my side mirror that two guns being aimed at my car, but not firing, they must be waiting until they get even with me to release their firepower. I jammed the brakes and watched as I came to full stop and they went by. They realized what I had done and jammed their brakes as well, but they were at least twenty five feet ahead of me. I leaned out of the window and aimed my gun directly at the back of the head of the driver and fired two shots.

The first shot shattered the rear window and ricocheted into the back of the seat. The second shot hit him squarely in the head. His head fell down on the steering wheel, and the car began to careen to the right. It finally hit the curb and bounced on its side and kept on sliding until it hit a brown electricity pole. I pulled over and ran toward the overturned car with my gun in my hand, ready for action. I found both shooters lying on their sides bleeding from their heads. I looked in and aimed the gun at the guy in the front seat and shot him through the head, and then I shot the other right through the neck. I turned back toward my car and began to run as fast as I could. I just wanted to get out of there before anyone would come by. I saw a couple of cars coming my way, but was able to jump into my car and continue along Corbin, until I reached a street that was busy enough for me to get into traffic. I turned right and went a couple of blocks and found myself back on Sherman Way. I took off toward Santa Monica and away from this carnage. I was a nervous wreck, but still alive and wondered when this would ever end! I was not a killer and did not have the stomach for this, but I had to defend myself no matter how many times I was forced to kill someone it didn't get easier. How I prayed this would end!

I arrived back at the house at about noon and went directly to my room. Vic came into my room and said, "What is wrong, Tom?"

"I just ran into a little problem today, and it has upset me. I'll be fine in a little while. All I need is a little rest," I said.

"Tom, you just relax and let me know if there is anything I can do. I'll be right here and will make sure you are not disturbed," he said.

I woke up from a deep sleep at around five and found Vic sitting in his favorite chair, watching TV. I had made up my mind that I must, in all fairness, confide the details of my life with Vic. He was a sincere friend and could be helpful because of his experience as a cop. I also felt that anything I would tell him would remain between us no matter what. After today's experience, I could not leave Vic in the dark and put him in any danger. I told Vic that I wanted to talk to him, so could we just order some Chinese and relax while I bring him up to date.

I spent the next two hours telling Vic everything from the beginning. I felt so much better when I had finished. It seemed like I was lighter now that I unloaded some of my problems. It also made me feel that Vic would have a magic formula that would make it all go away. Of course, I knew that was wishful thinking, but nonetheless, it made me feel better.

"Well, Tom, all I can say is 'what a story' you have just trusted me with. Thank you for your confidence. I don't know what to tell you about these people except that they are not very nice folks to go up against. In all the years I was cop, we never really wanted anything to do with the Mob. They are ruthless, as you can easily see by what has happened to you, and they have power. I commend you for your ability to defend yourself, but you realize this is a losing battle. You have to change your way of life as well as your appearance. They aren't finding you because you are leaving clues. They are locating you by following your pattern and then looking for events that take place within the geographical area that they think you are in. For example, Tom, you always run to a car dealer and buy a new car. By new, I don't mean a brand new car, just a car. You always try to buy the best, so there is one clue. The real big clue is the way you buy. You walk into a dealer and you drive out with a new car and you always pay cash and you are always anxious to get the deal done fast. They canvass all the used car dealers in an area they think you are in and find out who bought a car in the last little while and then they describe the way you buy cars. Because they are who they are, they easily get the name and address you gave the dealer and then they check that out. If the address is a phony, they find that out very quickly. If it is a real residence or office, they check it out. Just remember, Tom, they have the resources to do this and the time as well. When you bought the Oldsmobile, what address did you use?" Vic asked.

"I used this address because I never thought it would be a problem. I am truly sorry, Vic, really I have put you at risk," I said.

"I wouldn't worry about that, Tom, I am your best friend and I'd be happy to stand tall and fight side by side with you. If any of these bastards show up here, I'll blast them to kingdom come. You can count on me always. No one will know anything about your past from me, this you can be sure of," he said.

"Thanks, Vic, I really appreciate this and will move out because I may have caused you more trouble than I should have," I said.

"No way, Tom, no way at all. You stay put, and we'll fight this together as one team. I would not be very happy if you left, please believe that. Now let's not discuss this any longer," he said.

Wednesday, May 7, 1957

I woke up early and went into the backyard and worked extra hard at my exercise program. I was pumped as I thought of the events that have taken place in the last few days. I had taken every precaution to be someone else, yet these bastards kept on locating me no matter what disguise, address, or car I used. I thought I had discovered the problem. Vic was absolutely right about my habits and the small clues I kept leaving behind.

I certainly underestimated the Mob thinking they were so stupid. I believed I was much smarter than them, and in doing so, I left myself wide open to the brains in their organization. I would have to start thinking smarter and believing that they do have some brain power as well as some very sophisticated assistance from some very smart people. They buy the resources we had and used them to find out everything about a person. Something was wrong, and I thought I have now discovered what it was. Tina had no idea of where I am and what new name I am using, so she couldn't be one to give anything away. The Mob guys were clueless, or were they? No one knew who I was and where I was, except for Vic. I knew that their process of elimination seemed very logical and seemed to fall into place every time I get trouble. I trusted Vic with my life and knew he would not betray me. Not after I have seen how happy he was and how we have bonded.

I really was at a loss, but had decided that I would move out of Vic's place in the next day or two, even though Vic didn't want me to. I knew it would hurt him, but I couldn't take a chance and put his life in jeopardy. I would get rid of my car as well and get something different. Well, here I was, ready to repeat the same pattern once again. Get rid of the car, get another one, and so on. Why couldn't I learn that these actions were exactly what they expected me to take, and if I continued taking these repeat actions, they would find me once again in one or two weeks.

I picked up the *Los Angeles Times* that was delivered to Vic daily and found an article on page six. A small headline read, "Gangland slaying suspected" The article went on to quote a police source that the killings of three mobsters had all the earmarks of gang rivalry, The police suspected that a rival Mexican Mob is moving in and staking out their territory. The police were still investigating this further and were asking the public for any information they might have. So far it seemed that I was not involved, and there were three less warriors for me to worry about.

Thursday, May 8, 1956

I called Tina as planned and was very surprised to hear her very anxious voice.

"Bill, I'm so glad you called. I've got so much to tell you," she said very excitedly.

"I'm all ears, honey, please tell me what is going on," I said.

"Well, the other night I was with Luigi, when this guy stops by the dressing room to see him. They started to talk, and before I know it, I realized they were talking about you. This guy, his name is Sal Trevino, has been working on finding Harry Miller. He tells Luigi that this guy Harry Miller is in Los Angeles and they found out where he is, because a guy from back East was at the firing range in Reseda and saw a guy that looked like this Harry Miller, next to him, shooting his guns. He dyed his hair and changed some of this looks, but no doubt it was him. Luigi's man worked with Harry in New York and to be certain he spoke with him at the firing range. He asked him what kind of gun he was using and shit like that. He didn't want to give anything away and didn't want to make him suspicious. Once Harry spoke, he knew it was him, but played dumb. He followed him outside and watched what car he was driving and took down the license number as well. He was very careful and followed him home. He stayed well back so that he wouldn't give anything away. He found his place on Twenty-Eighth Street in Santa Monica. He couldn't tell which house exactly, but has it down to one block. They want this guy dead, and it has to be done now, that's what he said," she said.

"I couldn't figure it out! How the hell did they find me? Now I know, and I'd better get the hell out of here before it's too late. Thanks, Tina, thanks," I said.

"I'm not finished. Please, listen carefully. Yesterday three guys were sent out to get you, and they wound up dead. They are not fooling with you anymore, Bill, Harry. I don't know what to call you anymore!" she said, her voice breaking.

"I know, honey, I know, but please be my strength and help me. Above all, be very careful. If they knew you were speaking with me, you would be dead, so please take no chances. I love you too much," I said.

"Listen to me, Harry, don't go home and get rid of that car. Do it now even if you have to abandon it. You are a target because of that red convertible. I know because I heard Luigi tell Tony to advise everyone to be on the lookout for that car. Don't go home, they are watching the street, and they will shoot you down. It's not funny, Harry. They are close, and you know it. Get the fuck out of Los Angeles now! Please, darling, please leave now before it's too late," she was crying uncontrollably.

"I love you, Tina, and am getting out now. Can you get to this phone on Saturday?" I asked.

"I think so, about the same time?" she asked.

"Yes, I'll call you then. Don't worry I'll be extra careful, and I'll be okay." I hung up and started to get my plan organized.

I called Vic immediately and told him what I had found out. It wasn't so much the method I used, as it was the stupidity of careless actions once again.

I told him that I could not come home because the place is being watched and begged him to be very careful. I told him I would call him later and coordinate my movements with him.

I drove to the nearest used car lot and made a deal to sell my car. I took a loss of a few hundred, but what the hell! I had to get rid of it. I then went back to Valley by cab and stopped at Victory and Van Nuys. I then walked south on Van Nuys to a used car dealer and under the name of Tom Ferris bought a simple two door, black Plymouth. No frills, nothing to stand out, certainly not a car Harry Miller would drive. I had to get back to Vic's house to get some of my stuff as well as my money. I had forty eight grand hidden in the room and would need every penny.

I drove down Twenty-Eighth Street and saw two cars parked with people in it. One at each end of the street, watching every house and without doubt looking for the Red Oldsmobile. I decided it would be best to wait until tomorrow before going home.

I called Vic and explained that I would stay at a hotel tonight and would call him in the morning. I also alerted him to the fact that there were two cars, one at each end of the street, keeping a lookout for the red convertible. I begged him once again to be very careful and to be safe. I told him that I loved him and would not be able to live with myself if something happened to him. I finally hung up and went out to find a hotel room for the night.

Friday, May 9, 1957

I just couldn't get myself to trust a hotel room, so I stayed in the car all night and slept in the back seat, while it was parked on Wilshire near Sepulveda. I woke at about five just as the sun was starting to cast some light over the darkness.

I straightened out my hair and drove to Twenty-Eighth Street and turned down the street without stopping at the house. I was checking everything out to see if I could spot anyone watching the place. I noticed a big, black Buick parked at the corner of the street, perhaps about one hundred and fifty feet away from the house. I could see two heads and smoke coming out of the driver's window. Idiots, I thought if they want to be unnoticed, why do they use the same kind of cars and sit in them like they are invisible? I could never understand, but who cares if they are dumb, so much better for me. I checked out the rest of the street and did not find any other suspicious vehicles. I went around the back through an alley and parked behind the house. The alley was deserted, so I decided to break into the house and get my stuff and get out of there. I carefully climbed over the small wooden fence and went on to the rear porch. I tried my window, but it was locked. I didn't want to break it as that would wake Vic and who knows what he would do? I had to make a choice—wake Vic by breaking the window or knock on his window and wake him up.

It was getting bright, as the sun was coming up, so the odds of Vic turning on lights would be very small. I walked over to his window, which was located at the side of the house, but not visible from the street. I knocked on the window, no response. I knocked again; this time a little louder and listened. I heard some noise from the room and then there was Vic at the window. I held my finger to my mouth indicating silence. He got the message and slowly opened his window.

"What the hell's going on Tom?" he said.

"Shush, please do not make any noise. There are some people outside watching the street. They're looking for me. It's a long story, but I got to get my things and get out of here, Vic. I don't want you to be in trouble, and I certainly don't want to get my ass shot up. I can only ask that you forget me and say anything you have to protect yourself. In the meantime, you don't know me, never heard of me and so on. Please, Vic, please help me," I pleaded.

"Get your ass in here and get what you need. I'll watch your back. Now hop to it," he said.

I climbed into the house and went to my room and grabbed my bag and then took out the heating grate and retrieved my money satchel. I opened the rear door to leave and then went back to the living room to see Vic sitting with a shotgun in his hand.

"If anyone comes through that door, I'll blast them away. Now you go and call me when you can," he said.

I went over to him and gave him a hug and handed him ten hundred dollar bills and turned and ran toward the rear door. I hopped the fence and jumped into my car, and off I went. So far so good. Those assholes would sit there for a long while. Where to go from here? I hadn't gotten that far yet. I only wanted to get out of town. I had a bank account with the ten grand Moe sent me and thought it was best to leave it where it was. I could always write a check from Tom Ferris to whomever and remove the money. In the meantime, where should I go? I drove toward San Diego because I thought it would be safer to enter into Mexico there and head to Tijuana and then make up my mind where I want to go. At least, Tijuana would be crowded, and it would be very easy to get lost in the crowd.

Saturday, May 10, 1957

Tijuana, what a place! People everywhere looking to take your money. Hookers every where you look, hawkers selling junk to Americans, and bar after bar offering flesh and cheap booze. There was also the Mexican

Mafia, the real caretakers of this place and ruthless to the core. The Mob was considered kind compared to these low lives. I had to be extremely careful because news travels real fast in this hell hole. If anyone knew what I was worth dead or alive, it was certain I would be dead very quickly. This kind of money would make people do all kind of things, no matter where you were, but here in Mexico, it would make someone rich for a lifetime.

I decided that the dangers that existed here in Mexico were way too much for me, so I turned around and drove back to San Diego. I took a motel near the edge of the city and decided to stay there until, at least Monday. Let everything cool down as much as possible.

I waited until four and called Tina. "Hi, how are things?" I asked.

"Things change every minute since I last spoke with you. Luigi is acting like he has just made the deal of the century. He keeps saying that he has found one of the lowest assholes that ever existed. He told me that this guy is a rat, but he found him. 'By tonight he will be dead, and I'll be very rich,' he said to me. I just look at him when he talks this way and acts as if I don't understand. What did this guy do to you? I asked him, and he said that the guy was going to go to the cops and tell them things that were not true just to get even with some New York guy that fucked his wife. Is that true, Harry?" she said,

"Come on, Tina, do you think I'm like that? If some guy fucked my wife, I might get angry, but I wouldn't get the entire Mob after me for it. No it's not true. You know me, Tina. I hope that is good enough?" I said.

"Hey, I was just kidding you. I love you and know the whole story and just wanted to hear you say that it was bullshit. Okay, Harry, they are watching your house, I know that because I heard Luigi tell Tony to make sure they change guys every twelve hours. I also know that they are looking for your car and are watching the gun range in Reseda. Be very careful, Harry, very careful, please," she said with genuine concern.

"I'm not in Los Angeles anymore, so they are wasting their time. I will call you again on Tuesday about the same time. If you do not answer, I'll know something is wrong. I will then try that number again each day, the same time until I hear from you. I love you and miss you. You take care and don't get into any trouble with these guys." I hung up and went back to my motel to rest. I was exhausted. I spent the night in the motel watching TV and finally fell asleep.

Sunday, May 11, 1957

I decided to leave San Diego today and take a leisurely drive along the Pacific Coast Highway north. My goal would be San Francisco, but I didn't really have to get there at any special time. I felt very safe when I was driving, so this little trip would help me relax a lot. I passed Santa Barbara at around noon and just drove as if I didn't have a care in the world. When I arrived at Morrow Bay, I decided to spend the rest of the day on the beach and just look out at the Pacific Ocean and Morrow Rock.

There were a lot of people on the beach, enjoying the California sun. I stayed on the beach until the sun started to go down and decided to drive a few more miles and find a motel and spend the night.

I needed to rest after all this driving and being in the sun on the beach, I was really tired. I found a nice little motel near the Hearst Castle and spent the night there. My trip could resume tomorrow.

Monday, May 12, 1957

I had enough sleep and made up my mind that I would drive straight through to San Francisco and find a place there. I continued along the PCH all the way, as I was in no rush and wanted to take it real easy. I could easily see if someone was following me on this type of road. It was also a very nice route to take and who knows when I would be able to pass this way again. I didn't go into San Francisco, as it was late and I wanted to decide just where I would start again. So I stayed in Sausalito just this side of the Golden Gate Bridge. It was a wonderful sight to see, the bay, the bridge and the sunshine setting in a place filled with people who didn't care about me. It was good to rest a little and not think of anything.

I found a great place that overlooked the water that had a good looking restaurant attached. I had a great meal, watched a little TV, and then I walked a little way and called Vic.

"Hey there, Vic, how are you?" I said.

"I'm so happy you called. I missed your company and worried about you. Is everything okay, Tom?" Vic said.

"Yes, everything is just fine, and I do miss you as well. I'm truly sorry I had to leave. I was just starting to enjoy my new home, and of course, I found a real friend. Thanks for everything, Vic. You are a real pal," I said.

"Well, I feel the same way, Tom, and am sorry you had to leave, but I understand completely. I did check out the street a few times today and the cars are still there. I think they will get tired real soon, but you did the right thing, I'm very proud of you," he said.

"I have to go now, Vic, I'll stay in touch. Be well and remember I love you. I'll let you know when I'm settled, and we can organize some time together," I said and hung up.

Tuesday, May 13, 1957

I didn't go into San Francisco and drove directly to Oakland. I picked a paper and read in the classified that there were furnished apartments for rent at reasonable prices in San Leandro. According to the map I had, it wasn't that far from San Francisco. I called ahead and arrived around noon. I met this chubby and very happy woman, about fifty years old with blonde hair and big tits. She was smiling at everything, as she showed me around the building.

"This is a one bedroom with a very nice view of the pool. It will cost four hundred and twenty-five a month, and I'll need a month's security and some references.

I will need an additional five hundred deposit, in case you damage the furniture. As you can see the place has just been painted and new carpets were put in last month. This is a quiet building, so we don't want too many parties, if you get my drift?" she said.

"I'll take it," I said. "When can I move in?" I said as I started to count out the money.

"Well, Tom, that's your name, isn't it?" she said,

"Yes, Tom Ferris, Ethel," I said.

"That's right, Tom," she said with a big smile. "If you would like to move in today, I could arrange that," she said with a look of larceny in her eyes.

"Of course, Ethel, I want to move in now," I said as I handed her an extra five hundred for her. "I don't need any receipt for that, Ethel," I said with a smile.

"It's yours, Tom, by the way, there will be no lease required. It will be on a month by month basis. If you want to leave, you will have to give us thirty days notice, and that will be that. If there is anything I can do for you, Tom, just holler, and I'll be there. Just follow me over to my apartment, and I'll get you a key, and we can fill in the information sheet. A pleasure to have you, Tom," she said.

I settled in and then went out to call Tina. "Hi, how you doing?" I said.

"I'm singing up a storm and meeting with a record guy from Decca a little later today. It seems to be going great, except that I miss you. Do you need money? Do you want me to send you some?" she said.

"No, sweetie, no, thanks. But I appreciate your asking. Any news on the road to murder?" I asked.

"Luigi is gone mad. It seems that the boys who were watching the house missed their guy. No sign of him, and he is upset. They found the car dealer who bought your old car, but he couldn't tell them anything at all except what you looked like. They are checking with every used car dealer in Los Angeles to find out what kind of car you bought. If you did buy a car in Los Angeles I would get rid of it now and get another," she said and continued on, "then today Luigi got word from someone that you were seen in Tijuana so they have sent some goons there. I heard Luigi tell Tony to call some Mexican named Juan and let him know they are coming to look for you. I guess they are a few steps behind, but will get closer if you're not careful."

"Don't worry. I'll be fine, I'll call you on Thursday. Break a leg today with Decca. I love you." I hung up.

Things were getting very scary as these guys are just a few steps behind and do have a big army at their disposal. I went back to my new apartment and settled in. I'll take it day by day, as I always do.

I spent the rest of the day exploring the immediate area that I now reside in. I made sure I understood which road went where and what route I must take if I have to make a rapid exit. I am glad I bought the car in the Valley, but now that I thought about it I see where I had made another mistake by using the same name, Tom Ferris. That was stupid of me, but it's too late now. I had to have a talk with Ethel about my name, and I have to change my appearance once again. Of course, I might not be here that long if I felt there was any possibility of any heat at all. I felt shitty about not thinking clearly once again. When would I ever learn? I sure hoped it's before I died.

Wednesday, May 14, 1957

I spent the day driving around the area to get my bearings. I checked out some eating places, a couple of bars, and drove to Oakland, using city streets so that I could get very comfortable with life in this area. I also stopped at a used-car dealer to check out his inventory and see if I could swing a deal for another car. I did not want to buy anything today, but decided to make sure I would tomorrow. I then passed by a costume store in Oakland and purchased make-up supplies. I told the clerk that we were making a movie and we needed some costumes as well. The theme would be along the order of old English perhaps eighteenth century. I then made up my mind to see Ethel and have her dye my hair and help me change my appearance. I knew she could be trusted because of her love of money. Once she accepted my five hundred, she was my coconspirator for life or as long as the money kept flowing. Well, that was what I thought, and I hoped it won't bite me in the ass.

Thursday, May 15, 1957

I called Rachel to see what was going on, and if there might be any breakthrough in this mess. I was surprised when she told me that she had met someone and is moving forward with divorce proceedings. She would seek a divorce on the grounds of abandonment.

"Look, Harry," she said, "I still love you, but I can't live like this. I have needs, and I must try to think about the future. We will always have the memory of the love we shared and a child as a result. You won't be able to help me in bringing up our child. I understand that and hope you do to. I will never hurt you, and I'll always help you whenever I can. If you need money, just tell me, and I'll send all I can. I promise you, Harry, I'll always tell our child that you were a wonderful man. If you should ever resolve your problems and want to see your child, I'll never stop you. This I promise with all my heart. I would never rat on you to anyone, including my father. Please try to understand and help me get through this, please, Harry!" she pleaded.

"Rachel, I love you as well and always will, but I also do understand the situation and am not angry. If you want to get a divorce, then you have my blessings. Please give the divorce papers to Moe. He will accept them on my behalf. I'll gladly do whatever you want me to do. I mean you no harm ever. Please be happy, and if I need anything, I'll get in touch with you. And always remember, if you should need me, just contact Moe, he'll always know where I am. Leave your number with Moe so that I always know where to reach you. Thanks for everything. I'm sorry it just didn't work out the way we wanted it to." I put down the phone and felt relieved. It was like a million pounds was taken off my shoulders. It felt good, really good.

I called Tina a little later in the day and found out some more interesting things. One of the most interesting was that the Mob has raised the amount of the contract on me to a cool half million, dead or alive. That's a lot of money and loyalty does not always count at those high stakes. She also let me know that they believed I have moved to Los Angeles inner city and would be placing a large group of mobsters in that area. I told her I missed her and hoped things were going well.

All in all, the day wasn't too bad as I headed home to gather my thoughts and rest easy. I got in touch with Ethel and had her dye my hair from black to a light brown. I thought the color would be easier to maintain and now that I have removed my mustache, it was a lot simpler to keep the eyebrows the matching color. I looked different enough to get by and added a pair of glasses just as a final touch. I looked great, and I thought I was now a very different person, very unrecognizable, and was ready for a good night's sleep.

Friday, May 16, 1957

I decided I needed a little recreation to get my mind off this bullshit for a little while. I could not sit around like this day after day, just waiting for this to get whacked. I knew I was not a stoolie and was ready to live my life elsewhere and leave everyone alone. But how do I convince The Mob? How could I do this if no one would listen or trust me? And most of all how could I trust anyone? The only thing that the Mob knew was power and fear! I was only one guy and that didn't exude power nor did it generate much fear. Could I change all that? I really didn't know how just yet, but decided to take the weekend off and drive to Reno for some action. I needed a change of scenery, and I also needed to get laid.

I took the drive from San Leandro to Reno along the Sierra Nevada road. What a scenic and dangerous drive this was, along a winding road surrounded by deep gorges. I passed through the Donner Pass, where sometimes back in the 1800s a whole part of new settlers starved and froze to death on their way to California. There were even claims of cannibalism. I saw car wrecks lying deep into valleys, too deep to remove them and bring the vehicles back up. It was a very interesting drive and very scenic. I enjoyed it very much.

Saturday, May 17, 1957

Reno, Nevada, the small town gambling Mecca of the North, just a few miles out of Lake Tahoe. My kind of place to get lost and have some fun. Reno is a small version of Las Vegas, a very small one indeed. Who would look for me here? I felt that no one would care or bother as I walked down South Virginia Street, "The Strip" of Reno.

I felt that my new hair color and the glasses I was wearing would be enough to hide Harry Miller's identity. I felt that I was better off blending in by looking ordinary than by changing my appearance too much. This simple look of a pair of jeans, cowboy boots, a plaid shirt, mixed brown hair, and glasses made me look like any other joe looking for a little fun on a weekend. I walked down the street toward fourth, and entered a casino. The noise was just what the doctor ordered, slot machines ringing bells and good-looking ladies walking by in short skirts, offering drinks to all who played. The place was filled with hundreds of guys just like me, playing, looking, and having fun. I sat down at the blackjack table and played a few hands. I was very conservative and played a dollar per hand. After an hour of this, I left the table with a net gain of four dollars. I walked the casino floor for another thirty minutes, just looking at some of the very fine women who were walking around. I tried to make conversation with a few but was not very successful. Finally, I hit pay dirt, when I met Sally. A tall very striking blonde with big blue eyes. She was standing against the bar and looking out toward the casino floor.

"Hi, do you mind if I help you stare?" I said in a very easy and happy manner.

"No, go right ahead, you're not disturbing me," she said.

I sat down on a bar stool and said, "May I buy you a drink?"

"Sure, why not?" she said as she turned around and sat down on the stool next to mine.

"I'm, Tom, a pleasure to meet you," I said with a smile.

"I'm Sally, and it's nice to meet you. I'll have a martini, straight up with two olives."

"That's a real drink, Sally, how many of those can you drink?" I said in a teasing tone.

"I am not a champagne drinker. I like a drink with a little bite in it. If a martini is well made, it is a wonderful drink that can be sipped for quite a while, I just love them," she said in a bubbly and very soft manner.

"Well, Sally, martinis it is. I'll sip one with you. Do you prefer a special gin? Just say the word, and I'll make sure he does it right."

"Bombay, please," she said.

We had a great time, as we sat there for three hours and had three martinis each.

"Where are you staying, Sally?" I asked.

"I just arrived from San Francisco this afternoon and haven't had time to take a place yet. Where are you staying, Tom?" she said.

"I feel pretty stupid because I didn't make any arrangements either. How about staying with me, I'll get a motel room, and we can share the place. I'd love to spend the night with you, and promise you I'll be whatever you want me to be."

I took her hand in mine and waited.

"Let's do it, Tom. I like you, and I know I can trust a fellow martini drinker. Let's blow this joint," she said with a big smile on her face.

Sunday, May 18, 1957

I woke up at about noon and still had Sally at my side. She was still asleep, as I got out of bed and went to the bathroom to shave and shower. When I returned to the room, she was just getting out of bed and heading toward the shower. We kissed in passing, and I got dressed while she showered.

Sally came out of the bathroom and said, "I feel a lot better now. I feel alive and very happy. How are you doing, Tom?" she asked.

"I'm great and feel very relaxed. Why don't we get something to eat?" I said.

"Good idea, give me a minute to put something on, and we'll be all set," she said.

We left the motel and found a Howard Johnson and went in and had some breakfast and a little lunch. We decided to drive back to San Francisco together, seeing that Sally came to Reno by bus. We drove back and arrived at eight and agreed to spend the night at my place in San Leandro. She didn't have to be at work until 1:00 p.m. on Monday. She was a bartender at a club in the city, The Black Hole, a bistro type of bar that served finger foods along with drinks and plenty of ambiances for the working crowd. Lunch and early dinner were the busiest time. I told her I would drive her to work on Monday and see where it all happens. We spent the rest of the night at my place.

Monday, May 19, 1957

I drove Sally to work, arriving a little before one. She asked me to come in and meet the bartender on duty as well as some of the other people who worked there. I entered The Black Hole and found it to be a really nice bar. The tables were covered with checkered tablecloths that matched the chairs. The bar was as long as the entire place with bar stools that matched the tables and chairs. The floor was covered with sawdust, and music played all the time I was there. The place was well lit and gave off a very relaxed and safe environment. It was a fun place to hang out, and Sally was the highlight. Tall with long blonde hair and a disposition to match the relaxed atmosphere, she was an integral part of "The Black Hole." I liked the place a lot, because I felt at ease, and God only knows I needed a place where I could feel safe. This seemed like the perfect home away from home. I hung out for a couple of hours and returned home to San Leandro.

Tuesday, May 20, 1957

I spoke with Sally. She said she was working the three to eleven shift and would love to see me. She even offered to buy me dinner. I told her

I would be there this evening and went off to call Tina. She answered the phone after four rings, and her voice seemed a little nervous.

"Hi, honey, how are you doing?" I said. "Are you alone? Can I speak?"

"I'm a little busy now could you call me later?" she said. "Sure enough," I said and hung up. This was around one, so it seemed strange that she would not be able to speak. Of course, I could be reading a lot more into it than I should, but being paranoid was part of my life at this stage.

I called Tina again. It was about four. She answered the phone after one ring, I identified myself, and she went into a rapid conversation without any introductions, "I'm so glad you finally called back. I couldn't talk earlier as Luigi was here with a few of his guys. They were having a meeting about you, so you can understand my nervousness; I can't let them know I'm ever talking to you—"

I cut in and said, "I understand and appreciate your thoughtfulness. You are great, and I love you very much."

"I sure hope so because my ass is on the line with these Gumbas. They are hell-bent in finding you, because they want to look good in the eyes of the big bosses. They have no idea that my ex-manager and you are the same. I want to keep it that way for both our sakes," she said.

I didn't know what to say to her, but I knew I had to keep her on my team for as long as I can. "Thanks, honey," I said. "I will be careful, and I'll keep you updated on where I am always."

"Let me tell you where it's at. They know you are no longer in Mexico and think you are in Reno. It seems that somebody saw you or someone that looks like you along with some blonde playing in Reno," she said.

"Well, that couldn't be me, as I'm not in Reno. I also didn't go out with any blonde, so someone is mistaken. That doesn't change the fact that I have to be extra careful and trust no one. I wish this shit was over," I said with emotion.

"It will be over when you are dead, so don't let up for one minute. Watch your every move, and soon you will disappear. They can't spend the rest of their lives looking for you," she said with sincerity.

"Thanks, sweetheart, tell me how is your singing coming along?"

"I'm doing great and making a lot of money. I was singing last week at the Dunes hotel and got paid four thousand for the week. If I ever needed a manager, I need one now. Luigi takes care of all my bookkeeping. He has his man do it, and all I do is sing. I haven't looked into my bank account lately, but there should be plenty of money in there. I don't pay for anything. I've never seen a single bill and, of course, they all want to get into my pants. I'm okay. All I worry about is you. You are the one I love and want us to be together. That is what keeps me going, so please be careful. Call me on Thursday about this time, and I'll let you know what I hear. I love you, darling," she said and hung up before I could say another word.

"This is no life for me and has to change; I don't like it all, no sirree I don't like it!" I thought.

I spent the afternoon with Ethel as I had her dye my hair a dirty blond. She also dyed my eyebrows to match and showed me how to put on a few touches of make-up to change the color of my skin. I gave her two hundred for her help and made her promise that she wouldn't tell anyone about me. I told her that we would dye the hair another color next month when I play a different role. I like what I looked like and hoped that no one would recognize me now.

I arrived at the Black Hole at seven fifteen and sat down in the rear of the bar. Sally came over and sat down and said, "Tom, you look different. Are you in any kind of trouble?"

"Why do you ask?" I said.

"There was a guy in here earlier looking for someone who looks like the old you. He had a photo that looks something like you, and he made it known that he would pay a grand to anyone who can point this guy out. This guy is Mob, it's written all over him. If it is you, please be careful, you can't be here. There are too many people who would make that call, especially in a place like this," she said with a lot of concern in her voice.

"Look, Sally," I said, "I really can't explain it all to you, but please trust me. I'm not part of them."

"Who cares," she said, "they will blow you away and ask questions later.

Please leave the bar now. Be very careful and go to my place. Here's the key and wait for me. Trust me, I'll be there soon and will help you. Go now and don't look up. I love you."

With the key, she had written her address on a napkin and had folded it small enough to slip it into my hand. I left the bar and went directly to her place and waited. I parked my car a few blocks away and was very careful that no one was following me.

Wednesday, May 21, 1957

I must have fallen asleep when I heard a noise at the door. I jumped out of bed and grabbed my gun and waited for the door to open. It was Sally. She was alone and carrying a bag that she placed on the chair near the door and took off her coat. She turned and saw me there with the gun in my hand. She turned white and gasped, "What is that?"

"Oh! I'm sorry I didn't realize it was you. I must have fallen asleep, and when I heard the noise at the door, my instinct set in. Sorry about that," I said as I put the gun back into my coat pocket. "What time is it?" I said.

"It's a little after two in the morning. I had to close tonight and then I had to stop in and pick up something to eat for you. I knew you probably didn't eat, and if we are to resolve this problem, we have to stay indoors for a little while."

I looked at her and couldn't believe what I was hearing. Another female wanting to help me. What the hell is it with me? Why do I get all these people involved and expose them to harm? Why are they all willing to help me? Am I something special or what? Rachel, Tina, and now Sally; my head was spinning.

"Thanks, I really appreciate this, but I don't want to put you in any danger," I said as I looked in the bag to see what was there.

"I volunteered to do this, so don't start feeling mushy and guilty, I need the excitement as much as you do, and I hate those guinea bastards. You sure as hell don't look like you'd be one of them. If I'm wrong, please let me know. Otherwise, just be thankful I care about you," she said as she started emptying the bag with our hamburgers and fries.

"No, you're not wrong. It's a long story, so if you want to stay awake for a few more hours, I'll be happy to bring you up to date?" I said.

I proceeded to tell her the most important details. It was a little after five, when I finally finished. "That's it, I'm sorry to have kept you up," I said.

"You listen to me, Tom, Harry or whatever your name is. I'm on your team and will do whatever it takes to protect you. The biggest problem I see is that you can't leave this apartment. It's not safe for you right now, so what do we do?" she said. "We go to sleep and get some rest, later, when our heads are clear, we can work out some plan."

We slept until two in the afternoon, when Sally jumped out of bed and said she had to be at work at three. I reminded her that she must be very careful because the description they got from Reno included her and they might come after her just to find out if she knew anything. I could not go out, so I stayed at Sally's place again and waited for her to come home.

I realized that I could not stay at Sally's place too long as it is not safe. I just couldn't run out on her in the middle of the night, but would have to arrange my departure.

Thursday, May 22, 1957

It was around ten o'clock when I woke up and found Sally was still fast asleep at my side. I got out of bed and went into the bathroom to take a shower and let her sleep a little longer. I don't know what got into me, but I felt very uneasy in the shower. I kept thinking I heard noises. I left the shower running and carefully got out and quickly dried myself off. I had brought my jeans into the bathroom with me and still had my gun in the pocket. I pulled on the jeans and pulled the gun from my pocket, I thought I was being paranoid, but nevertheless I was not taking any chances. I heard a popping sound and then a footstep toward the bathroom. I waited behind the door as it opened slowly, then a heard two quick pops, as the shower curtain moved from the bullets fired at it. I slammed the door as hard as I could into the face of the guy standing there and jumped out and fired a shot into his chest. He was surprised and dead. His partner was bending over Sally to make sure she was dead. He turned around the moment he heard my shot, but it was too late. I shot him right between the eyes. I was in a panic. My hands were shaking and sweat poured down my face. Poor Sally, all she wanted to do was to help me, and now she was dead. I picked up my other clothes and wiped down the area as best I could and got out of there as fast as I could. Even though the guns had silencers on them, someone could have heard the pops. I left through the front door as quietly and as naturally as possible. As I approached the front door of the apartment building, I carefully looked out to see if there was another guy waiting for the killers. I saw a dark sedan that looked like a Cadillac parked near the building with someone sitting in the front seat. It seemed like this guy was either asleep or dead as he did not even glanced at the building. I carefully went out and walked quietly toward the parked car. I opened the door ready to plug this guy as well, but he didn't move. He just snored; he was in a very deep sleep. I thought it would be a super feat to just leave the gun in the car. I cleaned it off with my handkerchief and placed on the seat next to sleeping beauty and then turned left and walked very casually toward the corner. I turned the corner and walked another two blocks to my car and drove away. It was time I moved from my apartment to another place, another town, another state.

Friday, May 23, 1957

I quickly packed my few things and left the apartment. I found Ethel in her apartment, the look on her face was one of pleasant surprise as she must have thought I was coming to have my way with her.

"Hi, Ethel, hope you are fine," I said.

"I'm just great, Tom, what are doing out so early?" she asked.

"Well, Ethel, it's like this. I have an emergency I must attend to, so I must leave. You can keep my deposit even though you'll find everything in perfect order. Here's another few dollars for you because you've been so nice. Do me one favor, Ethel," I said.

"Sure, Tom, whatever you want," she said.

"If someone should come looking for me and shows you my picture just act as if you have never seen me. Please do that for me, and when I get back this way in a month or so, I'll drop off another bunch of money for you. Can you do that for me?" I said.

"No problem, Tom. You hurry back real soon," she said.

I left and drove directly toward Reno. I wanted to get out of California as fast as I could. With a little luck, I would out of California and Nevada by nightfall. I would feel more relaxed when I reach Utah and could then map out my trip with a clear mind.

I drove through Reno as I felt stopping was not in the cards, especially after being sighted when I was there last. I kept going until I reached Elko, Nevada, where I stopped to have something to eat and gas up. I was not taking any chances by staying in Nevada so driving through was my priority.

Saturday, May 24, 1957

I wanted to make it to Salt Lake City, Utah, where I would buy another car and move on. I thought, because it was a Mormon State with a great many rules the Mob would not have a presence there. Of course, this was a foolish thought, but at least it made me feel a little bit more comfortable. I decided to pull over at the first Howard Johnson I saw and take a twenty-minute nap and keep rolling along. I would drive all night and arrive in Denver sometime tomorrow.

Sunday, May 25, 1957

I arrived in Denver around noon and found a hotel just outside the city. I needed rest and most of all peace. I would continue my travels on Monday and get the car situation organized. I had two other sets of identification if I should need another driver's license. I went to sleep and slept right through to Monday.

Monday, May 26, 1957

I woke up early and although I was travelling east. I had not decided that I have to go back where it all started or pick another place that I thought would be good for a new start. They may not look for me in their own backyard. They would never imagine that I would have the balls to start again under their noses. New York or any area close by would help me because of the population density. It is a lot easier to disappear in a crowd than in an open area. Of course, if they saw me out in their home base, I'd have no chance at all, as they out number me.

Even if I show some real strength, I'm certain they would not back off. They would just send more soldiers into whack, and in time, they would get me for sure. It just made me feel better to think that I do have some chance against these odds, but deep down I understood that it was a losing fight.

I decided to call Tina, even though it was early and not on the appointed day. I needed someone to talk to, and she was it. My journals just didn't do the trick, when I really wanted to bounce something off someone.

"Hello, hello, who is this?" she asked in a very sleepy voice.

"It's me, Harry, sorry if I woke you. Are you alone? Is it okay to speak?" I said almost in a whisper.

"Yes, I'm alone and tired. I worked till four in the morning and drank a little too much. Never mind me. How the hell are you?" she said.

"I'm fine and on the move again. They tried to kill me in San Francisco. They missed as you probably know," I said as calmly as possible.

"I heard a lot of shit about that. It seemed that two guys were killed and some broad as well. Luigi was pissed because the third guy fell asleep and didn't know what happened. When the cops arrived, he was arrested. They found a gun in the car and another in his jacket and guess what? The gun in the car was the one that killed the other two guys. The guys were well-known gangsters, but no one knows who this broad was. It's a real mess, but I'm so glad you are alive and well. I miss the shit out of you and want to get out of here. It seems my career is going nowhere, as they are only using me here in Vegas. I think they just wanted to get into my pants, and now they don't know what to do with me. I need you. I really need you," she said with a little sadness in her voice.

"I wish I could just scoop you up and take you away, but I can't put you in danger. I love you too much. Are you really upset over your career?" I asked.

"Not really, it's because I am tired and want to see results already. I know it is a matter of time, but it will come soon," she said.

"What are they doing about finding me?" I asked.

"The last I heard they think you are in the San Francisco area, and they are stopping in at every bar and nightclub. It seems they found you through this broad that was working at some bar. The bartender fingered you and told them that you were staying at her place. Is that true, Harry, were you staying at her place?" she said.

"Tina, this girl was killed for nothing. She was a nice and kind person, and when she learned that people were asking about someone that fit my description, she suggested I stay at her place until she gets home. She gave me her key and directions how to get there, so I went to her apartment to get some rest while she worked until four in the morning. When she came home, she must have been followed, because they came into the apartment fifteen minutes later. I had just finished taking a shower when I heard some noise. Then I heard two pops and knew that someone was shot. They killed her for no reason. They are just animals. They began looking into the bedroom and saw the light on in the bathroom. They fired through the door and then kicked it down. I had started the shower running, as soon as I heard the first two pops and I hung my towel on the shower head, so it would look like I'm showering. I figured that a fast glance would be enough to fuck them up and give me my chance. I don't want to go into all the details, but it was horrible. I did what I had to do, and now I am on the run once again, I can't stand much more of this," I said.

"I know, sweetheart, please hang in there, and we will win out. I know we will. I love you with all my heart, I really do," she said.

"I'll call in a few days. If you are not alone, just say 'you have the wrong number,' okay? I love you," I said and hung up.

I went car shopping and bought a Ford Fairlane. I didn't give them my old car as I planned on scrapping it somewhere in Denver. I finally drove the car to the outskirts of town, removed the license plates and poured gasoline all over the interior of the car. I then left a cigarette burning with a book of matches attached. Once the cigarette reached the matches they will ignite and the car will burn. It also gave me time to make my way back to the center of the city so I may pick up my car and move on. It was a lot more prudent to destroy the car then to sell it and leave a trail. It was late to get on the road, but I wanted to move east so off I went.

Tuesday, May 27, 1957

Today, I drove through Nebraska, Iowa and on to Chicago. I was on a roll and didn't want to stop. But I was getting a little weary. I decided to take a motel outside of Chicago and get a few hours sleep and continue in the morning.

Wednesday, May 28, 1957

When I decided to go back east, I wasn't certain how far east I would go. After a great deal of thought and a lengthy discussion with myself I decided that my first stab at a new start would be Pennsylvania. I would start with a new identity, buy a property, and just meld into the local scenery. Once I was settled, I'll send for Tina, and perhaps, we could have a life of peace and quiet. They would never think of looking for me in a small town, especially one so close to Manhattan. This trip would take a few days, but it would be worth the wait and would get me the peace I desperately needed.

Thursday, May 29, 1957

I didn't rush as I felt there was no need to do so now that I have chosen my final destination. I drove through Ohio today and stayed the night near Cleveland. I had bought a map that included Pennsylvania and spent a good portion of the night studying it to help me select a good place to begin.

Friday, May 30, 1957

It was Memorial Day weekend, and here I am on the road and seeing parades, picnics, and flags flying everywhere. I spent the day in the Cleveland area, taking advantage of nice weather and lots of celebrations. I stayed another night at the motel and rested. I needed the rest and hoped tomorrow would bring me to my final destination.

Saturday, May 31, 1957

I spent the day driving from Ohio to Pennsylvania. I spent the night just outside Philadelphia.

Sunday, June 1, 1957

I finally decided, after reading the map, to drive from Philadelphia to the Poconos. This area was no more than a couple of hours out of Manhattan and was surrounded by big populations from New Jersey, New York and Pennsylvania. The Poconos was a famous vacation area known all over the world and was especially known as a honeymoon haven. I thought I could easily fit in and mind my own business, and perhaps, no one would pay any attention to me. It was worth a try so I drove toward the Pocono Mountains. I arrived in Stroudsburg, a small college town that was the entrance to the Poconos. I found a motel in a small town called Tannersville and spent the night.

Monday, June 2, 1957

I decided to take a trip to Harrisburg and explore the areas around there. There are places like Wilkes-Barre, Tannersville, Allentown, Bethlehem, and Stroudsburg, plenty of small towns in the area that will do just fine. I drove back to Philadelphia and drove over to the Jersey side to get rid of my Ford Fairlane. I sold the car and then took a bus back to Philadelphia.

I had to find a car, so I took a bus to Harrisburg and found a used car lot and for five hundred bought a 54 Chevrolet under the name of Joseph Smith with an address in Philadelphia. I took the car and drove to Atlantic City to get a little rest and check out the Boardwalk and beach before the season opens.

Tuesday, June 3, 1957

I had plenty of money with me and decided it was best if I stayed in Atlantic City and spend a few days on the Million Dollar Pier. The pier was preparing for the summer onslaught, and I hoped it would be easier to obtain a new set of identification papers, driver's license and whatever else I needed here rather than in the Poconos. I might even get lucky before I move on to my new location. I found a cheap hotel room a block away from the boardwalk. In another two weeks, this place would be packed with people from everywhere especially school kids once school was out.

I spent the rest of the day walking on the Boardwalk and looking for someone who might turn me on to the papers I needed. I walked all night, and at about 1:00 a.m., decided to go back to my room and get some sleep. Perhaps, tomorrow would bring some better news!

Wednesday, June 4, 1957

I called Tina from Atlantic City to get her reaction to the situation.

"Hi, honey, I'm so glad you called. I missed you and have been worried about you," she said.

"I was on the road and trying to find a place to settle down and make my stand. I'm tired of running, and I miss you a lot," I said.

"I miss you too," she said. "But things have changed a lot since I last spoke with you. My gig ends this Monday, and I'm heading to New York where I'm meeting with a record producer. Luigi arranged for me to make a few demos, and then we'll see where to go with that. I was supposed to be signed by Decca, but Capitol Records is making a better offer. This could be my big chance. What do you think?"

"I don't know what to say. I thought we were going to get together and settle down to a quiet life together? The other day you were very unhappy with these guys and now you love them again," I said.

"Listen, honey, I want to be with you, but right now I have the chance to be a star, and I want to take it. Please understand, I love you and want to be with you, but your situation is very dangerous and who knows what will finally happen. If I don't take this chance, I'll never know if I could have been that big star or not!" she said.

I got the message and felt quite lousy about it, but realized she was right and I had no business standing in her way because I was lonely.

"I wish you only the best and hope all your dreams come true. I won't be able to call you anymore because I don't have a number to reach you, and I can't give you a number for me. You just be good and knock their socks off. I'll find you when all this is over, and if you still want to be with me, you'll let me know. Please let's not make this any harder than it is. I love you and thanks for everything and having faith in me. It was great while it lasted, and I only wish it could have been different. My heart is with you always." I hung up before she could say anything. I closed another chapter and shall begin another as fast as I can.

There could only be one way to end this, a fight to the finish would not do as I would be the one that would be finished. I must disappear once and for all and start a new life; until I could get that going, I would think like them, be like them, and stay one step ahead. Survival would be achieved if I followed this formula to the letter, guaranteed!

Thursday, June 5, 1957

I woke up early and started my walk on the Boardwalk. The place was not crowded, but there were people on the boardwalk. Some were walking, and others were riding bikes and honeymooners were riding bicycles built for two. Then there were those who were just waking up. I walked for at least an hour, as the sun rose and the day stated to warm up. I was getting tired and discouraged when I met this young girl walking on the Boardwalk without any shoes and acting as if she was lost. She said she had been out all night and could use some help. I stopped her, and after a little bit of convincing, I got her to come with me and have something to eat. She was a good-looking girl under the dirt and grime of a night out on the beach. She stood about five feet two and must have weighed about one hundred pounds. She had a disheveled head of light brown hair along with big brown eyes and very white teeth. Cleaned up, I suspected, she would be a pretty good-looking young gal. She told me she was a native of Atlantic City and was out of work. She had nowhere to stay, as she had no money and was hungry.

After eating, I asked her where she lived, and she told me that at this time she was temporarily without a place. I invited her to my room to take a shower and stopped at a shop on the way and picked up a few new items of clothing that she could use after cleaning up. Once she was cleaned up and feeling a lot better, I found out that she knew a lot of people in Atlantic City. She said she could get me the set of identification I need and she said, "I can make a few dollars while helping you. I really need the money."

I know I am a sucker for things like this, but I felt she could be trusted and I did need the papers, and my heart went out to her. We agreed that for a fee of one hundred dollars she would arrange for me to obtain the new papers, I needed some help, and I rationalized that even if she ran away with the money, I would have done a good deed. I gave her the one hundred dollars and went with her to a Woolworth's five and dime store and took passport photos. She went off and promised to be back by five tonight with the papers. I gave her five hundred dollars to obtain the papers and told her I hope I would get change.

I spent the rest of the afternoon checking out the Million Dollar Pier and even went on a couple of rides. I bought some new clothes in Atlantic City and a big bottle of salt water taffy and went back to my motel and waited for this little girl I have trusted to arrive with my money. I could easily lose my six hundred by trusting a stranger. My faith in her was rewarded at five thirty when she arrived at my motel. I didn't even care if she didn't get the papers; all I cared about was that there was some goodness in her. She knocked on the door, and after entering the room, handed me a full set of identification documents starting with a Pennsylvania driver's license and a Social Security card and passport. She told me it had cost her an additional one hundred dollars. I gave her the hundred and an additional one to boot and thanked her for honesty.

I was happy that she looked good wearing her new clothes, and in my heart I knew the thousand dollar investment was well worth it. Sometimes, things do work out as they should, and one's faith in human nature proves to be rewarded.

I left Atlantic City in a great mood, as I drove north east into Pennsylvania. My new life would have to take roots in the Pocono Mountains if I am to stop this running. At least that was my dream, and I was willing to do anything to be lost in the Pocono Mountains.

I arrived in Stroudsburg, Pennsylvania around ten thirty in the evening—a one-road small town that didn't appear to have too many people. I took 611, the main road, and drove toward the resorts on that side. There were two sides to this area, as I was told at the local coffee shop. One was called Marshall's Creek, and the other side was Tannersville, where the famous honeymoon resorts were as well as the ski hill, Camelback, as it was called due to its shape in the mountain. I took a motel room on 611 near a town called Bartonsville and decided to get a good night's sleep and tackle my future tomorrow.

Friday, June 6, 1957

I woke up late as I must have been more tired than I thought. I showered and dressed and went to the Bradley's Diner for some breakfast. This place was filled with locals and was loud and full of old boy remarks and family style food. I felt a little out of place, as people looked at me as if I was interfering with their way of life. I understood at once that I wasn't welcome here. After finishing my breakfast, I thought I'd spend the rest of the day driving around and getting to know the area. This was where I planned to start fresh, and I needed to know the lay of the land. What made the local people tick and how did one fit in? I would make my stand here because it was remote and yet it was not far from

New Jersey, Philadelphia, and New York City. In two hours, I could be anywhere in either city and be back here again the same day.

This might be the right place for me, as long as I could slip into the scheme of things. I spent the day driving in and out of small roads that took you into the mountains. I went to Allentown and back to Stroudsburg and took back roads just to get the feel of the area. It was a far cry from the hustle and bustle of New York or Los Angeles, but it seemed to me it was what I needed if I was to get started on my way to a new life. I stopped in at Bradley's again, where I ate home-cooked food and met some very nice local folks. The evening crowd was a lot friendlier than the morning crew. I was able to gather a lot of information, while having dinner at this local eatery. They told me that this was a growing place as people discovered the peace and beauty of the Pocono Mountains. The summer was the busiest of the seasons, as people flocked from Philadelphia mostly. Kids were out of school, and the rental houses were all rented. Many business people brought their families here for the summer and made the trip every Wednesday and Friday.

It was like a ritual as the wives and kids stayed here and the husbands returned to Philadelphia or New York and went to work. The Wednesday procession seemed to me to be the most important trek, so their wives would not think they were having affairs while the wives were here.

The climate was great, and there were so many activities to keep everyone busy. It was a great place to enjoy the summer and to mix right in. I could not have picked a better place at a better time to meld right in. I was certain I would not be a suspect as there were so many new folks here for the summer. There was at least a tenfold increase in population during the summer.

There were summer camps, where folks sent their kids for the summer, as well as rental houses, where families spent three or four weeks of the summer. The hustle and bustle of the area was perfect for me to get assimilated and to establish myself. This was the perfect place for me. I was thrilled and felt a little more relaxed, finally!

Saturday, June 7, 1957

I spent the day searching out a motel that I could stay on a monthly basis. I would look for a house later as that would take time and I would need the time to get established properly. I didn't want to create any commotion about my presence here in town. I told myself to go slowly because this was a small town and news travel quickly. I also opened a PO Box in the Tannersville post office, even though I don't get any mail. I just felt it was best to establish some roots and get myself recognized gradually. I wanted to blend in, as if I have been around for a long time. I took the name of Aaron Van Johnson, as my new persona. My past history would show I was born in Sciota, Pennsylvania, and graduated from Penn State. I paid two grand to get these records posted with the credit bureau through my dear friend Moe Arnold.

Sunday, June 8, 1957

I finally found a motel located in Tannersville off route 611 and made a deal to rent the unit on a monthly basis. It was only one room with a bathroom and shower. I agreed to a maid service on a weekly basis in order to keep the price down. With this part of my new beginning being settled, I now could continue exploring the area and searching for the perfect house for me.

I spent my weekend driving around and trying to find an ideal place for me. I was looking at a little house just off Cranberry road that overlooked the Cranberry Bog. This area was famous for its wildlife and growth of various rare trees and plants.

It was a swamp, but spread out for miles and miles and guaranteed no one would ever build anything in the bog. Civilization in that area would always be limited. The piece of land I was looking at was just west of Cranberry road with a quaint little house sitting on top of a hill. No one lived behind me, as there was a power line running through and, much to my delight, an animal preserve just behind it.

To my left was an old farmhouse that was abandoned, and to my right was a nice cottage that was occupied. My only exposure to danger came from the right and left side of the property. I felt at once that protecting two sides was a lot easier than trying to cover all directions. I checked out the license plates on the cars in the driveway, and they were from New York. My conclusion was that these folks were weekenders and would not be a problem at all.

The real estate agent told me that no one has lived in this house for two years. She also stated that the owner lived in Germany and was anxious to sell. Once inside the house, it looked like it hadn't been lived in for many more years than two. For me, this was a perfect place. I could rebuild it to suit me. Yes, this was the place for Aaron Van Johnson to start anew! I could hardly contain my excitement as this property was ideal and with some work it can be fortress. I would call Moe tomorrow and discuss financing and see how we could obtain this great property.

Monday, June 9, 1957

I spent the day driving into Stroudsburg to see what the big city looked like and get a feel what life is all about in this rural setting. After taking a drive through the main street, I figured I have seen enough. There was the usual department store as well as the sporting goods shop and a super market. Of course, there were the ladies' shops and a furniture store along with two travel agencies. I spied at least two bars and plenty of cars, parked diagonally on the extra large main street. After my drive through Stroudsburg, I decided to explore the countryside. So I stopped in at one of the travel agencies and obtained a map to help guide me to Amish Country. I wasn't that far away from Pennsylvania Dutch Country, where the Amish settlers lived since migrating to America. I took a leisurely drive to another world, where motor cars and modern technology did not exist. It was a great experience for me and an enjoyable departure from being chased by mobsters. I enjoyed my day immensely and felt relaxed, more relaxed than I have felt in a long time. I tried Moe but he was in court all day. I stopped in at Bradley's for dinner and returned to my motel, where I slept like a baby. It felt real good.

Tuesday, June 10, 1957

I spent my day haggling with the real estate broker and finally came up with an offer for the property. I offered six thousand and five hundred for the house and land, although the asking price was a little over ten grand. I explained that the house had no value and had to be torn down, and the land hasn't been touched for years. I told the agent to tell the seller that this was a take it or leave it offer. I further explained that I didn't have time to waste, and if I didn't get a response today, I would look elsewhere.

Finally, after a few phone calls, we agreed to sixty-seven hundred for the place. I agreed, signed the offer, and gave a thousand dollar deposit pending the proper closing procedures to make sure the place was mine free and clear of any encumbrances. I now had an address in Tannersville, Pennsylvania, even though I really didn't know what it was yet. This was wonderful, and I felt great and spent what was left of the day at O'Reilly's Bar in Stroudsburg, buying drinks and having a real good time. I tried Moe again, but he was still in court. His secretary let me know that this case was taking longer than expected, but he should be in the office tomorrow. I did not leave a message!

I stayed at the bar until nine thirty and then went back to the motel for the night. I was floating on air, as I felt this was the start of my new life. A homeowner, who would have believed I could be so settled in the midst of this crusade the Mob was waging against me? Certainly not me, but here I was, at the start of something new.

Wednesday, June 11, 1957

I was given the name of Lew Brannigan as a very good and honorable attorney by Jan Fortu the real estate agent. His office was located on route 611 in Stroudsburg. I called his office and made an appointment for four that afternoon. I took a drive back out to the property and walked it from one end to the other. The lot was much bigger than I imagined, as it was fourteen acres in total. I could not figure out the property line or where it ended but who really cares? I would make sure I got a boundary map from the Township.

The day was very sunny and quite warm. There was wild flowers growing everywhere, and the smell from some of them was so sweet. Summer was around the corner, and the growth just made me fall in love with this place already. I began to imagine all the things I would do when I finally build the house that would be so very beautiful. My imagination ran away with me, and I got lost in time when I looked at my watch it was almost three thirty. I jumped into my car to get to Lew's office at four and drove off. I didn't know how long it would take me to get there as it was my first time making this trip from this location. I drove at the speed limit and arrived five minutes before the appointed time.

ALLAN BARRIE

I walked into a simple but well furnished office, with a very cute blonde sitting behind a receptionist's desk. She looked like she was no more than sixteen but had a pair of tits that made her look a lot older. Her smile was infectious, and her big blue eyes made me want to jump into her pants right there and then.

"Can I help you?" she said.

"I'm Aaron Van Johnson, and I have an appointment with Mr. Brannigan.," I said.

"Please sit down, and I'll tell him you are here," she said as she got up from her desk and moved like a goddess. She was dynamite. What a body! I wouldn't mind spending a few days with her. She disappeared through a door, while I sat there with my fantasies moving at breakneck speed.

It seemed like a million years until she reappeared, "Mr. Brannigan will see you now," she said.

"Thanks, by the way what is your name?" I asked.

"I'm Natalie, a pleasure to meet you Mr. Johnson," she said, as she extended her hand. I went into Mr. Brannigan's office with my head spinning.

"Welcome, Mr. Johnson, it is a pleasure to meet you," he said.

I extended my hand and felt a strong firm grip in his handshake. He was a tall man, must have been over six feet and wore a double breasted dark suit. He was very handsome with very dark hair and had a look of confidence about him.

"Nice of you to see me so quickly. Jan of the Fortu Real Estate Company recommended you. I have just placed an offer on a property located on Cranberry Road in Tannersville and would like you to represent me," I said. I handed him the papers I had and sat down on the super soft leather chair across from him.

"I'm very familiar with the area, Aaron. I think you made a good buy. By the way, please call me Lew. There is no need for formalities around here," he said.

"Great, Lew, I hate stuffy things like that. I am also interested in buying the property adjacent to this one. The building seems abandoned and would have to be torn down. It appears that no one has been there for a very long time." I handed him the notes I had on that piece of property as well.

"Where are you from, Aaron?" he asked.

"Well, Lew, it's a long story. So I'll just give you the important parts. I came from Los Angeles to the Pocono Mountains to start a new life.

My wife died in an automobile accident a few months ago. We don't have any children, and I just couldn't seem to get started with those terrible memories on my mind. We were only married for two years and were very much in love. It was a real shock when the accident happened. I loved her a lot and didn't really have a chance to enjoy much of our lives together. Being here will help me forget and meet new people and perhaps start a new life in a quiet setting." I enjoyed telling him this story, as it seemed so plausible and would—I thought—eliminate too many questions.

"I'm sorry to hear that," he said. "I'm sure you will find the peace and quiet you are looking for right here. This is a great community, and it is growing real fast. I'm sure you will meet some very fine people here. Please let me know if there is anything I can do for you. I'm at your service, and if you will allow me, I can introduce you to some folks here," he said very sincerely.

He told me not to worry and he would take care of the paperwork and make sure all is done properly. My interests would be fully protected and anything I say to Lew would remain confidential.

I left his office a little after five and went over to O'Reilly's Bar for a drink or two before heading home for the night. I walked in and went directly to the bar and ordered vodka on the rocks, with a twist of lemon.

"Hey, I'm Kelly, and I own this place," he said with a smile.

He was a little over six feet with blonde hair and big blue eyes. He was a big guy, must have weighed in at two hundred and thirty pounds, easily. Here was one guy I wouldn't like to meet in a dark alley.

"Nice to meet you, I'm Aaron. Nice little town you got here, Kelly. Is there any action around?" I asked.

"Aaron this is the place where all the action happens. All the great-looking girls come here for a drink and to look for some eligible guys. Stick around a little while and enjoy," he said.

"Thanks, I just may do that. I just bought a place in Tannersville on Cherry Lane.

I'm closing the deal next week and will start moving in. I guess I'm gonna need a good builder to help get the place back in shape. Maybe you can recommend someone reasonable and good? I guess I'll be a regular guy here," I said with a smile.

"Welcome to the Poconos Aaron, nice to have you with us. Let me buy you a drink to celebrate your new home and your arrival in the

Poconos. I know a few guys who are in the construction business and have been coming in here for years. Let me inquire and see who is free. You got a number where I can reach you?" Kelly said as he put down double vodka on the rocks.

"I'm staying at the Shady Rest Motel in Bartonsville temporarily, until my place is ready. I guess I can be reached there, I'm in room 191," I said.

I spent the rest of the evening talking with Kelly and meeting a few very nice ladies.

Thursday, June 12, 1957

I spent the day making sure I had all my ducks in order. I cleaned up my room and sent all my clothes to the cleaners. I went to the DMV to get my car registered with new Pennsylvania plates. I used my Pennsylvania driver's license, which I bought, and it worked perfectly without any problems. My little girl in Atlantic City did a great job. From there, I went to the bank and opened an account. I called Lew and asked him for an insurance agent so I can cover the car and the house. He recommended one, and I called and arranged to stop by their office in Stroudsburg and arranged all the coverage.

Finally, I got hold of Moe and told him about my purchase. He suggested I put the whole deal on a company name instead of my own. In that way, I would eliminate anyone from finding out the actual owner is. I gave him Lew's number, and he said he would call him and advise him about the corporation. He asked me if I had any particular name in mind, and I told him I leave it up to him. I gave Moe my new name and my address at Shady Rest Motel. I told him about the property next door and that I want to buy it as well. He thought that was a very good idea and reminded me that I have plenty of money in his account. He then brought me up to date about things in New York and Rachel. It seemed the divorce had been filed and will be official in a few weeks. She told Moe that if I needed anything, she would do her best to get it for me and that they should stay in touch. Moe felt she was very nice and still in love with me. But this was the best course of action for all of us. I promised Moe I would call him again in a few more days. I decided to take it easy and miss going to

O'Reilly's tonight. I needed to get a good night's sleep and get ready for the weekend.

Friday, June 13, 1957

Not that I'm superstitious but Friday the thirteenth, seemed like a day to really stay in bed and take no chances. It was a gloomy day with dark clouds ready to burst and a temperature of seventy-five muggy degrees. There was little I could do until the house was signed over to me so I decided to stop in at O'Reilly's Bar and see what action might happen. It was around 2:00 p.m. when I arrived at the bar. The place was half full with people who probably decided, just as I did, that the weekend was finally here, so let's party. I sat down at the bar, as Kelly gave me a big wave and a smile. Before I could warm the bar stool, a drink was placed right in front of me and the cutest little doll you have ever seen was sitting beside me.

"What are you drinking, Aaron?" she said.

"Vodka, how about you?" I said.

"Sure enough, I'll have martini, straight up with two olives, on the dry side please. By the way, I'm Heather Bigsby. It sure is a pleasure to meet you, Aaron," she said.

I guessed she was no more than twenty and looked like a china doll. She had a great big smile to go along with her dark black hair and hazel eyes. She was no more than five foot-two tall and wore a pair of very tight jeans and a bright red sweater that displayed her breasts to the maximum. She was just what the doctor ordered, and I knew I was going to enjoy this weekend.

"How did you know my name, Heather?" I said.

"Kelly told me about a good-looking guy who just moved into town. I know everybody who lives around here, so my curiosity got the better of me, so here I am," she said.

"Great, let's have another drink and get out of here. Maybe you can show me around, and we can get to know each other a lot better," I said. Friday the thirteenth wasn't always unlucky!

Heather and I spent the rest of day driving around the Poconos. She took me to Marshall's Creek and then over to East Stroudsburg and through the mountains. I saw a lot, as she didn't stop talking about the area and how proud she was of the place. We went out for dinner at the Beaver House. This place much to my surprise was a seafood restaurant in the middle of the Pocono Mountains. It was the place to eat for the tourists, but a little pricey for the locals. Heather was impressed that I took her here and loved the Maine lobster. I was amazed with the high quality of the food and service. Who would ever think that in the middle of a mountain there is a quality seafood restaurant? Wonders never cease! After dinner, we went back to my motel and had a wonderful night with my new found friend.

Saturday, June 14, 1957

Heather and I woke up around noon and went for breakfast and then returned to the motel and spent the day making love and just staying in the room. At about five in the afternoon, we decided to go for dinner but stopped in at O'Reilly's first. I gave Kelly a big hello and a thank you nod. We never left the bar, as we stayed and had a great and wild time as we ate, drank, and met so many people.

We helped Kelly close the place. I really don't know how I managed to drive back to the motel, but I did. The rest of the weekend looked like it was only going to get better.

Sunday, June 15, 1957

We decided to spend the day at The Delaware Water Gap, where they were having an artist's fair. We met many artists who displayed their paintings and other works on the streets of this quaint and very old Pennsylvania town.

We were just like tourists exploring this place and enjoying every minute of it. Heather knew everything about this place. She knew how old each building was and how the area has evolved into a haven for artists of all types.

We had a great day, and finally, our fantasy weekend had come to an end. Heather still had to go get her car that had been parked at O'Reilly's since Friday. I took her to O'Reilly's to pick it up and get home and prepare for work tomorrow. I kissed her good bye, and we arranged to speak to each other during the week and perhaps we will get together next weekend. I went back to my Motel to get a good night's sleep, I was bushed but happy.

Monday, June 16, 1957

I felt great and decided, judging by the people I had met, that life here in the Pocono Mountains will be great for me. As Aaron Van Johnson, I could really establish a new life and forget the old one. Maybe, my days of running and hiding are over, maybe!

Jan Fortu called me to let me know that she has gotten in touch with the people who own the abandoned property next door. There was twelve acres of land, and they would accept twenty-five hundred for the place.

"What do you think, Aaron? Do you want to make an offer?" she asked.

"I certainly do and will offer eighteen hundred. If that is acceptable, we can have Lew take care of the paperwork," I said.

She agreed to pass the offer along, and told perhaps we could make the deal. It didn't take more than an hour when Jan called me back and let me know they accepted my offer. She already called Lew with the information, and the papers were being drawn up as we speak.

"By the way," she asked, "who is Bom Holdings, Inc.?"

"Well, Jan, that is the company I represent and now owns the properties that I negotiated. The company wants to buy many properties in the Poconos as the shareholders feel that this is an up and coming area. If you should have any other properties that you feel would be good buys, please let me know, and I will pass the information along," I said.

She did not mention it again and hopefully it would be forgotten.

Tuesday, June 17, 1957

Lew called to let me know that the papers for the house would be ready for signature on Thursday at 2:00 p.m. He gave me the exact amount I would need to bring to the closing and that it had to be a certified check. He also told me that if I wanted I could go over to the property today and start planning whatever I wanted.

He had a letter of permission from the sellers, and in view of the fact that no one was in the house for many years, there would be no harm in my moving in anytime. Of course, I didn't want to move in just yet. There was a lot of work that had to be done before I could think of living there.

I went over to O'Reilly's and had a couple of drinks with Kelly and met some more local people. I was establishing myself real well; many people at the bar said hello as if I had been coming in there for years.

Wednesday, June 18, 1957

I got a phone call from a guy named Fernando Gotti who was recommended by Kelly from the bar. "I hear you're looking for a general contractor?" he said.

"I sure am. I just bought the Mulberry Place. It's on Cherry Lane facing the Bog, maybe you know it? It's been empty for years, so I need to start from scratch. How about meeting there sometime today?" I said.

"I know the place. I'll see you there about two this afternoon. Is that good for you?" he said.

"Great, I'll see you then." I hung up and was very excited.

I arrived at the property a little before two and waited for Fernando to arrive. I pulled my car in near the house so that he would be able to see it from a distance. I didn't have to wait long for a car to pull into the driveway. Fernando got out of the car and shouted to me, "Aaron, I'm Fernando Gotti. A pleasure to meet you." He was a big guy; he must have weighed in at 250 lbs. and was only 5'10" tall if he was that. He had very dark hair and looked like he hadn't shaved in a few days. He looked like a builder who got his hands dirty.

"My pleasure, Fernando. Welcome to my new digs," I said.

"What do you want to do with this place? To me it looks like you would be better off tearing it all down and starting from scratch," he said as we walked through the house.

"To be honest with you, Fernando, I agree with you, but I really don't know exactly what I want. I want a very nice place with a lot of light and a balcony that surrounds the entire house. I want the house to be up-to-date in design and to be well built. I will need a few different ideas with drawings if you can do that," I said.

"I'll get back to you in a few days with a few drawings of my own. Between your ideas and mine, I should be able to let you know what I suggest and then you can have me give you a bid."

"I need to know when you can start and how long it will take to build."

"I can't give you a definite time, Aaron, at least not until you give me an idea what you want. I can start in the next few days if we can agree on a style and the price," Fernando said. I thanked him and went to see Kelly and have a few drinks.

Thursday, June 19, 1957

After having something to eat, I went back to my motel and continued working on what I wanted to do with the house. Fernando said I was better off tearing it down and building a new house, it would be cheaper and faster. He was working up a price for me but couldn't really quote me until I gave him what I wanted. My only thought was to build a place that was secure. A place where no one could surprise me during the night or come up to the house without being detected. I didn't want to live in fear all my life, but I had to be realistic about being safe. No matter how comfortable I got, I could not let myself forget that there were big bucks riding on my head and every Mobster wanted a piece of it. So far I had been discovered each time because I was sloppy and didn't maintain a strict regimen. This time it had to be different. I couldn't allow myself any slipups. My disguise was good, and so far no one had any suspicions, but the Poconos was not far from New York.

I went to Lew's office at two as arranged and signed the papers for the first property. I left the funds with him, and he promised to have the deed filed within the next forty eight hours. He advised me that the papers for the next door property would be ready tomorrow, or I could sign them now and he would fill them all in and file it at the same time. I agreed and gave Lew the cash for the property. I was now a multiple property owner.

Friday, June 20, 1957

Fernando called me and asked me to meet him at the house at eleven. I showered and shaved and went over to my new house. It was early, but a beautiful day; the sky was dotted with a few white clouds with a great background of blue. It was a glorious day, and I wanted to enjoy every second of it. I spent the next hour walking my land and exploring the growth.

The land was just wonderful as it had every type of tree as well as flowers and plants that looked different and smelled wonderful. Aside from all this growth, there was an animal kingdom directly at the back of the property. It was wonderful to see a deer run by or a wild boar, and I just saw two raccoons walk by me as if I wasn't there. It was so awesome. I just loved this place and was so very happy.

Fernando arrived with a roll of blueprints under his arm. We went into the house and sat down on the floor where he spread out the blueprints.

"Aaron, here is a model of the house I propose. It is two stories with a basement of equal size and a two-car garage. I am including central air and three-and-a-half bathrooms, a spacious kitchen and party room with a large outside deck that will surround the entire house. The view from everywhere is just awesome as you can see the mountains from this side and the Bog from there and the preserve from the other side. All the bedrooms will be upstairs as well as a sitting room and an additional outside deck that surrounds the house from the upstairs and, of course, a fantastic view.

"I know it's kind of large for one person, but you have to look at it from the resale point of view. One day you may want to sell and move elsewhere. You will always get top dollar for this type of house—it's timeless. These plans are for a house that I just finished a few months ago. I figured this will give you an idea, and we can make changes from this while I build," he said with a great big smile.

"It seems like a lot of space for one guy! It sounds great, and I'm sure it will look super. What do think it will cost?" I said.

"Well, Aaron, I can do this entire job, including the demolition of the old house, the upgrading of the well, and the cleaning of the septic tank for fifty-seven thousand. If it turns out that the county does not approve your old septic, I will have to charge an additional thirty-five hundred for a new septic. Now I know that is a lot of money, but in years to come you will get back double that amount," he said.

"Does that include a stone fireplace in the family room as well as the basement?" I asked.

"I will include the fireplaces and guarantee the price not to exceed the price quoted," he said. "Let me check with Lew Brannigan, and I will get back to you on Monday," I said to Fernando and sent him on his way. He was building a palace, but did I really need a place this big?

Saturday, June 21, 1957

I spent the day shopping at the local hardware store. I bought a chain saw and a wheelbarrow as well as some other garden tools. I wanted to clear some of the land and doing it myself made me feel like I was a part of this venture. It made me feel good and satisfying.

Later in the afternoon, I went over to O'Reilly's and spent some time with Kelly and had a few drinks. I met a really nice girl who just moved in from West Virginia. She was tall, thin, with long blonde hair and big blue eyes. We had a few drinks together and then had something to eat. I finally convinced her to spend the night with me.

Sunday, June 22, 1957

I sent my beautiful blonde away as I dropped her off at her car and returned to the motel. I called Heather, and she came over to spend the afternoon with me. We went around the area looking at different homes that were just built. I wanted to get an idea of the type of structure I'd like, and this was the best way to find some architectural gems. We stopped in at a new roadside restaurant for dinner and then went back to the motel and spent the night.

Monday, June 23, 1957

I had asked Lew to look into Fernando's credentials and let me know. He called me early Monday to let me know that Fernando was well connected with the Mafia, but he had a very good reputation for fair dealing. The people he used did good work and he stood behind it.

If this is the type of house I wanted, then he asked me to go for it. Lew's news made me very uneasy. "Do I call Fernando and tell him I found another builder? Or do I go along with him and let the chips fall where they may? I wrestled with this dilemma for a few hours as I just could not decide what the best course of action was. On one hand if I called Fernando and told him I'm shopping around, will I cause any ill will?" Sometimes it was best to hide among those who were looking for you. I considered the fact that no one would think I was stupid enough to deal with the Mob when I was hiding from them. What should I do? What could I do? This was the place I wanted to call home and get a new start, now this! It was not an easy decision to make, and it wasn't any easier when I added one more fact to the equation! Fernando would make more money by turning me in than he would by building my home. Of course, he did not know I was Harry Miller and was not suspicious at all.

I decided to use Fernando, I felt it was the right move and would lessen any chance of his finding me. True, I was wanted by his buddies, but because he had no idea I was the guy, he would be the best cover for me. I also felt that keeping him close was the best thing for me.

It was the wisest decision for me to make, using the age old logic, "Keep your friends close, but your enemies closer." Using Fernando was my insurance policy. I called him and asked him to meet me tomorrow at ten at the property. I also asked him to give me an estimate as to how long it would take before I could move in. He said six weeks and I would be in. I liked that answer. It made me feel good!

I spent the rest of the day thinking about my decision but in the end felt it was the only choice I could make. I decided to go see Kelly at O'Reilly's and have a few drinks and something to eat. I stayed at the bar until nine and then went home for the night.

Tuesday, June 24, 1957

I met with Fernando and made some changes to the plans and finally settled on a price of thirty-one thousand. I asked him to contact Lew Brannigan to draw up a contract. He said he would need a ten-thousand dollar deposit to get started. I promised him that once the contract was cleared by Lew, I would give him the deposit, and he could get started. We shook hands and he left while I remained and cut a few more trees and just knocked around.

I left the property and went back to my motel and contacted Lew and asked him if I could come over and see him for few minutes. He told me to get there no later than three thirty as he had a four thirty conference. I agreed. As I was leaving the motel, I thought it over and decided to cancel the meet with Lew, so I called him, and we arranged it for ten tomorrow morning.

I took a drive to Allentown just to see the area and get a change of scenery. This was a really fast growing place and would be a major location in a few years.

The Allentown, Bethlehem, and Easton area was growing and there were opportunities here for me to invest and make some wise moves for a strong future. I drove back home and got in close to ten P.M.

Wednesday, June 25, 1957

The reason for my meeting with Lew was that he was my attorney, and I felt I must tell him the truth or else I could not expect proper advice when I needed it. It took me over an hour to explain the entire situation to him. Finally Lew looked at me and said, "That is some story. It takes my breath away. I'm glad you were up-front with me. I hope you understand that I am bound by client attorney privilege and cannot reveal this information to anyone ever. Please relax, Aaron, and we'll try to tackle the problems using logic wherever possible."

"Thanks, Lew, for your faith in me. I took the chance to tell you everything. I must admit I was worried that you might have told me to take my business elsewhere. I feel much better now and would like to move forward. You understand my reason for using Fernando?" I said.

"I sure do and agree with you one hundred percent. I think if you keep Fernando close to you, the threat he poses will be diminished. Good move, Aaron," Lew said.

We completed all the required paperwork and agreed that we would not ever discuss these things over the phone or anywhere; it could be overheard. Lew shook my hand reassuring me once again that I was in good and reliable hands.

I called Fernando and told him that the contract was ready, and if he would like, I'd meet him at O'Reilly's at five thirty with his deposit. I asked him to stop by Lew's office and sign the contract and then come over by O'Reilly's.

At five fifteen, Fernando came strolling into O'Reilly's and saw me sitting at the bar. We went over to a booth and ordered a drink.

"I signed the contract as well and left your copy with your attorney," he said.

I gave him a certified check for ten K to get the project started. It was agreed as per our contract that I would give him progress payments as he finished different phases of the house. Fernando was very happy with the deal and that he had landed a very nice job. I bought him a drink and shook hands to seal the deal. I said, "I can hardly wait for you to get started, and I can start seeing my dream house becoming a reality. It's so exciting, Fernando. Thanks for everything."

"I am pleased as well, Aaron, and I promise you I will do a very good job, and you will love the place. Let's get started, my friend," he said.

I remained at the bar for another couple of hours shooting the breeze with a few of the guys and gals that I had met over the weeks. I liked it here and felt very satisfied with myself.

Thursday, June 26, 1957

I went out to the old house early in the morning, and sure enough, there were people there who were unloading a back hoe and other construction equipment. As I parked the car, another truck arrived and a few guys started unloading lumber and bags of what looked like cement. I was so happy to see this project get underway. I could hardly wait to see the demolition of the old house. I waited around for another hour watching trucks come and go until I saw Fernando arrive.

He spoke with the man who was in charge of the project and work got under way. The men went into the old house and within an hour had stripped it of all material they could salvage. The next step amazed me as a tractor drove straight into the house with the plow and, within seconds, the structure collapsed. By noon, the house was gone, and the backhoe was digging a large hole in the ground. While all this was taking place, two other workers measured and placed markers and tied ropes to mark the area where the new house would go. It was a fast but an accurate method to get the project underway. Fernando saw me and came over to say hello. "We will have the area cleared by the end of the day, and by tomorrow we will start putting in the foundation. We work fast, Aaron, but don't get to excited. Tearing it down is quick, building it back up is slow, especially the finishing touches. Enjoy your day. See you soon," he said.

I hung around for another hour and finally left and went back to my motel. I was stoked just watching all the activities. I could not help it. I felt good. I went over to O'Reilly's and had something to eat and a few drinks before going home and resting.

Friday, June 27, 1957

With the contract signed and the deposit paid, I had very little to do other than drive out to my new home daily to see the progress being made. Today, I did this again for two reasons. I was anxious to see the progress, and I also wanted to enjoy each day as they passed without incident. I was expecting someone to accost me or to think I was the guy the Mob was looking for, but much to my chagrin, the days passed as if Aaron Van Johnson was a native of the Poconos. Before I knew it, we were into July, and things were quiet except for the madcap pace the construction crew was trying to maintain as they built my house.

July 1957

It was very much like a vacation time for me as it seemed like I didn't have to worry about anything.

Of course, one would think I was on vacation all the time simply because I didn't have a full-time job. Staying alive was job enough and took its toll. For the first time in many months, I was able to breathe easier and enjoy the hot days and wonderful nights.

I took a sabbatical on my writings as you can see by the omission of daily activities. I didn't feel it necessary to write about mundane things especially when I was at peace with myself. July came and went, and as you can see there was very little to write about. I was so busy with my vigil at the new house that I actually could not find the time for anything else. I was engrossed with the construction and made changes every now and then. Just watching the house grow in size was thrilling enough to satisfy me. I could not write anything on a daily basis as I was too excited and so involved in the construction and design of my new home. It was the best month I had spent since all this began.

I also spent a lot of time at O'Reilly's and really got close with Kelly. I met a lot of nice young ladies, mostly from Philadelphia and New Jersey, and had plenty of companionship. It was an exciting month for me filled with so much joy and anticipation. I tried to abstain from calling Moe for an update even though I wanted to know what was happening. I adopted the attitude of just enjoying the summer and letting whatever happened be!

Sunday, August 4, 1957

The house was getting closer to being a reality. It was built on the high point of the land so that it had a great view of the surrounding topography, and at the same time I would be able to see any approach from all four sides. Now that Fernando was nearly finished, I got in touch with Al Fogel, a security expert from Parsippany, New Jersey. He was recommended to me by my good friend, Moe Arnold, and, as Moe pointed out, was very discreet and trustworthy. I did not let Fernando know anything about Al and what I had in mind, because I didn't want the security additions to be known by anyone except Al and me. I also didn't want the intricacies of the security system used against me, if the occasion ever arose. Fernando's loyalties were with the Mob, and I'd be a fool not to recognize that at all times. Fernando had his hand into everything that went on from the Pennsylvania border at Del Water Gap to Harrisburg. I played the game as perfectly as possible during the time of the construction. It appeared to me that he never put two and two together and did not recognize me at any time. Thus there was no suspicion on Fernando's part. My goal was to maintain a strong and impregnable security zone in and around the property. An early warning system was essential as well as a secondary system that would thwart any attack. I also needed avenues of escape should the need arise. Although I felt my change in appearance was good enough, I still wanted to be certain that I had ample warning so that I could take steps to defend myself if for any reason I was discovered. Heaven only knows, I was discovered in the past even though I took every step possible to alter my appearance.

Monday, August 5, 1957

I met with Al Fogel at about ten in the morning. He arrived at the property in an unmarked van and looked like any other tradesman.

When he stepped out of the vehicle, I was amazed to see a giant of man. He looked like he was the biggest and most muscular man I had ever seen. He was about six feet five tall with strong black hair and thick eyebrows. His smile was very warm as he approached me and introduced himself.

"Hi, I'm Al Fogel. You must be Mr. Johnson?" he said.

"Nice to meet you, Al. Please call me Aaron. Did Moe explain what I wanted?" I asked.

"Well, he did express the need for confidentiality and asked me to treat you like you were my own son," he said with a big smile. He was old enough to be my dad as he looked close to sixty.

"Okay, Al, let me begin by explaining what I need," I said as we began a tour of the newly built house. "As you can see, the house was built on the highest elevation so we can get a good view of all sides. I have, as you can see, two set of balconies that surround the house. The upper one will give me a panoramic view of the property at all times.

"I need to be able to detect any movement covering three hundred and sixty degrees. I need time to put into place any defenses. I may need to defend myself should an attack take place. I'm speaking to you like you were my dad and placing a great deal of trust in your hands. My life and anyone else who may be staying with me could be in danger. I need an early warning system as well the most up-to-date weapons for protection that will hold off an attack until Police or other security personnel arrive. The response time may not be that quick to avert an all-out attack. I hope you understand my dilemma? I'm a one-man army, Al, and must always be prepared for the worst. I don't want my enemy to ever know how strong my defenses are at any time. In this way, I can surprise them long before they adjust to override the system or change their mode of attack," I said with a smile on my face as I wanted to make Al feel as relaxed as possible. Who knows how all this could affect him? "I get your drift and will do my best. Moe has recommended you as a first-rate guy who has been screwed. He also told me to give you my fullest cooperation, so please don't worry about offending my sensibilities. I am at your disposal. Secrecy is my first priority. My second is to provide you with the most up-to-date technology to protect your ass, no if's, ands, and buts about it. This is a big property, and there are a lot of problems because of the size of it and because it's a natural habitat for animals. We have to understand that there are animals like bears and probably deer just to name a couple of the critters that run around out there. Then, of course, there are the two-legged types that you are most interested in. It will take a few days to map out the area and prepare a plan for you. I'll need your help in establishing a perimeter that is acceptable and then I can proceed to lay out a plan. I will discuss the installation of the system with you, and we can then proceed from there. I will not have any other people working on this project other than you and me. In the meantime, let's keep our meeting private. I'll see you on Monday around the same time," he said as we started to walk the property together. As we walked the entire property, Al made notes and drawings. From time to time, he took out his tape measure and wrote down some numbers on his pad. Other times, he took out a small shovel that he opened into a large shovel and dug into the ground and wrote additional notes. I was amazed at the volume of notes he had written using his compass, binoculars, shovel, and Swiss Army knife for information I would never have given a thought to. I was impressed with his thoroughness and his methodical methods. He knew what he was doing, I was sure of that. It took us over five hours to complete the tour of the property. Al said good-bye and reminded me that he would be back on Monday to begin work.

I went to O'Reilly's to have a drink and shoot the shit with some of the regulars. This was a long day but very fruitful. I was very pleased with Al and promised myself I would call Moe tomorrow or the next day to thank him and update him on the progress.

Tuesday, August 6, 1957

I called Heather to meet me and spend the weekend with me. It has been a long time since I last saw her, so I apologized for not staying touch. She was pleased to hear from me and called me back in the afternoon to tell me that she had some vacation time coming to her and would be able to leave her work at two P.M. tomorrow. I thought that was great and asked her to meet me at my place, and I would surprise her with a real fun week filled with adventure. I told her to bring some extra clothing with her, because she was going to spend the rest of the week and weekend with me. I told her I would organize everything once we were together. It should be a lot of fun, and I missed her a lot as well. She was very nice to be around with and wasn't demanding at all.

I met with Fernando to go over some small details that required his attention and to thank him once again for a job well done.

Wednesday, August 7, 1957

Heather arrived at my place a little after four thirty. She looked great and was very excited to see me and spend some time together. After jumping her bones for about an hour, I told her that I had decided it would be great to spend a few days in Manhattan. It was only two hours away, and it would be great to enjoy some time away from all the tourists here and explore the city. It was summertime, and the city would be a lot quieter making it a lot easier to explore and enjoy.

We left the Poconos at six thirty and drove along route 46 to New York. It was great to leave the Poconos and see my City again. I had been gone too long. We drove through the Lincoln Tunnel and came into the city around nine thirty. It was just starting to get dark but was still very warm as we started looking for a hotel. We found a hotel, The Edison Hotel, on W Forty-Seventh Street between Eighth Avenue and Broadway. The hotel was centrally located near all the events that take place in and around Times Square. I wanted Heather to see the sights and so did I. I couldn't believe that she had never been to New York City. During all the time I lived in New York, I never did take a tour of the famous sights in and around the city. It would be fun for us both, and we looked forward to it.

We went to Lindy's for something to eat and have a piece of their famous cheesecake. After that, we walked for a little while along Broadway and then on to Forty-Second Street and Times Square. It was after midnight when we got back to our hotel.

Thursday, August 8, 1957

We got up early and decided to take a tour of New York City. This took most of the day as we toured Wall Street, the Bowery, and the Tribeca District. We went over the famous Brooklyn Bridge and saw the shipyards in Brownsville. We went through Hell's Kitchen and Greenwich Village and all the way up to Eighty-Sixth Street where the German migrants established themselves and onto Gracie Mansion where the Mayor and other city officials spent their days working. From there, our tour went to One hundred and Twenty-Fifth Street in Harlem and finally back through Central Park. We had a great time and got back to the hotel around six completely exhausted. We decided to spend the remainder of the night having dinner delivered to our room and just having fun.

Friday, August 9, 1957

I was very lucky to get tickets for a Broadway show at the Playhouse Theatre. *Simply Heaven* was a comedy that I hoped we would like and would help us enjoy the ambience of New York. How can you visit New York and not go to the theater? Unheard of. Therefore, I got tickets or my name wasn't going to be Aaron Van Johnson. We spent the afternoon at the Empire State Building looking out over Manhattan. We grabbed a fast bite at Carnegie Deli and went off to the theatre.

Oh, by the way, the show was great and very funny.

Saturday, August 10, 1957

We were still having a great time in New York. The weather was great and the City was not crowded at all. We walked around Greenwich Village and looked into shop after shop until I couldn't walk anymore. We went to Tavern on the Green in Central Park for dinner and walked back to the hotel. Life was good and no one recognized me in this busy city filled with Mob guys.

Heather and I were having a wonderful time and enjoying every second of it. We just couldn't get enough of the City and each other.

Sunday, August 11, 1957

All good things must come to an end so did our great little trip. We left New York around five thirty in the afternoon. We could not handle anymore time in Manhattan as were exhausted.

We had a lot of fun and talked about coming back real soon but really yearned for the peace and quiet of home.

We arrived back in the Poconos at about nine P.M. and were exhausted after having such a great time in the Big Apple. Heather didn't want to stay the night because she had to work tomorrow and wanted to sleep as much as she could. I was a little concerned for her because she was so tired but finally gave in and let her leave.

Monday, August 12, 1957

I arrived at the property at nine thirty to meet Al Fogel at 10:00 a.m. The place was so peaceful, I felt safe here. Promptly at ten, Al arrived, carrying rolls of plans and a briefcase. "Hello, Aaron, how are you?" he said cheerfully.

"Just fine, Al, I had a great weekend in Manhattan and am now ready for action. What have you got for me?" I said.

"Let me start by telling you that in order to overcome all the problems I had to use overkill. I have drawn my plans to cover the maximum risks and to provide protection of the highest degree. First, let's take the perimeter that is our first line of detection, and defense is most important and must be flawless," he said as he began to unroll one of the plans he had brought with him. Two hours later, we wrapped it up. I was in shock as to the many ways people could gain access to my house and how much danger I was in.

I decided to take the rest of the day off. This was too much to consume in one day. I told Al I would get back to him tomorrow as I did not want to move into the house until all security measures had been installed, tested, and retested. I headed off to O'Reilly's bar for a couple of drinks and some mindless chatter.

I took a few minutes off to call Moe and thank him for his help and recommendation of Al Fogel. "Hope you are well, Moe. I just wanted to thank you for all your help and for Al Fogel," I said.

"Hey, Harry, it was my pleasure, and I hope you are happy with Al. He is the best when it comes to security. I can guarantee you that no one can screw around with his stuff. He is good. As far as other things are concerned, there has been very little chatter lately. The last time they talked about you they had you located somewhere in San Francisco. I haven't heard another word since. This doesn't mean the heat is off. It is just a little respite almost like a summer vacation. Please, Harry, be careful, and keep your guard up always," he said.

"You know, I am settled in the Poconos. Things are going real well, and so far no one has even raised a single word about this guy the Mob is after. I hope it is the final road toward a new and peaceful life," I said.

"I certainly hope so, Harry, "Moe said.

I stayed at O'Reilly's for another few hours drinking and talking. I finally went home and went to sleep.

Tuesday, August 13, 1957

I spent the day going over the measures that were proposed by Al Fogel. He certainly made sure that no one could approach the house without an alarm being triggered from a distance of one hundred feet. At that point, lights would be illuminated covering the entire area. Because we had made sure that the entire area was cleared, there would be no place for anyone to hide, thus exposing the attacker. At a distance of fifty feet, an electronic beam would be activated. The beam would deliver a low-level shock that would serve the purpose of scaring the attacker rather than hurting them. If this line of defense did not scare away the attacker and they continued their assault, an electrical shock would be transmitted delivering a full one hundred and ten volts that would knock the attacker down. Recovery time would be five to ten minutes, more than enough time to take other offensive or defensive measures.

Further, we would have cameras mounted on poles that were at least twenty feet high. With the flick of a button, we would be able to activate an electronic fence around the entire house delivering a full one hundred and ten volts. At the same time, all windows would have steel hurricane covers that would automatically roll down protecting all windows. Of course, these steel cover plates would be bulletproof. We would also have an alarm system that would be activated automatically when zone three was violated and would alert the police directly that help was required. A redundant system would also be in place in case the main alarm system should be breached in any way. When building the house, I had the builder build a bomb shelter in the basement. This room would be able to sustain me for a period of ninety days without leaving it at anytime. The shelter was fully equipped with two bedrooms, a bathroom, and a kitchen. The shelter operated off a gas generator and could keep all appliances, lights, and plumbing operating for sixty hours before additional fuel would be needed.

We had an additional fuel storage tank of one thousand gallons which would easily sustain the quality of life in the shelter for at least six months. People all over the country were building bomb shelters in case of a nuclear attack. I was no different, so the builder did not think it was out of the ordinary to build this addition. The price tag for this system including total privacy was just under eleven thousand. A pretty penny, but one's life was worth a lot more than that. I called Al and gave him the go ahead. He told me he would start work at once and should be out at the property in a few days to begin installation. The job should be completed in three weeks, at which time I could start moving in.

Wednesday, August 14, 1957

I was getting excited about the move and the task at hand. I had to do furniture buying and a lot of other shopping to get the house ready to be lived in. This would keep me busy for a little while and keep my mind moving.

I went over to O'Reilly's to have something to eat and enjoy a few drinks.

Thursday, August 15, 1957

I spent the day in Allentown at the Sears store buying a bedroom set and a table and chairs for the kitchen. I also bought a complete living room suite, a hi-fi radio and record player with speakers all over the place. The television was the biggest I could find and was in a wooden credenza that looked like it was part of the furnishings. I spoke with Al Fogel about the television antenna, and he suggested that I let him install it as he had to install an additional antenna for the alarm and other electronic devices he would need. Also the antennas will be installed so that they could not be interfered with. I agreed and went on shopping for small things.

Friday, August 16, 1957

I spent today getting the few odds and ends I needed for the house. My motel room was starting to look like a storage warehouse. I was quickly running out of space to put the small things I was able to carry with me. I decided to bring the small stuff over to the house and leave it in boxes until I was ready for the actual move in. The house was getting nicer each day, and I loved it more and more. So far I did not see any Mob presence except for Fernando, but I was still staying very alert.

The back end of my land bordered a designated hunting preserve. Only members of the hunting club could look for prey and, of course, only during hunting season. This meant that no one would ever build on that land, and that suited me real fine. But it didn't mean that an attack couldn't come from that side as well. It didn't bother me that much because Al had covered that area in the plans he showed. His problem was being able to tell the difference between and bear and a Mob killer.

Saturday, August 17, 1957

I spent the day shooting at targets I posted on trees. I wanted to make sure my shooting skills were still top-notch. I went to O'Reilly's for a couple of drinks and just shoot the breeze. I finally had enough to drink and went home to watch a little television and get some sleep.

Sunday, August 18, 1957

I spent the day with Heather just hanging around the new house and exploring the land. We went for dinner and then I sent her home. We had a nice day together.

Monday, August 19, 1957

I wanted to visit with my folks who I had not seen in over six months. I was feeling restless and just wanted to have some semblance of a normal life. I felt it would not be risky after all this time. Surly these guys would have been tired of watching their house after all this time. I also felt they didn't think I was in this area and would never be so stupid as to show myself. The risk was very small, if any at all. Therefore I wanted to take the opportunity to see them.

I left the Poconos bright and early and headed for Fort Lee, a small town on the New Jersey side of George Washington Bridge. My folks bought a house in 1949 and have lived there ever since. This was where my brothers and I grew up and had a lot fun doing it. The trip took a little over two hours with the traffic going into Manhattan being a little heavier than normal. I pulled into their street and checked it out to see if there was anything unusual happening. Everything seemed quiet; most of the people were at work, so things were very calm. I parked the car in front of the house and went up to the front door and rang the bell. My mother answered the door, "Can I help you?" she said.

"Hi, Mom, it's me, Harry," I said as I quickly placed my hand on her mouth and motioned for her to go into the house. Once inside, she threw her arms around me and hugged me with her full force.

"Harry, I don't even recognize you. How are you? You look thin. You're not eating, Harry," she said.

"Mom, let's go inside, please," I said as we pushed our way farther into the house, finally reaching the kitchen.

"Where have you been? Are you okay? Have you eaten? My god, it's really you, Harry!" she said with tears running down her cheeks. "I can't stop crying, Harry. It's a miracle. Let me look at you. My Harry, oh my god, you look undernourished. You're not eating. What's the matter, Harry?" she could not stop. She was so excited.

"Where is Dad?" I asked.

"He went to see someone in Jersey City. A friend needed some help with a car. You know your dad. When it comes to cars, he'll go anywhere to fix them," she said with pride. We sat for an hour as I told her some of the problems. I didn't want to alarm her, so I kept the danger part to a minimum. She understood because my brother gave them some sort of explanation.

"Your dad will be so happy to see you. He loves you so much, Harry, even though he may not always show it. I'll call him so he can come home now," she said with such happiness in her voice. "You will stay with us, Harry. You can have your old room back, please," she said it in a sweet and truly loving tone. I begged her not to call my dad or anyone else thinking that her phone could possibly be bugged. "Give me the number and I will go to a pay phone and call him, or we can wait until he comes home and surprise him." We decided it was best to surprise him and not take any unnecessary chances.

My dad finally came home and was so surprised and taken with seeing me he cried. This was the first time I had ever seen my dad cry. I spent hours eating great Jewish food and just talking with my dad and mom. I had my dad move my car inside his garage so that no one would see a vehicle with Pennsylvania plates.

Tuesday, August 20, 1957

It was time to return to Pennsylvania. I found it hard to leave these wonderful people, but I could not take anymore risks, and I certainly had no right to put their lives in jeopardy.

"Look, Dad, I really have to leave. I don't want you to feel that I don't appreciate your great hospitality, but I have to get back to my life. Also, it would be dangerous if I remained too long. You never know who may come by or see me. Please understand. I love you guys so much and miss you terribly. Soon all this will be over and we can see each other often," I said.

"We understand, Harry, but why don't we face these people together and that will be that?" he said.

"Dad, it just isn't that simple. I really can't explain now. Have faith in me and love me, and soon it will all end, this I promise." By this time my mother was crying and dad was looking kind of sad.

"Please, folks, don't be unhappy. I'm just a few hours away and will give you my telephone number as soon as I have it. We'll visit often, so please don't worry. Just one thing, please do not tell anyone, not even your friends, where I am or that you have seen me.

"Be very careful what you say on the telephone. It may be bugged. If we stick to this plan, no matter how hard it may be, I'll be able to solve the problem quicker, and we will all be able to live our lives in peace and be very happy. Okay, Mom, Dad, put a smile on your faces and let happiness back into your hearts," I said as I kissed them both and left.

Wednesday, August 21, 1957

I was so happy that I did visit my parents and that it all went without incident. This was going to be my weekend to move into the house. I called Al Fogel to confirm that the security system was installed and in good working order. He confirmed that it was and he would meet me tomorrow morning at ten to go over the system and make sure I understood how it worked. He assured me that he would go over it a thousand times if that's what it took to make certain I was fully aware of how everything worked. I spent the rest of the day shopping for furniture for the house. While shopping at Belington's, a furniture showroom just outside of Allentown, I met Carol. She was beautiful, blonde hair, blue eyes, and was the right size and shape for me. She was about five feet tall and had a body that was just perfect and must have weighed about one hundred and ten pounds. I asked her out for a drink and, much to my surprise, she said yes. She gave me her number, and we agreed to meet for dinner and drinks tomorrow night. I was to call at six thirty so that we could coordinate. It was a great day all around as I got a lot of stuff done and met someone that really interested me. I had a great day, and I was thrilled with all the things I was able to accomplish and the fact that I would be able to leave that dull motel room and move into a nice and warm house.

Thursday, August 22, 1957

I met with Al and spent four hours learning how to set and undo the various alarm systems. The main alarm system was connected to the local Police station with an expected response time of about eight minutes. The redundant system was connected to Al's company who would monitor all the systems 24/7 at a reasonable fee, of course. Al explained to me that his people would be able to respond if need be but would take at least thirty-five minutes to get there. If such a thing should ever happen, I was to go to the bomb shelter and remain there until his men arrived.

A special code word was settled on, and only upon the code word being used was I to unlock the shelter door. Not only was this shelter bombproof it was also bulletproof, and the doors could not be breached. If they had the equipment, they could break the shelter door down; it would take at least five hours to accomplish this. This would allow us plenty of time to get there and take the situation in hand. It was close to three o'clock when Al finally left, and I was able to catch my breath.

My phone was installed earlier that morning as well as an additional line that was dedicated for the alarm system.

Another phone line was installed using a different telephone pole and was dedicated to the redundant system. Al obtained the second phone number from the phone company and ran that phone line underground on his own and made sure that no one would be aware that there was a second line. I was also unpublished, so if anyone would request a number for Aaron Johnson, they would only get his regular home number. I felt safe and secure as I was about to move into my own home and away from any civilization.

I spent the rest of day getting settled in the new house. I moved my clothing in from the motel, and although I did not have any furniture yet, I decided to try and get settled. I called Carol at six thirty, and we coordinated our evening date.

I met Carol at the Wayward Inn restaurant in Allentown where we had dinner and got to know each other. We had a wonderful time together and learned a lot about each other. We knew we liked each other and wanted to be with each other. I didn't want to take advantage of her in any way, but she was hot, and she wanted me. We decided to stay together for the night, and she came back with me to my motel.

Friday, August 23, 1957

I woke up with this beautiful woman at my side, sleeping like an angel. I knew I was falling in love. She just made me feel good and at ease. I was tired of being alone and I guess I was easily moved. It turned out it was Carol's day off, so we were able to spend the day shopping for things like dishes, towels, and other items required for a new house. I asked her to shop with the thought that one day soon she may move in with me, and I would hate to toss everything because she didn't like it. She thought that was real funny but got the hint and shopped with a great deal of thought. We went out for dinner and then I took her home so that she could be at work early Saturday morning. I must admit I had a wonderful time and was so happy that I met such a great girl.

Saturday, August 24, 1957

Carol called bright and early to say good morning and to remind me that some of the furniture would be coming today. She would call me when she knew just what was being delivered. We also agreed to have dinner after work. If I was lucky and the right pieces of furniture were delivered, Carol could spend the night at my new home.

The furniture arrived late in the day, but it did arrive at last. I was thrilled with the fact that my furniture did arrive and in an hour from this time I knew I would have some semblance of a real home. It was exciting to see the rooms fill up and to see a house become a home.

I had waited a long time for this and felt a little sorry that Rachel was not at my side to see it all with me. Of course, she had a new life, and all this was not important to her any longer. I was also happy to have met Carol and to share the joy that I felt in my heart.

The house was starting to look like a lived-in place and had some warmth to it. I wanted to call someone just to boast about the wonderful new home I had and how life was starting to treat me fairly. I could easily use my phone because Al had installed a device that could detect any bug that would be installed. My phone was clean, so calling anyone would not be too difficult, but I didn't because it was not a wise thing to do.

Sunday, August 25, 1957

I spent the day placing things in the house and waiting for more deliveries. Usually there were no deliveries on Sunday, but Carol had a friend of hers who had a truck pick up a lot of stuff yesterday and bring it over to my place today, his only day off from his regular job.

Carol came over to help me out. She had the day off, and the only place she wanted to be was with me. We didn't spend last night together because she had to be at church this morning with her folks, and she didn't want to disappoint them.

We spent half the day unloading the truck and the other half putting things away. I gave Carol's friend a few dollars for the use of the truck and his help. He left and Carol and I had dinner and spent the night breaking in the new bed. The house was great, Carol was great. Life was good!

Monday, August 26, 1957

I felt very strongly about telling Carol the whole story. I was deeply in love even though we had only known each other for such a short period. I didn't want to hurt her or deceive her in any way. I wanted her to come and live with me and marry me but could not do that without her knowing what the deal was. I called her and asked her to meet me after work at the house. We needed to talk.

She arrived at six forty-five and looked just beautiful with her hair up and wearing her baby blue sweater making her blues eyes look like stars. She looked super and made me want here even more than I thought could ever be possible.

"Hi, sweetheart, how was your day?" she said.

"It was great, but now that you are here it is fabulous," I said and took her into my arms and kissed her. "You must be hungry," I said. "Let me fix you a drink." I could not do enough for her.

"Relax, sweetheart, I'll make us both a drink, and we can go out to eat right after you tell me what is so important that it could not wait," she said as she went over to the bar and started preparing a couple of vodkas.

"Well, I don't know where to start, so please be patient with me while I try to tell you everything. First, I want you to know that I love you, and even though we have only known each other a short time, I want to marry you. Most importantly, do you want to marry me?" I said as she handed me a drink.

"Aaron, I just met you, and I too have fallen in love, but marriage is a little too sudden. Please don't get me wrong, but you know so little about me, and the same goes for me about you. I never felt like this before, and I want to be with you, but I'm afraid of what could happen if something went wrong. Please, sweetheart, let's wait a little longer," she said.

I was shocked as I thought I read her well and that she would be so happy to marry me. Now my mood changed, and I didn't want to tell her about me. What if things didn't work out? I'd regret this action. I also felt that it was very silly of me to expect her to want to marry me so soon!

"I'm very sorry you feel that way. I just felt that we had something real between us, and I wanted to get everything out of the way, so we could plan ahead," I said in an even tone as I didn't want to make her feel unwanted. We finished our drinks and I said, "Let's go for dinner and have some fun."

"I thought you wanted to talk to me?" she said.

"Of course, sweetheart, it was about our getting married. It's not a subject we can talk about any longer as you stated clearly you wanted to wait," I said as I took her in my arms and kissed her.

"Well, I didn't mean I don't love you, because I do very much and yes, I do want to marry you, but I'm a little afraid as we only know each such a short time. Oh, Aaron, let's go eat and get a little drunk. It will all work out. I know it will," she said as she took me by the arm and led me to the front door.

Tuesday, August 27, 1957

I spent the day getting the house in order and checking out the security systems. I was getting far too comfortable, and I didn't want to become complacent. Was this the calm before the storm? I knew that the boys would not quit looking for me. It was their way, and their reputation was at stake. They knew I wasn't that dangerous in regard to things I know, but I would be another chapter in the FBI's quest to put together a profile that organized crime and the Mafia does exist. J. Edgar Hoover had been saying for years that the Mafia exists and has infiltrated every aspect of legitimate business; he only needed an informer who will confirm these allegations and share with the FBI how the Mafia worked and the hierarchy that exists. For these reasons alone, the Mob wanted me out of the way, and the sooner the better. I could not and should not let my guard down, because the Mob won't stop.

The rest of the furniture finally arrived, and the house started to look and feel like a home. I spoke with Carol, and she told me how much she cared for me. She said she thought about our conversation a lot and after some real soul searching she decided she would like to get married whenever I felt it was right. She said that love was something that we had no control over, and when it came along, we must not let it get away. Even though it sounded very cliché, it was better to have loved and lost than never to have loved at all. I was thrilled with her attitude and her real feelings; her honesty made me love her even more. I felt as if I was on top of the world.

Wednesday, August 28, 1957

I was ready for a great weekend as summer was coming to an end and all the city folks were preparing to return to their permanent homes. It was the last weekend as Labor Day was always the symbolic end

292

ALLAN BARRIE

of summer. It would be nice to see them all gone and traffic return to normal. My plans were really very simple: Carole had to work on Saturday as well, so I would stay at home and tinker around the place and pick her up Saturday night in Allentown. We would go out for dinner and return home for a little fun and spend Sunday together.

Thursday, August 29, 1957

I went to the firing range at the back of my land and practiced my marksmanship. I placed bottles and cans on a few rocks and picked them off from different distances. I didn't want to become sloppy with my shooting ability. I also didn't want anyone to wonder why I was shooting on my property as it might arouse suspicions of some sort. Each time I went to the very end of the land, I brought my .22 caliber rifle as well as the handguns.

This was in case someone saw me, and because of where I lived, they would not think anything of my shooting practice. I lived in hunting territory, and most of the locals were avid hunters. I was always in a state of readiness; my instincts just would not let me relax.

I spoke with Carol and then made myself something to eat on my new stove. I watched TV for a little while and activated phase two of my security system so that I could have an easy night's sleep.

Friday, August 30, 1957

The house was set up, and I was getting cabin fever, so I headed down to O'Reilly's bar. When I arrived, it was about three P.M., and Kelly was behind the bar. "Hey, Aaron, long time no see! Is everything all right, my man?"

"Sure thing, Kelly. I was busy with the new house and other stuff. I'm now ready to wind down and get into the fall season. I am really looking forward to this Labor Day more than ever. It will be nice when the city folks leave, and we can look forward to some peace and quiet," I said.

"Hey, don't knock it. I make a lot of bucks off the casuals and the tourists, but to be honest, I welcome the quiet time too. Hunting season is just around the corner, and every nut with a gun will be here looking to shoot turkey and then deer. Once the hunters arrive, this place will be like a zoo. Then it will be ski season and Camelback will fill with weekenders, so let's enjoy the couple of weeks we have," he said with a big smile as he placed vodka in front of me. "So when are you going to invite me to your new place?" he said.

"Real soon, Kelly, real soon. I'm just waiting for a few pieces of furniture, and I'll be all set. You can look forward to a great night at my place real soon," I said with a big smile.

As I sat there nursing my drink, a big hulk of a guy came in and sat down at the other end of the bar. He sure looked like one of the Mob guys. He didn't look like a travelling salesman. I strained my ears to try and catch the conversation but just could not get it as he pulled out a picture and showed it to Kelly. He didn't buy a drink and finally got up and said nice and loud, "If you see anyone that looks like this, you give me a call fast. Vinnie will always be grateful for your help. Nice to meet you, Kelly." He got up and left.

I sat there for a minute and finally asked Kelly, "Who was that?"

"Just a guy looking for someone who owes some money to a friend of his. I'd hate to be in that guy's shoes if they find him. Seems he ripped them off for a lot of bucks, and they heard he might be in this area," he said.

"What would you do if that guy came in here?' I asked.

"Hey, Aaron, relax. I got no loyalty to any bum who owes them money. I'd call him right away and try to hold the guy here if I could. If I didn't, they would close this place down fast. They run the show everywhere, Aaron, so it is easy to decide which way to go. If they wanted me to be out of business, I'd be closed by now!" He leaned over and spoke in a hushed tone, "I pay them for peace and quiet. I get the right prices on beer and booze, and I make a good buck here. It's a live-and let live deal, and if I want to stay here I have to go along. And, Aaron, who the hell knows this guy they are after? I didn't send him to gamble or take their money. He may be a puke of the first order, no skin off my nose, I just want to survive." He straightened up and went over to clean a table.

"Hey, Kelly," I motioned to him, "I agree with you, man. You got to look after numero uno always," I said. I finished my drink and put down five dollars and yelled to Kelly, "See you later. I got to meet this broad. Better get on my way. Maybe I'll get lucky."

"See you, Aaron. Don't be a stranger, and don't forget our dinner," he yelled to me as I left. I was shaken up by this turn of events even though I always knew it was only a matter of time. I drove home and stayed there with all security systems on.

Saturday, August 31, 1957

I had a date to meet Carol at five thirty in Allentown to have dinner together. I was a little nervous about this, but I wanted to be with her, and I realized that the Mob would look everywhere. It didn't mean that they actually knew where I was, but if they threw out enough fishing line they might just catch a fish. I took my gun with me just in case and off I went. I picked her up and we went to Clancy's Seafood House in Allentown and ordered drinks and lobsters for our main dish.

"You look a little uneasy, Aaron. Is there something wrong?" she asked.

"No, I am just a little tired. I guess I was working around the house, and I started raking leaves not realizing that acres and acres of leaves cannot simply be raked," I said with a big smile on my face. Needless to say, I was very alert and made sure that I watched everyone in that restaurant. We finished our dinner and drove to the house in two cars. Carol felt it was unfair that I drive her all the way back to Allentown and then drive all the way back again. It was a mutual arrangement we had made, and she seemed fine with it. We watched a little television and polished off a bottle of wine and then went to bed. Of course, the entire security system was activated, and I was ready if anything did happen.

Sunday, September 1, 1957

We awoke around seven thirty to a beautiful sunny day. The air was a little brisk but warming up quickly. We decided to go to the Traveler's Inn for breakfast and then go shopping to fill the house with gourmet foods for us to enjoy over the next few weeks.

After breakfast, we spent an hour at the supermarket searching out some great delicacies. It was a lot of fun and very educational as a lot of the unusual foods come from Europe and other countries far away from here.

It was a little after two when we arrived back at the house and started unloading our purchases. It had become a habit to check out the surrounding areas a few times a day and especially when I first arrive. When doing this, I noticed a car parked on the main road. It was quite unusual for any car to be parked on that road as there was nothing there and no reason to stop unless your car had broken down. The car was a black Cadillac with white wall tires, and it just didn't sit right with me. It had the appearance of a Mob car, and when I grabbed my binoculars from the house, I could see two men sitting in the front seat of the car.

I unpacked the car quickly with one eye focused on the area near the parked car. I scanned the entire perimeter of the land and could not see anyone. Many leaves had fallen, but there was still enough on the trees to keep one hidden if they didn't want to be seen. I made sure that perimeter one and two were activated. I didn't like the feelings I had; it all seemed too surreal to me.

Carol was just walking around the area admiring the trees and growth when I yelled out to her, "Sweetheart, let's get these things put away. Would you please give me a hand?"

"Sure thing, Aaron, I'll be there in a minute. I just want to pick up a few of these big leaves," she said. I went into the house and just stood staring out the big living room picture window. I was scanning the area to see if there was any movement out there when all of a sudden I saw a reflection of light. I placed it about five hundred yards away and grabbed my binoculars at once to see if there was any movement. It was too far to take an accurate rifle shot, so they would have to come closer. Still, I didn't see anyone and could not detect any movements at all. Maybe these were just hikers, but I had never seen any hikers in this area, and there was really nothing that would attract them to this piece of land. I scanned the area again and again and still nothing. I began to think I was paranoid and wanted desperately to turn off the alarms, but I just couldn't do it. Carol finally came into the house which made me feel better. I kept up the vigil for a while but still could not see anything.

"What are you looking for Aaron?" Carol said.

"Just checking. I thought I saw somebody out there, so far I can't see anything. Let's get this stuff put away and relax for the rest of the day," I said.

The day passed with the car still parked and no movement at all. It was getting dark, and so were my suspicions as I wondered why that car was parked there all day? I knew that this type of car was the one the Mob used and, of course, my paranoia was justified after all the close calls I have had in the past few months. I decided to call Al Fogel and alert him that danger was at my doorstep and ask him what he suggests I do. He advised me to make sure the detection systems were activated for the entire night as a precaution and to go to bed. He assured me that no one could penetrate this system, so my safety would not be in jeopardy.

The hardest part of the evening was trying to act relaxed when I was actually uptight. Carol cooked a real good dinner, and we watched TV for a little while before going to bed. Carol had to work on Monday, so she would be leaving by eight.

Monday, September 2, 1957

Carol had gotten up early as she had to drive back to work. I walked her to her car and glanced over to the road where the black car was parked yesterday. It was gone. I had an uneasy feeling about all this and decided to call Al Fogel and see if we could get some manpower out here to help keep an eye on the house and me! I told him about my concerns, and he agreed that a little prevention was worth everything and having a couple of guards on duty wouldn't hurt. He suggested that they parked the car in the open to serve as a warning that they know who you are and it was just a matter of time before they make their move. He said he would send two guys who were very experienced in this type of situation and would work in shifts that would make certain I was always covered. This type of security was not cheap, but neither was my life. He gave me the pass codes these guys would use when they arrived. He assured me that these guys could be trusted one hundred percent. He also didn't feel anything would happen this day. The warning had been delivered and now they would watch my movements and see what the best way was to whack me. I was to think with clarity and relax and most of all not to panic no matter what happens, and I would always make the right decision. They did not know my next move, so I had to keep them guessing. He suggested that I should always have a driver, especially one who was familiar with losing a tail. Both of his men were well trained, so when leaving the house I had to always let one drive and the other remain in the car with me. "It is a simple strategy, Aaron, and will keep you alive," Al said. I agreed and hung up feeling a lot more confident now that I had some warriors with me.

I waited for about an hour when I spotted a car turning into my driveway. The car reached the gate, and the driver gave the agreed pass code, and I opened the gate. I introduced myself to my new bodyguards and showed them around the property and then made a tour of the house.

We spent the rest of the day hanging around the house and keeping an eye out for any unusual activity in and around the property. The day ended with nothing unusual taking place except that I now had two additional people for dinner.

Tuesday, September 3, 1957

I spoke with Carol and we agreed to have dinner at the house. She arrived at about seven. "Hi, Aaron, how are you doing?" she said with a big smile. She was wearing a great sweater and skirt; she looked like a college coed, so innocent and beautiful.

"I'm great. The day was filled with sunshine, and your appearance made it complete. I love you, Carol. I love you a lot," I said.

"Did you have something to drink?" she said.

"No, not at all," I said with a smile.

"I made some real good steaks ready for grilling along with a salad and a great bottle of wine, so let's sit down and enjoy each other while we enjoy this great feast," I said as I pulled out her chair. We ate and made small talk when I finally said, "Carol, I love you, and you know I want to marry you, and I want to be able to finally settle this matter now. There are things I want to tell you and I need you at my side to be able to deal with it all. If you love me and if you really feel good with me, why not say yes?" I said as I took her hand.

"Aaron, I love you and I want to marry you. I want you to meet my parents, and we can announce our engagement at that time. No matter what may be I love you and will be with you always," she said with a big smile. I got up from the table and filled her glass with wine. "Let's go sit near the fireplace and let me tell you a tale," I said.

I spent the better part of two hours relating the events of the last seven months while Carol sat there speechless. She just looked at me as if I had just written the greatest novel of the century.

"I can't believe it," she said. "Is this all true, Aaron? Or should I say, Harry?"

"Yes, my darling, it is all true and it's still happening. I want you as my partner, but I wanted you to know all about me and because there will be trouble ahead. If you decide now that you do not want to marry me, I'll understand, and I trust you will not reveal my secrets to anyone. If you decide to remain with me, we will live under my present name and hope and pray that life will be good to us. All I know is that I love you and will abide by whatever you say."

I sat down and took a sip of my wine and looked at Carol waiting anxiously.

"I do, yes I do," she said and jumped up and threw her arms around me. "I love you, Aaron, and always will. Let those bastards come, and we will send them off to hell, together."

I could not believe what I just heard from Carol. She was willing to put her life on the line for me. Most women would run the other way, but not Carol. She wanted to stand with me and face whatever may come our way together.

I explained that there were two other people in the house with us at this time. I explained that they were here because of the perceived threat that took place a couple of days ago. The guys were outside walking the perimeter and in respect of our privacy did not come into the house all the while Carol and I were talking. I signaled to the guys to come into the house, and I introduced them to Carol and explained that we planned to marry in the very near future. Carol and I spent the next hour talking with our bodyguards and listening to their advice about safety.

We finally went to bed and our bodyguards made sure the alarm systems were activated and they turned in as well. I was happy as the day and night went very well.

Wednesday, September 4, 1957

Carol called that she had set up a meet with her parents for Saturday night in Allentown. Things were great, and it seemed that the past was far behind. I spent the day around the house and called Al to report the inactivity.

He said he would withdraw the guards but cautioned that vigilance was the most important thing. Never take anything for granted. I called Moe Arnold and asked him to inquire discreetly if there was any news. He was thrilled to hear from me and promised to get back to me as fast as he could. In the meantime, I went to a shooting range in Scotia and made sure my gun handling was still sharp. I wasn't taking any chances, not now. I had come too far to relax now.

Thursday, September 5, 1957

I spent the day exercising and honing my shooting. I retained Al's guards another day; I felt a little extra precaution would not hurt. When I arrived home from the shooting range, they advised me that wasn't any action at the property today. They also told me that the people could come back at any time or it could have been a case of mistaken identity. I told them to report back to Al, and I would call if I need them again.

I spoke with Carol and told her that things were quiet and it seemed that it was a false alarm. I spent the rest of the evening watching television with all my alarms fully activated.

Friday, September 6, 1957

Things were really quiet in town and on the roads as the summer folks were all gone and only the locals remained. It was around noon when I saw the black Cadillac pull in at the side of the road. This time I saw a stocky guy with jet-black hair get out of the car. He was about six feet and must have weighed in at two hundred and fifty pounds. He parked the car in the same place and walked around the car and opened the rear door. He must have spoken to someone and then closed the door once again and walked back to the driver's side and got in. He backed up the car up a little and then turned into my driveway and stopped at the gate and spoke into the intercom, "We are here to see Mr. Van Johnson," the voice said.

"Please state your name and the nature of your business," I said.

The voice boomed back, "Mr. Harold Westerly is very interested in your property and would like to talk with you about a possible sale," the voice said.

"The property is not for sale. I have another appointment and cannot spare any time today. If Mr. Westerly would like to talk with me please give me your phone number and my secretary will set up an appropriate time," I said.

"Mr. Westerly will not be in the area for at least another week. Wouldn't it be possible to spare five minutes now?" the voice said. My deepest sense said I should let them in and get it over with. Maybe I could put them on another track and that will be that. Of course, I wasn't that naive, but I felt I was safe with only two of them.

"Okay, I can only spare a few minutes. Please proceed when the gate opens to the entrance of the house. Please come forward." The gate opened and the car moved very slowly toward the house.

I kept my eye on it all the way and had my gun at the ready. The car stopped by the house and the driver got out and went around to the back door of the car and opened it. A tall, handsome man around six feet tall looking quite fit at about one hundred and eighty pounds wearing a suit and tie got out of the car. His dark, greased back black hair was shining in the sun; he wore dark sunglasses and carried a briefcase in his right hand. He walked up to the front door and waited until I opened it.

"Hi, I'm Aaron Van Johnson. Please come in," I said.

"I'm Harold Westerly of Westerly & Smithers. We represent a client who is very interested in this property and is very willing to negotiate a fair price with you. May we talk for a few minutes, Mr. Johnson?" he said. We sat down at the kitchen table and I offered him a drink. "No, thanks," he said. "I'll come right to the point. Mr. Johnson, my client is aware that you have had dealings with a man named Harry Miller. My client is willing to give you two hundred thousand dollars for your property if you can deliver Harry Miller to us. We have it from reliable sources that Mr. Miller was seen on your property. My client does not want to harm Mr. Miller and is willing to guarantee your safety as well as his. As long as Mr. Miller leaves Pennsylvania never to return again my client will be satisfied. Mr. Miller will have to reveal himself to my client so we can be certain he does indeed leave the East Coast never to return again. My client wishes to remain anonymous and, as I said, wishes to avoid problems. I hope I have made myself clear, Mr. Johnson," he said.

"What makes you so sure I know this Harry Miller?" I said.

"Let's not play games Mr. Johnson. You are fully aware of where Harry Miller is and can easily reach him. If you want peace of mind and an end to this vendetta against Mr. Miller, you will make certain this arrangement is consummated. This is a one-time offer, I will not be back to make this offer again. I have been retained to help resolve an issue that I am not privy to. I am trying to save a lot of heartaches and allow you, Mr. Miller, and your lovely future bride the opportunity to live the rest of your lives in peace. There can be no second chances, Mr. Van Johnson, none whatsoever. You cannot be so selfish that you will not take advantage of this very sincere offer and certainly Harry Miller can't ignore this deal. My clients usually do not make deals like this, but the entire situation has gotten out of hand, and it seems Harry has proven his loyalty to the satisfaction of all those concerned. Please convey this message to him, and this entire episode can be closed. His silence has been appreciated, and in lieu of this an olive branch is being offered. This offer will be taken off the table very quickly, so don't put this off and resolve this while you can. Here is my card. I'll expect your call by Monday. Please do not take this gesture lightly. Thank you, Mr. Johnson." He got up and headed toward the door and got into his car and left.

I was shaken by this and didn't know what to do. Should I just tell him to go to hell or should I move on? I called Moe to find out what he knew. "Moe, how is it going?" I said, "Did you find out anything?"

"Harry, let me tell you, it's all bad. Somehow they think you are hiding out with some guy named Aaron Van Johnson somewhere in Pennsylvania, I think it is. They are going to raid the place in the next few days and kill Harry. I heard that an offer was going to be made to this guy Johnson to get Harry to reveal himself, and once that is done they will follow him and rub him out. My sources tell me that they just want Harry gone and whacking him is the best and final solution. Be careful, they got a lot snitches everywhere. The Mob guys are just as happy to see you gone, anywhere, but will kill you the minute they locate you," he said.

How the hell did they put it together? I couldn't figure it out, but I knew I had to make a decision fast! "Okay Moe," I said. "What do you think I should do? Please give me a little help with this, please."

"My recommendation Harry is simply guard against the worst thing that could happen. These guys are not too bright, and they'll just as soon shoot you as look the other way. If it serves you best to help you get away, then reveal yourself and then alter your appearance fast. Find a new location and start again. After all, Harry, they are giving you a good profit on your investment, and that is a nice nest egg to get started with elsewhere. Use it my friend, use it well," he said.

"Let me figure out a few things. I'll keep you posted on what happens. Thanks for the information and the heads-up."

"Not so fast my friend," Moe said. "I am your closest ally and will always be there to help. How they figured this out is beyond me but it is not important now. What is important is to make the right move. If you stay where you are, you will be killed, and they will still be looking for Harry. If you agree to sell and move on, you will not be harmed. This much I know, Harry, the problem is that they want to see Harry and that will be tricky but can be done. I suggest you take the deal and see what lies ahead. If you need me, just call and I'll be there. Good luck, Harry. You will need it."

I spent the next few hours at O'Reilly's having a few drinks and thinking. I just could not believe what had happened but understood clearly. They thought I knew where Harry was and could influence his decision to reveal himself. The purchase of the property was nothing more than camouflage to mask the payment of a reward for turning Harry in. They really didn't want to own a house, but this method gave them some sort of legitimate way of paying the money.

I called Lew to see if he could meet with me for an hour or so today. I told him it was very important, and he agreed to see me. I explained what had happened over the past few days and the offer. He agreed with Moe that it would be best to go along with the deal and reveal Harry and then disappear fast. I gave him Westerly's phone number and asked him to contact him today and arrange the deal. We agreed to the terms we would insist upon and I left. Lew said he would call me tomorrow just to confirm that all was taken care of.

Saturday, September 7, 1957

I called Carol to tell her that I would meet her about five to meet her parents. I spent the rest of the afternoon working on my target shooting and then went home to change and go meet the folks.

I must admit I had a great time meeting two very sweet people. Carol's parents were very down-to-earth folks. They seemed very happy together and had only one real concern, Carol's well-being and happiness. Her dad was a real nice guy who worked for a large paint manufacturer. He was tall and looked fit as he carried no fat. His blue eyes and dirty blond hair along with his pearly white smile made him look like a poster boy. Her mom was short next to her father. She stood about 5'3" and also had dirty blonde hair along with her baby blue eyes.

Here was a set of parents that didn't have an ounce of fat on them and looked and acted as if they were just married. They really were so very nice, and I sensed they liked me a lot. Of course, Carol was as nervous as could be as she wanted everything to go right and that we should all get along. There was no problem with that as things went real well.

I spoke with Lew earlier in the day, and he confirmed that he spoke with Westerly and the project was a go. We will go over the details on Monday.

Sunday, September 8, 1957

Carol came home with me and spent the night. When she awoke, I sat her down and told her about the visit and what I found out from Moe. She was shaken up but took it like a trooper. What should we do? We had to decide before Monday as I must call Lew and I guess Harold Westerly and give him my answer. I could fake it and let the chips fall where they may. It would only be a matter of time until they get to me and took me out. Yet I was tired of running and wanted this to end. After hours of discussion, Carol and I decided that it would be best to choose a battleground that would favor us, at least make it an even fight.

I called Moe again to consult. "I need your help," I said.

"Name it and if it is at all possible I'll do it," Moe responded.

"I want to resolve this matter without any killings, but I can't really trust them, can I?"

"No," he said.

"So what can I do? Fight a war! Kill a few of them! Run! It is really mind-boggling and I can't seem to come up with any real answers. Please, Moe, help me!" I said.

"Let me make a few calls and see if we can get somewhere. I'll call you back in about an hour. Just hold on and I'll try to get some answers," he said and hung up.

Carol and I sat around waiting for Moe's call. Finally the call came in. "Yes," I said,

"It's me, old buddy. Now listen to me carefully. I spoke with people I know who spoke to people they know and here is the skinny. The Mob guys think they got Harry cornered in your house or nearby. They have not connected that you and Harry are the same, but they really want Harry to disappear and they want it now. The big boys just want this over and are willing to pay to get you out of the way. Here is the real part. Once they know where Harry is they are sending a single assassin to kill him. Nice and quiet and end of story, and you are out of the picture.

"They will give you two hundred and fifty K in cash to get you out of the East Coast and never come back. As you can see, that is a little more than they offered you earlier. They want you out of the way. To make it legal, they want to buy your property. That way, they can easily defend the payment with a real estate purchase, and you will be long gone. Any sane person would run away with that kind of money, and they figure you will also."

"How do I get out of this, Moe?" I said. "I don't know if I can create another Harry that quickly, and I'm sure they will come after me anyways."

"I suggest you call their bluff. Tell them you will give Harry the message and give him the number to contact them directly. You cannot do more than that, but once you receive the payment for the property, you will leave as well and Harry will call them with his new address. In either case, Harry will be gone and will never ever speak about this again. Harry will have to reveal himself to one of them. Once this is done, he will have to fake his death and disappear and disappear fast. After that is done, no one should ever hear from him again. That should do it, and you'd better get your ass out of there and move on. Start again in Hawaii or California, but do not come east. I hope you hear me and follow my advice. Keep your eyes open all the time and watch your back. They can't be trusted, ever. The only good guinea is a dead one. Keep one hand on the trigger, always," Moe said and hung up. I repeated everything to Carol and began preparations. Carol reaffirmed her loyalty and love for me and agreed to stand beside me all the way.

Monday, September 9, 1957

I woke up very early as there was a lot to do. I got Carol out of bed and sent her on way home and back to work. I needed this day for myself to prepare and cover my ass as best I could. I called Lew to tell him that I would call Westerly and give him the terms. I called Westerly at ten A.M. and let him know the terms and conditions of the deal. He said he would get back to me in a couple of hours; I set a time for one

P.M. to call him and resolve this. In the meantime, I made sure I had all my weapons ready for war.

I called Westerly as agreed. "You're right on time, Mr. Van Johnson. I like that in a person," he said.

"Okay, let's cut the shit and get right to the deal. Do we have one or not?" I said.

"You've got a deal. Please arrange to have your attorney call me with the details on the property. We want to resolve this fast. Payment will be made by Wednesday in cash delivered to your home or to your attorney. Have your attorney act on your behalf so the property can be transferred without your presence. Once payment is received, we will expect your end to be completed within twenty-four hours. Simple and very clean. By the week's end, you will no longer be here. Do you understand the arrangements?" he said in a very stern voice.

"Yes, I am clear on it all. Please let my attorney know when the funds will be dropped off so I may be prepared," I said and hung up.

I called Lew to let him know what I had agreed with Westerly. Lew advised me that he would have the papers ready for my signature tomorrow. I told him I would be by to sign the papers. I then called Carol and told her that we would be leaving this area in a few days and that she had better quit her job and pack up a few things she would like to take along.

I reminded her to travel light, because we must be quick and versatile. "We can buy anything we may need along the way," I told her.

I spent the rest of the day removing things from the house that I would need and destroying things I wouldn't really need. I would be travelling light so there would be a lot of stuff I wouldn't need. I packed my car and took a load over to the local church and let them know I was donating these items for the needy. The donations I made were greatly appreciated as the local priest said.

I called Al Fogel and explained the deal the best way I could and asked him if he wanted to disengage the security system or leave it as was. He said it was of no consequence and to just leave it.

Tuesday, September 10, 1957

The day was very uneventful as I checked with Carol to start packing a few things and be ready as we would be leaving this part of the country by the end of the week or sooner. No extra luggage, just a few essentials. We can buy anything we needed; we would have plenty of money.

It was around eight thirty when I heard the noise. It sounded like leaves being walked on. I was very upset with myself as I didn't turn on the security system. I prematurely thought things were settled, so any danger was now eliminated. Wrong again. I switched off the lights and put on my jacket and waited in the dark. There it was again, the rustling of the leaves, I was certain someone was there. I waited and waited. It seemed like forever, but it was only a few minutes. I heard the door lock being picked and then it slowly opened and all I could see was a big shadow, then a crash as someone or something was flying through the window. The guy at the front door opened fire with an automatic machine gun spraying bullets everywhere. I could see where the bullets were coming from and fired a shot at that target and then another; a cry of pain came as that person hit the floor hard. I was on the move and tried to locate the second killer. He had the same problem, but I knew the layout of the house, he didn't. I was crawling on the floor toward a switch that I could flip on and make whomever it was an easy target. I reached the switch and hit it; the room was lit up with a searchlight. There in the corner of the living room near the fireplace was a big guy standing with a gun in one hand and a rifle in the other.

He could not see at first as he was looking straight into the lights, then he spotted me on the floor and was just about to fire when I rolled over to one side and started to fire directing the shots to his crotch. From the angle I was on, I could not take a chance to aim anywhere else but his crotch. My first shot hit its mark, and he fell at once clutching his privates. His gun fell on the floor, and he was crying in pain. I jumped up and shot him through the left eye, and he was still.

I checked out the rest of the house to see if there were any other attackers and found none. What a mess and now I had to clean this up. It was a good thing I would not own this house much longer, it was really fucked up with bullet holes and blood stains. I locked the doors and set the alarm by passing the broken windows and left the dead bodies where they were and went to sleep.

Wednesday, September 11, 1957

I was up at dawn and went out to the woods with my shovel. I dug a giant hole to accommodate the two bodies. I dragged the bodies out to the hole in my wheelbarrow and placed them in and covered them up. I placed a lot of loose leaves over the freshly made hole and went back to the house. I now took a walk toward the road to locate their vehicle that they must have parked nearby. I soon found a black sedan parked neatly on the side of the road. I had a set of keys I found on the big guy and tried them in the ignition; it worked and the car started to purr. I moved the car away from the road and parked it in the woods where it would be safe for a day or two. I then went back to the house and started to clean up as best I could.

I called Carol and asked her to drive over to the house this evening as there were a few things I had to do and I needed her help. I now waited for the money to be delivered as promised. It was near six when a big black sedan drove up to the gate and rang. "Package for Mr. Van Johnson, where shall I leave it?" the voice said.

"Leave it by the gate, please," I said.

"Okay, I'm leaving it now," the voice said. I waited ten minutes and then made my way to the gate. I looked around in all directions and sat behind a tree for an additional twenty minutes to make certain there was no one else waiting. The coast looked clear, and in plain view, next to the post box was a brown parcel. I went there and picked it up and returned to the house. I opened the package to verify, and there it was two hundred and fifty K in cash.

I called Lew who was waiting for my call to tell him that I had been paid and would vacate the house tonight. He told me he had a signed copy of the sale and would keep it in his files. I thanked him for staying up late and waiting for my call.

I told him I would be at his office tomorrow morning to settle my bill with him. I was to leave a set of keys in the mail box as I had already signed all the papers, and Lew had promised that I would do so.

Carol arrived at six forty-five, and after a quick look, she just wanted to run away. I calmed her down, and we packed my car with a few things. Next we went to get the car from the woods. Carol followed me to the shopping center in Stroudsburg where we left the car parked and returned to the house. We then picked up Carol's car and drove to Allentown to Carol's house to get our trip under way.

Thursday, September 12, 1957

Not being a professional at this type of stuff, I was seriously shaken by how easily I had taken two lives. I know I shot others who were chasing me, but I never stayed behind to dispose of their bodies and remove all traces of them. This was a calculating and methodical action that seemed to come to me quite naturally. What the hell had I turned into? I keep telling myself that once the threats against my life were removed, things would return to normal. What bullshit, how do you get the stench of death out of your nostrils? How do you know when your thoughts will be rid of these types of things? I just felt sick inside and could imagine how someone who fought in a war felt when they killed someone or when they returned home. It was not a good feeling, and it does change your point of view on life. On the other side of the coin, I now felt invincible; I felt I could easily defeat this arrogant army of assholes who wanted to kill me. Most importantly, I had to be certain I did not leave any clues that could be used against me. When the Mob rubbed out another member, there was usually no repercussions. I hope this carried through for me. My next step was to produce Harry Miller, even if it was for a few minutes. Carole and I were now ready for our trip. All we had to do was to get in the car and move out. I took my car to an Okay used car lot in the auto district of Allentown and sold it for twelve hundred dollars. I needed fewer possessions and had to rid myself of anything they could trace. Carol had told her parents that we wanted to elope and spare them the expense of a large wedding. It was an easy decision on their part as they gave us their blessings.

I called Moe. "Hey there, what's going?" I said.

"Everything seems to be all right. The paperwork has been signed and sent over by messenger to their attorney's office. The property is a done deal."

"Now what do you want me to do?" he asked. "I have to give them, Harry, so I thought I'd have Harry call them and arrange a meet. I'll then send Harry to the meeting from a distance and then let him disappear. I'll have kept my promise, and I'll also disappear. It will just take a few hours to change my hair color, remove the shoes, and change back to Harry. What do you think, Moe?" I asked.

"It's dangerous, but has to be done. Just be very careful, Harry. I need you alive," Moe said.

"I have their number, and I'll call them to let them know that Harry will call first thing tomorrow morning at nine thirty. I think that will keep them at bay for now," I said.

"Good luck, my friend, and stay in touch and stay safe. I love you and want you safe always." He hung up as I stood there with the phone in my hand. It was the first time it all sunk in and I was scared. Carol and I drove to Philadelphia and stopped at a flea bag hotel room for the night. Tomorrow would be the start of a new adventure.

I had called Westerly to let him know that Harry would call him tomorrow morning and they could arrange a meet. My part would be over and I would disappear into thin air. He laughed and wished me good luck!

Friday, September 13, 1957

I was not a superstitious guy, but the coincidence of this being the thirteenth and all the things I had to do today made my mind boggle. I called Westerly and identified myself as Harry Miller. Upon doing so, he gave me another number to call. I called the new number at nine thirty and identified myself and asked who I was speaking to.

"I'm Vinnie," he said.

"I was told to call. Well, here I am," I said.

"Hold the line and I'll get the man. It'll only take a minute," he said.

"Hey, Vinnie listen to me, I'll call back in five minutes when the man is ready. I can't stay on the line, you understand," I hung up. I called back in exactly five minutes and Larry answered the phone.

"Hey, there, Harry, how are you?" he said. What luck, Larry recognized my voice and maybe I wouldn't have to set up a meet. "I'm fine, Larry, but a little tired of all this bullshit," I said.

"I know you are a stand-up guy, so why can't we just come to some arrangement? Let's set up a meet and work this out once and for all. You know I hate this shit, Harry. I like you and would like to see all this disappear and let us all go back to living large. Don't you want the same, Harry?" he said.

"Listen to me, Larry. I have not talked to anyone and will not talk to anyone. I don't know anything and just want to live somewhere in peace. Call off this war and no one ever has to worry about me. If you want a war, I promise you I'll take a lot of you motherfuckers with me. I don't want that, so let's agree to agree and move on," I said.

"That sounds great, Harry. I still think we should meet and iron out the kinks so we both can go on without looking over our shoulders. There is no need to threaten anyone. We are all business people here and want a peaceful and profitable solution," he said.

"I'll call you back in five minutes, Larry," and I hung up. I had to make sure the call was not being traced. I called back again from another phone,

"It's me again, Larry, and remember why I am calling. It's to simply resolve all this now! I won't talk to anyone, and I promise you have nothing to worry about, end of deal. No need to meet, no need to try to hurt me as you have tried to do up to now. With all your guys trying to whack me, I still did not go in and talk to anyone. That should be proof enough that I'm solid and will not involve anyone ever," I said.

"Listen, Harry, you know I can't speak for the family. They asked me to make sure it was you. They decide what has to be done, and they thought it would be best if you came in and presented your case to them. It will make things easier and then you can go on your way. The hit will be removed, and you can live wherever you want. What do you say, Harry!" Larry said.

"I will not present this to them in person. If you want me to plead my case, set up a conference call of some kind, and I will talk to all of them by phone. No other way is acceptable, take it or leave it!" I said.

"I can't make that decision on my own. Call me back in one hour and we will conclude this. How is Rachel? I hope she is well and the baby is doing well. She should be due any day now. Please send her my love and tell her I care about her."

I said, "Thanks for asking, Harry, she is fine and both are doing fine. The baby is due anytime now and you can bet I'll give her your message." He hung up.

Carol and I checked out of the hotel and decided to drive to Atlantic City. Although the season was over, the pier was still a busy place. It was a different location than Philly, just in case they may have gotten lucky and traced the call.

We arrived in Atlantic City at eleven fifteen and decided not to take any hotel room as we may not stay here long enough. I found a phone and called Larry. "Hi, it's me, Larry, have we got a deal or not? I don't have much time to spare," I said.

"I spoke with the man and he said he wants a face-to-face. I explained that you will not accept a face-to-face meeting. He was pissed, but finally calmed down. He wants a meeting on Tuesday, you on the phone and the council on the other end. Call me on Monday at ten P.M., and I'll give you the number to the meeting and the time," he said,

"I think that is the best way," I said. "I'll call you Tuesday morning at ten and you can give me the number then. You see, Larry, I'm trying to protect you and the boys. I don't want any funny business. I just want this to be over." I hung up and got Carol and decided to leave Atlantic City. We'll head for Detroit where we would sell the car. I would get things done in Detroit under a new name that I had arranged earlier through Al Fogel. A new driver's license, passport, and utility bill in case. Alan Berry was ready for his new life and his new car. We also decided to get married in Atlantic City; it was only eleven thirty, so we had plenty of time. We went to one of those quick marriage places just off the Boardwalk and an hour later we were Mr. and Mrs. Alan Berry of Jersey City, New Jersey.

Saturday, September 14, 1957

I guess Friday the thirteenth was not so unlucky. Here I was a new man, married and on my way to Detroit with more than a quarter million dollars in my car. Life was not that bad and with a little luck it would only get better. Of course, I never looked into the divorce Rachel was handling. I just might be married to two women although my marriage to Carol was under a different name. I wondered what the law was under those circumstances.

Sunday, September 15, 1957

We arrived in Detroit and stayed in our hotel room all day. We had room service sent up and made love. There was no reason to go anywhere and risk being seen; I reminded Carol that there was still a hit out on Harry Miller. It was great to just stay inside and enjoy each other's company for a change.

I took out my make-up bag and with Carol's help changed my hair color once again and added a mustache. Carol had a great time making me up. It was now a game for her, and I was thankful she felt so relaxed.

Monday, September 16, 1957

With my new look and time to kill I put on a big fedora as we took a sightseeing tour of Detroit. We visited the General Motors plant in Dearborn and saw a lot of other sights. We decided to go Windsor, Ontario, just over the bridge on the Canadian side and have dinner there. We just had a great day without incident!

Tuesday, September 17, 1957

I called Larry at ten, and he gave me a number to call at exactly noon. I found a phone that would be out of the way and made sure I hade plenty of change. I picked up five rolls of quarters; fifty dollars should be more than enough. Carol was with me as she waited in the car next to the pay phone.

"Okay, Larry, it's me, Harry. What's the deal?" I asked.

"I want to make sure you don't turn against us in any way. I want a meet so we can cement a deal and move on. What do you think of that, Harry?" he said.

"Let me give it to you straight, Larry. You guys have been trying to kill me for a long time now. There is a hit out against me sanctioned by the council. I have been able to hide away from you and your boys, and I haven't once gone to the law and said anything against you. If this is not enough proof to you and the council that I am not going to talk to anyone and just want to be left alone, then I guess we have to continue this war. I don't trust you and you don't trust me, yet I have proven one thing to all of you—I am not a stool pigeon. What more can I do that I have not done up to now? A meeting will not be a face-to-face meet, not today, tomorrow, or ever. Let's just agree that I will leave you alone and you will leave me alone! No other way, capish?" I said with authority.

"Please deposit another five dollars or your call will be interrupted," a voice spoke into the phone. I deposited the coins and continued my conversation with Larry.

"You must be nuts to think we will just walk away and forget you, Harry," Larry said.

"Then there is no further reason for us to continue this conversation any longer," I said.

"Harry, be reasonable, all we want is to meet and agree in person then you go your way and we'll go ours. We just can't forget this so easily because you said so. Omertà is our motto, and we respect your continuing to follow that path. So why not meet?" he said with a little anger in his voice. There was no doubt he was getting hot, and if I was in front of him, he would have killed me then and there.

"Look, Larry," I said raising my voice a little. "I will call you back tomorrow at this number at noon and give you my answer, I have to run now." I hung up and jumped back into the car. "Let's go, honey; I don't want to hang around here any longer," I said. Off we went to the hotel to check out and move on. I thought it would be best if we went to Toronto and called from there, just in case there was any trace taking place. This war was far from over, and it was time to be on my guard at all times.

Wednesday, September 18, 1957

Instead of Toronto, we went to Niagara Falls and went over to the Canadian side and spent the night there. I was ready to call Larry again, and this time I would tell him that if he wants a war he'll get one, or he could easily work it all out, and we could both live in peace.

I waited until noon and called the number once again, Larry answered the phone on one ring. "Harry, I see you are on time. Did you decide what you want to do?" he asked.

"Here is the deal, Larry. No changes, no discussion. Is your council there? I want to talk to all of them at the same time as we agreed," I said.

"The council is all present and listening. You are talking to them all, please go ahead," he said.

"If you want an agreement in writing, you can draw one up and forward to it to my attorney, and he will review it, and I will then sign it. After I sign it, he will return your copy to you and we will all have copies. You go your way and I go mine, and that is the end of it. If we are to be honest with one another, then answer this simple question. Since when did you people need a signed contract? If you feel that an agreement will prevent me from ever testifying or cooperating with the feds or anyone else, then please make one up, and I will sign it without hesitation. I will go live my life under another name, and you will never hear from me or about me again," I said loud and clear.

"Well, that sounds good, Harry, but you have to meet with the council. They want to see you and make the terms and conditions very clear, no other way will do. If you don't do this, Harry, you will have the full force of the council against you, and I guarantee you, winning will be impossible. I don't want to see you all fucked up, so agree and we will set up a meet," he said.

"I don't agree with that logic, but if that is the only way we can end this, then I am willing to organize a meeting. I want you all to see that my desire to resolve this is real and must be fair for both of us. I never asked to be picked up by the feds, and I never agreed with them or anyone else to give them any information. The funniest thing is I know so little about your operation that I could not, even if I wanted to which I don't, give them any information at all. I'll call you back tomorrow at this number, and we can see what we can do about this." I hung up and went back to the hotel to talk to Carol. I called Moe and told him the story and asked his opinion. He said I should wait until he made a few calls and get back to him tomorrow morning.

Carol and I went out for dinner and talked about all the possibilities. It was quite a burden for her as she never had to worry about such things like life and death before. She was a trooper and did her very best to understand just how serious all this was.

Thursday, September 19, 1957

We checked out of the hotel and drove on to Toronto where we felt we could disappear a lot more easily. I called Moe at nine thirty, and he took my number of the payphone and called me back instantly.

"Hi, Harry, how are you?" he said.

"I'm fine, Moe. I just need a little guidance with all this," I said.

"Okay, here is the best I can do. I spoke to some very powerful people and they all tell me the same thing. If you do not meet with them, they will organize their entire organization to rub you out. They will offer one million for your death, and it will only be a matter of time. If you go to a meeting, you will not be hurt. These guys are proud of their word even though they are known to kill people. They have never personally killed anyone, or that is what they would like the world to believe. I think they want to see you, to see your face, and to make it clear that you are a dead man if one word is uttered by you.

"Remember, Harry, they have their hands everywhere, and one day they will find you especially when you feel safe and it will be easier to kill you. I suggest you organize the meeting with them and get it over with. You can easily take your time. Set it up for next week. You can request that you bring me along and see if that will fly. If they want you dead, they certainly don't want it at a meeting of the council," Moe said.

"Wow," I said, "that is a mind blower, Moe. I just can't see myself going into the lion's den. I understand what you want me to do, but I am very nervous about it. It scares the shit out of me!. Let me think about it and call you back in a day or two." I hung up and went back to discuss this with Carol.

Friday, September 20, 1957

I spent the day with Carol just hanging out and talking about the proposition. I felt it was time to stop running and to try to settle things right and maybe I could finally start a new life. I had plenty of money and could easily open a business or just get a good job, but in either case I could start to breathe and think about having children and starting a family. On the other hand, I also felt that I couldn't trust these guys with anything. What a dilemma. I called Moe and told him that I would set up the meeting and would let him know what day. He agreed with me as he felt it was the right thing to do, and the chances of getting killed were just about zero.

Saturday, September 21, 1957

End of summer and I was looking to end all this violence and living like an animal. I had to reinvent myself so that when I do meet with them they'll see the real Harry Miller. Carol and I spent the rest of day removing all my make-up. She was finally able to look at the real Harry Miller, and she was not at all disappointed.

Sunday, September 22, 1957

We went back to Niagara Falls to see one of the wonders of the world again. We had a great time and then had dinner at one of the restaurants near the falls. We wanted to see the falls lit up at night, so we stayed until after dark and had a great time seeing the falls in all their glory.

Monday, September 23, 1957

I called Moe and told him I was still trying to reach them and would call him back as soon as I set up a meeting date. I assured him I was fine and that we were safe. We spent the rest of the day driving in around Toronto seeing things that we probably would never see again.

Tuesday, September 24, 1957

I contacted Larry Casparizzi, no matter if he liked it or not.

"Hello, Larry, it's me Harry. How are you?" I said.

"Well, blow me down," Larry said. "What is the occasion that you honor me with a phone call? After our last conversations, I thought you were going to talk directly with the council?"

"Well, let me get right to it, Larry. All of this shit began with you and hopefully it will end with you. I have tried to get in touch with the council but no one answers the number I had. You will have to be the moderator and handle the details and help get this circus shut down once and for all. I will bring my lawyer with me to any meeting we set up and we can conclude everything with one meeting. The situation is this as you already know, I have shown that I have no interest in talking to the feds or to anyone else and this crap of having a contract out on me is wrong. The council wants to meet face-to-face to resolve all this and I agree. The key point is that The council will stop this nonsense and useless violence directed against me, and we can each go our separate ways. Easy enough, isn't it, Larry?" I said.

"It sounds that way, Harry, so why call me?" he said.

"As I said, Larry, I want you to set up the meeting at a place that is safe for all of us. I will bring my lawyer with, and we will have a sit down and get this worked out. I just want assurance that my life will be safe," I said.

"How will I get in touch with you, Harry?" he said.

"Don't worry, I'll call you on Thursday at ten A.M., and you can tell me the day and time. We will set up another call to get the location fifteen minutes before, so there will not be any fucking around by anyone," I said.

"Hold your hat, Harry, how do you know I'm not full of shit?" Larry said.

"I don't, Larry, but I have to trust someone, and I have picked you. In all the time I have known you, I know that your word is good. Call the big bosses and let them know that I called and am ready to meet! Let them know that we are operating on our word of honor and shall be honest and above board at all times," I said.

"That sounds good to me, Harry, I'll get in touch with them and we will arrange everything. By the way, Harry, Rachel is due any day now. I think it may be today or tomorrow. When you call me, I may have news for you," Larry said.

"I got to go, Larry, just do your job and things will be fine." I hung up and left the area at once. I grabbed Carol and got the hell out of Niagara and drove back to Toronto.

Wednesday, September 25, 1957

We decided to get moving and begin our drive back to New York. There was no reason to hang out in Toronto. I called Moe and told him our plans, and off we went. It was an eight-hour drive, and I wasn't in any mood to take forever to get there. I also didn't want a ticket so we kept to the speed limit and arrived in Yonkers at about six.

"I think we should find a place here in Yonkers and relax tonight. Tomorrow, I'll call Larry and then Moe and make the arrangements for our meeting. It'll all be over in a week or less, sweetheart," I said as I leaned over and kissed her gently on the cheek.

"Harry, I'm scared," Carol said, "How do you know you can trust these people? I'm very nervous about all this and want it to end. I thought it would be easy, but these people scare the shit out of me."

"I know how you feel, sweetheart," I said softly. "But this is the only way out for us. Once I get the agreement from these goons, we will be able to go away and start a new life. We have plenty of money and each other, and all we need is some peace of mind and we could possibly be starting our life together without looking over our shoulders. Be brave and trust me. I won't let anything happen to you, I promise."

"Harry, I do trust you. It's the Mob I don't trust. They are killers, murderers, and psychopaths and have no word of honor. They kill people for less reason than you can imagine. I heard about them cutting off people's balls and stuffing it in their mouths. This is not the way nice people act, so please don't tell me not to worry, please, Harry!" she said as tears began running down her face.

"You're right Carol, they are bad people, but they also have a code of honor that they do pride themselves in keeping. Don't ask me why they act that way, but they do. As a matter-of-fact, I'm not sure I could trust our government anymore than I can the Mob," I said.

We pulled into a motel just off route 87, and I registered a room under the name of Mr. and Mrs. Arthur Morgan of Albany. I put down some bogus address and paid for one night in full. We went to a nearby Howard Johnson for dinner and ate in almost total silence, then returned to the motel. Once in the motel, I walked around the cabin to make sure there were no suspicious characters hanging about.

I parked the car at the opposite end of the lot and returned to the cabin. I could not relax and felt very uncomfortable; I kept pulling apart the drapes and looking out the window to see if anyone was about.

Finally, I said to Carol, "I am not happy at this place. I just feel it in my bones. Let's get out of here and find another place to stay. I think they may find us here, and even if I am wrong, I still don't feel good about this place. Let's move *now*, Carol."

We packed our one small bag and moved slowly down the parking lot toward our vehicle. No one was around, so we jumped in and pulled out and drove into New York. I took the Fifty-Ninth Street Bridge to Queens and found a motel on Queens Boulevard in Flushing. We parked the car on the street and walked back to the motel. I felt a little more at ease, but not relaxed. I needed peace and hoped we could get this resolved fast.

Finally, I started to relax and said to Carol, "I know they are very bad people and that they don't give a shit about anyone but themselves. Let me tell you, Carol, when I was working at Larry's, there was this guy, who was a compulsive gambler and borrowed three grand from Larry's racetrack bookie. Of course, he lost it all, and now his total debt was over ten grand. With their method of interest, it wasn't long before he owed double. He brought cash over to the office daily, small amounts like five hundred, three hundred to help keep these guys off his back. One day he disappeared. No one knew where he was. His wife was frantic, and she finally called the cops and reported him missing. They found him in a garbage bag at the dump. He had his balls stuffed in his mouth and was dead as can be. He had been shot through the head, the balls was the message loud and clear as to what was in store to anyone who tried to stiff the Mob. It wasn't a mystery who killed him! I don't know for sure who actually killed him, but I can guess. A week later, his wife received a visit from one of Larry's boys and was presented with an IOU for thirty grand signed by her husband. They knew he had a life insurance policy and that she was going to get paid very soon. They let her know that they expected payment in full, and by the way, they mentioned how cute the kids were. She didn't need a clearer message—take care of this debt or else. Guess what the total of the insurance was thirty-five K, yes they wanted most of it, and they got it. So if you want to know who we are dealing with, these guys are the type of people we have to deal with.

"Ironically, they were approached by our government during World War II to spy for them in Italy and get them information that was vital to the war effort they did so and kept their end of the bargain, and the American Government did not keep theirs. So we have people that have two sets of rules and one must understand them. The case of the father who was eliminated shows their reaction to being directly harmed and setting an example. He took them for money; no one can get away with that as it would ruin their reputation. Fear is their bosom buddy, and as long as everyone respects that there is peace. They paid him back, and no one else was involved or in danger. In their opinion, this scumbag, if he truly loved his family, would never have sunken to the level of losing so much money that he would put them in danger. They killed the rat because he was nothing more than the lowest of the lowest and fucked them and everyone in his path. Would they really hurt his kids? Who knows? But the fear factor is there. So the debt is paid. Most of the time, these Mob guys do not kill people who were not involved one way or another. I should make that a little clearer, intentionally is the proper way of putting it."

"Well, Harry, what that tells me is that these low life's are scum and we better stay clear. They don't make deals with those who directly affect them. Your words and your story can tell me that we should be very careful how we take all their actions," she said.

"I guess you are right about that, and that is the reason I want a face-to-face meeting so that we can eliminate this conflict and prove I'm not a threat," I said.

"Just great, Harry, they will agree to anything and kill you later. Don't you understand? You are a liability as long as you are alive. They don't know how much you know. They assume you know a lot more than you should," she shouted at me. "Harry, wake up. It's war, a matter of survival, and we are in the middle of it, like it or not."

Sleep didn't come easy, but we had to get some rest or we would be screwed. We couldn't fight amongst ourselves as that would lead to us losing all reasoning and allowing them the advantage. No way could we give in, and I won't let them win no matter what.

Thursday, September 26, 1957

I woke up very early, as usual, and decided to let Carol sleep. I showered and dressed and took a long walk on this beautiful morning. The leaves were turning yellow, red, and brown. The air smelled fresh and the sky was clear and blue. It seemed like this would be a great day. I walked along Queens Boulevard, always alert to my surroundings. This early in the morning, traffic was light, and I was able to see a car a little distance away that looked like it could be one of the Mob cars. It was black with whitewall tires and had every appearance like a black Cadillac. Of course, the car was at least three or four hundred feet away, so I could not be certain.

My gut feeling was that this car was dangerous. My attention was further aroused when the black Cadillac got a little closer and was moving at a very low speed. This section of Queens Boulevard is a divided roadway with service roads as well. I was walking toward the Fifty-Ninth Street Bridge, and the car was on the other side of the median going toward Long Island. It was coming toward me on the other side of the boulevard and really moving very slowly. I didn't like the look of it, so I turned off Queens Boulevard on to Reid Street and made sure I would be able to keep the car in my sights. I walked at a leisurely pace so that I could check on the car. I made another turn and stopped behind the corner of an apartment building and peeked out toward Queens Boulevard. The car increased in speed, and at the first break in the median, it made a U-turn and started to come back toward me. I knew that my expectation of this being a great day was to be short lived; it was going to be a bad one.

At first, I thought they could not be after me. No way could they be that smart, they didn't know that I was here in New York. Then I realized that I was Harry Miller, no disguise, no hiding, just plain old me. I never gave it any thought, but they must have circulated my photo to every hotel in New York and the Burroughs. They must have offered a nice reward for anyone who would call to advise them that they have located me. Because of the upcoming meeting, I was staying as Harry Miller for the council and never gave it any thought. It turned out that I was safer in Yonkers than New York City. What a fool I was!

My choices were to stand my ground and let it play out and fight it out or I run and hide. I was very uncertain what to do. In the first place,

I didn't know how many people were in the car. I also didn't know if they have spotted me or not? Did they turn around because they wanted to stop at the hotel I am staying at to see the informer? Did they turn around because they saw me and now want to whack me and collect the reward?

My second thought, I was only one against more than one for certain. I was in an open space, where I was an easy target. As my heart was pounding and I was trying to gather my thoughts, I noticed a small alley. One problem it had a steel gate and it was locked. I made the only decision I could in the limited amount of time I had, like less than ten seconds, to climb the gate. It was only about eight feet high, but I was agile and scared out of my mind, and it was the only chance I had.

My adrenalin came was at its highest peak and I also didn't have any other choice I had to get my ass out of there now! I jumped on the gate as high as I could and grabbed a cross member. I pulled myself up with every ounce of strength I had and was able to reach the top. I hung over the other side and dropped the remaining three feet to the ground. I hit the ground running as I was just able to reach a row of metal garbage cans. I ducked behind the farthest one, held my breath, and waited as the car appeared moving very slowly. The car continued past the building, I lost sight of it and could not chance moving.

I waited for what seemed like a very long time and was about to move when the car reappeared and parked a few feet from the locked gate. I could easily see the street and the car as two very large and menacing-looking guys exited the back seat. I could hear them clearly that was how close they were.

"You stay in the car and honk the horn if you see anything. We are going to check out the buildings. He has to be here somewhere. He could be living in one of the apartments under any name, so be careful and find the bastard. We are not leaving this street until we find him. Let's get to it and, Vinnie, remember there is a lot of bread riding on this guy's ass. Angelo said when he called us that he saw this guy on Queens Boulevard. and wasn't sure where he lived, so we have to check everything out in this area. I also think the guy we spotted walking along the Boulevard was our mark, so be very careful, he is around here somewhere," he said.

"This was great. Here I am in a box, and I can't move. I also have to call Larry at ten and can't miss that, shit, shit, and shit."

In everyone's life, there are times when luck plays a part, I could use some now. As I stayed crouched I heard a noise behind me, I turned back to see what was up when I saw the service door to the back of the building begin to open. I move to the other row of cans and stayed very low as the rear door opened. I had my gun in my hand and was ready to blast my way out if I had to. A short, stocky man appeared carrying a pail of ashes. He opened one of metal pails and dumped the ashes into it. I saw an opportunity that may not be there in a few seconds, he had left the door open, and I slipped quickly and quietly over to the door and went inside. I stopped, as my heart was pounding as I heard voices, It was coming from outside, and it was a conversation between the short guy and one of the Mob giants.

"Hey did you see a guy about six feet tall, one hundred and eighty pounds, wearing a blue jacket and khaki pants anywhere around here?" The Mob guy said.

"No, I don't see anybody," he said.

"Do me favor check behind those cans and see if there is anyone hiding there."

"No one be here, the gate is always locked, and I have the key. No one here," he said as he walked toward the garbage cans and looked. "See no one here, what you want with this guy?" he asked.

"He owes me some money and I thought he might live here in this neighborhood," the Mob guy said.

"No new people here same tenants for years, no new people," the guy responded.

"Thanks for your help," the Mob guy said and left. I ran down the hall and ducked into a stairwell when I heard the rear door close and lock. His footsteps were getting closer to where I was. I frantically looked around to see if there was any place for me to hide.

I noticed a door and a sign that said, "Stairs." It must lead to the basement or the upper floors, good or bad I had no choice but to take it. I ran up the stairs and into another hallway with doorways every ten of fifteen feet.

I was in the apartment building hallway with nowhere to go. I walked down the hallway toward the elevators and saw a door with no number on it but a sign "Incinerator" I took a chance and opened it. There I was looking at a garbage chute where everyone drops their bags of refuse. I remained in that small room for a few minutes, even though I could be discovered at anytime I had no choice once again. I remained in the incinerator closet and waited in the dark. It seemed like I was there for hours, but it was actually only twenty minutes when I heard footsteps approaching. I immediately stood with my hand on the garbage chute door as an elderly woman opened the door.

"Oh my, I am sorry. Did I frighten you?" she said.

"No, not at all. I was just finished. Let me get out of your way," I said as I walked out into the hallway.

I made an attempt to fumble in my pocket, as I stood in front of an apartment door. "Oh my god, I must have left my key inside, and no one's home," I said as the woman closed the garbage chute door and looked directly at me and said, "Young man, that is terrible. But if you go see Ivan, he will be able to let you in. He is in apartment fourteen in the basement."

"Thanks a lot. I feel so stupid, Mrs . . . . I am sorry I never got your name. I'm Richard Smith," I said.

"Margaret Swenson, a pleasure to meet you. If you should need anything at all please knock on my door no. 233," she said.

"You are so kind, Mrs. Swenson. Thank you very much and have a very nice day," I said as I walked toward the stairway.

I descended to the ground floor and proceeded to the front door, as I wanted to get a look at the situation on the street. I had to get out of here fast. The car was still there, and there was a guy sitting behind the wheel. He appeared to be asleep, but I didn't think I could take the chance to try walk out of the building. I decided to remove my jacket and take a chance at leaving the building through the front door. I figured they must have searched the front of the building already, and if they weren't near this one, they might be up the block. I could not stay in the vestibule forever. I made my way out the front door and turned toward Queen's Boulevard. The guy in the car didn't move, and I could not see anyone up the street. I turned the corner and started to jog as I wanted to get out of the area as quickly as possible. At the first light, I crossed Queens Boulevard and hailed a cab. That was a close call. It took all my strength away as my heart beat faster than ever before. I have to call Larry and get things set up. It was eight forty; I still had some time.

I had the cab drop me off on Queens Boulevard, three blocks away from the hotel. I walked the rest of the way and wasted no time in hustling Carol out of the bathroom. I explained very quickly what had happened and started packing the few things we had in the room.

"Let's get out of here now. I don't trust anyone and cannot figure how these bastards had a clue that this area was where to look. I just don't buy the coincidence factor. It's too easy, way too easy," I said as I picked up the suitcase and gave Carol that hurry up look! We left the hotel and walked the few blocks to the car. We proceeded along Queens Boulevard to the Fifty-Ninth Street bridge and crossed over to Manhattan and proceeded north to the George Washington Bridge and crossed over to Fort Lee in New Jersey.

It was now nine thirty-five, so I decided to stop at a Howard Johnson for some breakfast and make my call to Larry. Where we go from here will depend on the results of this call.

I called exactly at ten, "Hello, Larry, hope you have some real good news for me," I said.

"Sure do!" Larry said. "We want to set the meet up for Saturday around one P.M."

"Where are we meeting? Who is going to be there? Larry, give me some details, I need the truth, now!" I said.

"I can't tell you the location today for security reasons. I'm sure you understand that. You will call me on Saturday about fifteen minutes before the meet, and I will tell you where to meet me, and we will proceed from there to the rendezvous. There cannot be any discussion on this. We cannot take any risks and will not. The council will not be there, but their representatives will be. They will have received their instructions and can speak for the bosses. There will be no tricks, no bullshit. We will try to come to an agreement and you walk, simple as that," he said.

"Wait a minute, Larry, it all sounds so easy, but what protects me from getting whacked once we are alone or anytime?" I said.

"I thought about that, Harry. So we will set up an easy guarantee to make sure you are safe. I'll tell you about it when you call on Saturday. I'm sure it will work for both of us and get this bullshit out of the way, and we can all move on. Harry, let's get this shit done with we all have things to do other than chase each other. We have a history between us, even though you think I'm full of shit, I still don't want to see anything happen to you. Trust me, Harry, it will work out," Larry said very convincingly.

"I'd love to believe you, Larry," I said. "But if we are on the brink of an agreement, why are your guys still out there looking for me? I thought the hit was called off? I'm ready to blow away anyone who tries to hurt me. Believe me, I have the weapons to do it and am very good at it. We don't need a war, but if you want one, you'll get it."

"Harry, hold on to your hat, no one is out there looking to whack you. Word went out a few days ago that the hit is no longer valid," he said. "I can't believe anyone would be trying to fuck with us. Take my word, Harry, the hit is off, but I'd still be careful because there may be some renegade who thinks he can make some brownie points by whacking you. Protect yourself at all times, even though I know the hit was cancelled."

"I hope you are straight, Larry, if you bullshit me, I swear I'll hunt you down and kill you and everyone near you. I want peace and won't be fucked over by anyone, trust me, Larry. I have the means and will carry it out no matter what happens to me. I'll call you on Saturday at twelve. Let's get the show on the road."

"I got it, Harry, and congratulations! You are a father of seven-and-a-half-pound baby girl. Rachel had the baby last night, and both are doing well. She sends her love and wants you to know that she will always be there for you. Your daughter is gorgeous, and she is going to be a stunner. You guys certainly know how to make beautiful kids," Larry said.

"Thanks, Larry, for the update. Please send my love to Rachel and tell her I will get in touch once I am settled. Please give her and the baby my love," I said and hung up as it was no longer necessary to repeat the same crap over and over.

We left the Fort Lee area and proceeded along route 80 to Pennsylvania. It was my feeling that the last place anyone would look for us was where we began, so we might as well spend the next couple of days somewhere near out of harm's way.

Friday, September 27, 1957

We spent the night in Stroudsburg, Pennsylvania, in an obscure hotel off the main street. Nothing fancy, but effective for our purpose—to stay out of sight and get ready for tomorrow and the big meeting. I took Carol to the Pocono archery and gun range, as we practiced our shooting skills for more than three hours. I didn't know that Carol was such a good shot, but she was. She let me in on the secret that she went hunting with her dad many times and learned to shoot when she was just ten years old. Our guns were, hot and we were good at it, we were ready for the Mob, to bring them on!

Saturday, September 28, 1957

It was raining pretty hard when we woke at seven forty-five. We dressed and packed our things, as we had to get on the road very soon.

It was at least a three-hour trip back to Manhattan. We didn't want to rush it and wanted to be fully relaxed. If we took our time, we could think clearly and eliminate errors in judgment as best we could. We had to deal from strength. These assholes only respected power, and we had to make certain we displayed that at all time. If we showed any signs of weakness, they would take advantage of us and probably whack us. I explained all this to Carol last night, and she understood this very well. Even if all was an act, it was one that had to be played out if we were to succeed. There was no room for error, and I was determined to make sure we didn't make any.

We arrived in Manhattan at eleven thirty through the Holland Tunnel and proceeded to Tribeca, where things were very quiet on a Saturday morning in comparison to weekdays. We found a phone booth and parked nearby. It was noon. We had a little time on our hands. Just enough to ready ourselves and make us more composed for the meeting.

At twelve thirty, I called Larry to get the details. "Hi, Larry, how are you doing?" I said.

"I'm okay now that you have called. Let's get down to details. We will meet at the corner of Eighty-Third and Third on the Northwest corner. I will meet you there, and we will then proceed to the meeting place. I know you wanted to bring your attorney with you, but I don't think that is a good idea. The insurance factor is very simple. We will have Frank Costarino escort you to the meet. As you know Frank is now retired, but he is a well respected person with the Mob. You know Frank is a very well-known person and has a reputation of being a man of his word. He has agreed to be the guarantor of your safety and, as you also know, Frank does not like to get involved in stuff like this, but he has agreed to do so. In this way, there will not be any deceit on anyone's part. He lives on Eighty-Sixth Street near Lexington, and your wife can stay at his home while you are having your meeting. I think that is a sign of good faith and should make you happy," he said.

"Okay, Larry, I'll accept this token of good faith and will meet you. I want you to understand one more thing. I have left a full accounting of the operations of the loan business and anything else I may know about the Mob. I have left this with very responsible people who will turn it over to the proper authorities if anything should happen to me. If all is okay, it will be destroyed once I have left town. Now that we understand each other, what time do you want me to meet you?" I said.

"I want you there by one fifteen. I will wait until one twenty and then leave. Don't be late." He hung up.

I drove as fast as I could as I took Third Avenue all the way uptown. Because Saturday traffic was lot lighter than during the week. We made it by one ten, as I parked on Eighty-Fourth Street between Lexington and Third Avenue. We walked to the corner of Eighty-Third and Third and waited no more than a minute when Larry showed up.

"Well, Harry, you haven't changed a bit," he said.

"Neither have you, Larry. Is it all set?" I said.

"We will meet with the big boys in one hour. Leave the broad here or we can take her over to Frank's place. We can't take anyone else along. You are the only one that can meet these people," he said.

I went over to Carol and spoke with her softly, "I'm going to go with Larry now, I can't take you with. I'm sorry, but they just won't go for that."

"Harry, I'm afraid. I have this feeling I may never see you again. Please, don't go, please," she pleaded.

"Listen to me, Carol, I must play this through, or there will never be any chance of peace. You leave the car where it is and come with us. We will drop you off at Frank's place. You can wait there, and I'll be back as soon as I can. Do not worry. Nothing is going to happen to us. They don't want any shit to start to fall. I know it will be all right. Please, don't make waves now. We are real close to finalizing this. It was all a mistake from the start, and I believe I can get it all put to rest, please, trust me, please!" I pleaded in the gentlest voice I could muster.

I was nervous as hell, but I wasn't going to let her know. I needed her to be strong and believe that all will be okay very soon.

"Okay, Larry, let's get going. We'll drop Carol off at Frank's," I said confidently.

Larry raised his arm, and like magic, a big, black limousine appeared.

The driver jumped out of the car and opened the rear door so that we could get in. He was a giant or at least appeared to be at least seven feet tall. He was as wide as he was tall with hands the size of basketballs.

We got in to the limousine, as I tried to relax, especially for Carol's sake. "Great looking limo, plenty of room. I'm glad I command a car like this," I said with confidence. We drove a few blocks as we took Third Avenue to Eighty-Sixth Street and turned left. We drove a couple of blocks and pulled over. The giant left his driver's position and opened the passenger door. He spoke to Carol, "Mam, will you please follow me?"

Carole said nothing, as she looked at me. She was frightened but committed to carry this through. She loved me a lot and was willing to put her life on the line if need be.

We waited fifteen minutes and the door opened once again, and this very distinguished man entered. Larry made the introductions, "Harry, Mr. Frank Costarino," he said.

I extended my hand and was gripped by a strong and confident handshake. "A pleasure to meet you, Harry. I do hope we will have pleasant and fruitful meeting?" he said very pleasantly.

He was dressed in a very expensive looking suit, a white shirt, and tie. If this was the picture of gangster, then the public was very misinformed. This guy could have passed for a bank president, an attorney, a doctor; he was very distinguished.

"Let me make as few things clear, gentlemen," he said in a very soft but firm tone. "I was asked to be the guarantor in a dispute I know nothing about. I agreed to guarantee the safety of Harry and his wife and this I will do. I was also asked to listen and give an opinion to the council. This I will do. And I will be fair and unbiased in listening to both sides of the dispute. I am guaranteeing your safety, so you have nothing to worry about. Tell the truth, and all will be fine. You will be returned to Manhattan unharmed regardless of my decision. You have my word on that. We will conduct this meeting in a civil and respectful manner at all times and will not let personal feelings get in the way at any time. I hope I have myself clear? By the way, gentlemen, if you have any questions, please feel free to ask them," he added.

We drove for at least another forty-five minutes. I could tell we crossed over a bridge and drove at some pretty high speeds. The windows in the limo were so dark that I could hardly see out and I was not able to look through the windshield because I was sitting in the jump seat facing Larry and Frank. As time went on, I tried to make conversation with Frank Costarino.

"It is a great pleasure to meet you Mr. Costarino. I really appreciate your taking your time to help resolve this. Do you know how much longer it will be until we get there?" I said.

"I'm sorry, but I don't know where we are going either. I'd be happy to tell you if I knew," he responded in a gentle tone.

Finally, we arrived and Larry advised me that I would have to wear a blindfold. He produced a large black cloth and carefully placed it over my eyes.

"Okay, let's go," Larry said. We left the limo and walked about one hundred yards. I paced them off, just in case I need to know where I was sometime in the future. We entered a large room that was devoid of any furniture at all. I could tell by the sound of our footsteps as there was an echo. That signified to me that the room was void of any furniture. We walked a little further, until I heard a door close and another door open. We had walked into another room. Once we entered the final room, I heard the door close and my blindfolded was removed. The room was windowless and had nothing in it other than a large table surrounded by fifteen chairs. There were four people sitting at one end of the table. On the other side, there were two very large bodyguards in black suits, and two more were on the other side.

"Sit," one of the big giants said to me pointing to a chair near the far end of the table. I sat down and just stared ahead at the faces of those at the other end. If they wanted to kill me, this was the place and the time. There was no way I could get out of this place, and I did not have any weapon with me.

I sat there mesmerized by the surreal scene that has unfolded before me. Wow, what a way to go! I thought. I was so deep in thought that I didn't hear the door open behind me as a tall man wearing a beautiful suit with an open-collared shirt walked in and nodded to everyone.

"Are we all set here? Let's get this show on the road. I got things I gotta do!" he said.

I still didn't know who he was and who the others were, as no one bothered to make any introductions. I didn't say a word in the last fifteen minutes. I just sat there in a daze, wondering how I am ever going to get out of here alive.

"Harry, what is this shit we hear about you?" the new guy said.

"I don't understand what shit you are talking about. And I don't like having a hit put on me. I'm not any threat to anyone and know even less. Why am I being singled out?" I asked as firmly as I could.

"Cut the crap, Harry, you know why we are here, and all we want to do is resolve this so that we can all go back to our peaceful lives and enjoy what we have. You were going to talk to the cops. We know that and we can't have that. You know our agreement is to keep our business private at all times. No wives, no friends, no one knows what you or anyone else does. I'm sure that is very clear, Harry?" he said in a very menacing tone.

"Let me talk for a minute, okay?" I said.

"Talk," the big man said.

"I woke up one morning and two cops were at my door with some phony papers placing me under arrest. They told me I have to go with them and have no other choice. They wouldn't give me anymore details, and I could not make any phone calls. They took me to a place on Broadway and Sixteenth Street. No one was there. It was a fucking old station that was abandoned. They tried to offer me deals of every kind if I would agree to tell them everything I know about Larry's operation and who is behind it all. They said they have films of what goes on and can put me away for life if I don't cooperate. I told them they were full of shit, as I didn't know a thing. I finally agreed to cooperate with them if they allow me a call to my attorney. That was a move to get an attorney, so this bullshit would stop. In the meantime, my wife had called Larry, and he called Arnold Vignola. I called my wife, and she told me to hang in there and that help was on the way. A few hours later, Vignola arrived, and we talked. He advised me to leave it to him and he will get me out of this hell hole. So far I have said nothing and didn't intend to!

"Vignola promised them that I would return on Monday and I would cooperate with them, but it would be in the best interest of everyone if I was allowed to return home and voluntarily return on Monday. I did all that and returned to the cops on Monday and led them to believe that I would cooperate. All the while, the plan was to straighten this out and get me off the hook. But you guys thought I was a snitch and sent some goons out to kill me. At the same time, the cops sent people out to get me as well. Now where was I? In the middle of bunch of shit that was getting way out of hand and nowhere to hide. I had to fight back or die. Given the choices, I would much rather fight back. If I was going to talk, I would be in the protective custody of feds by now, who are dying to break your back. If I had intended to screw you guys, I would not have changed my name and tried to hide out. If I did something wrong, then I agree with you that you got a beef with me and must put a hit on, and that is that. If I did not do anything wrong, it should be a demonstration of my loyalty and my desire to be left alone. I know nothing, and I am not a threat to you or anyone else, and I am tired of hiding and running. I will disappear after this meeting, and you will not ever hear from me again and neither will the feds. I don't want a war, but if I am left no other choice, I'll fight back to my last breath. I am not a person who would pull a double cross, and I don't bite the hand that feeds me. So give me a break and let's leave the bullshit behind and move on with more important things. I'm not your enemy. Believe me, I am not!" I stopped talking and sat back exhausted. I had just pleaded for my life and felt out of breath and strength—what pricks these guys are—and I was begging them.

"Thanks for the nice story, Harry. We will think about it and get back to you by tomorrow. We don't usually do things this way. If you fuck us, we will kill you. That is the way it's done. Out of respect for Larry, and the fact that you had Moe Arnold speak on your behalf, we granted you this meeting. Do you think we invite those who fuck us to a meeting before we teach them a lesson? No we don't, and we never will. Keep to the rules, and we all live well and long. We're not animals, even though the feds would like the world to think we are. We are business men who play by rules. Fuck up and pay the penalty. Have a nice day, Harry. We will be in touch." He got up from the table and walked to the door and was gone in a flash.

My blindfold was put back on, and I was walked back to the car. A minute later, Frank got back into the car and sat next to me. After a few minutes of driving, the blindfold was removed and we were speeding along the Parkway.

"So, Harry, do you feel you had a good meeting?" Frank Costarino asked in a very soft and calm voice.

"It was an experience that I don't ever want to have again. I felt very scared, but I couldn't let them know it. Thanks for coming along and keeping your word about my safety. I feel we might be able to resolve this without anymore violence, I sure as hell hope so," I said with resignation.

We arrived at Frank's apartment. "I'll send your wife down in a moment. Make yourself scarce for a while, as there isn't any reprieve until one is issued. Be careful, that is all I can say. Nice meeting you, Harry, I hope to see you again." And off he went.

Carol appeared at the front door and was smiling from ear to ear. "Let's get out of here now!" she said as she hugged me tightly. We were dropped off on Lexington and Eighty-Third Street and picked up our car. The plan was to drive out of the city at once and to make sure we were not being followed. I glanced at Carol and could see that she was stressed and deeply concerned about what may happen in the future. Right now we have to get out of Dodge before it's too late. We drove along Lexington to Eighty-Second Street and then turned back and took Third Avenue north toward the George Washington Bridge.

"Let's get out of this place fast and find a safe area," I said. "Keep looking out the window and check on all traffic behind us. I want to be sure we are not being followed and being set up. It's real easy to whack us and then say, 'Oops, we didn't know the hit was off.' No, sweetheart, nobody will mourn our passing. I swear, Carol, if they are trying to double cross us, I will kill them all."

"Harry," she said in a very strong voice, "cut the shit. We are dealing with garbage, and no matter what they say they still can't be trusted. We just have to make sure we are always very careful and don't let anyone know who we really are, ever!" We had just crossed the Bridge and passed Fort Lee on route 80.

So far we could not detect any suspicious car behind us.

"Here is what I propose, Carol," I said. "I want to change our appearances as quickly as possible. I want to get rid of this car in the next hour. Who knows if they planted a bug in the car while I was at the meeting? They knew what car we were driving and where it was parked, so it would have been easy. No need to follow us when they have us tracked to within a few miles. We are dealing with animals that don't care about rules, money, or human rights. They are cruel and will do anything and so must we. If they want a war, they are going to get it. I'm giving them every chance to bury this thing and move on. I sure as hell hope they take the easy way and close the issue," I said to Carol with firm indignation.

As we drove, we saw a large billboard for a Chevy dealer, Honest Carl Smithers wanted to put you into a new car. All we had to do was to take the next exit. I took it and drove a half mile and on my right off the service road was Honest Carl, a very big lot filled with new cars, and right next to it an even larger lot with used cars of every make.

"Here is what we will do," I said to Carol. "You will buy the car on your new name. Use the license we got last week under the name of

Carol Washington. Make sure you remember the address listed so that there will be no suspicions. I will not come inside with you, as I don't want anyone to see this car or me if they should track anything to here. Here is three grand, look at a used car first then buy a new Chevrolet. It should cost less than two grand and you want to drive it out now. Do not wait until tomorrow, you want it now and will wait while they prepare the car. Take your time and act like it's no big deal. You just want a car because your husband just left you and you are starting a new life. Don't leave too many impressions behind. You want them to forget you as quickly as possible. Got it all?" I said.

"Harry, I'm not stupid. I can handle this. Just drop me off, and in a couple of hours, we will have a new car. I love you," she said as she leaned over and kissed me. I dropped her off in front of Honest Carl and drove off.

I found a pay phone about a mile down the road and call Moe.

"Any news through the grapevine?" I asked.

"Nope, not a thing, but I'm sure I will hear from Larry very soon. Stay out of sight and keep your hat on. Things will work out very soon," he said. I hung up the phone and moved on. It was very important for me to find a place to ditch the car. I decided to wait for Carol and her new car and move on to Newark, where I will get rid of the car and then proceed to Pennsylvania. I don't think they will be looking for us just yet and with our new appearances and new car, we should be safe. It was the best we could hope for. If there is no truce, the war will be ugly, very ugly.

Sunday, September 29, 1957

We stayed at a motel in Parsippany and slept until nine. We were exhausted. Saturday was a long day for us and drained us totally. "Wake up, sleepyhead. Rise and shine," I said to Carol. "Oh, honey, let me sleep a little longer. I'm so tired," she said.

"Okay, you got one hour and it's up and on our way. We have to organize our next step and make haste. Love you," I said and went out to make a phone call to Moe.

"Any news?" I said to Moe without any preamble.

"No, nothing yet, but I think I will hear sometime today. Regardless of what I hear, I suggest you make yourself scarce and take every precaution you can. Call me later this afternoon, and we will see what happens."

He hung up before I could say another word. I returned to the motel and shook Carol awake. "Okay, sweetheart, let's get on the way. We've no time to waste. Let's get our shit together now." I packed up the few things we had with us and wiped down the room. I waited for Carol and then went back into the room to do a final cleanup. I wiped down the bathroom and gave the room a once-over just to make sure. "Let's go," I said as I started the car. "We will go to Atlanta and then decide our final destination. Today we have to change our appearance. Let's stop in Stroudsburg and pick up the supplies we need and then head to Scranton where we will stay the night and change our looks so that no one will recognize us. We can't afford any mistakes here, honey. Our lives depend on it. No matter what happens and what you may see don't get shocked. I will do what I must do to protect us," I said with conviction. We moved out and drove to Stroudsburg and promptly went about our shopping. We then left Stroudsburg and proceeded to Scranton. It was now after twelve noon.

We arrived in Scranton a little after two and immediately checked into a nondescript motel. We went right to work changing our appearances. Three hours later we were a new, happily married couple. I now sported dirty blond hair with a mole on my left cheek. Carol was a redhead and looked great. Our new names were Dan and Carol All right out of Utica, New York. We had New York driver's licenses as well as new social security cards. Once this was completed, we checked out of the motel, and once again I wiped down the entire room. We were finally on our way with hope and dreams in our hearts. It's time we started a new life without violence and without any threat of Mob retribution.

"We look good, really good!" Carol said as we drove.

"I hope we will not have to be living like this too long. It is a pain in the ass and worries me that we have to watch our every move always being fearful of making a mistake. We have to remember that anyone we befriend can be a potential enemy. We must be careful as to what we say and what we do at all times. It would be best if we did rehearse who we are and what story we may weave about our lives so that we don't make any mistakes. Most people who have gone underground and then discovered was a result of becoming lackadaisical and making very silly errors. If we don't know what to say, then don't say it. We have to be like politicians and never answer a lethal question. Always find another way," I said as we drove along the highway. We stopped for gas around five P.M., and I called Moe to find out if he had heard anything at all.

"Hey, Moe, how are you doing?" I said.

"Just great, my friend. I heard from Larry and listened to the bullshit I expected. The hit has been lifted and will stay that way as long as you stay hidden. He added that they believe you are not a threat, so there is no need for a battle. Let me translate this into real English for you, my dear friend. It means that they will blow you away when you least expect it. They want you to relax, and they will find you and take care of you. End of story!" he said.

"Wow, Moe! That is not what I really thought, but it makes sense, boy. I'm fucked," I said.

"Let me give you some advice. Please listen. Change your identity, change your lifestyle, and move where you are just one of the people in a large population. Be very careful, and do not let anyone know where you are. They will look for you, and they will try to kill you. So be ready. The difference now is that the entire Mob will not be looking for you any longer. Once they locate you, they will send an elite crew of killers to whack you, because it is easier, and you will be off guard. You must always be vigilant, and be very careful. I can only tell you the truth and let you know that I'm always here for you. Trust no one except me. Please follow that advice, and you have a chance to beat these bastards," he said.

"Okay, Moe," I said. "I'll keep in touch. Thanks for everything. You are the best." I hung up.

Monday, September 30, 1957

We slept late as we were both very tired from the ordeal we had just been through. The last few days were very hectic with little time for sleep.

"Where to from here, Dan?" Carol said. "I am just getting used to your new name, but I am getting very tired of running. Let's settle somewhere, at least for a while."

"I'm just as anxious as you are and am as tired of all this shit as you must be. Would you rather find me dead? I am sorry for saying that it is unfair to you and you didn't deserve that. I know this is bullshit, but we discussed this before, and you agreed to accept the conditions. This does not mean you have to stay with me if you feel it is too much. I love you and will respect any decision you make, but make no mistakes, Carol.

We have to be vigilant at all times. Things are not going to change real soon. I am pretty sure of that," I said.

She looked at me with surprise in her eyes as she tried to find the words. It was clear she was having a very hard time putting her thoughts together. I could see it in her eyes. It broke my heart. I took her hand and held it gently and pulled her close to me.

I whispered in her ear, "I love you with all my heart and will do anything for you. Just tell me what you want." I kissed her gently on the lips and held her close. I could feel her body tense up as she tried to speak. Instead tears filled her eyes, and she just pushed me away gently and looked into my eyes—a piercing look that made me feel she had just seen inside me. She was so beautiful, red hair flowing, tears running down her cheeks, an innocence that I just cannot describe, a feeling you get once in a lifetime! I just wished I could switch on the sunshine and look out at a white sandy beach and watch the ocean gently come ashore with her at my side forever. It was euphoric, an inexplicable feeling of peace and love.

"Carol, please talk to me. I need to hear from you and do what is right for you. Please, my darling, talk to me," I said in a very gentle tone.

"Harry, sorry I meant to say, Dan, I love you with all my heart. The life we may have is filled with adventure and love. An excitement that is impossible to describe, and I am so lucky to be part of it. My heart skips a beat every time I see you, and your voice makes me feel so warm and safe. But I don't know if I can live with death hanging over our heads daily. I don't know if I can ever feel safe and settle down, have a family, and live as normal a life as possible. I am torn by two desires and really don't know what to do. I don't want you to talk me out of my feelings. It has to come from me. I don't know if I can go through life without you, but I also don't know if I can with you. I just don't know what to do, Harry. I just don't know," she said.

"I understand and will not try to talk you out of any decision you make. I shall love you no matter what course you choose. Of course, I'd feel so much better if we could face the future together, but I do understand completely. There may be bloodshed, if they should come after me. This I cannot deny. There will be pain and suffering, and once again I cannot guarantee this won't happen. I'll not go easily and will take as many of those bastards with me, but that doesn't make it any easier for you. The difference today is that I am no longer afraid of these bastards. I am now proficient with a gun. I understand how these bastards think, and that is not saying much. I know I can beat them and will if a war starts, because I am smarter and stronger. Of course, that is no way to live and is a lousy future for you to share. Love does fill in a lot of blanks, but no matter what, it can't make it all go away. The future, at best, is filled with doubt, with uncertainty, and a real danger to us, and if kids are involved, it would be a lot more worrisome. I knew in my heart when you agreed to marry me and join me on this journey that you could not really know what it was like. Not until the real thing came along could you understand what the sacrifice really was. Perhaps you are right, and I should face this alone. Not that I want to, but, Carol darling, I have no right to put you in harm's way. I should have known that from the very start and not have been so selfish. I am sorry but grateful for the days we have had together." I turned and walked out of the motel room for some fresh air. The subject had been beaten to death, and it was time to turn it off once and for all. I had no control over it and over her decision, but deep down inside I wanted her to leave. If something happened to her, I would not be able to forgive myself. I'll give her a little time to think about it alone. I stopped at the telephone booth at the end of the parking lot and looked up "shooting ranges" and found one listed. I asked the clerk for directions and left for a little target practice. I'll get my frustrations out on the firing range and will also make sure I am still as sharp as ever.

I returned to the motel two hours later and found Carol all dressed and sitting at the table putting on her lipstick. "Hi, how are you feeling?" I asked.

"Much better," she said. "A little time alone helped me think and put things in the right perspective. I have decided to leave you, Harry," she said in a matter-of-fact way.

It was like a dagger was thrust through my heart. I felt weak and sad but relieved that she had made the right decision.

"It's not because I don't love you, it is because I do. Life without you will be very hard for me, but at least I will have left you alive. Life without you when you are dead is very final and more than I could handle. This way is best for us both. Please believe me, my sweetheart. As hard as it is for us, it is best. I thought I could take it easily. I thought love would conquer it all. I was wrong. The ache in my heart is the worst pain I have ever experienced. This decision was not easy and will always haunt me, but Harry, I must move forward with hope that you will resolve this issue and come and find me. I will be waiting. No one can take your place in my heart or mind. Please, Harry, stay alive, please. I love you so much," she said as tears rolled down her cheeks.

I stared at her for what felt like a long time but was probably no more than a minute or two. I could not believe what I had just heard even though it was true.

"You don't have to go this minute. Please stay a while," I pleaded.

"No, Harry, it's best I go while I can. If I stay a little while, I'll never leave, and it will be bad for us both. Please let me go, Harry, and let me begin my vigil, waiting for you to return to me. Please drive me to the bus station and help me be strong. Harry, please, help me do this. Be my strength, please!" she cried.

Her tears made her mascara run, but it made her look stronger and more determined. She went to the bathroom to repair her face and then said, "Let's go. I don't want to miss the bus. It leaves at four-fifty for Allentown." We drove to the station in silence. There was nothing more to be said. We were married, but she could get an annulment easily as we had only been married for a very short period. We still loved and cared for each other a great deal, but survival was number one for both of us. With a heavy heart, I kissed her good-bye and waited until she was safely on the bus. I placed five K in her pocket so that she would have a few dollars. I whispered good-bye to a part of my life—a part that I knew I'd never see again. It was one of the hardest things I have ever done in my short life, but it gave me strength and renewed my motivation to go on with this battle once and for all. The day was shot, so I returned to the motel and hunkered down for the night. Tomorrow will be a new beginning, and I'll be ready for it. You bet your life I will.

Tuesday, October 1, 1957

I awoke at six in the morning feeling great. I jumped in the shower and got ready. Today was the start of new way to fight this situation that I knew I would win. I had decided to return to Manhattan for a few reasons. This is where the war was being fought, and if I am to win, I must be on the battlefield, not in hiding.

The best defense is a strong and powerful offense; I'm on the offensive from now on. Don't fuck with Harry Miller; he'll kill if you do. That was my motto, and it had better work. In the event it didn't,

I would not be any better off than running like a scared rabbit. Of course, I would still use disguise, and I would not go out of my way to help them find me. My plan was to find a place to live in Manhattan and to resume a life as close to normal as possible. I'll use my new name, Dan All right, and establish a new life under that. If they are going to look for me, I believe they will look everywhere but under their very noses. I had my papers that easily established me as a real person. I'll choose my friends very carefully and shall remain very low-key at all times. Yes, this was the best way to handle it, and only Moe will know my location. I packed the car with the few items I had and left: New York City, here I come.

Wednesday, October 2, 1957

I spent the night in a motel on the Jersey side and drove into Manhattan at ten thirty, missing the heavy traffic. Where to begin was the big question. My calculations were very simple; these guys hang around Brooklyn and the Lower East Side. Little Italy was their place to dine and be seen by other families. I figured it would be best if I started my new life on the Upper East Side. Manhattan, although small in square miles, is as big a place you would want to get lost in. With over seven million people coming and going each day, it was a perfect place to blend in, and that is exactly what I was doing.

I began apartment hunting in the Upper East Side area from East Seventy-Ninth Street to East Ninety-Sixth Street between Lexington and First Avenue. I found many signs posted outside buildings, so I decided to walk and stop and look. I went into building after building looking at apartments but didn't find anything I would like. I needed a place that gave me security first and comfort second. I finally found a very nice place on Ninety-First Street and Second Avenue. The super was a nice old man, probably from Russia. His English wasn't that good. He showed me an apartment on the fourth floor and another on the sixth floor. The building only had six floors, but it had an elevator and was pretty nice. I decided that the sixth floor apartment would be best for me. There was only one way in and that was through the front door, yet there was an alternate way out. If I was faced with an attack, I could easily leave through the front window that led to a fire escape that would drop me directly in front of the building and on Ninety-First Street. If someone wanted to pull down the fire escape from the street, they would need a ladder first. When descending the building, the weight of one's body will force the fire escape to drop to the street. I filled in a rental application and gave him a hundred dollar deposit as requested. I also gave him a half of a hundred dollar bill and told him he'd get the other half when I get the apartment, and I'd like to move in today if possible. We reached an agreement on the rent. He said I should return after twelve because he needed a little time to get the lease prepared and have the owner sign it. This place was just right for me, because it was on the top floor. It was not possible to get into this apartment from the roof or the windows as they were fronted by Ninety-First Street and would require Superman to get to them.

Further, the windows had iron bars on them, thus it was very unlikely anyone could or would even try to gain access via this route. I could unhook the iron bars from the inside if I needed to use the fire escape route. The solid steel front door was in a steel frame; breaking it down would be difficult. There was no other way in or out for that matter. Although it did represent a problem for me if I had to get out in a hurry, it was still a great place for me to settle. The pluses far outweighed the minuses and made me feel quite secure.

I spent the next two hours walking through the neighborhood to Eighty-Sixth Street and found that everything one needed was located right here within a few blocks. This area was called Yorkville and was filled mostly with German and Irish immigrants.

A person could live in the ten-block area from Ninety-First Street to Eighty-First Street without ever leaving that area and having everything they ever needed. It was ideal for me and allowed me the chance to start again without any suspicions.

I returned to the building a little after noon and went directly to the super. "Hello there. How is everything?" I asked.

"You have been approved and can move in today. I convinced the owner that you were a good man and would be responsible. A five-hundred-dollar deposit is required and the first month's rent. You will have to sign this lease, and remember, it renews each year automatically with a minor rent increase set by the city of New York as this is a rent-controlled building. I have to tell you these things. It is my job. If you need anything, please let me know, and I will get it for you if I can," he said as he slipped the lease under my nose with pen in hand. I signed the lease and initialed where he indicated. I gave him the other half of the hundred dollar bill. I told him that there are many more of those if he works with me when I need something done and then asked if I may use his phone to call the phone company, the electric and gas company. I arranged all this and went to the apartment to assess what I must do to get it in shipshape. I went out to Eighty-Sixth Street and walked to Lexington where there was a Gimbles' department store. I bought a bed and a mattress and a small kitchen table. The condition of my purchase was that they deliver today as I needed the bed to sleep on. Seeing that Macy's was across the road, they agreed to deliver. Tomorrow the phone would be installed. The gas and electricity will be operational and the existence of Dan All right will be complete.

Thursday, October 3, 1957

I woke up. It was still dark outside, so I went back to sleep. I jumped out of bed at seven as I had to be ready for the phone guy who was coming sometime between eight and twelve. The gas and electric was already on and, I'm sure the billing had already been changed. I will get to the license bureau after the phone is in to change my license to New York. I will give them my Pennsylvania license as a proof of identity. It wasn't difficult to establish one's proof of life; at least, I didn't find it so.

In a day or two Dan All right will have existed since the beginning of time, especially now that he has a Gimbals' credit account. I opened one the day I bought the furniture. The phone guy arrived at ten thirty and spent about an hour connecting the phone line. He had to go the main phone room to connect the line. I also gave him a twenty to put in a couple of jacks in case I wanted to add more phones. I then located the License Bureau somewhere in the Bronx and got my driver's license changed to my new address. I then went to the Chemical Bank and opened an account. It took all day, but now I had all sorts of ID and was well established. It was as if I had been around for a long while. I stopped in at a carpet store on Third Avenue and Eighty-Third Street and picked out new carpets for the apartment and some tiles for the kitchen floor. They needed to confirm my measurements and would install on Saturday. My apartment was now ready to be called home as I filled it with clothes, furniture, dishes, etc.; I was for real and felt I could now move forward and try to find some kind of business or a job.

Friday, October 4, 1957

I spent the day fixing up my apartment and filling up my new fridge. I was now a real person in a big city and ready for things to happen. I went out for the first time that night. It was a great night, quite mild, so I walked to Third Avenue and Eighty-Third Street where I noticed a bar called O'Reilly's. It reminded me of Kelly's place in Stroudsburg. I went in and sat at the bar and looked around. It was about six thirty and the bar was pretty full. I figured it was happy hour as a lot of the offices nearby closed for the weekend and others were returning home to their apartments. There were a lot of women crowding the bar, I presumed, looking for guys. I struck up a conversation with the bartender, Mike, and introduced myself. I told him that I had just moved into the neighborhood and really would love to get to meet some nice people. I slipped him a twenty and knew he was my buddy right away. A few bucks certainly go a long way, no matter what city you are in. Ten minutes later, he brought over this really good-looking gal—blonde hair, blue eyes, about five foot two, and one hundred and twenty pounds with a smile that would melt an iceberg. "Kathy, I'd like you to meet a friend of mine, Dan. He is new in the neighborhood," he said as wiped the bar and moved over to another drinker.

"Hi, it's real nice to meet you, Kathy. Can I buy you a drink?" I said in my most cheerful tone. "Sure thing, Dan, it's really nice to meet you as well. You're new here Mike said. When did you move in?" she said with a slight Irish accent.

"I moved in last week from Scranton, Pennsylvania. I thought it was time I came to the big city and found some work. I have a place on Ninety-First Street and Second. I'm just getting to know this city even though I haven't been out of Yorkville yet," I said with a laugh. "Mike, please give Kathy another, what were you drinking, Kathy," I said.

"Chevas on the rocks, please," she said. "Thanks, Mike," I said.

Kathy and I talked and drank for another hour until I suggested we have something to eat. She was all for that and suggested a little place on Eighty-Sixth Street that was quaint and quiet. We ate and talked and really got to enjoy each other's company. I suggested Kathy stay at my place tonight, but she said no. She gave me her number, and I gave her mine and asked if she was free tomorrow night. She was busy, but Sunday was good. I suggested we meet early, around noon, and go for brunch because there were so many good places that feature great brunches. We agreed, and she said she would call me Sunday morning. I offered to take her home, but she said she would prefer to go alone. I had a great evening and didn't worry about anything.

Saturday, October 5, 1957

I waited until nine-thirty when the carpet guys arrived. They went through the apartment and then back to the truck to bring up their tools and the carpets. They worked real hard until two when the job was finally done. I got to meet the chief installer, a black man named Jimmy from North Carolina. He was really a great guy, and we hit it off real well. "Hey, man, if you ever want to party, I live in Brooklyn, and we have some real super times there. Here is my phone number. Give me a call whenever you got nothing to do. It was great meeting you, Dan," he said as they left.

I spent the rest of the day wandering around the city looking for stuff for the apartment and getting acquainted once again with the city I loved. I stopped in at a bar called The Blue Parrot on Fifth Avenue and Twenty-Third Street. It seemed like a nice place, and it was nearly five in the afternoon. I also needed to expand my world and see if I can meet some nice people. What surprised me most was how easily I forgot Carol. I guess when in the environment of small town US, relationships have different meanings. I still cared for her a lot, but New York seemed to keep me so busy that I didn't have time to think about it. I understood that life must go on, and I must remain alert and could not have any distractions. I sat down at the bar and ordered vodka on the rocks and sat there nursing my drink. I was taking it all in; a great bar with a lot of tables. It was very quiet, but it was early, and I figured being Saturday the place would fill up in a few hours.

I introduced myself to the bartender, "How you doing? I'm Dan All right. I just moved into the city. How's the action here?" I asked in a very genial tone.

"Welcome to the city and to our bar. I'm Ron, and I'm one of the owners. Hope to see you here often, Dan. A pleasure to meet you," he said as he extended his hand.

We shook hands and I said, "Do you serve any special kind of food here?"

"We try to specialize in seafood and have different special nights. For example, Thursday we have all you can eat snow crab legs for $7.95 and Sangria for only $2 a pitcher. Not a bad deal, Dan. We also have all the lobster you can eat on Fridays for only nine dollars and ninety-five cents, and all drinks upto 7:00 p.m. are only a buck. If you look over there, you see the board on that wall?" He motioned to my left. "Those are all the specials we feature each night. This is a great place to meet, greet, and eat, not to mention drink," he said with a smile. Ron was about thirty-five with serious blond hair and great blue eyes. He was about six feet tall and was in great shape. His personality was super as he laughed and smiled and was always polite. I liked him and felt very comfortable in this place even though it was a bit far from the apartment.

It was about seven thirty, and I was getting hungry and didn't want to continue drinking on an empty stomach. I had met a few people who sat besides me at the bar when a tall, good-looking guy sat down next to me and ordered a drink. I called Ron over and asked if it was okay to eat at the bar or should I sit at a table.

"Hey, Dan, it's up to you. We'll serve you anywhere," he smiled and went over to another drinker at the bar.

"Hey there, I'm Larry Robbins, and I couldn't help overhear that you are ready to sit down and eat. Well, so am I. Maybe we could eat together. It would be my pleasure." He extended his hand as I said, "I'm Dan All right. A pleasure to meet you, Larry. It would be very nice to meet someone new. I'd love to join you. I'm new here in the city and would welcome the company," I said as I shook his hand.

"Hey, don't get me wrong, Dan. I'm not a homo or anything like that. Just thought it would be nice for us both," he said.

"Never entered my mind, Larry. Let's get a table while the getting is still good. I'm starved."

Ron came over and asked, "Can I get you another drink?"

"No thanks, Ron. Dan and I are going to eat. Can you get us a table, please," Larry said.

"I'll have it set up. Give me five minutes, and we'll move you over, Larry," Ron said as Larry palmed him a bill.

"We know each other quite well. I'm a regular here as my studio is only a few minutes away on Twentieth and Fifth. Let's go. Our table is ready," Larry said as he got up and started walking through the crowd. "Hi there, Larry. How are you doing," some good-looking girl said and I noticed many more saying, "hello, how are you, etc." I guess Larry was a well-known person here and quite a guy. We sat down at a table and looked at each other. What a strange way to meet, but what the hell, it's better than sitting alone, and who knows, this might help me open new doors. We ordered our food and I said, "Larry, do you live near by?"

"I live and work on Fifth and Twentieth Street. I am a film producer and was lucky enough to make a deal for this vacant factory space. The rent is dirt cheap, and it is great for my work. I had to adjust my life a little because the building was designed for manufacturers and was usually closed on the weekends. Because of that there is no heat on Saturday afternoon and all day Sunday. The price was right, and God knows, I need any break I can get," he said.

"Wow! That sounds exciting. What kind of films do you make?" I said.

"I make XXX-rated films that you see in the theaters. It's a very hard business as they don't like to pay too much for each film," he said with a smile.

"It must be very exciting. I'd love to see your studio and see how you do it," I said excitedly.

"Are you a cop, Dan?" Larry said.

"Hell no, Larry. A fine time to ask after you've told me what you do. Didn't you know you had to be careful as to what kind of movies you make? A cop? No way, Larry, but if you would feel better, I'll pass on visiting your place. I feel we are going to be good friends for a long time, so there is no rush," I said.

"Dan, sorry if I offended you, but a guy in my business has to be careful. I have never heard of the feds ever busting a filmmaker, but one can't be too careful," Larry said as he ordered another drink. "Let's finish our dinner and stop by the place. I feel the same as you do that we will be friends for quite a while, so let's not worry about any bullshit. What do you do, Dan?" he asked. I ordered another drink and said, "Well, Larry, I just arrived in town and rented a condominium on Ninety-First Street and Second. I was married, but my wife and I are now separated. I used to be in construction. I built homes in Pennsylvania, but that went south. and I'm now in between something.

What that something is I really don't know yet. My first job was to get used to living here in Manhattan. I am open for anything, Larry. Maybe it was fate that we should meet and find each other," I said with a big smile.

"Let's get out of here and take a look at the studio. I am excited to show it to you," he said. We left the Blue Parrot at nine forty-five and walked the few blocks to Larry's place. Along the way, Larry pointed places of interest and how quiet the street was during the weekend. We arrived at the building, and sure enough it looked like any other factory with multiple floors. We went into the small lobby, and Larry used a key that opened the elevator.

He inserted a key into the elevator panel and the hum was heard instantly. "I am on the sixth floor. The entire floor is mine. Each floor is rented out the same way. Above me there are two chicks that are really very nice, but I don't know exactly what they do. There seems to be a lot of action on the weekends as I see many guys going in and out, but all is quiet. On the ground floor there is friend of mine, Harry Looming. He runs a club for couples who come there for fun and a little switching around. All of this stuff has to be on the quiet as society is not ready to openly admit that sex is here to stay. Nothing illegal, because the people are just gathering for a party, and what they do with each other is their business. He makes his bucks as he charges each couple seventy-five bucks every time they attend a party. He's doing real well as there about one hundred couples who party four times a week. Tonight, the place is full and you'd never think anyone was here. Quiet, isn't it?" he said with pride. The elevator stopped and the door opened to a wide open space. To the left the windows faced Fifth Avenue; the space continued to what seemed forever. I could not see the very end, although it was only one-hundred-and-twenty feet away. The place was cluttered with an array of sets, blankets, pillows, and just unbelievable curtains of every color. In the front end there was an unmade bed, and a table with a typewriter in the center and a solitary chair. This was Larry's studio/home, and although it was not luxurious it had a mystique about it that excited my wildest imagination. I could imagine women and men making love, the excitement was surreal as I thought I could actually smell sex and hear the groans of ecstasy. It was the most exciting thing I have ever experienced and could hardly wait to meet a porn star.

"Well, Larry, this is something. I really could not imagine what your studio would actually look like. I'd love to watch a shoot. Tell me the truth, Larry. Do you fuck these women?" I asked. "Dan, I'm human, and each and every day I am on the hunt for new talent, but I am also looking for me. If she is no good in bed with me, she won't be any good on the screen, so I've got to test them out. People think that porn is easy, but that is not so. If a movie star doesn't display emotions, the movie will fail. Good looks alone will not do. A girl has to love her work, and it has to be transmitted to the viewer. Tell me, Dan, would you like to screw someone who just lies there and does nothing or very little, or would you rather screw a broad that moans and groans and tells you when she comes? Of course, you would rather have the action, and in porn the same reaction is expected and turns the viewer on," he said as seriously as possible.

Here we were discussing sex in a manner no different than what kind of lumber would be better in making a building. It was great and exciting; I was on cloud nine and could hardly wait for tomorrow. I told Larry that I want to come back when he does have a shoot and agreed to meet him tomorrow for brunch. He had a meeting with a couple of girls who wanted to be in a movie he was about to shoot, and he would love to have me come along. I was stoked, I could hardly wait.

We exchanged phone numbers, and I said good-night. It was after midnight, and I didn't even know where the time had flown; I had a great time and felt that this would be the start of a new career. I was excited!

Sunday, October 6, 1957

I could hardly sleep as my mind was racing with thoughts of meeting a porn star. I was excited in every way possible and could hardly wait until I would hear from Larry. I was up at seven and just waited for the phone to ring. We had agreed that he would call me and tell me the time and place where to meet. It was truly an experience that perked up my senses and made me feel alive.

If I would have told anyone how I felt, I am sure they would have thought I was a pervert. I just couldn't help the way I felt; it's hard to explain but it was a nice feeling. After all the shit I had been through in the last seven months, this was a new experience, and a very welcome one for me! In my excitement, I had forgotten that Kathy was supposed to call me as well for a tentative brunch. So far she hasn't called, and I was hoping she wouldn't.

At eleven thirty the phone rang. I hesitated to answer hoping beyond hope that it was not Kathy. Finally, I picked up the phone, and much to my relief, it was Larry. He asked me to meet him at the Flower Hotel on the West side, at Fifty-Seventh and Seventh. "They have a great brunch for nineteen ninety-five that include shrimp, lobster, smoked salmon, roast beef, and all the champagne you can drink. Let's meet at 10:00 p.m. Wow! Very exciting," Larry said.

"Larry, what shall I wear?" I asked.

"Dan, it's Sunday. You can dress casual, enjoy the day, and let's have some fun," he said. I put on a pair of blue jeans and a nice shirt and a sweater for later in the day when it cools down. I had decided to walk to the Flower Hotel; the day was beautiful, the sun was shining, and it was seventy-four degrees. I left my place and walked to Fifty-Seventh Street along Second Avenue. It was a great walk as I floated along the sidewalks and crossed the city to the West side and arrived at the Flower Hotel seven minutes before one. I waited in the lobby until one and then went into the dinning room where brunch was being served. I spied Larry and a very cute looking woman at a table and immediately went over. "Hi, sorry if I kept you waiting. It is such a nice day I walked here," I said.

"We just arrived. Dan, I'd like you to meet Sasha. Sasha, this is Dan All right," Larry said with a big smile.

"A pleasure to meet you, Sasha," I said as I pulled out a chair and sat down.

"Are you in the movie business, Dan?" she said.

"I sure hope so if you are any indication of the beautiful women I'd get to meet," I said with a big smile.

"I'm working out a deal with Dan, and I'm hoping he will join me in my new venture. 'Over the Top Films' is a new film company I am opening. It will make documentaries and children's movies and, with Dan's help, will be a major studio in a short while. We are organizing the entire operations as we speak. We hope to have studios in Hollywood and here. Maybe you will be one of our signature stars, Sweetie," Larry said with wink in my direction.

I thought it sounded great but was under the impression that Larry was saying this to impress her. It didn't bother me; I was along for the ride. We enjoyed our brunch and left the hotel a little after three.

"Larry, what's on the agenda?" I said. Deep down, I wanted to get laid with Sasha, but I didn't know just how to handle it.

"We are going back to the studio. I have two other girls coming over at four to audition for the next movie. Do you want to come along?" he said.

"Do I want to come along? Of course, I do!" I said.

"All right let's grab a cab and get there a little early and be ready for the auditions," Larry said. Sasha joined us as we jumped into a cab and set off to the studio. While in the cab, Larry sat in the front, and Sasha and I sat in the back. As we sat in the cab, she slid her hand on my leg and kept on rubbing it. I was getting excited and could hardly wait to get out of the cab and take her to bed. I didn't want to offend Larry in any way and still did not understand the ground rules. So I felt that no matter how much I wanted her I'd better show some restraint.

We arrived at the studio ten minutes before four and took the elevator up to wait for the others to arrive. At four fifteen, we heard the bell ring, and Larry sent the elevator down to pick the girls up. When the elevator door opened, two unbelievably good-looking girls exited. They were wearing very tight skirts and tight sweaters with no bras underneath. They were stunning with long legs, stiletto heels, and leather bags hanging from their shoulders. "Hey there, Larry. How are you?" The first girl said as she went over and kissed Larry on the cheek. "This is Penny. She is new to the industry, but she knows what she is doing."

"Real nice to meet you all," Penny said while chewing gum.

"Let me introduce you to everyone. This is Dan and Sasha," Larry said. "Oh, by the way this is Lori. We have worked before," Larry added as we all said hi.

"Okay, guys, first I need Penny to get undressed and pose for some nude photos. I need to see how photogenic you are," Larry said in a matter-of-fact way.

I was in heaven as this ritual unfolded before me. Wow! What a way to make a living, I thought. Larry went through the photo session in a very professional manner and made Penny feel like she was a real actress. He did the same with Lori and Sasha and explained to me later that even though Sasha was in a movie previously he had not seen her in her few months and must see if any changes had taken place. It was a little after six when the girls left and Larry and I were alone.

"You start shooting on Wednesday, and you say it takes only two days to complete the film?" I asked.

"Yes, Dan. It only takes two long days to get all the scenes done. That concludes the shooting part and then comes the hard part. I have to edit the footage to make a real story out of it and that takes weeks. It isn't as easy as the finished product may indicate. Seeing that I am the director and the editor, I understand beforehand what the final film should look like, and it makes the editing part a little easier. When a major studio makes a movie after the shooting of the film is done, the editor and the director sit down with the notes they have made while each scene was being shot, and the director instructs the editor exactly what scene should follow another and how the flow of the film should be. If this wasn't done, it would take an editor a very long time to finish the movie, and no one would really know—especially the editor—if this was the intent of the movie. So as you can see, there is a lot of work behind the scenes to get the film finished right. Most people have no idea how a movie comes together, and how much hard work it takes. Just a play on words, 'cums together,'" he said. We both laughed, and Larry went to a file cabinet and took out a bottle of vodka.

"Let's have a drink, Dan. It's been a long day," he said as he walked over to the fridge on the set and took out a bottle of orange juice. We settled back and Larry said, "Well, Dan, what do you think about the movie business?"

"I really can't give you a real good answer. The broads are great, the action is exciting, but how about the business end of it all? Who buys these movies? How much do they pay? How much do they cost? There is so much I need to know in order to answer your question. Give me a clue, Larry, because I am very interested. I'd love to be in your business and to be your partner."

"Well, Dan, let me be perfectly honest with you. I may not be rich, and I may not be the most successful director around, but I have a lot of fun and enjoy life to the maximum. I pride myself on being an honest dude and have never cheated or lied to anyone except a little white exaggeration when I am talking to a girl. Everyone in this business who knows me knows that my word is my bond and badge of honor. I am not doing well financially as things have been very tough lately. This business is not considered legal by the feds. They use the fact that we make movies in New York and take them across state lines. Of course, we have many clients that want these movies and live in states outside of New York. Once you do that, it becomes a Federal offence as you have crossed state lines with obscene material. The stupidity of it all is that the government spends fortunes on trying to stop this industry when the fact is that people like to watch X-rated films. That is one factor we have to contend with. The other is the fact that the industry is controlled by the Mob, and they never put themselves in harm's way. They use shills all the time but are always taking the lion's share of the money. The feds are always using undercover guys to buy movies and then bust you. They set up meeting places like a shopping center or a parking lot, and as you open the trunk of your car to hand over the porn films, they bust you for taking obscene material across state lines. The government will look pretty stupid one day when this becomes legal, but right now we are basically underground. The one thing the feds have done was to help keep the prices high and help all those who make the films, even the Mob, make more money. If the feds stopped for a moment and figured it out, they would realize how futile and costly their efforts are and that in the end they will never end this lucrative industry. There is good money in this business, but the Mob controls it all. If they want me out of business, they starve me out; if they want me to make money, they give me plenty of projects. If I don't have money for rent or to pay the actors, they give it to me and own the movies for next to nothing. I work for them and can't get ahead unless they let me. The biggest problem is that none of the producers have their own money, and most are so busy partying they really don't care, so they need the Mob's money. The Mob doesn't want to change anything because they own every theater. They are pretty smart about these operations, because they never put the theater in their names. They find some guy who needs work, and he is now the manager of the place, and when the theater is busted, he takes the fall. They pay all the fines, and if there is any jail time, which in most cases there isn't, they pay him for as long as he sits. Some people wish there would be jail time because they get paid real well, but usually there is none, but it could happen. You see how stupid this is, Dan. Running a theater that shows X-rated films is a misdemeanor, so the maximum is a fine. A second offense carries up to six months that is why they always appoint another manager/owner so that the records will always show one conviction against that person. They have it all down pat and use all the loopholes the government built into the law. Needless to say, I'm broke; it really hurts me to admit this to you, Dan, but I have to be honest. In order to shoot the movie on Wednesday, I will have to borrow money from them. If I do that, they will own the film and dictate the selling price, and that won't be very good for anyone except them. I'm sure you understand how their money lending rates are. They charge an outrageous amount of interest because they are the loan company of last resort. You pay or you stay broke, and that is not a very good option. If you came in, we would not need to borrow any money, and we could get to keep all the proceeds we get from the film. A typical movie costs about twenty K, sometimes a little more. We get back twenty-six K for each one. All our dealings are done in cash because once again the feds have made the buyers do business in this manner. It's obvious that they don't want anyone to know who bought the movie and from whom. If a movie was made in New York and bought in New Jersey, it would become a Federal offense, and the FBI would be able to try to prosecute. The local law doesn't care to prosecute anyone except the theater owner, and I explained what steps they take to cover that. In order to avoid any records of where the film was made, we deal in cash—no bills, no receipts, and no records at all. We don't even put a name and address of the studio on the film, and all the credits are for people who use stage names only. If we create a superstar, we can get an additional 10K or more depending on what following she creates. They make about $200K per film. Not a bad return for your bucks, and if we play our cards right, we can get a lot more when we find the perfect girl, and that's not very far-fetched, Dan. If we make a real extravaganza, we can really clean up, but first we have to be able to cut the ties with the Mob. I will make you a fifty-percent partner in a new company that will distribute the films. Of course, neither you nor I will appear on the documents of the company in case there is ever a bust. We will have someone else sign the papers, and we'll have the checks signed with a rubber signature stamp. We can get a bum and give him a few hundred, and he will sign anything and then disappear back on the streets again. We can make a lot of money, and there is plenty of pussy. I know you wanted to fuck Sasha, didn't you?" he said with a smirk.

"I really did want to strap her on, but I didn't want to offend you in any way, so I let it pass," I said.

"Thanks, Dan. It was very considerate of you but go at it at any time. If I don't want you to get involved with one of them, I'll let you know. Otherwise, go at it my friend. How about our partnership? What do you think?" he said. "How much money do we need to get going?" I said. "With twenty-five K, we can shoot the next movie and pay off the old debts. You can get your money back in a month or so, and we can get some additional movies shot and ready for editing," he said.

"Okay, Larry, I just have a feeling this will work out for us both. Let's do it. I'm in. We start tomorrow. What a great day. I'm very excited," I said. I left Larry at about nine and took a cab home. It was a good day; one of the better ones in a long while.

Monday, October 7, 1957

I called Larry at about eight-thirty and told him I would be at the studio by ten A.M. and was bringing the funds. I went to my cash stash and took out fifty K just in case additional funds were needed. I was floating on cloud nine as I was so thrilled to be involved in something like this and get my mind off the Mob.

Of course, I knew that the Mob was behind this business, and the time would come when I would come into to contact with one of these guys. I just could not let this rule my life any longer; when the time came, I would cross that bridge then and do what I must do. I will not run any longer as I must get my life in order, and this is the best way to get it started.

I arrived at Larry's place at about ten A.M. and found him sitting at his little table pecking away at his typewriter, one finger at a time, writing the script to the next film—our first under the partnership we had agreed upon.

"Hey there, Larry," I said. "How's it going?"

"Pretty good. I have been writing a new script for our first full length feature," he said. "Great," I said. "I can hardly wait to read it," I said smiling from ear to ear. "Larry, I brought cash and hope this is okay. We can pay the actors in cash for this movie as well as any props we may need. I just want you to understand that we are now partners, and I trust you all the way. We don't need any contracts; our words are our bonds and shall always remain so. Honor will rule our relationship and will always allow us to be truthful between ourselves," I said.

"I agree with you, Dan, and hope we should never argue or ruin our relationship over money," he said. "I love money, Dan. Don't get me wrong, but friendship is far more important to me. I have made and lost money many times. I can live in my car, when I have one, and endure almost anything except bullshit in friendship."

"I know what you mean, Larry," I said. "I feel the same way. There are a lot of things I haven't told you, and they will have to wait until we are settled down. I'm sure there are things you have to tell me as well so that I know what it's all about. One day we will sit down with a bottle of vodka and tell each other all about our sordid pasts and know that we, above all people, know the whole truth about each other." I counted out twenty-five K and gave it to Larry.

"Dan, I need to use three K to pay the landlord some back rent and next month's as well. I should have mentioned that I was behind on the rent. If you would like to reconsider, you can have this money back, and we can cancel the partnership. Sorry, Dan, I did not mean to hold that back," he said.

"No way, Larry. I knew you were broke but too damn proud to admit it. I knew you were hurting, so please pay the landlord and any other outstanding bills, and let's get the show on the road. If there are any other bills that need paying, let's pay them today. Phone, power, anything that may impact our operation. Larry, it is our show now, and we are going to make it work and make some serious money and have a lot of fun at the same time, so let's get the show on the road," I said as I got up and gave him a big hug.

"Let's go out for a power lunch, right after we take care of our stuff. Today is the start of a big and wonderful future. We need to name our film company. Let's do that at lunch. No more business today except our new name and our new beginning," I said as we both laughed and knew a relationship was born that would not easily be broken.

Larry took care of the landlord and then went over to the bank nearby to pay the electric bill and buy a bank check for the phone company. We then went over to O'Meara's, a great bar and eating place located on Third Avenue and Fifty-Second Street.

"Here is where we will start the newest and best film company and grow into the largest of them all," Larry said. We sat at a table near the back end of the restaurant where we would not be disturbed and could enjoy our drinks and food. After an hour of drinking and snacking on some very delicious appetizers, we finally came up with a name. The criteria for a good name were that it would be easily remembered and associated with the type of films that the studio produced. Climax Films was our final selection as it was easy to remember and easily associated with X-rated films and could be used for legitimate films as well. Some of our logo suggestions were just great. We finally settled on "Cum and Enjoy another Climax Film." The film would always have a picture of a cumshot across the screen, like a fire hose spurting out its first stream of water. We felt it was risky enough for our times and would drive the feds crazy. They would pull their hair out trying to figure who owned Climax Films, because we would never register it as a company. We also made sure the address of Climax Films was not found anywhere on any of the films for obvious reasons.

We felt like we had just conquered the world and would be remembered as pioneers in the adult movie genre. Instead of making our films appear like our competitors' films, we decided to make this genre legitimate by openly demonstrating what the films were about. Our films will have story lines and will have some redeeming values that will compete with the best dramas ever produced. In regular movies, the viewer must use their imagination when any intimate scenes were about to take place. In our films we will have a plot in the same way that a story is revealed in a Hollywood movie. The difference in our movie will be when an intimate scene is part of the film it will be shown in its true to life way. When one of the actors stays overnight at another's place, the scene will show everything that really happens with full love making. Of course, we didn't expect the censors to place their stamp of approval on our films today or perhaps in the near future. Here we are two guys that are going to make film history and have a great time doing it. We ate and drank until after seven. "Well, Larry, I think we have accomplished a lot today. I am completely bushed and can hardly stay awake. I'll grab a cab and head home. What a great day this has been. I know we will do very well. I can feel it in my heart," I said as I grabbed my jacket.

"Thanks, Dan. It was a great day, and I feel we are on the way to success and a lot of fun. Great stuff," Larry said. "See you tomorrow, partner," I said.

Tuesday, October 8, 1957

We met again at the studio, and Larry gave me a set of keys for the elevator and the doors. He spent an hour with me showing me what to do with the elevator and so on. Larry had to show me step by step how to do it; he was a stickler for detail. We then sat down and read the new script, a thirty-page extravaganza that sounded great.

Larry wanted Heather Willis as she was a known star to headline this film. She had a great name in the business and would guarantee a full theater as well as top dollars for the film.

At the same time, we wanted to start our search for our own exclusive stars that we will place under contract to Climax Films. We had to start development now as it would take about two years to build up our own star and expose her enough to create a demand. It was our belief that the so-called blue film business would become accepted soon, and as the demand grows, the feds will have no other choice but to allow it. The film company with the best superstar will reap fan loyalty. This will equate to bigger and better box office receipts and, of course, a lot more money for all of us. Mob or no Mob we will be leaders in this field, and they will work with us because no one else will be able to give them the quality shows and the superstars the public wants. No matter what the Mob is, it is not stupid; they want to make money and will ride a winning horse all the way to their bank.

The casting for the films was to be handled by Larry, and I was to observe so that I could help with it in the future. I could not argue about this as I did not have any experience and felt it best to learn from the sidelines. I was good at financial issues and organizational tasks and not at handling women who had many different agendas. Climax Films was going to be known as a great studio putting out the highest quality films at all times even if some were porn. "Okay, Larry, when do we start?" I said.

"I will have a casting call on Thursday in the afternoon. Until then, I have to get Samuel Polter to get the shoot ready. The problem is how to find him. He doesn't have a permanent home as he doesn't have any money. I let him stay here for free, and he works for free. But he met some broad last week and hasn't been back since. He'll show up eventually, but we need him now if we are to get started soon," he said.

"Okay with me, Larry. Please don't feel any pressure. Take your time. We could put off the shoot until all loose ends are taken care of and your mind is not filled with distracting garbage. Whatever it takes to move forward, we'll handle it all. I don't want you to feel our relationship will fall apart if things are not done quickly or on schedule. I'm in and that is it. No ifs, ands, or buts, capish?" I said.

"Yes I do, and I appreciate your being so above board. I will also be that way, I promise," Larry said. "Okay then, Larry, what else is there in the way so that we can move on?" I said.

"Let's have a drink, Dan, and get the rest on the table." While I prepared two screwdrivers, Larry called a few places to find Samuel. He left word around town.

"Okay, Larry, what's left?" I asked as I set down the drinks.

"Well, I owe the boys about five K, and I must pay them. I was going to take care of it right after we got paid for the first film. Of course, this debt is mine and will come out of my end. I also owe Samuel about five hundred for some work and feel kind of shitty about not paying him," Larry said hanging his head down as if he was ashamed.

"Let me explain this to you one more time, Larry. We are committed to each other, and no matter what the problem may be, I will be there at your side. My loyalty cannot be compromised, and I am not judgmental, so forget this shit, and let's clear it all up and move forward. I really don't care if it is one dollar or a million dollars. I am in and at your side, okay?" I said as I slapped his back and drained my drink.

"Who is the Mob guy that you owe the money to?" I asked.

"Lew Carlotti is my contact. The problem is that his boss thinks he owns me, and whenever I make a film, he wants to own it. He takes the film and forgives the debt. That leaves me without any money to pay anyone, and I'm right back where I started. He then will lend me what I need and takes the next film. It never ends," Larry said without emotion.

"Larry, is his boss Carmine Velone?" I said.

"How did you know, Dan?" Larry said.

"Seeing that we are laying the cards on the table, let me tell you a little story. Please don't interrupt until I'm through. Got it!" I said and proceeded to tell him all about my adventures. When I was through, he just sat there. He couldn't believe what he had just heard, yet he knew in his heart it was true. "I want you to call your guy Lew and tell him you have his money in full. Tell him you want to meet with Carmine and give him the bread, and you want to do it now. Then you tell Carmine that you will not need his money any longer as you have sold half your business to some legit guy that has a few bucks and will fund the movies from now on. You tell him that you will give him first right of refusal on every film you make. The terms will be cash. You tell him that you are clearing up any debts you owe including his. Assure him once again that he will have first call on all the movies you make. That's what you tell him, and let's see where he stands. In my opinion, he will take his money and ask for interest, like another five K, but he will not cause you any problems. If he asks for additional vig tell him that you probably can get it from your new partner, but you will need a few days because you have to add it to the budget of your new film. This way, the guy won't ask too many questions, and I'll get you the bread. Just do it and let's see!" I said in a very hard tone.

"I will, Dan. Yes I will, and thanks," Larry said.

Wednesday, October 9, 1957

I was filled with plenty of hate for these Mob guys and vowed to get them, but for now I would have to remain in the background as much as I can. I called Larry who told me he was meeting Lew at noon, and he would see Carmine right after. He needed some money, so could I please bring him some. I jumped into a cab and went to the studio and gave him ten K and told him to settle for as little as he can but spend it all if has to. "Carry the money in bundles of one thousand each as that way you can act like it's all you have, and Larry don't keep it all in one place. Spread your money out in your pockets and in your beautiful briefcase. Good luck, Larry. I'll be here waiting for you," I said as he jumped into a cab and left for Brooklyn.

I waited for five anxious hours for Larry to return; I was very nervous for him and hoped all would be resolved. "Hey there, man, how'd you do?" I said. The smile on Larry's face said it all.

"It went great. I could not believe how easy it was and how everything you said hit home. I gave him five K, and he cried for a few minutes about all he is losing. He then said how much he likes me and does not want to stand in my way to make it big. He made sure I understood that he is the first and only buyer of the films. I gave him two K additional as a bonus for all his help. I told him that was all I had and needed a break.

"He said how much he cares about me and bought me lunch and kissed me on both cheeks and welcomed me to his family. Boy, this fucker really thinks his shit don't stink, but I wouldn't like to get into a battle with him. He was surrounded by at least ten guys, all wannabes," Larry said with some pride.

"That is great. We now move forward, and let's not think of him. We are the new team in town, and if we have to, we'll blow their heads off. You got any problem with offing a few of those guys?" I said.

"No problem, Dan. I hate those fuckers and would love to get rid of a few. I'm ready anytime," Larry said.

The day was shot. So Larry and I decided to go to the Blue Parrot and get a bite to eat. If we were lucky, we would find a couple of chicks and maybe get laid tonight.

"Let's make sure we are always on the same wavelength, Larry. The way people get screwed is how they act and what they say. We have a common enemy—the Mob. No matter what you say, these guys will always want a piece of the action. If we keep our mouths shut about the movie business, we will be better off. We certainly can talk about films and movies but not about porn, because we don't know who the stoolies work for—the feds or the Mob. Every bartender has his source of information and makes a bundle by passing along information.

"The only thing we don't know is if they are passing it to the feds or the Mob. Bartenders are the worst of all, and next are the fringe gangsters who hang around bars and clubs hoping to make a name with some meaningful information passed along to the right Mob boss. As long as we keep our business private, we will be ahead of the game. We need women, and we will recruit them, especially after we fuck them, but not in a bar because our lives are far more valuable. Okay, partner?" I said.

Larry came over to me and put his arm around my shoulder. "I am so glad I met you, Dan. This relationship will always work. Thanks, buddy. Thanks for everything. I got your back, always." Off we went to the Blue Parrot.

When we walked in, Ron, the bartender, called out, "Hey, Larry, how's it going?"

"Just great, Ron. You remember Dan?" Larry said. I put my hand out to shake Ron's. "Great to see you again. Any action tonight, Ron?" I said.

"It's filling up fast. Why don't you guys sit here at the bar, and I will give a heads-up when some real action comes in. In the meantime, what are you drinking?" he said.

"Two vodkas on the rocks with a twist," I said. We sat at the bar nursing our drinks and looking over the action. Finally, two great-looking chicks walked in and sat down at the bar. We decided not to wait too long and get to the bottom line.

"Hi, I'm Larry, and this is my friend Dan. Can we buy you girls a drink?"

"Sure thing. I'm Natalie, and this Stephanie. Nice to meet you guys," she said. Here we are looking at two stunners. Natalie, a blonde with blue eyes and a face of an angel. She was about five feet two inches tall and was a knockout. Stephanie was a little taller with extra long hair and a body that was model material. She had brown eyes that went along with her brown hair just perfectly. These were two goddesses, and we were lucky enough to meet them.

"Are you from the city?" I asked Stephanie.

"We just moved in a week ago. We live in the village and are just getting acquainted with the city. We are from a little town in upstate New York, Lake George. It's a great place, but nothing to do once you get to our age. So we packed up our car and moved here."

"Welcome to New York City. It is your lucky day that we met. Have you eaten?" I said.

"No, we haven't. Are you inviting us for dinner?" she said.

"You got it. Ron, can you get us a table?" I said as I threw down a ten dollars for him. We were seated right away, and Larry ordered a bottle of champagne. I guess the next film will be a little more expensive. "Well, Stephanie, tell us a little about yourself. What did you do in Lake George? What will you do in the city?" I said as Larry was lifting the champagne glass for a toast.

"To a lucky break for all of us, meeting here, and having some fun. Drink up and enjoy," Larry said.

"Well, let me tell you about us. It really isn't very interesting. Growing up in a small town like Lake George was very boring. The place rocks in the summer when tons of people spend time boating and swimming. They rent houses for the summer season and leave the family there to have fun and stay out of their hair. The day after Labor Day, it all ends and it becomes a morgue again. Winter was very boring even though we are not far from Lake Placid. After getting out of high school, we were going to go to college but just never got around to it. We started working at the Orange Jug, a drive-in that was open in the summer only. We were car hops and made a lot of money but were going nowhere. This year we decided to get out and make our way in the big city. We made a few bucks and have enough to last about six months. We feel we will be able to get into acting and modeling and, if we get a break, start making some money before the six months run out. There, you have it in a nutshell," Natalie said.

"Well, girls, I hope you believe this. Today was meant to happen," Larry said with a big smile. "We are in the movie business and are always looking for some real talent. I know you think I'm just making this up, but it's true. We are in the movie business, and maybe we can help you get started. How old are you, girls?"

"We are nineteen years old and it's true. We can sing, dance, and, we think, act as well," Stephanie said. "All we need is a break, and that's why we're here in the city. We just don't want to be screwed over by anyone. You know what I mean?"

"Let me tell you, girls," I said. "Every guy who meets you will want to take you to bed. There is no question about that. You are both very beautiful and look great in every respect. If I would tell you I didn't want to take you to bed I'd be a liar, but that is not what I will do because I like you and really want to help, and I'm sure Larry feels the same way. We are only human, but we are also business people, and with girls as beautiful as you are, we are certain we can get you some work, and we both can make some money."

"Well, that is a relief," Natalie said. "Can we eat now? I'm starved." We ate and drank and had a great time. It was now nine thirty, and Larry suggested we go back to the studio. We were all feeling no pain as we walked back to Fifth and Twentieth and just having a lot of fun. When we finally got up to the top floor and went in, the girls were convinced and excited that indeed we were for real. Larry gave them a tour of the studio.

"Here are some of the sets we use. See how simple it is to create an atmosphere," he said. "Wow! That is neat," Stephanie said, as she inspected the cameras. The klieg lights really got them excited, and Larry's director's chair sealed the deal.

The girls were putty in our hands as they wanted to get involved in show business. It was obvious that they were not aware that we made porn as their innocence showed through and through.

"It's getting late," Natalie said. "Don't you think it's time to go home, Steph?"

I spoke up at once, "Let me call you a cab and get you on the way. How about your number? How can we get in touch?" They gave us their number, and we promised to call them tomorrow, and perhaps we could have some fun and discuss how they could get into the show business. I went downstairs with them and put them into the cab and gave the driver a twenty.

Thursday, October 10, 1957

I called Larry. It was about ten in the morning. "Hey there, how are you doing?" I said.

"I feel great and just spoke with Natalie. They want to get together later today for a few drinks and maybe a little information about the movie business. I'm writing a new script that will have them both involved," Larry said and continued. "I think they will be big hits in the business. They are good-looking, and that's what the viewers want—someone nice and easy to look at. Most importantly, they want to feel that they could be the lucky guy sleeping with that woman. These girls have that air about them."

"I agree with you. Even I feel that way, Larry. What time do we meet them?" I said with anticipation.

"Get here about noon, and I'll set something up for a late lunch or an early dinner. This is going to be great, Dan. I can feel it," Larry said.

I hung up and was so excited I felt like I was walking on air. I could easily relate to Larry's description of what made a true porn star. I wanted to get laid, but I also wanted to get the show on the road. I reminded myself that I was still a wanted man and should take everything very slowly and be cautious. I must be aware at all times of my surroundings and always carry my gun and always be ready. I felt a little down as the reality of the situation dampened my desires a little, but after a long shower and putting on some dandy-looking clothes, I felt revitalized and ready for action.

It was about seventy-five degrees, a very warm day for October. The sun was shining, and everything seemed almost perfect. I jumped into a cab and rode down to Twentieth Street to Larry's. I arrived close to noon and went upstairs to the loft to get the day started. When the elevator door opened, I had a feeling something was wrong; Larry was not in his usual place up front. I noticed that Larry's typewriter and table were lying on the floor in the far corner of the room. I immediately removed my gun from its holster and took a very defensive position.

I crossed the office toward the back of the loft where all the sets were and saw two heavyset guys dragging Larry toward the bathroom. I carefully made my way past the sets and lights; obviously they hadn't heard the elevator and didn't know I was there. I could hear them speaking to Larry, "Carmine wants you to know that you can't shoot anymore movies unless he gives you the okay," the very big guy said. He must have been well over six feet and weighed in at about three hundred pounds. His hands were so big that Larry's face was hidden behind it.

"Go fuck Carmine and you as well," Larry yelled. The other guy who was not much smaller hit Larry in the ribs, and Larry went down on all fours and cried in pain.

I didn't want Larry to be in any danger, and I didn't want these bastards hitting him again. I jumped up from behind a set piece. "Hey, you fuck faces, get away from him or I'll blow your heads off," I yelled as I aimed my gun directly at the bigger of the two guys. I'll make you shit your pants, and then I'll kill you, nice and slow. You go tell Carmine that the next bullet is for him. That rat bastard was paid in full. What the fuck does he think he can do now? Muscle won't work with us. Now get your asses out of here, or you will never leave here alive, and never come back here."

"Fuck you," the big guy yelled. "I'll kill you before you can even fire that gun, you little prick. Drop the gun and I'll just beat the shit out of you. Keep it up and I'll kill you. You make up your mind, asshole. I'll kill Larry with one squeeze of my hand, capish?"

I looked at this prick and could not believe my ears. I fired directly into his face and down he went.

"Please don't shoot," the other mobster cried. "I didn't know you had a deal with Carmine. If I did, I would never have come along. Please don't kill me."

"Fuck him," Larry said as he recovered his balance and some degree of composure. He turned toward this guy and hit him as hard as I have ever seen anyone hit someone.

"That felt good, you son of a bitch. You should be killed. Now get the fuck up and give me your gun, now!" he yelled at him as the guy held his nose as it bled everywhere. He handed Larry his gun and just stood there in fear.

"What do you want to do, Larry? Give me the word, and I'll blow him away," I said.

"Pick up your buddy and drag him along," Larry said. He had the guy drag the giant to the back of the loft where the freight elevator was.

"Now get those burlap bags over there and wrap him up in them, fast. I don't have all day, asshole," Larry said.

He began wrapping the body as fast as he could. He was shaking and bleeding and mumbling to himself, "I didn't sign on for this. What the hell am I doing here?" he mumbled over and over.

"Where is your car parked?" Larry said.

"Just around the corner on Twenty-First Street," he said.

"Give me the keys, and put your buddy on the elevator, fast," Larry said. "You keep your gun on this guy. If he fucking moves, kill him. I'll go get the car and pull it around the back so we can get rid of the body. Don't take any chances with this prick," Larry said to me as the elevator appeared on our floor.

The goon started to speak, "The keys are in his pocket. Let me get them for you. Please don't shoot," he said nervously as he slowly bent down and started to go through his dead friend's pockets. "Here, here they are. Here!" He was very nervous and just peed in his pants. He handed the keys to Larry and started loading his buddy on the elevator in the burlap bags, and we all went down to the loading dock.

"Okay, you guys wait here. I'll be right back. If you want to live, you'll do what you're told, and then you can go tell Carmine to get fucked, you understand?"

"Sure thing, I understand, boss. I won't make any trouble," he said. Larry went to get the car, and I stood watch over the piece of shit.

"I really don't understand why you would put the muscle on Larry. He paid his bill, and he agreed to offer every movie to Carmine first. What the fuck is wrong with him?" I said in a very menacing tone.

Larry came around the corner driving a large, black Caddy around to the back of the building and backed it into the loading dock.

"Get that bag into the trunk. Come on, hurry up," he said. I kept the gun aimed at the big guy as he lifted the body and placed it in the trunk.

Larry went back inside and came out with a shovel in his hand. He placed it in the trunk. "Okay, get in the car. We're going for a ride and get rid of this garbage, and then you can tell Carmine that if he pulls this shit again, he will be the next target. Give us any trouble, and you won't be seeing anyone ever again," Larry said.

I got into the backseat, and the big Mob guy sat next to me. "If you want to live, then I'd suggest you look out the window and enjoy the trip. No funny stuff and no conversation," I said.

We drove out through the Lincoln Tunnel into New Jersey, when Larry said, "Give me the gun, and I'll cover him. You blindfold him until we get there."

We kept going until we got to the Delaware Water Gap and moved into Pennsylvania. The drive took us two hours, and now we were in real deep country. Larry finally turned off Interstate 80 and took route 611 into a town named Bartonsville. I knew this area well as I had a house and a wife here in another time. I wasn't going to tell Larry as I felt this was not the time. He then veered off and took some back road until we were deep into the woods. There were no houses for miles, just trees and growth. He pulled into the forest as far as the car could go and got out.

"Everyone out," he said. I took the blindfold off him, and we all got out as he opened the trunk and said, "Get the bag and follow me. Dan stay back a little and keep this goon covered," he said as he grabbed the shovel. Finally, he stopped and said, "Put him over there and cover him with leaves and bushes. Let the animals find him if they are hungry." The big goon did as he was told and then looked at both of us and said, "Okay, can I go now? Please don't kill me. I was never going to hurt you, please!" he pleaded. Larry took the gun from my hand. He turned to this guy and said, "Sorry, man, I can't afford to let you loose. You guys had a real offer when Dan asked you to leave, and you guys threatened to kill us. You chose this life and knew the consequences," he said as he fired one shot through his head just above his left eye.

"Now let Carmine wonder what happened to his men. We'll act as if we never saw them or know what he is talking about. Now let's cover this guy up and get out of here. We'll ditch the car in Manhattan and hope someone steals it." We went through their clothing and removed all forms of identification as well as their money and covered the bodies up and jumped back into the car and drove back to town.

It was five-thirty P.M. when we finally got back to the loft. Larry said, "Let's call the girls and see if they want to have dinner and a few drinks. Maybe we will get lucky." He called the girls and spoke with Stephanie. "They'll be here about seven. Let's get ready to party, my friend. Tonight is fun and only fun. No other problems on our minds."

I said to Larry, "We better clean up the blood at the end of the loft. There is no need to leave any evidence around even though I think it will be a long time before they are found. We took a pail of hot water and bleach and scrubbed real hard. Lucky for us the area where the blood hit the floor was covered in loose linoleum. This made the clean easy. In a few minutes, all signs of what took place were gone. I took a cab home, showered and shaved, and met Larry and the girls at the Blue Parrot a few minutes after seven.

The events of the day were things of the past; I didn't feel any remorse at all as these guys would have killed us both without a thought. I don't agree with cold-blooded murder, but in this case I didn't feel it was wrong; it was self defense. Now it was time to enjoy the night with people I liked and cared about.

"Hi everyone. Sorry, I'm late. It took a few minutes to get a cab," I said with a big smile. I leaned over and kissed the girls in the cheeks and gave them a little squeeze. "Let's get a little drunk and have a super meal and party till dawn," I said.

"Sounds good to us," Natalie said. It seems that Larry had his eye on Stephanie, so I was left with Natalie. Not so bad; she was a looker and I liked her. I had no objections to this at all. We ordered a bottle of Dom and some great steaks and ate like this was the most enjoyable day of our lives. We laughed and drank and finally decided to go back to the studio, "Let's make a movie," Stephanie said as she laughed and kissed Larry.

We went back to the studio and locked the elevator door so that no unexpected guests could intrude. It was action time, and why not, we had plenty of energy to release.

"Why don't we talk about the movies?" Natalie said.

"Okay, sweetie, where do you want to start?" I said.

"Let's first get comfortable and have a drink," Larry said. We removed our shirts and took off our shoes and just lounged on one of the beds with a drink in our hands.

"Listen, girls, there is no room here for bullshit. I'm sure you realize that we make adult films? We are not into the Hollywood type of movies even though we have had more innovation in movies than anyone. We make adult films and take each and every project very seriously. You can make a lot of money and get very famous doing something you like to do. It is not a sleazy business as many people would like you to believe, but it does make heads turn and you can't always tell your friends what type of movies you star in, "Larry said very seriously.

"I thought so," Natalie said. "But I still want to try it out. I think I can be a big star in these films and maybe move on to some straight films. In any case, I like you guys, and if the people in this industry are like you two, then it is okay with me."

"Well, that's a mouthful," I said, as we all laughed at the double meaning. "Thanks for the vote of confidence, but let me warn you, not all the people in the industry are as nice. Regardless, not all the people in any movie business are nice. Most importantly, we try to be good to others and build a good name for ourselves. If someone can't handle the type of movies you star in, then it's their problem not yours. It's not an easy job like people think. The only thing is that most people never get past the first ten minutes of any porn film. No viewer wants to see anyone getting laid if there is no emotion involved. You have to suck the viewer into you like any good film with a story so that they feel they can identify with the character you are playing. It's not easy but damn rewarding when it works. The world is your oyster once you have established that magic between you and your fans."

"I'm ready," Stephanie said.

"So am I," Natalie countered.

"One thing I want to make clear. You will both have to sign an exclusivity agreement. That means you will not be able to star in any movies other than ours. If we grant permission for another film company to use you in a film of theirs, we will be certain to get a good price. This agreement will keep you from being used by many other companies and diluting your popularity. I also want to be your manager," I said.

"Are we making a mistake here, Dan?" Natalie asked.

"No, as manager, I will protect your interests at all times. I will make sure you are properly paid and that anything you do is in your best interests regardless of any personal feelings," I said.

"Look, guys, you have us because we don't know anyone else," Natalie said. "You can screw us easily or you can be honest and take care of us. Yet I come from the country, and the only thing I ever knew out there was trust. If I felt good about a person I trusted them, and that is how I have lived all my life. I trust you guys and am ready. I'll sign anything you ask me to, and I'll be a good actress. This I promise. All I ask is that you tell me everything all the time. Don't treat me like a bimbo. I am smart and loyal and will always treat you with respect and expect the same from you," Stephanie said.

"Wow! That was some speech, but I will always respect both of you and never lie to you. Welcome to a new career. Starting right now, both of you are working for Climax Films," I said with a big smile. "We now have to find some real good names for you both. In this business, we need sexy names especially when we have such gorgeous women as you are!"

I didn't waste anymore time talking. I took Natalie home with me and spent the rest of the night making love to her.

Friday, October 11, 1957

When I woke up, I found Natalie at my side fast asleep. It was about eight A.M. and time for me to get out of bed and start the day. I called Moe Arnold and told him what I was doing. "Are you nuts? What the hell are you doing here in town?" he yelled into the phone.

"Calm down, Moe. I think the best place to hide out is in plain sight. I'm low-key and live under another name and have changed my appearance so that no one would recognize me. I am now involved in the adult film business with a friend of mine. I am not a front man. I work in the background and will never deal with anyone from the Mob. Moe, I need to be busy and make some money as well. This does it all for me, and I promise I'll be very careful. Please trust me on that. I know you have my best interests at heart, and I love you for it. Here is what I need—a contract that binds actors and actresses exclusively to Over the Top Films. They cannot work for any other studio nor can they perform without permission by us. I also need a manager's contract, because I want to represent some of the stars as their manager. I want to decide what is best for them and, of course, I want my fifteen percent fee. Can you do this please?" I said. "Oh by the way, Moe, please bill OTF for the contract and any other work we may ask of you."

"All right, Harry, you sound excited, and that's most important to me. Your contracts will ready on Tuesday. Call me and we'll arrange a meet or something. Are you okay? Harry, what is going on with your marriage?" Moe asked.

"It's over, Moe. Carol and I agreed that it would be best if we did not stay married. She returned to her parents in Allentown, and I guess is preparing to annul the marriage. We agreed that she will get in touch with you when all is ready, and you will get in touch with me. Things are good, and life seems to be getting better and better all the time. Wow! Married twice in the same year. It must be a record? I'll call you Tuesday and then we can meet at your office, after all I am Dan All right, just another client," I said with a laugh as I gave Moe the address of OTF. I hung up feeling a lot better now that things were back on the right road.

I woke Natalie. "Get up sleepyhead. Let's go and have breakfast," I said as I kissed her gently. "I know you didn't have much time to think it over but have you thought about a stage name?" I said as I handed her the jeans I just picked up off the floor.

"No, silly, I was too drunk and then asleep, but this will be my project for today. Let me grab a fast shower and put my face on, and we'll go have something to eat. I'm starved," she said with a big smile.

We grabbed a cab and went to the studio where I thought we would surprise Larry and Stephanie. When we arrived, I signaled Natalie to be quiet and let them sleep as I walked slowly over and took her hand and led her to the rear area. We had left a few things there last night and quietly tried to retrieve them and make our way toward the elevator when Larry's voice seemed to float over the high ceiling, "Where you going, pal?" he said. I looked back and there was Larry sitting up in bed and smiling, "So where are you guys off to?"

"We are trying to go have something to eat and not wake you. I guess we did a lousy job of it!" I said.

"Aw, come on, Dan. I'm only kidding. You didn't wake me. I was getting up anyways. Hang in there, and we'll join you guys. Give us ten minutes," Larry said with a big smile.

"No problem," I said. "We'll wait, but we are hungry, so get your ass moving," I said laughing.

While Larry and Stephanie showered we sat around and started to throw names around. "What do you think of, Shirley LaRue? Or Sandra Nicely? How about Pussy Willow or Queenie? Boy, there are so many variables. I think we need to get a connotation of sex into the name. This will insure instant recognition by the viewers and make it real easy to build a following. What do you think, Nat?" I said.

"I think you are right. That's why I want to take my time and use a name that will be just right. There is no need to rush into it when another day or two will do. It's like I want the guys to know who I am but not my folks, even though they would never watch XXX-rated movies. It's not easy, Dan, not at all," she said as she squeezed my arm and kissed me.

I was very happy and wanted this time to stay with us forever. I wanted her to be a big star and to be happy. I realized that life will not always be as much fun as it is now. This is the beginning, and she will grow and will be exposed to other guys, so getting carried away will only hurt us both. I would do my very best to enjoy her for as long as possible; business first and fun later. I did feel lucky because of where I was. I was in a great business. Each day was fun and filled with experiences that very few people can honestly say they may have. I was going to enjoy this to the maximum and would always be grateful for the pleasures I experience.

We left the studio and went for breakfast—a breakfast that took over two hours as we discussed the first movie that will feature the girls. We threw many names around as the girls were very serious about this. Finally Stephanie decided on Mary Lou; she felt she looked like a Mary Lou would look, and her babyish voice would add to her sexual appeal.

She was so excited and could not contain herself as she explained to Larry and me that she wanted to make her name a famous one.

"I'll need photos that I can sign for my fan club. I want my own color scheme. Everything I own will need to have pink in it, the color of my pussy. I want towels with ML embroidered on them in pink. I'll need short shorts in pink and ML in white embroidered on them. You understand what I want and need. If I am to create the impression I am Mary Lou I'll need to live my life as Mary Lou," she said with a big smile on her face.

Larry sat there and smiled as well as he was, without doubt, turned on by Mary Lou's color scheme and her dress code. Larry loved young girls over eighteen but below twenty-four, and if he could, he would have all of them dress up in short little white dresses. The Mary Lou persona was a gift from heaven; he loved it.

Natalie was as excited as Stephanie was as she piped in, "You'll look great Mary Lou. I can hardly wait. Let's go shopping today and get the new Mary Lou on the road to stardom. Boy, I can hardly wait," she said with sincere enthusiasm.

So far we had not found a name for Natalie, but Mary Lou was born as she said, "Don't call me by any other name any longer. From now on, I'm Mary Lou all the way except in my private life. When we go home for a visit, I'll be Stephanie again. Now let's go shopping."

Larry gave her five hundred dollars and told her to make Mary Lou look exactly as she wanted. Natalie and Mary Lou left for their shopping spree, while Larry and I went back to the studio to go over our plans.

It was close to six when the girls came back to the studio with both of them carrying bags of stuff they had bought. They were excited, and Mary Lou could hardly wait to show us her purchases. She tried on her little white dress and her short shorts all with the initials, ML. She was as happy as we have ever seen her. She fit right into her new identity and loved every second of it.

"Well, I'm glad you only had five hundred," I said jokingly.

"Come now, Dan," Mary Lou said with a big smile. "I could have spent three times that. Tell me the truth, do I look good or not?"

"You look great! You are Mary Lou, and you will be famous. This I can assure you. I'm real proud of you, and now all we have to do is to find a very special name for Nat and we are all set. What do you want to do tonight?" I said.

"I'm beat," Nat said. "I'd like to go home and just relax. We haven't been home in two days, and I need a little rest. Let's get together tomorrow for dinner and present Mary Lou with her first public appearance. Sound good to you, guys?" she said.

"Okay with me. Let me get you a cab," I said. The girls left, and Larry and I welcomed the quiet time we now had. We were getting worn out. It wasn't easy keeping up to these girls who seemed to be able to party forever. I finally went home just to get some sleep and get my strength back.

Saturday, October 12, 1957

I woke at around eight and cleaned up my apartment. The day appeared to be nice but cool. I waited until noon and then called Larry, "Hey, how are you doing?" I said,

"Great and you old man?" he replied.

"I'm ready for some action tonight just to see how Mary Lou will be received. Have you picked out a place for tonight?" I said.

"No, not yet, but I think we should skip the Blue Parrot and perhaps do Tavern on the Green in Central Park. I know it's a little expensive, but I think we'll cause a buzz with the girls.

Let me give them a call and I'll call you back. Stay by your phone." And he hung up.

An hour later Larry called, "Okay, we are set for seven tonight. We have to wear jackets. I'm certain the girls will raise some eyebrows as there will be some celebrities there. We'll do the Carlyle Hotel another time. Tonight it's the Tavern on the Green. I called the girls and told them about our night out. They are very excited and can hardly wait. Natalie is still trying to come up with the right name but will wear some very provocative stuff tonight. I told them to take a cab directly to the restaurant, and we will meet them there at seven," he said.

We met at Tavern on the Green at exactly seven as Larry and I arrived right on time. We advised the maître d' that we were just waiting for our girls to arrive. At once he knew who we were and asked us to follow him to the bar area. Sitting at the bar were two beautiful girls that seemed to stop all traffic as each waiter could not help themselves from gawking at them.

"Your table will be ready in a few moments, Mr. Robbins. I'll come and get you," he said. Larry had just given him a twenty, and he was thrilled. "Thank you, sir. If there is anything I can do for you please let me know," he said with a big smile.

The girls looked unbelievable. Mary Lou looked stunning in her white dress with pink piping. Her cleavage was a thing of beauty that made everyone look and look once again. Nat was a little more subdued but not very much as she wore a black dress with an open back and her hair up in bun. She looked like she had just left the movie screen and walked into real life. Her beauty was radiant as was Mary Lou's glowing. We had two winners here, and we knew it. Once seated at our table, people could not help but stare and wonder who these people were. While we were having an after-dinner drink, a man came over to our table to introduce himself.

"Hello, I am Rudy Valle. I just could not help it. but I had to say hello to you folks. I don't normally do this as I appreciate being left alone when I am out on the town, but I could not help myself as you are such a handsome group of people. Are you in show business?" he said with a big smile and a very poor toupee.

"Yes we are in town to begin shooting a new film. This is Mary Lou and Natalie More. My name is Dan All right, and this is Larry Robbins, the director. A pleasure to meet you, Mr. Valle. Would you like to join us for a drink?" I said very respectfully.

"That is very kind of you, but I am with a party and must not leave them alone too long. Here is my card. Please give me a call when you do have some time, and perhaps we can have dinner together," he said. We said our good-byes to Rudy Valle and could hardly wait to laugh at this most bizarre incident.

Although Rudy was old school, just his act of stopping by made everyone wonder who we were. Most everyone thought we were very important people from Hollywood.

The girls looked great, and we wanted to take advantage of our good fortune and continue our evening of fun. Tomorrow was Sunday, so we could sleep late and take all the time off we want. We decided to go to the Café Carlyle in the Carlyle Hotel. George Feyer, the jazz musician, was playing there, and we figured there should be a few celebrities on hand. We took a cab to the hotel and went directly to the Café. The

ALLAN BARRIE

maître d' almost did a double take when he saw the girls; he just couldn't take his eyes off them. "Yes, sir, can I help you?" he said.

"I wonder if there is room for us," I said as I slipped him a twenty. "I am not certain if the studio did make a reservation or not, because we only decided an hour ago that we would like to have a few drinks here and listen to George," I said.

"No problem, sir. I believe the studio did call. Your table will be ready in a few moments. Would you like to sit at the bar until we make the table ready, sir?" he said. "No thanks. We'll just wait here if it's all right with you," I said I slipped him another twenty.

"No problem, sir. It won't be long," he said cordially. Once again we were seated and enjoying a bottle of champagne as people looked at us with a stare of recognition.

"I like your choice of names, Dan," Nat said.

"I just didn't want to introduce you using your real name fast on my feet, so to speak," I said. "Well, I like it and maybe I should use the name Natalia More? It sounds good with a little intrigue in it, and of course, once they see me they will never forget it. I like it. What do you guys think?" she said.

"I think it's great," Larry said.

"So do I!" Mary Lou said.

"I guess that settles it. From now on you're Natalia More, femme fatale," I said. "A drink to seal the start of a new name and a new career. Let's get the show on the road," I said. We finally left the Carlyle as Natalia and I took a cab to my place on Ninety-First Street and Larry went to the studio. We had agreed to get together tomorrow for brunch if we got up in time.

Sunday, October 13, 1957

We woke at about eleven and felt real good. It was amazing how nice we were feeling after drinking so much and having a lot of sex. We were ready to attack a new day especially Natalia as she would be known from now on. Of course, Natalie understood that each time she went out in the public eye she had to look her best. If she was to build a reputation, it was clear that the fan base wanted their star to be perfect, always.

I called Larry, and we agreed to meet for brunch at the Mayflower Hotel on the West side at one.

"Hurry up, Nat. We are meeting Larry and Mary Lou at the Mayflower Hotel at one," I said. "Dan, why so early?" she said as she laughed on her way to the shower. It was about twelve thirty when I yelled out to Nat in the bedroom.

"Are you ready? We have to catch a cab and try to be there on time."

"Okay, sweetie. I only need another minute and we can go," she said as she walked out of the bedroom looking like a goddess. I was moved as I looked at this gorgeous woman—sexy, tall, and just a super good-looking woman, but now a movie star.

"Wow!" I said. "You are beautiful!"

"Thanks, honey. I am trying to look good for my public. Now that I know you like it, it's fine with me," she said as she kissed me on the cheek.

"Smashing. I just can't get over how great you look. Delicious," I said as we made our way out the door. We hailed a cab on Second Avenue and headed for the Mayflower. As we drove through Central Park, I thought: Is the World ready for her? She is a stunner and heads will turn. Am I doing the right thing? I don't need talk. I don't need attention if I am to keep a low profile. Although she was a super beautiful woman, she was also a recipe for disaster, especially for me. I decided I will have to stop making public appearances. I'll have a heart to heart with Larry about this tomorrow. Today was already under way. So make the best of it, and we'll change it all tomorrow.

We arrived at the Mayflower, and I knew the minute she stepped out of the cab that this was a mistake. People stopped in their tracks and just stared at this goddess as she started to walk up the stairs into the hotel. Heads turned as she walked with confidence and a big smile on her face. I knew right there and then that this type of exposure was great for her but not so good for me. I thanked my lucky stars that she did not wait for me as I paid the cabbie and walked directly to the dining area where she spotted Larry and Mary Lou.

"Natalia, here we are," Mary Lou yelled and waved the second she walked into the dining room. Nat acknowledged her by waving back and walking slowly and very deliberately to their table. Everyone in the dining room stopped whatever they were doing and just stared at Natalia—it was a sight to see.

"Sorry, I'm late, guys. There was a little more traffic than anticipated," she said as she sat down. I arrived a moment later and kissed Mary Lou and gave Larry a pat on the shoulder. "What a day, isn't it?" I said. "I think we have created a couple of superstars here. Did you see the people in this room?

They all, and I mean all, stopped and stared first at Mary Lou and now at Nat. "These girls are stunners. I think we have created something here," Larry said with a big smile.

The waiter came over to our table to take our order and asked, "Can I get your autographs, please?"

"Of course," Mary Lou said. "What's your name?" "George O'Malley. Thanks," he said. Mary Lou signed a photo she had in her bag and then gave the pen to Nat who followed suit.

"Gee thanks. By the way, are you actresses?" George asked as he poured the champagne. "Yes we are," Mary Lou said. "How did you guess?"

"I just knew it," George responded. "I have an eye for movie stars. Is any of your movies in the theaters now?"

"Our first movie will be released in January. We don't know the title yet as we just finished shooting the last scene yesterday. We'll see you again George, and I'll be able to give more details. It's great to meet you, George. How about a little more champagne!" Nat said with a big smile. George floated away with a big smile on his face. If this was an indication of the reaction of men, then we have two winners here. I knew we would be rich with these girls; they were pure gold. Let's see if I could have it both ways and not get my head blown away.

We spent the next two hours enjoying our brunch but liking the reactions of the guys even more. These girls were dynamite, and every guy who met them wanted to get into their pants. Success was around the corner; I could feel it. We finally left the Mayflower and decided to go back to the studio.

"I hate to be a party pooper, but I must work on the script if we are to ever get a movie started," Larry said.

"Can't we help?" Mary Lou said. "We can give you some ideas and maybe we can all contribute a little. Come on, Larry, let us help, please." We took a cab to the studio and didn't give Larry much choice as we all took the elevator up to the studio.

We left Larry alone so that he could sit by his typewriter, and with his famous one-finger pecking system, he started to pound out a script. In the meantime, I sat with the girls in the set area as they wanted to take a nap.

"All that food and champagne knocks the shit out of you. I can see it your eyes," I said to both of them. "There are plenty of beds, so take a little nap. I'll wake you later."

I woke the girls at six thirty. I was afraid that if they slept any later, they would not be able to sleep tonight.

"Hey. What time is it?" Mary Lou said as she sat up rubbing her eyes.

"It's six thirty. Night has fallen, and Larry is still hard at it. How do you feel?" I said.

"I feel a little groggy, but I don't want to sleep any longer. It will screw up the rest of the night," she said. We all got moving around, and soon we were talking about the day. I decided that I must explain to these girls that there is danger lurking about. I changed the story a little but did deliver the message.

"Maybe we shouldn't get into this business?" Natalia said.

"I don't think that you girls have anything to worry about. You are not in any danger. The actors and others who make the movies are not in any danger at any time. The people who are in the path of being fucked up are the filmmakers. Remember, the adult industry is still a growing genre. Of course, this form of entertainment has been around since the beginning of time and will be here long after we are gone. The problem is simply this, while it is an industry in the grey area, the money that is being made is big. The Mob wants their piece of action because that is the way they operate. They also control the theaters and almost all other avenues of distribution. They don't want to get their hands dirty, so they don't make the movies, but they want all the movie distribution to go through them. This is the way they control the industry, and they take the lion's share of the money. If they don't like you or feel you are trying to fuck them, they will try to do serious physical harm to you or just get rid of you. So actors, directors, grips, or anyone else other than the actual filmmakers need not worry. What concerned me today is that wherever we went heads turned. All privacy was shot out the window, and it made Larry and I easy targets. You can be sure that the Mob is already aware of the two gorgeous femmes fatales that are the newest movie stars to hit the scene. Of course, they do not know just yet that you are in the porn films they will buy, but once they find that out, they'll love it and will make more money because everyone will want to go to the theater to see these beauties. Cash registers will be ringing, and the Mob will love it. As long as Larry makes movies and as long as the theaters are filled, there will be no trouble. I tell you all this because I can't be out in the limelight. I'm only making myself a target and this is not what I want to do. I don't need to feed my ego to be seen in public with you girls. Sure I don't mind all the publicity, but in the end, it can't do me any good. So from now on, you will have to leave me in the background.

"I'll still be involved with the entire operation, and I'll still be in love with you, Natalia, but I have to abstain from public appearances. I sure hope you understand and will work with me to keep us all healthy and allow us the opportunity to spend the money we will make," I said.

Monday, October 14, 1957

I woke early as the trash collectors were throwing around the metal garbage cans. It seems it is their job to wake the entire city via garbage collection. I showered and jumped into a cab and rode to the studio. Larry was already awake and busy typing on his little typewriter. "Top of the morning to you," I said to Larry. "I sure had a good time this weekend and am convinced that we have some super girls and can make them into very popular stars."

"Well, aren't we full of great dreams today," Larry said. "Let's get off cloud nine and look at the facts, Dan," Larry said. "First, you know that the cops, especially the feds, are trying to bust porn everywhere they can. Sure we won't be grabbed, but we have to operate underground while the atmosphere is like it is. The Mob rules the distribution network. Without them we are dead meat. We can sell our films in Europe, but it is hard to ship the films out of the country. If the customs guys find them, they will confiscate them and destroy them. They can also charge the sender with distribution of obscene material, but that can be avoided by using a phony name. The world is changing fast, and soon porn will be accepted, and it will no longer be a tool to be used to prosecute, but right now it is good publicity for politicians to bust a porn filmmaker as it makes good headlines. Sex has been around since the beginning of time, and no matter what they do, they cannot eliminate it and never will. Yes, the girls are great and can turn every head whenever they want to, but can they act? A film has to have some feeling in it, and sex is no different. If the viewer sees that there isn't any sparkle in her eyes and the sex is not real, he will look elsewhere for his sexual fantasies. It's hard to jerk off in a theater, so the feel of sincerity and real emotions needs to be there. There has to be communication between the actor and the viewer. Did you ever go to a strip show? Well, if you did, you know damn well that you and everyone else thinks she is turned on by you. That you are the one whom she likes and you are Mr. Right. How many times have you said, "She is looking at me" "I know she likes me," and once you feel that way, the bucks come out, and she has you in her pocket. Take my word for it, old buddy," he said.

"I know you are right, Larry, but I'm no different than any other man. When you see a beautiful woman with a body to die for, the rest of me can only think of taking her to bed. Seeing her on the screen will only heighten that desire. Yet I know how fucked I am and now you as well. We offed two guys that Carmine sent after us. Half the Mob is looking for me, and there is a price on my head that is probably about two hundred K

"Yet I'm the biggest asshole of all, because instead of being low-key, I'm out with two beautiful broads and making sure everyone knows it. I must have a death wish, and now, all because of pussy, I have placed you in harm's way. I suck, don't I?" I said.

"Look Dan," Larry said. "I made a deal with you, and I was very much aware of all the baggage you came with. I don't give a shit about the Mob and will go to war if we have to.

"I care about you, and of course, I care about myself as well, and I agree with you about this exposure route we have taken. Let's change our way, and let's move forward. If the Mob wants a fight, bring them on. I have plenty of guns here and will gladly use them on these guys until they kill me, or we kill them all. Don't worry, Dan. You are my lifetime partner and that is final," he said. I felt good about Larry's attitude and felt we were on the way to the path of success. I only hope that all the shit I left behind stays behind.

Larry went back to polishing his script while I was working on the sets in the back of the studio. It was nearing one, and I felt a little hungry. I started toward the front of the studio when I heard the elevator door open. I stopped in my tracks and moved a little to my left where I would not easily be seen. Two giants stepped out of the elevator and walked directly toward Larry; it didn't look good at all. I inched along the wall until I came to a desk that is used in the films; this caused a small problem as I had to go around the desk and risked exposure. I had my gun with me and held it in my right hand as I decided to get on the floor and crawl around the desk. I moved very slowly and very quietly, always keeping my eyes zeroed in on those two guys. As I got closer, I could hear the conversation. The first guy said, "Larry, we came over to see how you are. Last week, we sent two guys out here to meet with you, and they never returned. Do you know anything about that?"

"Excuse me, who are you guys?" Larry said. "I don't know you. Why are you here? Come on guys, what's this all about?"

"You are a real smart ass, aren't you?" the giant said. "Carmine sent us over, and we aren't leaving here without some answers, or we'll beat the shit out of you. Now cut the crap and get with it, asshole!" At that moment Larry stood up from his little typewriter table and stood face-to-face with the giant and his stooge. The giant grabbed Larry by his shirt lapels and lifted him off the ground as if he was a fly.

"Listen to me, you piece of shit. I'm here to find some answers. Fuck with me and you will be sorry. Very, very sorry," he said as he put Larry back down. It was hard to believe that this guy could lift Larry up like he was nothing. Larry was at least six feet tall and weighed close to two hundred pounds, yet to this guy he was as light as air. "Now shut up and listen, you asshole," the giant said.

Larry just stood there staring this guy in the eye showing no fear and ready for a fight. I watched all this in awe as these two guys were big and nasty-looking. "Now, Larry, did you see two guys last week? The giant said.

"I didn't see anyone, and why should I see anyone at all. I have a deal with Carmine. We settled everything last week, so why the hell would he send you or anyone else?" Larry said with authority.

"Well, here is the message. Carmine needs some shows. Get them done as fast as possible. Just remember, you can't shoot any movie without Carmine's okay. When you are ready to shoot, you call Carmine, and he will give you the okay. There will be a movie fee that has to be paid up front. I hope you got that straight? You don't want anymore trouble, and you don't want us back, capish?" he said.

"Fuck you and fuck Carmine," Larry said. "We won't pay any movie fees, and if Carmine wants to play this game, there won't be any movies at all. What will he do when his theaters are running out of new movies? I just don't understand why you guys aren't satisfied with a smooth running deal. I just don't know. Get the hell out of here and don't come back," Larry screamed at the top of his lungs. Once the goons left, Larry and I decided to go to the Blue Parrot for a drink or two and discuss the future.

We found a nice table as it was pretty empty as the lunch crowd had left. We ordered a couple of drinks as we got into the serious side of what we should do about the Carmine situation. "Look Larry," I said.

"I'm ready to go to war with this ratbag once and for all. I can easily give you some names of some very powerful Mob bosses, and you can set up a meeting and state your case. You can't ever take me to any meeting as that would cause some serious fireworks, but you can tell them what is going on. I don't know if they would support you. It all depends on how much they like or dislike Carmine. In any case, it could cause a war. It could cost you your life, or it could be resolved. In either case, it is a crap shoot, and I'm with you all the way. If there is a war, I'll be fighting alongside, and we will kill those bastards, but that will end your film business here in New York."

"Wow! That's a lot of ifs. I don't want to give up the film business as I love it, and it is all I know. I don't want to give in to this bastard, so I must make a stand. What the stand will be, I can't honestly say. Let's have another drink, and maybe I'll think of something," Larry said as he signaled the waitress for another round.

"Listen, Larry. I know a guy. He's an attorney, and I'd trust my life with him. He can easily speak to the powers that be on your behalf and maybe get some resolution. Let me call him and see if he will agree to help us," I said as I got up and went to the pay phone at the rear of the place.

I called Moe from the Blue Parrot, "Hey, Moe, how are you? Thanks for taking my call. I need some help and hope you can handle it," I said.

"So what's new?" Moe said. "When don't you need my help?" I told Moe the story of how Carmine was leaning on us and suggested I send Larry along to meet him and perhaps he could set something up.

"Listen, Harry. I'll be happy to talk to one of the bosses on behalf of Larry Robbins. Your name will never be mentioned. Of course, I may talk about Dan All right, but it will be very passively. You don't have to have Larry come see me. Just tell him I will handle it, and we can see what comes out of it. I'll bill you and take it from your funds. I'll also send you a detailed bill made out to OTF. I'll cover your ass as I always do. By the way, Dan, your management contract and the agent agreement is ready. I'll see you tomorrow at my office at about noon. Check it out, and see if it has all the items you want and need. I'll get back to you on the other matter as soon as I can. Take good care of yourself, old buddy." He hung up.

"Okay, I spoke with Moe, and he will get in touch with the bosses and get back to us. You may have to sit down at a meeting and maybe not. Just wait and see. I'm sure if anyone can get this thing straightened out. Moe can. In the meantime, let's get a little hammered and relax. We have had enough excitement for today. Do you want to call the girls?" I said with a big smile. "Let's pass on them today. I think it will do them some good to be without us for a day. They will love us even more tomorrow and appreciate us a lot more," Larry said. We spent the rest of the day drinking and finally decided to go home and get some sleep. Tomorrow should be a busy day.

Tuesday, October 15, 1957

I woke early, and my head felt like a large watermelon. Boy, we must have had quite a few drinks. I didn't want to ever have another drink if this is the way I have to feel. I knew this would pass, and I would be drinking again but not as much. I waited until ten thirty and called Larry to see if he was okay and try to plan out the rest of the day. "Hey, Larry, how are doing?" I said as cheerfully as I could.

"My head feels like it weighs a hundred pounds, but I'm slowly feeling alive. What is the plan for today?" he said.

"I want to wait for the mail. The first delivery gets here in a few minutes. I'm waiting for the contracts for the girls and want to review them to make sure there are no errors. I have to meet Moe tomorrow and want to make any changes that are necessary. Why don't you call the girls and have them meet us at the studio sometimes this afternoon? I should be there by one. If there is any delay, I'll call you," I said as I hung up.

I waited another thirty minutes and then went down to mail room to see if the contracts had arrived. Of course, true to his word, Moe's large envelope was stuffed in the mail box. I retrieved my mail, and as I headed back toward the elevator I noticed two guys looking at the names of the tenants. These guys didn't look like census takers; they were Mob guys, without doubt. I jumped into the elevator and went back to my apartment where I had left my gun. I picked up the phone and called Larry.

"Hey, listen to me. There are two guys downstairs trying to find out who lives in this building. These are, without doubt, wise guys, and I guess they are looking for me. I'm okay. Just wanted to let you know in case I am delayed a little in getting to you."

"Should I jump into a cab and get to your place in case you need my help? I can be there in ten minutes," he said.

"No, Larry, and thanks for the offer. I think I can handle these two guys. I'll just be delayed a little. See you soon, and don't worry, I'll be fine," I said as I hung up. I immediately put on my jeans and a sweater. I grabbed my jacket and took my mail from Moe and left the apartment. I went down to the end of the hall and knocked on the door.

"Hi, Jackie, how are you? I hope you don't mind, but I need to make a phone call, and my phone is not working. They are coming this afternoon to repair it. Am I disturbing you? I hope not," I said with a big smile. Jackie Rosella was a really very attractive-looking redhead that was a hostess at a leading restaurant. I have known her since I moved in and have always been very nice to her.

She always appeared to have an eye for me, but I didn't have the time for her, although I have always been very polite and nice to her. I had helped her with her bags from the grocery store a few times and invited her over to my apartment for drinks one evening—it was the neighborly thing to do. I wanted to be at this end of the hall so that I could keep an eye on my apartment and see if these wise guys came knocking at my door.

"Come on in, Dan. Of course, you can always use my phone. Excuse the place. I just got up and haven't had time to straighten up yet," she said.

"No problem, Jackie. I'm sorry to disturb you," I said.

"Dan, please don't worry about it. You're always welcome here. Make yourself at home, please. Can I make you a coffee? Perhaps a stronger drink?" she said.

"No thanks, Jackie. I can't stay very long. I have an appointment to keep. Maybe we can have dinner one night this week and have a little fun? I'll knock on your door tonight if I get home early enough or in the morning," I said with a big smile and a lot enthusiasm in my voice. "That sounds great, Dan. I won't be home early tonight as I must visit with my parents, but let's see if we can organize it for Wednesday. It will be a lot easier to do that now, don't you think?" she said.

"Wednesday for sure. How about if I pick you up at seven, and we can decide then where we will eat?" I said.

"Great. It's a date," she said. I opened the door a crack and could see these two guys standing by my door. They rang the bell again and again and then finally turned around and pressed the elevator button. I watched as they got into the elevator and the doors closed.

"Thanks, Jackie. I'll see you Wednesday. We'll have a good time," I said as I made my phone call to myself and then left her apartment. I took the stairs to the street and got there just as the two goons left the front door and turned toward First Avenue. I went outside and carefully stayed back about fifty feet and walked slowly as they walked and talked. They continued down Ninety-First Street toward First Avenue as I kept my distance steady. I wanted to keep them in my sights so that I would be prepared for any changes in their habits and wouldn't be surprised. It is so easy to get screwed when you are following someone when you fall into a rhythm and let your guard down. You never know if the people ahead of you are aware of being followed or not. I kept walking and trying to be as inconspicuous as possible. Near the end of the block on the north side of Ninety-First Street, the school was just about to break for lunch as the time was approaching noon. All hell will break loose if the kids all came out at once and crowded into the street. I saw the crossing guards placing the wooden barrier across the street so that no cars would be able to enter while the kids were on lunch break. I had to move a little faster but could not really do so as the pace was dictated by the goons in front. They reached First Avenue and turned south toward Ninety Street. I turned the corner as well and surmised that they did not have a clue they were being followed. Half way up the block, they stopped in front of a black Buick that was parked on First Avenue. They stopped and looked around haphazardly, and one of the goons opened the passenger door and got in while the other walked around toward the driver's side. This was my moment to act. Just a few more seconds, and I'll be passing the car. I needed to see the other goon get into the car. This way I had both in a confined space and would be able to complete the job I had to do. The goon reached the driver's door and opened it and slid in.

As he closed his door, I grabbed the handle of the rear door and in one swift motion opened the door and was in the car. "Don't move a muscle," I said. "Who sent you after me?"

"Who are you, asshole?" the goon in the passenger seat said.

"I'm the guy you are looking for," I said in a very menacing tone. "One fucking move and I'll blow both your heads off. Keep your hands on the dash and the wheel where I can see them. Move one muscle and you are dead meat, capish?"

"What the fuck do you want?" the goon said.

"I'll repeat the question for the last time. Next time I shoot you through the head and move on. Who the fuck sent you to find me that is the sixty-four-dollar question?"

"No one sent us. We saw you at the Carlyle the other night. We followed you home with the beautiful broad and finally worked out which apartment was yours. We just wanted to find out who you are. No one sent us, I swear. No one," he said. I knew these guys were telling the truth as they were scared to death.

"Well, if that is the case, what am I to do with you guys?" I asked in a very gentle tone. "I just can't let you go because you will be back again and try to shake me down. I don't like killing you guys, but you don't leave me much choice. What do you think I should do? You should really find another way of making a living," I said.

One of the goons started to shift in his seat. This made me very jumpy and I yelled, "One wrong move and I'll off you both right now. So just take things easy. Open your window a little so that we can get some air in here. Now what are we to do?"

"We won't say a word, and we'll never come back. I promise," the goon on the passenger side said. "You let us go, and we'll forget this ever happened. You got our word on it," the driver said, like he had to back up his buddy.

"Here is what we are going to do. One at a time take your guns out and give them to me. No fucking funny business or your brains will be all over this car. Now you first give me your gun, slowly," I said as I watched him take it off his pocket. "Two fingers only. Just hand it over here and put your hands back on the dash. Now you do the same. Keep one hand on the wheel and use two fingers and give me the gun." He did the same, and now I felt I finally had control. "Okay, start the car and pull out. I'll tell you where to go and hope, for your sake, you follow my instructions. If you do as you are told, you will live. I hope your word is good. If not, I'll find you and kill you on sight. Now let's move," I said. We drove along First Avenue until we reached the George Washington Bridge and then turned onto it and took route eighty for a few miles. When we reached an area that was heavily forested, we turned off and drove another five or six miles. We were now in the country with nothing but fields.

"Pull in over there by those trees. It looks like a road here. Let's take that for a little while and see where it gets us!" I said. Finally, we reached a small clearing that was situated before a large forest.

"Stop here and shut the motor. Okay, give me the keys, and you get out," I said pointing to the driver. "You stay in the car. Do not move out or I will shoot you." He got out of the car and just stood there looking at me. His legs were wobbly and his pants were wet; he must have pissed in them a little while back. I thought how ironic that was: Mafia tough guys pissing in their pants. Who would believe it? I opened the trunk to see if there was any rope in there. All I found was some stains that looked like dried blood. These guys must have taken a few people out before. What low lives these guys were! "Okay, you get out and walk this way. Walk, do not run, and don't try anything at all.

We walked about a mile into the dense wooded area.

"Okay, far enough guys. Let me tell you a little story so that you will understand. You two guys have been out and about killing, beating, and roughing up people for a long time. You two are tough guys when you have a gun and an army to back you up. Alone you are shit, but most of all you must have realized that one day someone will come along and give it back to you. Payback, Karma, whatever you want to call it, and now is the time to pay your dues," I said.

"Hey, man. We made a deal, you promised. We won't tell anyone. We'll leave town. Please we don't want to die," the goon said.

"How many times has someone said that to you, and all you did was pull the trigger anyway," I said. Just as I finished, the driver goon lunged at me. I stepped aside, and he missed me. I fired two shots into his chest and turned to see the other guy running in the woods. I gave chase and easily caught up with him and fired two shots into his head. I carefully went through both their pockets and took their wallets and money. I left them dead and without any form of identification; let the cops work a little. I walked back to the car and drove back to the city. On the way, I threw my gun off the GW Bridge as well as the two I took from the goons. I drove the Cadillac back to Manhattan and left it parked on Broadway near the Bowery. It was now close to six, so I called Larry and told him I was on my way to the studio. I also called Moe and apologized for not keeping my appointment at noon. The papers were just fine, and I would get in touch in a day or two.

When I got to the studio, I was just starting to settle down after the day I had. Larry said as I walked in, "Where have you been all day?"

"You really don't want to know, and you probably won't believe me anyways," I said. "Let's get a drink, and I'll tell you all about it." "The girls are coming over in about an hour, so tell me now while I make us a couple of drinks."

I went through the entire day with Larry. I left nothing out including Jackie and my date with her tomorrow. While I told Larry the story of my day, we managed to polish off a couple of drinks. The recounting of the day's happenings made me feel better and helped me relax a little before the girls arrived.

"Let's have a good time tonight. I need it," I said. "I also wanted to add a little about our conversation last night. I don't like this Carmine character and think it would be best if we start planning to leave New York and start shooting our films in Los Angeles. I think we can work easier and get rid of this piece of shit. Think about it, Larry! I also need another gun as I had to throw mine away. Have you got any that is clean and I can use?"

"Of course, I have one," Larry said as he got up and went into the back and returned with a handgun. I made sure my silencer fit. It did, and I was set to go once again.

We met the girls and went to the Blue Parrot and had dinner, and I spent the night at Natalia's place.

Wednesday, October 16, 1957

I woke bright and early once again, but this time I was in Natalia's place in the village. I guess we drank a little too much last night once again and ended up here.

Not so bad at all. It was a pretty nice place with two bedrooms, a small kitchen, and eating area. The living room was small but cozy with a fireplace; a nice touch for a cold winter night. Natalia was fast asleep besides me. It looked like the world could not be more oblivious to her. She was beautiful and I guess very happy. I dressed and left a note explaining that I had a few things to do today, including picking up the final contracts for her and Mary Lou. I also had a very important meeting tonight, so I would see her tomorrow. I told her I had a great time and loved being with her and off I went.

My first stop was at my friend Seymour's furniture store. I knew Seymour for at least five years when I was Harry Miller and partied with him many times. He was also a great gun connection, and even though Larry gave me a gun, I needed a new one and one that was clean. I didn't want to go a day without being armed; my life was much too important. Seymour Gable was the spitting image of Phil Silvers and was a great guy. He was in trouble with the cops back in 1948 when he was arrested for collecting all kinds of guns and then shipping them to Israel. He was very pro-Israel, and they needed guns to defend themselves against the Arabs. No one else in the world seemed to help Israel when they were fighting for their very lives. Even wonderful America, the land of the free, made it illegal to send guns to their aid. Seymour was about fifty years old and had come to the United States in 1946 directly from a refugee camp after being liberated from Auschwitz where his entire family was wiped out by the Nazis. He arrived in the United States, as he tells it, without anything except the numbers burnt into his arm. His heart was filled with hate and the desire to kill Germans. He was proud of the Jews that they could fight against all odds and establish a homeland that would absorb Jews from all over the world and that never again will they be slaughtered. He went to work for Arnold Weissman who was in the furniture business and worked his way up to manager. In 1956, Arnold died of a sudden heart attack. When his will was read, it was revealed that his business was left to Seymour. Arnold was married but had no children and provided his Becky with a lump sum that would take care of her forever. The store went to Seymour, and he worked hard and long to make certain it prospered. He was a good friend and always would help me out if I called upon him. Of course, I knew I could trust Seymour with my identity; he was as solid as the Rock of Gibraltar.

"Seymour, how the hell are you?" I said as I walked into his office on the mezzanine of his Fifth Avenue store.

"Who are you? Do I know you?" he said.

"It's me, Harry. I'll explain it all," I said.

"Boy, you a sight for sore eyes, and you sure look different. Where have you been, boychick? Why have you been hiding from me?" he said as he hugged and kissed me on each cheek. "Have a coffee and tell me what I missed."

I spent the next hour telling Seymour all about the last nine months. He just sat there in a trance; he could not believe his ears. Finally he said, "Listen, Harry, I am your friend and would give my life for you. Please be very careful. Trust no one and watch who you tell this to. Is there anything I can do for you now? Anything at all, please let me know," he said.

"I need a gun," I said.

"That's very simple. Come with me," he said. We walked along the mezzanine until we reached the very end, a solid brick wall; there was no evidence of a door at all. He removed one brick and pressed something inside the space, and the wall began to open. We were now entering a small space no more than five feet deep by eight feet high and six feet wide that had every conceivable weapon you could imagine. I spied hand grenades, pistols, and automatic weapons, and noticed with great astonishment the absence of ammunition.

"Go ahead, Harry. Take your choice," Seymour said.

"I am amazed by this collection, Seymour," I said. I checked out a few guns and finally selected a Baretta and asked, "How much Seymour? Is it a clean one?"

"You don't have to worry. It is unregistered. No one can ever trace it back to you or me. This one is three hundred dollars and is a deal," Seymour said.

I peeled out three one-hundred-dollar bills and gave it to him. "I need some ammo, my good friend," I said.

Seymour took the gun and looked at me and said, "I will put the firing pin in, and you will have plenty of ammo." I looked surprised when he continued, "I take out all the firing pins for two reasons. One, if I am busted, my defense is that I am a gun collector, and the other is that it stops anyone from shooting me. I also do not keep any ammo here because the buyer could be a nut and try to turn the gun on me. Even though I don't deal with anyone who wasn't recommended, I still do not take chances."

He stepped back on to the mezzanine and pressed the magic button and the wall returned to being nothing more than what is was before he removed the brick. I followed him back downstairs as he motioned to me to take seat. "I'll be right back, Harry," he said as he went through a set of doors in the back of the store. A moment later, he returned with a shopping bag that looked heavy.

"Here, Harry. Take this bag, and here is your gun with the pin in. I suggest you put it away in a safe place. I also included a silencer in case you may need it."

"Thanks, Seymour. You are great and as always there for me. By the way, please don't call me Harry. I'm now known as Dan, Dan All right. It's safer this way as I never know who is listening," I said. I got up and gave Seymour a big hug and walked out of the store. I jumped into a cab and went off to Moe's office to pick up the management contracts I should have gotten yesterday.

When I got to Larry's place, I found him busy at work on his little typewriter. "How you doing, old man?" I said.

"Glad to see you, Dan. I almost got this script finished. I think we can start shooting on Monday. I'll put together a list of props we will need, and we can get Ralph started on putting it all together. I'll get the model releases done so that you can have copies and make sure that each actor and anyone else involved with the movie signs off and releases us for any future claims etc. I like to make sure we always have proper records so that nothing or no one can come after us and bite us on the ass. One of my biggest problems is taking care of things like this. I don't remember where the hell I put all the releases from past shoots. I'm really lousy when it comes to record keeping. I don't know why, but I am just a schmuck. No matter, they don't know I lost them, so there will never be any problems. From now on, it's your problem, Dan. Keep those records straight and in a safe place. I'll get in touch with Ralph today," he said as he turned back to his typewriter and began pecking with one finger.

I went into the back of the studio and sat down and loaded my gun. I then put the bag of ammunition away securely. I felt better now that I had a gun again.

The day had gone quite well as I was busy with little things around the studio as Larry was busy putting the finishing touches on the script. It was nearly five thirty when the phone rang. Larry picked up the phone and spoke for few minutes and then hung up. I paid no attention until Larry called me, "Dan, got a minute?" he yelled out to the back of the studio. I walked up to the front end, "What's up, old buddy?" I said.

"I just got a phone call from Carmine. He wants a meet tomorrow. He said we got to clear up a few misunderstandings, and it's best if we do it face-to-face. I don't like it, Dan. It smells, and when something smells, I usually stay clear," he said very seriously.

"What you tell him?" I said.

"I told I'd call him tomorrow at eleven, and we can set up a meet. What else could I say?" Larry said.

"Okay, Larry. Don't worry about it. We are in the driver's seat. He needs movies, he needs you. All he wants to do is show you that he is the boss. String him along, and let's get some movies done. Once he sees them, he'll kiss your ass. You're going to make him rich and ourselves as well, you mark my words, and he'll kiss your ass," I said with confidence.

"I hope you're right. I just don't feel comfortable when these assholes are involved," Larry said.

"Let's call the girls as I have the contracts and need them signed so that we can move forward. Also remember this. Once we have the girls under contract, we will control a great deal of the market. These girls are going to be stars, and everyone will want them, especially the dance clubs, and we will own their rights, lock, stock, and barrel. It would be very smart if you told Carmine that your new stars are the most beautiful girls you have ever seen and will make him rich. Don't forget to tell him that as I think it will cement the deal. Always deal from strength, Larry, and you will always be the winner," I said with a big smile. Larry called the girls and told them to get over here, and we'll get the contracts signed and then go out and celebrate.

I called Jackie to beg out of dinner tonight. I told her that I was called into an emergency meeting and would not be able to make it. She understood and thanked me for calling.

It was seven twenty-five when the girls arrived. "Hi guys, how are you all doing?" Mary Lou said in her exaggerated southern drawl.

"Not bad at all, but a lot better now that you girls have arrived. We missed you. Let's see, it has been about twelve hours, hasn't it?" I said with a big smirk on my face. We spent the next half hour going over the contracts and getting them signed. The girls were thrilled that they were now under contract and will be getting paid each week. This was their beginning to stardom and, I felt, their satisfaction with Larry and I was evident in every move they made. They believed in us, and we could not ever let them down in any way.

"Let's party tonight. Where do you want to go?" I said. "Let's go to the Palm. I haven't been there in a long time, and a juicy steak will go a long way. What do you guys think?" Larry said. "Listen to me, you all know my problem. What we need is a solution to this problem as I like to enjoy being out there and having fun. We are in the movie business, so making me look different should not be very hard. Girls, get your best efforts together, and let's make me look different," I said.

The girls were thrilled to be able to make me up. They started with a wig and a matching mustache and went to eye makeup. In less than ten minutes, I looked like another person. We were thrilled with the results and laughing all the way. We were off to the Palm restaurant to have some fun and to celebrate the start of a new phase in their lives. Who cared who saw me because now we had found a solution, and each time we had to go out I would be made up differently. No one would be able to say that she didn't have a lot of different boyfriends. We took a cab to the restaurant on Second Avenue in lower Manhattan. Well, it was a sight to behold as we walked into the Palm with the two most gorgeous women you had ever seen. Every eye, male and female, looked at us as we walked to our table. This place was known as the watering hole for celebrities, and many in this place could not help but wonder who we were. We ordered champagne and plenty of food.

"Girls, if you don't know what to order, please allow me to handle it for you. There are a great many wonderful dishes here that you probably never heard of. Let's have fun and eat like there is no tomorrow. Just remember, we start shooting your first movie on Monday, so party while you can. After tonight, it will be work and more work," I said.

People were looking as hard as possible without appearing to be staring and wondering who we really are. We ate and drank and enjoyed ourselves a lot. Most importantly, no one could recognize me; this made me feel real good. Safety was my only concern, and I wanted to have fun as well, so this change of identity was exactly what the doctor ordered, and Natalia understood that real well. I perused the entire restaurant and noticed a few people who looked like wise guys, but I couldn't tell for sure. Just as we were about to wrap it up, a man walked up to our table and addressed Larry.

"Larry Robbins, I haven't seen you in a long time. How the hell are you, my friend?" he said. "Hey Stan, how are you? Nice to see you. Let me introduce you. This is Natalia More, Mary Lou, and Jack Reed. The girls are in town to shoot a new movie. We are starting the shoot next week. The film should be great, and these girls are, as you can see, super." Stan shook hands with everyone and could not take his eyes off the girls.

"It is great to meet you all. I can hardly wait to see the movie. I hope you don't mind me telling you girls that you are very beautiful. Your movie career will be very successful I can assure you. Where did you find these super beautiful ladies, Larry?" Stan said.

"I'll give you a call tomorrow, Stan. We can talk about it then. Thanks for stopping by," Larry said. We watched Stan leave and then paid the check and left.

Thursday, October 17, 1957

I awoke with Nat still asleep besides me. I was very careful not to disturb her as I showered and dressed in the bathroom. I called Larry at nine thirty hoping he was awake as I wanted to get the day started by getting things ready for the shoot on Monday. "Hello," Larry sounded very groggy, "I guess I woke you?" I said.

"No shit, Dan, why couldn't you wait until morning?" he said.

"Sorry to disappoint you, Larry, but it's almost ten, and I figured you wanted to get started on making ready for the shoot on Monday. I'll call you later if you prefer," I said.

"No need. I'm already awake and won't be able to get back to sleep. You're right. I have to call Ralph right now. We need to go shopping as we need a lot of small shit as well as the film which I did order and will need the bread to pay them when I pick the film up. I don't have any credit any longer with them. Oh shit, I just remembered. I got to call Carmine as well at eleven and set up a meet. Hey, thanks Dan. Thanks for calling. I didn't need to piss Carmine off and add more fuel to the fire," he said.

"Do you want me to meet you at the studio, or do you have somewhere else in mind?" I said. "Why don't you take a cab here, and we can map out the day together. See you when you get here." And he hung up!

I left a note for Nat to call me at the studio when she wakes up. Maybe we will have lunch but still call. I was ready to go downstairs to grab a cab and remembered that I fucked up. I was supposed to take Jackie out last night and didn't. I knocked at her door ready for some real ass kicking when the door opened and she stood there looking just stunning in a pair of panties and a bra.

"Hi, it's me!" I said. "I'm sorry about last night. I was in the middle of signing a contract and went for a few drinks to celebrate the deal and before I knew it the night was gone. I'm truly sorry and am here with my hat in my hand."

"Come on in, Dan. All is forgiven. I know you must have had a lot of drinks because you did call even though you don't remember. I know I should be pissed but I'm not. Now are you staying a little while?" she said as she unbuttoned her bra. "I'm real horny and could use a quickie. So stay a little while and let's play." I was ready for action and could not help myself. I took her in my arms and kissed her. She pulled me toward her bedroom as she began undressing me.

"Take off your clothes, sweetheart," she said as she dropped her panties. In a minute we were in bed making love.

She was wild and knew no limits. I thought I had fallen in with a nymphomaniac; there just wasn't enough for her. I spent the next hour doing everything I could to satisfy her. Finally, I said, "I got to run, Jackie. I have things I must do today and people are waiting for me. I had a great time. You were great," I said as I got dressed.

"Look, Dan. I'm your neighbor and your friend. Please don't think you have to cater to me. If you can stop by every once in a while, we can make love. No commitment, no ties, just friends. Please believe me, Dan, I think you are a super guy, but I need more than one, and my real love is my girlfriend Lisa. You're just a side dish, and you taste great. Can you live with this?" she said with a very straight face.

"I certainly can, and as long as we keep this arrangement between us, we will all benefit and always have fun," I said with a big smile.

"I also want you to know, Dan, that I am a rock. I'll never tell anyone anything about you no matter what they may do to me," she said.

"Whoa Jackie! What are you talking about? You're scaring me a little. Please enlighten me," I said. "Well, Dan, the other day two guys came by and knocked on your door. You were here when they did that and then you left and they did as well. Two days later, two more guys came to your door knocked again. Of course, no one answered, so they knocked on every door on this floor. They asked me if I knew a guy named Harry Miller, and I said I didn't. They asked me who lived there in six C and I said Dan All right and I've seen him around for a long time. They showed me a picture of Harry Miller, and it did look like you a little, of course. I said I never saw that person. These guys didn't look like very nice people. What's the story, Dan?" she said.

"Jackie, it's a long story, and I really don't want to get you involved. It could be dangerous," I said.

"I'm already involved, and I don't give shit about danger. I care about you a lot, so all I ask is that you be straight with me. You don't have to worry about getting involved with me, Dan. I'm a lesbian and prefer girls, so it'll never happen between us. Even though the sex is great, there is no chemistry, and that is what I need," she said.

I told her a small portion of the story and begged her to remain mute on my real name. She could easily get me killed by saying the wrong thing to the wrong person. I was screwed but could not change what she knew and could only hope she would be a friend. I believed her when she said she was my friend and would always be solid. Sometimes you meet people that just are strong and true in their friendships; she was one of them. I left her with a heavy heart and a lot of worries as I jumped into a cab to go to the studio. I paid extra attention like in the past to see if I was being followed; the recent events with Jackie made me more nervous. If they sent around another couple of guys, they must have some suspicion that Harry lives here.

I checked the back window several times on our way to the studio and did not detect anyone following us. This didn't mean I was right, so I had the cab drop me off on Twenty-Third Street and Broadway. I figured I'd walk the rest of the way. If anyone is following me, I will be able to spot them easily when walking. I had my gun with me, which made me feel a little better. I was careful as I walked leisurely toward Fifth Avenue. I took Twentieth Street and walked very slowly so that I'd be able to spot anyone who may be following me. So far, no one seemed to care about me, and everyone I encountered seemed to disappear without a single glance at me.

I arrived at the studio and found Larry standing by the elevator waiting for me. He looked a little pissed off. "You wake me three hours ago and then waltz in here like it's all okay," he said, "Let me hear what happened now,"

I told him everything including my strapping on Jackie.

"I'm not happy about all this Dan. There are far too many people who suspect that you are this Harry Miller. We have to settle this thing once and for all. If not, we are going to run into more trouble than we can handle real soon," he said.

"Okay, Larry, I'm with you. What do you suggest?" I said.

"Here is how we are going to resolve all this. After all, we are in the movie business and make anyone look like any person we want to. As of today, you are not going out in public as the same person. You are going to look different every time you leave here or your apartment. Let's imagine we are making a movie and your character is an old man. We can make you look old to fit the part and no one would know.

We'll make you up and then when someone comes in contact with you or to your apartment, you will greet them and they will find someone very different than what they expected. We will do this all the time and shall make you up as Jack Reed when you are on the shoot so that no one can ever leave the set and identify Harry. He never existed. It's the only way, and we start now. I'll call Ellie now and have her come over," Larry said.

"No, Larry. That won't work at all. It will just involve another person and who needs more people in the loop?" I said. "I suggest we call Nat and let her do it. She is very good at this, and we avoid bringing in any other people."

"Great idea, Dan. Where is she?" Larry said. "She's at the house. I'll give her a call and tell her to come here," I said.

"No way. I don't trust your phone either, so until we resolve the identity issue, let's do it another way. I'll have Mary Lou call her and tell her to meet at the studio as there is a casting call at the studio. In case anyone is listening, it will mean nothing more than what it sounds like. In the meantime, you stay put. No going out until Nat arrives and does her thing. What do you think?" Larry said.

"If you really think the phone is tapped, why don't I call Jackie and ask her to go over to the apartment and tell Nat to get her beautiful ass down here?" I said.

"Good idea," Larry said. I called Jackie and asked her to do me a favor. She readily agreed and was happy to be able to meet Nat as well. A few minutes later Jackie called, "Dan, it's all taken care of. She is just wonderful. Thanks for introducing her to me. She is just beautiful. Do you mind if I make a play for her?" she said.

"No not all. Go for it, babe," I said. "And thanks for taking care of this for me."

"She will be there in half an hour. See you later, Dan." She hung up.

Larry was speaking on the phone for quite a while, yelling every now and then. When he finally got off the phone, he called me over and said, "I just got off with Carmine. He will have one of his boys call me to set up a meeting. I reminded him that he was the one who wanted a meeting. Right now he is too busy to see me but agrees that we should have a sit-down and get all this settled. It's amazing that this guy can't remember what he said from one day to the next. In the meantime, we proceed with our shoot on Monday, and we'll handle that piece of shit when he calls." I agreed with Larry and went back to puttering around the studio.

It was close to two when Nat arrived. She looked unbelievable, wearing a pair of short shorts and a see-through blouse. Boy, she was hot, and she knew it, and so did everyone else. Larry and I sat her down and explained what we needed. She was excited beyond belief to be part of this project.

"Makeup has always been my first love, and now I can do it for real. I need supplies. Is there a makeup supply store nearby?" she asked Larry. He wrote down the name and address and said, "Where is Mary Lou?"

"She is just waking up," Larry said.

"Let me get her ass out of bed and take her with me to help me shopping. We are going to have fun. I'm so excited," she said.

It was close to five when Nat and Mary Lou returned with two big shopping bags completely filled with makeup material.

While they were out shopping, Larry and I made up two different sets of driver's licenses as well as social security cards and a few other matching items that would serve my new characters. All we had to do now was to create a new guy, and Nat was ready to do that. For the next two hours, I was under the lights while Nat did her job.

My hair was changed, and we made my eyes smaller. I was different and did not look like Harry or Dan at all. Tonight, we would put it to the test when I go home and wait for anyone who might want to knock on the door just to see Harry Miller. I would never be without my gun even though I didn't really think I would need it with my new disguise. We spent the rest of the evening making a list of things we would need for the shoot and then have dinner over at the Blue Parrot. The girls went home, and I went to my place to see if anything was happening.

Friday, October 18, 1957

I woke up early, as I usually do, and made myself an egg and toast. I heard a knock at the door and went over to the peephole to see who was there. I spied two large men in suits, easy Mob guys; it was written all over them. I opened the door, "Yes, can I help you?" I said.

"We are looking for Harry Miller. We were told he lives here," one of guys said.

"I'm sorry. There is no Harry Miller living here. What is this about?" I said. The guy pulled out of badge that appeared to be an official FBI badge and said, "May we come in Mr.?" he said. "I am special agent, John Hardy, and this is my partner, special agent Watson."

"A pleasure to meet you. I'm Dan All right. Certainly, please come right in, Officers," I said. Both guys entered the apartment and looked around. The apartment was not very big, so it wasn't hard to check it all out at one glance.

"Well, Mr. All right, we have a report that you have another person living here," he said.

"Well, that's not so except for a girl I bring home from time to time. I live here alone, and I always have," I said.

"Can you show us some ID, sir?" he said.

"Certainly," I said as I took out my driver's license. "Did I do something wrong, sir?" I said.

"No sir, you haven't. We are looking for another person, and it was reported to us that that person was living here. Evidently, that is wrong. Sorry about this and thank you for your cooperation," he said as they started to leave. "By the way, if you should here from this person, be very careful. He is dangerous and armed. Here is my card with a special number on it. Just call that number, and we'll handle it from there. By the way, there is a reward of twenty-five K to anyone who spots this guy." He handed the card to me and turned and left the apartment.

My hope was that the disguise and slight accent fooled them. I was certain that they were Mob guys posing as FBI agents and just wanted to get into the apartment to verify that Harry Miller didn't live here. I decided, just to keep myself sane, to call the number. I did and a man answered with a plain "Hello." I asked for some fictitious person and was told that there wasn't anyone by that name. I asked if they could tell me who was at the other end, and they told me it was none of my business, and I'd better stop annoying them, or they would report me to the phone company. I apologized and hung up.

This made me feel a lot better knowing that the FBI was not involved but gave me reason to be careful once again as it confirmed that they would stop at nothing to find me. I only hoped that they were satisfied that Harry Miller didn't live here and would not bother me any longer. Evidently, these goons never seemed to give up; they just kept on coming. What really got me worried was how they zeroed in on this building! I always was in disguise and always used the name Dan All right. I wondered what was going through their minds about the guys who never reported back. Didn't they wonder? It isn't hard to understand the thought process of the Mob bosses—business as usual. Harry Miller certainly had demonstrated that he was not a threat to them. If he was, he would have made contact with the feds by now, and things would have been loud and clear. People would have been indicted and arrested by now. With all the informers, they have they would have gotten the news that the fat was in the fire. Even though all this never happened, it doesn't seem to matter now. All they cared about was that they get rid of Harry Miller as an example to all who may think of defecting.

I called Larry to verify what time he needed me for the first day of the shoot. "Hey Larry, how are you? What time do you want me there?" I asked.

"How about now. It would be great if you got here early so that we can get ready and go over what has to be done. Sam is already here getting things in order. I expect the people to get here about noon and would like to have makeup done by two and start shooting by three at the latest. So if you can get your ass over here now, you can be a big help," he said.

"Okay, I'm on my way. I'll leave in five minutes. See you soon," I said. I spent the next few minutes going over my apartment once again to make sure that there was nothing out of place that would lead anyone closer to Harry. I had made sure I had nothing of the past, so this exercise was really not necessary, but I needed to keep myself sane, and this was one way of doing it. There was nothing left that contained any reference to Harry, but one more search wouldn't hurt. All my bills were under the name of Dan All right, so leaving papers around and other stuff that said "Dan All right" was fine. Everything seemed in order as I left and hailed a cab on Second Avenue and went off to the studio. During the ride, I continually checked in the rear window to see if I could spot a tail. I couldn't, but that didn't convince me. I was paranoid, and who could fault me for it? I called Natalia before leaving reminding her that I need a complete makeup job before I arrived at the shoot. She suggested I stop by her place where she would make me over before I arrived at the studio. I told her that I needed this quickly as I promised Larry to get there very soon. She guaranteed it would only take half an hour.

Nat was right on schedule as she got me in and out in a little less than twenty minutes. I arrived around eleven and took the elevator up to the studio. "Hey, guys, how's everything going?" I said as I walked in ready for my first film shoot. I could feel the excitement and anticipation; it was on everyone's faces and certainly must have been on their minds.

"Hey, Jack, a pleasure to meet you. How are you?" Wally Judson, the cameraman yelled out from the back end of the studio.

"I'm great and ready for action. Let's make this film the best we have ever done. For me, it's easy as it is my first, so it will be the best. I am stoked, guys, really stoked about the whole film. If you need anything, please let me know. I need you all to see me in about ten minutes to sign the model releases and any other crap we have to get done with, then on to having fun and making a great film," I said with a big smile.

I called Larry ahead of time to make sure I was introduced as Jack Lamm for this movie shoot. My disguise would eliminate anyone from knowing who I really was, and thus there wouldn't be any chatter in and off the set. I parked myself at a little table that Ralph had set up in the front area and began getting all those present to sign the model releases and the appropriate tax forms and independent contractor agreements. It was my job to protect the shoot from any shortcuts that could cause problems with the government man. The IRS would love to grab us and charge us with one violation or another. My job was to make sure that this was never going to happen. By protecting ourselves, we were also protecting each actor. I had my checklist, and once a person signed the proper forms, I checked them off the list and onto my payroll sheet. All personnel were paid in cash and had to sign a receipt upon payment. Even though they were paid in cash, we sent them a proper IRS tax form.

Mary Lou and Natalia had not arrived yet, but most of the others were there. Ralph had picked up a lot of food and had a great spread in the front area of the studio. He did a great job within the budget laid out by Larry. Everyone was eating and enjoying themselves as Larry handed out copies of the script. The elevator opened once again, and in walked a big, very fat lady with flaming red hair. She was about five foot two inches tall and just as wide as she carried her bag and yelled out, "Hello, everybody. I'm here and ready to make all of you beautiful people even more beautiful. I'm Marilyn, your favorite makeup person."

Right behind her, a super nice looking girl followed. She was as skinny as Marilyn was fat with blonde hair. She was about fifty-five and had a tight skirt on that just covered her pubic hair.

She was really a very good-looking girl. Maybe she was one of the stars? Marilyn yelled out once again, "I want to introduce you to Vicky West. She is my assistant and is very good at making you look beautiful."

"Larry," Marilyn went over to him and gave him a big hug and a kiss. "Where is my station?" "Follow me, sweetie," Larry said as he put his arm around Vicky and started walking toward the front of the studio where he had set up a room with a table and a Klieg light to illuminate her work and a couple of chairs.

"Set yourself up here, and let Jack know if you need anything. We'll get it for you," Larry said as he kissed Vicky on the cheek and helped Marilyn set her bag down in this little room. "Don't forget to see Jack, and get all the papers signed, and let's get to work," Larry said as he made a beeline to Wally to talk about the camera set-up.

I was at my desk when Marilyn and Vicky came by and said, "Is this where we sign the papers?" Vicky said with a smile.

"Sure is. I'm Jack Lamm. A pleasure to meet you," I said as I placed the papers neatly on the table and indicated where to sign. Just as I was wrapping up the latest group to sign, the elevators opened and Mary Lou and Natalia stepped into the Studio.

All heads turned their way as Mary Lou said with a big smile, "Hi everyone, I'm Mary Lou and this is Natalia More. Are we in the right place?" she laughed as the joke went over quite well.

"Hi Larry, Jack, how you all doing?" Natalia said as they walked over to the food table and picked up a soft drink.

"Hey, there girls. Nice to see you. I need you over here to sign some papers and then off to see Marilyn in makeup. Chop, chop, let's get it together. Time is important," I said.

I checked my list and spoke with Harry Teems, "I need you over here, Harry. Your papers are ready."

"I'll be right there," he said. I finally got everyone signed up and then asked the entire crew to listen as I explained the way we would operate.

"Please pay attention as I will only say this once. We are here to have fun and make a super good film. It is important that everyone works together and follows their cues. Once you are finished with your part, please wait for Larry to dismiss you. He will check with Wally to make sure the shot was right and then you are done. Please stop by and see me, and I will pay you in full. Once you leave the set, your services are over until the next film. Of course, we will call you if the part suits you. Please have fun, and let's get this shoot done with as quickly as possible. Thanks," I said.

It was nearing six, and the shoot was going quite well. John Boner who was scheduled for two sex scenes was having a little trouble staying hard. His dick was enormous; it was hard to imagine deep throating it. Harry Teems was no slouch either; although not quite as big as John, he was still very well-endowed. Watching the film being made opened my eyes to how much work was involved. Mary Lou was playing the part of a very young college coed having an ice cream soda in her short little cheerleader skirt when along comes John Boner, and they start to play with each other in the soda shop. The scene had to be shot over eleven times to get it just right. Larry was a very compulsive director and was very concerned with perfection. The cumshot alone had to be shot three times because he didn't like the way it looked. It was not easy to do the third one in such short order, so we had to use milk to simulate the final cum shot. It was an education for me and shot the hell out of my fantasy that a porn shoot was all fun and games; every indication was that filmmaking was hard work no matter what kind of film it was. We continued shooting until after eleven when Larry announced that we would wrap it up for today and meet me here tomorrow at eleven thirty A.M. to prepare for the continuation of the shoot at one P.M. "Please do not be late. It is very important that we get everything ready and get started on time. If you are late, your part will be given to someone else, and you will lose all of your wages. Let me repeat this everyone, *you will lose all of your money if you are not on time!* Thanks for working so hard, and have a good night. Go directly home. No partying. It can wait another day or two. See you tomorrow," he said.

After everyone was gone, Larry and I sat down with Mary Lou and Natalia and just breathed a sigh of relief.

"Thank goodness that's over. I never thought it would be so hard. I am whacked out, I really am," Mary Lou said.

"I had a great time. I'm tired, but it was fun and will be a lot more fun in the future when I get used to the routine. I am tired, but it's an exciting tired," Natalia said. I was surprised to hear her say how much she enjoyed the shoot.

"I didn't think you would take to it so quickly. I'm glad you enjoyed yourself. The making of a real superstar is the fact that they can enjoy what they are doing and you certainly did," I said with sincere enthusiasm. "I guess we'd better get home and get some sleep. Tomorrow will be here quicker than you can imagine. Are you coming with me, Nat?" I asked.

"No, Dan. I'm going to crash with Mary Lou. I'm excited but very tired. If it's okay with you, I'll see you on time tomorrow," she said.

"That's fine with me," I said as I kissed her and headed for the elevator. I'd better get some rest as well as there will be plenty of work tomorrow.

Saturday, October 19, 1957

Larry explained to me that shooting a film on Friday, Saturday, and Sunday is a little less costly and a lot safer than during the week. Although a permit is required, it is impossible to get one for a porn film. That department does not work on Saturday and Sunday, and Friday they only work half days so that they could have a pleasant weekend.

Seeing that the city of New York doesn't like porn shoots in their city, the weekend takes the pressure off as most of the cops involved in that department do not work. The weekend is a great equalizer and understandably much quieter. The paperwork involved is too much for those guys and could ruin their weekend. The cameras and other rented equipment cannot be returned on Sunday because the rental place is closed; therefore, a free day.

I jumped into the shower and called Larry as soon as I was through. "Good morning, I'm on my way. I'll be there in twenty minutes. Do you want anything?" I asked. "Pick up a couple dozen doughnuts, and get your ass here—make that three dozen," he said. I jumped into a cab and picked up the doughnuts and arrived at the studio twenty-five minutes later. "Good morning everyone. I hope everyone is here and ready to get to work?" I said smiling.

"Hey Jack. Welcome to day two of the Rockem High School Reunion shoot. We invite all the new and old alumni to get undressed and join the party," Larry shouted out from somewhere behind the set. "Just kidding, old buddy. Let's get to work!"

It was still a little early, but most of the people had already arrived and were ready for work. I guess no one wanted to lose their paychecks and gain the reputation of unreliability as well. I looked over toward the elevator and saw Mary Lou and Natalia arrive; it made me feel good to see them both. I wondered if I was getting too involved. After all, I'm now in this business for the long haul.

"Hi girls," I shouted from the rear of the studio. "Hope you had a good night's sleep?" "Sure did, Jack, and guess what, I thought of you all night long," Nat said with a smile and that sexy look in her eyes.

"I missed you as well, babe. It was hell sleeping alone," I said.

"Okay, you guys. Enough of this lovey-dovey stuff. We have work to do," Larry yelled out.

"Is Marilyn here? Please show yourself," Larry cried out. "We need to get started with makeup. Wally, get your cameras set up. We'll be doing scene forty-three today with Mary Lou and John. I want some close-ups, real close-ups. Let set the world on fire and get the closest shot of a clit ever photographed. I want the viewer to see it so close that he imagines that he could taste it. If we need to mount the camera and get an overhead shot, let's do it. I want this feature to be the talk of the town with shots that have never been done before in any porn shoot anywhere. Got that, John?" Larry said as he started to walk toward the makeup section.

I was so excited about being on a movie set. It was a beehive of activity and just watching how things were done was very exciting. The entire studio smelled of sex and excitement; just the very thought of it all turned me on. Of course, I had to come to my senses and get to work and make certain that every form was complete and each person involved received their pay as agreed. I had a large amount of cash with me, so I could pay everyone and take care of my duties properly. Work, work, work. We were always working, except the working conditions were quite different and very pleasant. Here I was working with John Boner, a legend in the industry, and two new great stars in Mary Lou and Nat. Everyone was so gracious and happy and hard at work. We were at it well past midnight, and finally, Larry announced that the shoot was over and ready for editing.

"Thanks to you all for your hard work and great acting. This film will be a great hit, thanks to you all. Have a good night, and see Jack on your way out. We'll be calling you when we are ready to make the next smash hit. Until then, goodluck, and don't party too much."

I spent another hour paying each one in cash and getting their signatures on the receipts. It was about two thirty in the morning when everyone had left, except for Mary Lou and Nat. "I'm whacked. What a day! I never thought shooting a movie was this much work. It seemed like so much fun when you watch the finished film," I said. "Nat, let's get going. I think I can sleep for a week, how about you?" I said. "Larry, I'll call you tomorrow when I wake up, not too early. Maybe we'll have brunch or dinner? See you buddy. Great shoot," I said as we left and grabbed a cab on Twenty-Third Street and Fifth and went home.

Sunday, October 20, 1957

We were too tired to make love and fell asleep in five minutes. It was eleven thirty Sunday morning, and we were just starting to feel alive enough to meet the new day. "I can't feel my legs, Nat. Do you think I left them at the studio?" I said.

"Me too," Nat said as she stretched her arms out wide in the bed and pulled me closer to her. "What do you think, Dan? Can you find the strength to make love to a desperate young lady?" she said.

We spent another hour in bed having a great time and just enjoying each other. I jumped into the shower and felt renewed and ready to face another day in the Big Apple. "Dan, do you have anymore shampoo? You didn't leave any in this bottle," Nat yelled from the shower. I reached into our pantry and found another shampoo bottle and handed it to her.

"Here, honey, enjoy your shampoo and make that head of hair look real good as it always does. Let's go for brunch if we can ever get out of here," I said.

I called Larry. "How are you doing, Larry?" I said.

"Well, I think I'm awake, but only time will tell if I'm really there yet. That was a marathon session yesterday, much too long for us all," Larry said.

"I know how you feel. I feel the same way. Are you up to going for brunch?" I asked.

"Sure thing, where do you want to go?" he asked. "I really don't care as long as it's easy, and we can just lay back and eat. I think I'll get to sleep tonight real early, but until then, I need to eat and so does Nat," I said.

"Okay, I'll meet you at Gallo's in thirty minutes. I hear they have a great brunch and it lasts until five. I'll see you there," Larry said and hung up.

After brunch, we were too tired to do anything else except go home and go to sleep. Nat came home with me, and we watched the Ed Sullivan show and then went to sleep.

Monday, October 21, 1957

I was very tired when I went to sleep and must have slept real well. I was woken by a loud banging on my door. I jumped out of bed and checked to make sure my gun was handy and went to the door. I looked through the peephole and I saw a very agitated Jackie, my next door neighbor. She was about to bang on the door again when I yelled, "Hold on I'm coming," and opened the door. "What's the matter, Jackie? Come on in, please," I said as I closed the door.

"Listen, Dan, there was some strange and very ugly looking guys hanging around the building yesterday. They were asking a lot of questions about you. They knocked on my door and asked if I knew you. I told them that of course, I knew you and that Dan was a great guy and has always been very nice," she said to me and continued. "They kept on asking if I knew someone named Harry Miller. I told them I never heard of Harry Miller. I know they went to see the Super, Manuel, and he told them he didn't know any Harry Miller either. I spoke with Manuel later, and he asked me if I knew what it was all about. I told him that it was a case of mistaken identity. In any case, Dan, they look mean, and they look like serious trouble. Please don't stay in your apartment for a little while. You can stay with me or anywhere you want, but please get the hell out of here. I can feel it my bones. They'll be back, today, tomorrow, but soon. Please, Dan. I don't want anything to happen to you," she said. The noise of the banging on the door and our loud conversation finally woke Nat. "What's going on out there?" She yelled from the bedroom.

"Hey, Jackie. Thanks. I appreciate your concern, and I'm so glad you care. Please try to relax, and don't worry. I'll be very careful, and I'll stay away for a while.

It's no use staying with you, because if they are watching the building, they'll see me come and go. I really appreciate your help, thanks," I said as I held her close and kissed her head. "With friends like you, I really don't have to worry." Once again Nat yelled out, "What is going on? Who is with you, Dan?" I responded, "It's only Jackie. She came over to give me some news. I'll fill you in shortly."

"Dan, please leave the building now. Go out through the back. It will take you out on to Ninetieth Street. They could be watching the building now. Please listen to me and do it," she said. "I'm certain they gave fat Jerry a few bucks to watch the building as well. He has nothing to do with his time except kick his wife around and try to act like some big shot. Be careful, Dan. You've got no friends here besides me. I love you and care, Dan!" she said.

"Okay, Jackie. I'm on my way. I'll be out of here in ten minutes. Now go back to your apartment and act as if nothing has ever happened. I'll call you later today," I said as I kissed her gently on the lips and squeezed her arm.

I went into the bedroom and told Nat that she must get up at once as we were leaving the apartment and we were doing it now. "This is not a drill. This for real," I said as I grabbed a few things I will need and my personal papers. I took Nat by the hand and went out of my place and knocked on Jackie's door.

"We need to get out through your place. My place opens to the front of Ninety-First Street. Your place faces the back, and we can leave through your back window without anyone seeing me," I said.

"No problem, Dan. Do it now. I just have a bad feeling about these guys and know they'll be back," she said as tears ran down her cheeks.

"No need for any tears, Jackie. I'll be okay. I'm sorry to have involved you in all this, really I am," I said.

"Shut up and get down those stairs before it's too late. Please be careful, please. I love you both," she said. I opened the rear window and stepped out on the fire escape as Nat followed me closely. We started to climb down to the street level. I reached the last floor and had to put all my weight on the ladder to get it to drop to the ground. The back alley would lead to either Ninety-First or Ninetieth Street. I dropped to ground and then waited with open arms to catch Nat. I checked the area out quickly and didn't see anyone. We turned left and went to Ninetieth Street and walked along to Second Avenue and hailed a cab. We were out and safe again but for how long? We went to the studio and relayed to Larry what had happened. "Well, what do you think I should do, Larry? Come on. Give me some advice, will you, please?" I said.

"You can't kill them all, and it seems to me that you can't make peace with them no matter how hard you try. Seeing that you enjoy living, we must find a way to carry out that wish. First I suggest you move in with Nat for the time being. I'll handle cleaning your place out, and whatever we can't move, we will just leave it there. Fuck it, we don't need material things. We can buy new stuff. We will move the studio from Manhattan to Los Angeles, and we will start all over again. They don't have the power in Los Angeles that they have here, and in time you will be forgotten. We have to do all this slowly so as not to arouse any suspicions. We will set a date, let's say January first, to be in Los Angeles and forget snow once and for all. I'll start shipping my stuff right after the next shoot, and we are on our way. Let's blow this place and start all over in warm Los Angeles. That's my advice, what do you think?" Larry said with a big smile.

"I agree with you about leaving town. I think we should rent a trailer and haul everything ourselves. That way there is no one who can track us through our equipment, and the equipment will arrive in good order. I also think we should leave right after the next shoot is done and not wait until January. I also want to take Mary Lou and Nat with us as they are our tickets to fame. What do you think?" I said.

"I agree with you. Let's do it. We must be careful until we do leave as they might try to come here. Also with Carmine on the warpath, we will have our hands full. I love this shit, Dan. It's exciting and sends a rush through me. Great stuff!" Larry said with a big smile.

Tuesday, October 22, 1957

I spent the night at Nat's place which I enjoyed a lot, and we agreed that I should remain there until we leave Manhattan. The girls were very excited about moving to Los Angeles. They could not contain themselves and could only keep repeating that they couldn't wait for us to get going.

I warned them not to reveal our plans to anyone regardless of how much they may feel they could trust them. We decided that we would not talk about the trip while in the apartment. I knew I was paranoid, but the walls seemed to have ears, and somehow someone always seems to hear things they shouldn't. These Mob guys have money and fear going for them, and they know how to get information from people—they are quite adept at it. The girls understood what was at stake, and if they were to enjoy this adventure, it would be best to be very cautious, or the trip may never happen. I wondered what excited them more: going to Hollywood or my staying with them. It was like a movie to them, a big game and lots of fun. Nat was at the apartment when Jackie, my next door neighbor, knocked on the door and displayed her concern that these guys were dangerous. Even with that in mind, it didn't seem to make the impression I hoped for. This was still very much like a movie part to both Mary Lou and Natalia. One shot from a Mob gun or the killing of one of them would scare the hell out of the girls, but until that happened they were having the time of their lives.

Larry was waiting for the film processing to be complete from the last shoot and then the editing could begin. We were facing another six weeks of hard work in editing the footage before the film would be in the can. This schedule was far too long and would cause us to have a very difficult trip across America when winter would set in. I had decided to talk to Larry about this and see if we could get the editing done in California. If we could leave now, we would be gone before Carmine and all the other Mob guys realized that we were not here in New York.

I went to the Studio to see Larry and see if there was any way possible to accelerate our migration. "Hey, Larry, how are you doing?" I said as I tossed my jacket on the chair.

"I'm fine, old man. How was your night with the girls?" he asked with a twinkle in his eye.

"It was a comfortable night, and Nat, as usual, was great. Mary Lou was a real trouper as she slept on the pullout sofa so that I could bunk with Nat. The girls are excited about our move and can hardly wait. The intrigue of Hollywood has them mesmerized even though they think it's a game. I tried to tell them how serious this was and that it was imperative they do not tell anyone. I told them that we can't trust anyone, no one at all. I hope I put the fear of God in them. They are so excited about going to Hollywood, and once again I stressed how important it is to keep this quiet. I think they got the message," I said.

"I hope so," Larry said. "I'll talk to Mary Lou again to make certain that no one knows our plans, and she knows how serious this thing is." I played the music a lot louder as we spoke, a practice we had been doing since we were not sure if the place was bugged.

"I wanted to talk to you about our plans," I said. "I think the sooner we leave, the better it is. We will have a lot of trouble getting to Los Angeles when winter hits. Also, it is just as easy to edit and distribute the films in Los Angeles as well as shoot new ones. So I don't think we should delay. It will not impact us in any way. Financially, I will keep us afloat, so money will not be our problem at all. Fuck, Carmine. I am reading your mind, and I can see through the smoke that you are concerned about him," I said.

"Well, I am, a little," Larry said.

"I'll repeat myself. Fuck him. He does not care about you or anyone else. He wants the movies and will have to pay or he doesn't get them. The way things have worked in the past, you probably wouldn't be paid because he is a fucking puke and is always looking to screw everyone especially you. He wants to control everyone through fear and money. It's his way, so Carmine is nothing for us. If he wants to buy a movie, he will have to pay cash for it. I think I can have a broker handle it—in this way, it is cash up front. If he comes with muscle, we'll kill the bastard once and for all. I don't think he will try to muscle you and will work with you in a proper businesslike manner. In any case, I think it is time we struck out on our own and built a strong and secure business. The

Mob is not as strong in Los Angeles as it is here. Of course, I know it is in my best interests as well to get out of here, but it is also in yours as well," I said.

"I guess you are right, Dan. Let's start getting ready. Can we handle a shoot as early as next week?" Larry said.

"No problem. If all you need is money, then it's handled. You take care of the talent," I said. "Okay, let's get started," Larry said.

"Okay, partner, but remember, Larry, we need to shoot and leave. No waiting for anything. We shoot the film and disappear—all within twenty-four hours," I said.

I left Larry and returned to the girls' place and spent the rest of day there and started putting our plans together for our departure. I had no trouble getting the cooperation of the girls with this project. They were walking on air and excitement—Hollywood, here we come!

Wednesday, October 23, 1957

"I spoke with Jackie last night, and she promised to pack up the stuff that I requested from my apartment today. She will keep the stuff in her apartment, and we can pick it up whenever we want," I said to Nat. "I want you to call her and coordinate the pickup of the stuff from her apartment. Also tell her that I instructed you to advise her to keep anything she likes from the apartment and sell the rest. Tell her she can keep the money as payment for all her help. We'll get in touch in a little while. In this way, I will never be seen in case they are watching the building."

The list I made for Jackie was only things I felt I needed and should fit into one suitcase—anything else, I didn't want or need. I gave Nat Jackie's number, and off I went to the studio to get organized for the last shoot and the move to Los Angeles.

I got off the elevator and found Larry working on the final touches of the script. "How's it all going, old man," I said.

"I am almost done with this script. It's in its final stage. This will be our final film in New York, and I want it to be a memorable one. I will need some exterior shots, like the Statue of Liberty, Ellis Island, and the Empire State Building. I'll call Wally to get his camera working and get these shots today or tomorrow. What do you think of sex on the stairs of the Statue of Liberty?" Larry said with a gleam in his eye. "I also need a scene of a wild orgy on the observation deck at the Empire State. You always need new material and stuff like this will fill that bill. This will be an epic, a final tribute to New York, and the last of the real porn shoots ever shot in New York. What do you think, Dan?"

"I love it. It sounds exciting and fun. Of course, we will have to charge a little more for this film to recoup our costs and make some profit. "Profit" that's a special word that translates to survival. Larry, please don't go overboard. We can't afford to go broke." I laughed and laughed until I nearly wet my pants.

"Larry, not to put a damper on all this, but we still have to be on the alert. Carmine could easily send some of his goons after us. He wants your movies, and he doesn't want to lose control, so please be careful, please!" I said.

"I will be very careful. Now let's get to work," Larry said.

"By the way, Larry, why can't we call Stan and offer him some distribution deal. I know he will deal a lot better with us than Carmine, and his brother Peter can straighten out things between Carmine and us if need be. Come on, don't you think we should give it a try?" I said.

"You're right, Dan. I don't know why I didn't think of it. Stan is the perfect one to trust. Let's shoot this film, and then I'll call him and maybe we can get the hell out of this city in one piece and some real bucks?" Larry said as he went back to his script.

I called Nat and she informed me that Jackie had already removed my stuff. She would meet with Nat tonight at Oliver's on Second Avenue and Eighty-Third Street and give her the suitcase with my stuff. She would also get rid of everything in the next few days. I would call the utility companies and cancel the services as of the end of the month. I then filled in a change of address card using an address of an empty lot in Brooklyn. Now all traces of Dan All right would be a thing of the past. Finding him would not be easy for anyone.

Thursday, October 24, 1957

After a great night's sleep with Nat, I was ready for a full day of movie making. Before I could get started, I had to call Moe and tell him of my plans. I also decided on a name change. I thought it best that I would fare a lot better in Los Angeles under a new name.

"Hey, Moe, how are doing?" I asked.

"Just great, Harry. How about you, my friend?" he responded. I told Moe about leaving the apartment and getting ready to leave for Los Angeles.

"All that is left is to complete this last movie, and then we will drive west. I'll get new papers and change my name so that getting settled in Los Angeles will be easier. I'll advise you what my new moniker will be as well as my address and telephone number, of course. As always I trust you will not release that information to anyone. I'll need about two hundred K in cash. How's my money holding out?" I asked.

"No need to worry. You still have more than two million left with the two hundred K we got from the sale of the house, and seven hundred and fifty K Rachel's dad left for you when he thought you both would be together. He does not expect any of it back. Plus the cash you left me leaves us with about a two million balance plus interest, so don't worry about it. I think the interest alone will cover your expenses. Of course, you will have to start seeing some profits from your new enterprise as making some money is a good habit to get into. I only mention this because your money won't last forever. Meanwhile, when do you need the cash?" Moe said.

"In one or two days. I'll keep you posted!" I said. "I'll call you on Monday, and we can arrange a pickup. Moe, I really don't know how to thank you. You have been so good to me, thanks."

"Okay, Harry, call me on Monday, and please don't worry about this. I knew your dad for years—a nicer man never existed. I don't know if you are aware that he paid my way through law school as you know my folks couldn't afford anything at all. And after all that he helped me start my own law practice. He brought me clients and made sure I was always paid and never once did he ask for one penny back. Good people deserve good things, and your dad was one of the best. This is the least I can do. And by the way, Harry, you're not so bad either." He hung up.

I felt good in my heart to know how great my dad was. I always thought he was just a hard working guy who didn't care about anything and never really was a success. I guess success is revealed differently in many people. My dad was the best, and I was so sorry I did not stay in close touch with him. I was sure he understood the circumstances, and knowing what kind of guy my dad was made me feel he understood me even better. I loved him very much and wished I could just call him and tell him so. Under the present circumstances, I could not call him, and I couldn't spend any time with him. Our last visit a couple of months ago said it all. He understood one hundred percent and assured me that he loved me more than anything and would always be at my side. He told me to do whatever I had to do and not to worry about him—he would always be there waiting for me.

I was feeling on top of the world when the phone rang. "Hello," Nat answered. "I am sorry, there is no Harry Miller here. You must have the wrong number," she said and hung up.

"Who the hell was that, Dan?" she said, "And how did they get this phone number?"

"I really don't know, but I don't like it. I think there is someone who works at the studio that is giving these people information. Where else could they have gotten your phone number? The phone is actually on Mary Lou's real name, so how would anyone know?" I said very concerned. "There has to be a mole in the employ of Larry. I'll get to the bottom of it, but be careful, and Nat, you did the right thing with the call," I said.

"By the way, girls," I shouted as I was preparing to leave for the studio, "Please watch what you say, and be very careful. Always pay attention to see if you are being followed. Always pay attention around the apartment. Once we leave here, we won't have to worry about this, but for now, please be alert and very quiet about our plans. If you have to tell your parents, please do it by pay phone and ask them to keep it quiet. Tell them you are scheduled to be in a movie in Hollywood and must keep it very quiet. They will be excited and proud, but assure them that if they talk about your trip they can easily screw up your deal. This is the big break you have been waiting for, so they must keep quiet. Secrecy is the name of the game. Let's not regret a bad decision, please," I said.

I jumped into a cab and went directly to the studio. When I arrived, I found the area downstairs to be deserted. I looked everywhere to see if someone was watching the place and could not detect anyone. I took the elevator up to the studio and found Larry talking on the phone.

"I don't care what you do, Harry. You've got to make time. I need you for a couple of days starting on Monday. If you are committed, please tell me now as time is of the essence. This is going to be the movie of the century, and I would like you to be in it. It will do you a lot of good when you need work, believe me, Harry. I wouldn't bullshit you!" Larry said.

He finally hung up and saw me standing behind him. "Can you believe this shit? I help out these people whenever I can especially when they are out of work and need money. Now when I need a rush job, I get excuses. Fuck them all. We'll find new people to play the parts."

"Listen, Larry, I have to talk to you. It's very important. It seems we have a mole who is working here. I wish I knew who it was, but the Mob called Mary Lou looking for Harry Miller. There is no way we have given her phone number to anyone. The only place it is available is on the bulletin board in the back of the studio. I just feel we have to watch our steps and be very careful. If we don't, we will be in the middle of a fucking war, and I don't want you to get hurt," I said.

"Are you serious, Dan?" Larry said. "It's hard to believe that anyone here would be a mole for the Mob. I just can't believe it."

"I have an idea that I think will serve us all very well," I said. "Let's get out of here and go have a drink, and I'll tell you all about it. I can't trust this place at all. It could easily be bugged," I said.

We left the studio and proceeded to the Blue Parrot where we took a table in the far corner. We ordered our drinks and settled back while surveying the area to make sure there weren't any strangers in the area. I even looked under the table to see if there were any listening devices attached underneath. I finally said, "Okay, it all looks clear to me, so here goes my plan. Forget shooting the movie here. We have the females, and they are the main stars, and getting guys will not be difficult in Los Angeles. You have already shot all the exteriors, so the theme for the movie is all set. Shooting the rest in Los Angeles will be a breeze, and we can work in a relaxed atmosphere. This place is too heavy and too volatile, while in Los Angeles it is an easy shoot with nothing more than sunshine and lack of fear. My idea is to pack up everything we need and shove off. Tell no one except the girls, and let's get out of here. I will rent a trailer that will handle all our stuff, or if you think it best we can scrap everything and just buy new ones once we get to Los Angeles!" I said.

"Well, Dan, I'm not sure that would be a good idea," Larry started to say.

"Hold on to your thoughts, and let me finish, Larry," I said. "We can have the girls meet us in Chicago or someplace like that and pick them up on the way, or we can just fly to Los Angeles and get things organized there while the girls meet us in a few days. I will get us new identifications for Los Angeles, and we can start afresh under new names and a new company name and sell our films through a distributor. That way, Dan All right and Larry Robbins will disappear, and we can begin a new life and work with clear heads. Please don't get me wrong, Larry. I can easily kill these bastards, but I'll run out of bullets long before they run out of guys.

"They will get us sooner or later, and it will be too late then. Making movies will be impossible as we will be too busy fighting, and in the end we shall lose. This way our chances are a lot better, and you have the opportunity to establish yourself in the porn industry in Los Angeles where very few companies exist at this time. It is the future home of the porn industry, and you should be a part of it. I feel this is best for both our goals and will make life easier for us all. Think about it. We don't have much time. I can feel a war on the horizon. It's coming, Larry. It's coming very soon!" I said.

"I hear you, buddy," Larry said as he signaled the waiter for another round. "I like the idea, and I think we can scrap most of what we have here. There is no use in taking sets with us. We can easily buy or build new ones. My typewriter takes up very little room, and I would love to start afresh with a new name. Why not? I can be the new director who has just been discovered. Yes, Dan. I like the idea. Let's do it. Fuck these prima donnas, and let's start the new 'Erosion Studios of Hollywood, California.' When can we leave?" Larry said as he tried, unsuccessfully, to contain his enthusiasm.

"Well, I'm all set as I've nothing left at my apartment. Nat is picking up my personal stuff as we speak. She's meeting Jackie and getting my suitcase," I said. "The girls rented their place fully furnished, so there is very little they need. We will use my car, and I'll get rid of it somewhere in Los Angeles and buy another. I need to get our ID all set up and can do that right here in Manhattan. I will get yours as well as the girls. If we are to start new, let's make sure we are on the same page. Please let me know if you have a special name you want to be known by, and it will be done. I need to pick up some cash on Monday so that we can leave anytime after lunch. In the meantime, I think we should not tip our hand to anyone. Business as usual and we'll be way ahead of the game," I said.

"Agreed. Let's get to work once and for all. I'm so excited, Dan," Larry said.

"I have to get in touch with the editing company and see how far they've gotten with our first film. If they are close to completion, it would be best to wait until the film is done and then take it with us. I'll change the names on the films when we are in Los Angeles," Larry said as we walked back to the studio. I guess I'd better come up with a new name. Help me out, Dan," Larry said.

"How about Richard James? I think it has a great ring to it. What do you think Larry?" I said. "We need an address in Los Angeles, and

I'll need three or four photos for your passport and license. I think California has started using photos as well as a thumbprint. I'm not certain, but I'll find out."

"I'll get started right away and get the photos. I love the name Richard James. Most people will call me Dick, but that sound's great. Let's move forward," Larry said.

"Shall do, and while I am at it, I'll get new IDs for the girls. It'll make it easier for them and easier for us. Keep your eyes open, Larry. We only have a few days," I said.

Friday, October 25, 1957

I had an early meeting with my contact for new identifications. I had told him I needed four sets of passports, driver's licenses, and Carte Blanche credit cards. I gave him the names he would need. My new name would be Ron Majestic, and Larry would be Marty Loomis; the girls would be Mary Lou Johnson and Natalia Petrov as we wanted to retain their theatrical names. I didn't have an address in Los Angeles, so he said he would find one for us. We could change it when we were in Los Angeles if we didn't like it, but in the meantime it would do. We all went to a Woolworth store where they had a passport photo machine and took our pictures.

Each document had to look perfect and pass any test it may be put through. As far as my guy was concerned, California did not require any photo, so all we needed photos for were the passports. I left the house at seven and took the train to Forty-Second Street and then walked the few blocks to Forty-First and Ninth and met with him. I carefully noted which picture belonged to each description and correct name along with five hundred to get things started. The total price was an additional eight-fifty for all four of us, and it would be ready on Sunday.

I then went to the studio and woke Larry up and prodded him to get his ass into gear and start the ball rolling. We agreed that it should appear as if it was business as usual so that no one would suspect a thing. We would leave sometime on Monday and drive as far as we could the first day and spend the night along the route.

We decided to take the southerly route as it would be safer in the event of bad weather. We estimated it should take us about five days to get to California, but we all agreed we were in no rush, so an extra day or two wouldn't matter. In the meantime, we gathered up all our important stuff and placed them in suitcases that would fit in the trunk only. Anything else we may need, we will buy along the way or in Los Angeles. "Okay, Larry, get all your shit together, and let's get ready for the shoot," I said with a wink. We decided that we will not say anything out of the ordinary in case the studio was bugged.

"Is the script ready?" I said.

"It sure is, Dan, and we can start shooting on Tuesday. I spoke with Suzie and John, and they will be available on Tuesday. We'll start after lunch and should wrap it up by Thursday. This one is going to be the biggest and best ever. I have Wally shooting exteriors all weekend and should have some prints by Monday. I will then decide where to shoot what scenes. It's going to be the best movie I have ever made and the most costly," Larry said. "How about lunch, Dan? Let's go to the Blue Parrot. I'm buying."

We went off to the Blue Parrot leisurely enjoying the beautiful warm day as we walked along Fifth Avenue. "Hey, Dan, don't look around. Just keep your head looking forward, but I think we are being followed. They look like Mob guys. They're trying real hard to look like the rest of the walkers," Larry said.

"Okay, Larry, let's see if they follow us into the Blue Parrot. How many did you count?" I asked. "I see two on this side of the street and one on the other side. They are easy to pick out, but why are they following us, why?" Larry said. We entered the Blue Parrot and took a table that gave us a perfect view of the front door.

We could see anyone who came and went; it was easy to follow what these guys were doing. A waiter approached our table and Larry ordered, "Thanks, we'll have two vodkas on the rocks with a twist of lemon."

"So what do you think, Larry? What should we do?" I said, "Maybe we should blow them away before they get us."

"Maybe you are right, but why me? I didn't do anything to them yet, so why me, or am I just collateral damage?" Larry said.

"They could be from Carmine, and I am the collateral damage, so don't be so quick to think it's the Mob after me! Fuck them. Let's enjoy our drinks and then on the way back to the studio why not give then a run for their money. So far, no one has come inside, so if we leave by another way, we could possibly lose them, but they will still come after us. I think we should take them out near Twenty-Third Street and Fifth. There is a lot of traffic, and it will inhibit their ability to do much. Most importantly, their anonymity will be over, and we will have the upper hand," I said.

"Okay, Dan, let's not rush. Fuck them. We might as well enjoy ourselves while they sweat."

"Okay, let's just have a few more drinks, and shit, if they want war, we'll give it to them," I said.

It was around five when Larry and I decided to leave the Blue Parrot. We couldn't find an alternate exit, so we left through the front door, and sure enough, these assholes were outside waiting for us. We just stood there and laughed as we started walking back toward the studio. It was starting to get dark, and we figured if we walked slowly by the time we got to Twenty-Third. Street, it will be getting close to real dark, and their vision will be affected more than ours. It's like a football player running for a touchdown with only one person in the way; the advantage goes with the runner because he knows exactly what he is going to do while the other guy can only guess. They continued to follow us; two on our side of the street and one on the other side. Of course, they did not know that we were on to them.

"Larry," I said. "You cross the street and take out the guy on that side while I take care of these two. Don't worry about me. Worry about yourself and off the fucker if you have to. I forgot to ask you if you are carrying a gun. Do you have a silencer on it?" Larry laughed and said, "Does Macy's ask Gimbles?" I watched Larry cross the street, and he continued walking south while I stayed on my side and continued south as well. As soon as Larry crossed the street, the other two got a little panicky. I slowed my pace so that they could catch up and waited by a store window as they approached. Traffic was pretty heavy on Twenty-Third Street as it was Friday night and rush hour. They went past me and continued as if they were two people talking and walking with a destination in mind. Now the advantage was on my side as I was behind them. When we reached Twenty-Second Street, I turned right and ducked into a doorway. I saw them panic as they thought they'd lost me. As they came down Twenty-Second Street, I stepped out of the doorway and spoke, "Why are you following me?" I said as I leveled my gun at them. "Don't try to bullshit me, or I'll kill you right now," I said.

"Hey, man. We aren't following you. What gave you that idea?" one of the guys said.

"The fucking trouble with you assholes is that you don't know how to follow someone properly. Well, all I can say is fuck you," and shot the first guy in the knee.

"Oh, that hurts like hell, you motherfucker," he screamed as he dropped to the sidewalk holding his knee.

"Okay, let me shoot out the other one if that is what you want? Now answer my question or you are both history. Now, buddy, my patience is running very thin. You hear me?" I yelled.

The guy who was not wounded said, "Okay man, listen to me. We were sent by our boss to follow you and report back. We were not asked to hurt you ever, I swear."

"Okay, I believe you. Now give me your guns, or I'll blow you to shit." They both took out their guns and threw them toward me. I bent down to pick them up, and the guy on the ground found another gun and was aiming it at me. I spun around and in a split second pumped three bullets into him. He fell over dead right there on Twenty-Second Street. The other guy yelled out, "Please don't kill me. I don't have another gun. I am married and have three kids, please!" "Who sent you out here, and don't bullshit me. I know a lot more than you think, you fucking rat bag," I said.

"Carmine wanted us to follow you. He said you were trying to run out on him, and you owed him a lot of money. I was just doing my job. Please don't kill me, please," he begged. "I guess you had no intention of killing me, that's why you brought guns along. What sad fucks you are," I said and pulled the trigger and watched the bullet leave a small hole just above his right eye. He fell to the ground dead. I pulled both of them into a small alley and left them there and went back to Fifth Avenue to continue my way back to the studio. I looked across the road to see if Larry was okay and saw nothing. I just kept walking toward the studio at a very leisurely pace. I stopped outside the studio to wait a few minutes for Larry to show. When he came around the corner, he was smiling from ear to ear.

"Hey, man, how are you?" Larry said. "That was the greatest experience I ever had. No more conversations in the studio. It is bugged, and it is obvious they are trying to put me out of business so that Carmine will own me. I'm glad we did what we did. It feels good. Let's get our shit together and get the hell out of here, *asap*."

"I think we should start on our trip first thing in the morning. In the meantime, let's get whatever shit you want out of here and stay over at the girl's place tonight," I said.

We went back to the studio where Larry gathered up the papers he wanted to keep and threw the rest into a burlap bag. He grabbed his typewriter, and we left the studio and went over to the girl's apartment to spend the night.

Saturday, October 26, 1957

We woke early and packed the car with as much as we could without causing us any discomfort. We had a long drive ahead of us and wanted to be as comfortable as possible. I had plenty of money that I picked up from Moe on Friday. I gave Moe as much of the particulars as I could and the details regarding Carmine's guys. He agreed that the trip to Los Angeles was in order and was glad that we were leaving so quickly. We still had to pick up our new paperwork on Sunday, so we decided to drive to the Catskills for the day and sleep over at a motel.

It was not tourist season, so we figured we wouldn't have any trouble finding a place. The reason for all this was safety. We felt that if we stayed in Manhattan we would run into the Mob, and we don't need another battle right now. We had a great time driving around and stopping in at Grossinger's. We told them we were interested in checking the place out for our next vacation. They were very accommodating as they showed us around. The place had everything one would want on a vacation. Tennis courts, golf course, volleyball, dance floors, and plenty of places for entertainment. There wasn't a lack of things to do and food galore—all you can eat. What a great place to forget your worries and party all day and night.

Sunday, October 27, 1957

We stayed at a small motel near a stream. It was cozy and very reasonable, and we all had a great night's sleep. We left the Catskills at about ten thirty and arrived in Manhattan a little after lunch. We drove directly to my source to pick up the new identification papers. I went in and examined them to make sure they looked real and paid him the balance and left. We were now ready to leave New York behind and head out to Los Angeles. We took First Avenue to the George Washington Bridge and felt a lot better once we crossed into New Jersey. We were on our way and would probably stay somewhere in Pennsylvania tonight.

Monday, October 28, 1957

We got on the road bright and early and headed toward Ohio. We hoped we could make Indiana tonight and rest easy. The girls were excited as they looked out at the countryside of places they had never been to. Of course, they were also so excited about getting to Las Vegas and playing those slots and checking out the shows. The thought of settling down in Los Angeles was very exciting to everyone except me as I had lived in Los Angeles previously. I didn't want to dampen anyone's enthusiasm, so I kept my thoughts to myself. What they didn't know was the layout of Los Angeles and how spread out the city was. The weather in Los Angeles would be a great improvement over New York, but the size would be overwhelming. The thought of our new environment excited me more than anyone could imagine. The thrill of it all was overwhelming and gave us all a rush. All along the way, the conversation was all about what would do when we arrived in Los Angeles.

Larry and I had been sharing the driving, which allowed us to drive longer and make up some distance. We were very concerned about using my car, but as we drove and discussed the situation, we all agreed that it was unlikely anyone would know what kind of car I drove. The reasoning behind our thoughts was the fact that while living in New York I never used the car and had it parked in an indoor lot. Also the car was registered in another name, so there was no connection to Dan All right. After a few hundred miles, we all agreed that this car did not present any risk whatsoever. We agreed that once we were settled in Los Angeles, we would buy a new car under the names we would use in our new location. We could hardly wait until we got to Los Angeles.

Tuesday, October 29, 1957

Our trip had been going real well, and we were making up some real distance. We should be in Denver today and then on to Utah. I promised the girls we would stop at the Salt Flats and, if the temperature allowed it, we would swim in the Great Salt Lake. While on this trip, I promised the girls we would try to see as many sights as possible but not forget that the reason we left New York was to escape the Mob. We certainly didn't want to give them a clue where we were.

"Fun is fun, girls, but we have to take into account that we are taking care of our futures and that is most important to us all. Remember, your careers are in the balance, and Los Angeles will be a great place for that. I think we should decide on a proper story that will be used as our past so that we will all be on the same wavelength. We cannot ever talk about the past in New York, and we can't trust anyone. You don't know who your friend is and who is not, so please be careful. I don't care how often I remind you of this. It's your lives I'm trying to protect, and they are very important to me. So while we are all in one area like this car, let's make up a good past that will be easily believed and can always be used. Once we settle on an agreeable past history, we will remember it always. Thus we will have eliminated any problems of slipping up," I said as we drove along toward our ultimate destination. We continued the drive well into the night as we wanted to put some distance between us and New York and get to Las Vegas as soon as possible.

Wednesday, October 30, 1957

We continued our drive with very little sightseeing as we passed through Denver and on to Salt Lake. The temperature was a little too cold to swim in the Salt Lake, so we took a ride on the Flats where all the land speed records were being set and continued on to Nevada. We arrived in Reno late at night and found a motel. We would look around tomorrow. Right now, we needed sleep.

Thursday, October 31, 1957

After a relaxing breakfast, we decided not to spend any time in Reno and to drive on to San Francisco and then take the Pacific Coast Highway to Los Angeles. We all agreed that exposing ourselves in a gambling town like this would the same as placing an ad in the newspaper that we had arrived. We also decided that we would not drive to Las Vegas either for the same reasons. We'd come this far without any incident and wanted to keep it that way.

We left around ten and made our way to San Francisco passing through Lake Tahoe and on through the Sierra Nevada and looking at the Donner Pass. The girls didn't know what the significance about Donner Pass was, so we used the time to explain the history behind it.

This was where a wagon train in 1846 got stuck in an early snowfall on their way to California. It was a great tragedy as they eventually ran out of food, and as the story has it, some of those travelers resorted to cannibalism to stay alive. You could see how difficult the Sierra Nevada was when we were driving in a car; you could just imagine how hard it must have been in the days of wagon trains. We also saw a few car wrecks way down in the valleys and gorges in the Sierra Nevada. The depth of the gorges were so deep, they just left the wrecks where they were. Well, at least we saw some sights on the way. We arrived in the early evening and thought it was best to have something to eat and stay the night in or near Oakland and proceed early tomorrow. We found a small hotel in Oakland and stayed the night with a wake-up call for eight A.M.

Friday, November 1, 1957

The girls insisted that we stay an extra day in San Francisco because they had never been here and very much wanted to see the city. After a little discussion, we agreed and spent the day in San Francisco seeing the town. We went to Fisherman's Wharf, Lombard Street, the most crooked street in the world. We were able to see Alcatraz when we crossed the Bay Bridge. It was a sight to see as it housed some of the most dangerous criminals in the United States. We then decided to go to Chinatown for dinner and take a walk through the streets. It was fun for us all, but we had to move on and get to Los Angeles. We planned to leave first thing in the morning for Los Angeles and should arrive by nightfall. We agreed we would leave via the Golden Gate Bridge and through Sausalito and then on through Marin County. We would pass another prison, San Quentin, and on through the Big Sur and on to Los Angeles. The last four hundred miles of our trip would be along the Pacific Coast highway and was to be the most exciting stretch of the drive west. The trip was great and finally came to an end.

We could now start to get serious about finding some decent housing and settling down. It was exciting, but we all remembered that the trip was to establish new identities and forget New York.

Saturday, November 2, 1957

The trip along the Pacific Coast Highway was everything we had expected and was by far the most exciting part of our trip. Of course, being the last leg and the anticipation of our new beginning added to making this segment wonderful. While on the drive, we rehearsed our background story over and over again, and all agreed that we had it down once and for all and would not have any problems.

We arrived in Los Angeles in the early afternoon and continued along the ocean drive past the Santa Monica Pier, where there were many motels and a lot of activity including traffic.

We found a motel in Santa Monica on Ocean Drive, right on the beach near the Santa Monica Pier. The air was clear and quite warm and a lot of people were on the beach enjoying the warm sun. Life seemed great. This was going to be the best move I had made in the last year. Marty and I went out to scout around and see if we could find a suitable office/studio to begin the film business.

"So what is your take on all this, Marty?" I said.

"I think we have to find out if there are other XXX-rated companies operating and just where they set up shop," Marty said.

"Let's stop in at a bar and make some very discreet inquiries. It won't take long, Ron, let's go." "I'm with you, old man. Let's get started," I said as I opened the door to our motel room.

"Girls, Marty and I are going to scout around. Make yourselves comfortable. Go out on the beach. It is such a gorgeous day. Enjoy yourselves, but be very careful what you tell people. See you a little later, and remember, I love you."

We went along Ocean Boulevard and turned east on Pico. We soon reached Lincoln Boulevard and saw a bar a little beyond Lincoln on Pico on the south side. The "Rear Entrance" seemed like a good place to start.

"This looks like a good place to start," Marty said. "Pull in here, and we'll see what is going on." I turned the car into the rear parking lot, and Marty and I went into the bar to see if we could get some information.

"Let's sit at the bar and have a drink. We'll get all the news we want in a few minutes," Marty said. The place was empty except for one lonely looking guy sitting at a back table nursing a beer.

"Hi, how you doing?" Marty said as we sat down on a worn-out stool at the bar.

"Just fine. What can I get you?" the bartender said with a smile.

"My name is Marty Loomis and this is my buddy, Ron Majestic. A pleasure to meet you. We'll have two vodkas on the rocks with a twist, please."

"Coming right up, Marty. By the way, I'm Albert. Are you new in town?" he asked.

"Yes, we just arrived, and we love this place. This is the only place to live. Too much cold weather and snow to deal with in Fargo not to mention that the opportunities in the motion picture business are not too big over there. We are going to make a name for ourselves here in Hollywood. This is our first stop. We are going to the moon from here, Albert," Marty said.

As soon as Albert heard the word motion picture, he perked up at once. "Are you guys really in the movie business?" he said.

"Sure are," I replied. "And plan to make it big in here. A little hard work and some decent connections and we will be on our way."

"A pleasure to meet you, guys," Albert said with enthusiasm. "If there is anything I can do to help you guys please don't hesitate to ask, I'm at your service. Wow! This is great."

"Hey, Albert, give me a little heads-up on the lay of the land," Marty said as Albert set our drinks down in front of us.

"What do you want know, fellas? I meet everyone here and have my fingers on everything that's going on," Albert said.

"Well, Albert, is there an X-rated industry here besides regular moviemakers?" Marty asked. "Don't tell me you guys make porn flicks," Albert said.

"We have some of the most gorgeous stars you have ever seen under contract to us. We plan on being the largest XXX company in the world, Albert," Marty said.

"Well, as you know, it is very hard to be public about XXX movies. Most of the people who do make them have their studios in the valley. The reason is that rents are a lot lower, and if you have to close up shop, it is easy to find another place. There are plenty of busts that take place, and most of them are in the Valley. It's not more than a thirty-minute ride over Mulholland to get to the valley. Did you know that most of the westerns are also shot in the San Fernando and Simi Valleys?" Albert asked with a big grin on his face.

"No, I didn't, Albert. Are you serious? I'd like to watch one being made," I said.

"Hey, why don't you guys come by around five this afternoon, and I'll introduce you to a few guys who are in that business. You'll like them. They are good guys," Albert said.

Marty took out a twenty and slipped it to Albert. "Thanks for your help. Keep things hopping, and we will see you about five tonight. We'll bring along a few of our stars so that you see can see the quality of our stuff," Marty said.

We left the bar and decided to drive to the Valley so that we could scope out the place. The Valley was not a place that either of us had ever heard of before. We felt that we should check it out right away, so we jumped into the car and off we went. As we drove along Sepulveda Boulevard, we passed through hills and mountains and large ranches everywhere. It looked like farmland to us, but we continued on. We arrived in Encino and took Ventura Boulevard toward the deeper parts of the Valley. As we drove, we started to pass a great many stores and a lot of warehouse-type buildings and found that there were a lot of people living here in the San Fernando Valley. The Valley was quite a different place than what we had imagined. The main street, Ventura Boulevard, was lined with retail stores, and beyond that, there was nothing more than open range. We drove along Ventura until the road sort of ended and more farms started to appear. We took De Soto Boulevard and drove north, always looking at the area to fully understand where a good location could be found. Of course, we were operating in the dark as we didn't know exactly where to look and could not understand the lay of the land.

We finally came to a street named Roscoe Boulevard, and as we approached the intersection of De Soto and Roscoe, Marty yelled, "Turn left, Ron, turn here." I almost missed the turn but, with a little effort, turned the wheel and got into the left turn lane. Once we turned on to Roscoe Boulevard, Marty said, "Ron, with a name like 'Roscoe' I just had to turn on it and see what is going on here," he said.

"Look, there is a bar on the right. I'm going to turn in there," I said. We pulled into this dingy-looking bar in the middle of a few stores. Outside the bar we saw a guy sitting on a chair next to the front door. To all who may pass by this establishment, it would appear that they were very desperate for business. We got out of the car and approached the bar "The Shed," and let me tell you, the name was quite explicit.

"Hey, welcome to The Shed," the guy on the chair said as he opened the door for us. The place was empty and smelled like a beer factory—a stale beer factory. The lighting was, to say the least, on the dark side. The place had about ten tables and a long bar with at least twenty stools.

"What's happening here in the Valley? Are we too early? Maybe everyone sleeps late," Marty asked.

"What you see is what you get man, quiet and quieter," he said.

"My name is Ron and this is Marty. We are new in town and looking for some good space to set up our business. We are in the film business, and this area looks like a good place to set up our studio. We were told that the Valley was the place for studios that make XXX-rated films," I said.

"I'm Arty. A pleasure to meet you, guys. What kind of movies did you say?" Arty said with great interest.

"All kinds, Arty. Right now, we are getting ready to shoot a XXX feature. The warehouse we need has to be discreet as we don't want to offend anyone. We need a large enough place to build sets and operate at odd hours," I said.

"There is a building on Remmet that is available. I heard the landlord talking the other day when he was in here for dinner. Yes, guys, we serve food every day after four. There isn't enough business to do lunch. I'll give you his name and number, and you can call him and go see the place," he said as he took out a pad and started writing the information for us. "If you like, guys, I can call Charlie right now and see if he is in. What do you think?"

"Please, Arty, call him. It would be great to see the place and see what is available. Thanks," Marty said. We sat around the bar as Arty made his call.

"He is coming over to meet you guys. His name is Charlie Breakwater, and he is really a very nice guy," Arty said.

"Thanks, Arty. Could you get us two vodkas on the rocks with twist? We might as well refresh ourselves while we wait. How far is this place from here?" I said.

"Not very far. It's just a block away, so if you do move in, we will see a lot of each other," he said as he placed our drinks in front of us. Marty pulled out a fifty and gave it to Arty.

"Keep the change, man, and thanks for your help. You really don't know how important it is to have some help when you move to a new place. You've been great, man, thanks a lot," he said.

We sat at the bar for another ten minutes when the door opened and in walked an elderly man who stood about six feet tall and looked like he weighed in at about two hundred pounds. We could easily tell that this was Charlie just by looking at the expression on the face of Arty. "Hey, Charlie, over here," Arty yelled out. "Charlie, I want you to meet Marty and Ron," Arty said. We extended our hands and shook Charlie's with vigor.

"A pleasure to meet you," Charlie said.

"Thanks to Arty, we are now able to speak with the owner directly. We are looking for a building that will serve as our office, warehouse, and storage facility. We are in the movie business and need a reasonably-priced space," Marty said.

"Well, fellas, I have a building just a short way from here on Remmet. It is about 9,000 sq. ft. with high ceilings, and I'm willing to let it out at a very reasonable price," Charlie said.

"Sounds great, Charlie. Why don't we go over and take a look at the place. We can negotiate the rent after we see the place," I said.

We left the bar and walked along Roscoe until we reached Remmet and turned left. We got to the end of the block and Charlie said, "This is it. Let's go in and check it out. No one has been in the building for a long while, so please excuse the smell. It is a little musty, but this place can be the best deal in town," he said.

We walked in and found a building that needed a lot of work. The shipping area in the back of the building was easily accessible, and the building had plenty of possibilities; the only issue was the rent and for how long?

"Okay, Charlie, what's the deal with this place?" I asked.

"Listen, guys," Charlie said. "I don't know much about you, so let me ask you a few questions. I am told you are in the movie business. What kind of movies?"

"I'm not going to bullshit you, Charlie. We primarily make XXX movies. We make them very discreetly and want to make sure the integrity of the building is always paramount in our dealings. We never release the address of our offices and hope you will always maintain our confidentiality. We will be good tenants and will take good care of your property," I said.

"Can you guys afford the rent?" Charlie asked.

"Charlie, you haven't let us in on that little secret yet. What is the rent you are asking?" I asked.

"Well, guys, I want to be fair, and I want to see you succeed. I don't want new people in here every few months, so here is my offer. I want fifteen hundred per month for the first year and then I want an increase of one hundred per month for each additional year you stay on. That means you pay fifteen hundred this year, and next year you pay sixteen hundred, and in the third year you pay seventeen hundred. You pay all the expenses of the building except the roof. I'll pay the taxes based on the present taxes. If there is a tax increase, only the increase will be passed on to you. I think that is fair and could make us good working partners," Charlie said with a smile on his face.

"Okay, Charlie, I think you are fair, and what you have laid out sounds reasonable. Let's see if we can work out a deal now and get the show on the road. We need to spend considerable funds on fixing this building as it is in shitty shape, so let's do it this way. We'll give you what you have asked but need the first six months free. You will start the lease at once with the first payment due six months from today and the lease actually starting now. I will give you nine thousand now to represent the last six month's rent. That means the first year will be fully paid for. To be clear, the next rental will be due on December 1, 1958, at the sixteen-hundred-dollar rate. The reason I am willing to pay the last six months in advance is to show good faith that we will be here for a long time. What about it Charlie? Let's close this deal now and be done with it. The balance of this month will be a bonus as we will need a few weeks to get started anyways, deal!" I said.

"Boy, you know how to drive a hard bargain. You're a grinder, Ron, but you know, I like you guys and need someone in the building. I feel real good about you boys, so let's do the deal, and let everything begin as of December 1957, but I'll give you the key today, deal!" Charlie said.

"Deal. Let's get this on paper and start a long and good relationship," I said.

We spent another hour while Charlie typed out a standard lease. Once that was done, I gave him nine thousand in cash, and we were in business. All we needed now was a place to stay, close to our new offices. This was great, and it was only four P.M.

"Let's get started back and tell the girls that we are on the way to stardom. The place will be great, and we will be on top of the world very soon. Now let's be careful, and get the show on the road," I said.

We arrived back at our motel at five and told the girls to get dressed for the night as we are going out to celebrate. We arrived at the "Rear Entrance" at six thirty. Upon entering, Albert spotted us at once and motioned us over to the bar.

"Hi guys," he said. "I have a table reserved for you. Follow me."

"Albert, I would like you to meet Natalia and Mary Lou, stars of the future," I said. Albert lost it the minute I mentioned the girls' names; he could hardly speak as he seemed to fall over himself. We spent the rest of the night at Albert's bar and drank champagne and ate some great steaks. The girls had a great time and so did Albert who went off duty at six and joined us until we left. When the time came to pay the check, Albert insisted it was on him. I don't like that kind of stuff as it brings attention to oneself, but I could not refuse Albert's hospitality. I made up my mind that I would have to straighten Albert out later this week in case anyone inquires about us. Will this ever end?

Sunday, November 3, 1957

Last night, we had a long discussion amongst ourselves along with a map of the San Fernando Valley. We wanted to understand where we were in regard to our office and whether we should live nearby or in Los Angeles. We tossed around the good and bad points and finally agreed that although the Valley is at least ten degrees hotter, it would be better for us. It would eliminate all that travel from Los Angeles to the Valley, thus lessening our exposure to danger and cost of travel. We also felt that we would be less visible in the Valley and our lives would be less stressful. We decided to spend the day in the Valley looking for a house that we could be comfortable in and call home.

We left early in the morning and arrived in the Valley at about nine fifteen. We decided to stop for breakfast and then start looking for a place. We had called a real estate agent and met her at her office on Ventura Boulevard and Corbin. She wanted to show us a few places in Woodland Hills, Tarzana, and Encino. All were upscale areas that, according to our agent, we would love. We needed a house with enough rooms to accommodate all of us. We needed at least 4 bedrooms, a pool, and a two-car garage after all this California where the sun always shone, and being in the show business, we needed an impressive place.

After looking at one house after another all day long, we finally found a beautiful house on St. Louis Street just off Topanga Canyon Boulevad in Woodland Hills. The house was just right and so very charming with a big brick fireplace in the family room, four bedrooms, three bathrooms, and a great kitchen, dining room, and living room. There was a great looking swimming pool and a hot tub attached to the pool. The garage was a little tight for two cars as the previous owners built large storage cabinets on each of the walls that cut down the size. We could remove the cabinets, and there would be plenty of room for two cars. They wanted six hundred per month that included the gardener. We had to take care of the pool on our own, but the place was immaculate and very private. We loved it and completed the rental application and told the agent to call us at once. We offered two months' rent in advance as well as a one-thousand-dollar security deposit refundable at the end of a three-year lease. It was a sweet deal all the way around. We kept our fingers crossed that it would be approved; the girls were crazy about the place and so were we.

We went back to our motel in Los Angeles and went out to a restaurant in Santa Monica and had a nice Italian dinner and went back to the motel to relax and get some sleep. Life was starting to feel good; at least we were very relaxed.

Monday, November 4, 1957

We called the real estate office at ten A.M., and we were told the lease was approved but was only for one year and will automatically be renewed each year with a small increase in the rent not to exceed five percent per year for as long as we wished to remain in the house. They asked us to be in their office at two so that we could sign the official lease and pick up the keys. We called the appropriate utility companies to make sure the electricity and gas service would not be interrupted and arranged to have a couple of telephones installed with a few extensions. We also organized the telephones and utilities for our new offices.

We were establishing ourselves which felt very good and made us feel that we were on the way to success. It was a busy day, but one filled with fun as we were settling down to a more stable life. After the signing of the lease, we went over to the house to measure the sizes of the rooms so that we would know what size furniture we would need. We spent the rest of the day buying furniture at a big furniture outlet. We met the owner, Ralph Meeks, and when we told him that we were in the movie business, he went wild. We made a deal to trade fifty free copies of our next ten releases in exchange for the beds, mattresses, linens, lamps, and end tables as well as our living room ensemble and kitchen set. The girls were very excited that they could select the furniture including the kitchen set and dining room suite. All in all, we furnished the entire house without spending a dime. We also promised Ralph that he would be invited to at least one shoot. Delivery was set for Wednesday, and all that was left was office furniture for our new offices/studio. That would be tomorrow's job while the girls could spend the day preparing the new house for the furniture delivery.

Tuesday, November 5, 1957

I spent the first hour with Natalia changing my appearance so that no one would be able to identify the guy who was with Marty when they bought furniture and other things. I didn't want the real problem forgotten and constantly reminded everyone that it still existed.

Marty and I spent the day laying out the offices and studio sectors of the new building. We went shopping for office furniture from a used office supply company located in the West Valley. We went to the office early in the morning and made an extensive list of things that had to be done to bring the building up to the standard we wanted. We needed new carpet and found a sale going at a carpet company.

"Well, what do you think, Marty?" I asked.

"It's all so great. I'm so happy we made this move and a new start. Over The Top Films now has a real home and will begin to produce fine adult films. I promise you, Ron, we will be the best and the largest adult film company in the world. I can just feel it in my bones," Marty said with a smile that was a mile wide.

"One thing we must really keep in mind, Marty," I said. "We cannot forget for a moment that the Mob will be looking for me and perhaps both of us. A low profile is the most important thing we must do. We are in a business that is not legal, so there is a great deal of risk out there from the feds. We are out on a limb as Carmine will not accept being made a fool of so very easily, and the Mob will do anything to get to me. And, Marty, never forget that the cops are looking for me. They still want me to testify, and they think they've got the real thing with me. If they should ever catch up with me, they will never let me go again. It is our job to protect everything we own and eliminate the past. Our new identities must be foolproof, and that can only happen if we both maintain a very cautious way of life," I said. "I hope I am clear on all this?"

"Ron, please don't worry about a thing. I promise you we will always be very careful. We are brothers and will face each day together and no one will ever come between us no matter what the danger may be. We must forget everything about New York so that no one will be able to trick us into revealing that we came from there," Marty said. "My cover story is simple. I am an orphan from Minnesota. No way anyone can look for me as it is a dead-end and will stymie any investigation. As a matter of fact, let's make sure we get new Social Security numbers. We'll tell them we lost ours in a fire, and we will have legitimate ones."

"Okay, Marty, my story is also as simple. I came from Northern California and moved here when I was six years old. My folks are dead, and I have no brothers or sisters. Nothing more for me to say as it is no one's business and that is that. I will make sure my hair is always jet black, and you make sure you are always blond. I'll do a little makeup to change my features, and I suggest you do the same and then we are off to the races," I said. "One more thing, Marty," I said. "I will not ever appear at the offices. I will work from home or rent a small office elsewhere. They will be looking for the two of us to be working together as a team. By keeping ourselves apart, we will keep anyone who is checking on us realizing that we are not the people they are looking for. The only weakness in our plans is the girls as they are the type that people do not forget easily. Because you and I are seen much too often with them, their presence could make someone suspicious. Of course, if someone is going to look that hard, we will get news of it pretty fast and we could easily take the appropriate action."

We picked up the girls at the house and went for dinner and made the final trip back to the motel. This drive was proving to be much too much for us all. We were so happy that we made the decision to move to the Valley.

Wednesday, November 6, 1957

We moved out of the motel and went directly to our new home. The furniture arrived around ten in the morning, and the girls set about instructing the delivery guys on where to place each piece. The delivery guys were so taken by the girls that they would have moved the entire house for them if requested. A new life was emerging, and we were all very excited about it. The offices were also a beehive of activity as tradesmen were busy building, painting, and repairing.

Through Charlie, we were able to find reliable tradesmen and at very reasonable prices. Each hour, the future was starting to look brighter and better. "Over The Top Films" head office, what a thrill, especially to Marty. We worked late into the night as we wanted to complete as much as possible. Finally we quit for the day around eleven as we were exhausted.

We came home at eleven thirty and found a transformation of our castle completed. The girls did a masterful job and made the place warm and welcome. Marty and I were both exhausted after the long day, but we made the effort to have one glass of wine with the girls in celebration of a job well done and in appreciation of their dedication to our happiness.

Thursday, November 7, 1957

This was going to be the first day of work for us even though our offices and warehouse were not quite ready. Marty insisted we start making contacts and get word out that a new film company was in town, and we will start shooting in two weeks. Marty spoke with a good friend of his from New York and was given the name of Jeb Johnson who was the number one agent for models and actors. Jeb handled people for all type of roles including XXX films. One could not deal with Jeb unless he was well recommended, and in this instance, Marty was able to drop the name of his buddy, Eric Samson, from New York and the door to model heaven opened wide.

"Where is Jeb's office, Marty?" I asked.

"He is located on Ventura Boulevard near Van Nuys Boulevard," Marty said. "I spoke with him a little while ago and have an appointment to see him at his office at four this afternoon. I need to make contacts so that we can have access to cameras, lighting, actors, and makeup people. I also need a very good photographer to shoot our posters and advertising pieces. I cannot just call anyone, so I'll use Jeb as my entry. Once I know my way around, I'll handle all these things more discreetly, but until then, Ron, we have to take some risks. It can't be helped," Marty said. "I guess you are right, Marty, but keep me in the background. The less people who see me the better it is. You can make all the connections and friendships, but please keep me in the background as much as possible. I am the silent partner that no one needs to see or hear," I said.

Marty and I went about the rest of the day getting things organized in the office. At around three thirty, Marty left to see Jeb, and I left to find a bank. I had heard while at lunch that The American Trust Bank was now accepting accounts from adult film companies. It seemed that the bank wanted to get its new branch firmly established in the Valley and would do business with adult filmmakers. It was almost impossible to open a bank account if you were in the adult business because of the risks involved.

Banks did not want to be associated with adult companies, so most of the XXX companies had to use fake names and personal accounts to put their money in. Not only was the content of the films out of bounds, the reputation of the operators was also very bad as many of them were folks who did have a minor skirmish with the law in the past. Insurance coverage was almost nonexistent due to the fact that mobsters and other crooked operators had set fire to their warehouses and then made some very large claims under their fire coverage. Only two weeks earlier, an adult rated operation burned to the ground during the night and nothing was left. The owners claimed a cool one million in inventory and fixtures. Upon further investigation, the fire marshal could not find enough evidence in the ashes that there was any stock at all, but he also couldn't find sufficient evidence of arson. In another case, there was a warrant for the arrest of the owner of another adult company, a Larry Bellini, on charges of arson, fraud, and grand theft. The XXX business was going through a tough period and was being pummeled from all sides. Finding an insurance carrier to cover us as well as a bank was by no means an easy task, especially under the shady environment the industry seems to be under.

I went to the bank this afternoon and met Sally Thornton, the manager of this branch. I knew at once that we would hit it off as she was a swinger, and I knew she was movable—I just had that feeling. She was outgoing and had a personality so different from the typical bank manager. I liked her a lot.

"Hi, I'm Ron Majestic of Over the Top Films. It is a pleasure to meet you Mrs. Thornton," I said as I shook her hand.

"Please sit down, and please call me Sally. Would you like a drink, water, tea, coffee?" she said.

"No thanks. Perhaps later we could have a drink. Right now, I'd like to get some information about your bank. I would like to open a few accounts for our film company as well as my personal one and would like to know if our money will be secure with you. I want us to work together and grow," I said. "This is a new branch, and our film company is a new company, and I know we will be growing by leaps and bounds and quickly too!"

"Well, Ron, may I call you Ron?" she said.

"Of course, you can, Sally. Let's eliminate any formalities. I want you to have faith that we will be great partners," I said with a big smile.

"Well, Ron, it is true we are new and we want to grow, but one of my directives is not to accept adult companies as clients. The risks are far too big. That is the opinion of the president of our bank," she said in a very respectful tone.

"Listen to me, Sally," I said. "Banks flourish if people put money in, and if the accounts are large and the activity is good, the bank makes a lot of money on fees and the use of our money. If you want to know where the money is all you have to do is look at the adult industry—the amount of money is mind-boggling. Like any other industry, there are risks, but most of the people in this business are honest and only want to operate without hassles. There are a few fringe players in this industry, but they are being weeded out, and you will find the new breed of adult filmmaker to be one of integrity. I promise you that I'll bring you a lot of new accounts, and most of them will be great. They will make your bank grow beyond your wildest dreams and make you a big star with your president," I said.

"Well, Ron, I fully understand and want to agree with you, but I could lose my job," she said.

"Now, now, Sally, that is a little extreme Your people are only going to reward you for such growth. You wait and see. Now I'd like to deposit fifty thousand in our new today as a token of good faith. There will be plenty more in the next few weeks as well as the many other accounts I can recommend. Let's take care of this now and then let's get out of here and have a drink together," I said as I placed bundles of cash on her desk. Once she saw the money, it only took a few minutes to complete the paperwork and get the account open.

We left the bank and went to a local bar and lounge on Ventura Boulevard in Tarzana. "Isn't this a lot better, Sally?" I asked.

"It sure is, and I'm glad we are having a few drinks together," she said. "I really want my decision to be right, Ron. I have been with this bank since it began, and we do need as many new clients as we can get. Can you really get me some of the big money accounts?" she asked as she finished her Makers Mark on the rocks.

"I sure can, but it won't be overnight. I promise you I will bring in the money guys, and all I want from you is to give them the greatest service of all and we should always be friends. No bullshit, just good friends and good business. Of course, we can go out and have some drinks together every now and then. I just hope your husband won't be jealous?" I said in a joking way. We remained at the lounge for another hour and after four rounds it was time to make our way home.

"Can you drive, Sally?" I asked.

"Of course I can. I hope you can, Ron? I can easily drink you under the table but not tonight. I have to get home and make supper for my husband," she said.

We parted ways, and I felt good. Now we were well established in a bank and could operate like any legitimate film company. Even though I couldn't deliver a single account to Sally, I knew in time I would be able to do so. I needed this ace in the hole to get our account opened, and I knew it would stand me in good stead in the future.

My college education, especially my major in psychology, helps me understand what buttons to hit when making deals with people. With Sally and the bank, they needed to feel comfortable and to be assured that they would not be embarrassed by an adult company and could look to the future—a little promise and a pot of gold at the end easily sealed the deal. I will use this connection to gain favors in the future. I will be able to be a power broker real soon, and the name Ron Majestic will be one that people will respect.

No better way to remain incognito than to be one of those that can get things done for you and remain in the background all the time. Very few people will know who Ron Majestic is or anything about him. It is my goal to bring Marty to new heights and teach him responsibility and how easy it is to make a fortune if he follows the accepted rules of society.

I arrived at the house a little after seven and entered a palace. The girls had done a great job. The place looked just beautiful. "Hey, what's up girls?" I said.

"What do you think, Ron? Isn't the place great?" Mary Lou said.

"Great isn't the word for it. You have understated how beautiful and comfortable you girls have made this place. I love it," I said.

"Thanks, Ron, we love it too, and soon it will be the greatest home in the Valley. Maybe we can have a party in a few weeks?" Mary Lou said.

"Don't forget, girls, we have to be careful. Let's take it slow, and we will live a lot longer. Did Marty call?" I asked.

"No, we haven't heard from him. What are we doing for dinner?" Natalia asked.

"I guess we'll go out, but first, we have to wait for Marty. I hope he gets here soon," I said.

"I was wondering if we should get some real good-looking furniture for the pool area or should we stick to low-priced stuff from Woolworths?" Natalia said.

"Listen, girls, this is our house for now. Make it shine any way you would like, but don't make it stand out like a sore thumb. We are going to make a lot of money together, so when spending please realize that you are blowing yours as well," I said with a big smile.

"How about making me a drink?" I asked. "The usual," I said as the door opened and Marty walked in.

"Wow! This place looks great. Am I in the right house?" he asked with a big laugh. "I can't believe my eyes, guys. This place is a palace, and I love it."

"We worked hard and spent your money on making this house a home and a warm, cozy place for us to enjoy when we are here. We work hard enough as actors. In here, we will be ourselves, always," Mary Lou said.

"You hit it on the head, sweetheart. This is our private place for us all. Thanks for the great job you both have done. We could never have had this place looking like this on our own, thanks again," Marty said sincerely.

"How did things go with the agent?" I asked.

"This was the best connection I could have ever made. He has a small place in Van Nuys, but he has plenty of talent from all over the place. He charges one flat fee of twenty-five dollars per actor/model each time you shoot and use them. If you use four, you owe him one hundred, and he has a casting call every Thursday at four o'clock. If you need someone for a shoot in two weeks, he will organize the whole thing. If the model doesn't show up, he will replace her with another at no charge. He also has makeup people that he can recommend, and he has turned me on to a great photographer who is reasonable. He can arrange locations for us—each one is negotiable, of course. Every Tuesday night, he plays poker in his back office and has invited me to play. It will be a great way to meet the other guys in the film business and set up some contacts. I think we have hit a home run with Jeb," Marty said with enthusiasm.

"Did you mention me to him at all?" I asked.

"I told him I have a silent partner who supplies funds and has some great connections. I told him that my partner stays in the background and does not get involved with the talent and keeps out of the way during a shoot. With my partner I never have to worry about the paperwork, model releases, and so on as he takes care of it all, I also said," Marty added with a smile, "Yet I never gave him your name and he never asked."

"I'm glad to hear that. Let's keep it that way. Did you hear that, girls?" I said a little louder. "What about dinner?" Mary Lou asked.

"I was told by Jeb that there is a great Italian place on Ventura Boulevard called Gina's. They have great spaghetti and other stuff. Let's go and eat and drink ourselves to death," Marty said.

We arrived at Gina's a little before nine; the place was small as there were only fourteen tables. On the left side as you entered they had a pizza oven and two chefs in white aprons busy with various dishes. There wasn't any bar, yet they displayed bottles of wine on the counter. This was an old storefront with the two big glass windows looking out on Ventura Boulevard. They did a good job in converting it to a family-style restaurant with some great Italian operas playing in the background. The tables were covered with red-and-white plaid tablecloths, simple but very appropriate for a family-style Italian restaurant. We had to wait about ten minutes before we were able to be seated. The people in the restaurant looked Italian, and some of them even looked like the old Mob boys from New York. "Hey, this looks like a nice place, nothing fancy. It looks like everyone is enjoying their food. The only thing I don't like is that some of the people eating look like Mob guys from back East," I said in a hushed tone. "You are so paranoid, Ron," Marty said. "You're just seeing things that don't really exist. No one knows you and who cares here in Los Angeles?"

"Let's order a bottle of Chianti," Natalia said as she grabbed my hand and gave it a reassuring squeeze.

"Okay," Marty said as he signaled the waiter. I sat there a little nervous as I felt there were people who were looking at me with questions in their eyes. No doubt Marty was right—I was being paranoid!

Friday, November 8, 1957

It took a little effort to wake up early after all that heavy food and wine last night. We polished off two bottles of Chianti, and after eating like there was no tomorrow, I was a little slow in greeting this new day. The girls were dead to the world, and Marty never got up too early. He liked to stay up until the wee hours of the morning, and being in the film business allowed him that luxury, especially because he was the director. I had decided that we must settle the car issue and also need to buy another car so that we could all be mobile. One car amongst four of us did not work out to well. Woodland Hills was a very nice area. It had a lot of beautiful homes with the Santa Monica hills looking down on it.

Mulholland Drive, the very famous street where lovers hung out, was just above our home. Early in the morning when the sun was rising, there was a mist that seemed to linger there for a few hours each morning giving the whole mountainside a peaceful start to a perfect day. Our world was magical when the sun set and nighttime appeared as the air seemed to have a magical aroma about it making the world seem so very peaceful. This was paradise lost and now found. I was at peace for the first time in almost a year. I took an early morning drive along Mulholland Drive and went up high in the hills and looked down at our new home and the surrounding terrain; it was breathtaking. I could easily run every morning here and love every second of it.

When I returned home, the girls were just getting up and discussing their plans for today.

"I think we should go to the shopping center and look for patio furniture," Mary Lou said.

"That can wait. I think we should get our house stocked with plenty of food and other supplies so that we can stay at home and make dinner and get crazy," Natalia said.

"This will probably be our last weekend of fun before we start back to work. Let's ask Marty when he wakes up. Did anyone see Ron this morning?" Mary Lou asked.

"Hey, girls, I'm right here in the kitchen and heard every word you said," I said. "I think you will have to ask Marty what the schedule is, but we will have to get back to work real soon. We need the money."

"You make me laugh, Ron. You always worry about money, but it seems there is always enough. If we run short, let me know, and I will give you all that I have. It isn't much, but it's all I possess," Natalia said with a big smile.

"Girls, I want to take you both to meet Sally at the bank. She is great and will help you open up bank accounts and start saving some money for the future. I won't always be around, and if something should happen to me, it would be best that you both have an established record and some funds available. You'll love Sally. She is great, and you won't feel uncomfortable with her. She is a friend and not at all like most managers that you would meet at any other bank. I'll give her a call and set something up," I said.

I spoke with Sally and made a date to meet for lunch at Gina's. Marty finally woke up, and I convinced him that it would be best if he met Sally and opened an account as well. We met Sally at Gina's at about one and sat down and ordered a bottle of Chianti and a large pizza. The girls loved Sally the minute they met. They felt relaxed and enjoyed their experience of talking and eating with the bank manager—something that they never did in the past. Marty also fell in love with Sally and thanked me for introducing him to her. After lunch, we all went back to the bank, and Sally opened up four new accounts and took in over $100K in deposits, and guess what, we didn't have to pay for lunch.

"Thanks, Ron. You are a man of your word, and this will go a long way in convincing my boss, Frank Whalen, that the adult industry will be good for the bank's growth. I have had a hell of a time since opening your company account convincing him that it was a right move. He hates the adult industry because of the many negative articles in the press, and he hates gamblers because he feels they are addicts and can cause the bank embarrassment. This influx of your accounts will help seal the deal. Bring me more, my man, please do," Sally said.

It was three in the afternoon, and the day was shot.

"Let's stop by the office and see how the workers are doing," Marty said. When we arrived at the office, things were wrapping up for the day. The offices were coming along fine and would be ready for occupation by Monday. The furniture we bought was ready, and all we had to do was call and give them one day's notice and it would be delivered. The back section of the building where we would keep the sets and inventory of films would not be ready for a little while longer. The rear section required the installation of ceiling lights and tracks for the microphones and cameras to run on. The rest of the sets were things that would be used to create scenes for each movie.

We now had to hire a full-time secretary, a warehouse manager, and a couple of grunts. We were slowly building a proper studio that would be able to produce first-class productions. It was all starting to look real good.

"I would like to buy another car or two," I said. "I think we need to be able to get around, and one car won't do. We don't have to spend a lot as long as the cars run and get us to and from. I saw a place on Roscoe not very far from here. Let's go over and see if we can make some friends and buy a couple of cars."

"I didn't want to bring that up, Ron, but you are right. We need to be mobile," Marty said.

We left the office and went over to Don Coleman's Chevrolet. We walked into the showroom, all four of us, and must have given the staff a hell of lift.

"How can I help you? I'm Don," he said as he put his hand out to shake.

"I'm Ron Majestic and this is Marty Loomis. We just moved into the area and need a couple of cars. We're looking to establish ourselves with someone we can trust and, of course, get a good deal to boot. After all we are neighbors," I said.

"Well, you came to the right place. What business are you in?" Don asked.

"We are in the film business and want you to know, Don, we can easily bring you a lot business, so make us the best deals you can, and we can move on from there. By the way, the girls will also need a car or two. These girls are two rising stars and will be featured in our next film," I said.

"You can count on me, Ron. I own this dealership, and I'll make sure you always get top-notch service and the best deal possible. What kind of cars do you want?" Don asked. He could not take his eyes off the two girls. I knew he was hooked, and we would make a good deal. It took a little haggling, but in the end, we settled on two 1957 Chevy Impala Convertibles for the girls. These were brand-new cars, and Don was giving us a deal at eighteen hundred each.

"Remember, Don, you're coming to the next film shoot, and you'll be getting many customers from us. I want to always walk in here, buy a car, and walk out—no need for haggling anymore. If I find you did not give us the best deal on the planet, it will be the last car you ever sell us. Now let's get another car for Marty."

After my little speech, Don said, "I'll let you have both cars for thirty-three hundred, and that is rock bottom I assure you."

We let Marty work out his own deal for the car he loved. We left the showroom and took Don along with us and went for dinner at a nice little place located on Topanga Canyon Boulevard and Sherman Way, the Whales Corner.

This was Don's favorite seafood place, and it had a great bar. Marty was giddy because of his new car, a 1954 White Corvette Convertible. Don had one on the lot and promised to have it completely checked out so that Marty would not have any problems with it. Marty was so happy he could hardly speak, and the deal was super. All Don wanted was eight hundred for the car and a promise that he could take one of the models out for dinner one day.

"What a deal, Don. I just hope this car doesn't crap out on me. I always wanted a Corvette," Marty said.

"You don't have to worry about the car, Marty. If there is anything that goes wrong with the car, call me, and my service guys will take care of it. You have my word on it. We are friends, and you don't fuck your friends," Don said.

We had a great meal and drank a few too many to celebrate the new cars we had just bought. The girls were going to pick up their cars tomorrow morning. Their excitement was electric, and along with Marty's dream come true, no one could wait until morning.

Saturday, November 9, 1957

I was up early as usual and went for a run to help settle all that food we ate last night. As I ran along the side of the road, I noticed that most of our neighbors were still asleep. Of course, this was suburbia at its best with large lawns and backyard swimming pools and BBQ stands, and it was Saturday morning. This place will be busy with all these folks cooking burgers and steaks later today and tomorrow; a real bee hive of activity. This is the weekend, and this is the way of life in suburbia. I wondered what most of these people would say if they knew what kind of films we made. These people who swap wives and do things that are supposed to remain very quiet. Behind the doors of suburbia is hidden the best adult film subjects in the world. An idea just popped into in my head; the greatest stage ever created was right in front of me. I wondered how I could get these people into the act; it would be great to produce some films without actors, just real people doing what is natural. Amateurs at play—what a great name for a series, but how could I get these people to participate in the creation of a new form of adult films? I completed my run in record time as I floated through the five miles as if it was a sprint, I was floating as I was deep in thought as my mind was so wrapped up in this amateur theme. This was a winner and I could hardly wait to talk to Marty, this was it and I was stoked.

I entered the house at about seven thirty and yelled out, "Marty, get up. I need to talk to you. It's very important."

"Shut up, Ron. You'll wake the girls. What the hell do you want? What time is it? It's the middle of the night. Can't it wait a little while?" Marty said as he sat at the edge of his bed.

"Come on, Marty, get up. This is important, and it will establish you as one the greatest directors ever," I said.

"Okay, pal, let's go get some coffee and see what this all about," Marty said as we walked toward the kitchen.

"Marty, I'll make the coffee. You just relax and listen to me. Don't speak until I'm through, please," I said.

"Okay, Ron, let's get it over with. This better be good now that you have fucked up my sleep. If it isn't, I swear I'll kick your ass," Marty said with a wry smile.

"Okay, my friend, listen to this. The adult business is growing, and each day more and more people are buying films to watch at home and at parties. The problem is that after a little while the public will get bored with ordinary sex and sales will fall. This is inevitable in any business. Innovation is always needed. We are no different and have to think about the future. Every day, new people are trying to open their own adult operations. As the field gets more crowded, it will become more difficult to sell our films, because they are all trying to sell the same product. I have a brand-new take, and I think we can cash in now before everyone jumps in on it. I was out running this morning, and I was thinking, just look at all these houses filled with party people. Why couldn't we find a way to recruit all those who like to have sex and participate in the filming of their parties? We can call our films *The Amateurs* or something like that and be the first film company to show how the other half of America lives. We don't need any sets. We don't need any actors. All we need is the actual scenes and there is the movie. If we can get a few couples to agree and offer them a few hundred dollars, we would be business. We will need a cameraman, but that is about all we will need. What do you think, Marty?" I asked.

"Are you nuts?" Marty asked very seriously. "Do you want to go to jail?" Marty yelled.

"What are you talking about, Marty? Why jail? There is nothing illegal here as long as everyone consents to allow the filming of their actions, whether it is sexual or not!" I said.

"Also, remember, Ron, when you start to speak to someone who is a prude or gets easily insulted, they will want to call the police and report us," Marty said.

"No way, Marty. We can only do this by first making friends with people in our neighborhood and being invited to one of the many parties they usually have. We bring our girls with us so that if there is any switching going on we participate as well. Of course, some of the wives might get upset, but they will get over that once they have a taste of us. All we need is to choose a few of the people and ask them if they would like to put this on film. Those that say yes are perfect candidates, and once agreed, we can offer them a few hundred for their participation. Now you can do what you like to do and make some money while doing it. One film may cost us three thousand dollars, and that is next to nothing when we can get fifty dollars per film, and I know we can sell at least five thousand copies of each film. That is a hell of a profit and with very little effort. I'll have everyone sign a model release, and we will be home free. In the future, we can run ads for fun-loving couples who want to record their lovemaking on film and make a few dollars as well. I think the field is unlimited, and we had better be the first ones to do it. We can set up another production company that will produce these films using dummies as owners in case there is ever any feedback. Tell me, Marty, what do you think?" I said as I could hardly contain my excitement.

"Now it's starting to sound very interesting, Ron. I know we can do it, but we have to think this out carefully, and let's get a real good lawyer on our team so that we can make sure we cover our asses at all times. Yes, sir, I like it. I think we can do it. Let's get to work on this now. Let's start by meeting some of our neighbors and getting invited to a party or two. That is our job today—meeting our neighbors. Let's get the girls up and get them started on meeting the other wives on this street. I'm excited, Ron, you have really come up with something unique. Wow!" Marty said as he drank his coffee.

We woke the girls and gave them a little pep talk about meeting our new neighbors.

"Now, girls, if you are asked what we do for a living, just tell them we are in show business. You are actresses, and one of the guys is a director and the other is a producer. We just moved in, and we are so happy to meet new people. In regard to films you have done, all you have to say is that so far you have only been extras in some recent films. You are now reading for a part in a major motion picture. You can't talk about it as the producers want everything to remain very quiet until all the contracts are signed and shooting is well under way. As soon as I can, I will get you a stage pass so that you can watch a film being made. That is all you have to say, and they will be eating out of your hands and want to be your friend. This is your biggest part you have ever played, girls. So do it very professionally," Marty said. The girls were very excited and could hardly wait to get started.

I also reminded the girls that today they must pick up their new cars and what better way to get your neighbors to be talkative than showing off your new cars.

It was approaching noon when we all got ready to face the day and leave the house. Marty and I had to go the office to check up on things. "Girls, we are going to the office and then over to the Don's to see if Marty's car is ready. If your car is ready to be picked up, we will call you, and either we'll pick you up or Don will send a driver over to get you. Once you park your car and the Corvette is in the driveway, you will not have problems meeting your neighbors. Love you, guys," I said.

We went to the office to see what progress had taken place since yesterday. They did get quite a bit done since yesterday, but it didn't look like we would be ready to open on Monday. We then went over to see Don.

"Hey, Don, how are you doing?" Marty said. "Is my car ready for me to take home?"

"I think it is. If not, it will be in less than fifteen minutes," Don said. "Boy, wasn't that a great dinner last night? I enjoyed myself, guys. I really did."

"It was great food, and the company was superb. We'll have to do it again sometime real soon," Marty said.

"How are the girls' cars coming along? Can they have them today?"

"I'm sure their cars are ready. Let me check," Don said. A minute later Don came back with a big smile on his face. "Both cars are ready. What would you like to do?" Don said.

"Let's drive home now and pick up the girls, and they can drive their cars back home. Ron, you can drive the Corvette, and I'll drive my own car. Don will follow. Okay with you?" Marty said. "Let's do it. The girls will be very surprised and happy as well," I said.

"Okay, Don, follow me, and we are off, and by the way, thanks for the great service. Do you want to drop by the house a little later for a drink or two? You are most welcome, and I know the girls would love to have you," Marty said.

"By the way, Don, where do you live?" I asked.

"I have a house in Tarzana. A nice place. I'll have you over one day, and you will see how the other half lives," Don said.

"Well, we are just getting used this area and are always looking for places to party and just have fun. Maybe we will throw a party in a week or two. You will be invited along with your girlfriend, of course," I said.

When I pulled the car into the driveway, our next door neighbor was standing there looking at this procession as Marty pulled into the driveway in his Corvette.

They watched as I ran to the door and yelled, "Anyone home? I'm back and have a big surprise for you!"

"What is all the fuss, Ron?" Mary Lou asked as she opened the door. "Oh, nothing, my sweet. Just a little gift for you girls," I said as Natalia came to see what the noise was all about.

"Come, look what is in the driveway. Bet you will be very surprised," I said teasingly. "My god, your car looks great. It's beautiful.

"Drive it well. I just love it. Wow!" shouted Mary Lou as she ran out and opened the car door. "It looks great, Ron. Throw me the keys," yelled Natalia as she sat on edge of the front fender. All this time our neighbor was standing there watching this and slowly walking over to us.

"Hi, I'm Cathy Willets, your next door neighbor. What a nice car. Use it well," she said.

"Thanks and nice to meet you. I'm Mary Lou Johnson, and this is Natalia Petrov. We've just moved in," Mary Lou said.

"Is this your new car?" Cathy asked. "It looks just beautiful."

"Ron bought it yesterday. He always loved a Corvette," Mary Lou said. "We also bought two new cars and are about to pick them up. We are actresses and need to have transportation as we have to go to different places," Mary Lou said.

"How about coming into the house?" Natalia said. "This is my guy, Ron Majestic."

"I'd love to come in. Welcome to the neighborhood. Where are you guys from?" Cathy asked.

"We are from Minnesota and so happy to be here in warm California," Natalia said as she walked in from outside. "We are here to work on a movie, and we decided to remain here because we liked it so much. Marty Loomis, our director, is the guy in his new, or should I say vintage, Corvette. He just loves Corvettes and couldn't resist this little beauty. So where are you from, Cathy?"

"My husband, Irving, is from New York, and I'm from here—born and bred in the Valley. I'm a hairdresser and met Irv at the shop two years ago. We got married last year and bought this house three months ago. Irv is in the movie business as well, except," she bent her head closer and lowered her voice, "he makes adult films. I hope you don't mind?"

"Of course not, Cathy. We also make adult films and don't think it is wrong in any way. The world is changing and so is the film business," Natalia said.

"What a small world. You move into a new neighborhood, and can you believe it, you meet another filmmaker just like you! It's so amazing. Irv will be so surprised when he gets home later. How about having some drinks with us tonight? We are planning on going out to Masters Steak House. Would you guys like to join us? Please say yes," Cathy said with a big smile.

"Oh, I'm sure we'd love to," Mary Lou said. "What time do you plan on going?"

"About eight. We will have to leave here about seven fifteen. It is a little bit of a drive over the hill, and traffic can be tough. I'll call and add four more for dinner. This is great. Irv will love it!" she said as she ran out the door.

"Boy, that was coincidental, wasn't it, honey?" I said. "I sure hope Marty won't be upset about our dinner tonight?"

It was about one P.M. when the girls arrived in their new cars. You could see the pride on their faces as they parked their cars in the driveway. They stood there staring at the cars and walking over to the hood and cleaning off a speck of dust. No doubt this was their pride and joy and let no one come between them and their cars. "Hey there, girls, what beautiful cars you have there," I cried out. "Use them well. These cars suit you, girls. It's like they were built especially for you. Great cars. Maybe one day you will honor me with a drive?"

"Ron, you can drive it any time you want to, you know that. What's mine is yours, so don't think twice about it. It handles great. What power, and it looks great. Plenty of people gave us the right looks. I know I'll be happy with this. What's up?" Natalia said.

At that moment, Marty walked out to check out the cars, and Mary Lou couldn't wait to tell him the news. "Well, we've met our neighbor next door, Cathy Willets, and guess what? Her old man is in adult film business. I didn't get the name of the company, but we'll know that later. We're going out for dinner tonight with them to the Masters Steak House. This should be a very interesting evening. Don't you think, Marty?" she said.

"I bet it will be," I said to both Ron and Mary Lou.

"Wow! You guys work fast. It is good for us to meet new folks, and if they are in the business all the better. We have to learn who is who in the business here in Los Angeles and get ourselves into the groove. The more you know, the better it is," Marty said.

"I'm just going to hang in for the rest of day and clean my new car. I'm also going to clean up the backyard and see if I can make it beautiful as well. I think we should throw a party in a couple of weeks and invite some of the movers and shakers," I said as I went out the back door.

The girls started getting ready for dinner at about five thirty as they had to shower, put on their makeup, and select the proper dress for tonight.

Mary Lou said it best, "It is Saturday night, and anyone who is anyone will be at the restaurant. I need to look my best so that they'll never forget whom they met. Natalia also feels the same way. So stay out of our way while we get ready." And so the show began.

Cathy and Irv drove a big station wagon as well as their regular cars. The wagon was for Irv's fishing and hunting trips and was rarely used in town. Tonight, they wanted us to drive with them in their wagon, more fun for us all. We met Irv when he came over to the house at about six fifteen and introduced himself. He was a tall guy with thick black hair and deep brown eyes. He had a very good build; looked like he worked out a lot and looked very strong. He was a very handsome man and probably used his good looks to procure plenty of female stars. He told us a little about himself. He was a construction worker in Los Angeles until last year when he met his partner Steven Paul, who had just arrived from London, England. They met at a bar in the Valley and hit it off at once and became pretty good friends. One day, Steven suggested to Irv that he quit his job and join him in his plan to open an adult film company. Although Irv knew nothing about the film business, he did know a lot about the female creature. His wife, Cathy, was once an adult actress and was very supportive of this venture. They attended a few swinging parties, some at their house and some at friends' houses and said he would invite us to their next one. So far, the pieces were falling into place as we were learning all about the adult business in Los Angeles.

The girls looked smashing as did Cathy as we all piled into the station wagon and took off for dinner. We arrived at the restaurant, and Irv gave the valet the car. "Welcome, Mr. Willets, how have you been keeping?" the doorman asked. I could see that Irv was very proud that he was well-known at this place.

"Just great, Jose. Thanks for asking," Irv said.

We entered the restaurant and walked directly into the bar area as the maître d' said, "Your table will be ready in a few minutes, Mr. Willets. Would you like to have drinks at the bar?"

"No thanks, Robert. We'll wait and order some wine when the table is ready," Irv said.

We were shown to our table in less than two minutes. Once we were seated, Irv asked if we wanted to enjoy a good bottle of wine or if anyone would like a drink. It was like sitting on a stage as people looked at us in awe as we had three beautiful women at our sides. It was easy to see that many people were wondering who we were and would love to have a reason to meet these beauties. We decided on a bottle of Dom Perignon to celebrate the purchase of our new cars and the chance meeting of a new filmmaker. As we sat there sipping our champagne, the waiter came over with another bottle of champagne.

"Excuse me, Mr. Willets, this bottle is from the gentleman over in the far corner. He said to give you his compliments and perhaps he could join you for a drink." We looked over and there was Clute Gallagher smiling at us and slowly getting up and making his way to our table.

"Thanks for the champagne, Mr. Gallagher. It was very nice of you," I said.

"You are more than welcome and please call me Clute," he said.

Irv jumped up and said, "Let me introduce you to everyone" as he presented everyone at our table.

It was obvious that Clute was smitten by the women and was clearly disappointed when Irv introduced Cathy as his wife. His attention immediately switched to Mary Lou and Natalia. Clute was in a lot of westerns, and although he was not a star like Roy Rogers or Gene Autry, he was still very well-known, and as far as he was concerned, he was a superstar. He was a supporting actor to Marlon Brando, Randolph

Scott, Roy Rogers, and so on. He was very slick, with blond hair slicked down with Brylcreem. He made himself at home at our table and spent the rest of the evening with us. There was hardly any room at the table for anyone else as his ego took up a lot of space. Irv and I could not discuss anything in detail about the adult business due to Clute being at our table, but we agreed that we would spend some time tomorrow in one of our backyards and talk about the business, and we could help one another. Everyone had a great night even with Clute's presence at our table for the entire night. The fact that we met a lot of people made me a little cautious as it only brought attention to our group. It wouldn't be long before people would be talking about the new film company and the beautiful stars. The girls were the common thread that could connect old contacts from New York. I was glad when we finally left and went home. I couldn't help myself from wondering if anyone followed us. I tried to keep an eye out as we drove home without making it obvious; it wasn't easy. Once we arrived home, I waited up for another hour checking the street making sure we were all safe. It was a wasted effort in the end, but my paranoia could not be cancelled out so easily.

Sunday, November 10, 1957

I was up real early as I was still concerned over our evening out and the blatant display last night. Everyone else slept late except me as I just couldn't seem to stay in bed no matter what time I got to sleep the night before. I went for a run and was able to get seven miles in before I felt it was enough, especially after the night before. When I returned to the house, everyone was still asleep, so I jumped into the car and went over to Ventura Boulevard to pick up some lox, cream cheese, and bagels. I picked up some for Irv and Cathy as well and went home for a breakfast that would make everyone very happy. It was nine thirty. So I felt safe about waking the Willets. I knocked at their door and let them know that we had bagels and lox at our house. "Come on over, guys, when you are ready, and we'll have some good eating," I said.

After breakfast, Irv said, "Let's sit down and talk a little about the business."

"Okay, Irv, Marty, get your ass over here and let's talk a little," I said with a smile on my face. We went out to the backyard, and Marty came over and pulled up a couple of lawn chairs. "Well, Irv, I hope you don't mind, but we can use all the help we can get. We got some great scripts, and we are opening our offices in Canoga Park and should be ready to start operation next week. How are things run here?"

"Just like anywhere else we make the movies and we have to sell them to the Mob as they are the only game in town. The problem we have out here is that the Mob runs the distribution end of it. The cops want us out of business because the Mob is involved, and we want the Mob out of it because they are pieces of shit and try to make all the bread and leave us with as little as possible. The retail adult stores are owned and run by Nate Schwartz, who we think is a front for the Mob guys. No adult store in the United States operates without the Mob's okay, and Nate owns them all. That means all the movies go through them, and all they want is content for their peep shows. We have to put the film on a loop so that it plays over and over again. Those quarters add up, and Nate and the Mob seem to have it all locked up," Irv said.

"That sounds like Minnesota and I guess the East Coast as well," Marty said.

"Basically the same except here they leave us alone because of the heat and simply put there is no other market. They don't want to pay a lot for the films, so they keep the prices pretty standard. If we need cash for the shoots, they are ready to loan it to us for a discount when they take possession of the film. The Mob owns every theater in the country, so our options are limited. We can market our films in Europe, but if we get caught shipping porn out of the country, the fines are big and jail time is mandatory. We have to smuggle out our productions if we want to make some more money. The industry is changing, and soon this cartel will be busted up, and we'll be able to start making some real bucks. The theaters, as I said, are all run by the Mob, and that is where the big bucks are right now. It would be great if someone else would open a few theaters and give these guys some competition. The problem is that anyone who would do that would probably be dead in a week," Irv said.

"Well, we can make some changes and start making some bucks here. I went to see Jeb the other day, and he said that all talent goes through him. Is that what you do, Irv?" Marty said.

"It's a lot easier to let Jeb handle the talent. He runs the ads and has a casting call once a week. It is also good because we get to meet all the other players and can easily organize our businesses so that no one steps on anyone's toes. It makes one part of the business easier and allows us a little window of cooperation, and maybe we can overcome all the problems the Mob causes us. We have a lot of bullshit to contend with and have to spend more time negotiating than actually being creative. There are seven companies in the Valley and one in Los Angeles proper and another in Vegas. The Perronies run the Vegas scene and the rest are in Los Angeles as they have a lock on the market. We are just the peripheral companies that are allowed to survive. If there was no Mob involved, we would be better off. Just be careful, Marty. These guys play for keeps. You've got two of the most beautiful models we have ever seen in the adult business. This is going to make your life difficult. I'm not saying this to scare you, but they will want the films, and they will make your lives hard. Remember, Marty, they want to control you all the time. Just be careful. I like you guys, and now that we have become friends, I would like our relationship to last," Irv said.

"I feel the same way, Irv," I said. "We are here to stay and build this business into the largest adult operation in the country. I know that's a tall order, but I know we can do it by producing quality shows and making a name for ourselves. Europe is ripe for our material, but we will have to shoot special scenes for the European market only, but we can do it. Getting the masters over to the other side will be the job. We have only begun, and I promise you we will find ways to beat those assholes. In the meantime, if there is anything we can do for you just name it, and I'm sure it will be likewise."

"I want us to be friends and not ever let the business get in the way of that friendship. Competition is good for everyone, so let's be up-front with each other at all times, no matter how distasteful it may be," Marty said.

"Okay, guys, how about a drink?" Mary Lou called out from the kitchen window. "I'll have the usual," I said. "How about you, Irv?"

"I'll have a Bloody Mary, spicy if you can," Irv said.

We had a few drinks and talked shop until we realized that it was close to five. We had killed the day with our chitchat without realizing it. Irv suggested we go for Chinese food as he left for home to get Cathy ready. He had a great place on Reseda and Sherman Way, not much in the ambience department but super great food. We agreed, and I changed into a pair of jeans and a sweater, and off we went.

The food was phenomenal, and we had a great time. While we were having dinner, Irv started to tell us about the Mob in Los Angeles. They wanted to control the adult business but could not get a hold on the market. The cops didn't want them in Los Angeles and a war was about

ALLAN BARRIE

to start. This business was too lucrative to just walk away. Yet they could not make movies like we did, and this aggravated them. There wasn't any use in running us out of the business, because they wouldn't have any movies for their theaters. There was also the Mexican Mafia that was trying to take over the numbers racket, so the Mob had its hands full.

"It would be nice if we could just get the Mob out of this business. This would remove the heat from us and allow us to move forward and make the business a lot more legitimate," Irv said.

"Well, Irv, we are not in a position to go to war with the Mob. We have to bide our time and let the feds do it. Our time will come. Just sit back and relax. They will screw themselves," I said.

"Easy to say, Ron, but remember they still rule the business. Las Vegas is a great market for our films, but because of the Mob, the real money is made by them. They send in Andrew Gills, and he offers us an advance of fifty K, and then he takes the movies in payment and controls the Vegas market for almost nothing. By the time we pay off the fifty K, we are left with very little profit and must borrow another fifty K and the cycle starts over again. We can't make a lot of money this way," Irv said.

"Why take the fifty K? from them when you can use bank money. The interest the bank gets is really very little in the whole scheme of things and allows you to make a larger profit and keep it. If Andrew wants to pick up movies for the Mob, he will have to pay the going rate. The Mob still makes plenty of money, but we also make a lot as well. Of course, the Mob won't like this as it cuts into their take, and we risk some reprisals. No matter. I feel we will win because they still need movies, and we are the only companies that are producing good films and keep their theaters full. The only company that they own is Bijou Films, and they haven't produced a decent film for over a year. Remember, Irv, the viewer doesn't know jack shit about the Mob. All they know is that they want to watch a good adult flick that they can jerk off to, and Bijou hasn't been able to do that in a long time," I said.

"You know, Ron, I love what you say, but you don't know anything at all. You're not being realistic, I hate to tell you," Irv said. "What bank will deal with an adult company? They won't even let you open a bank account unless you lie and say you make cartoons or straight movies, and then if they should find out that you deal in smut, they will close your account fast! You're just in dreamland, old buddy," Irv said as he finished his drink and signaled Mary Lou for another.

"Maybe so, Irv, but if I could arrange a legitimate bank for you what would you say? How much would it be worth to you?" I said.

"Let me tell you, Ron, if you can do this I will call the other companies and set up a meeting so that we can see if we can work together. I know we will all be very grateful to you. It's a big problem for us all, and we need to take care of this now," Irv said.

"Okay, Irv, get the meeting set up, and let me know where and what time. Here are the rules. Please follow them as it is very important and will avoid problems. No one is to know who I am, so please keep my identity very quiet until after the meeting. Use the term that you know someone who can help us. Please emphasize that this person wants to remain silent, independent, and in the background. No mention about my connection to Marty's company. This is very important as I don't want any conflict of interests or anyone to think there is any collusion involved. Marty will not benefit anymore than any of the other companies at any time, I guarantee it. Marty will be there representing his own company and will always conduct himself in an aboveboard manner. If the meeting goes over as I think it will, you will be able to do a lot of great things for all the companies. I have a lot of clout with a bank, so you will not have to hide the fact that you are an adult company. Things will turn around very quickly for you all. I want, in return, that Marty always be part of the group and that all decisions regarding the standards of the industry are agreed to by all. We have to work together at all times, and we will easily make this into a billion dollar industry in a few years. I also want first crack at all new releases for the next three years. If I buy the release, then the Mob doesn't get it. I'll buy the release for a fair market value or on a sixty-forty basis, I keep the sixty and you get the forty from the gross receipts from my theaters. Presently, I do not own any theaters but will within the next two to three months. If we have a deal, I will get the ball rolling with the bank at once," I said with confidence.

"How do you know you can deliver, Ron?" Irv said.

"If I cannot deliver, then you don't have to work with me, and all deals are off. I know I can deliver and best of all, Irv, what the hell have you and any of the companies to lose? The way the situation is at this time, it's only a matter of time until you all are out of business. You are not gambling in any way at all, believe me!" I said.

"It sounds like a good deal for everyone, and I'm sure the boys will go along with it without hesitation. You are right, Ron, there is nothing to lose, so why not go for it. I will contact them and get their agreement within the next few days. I'll set up the meeting. Please tell me when and where, and I'll get them all on board. This will help put them on the map once and for all. I'm very excited about this. Let's go home. I'm bushed," Irv said.

Monday, November 11, 1957

"That was some speech you made last night," Marty said as we drove over to the office to see what the progress was and if we could start operating.

"Not really, partner. It is all true, and I can deliver. If they all come to the party, I will have Sally get to work and open accounts for them all. This will allow them to be legitimate and allow them to operate as a real business would. They'll pay their due to us, and we will make a fortune in the theater business and have a great distribution network for our own films and theirs. There might be a war, but we're up to it. We're going to have to fight Carmine and his boys sooner or later, why not take full advantage while we can? I want to set up an organization that will contain security and also a business plan that will make us very wealthy and keep us alive at all times. What I really want is to protect you and keep the organization separate from your film company. My identity must remain secret at all times due to the dangers that exist. Let people think what they may or that it is one of the families. Maybe we'll get lucky, and they will start killing each other. In other words, Marty, you are one of the people who need this deal, and I need you to agree to the terms of the deal. They must never know of my involvement in your film company and your involvement in the theater business, never. Of course, you will be making the same money as I make as we are always partners. Leave it to me, and I think we can just about control the adult industry for the foreseeable future. And when I say control, I am not trying to act as if we are like the Mob. Control means leadership and direction in the right way to operate and make the most profit possible. It will also eliminate the Mob from the business in time," I said as we pulled into our parking lot at our office. We made a quick inspection and found that we could start working; the bulk of the renovations remaining were in the warehouse section. We called the phone company and had all our phones connected along with our burglar alarm. We were ready for action and placed our ads for personnel.

This would be my last visit to Marty's office unless I come in the side door directly to his office. I cannot have anyone see me there at anytime and would not want the staff he is hiring to know anything about me. What they don't know, they cannot say and it is best that way.

I left Marty at the office to organize his next film shoot and as I took a trip along Sherman Way and De Soto, I noticed a few buildings for lease. I called our real estate agent who helped us with the building on Remmet and let him know that I was very interested in leasing a few buildings that I would convert to theaters. I would need to be able to get the zoning that will allow a movie theater. Each building will be leased under a different name for legal purposes. He told me he would have different locations ready for me to check out before the day was complete. I then went home as I wanted to speak to the girls when things were quiet.

I found the girls watching television out at the pool. Life seemed quite good for them.

"Hi, girls, I see you are enjoying the sunshine of California," I said with a big smile. "I wanted to sit down with you and explain just what is going on so that there will never be any question as to what is what. I am doing this because I care about you, and we do live in the same house. Things will get a little scary if we do not know what the dangers are."

"Ron, are you trying to scare us?" Mary Lou said.

"No, not at all. Just trying to prepare you for what I believe is the inevitable," I said.

"Okay, Ron, you have scared the shit out of us. Now tell us what this is all about," Natalia said.

"In the first instance, you know why we moved here," I said. "It is only a matter of time until they figure out who we are. How many guys have two of the most beautiful movie stars living with them? How many companies can boast having two of the most beautiful and most popular stars in their films? So we must agree that it is a matter of time until they figure it out, and once they do that, there will be shit to pay. My goal is to keep you safe always—being aware is the first step in that direction. I want to make sure that my identity is never revealed, so I will no longer be going out with you guys for dinners and other public places and events. I know we disguise my appearance, but I am paranoid and feel it is just a disaster waiting to happen. The Mob is after me. So if I stay out of the limelight, they will have a harder time putting us together, and it will keep you guys out of danger. Natalia and I will still be lovers, at least I certainly hope so, because I love her a lot, but I will not go out in public. I will move out and find my own place so that if they are looking for me, it will be at that address and not here. I probably will not spend time here, but if I do, it will be very private and only be between us and not anyone we know will be able to put us together. When we shoot a film, I will handle all the paperwork as I used to do, but I'll be wearing a disguise so that no one on the set will be able to recognize me. Eventually, Marty will hire a manager who will take care of the paperwork, and I will not have to expose myself on a set. The more I am in the background, the better it is for us all. I know this sounds very melodramatic, but staying alive is very serious stuff, especially to me," I said with a big smile.

"Wow! You are serious," Mary Lou said. "Look, Ron, we are your friends, and we can't ever forget what you have done for us. We'll be at your side, no matter what the danger is. Friendship doesn't come and go like the weather. With us it's for real. Don't you forget that, ever."

"I understand and appreciate your loyalty and trust, but I have no right to put you in harm's way. If I can avoid it, I want to make sure I do all the time. We can accomplish everything by being up-front with each other and making sure we protect each other. Lying will bring terrible results. I plan to be around a long time, and I have you in those plans as well. So let's not bullshit each other and take the steps that are best to keep us all safe. In a year or two, this will all be a thing of the past, and we will be so thankful we did this the right way and laugh at it," I said. Tonight when Marty gets home, I want to discuss it all and make a decision—a decision that will protect us all."

"I'm not so scared now that I know what it's all about. Let's get it all resolved tonight. Now, Ron, let's go take a little time out for some fun," Natalia said with that look in her eye.

"I'm sorry, love, but I have to meet a real estate agent in a few minutes. Can I take rain check?" I said as I kissed her on the lips and held her close and left.

I went over to Don at the car dealership and explained to him that I wanted to trade my car in for a new car. He had an Oldsmobile Super 98 that was just traded in with less than eight thousand miles. This was a honey of a car, and the deal would be one I couldn't turn down. We made a deal and registered the car using a name that was selected from the phone book and the address that was the empty lot next to Don's dealership. Don arranged the insurance coverage so that the car was basically untraceable. I kept the old car while Don thoroughly checked out the Olds to make certain nothing was wrong. Making Don our friend had paid off in spades and had proven how essential a role he played in keeping us all safe.

I then went to see an apartment on Gresham Street in Canoga Park. It was located near Parthenia and De Soto and was in a very nondescript building. Lost in the crowd was what I wanted, and this place was right. It had two bedrooms, a living room, and a small dining room with a good-sized kitchen. The rent was very reasonable, and they were willing to give me free rent until January 1958. I took the place and paid six months' rent in advance. No security deposit was required. I was pleased with the place and would get it furnished in the next week or so. I used another name so that anyone inquiring would never get a match on Harry Miller or Ron Majestic. The apartment owner didn't care what name I used once I said I'd pay six months in advance. I was starting to feel a lot better as things were starting to fall into place.

I called home and asked what the schedule was for dinner tonight. They had none, so I suggested I'd pick up Chinese and bring it home, and we could all enjoy being together at home tonight while I talked to Marty and I didn't want any ears when we talked tonight. Of course, I wanted everyone to be there. I arrived at about seven fifteen with a bag full of delicious noodles and egg rolls with fried rice and shrimp dishes. Marty had just arrived and was happy to relax and have something to eat. We opened a bottle of Chateau Laffite Rothschild, a 1936 vintage wine, and ate Chinese.

"I'd like to speak to you all about our future. I know I spoke with you girls this afternoon, but I want to review and set the record straight when we are all together. It is imperative that we are all on the same page and work as a team to make every aspect of our future succeed. I think my plan is good and welcome any criticism as long as you can find a better way. Let's get down to specifics and get the plan into effect," I said as we lifted our glasses.

"We are friends, lovers, and business partners. We also love one another and respect each other's opinions. The facts are as follows. In regard to me, the Mob is after me and still would like to kill me. This is not going away. These psychopaths can't be reasoned with no matter what I may do. I keep thinking that in time if there are no incidents, they will forget about me, but that is only wishful thinking and probably won't ever happen. Regardless of all this, there is a two hundred and fifty K price on my head. The only thing keeping me alive is the fact that they do not know where I am, yet! The other group that is looking for me is the feds as they want me to be a witness for them against the Mob. They also don't know where I am, but I am not too concerned about them as I am not a priority any longer. They are confident that time is on their side and soon I will surface. Hopefully I will stay alive and still be useful. Then there was a new twist when I joined Marty in New York and we stood up to Carmine and his crew. We took the adult business out of their hands and made the market a lot more profitable. Carmine will not sit back and let this happen. War will ensue. When and where is hard to determine, but eventually he will find us, and he will try to get his piece of the action. He has to save face, and he will try. It is real easy to put the pieces together when Carmine sees the films that star Mary Lou and Natalia. You girls are, without doubt, the most beautiful and sexiest girls to have hit the big screen in many years. He and anyone who knew Marty in another life will put two and two together and figure it out that Marty Loomis is my man, and I'd better get the bastard. They will look at Marty and see if he is Larry under another name or a new guy on the block. If he thinks Marty is not Larry, then I think he will cease to be a threat as his power in this part of the world is not strong enough," I said very carefully.

"The solution to our problem is as follows. Please understand that I have given it a lot of thought and feel this is the right plan. I will listen to your opinions only after I have laid out the plan, so please allow me the chance to complete my plan. In the first instance, I feel it is best for us all that I move out of this house and live elsewhere. To that end, I have taken a place in Canoga Park that will suit this purpose. By doing this, it will give us separation, and in case your house is being watched, they will not see me come and go. So connecting Harry and you guys will be impossible. Also, it will give us time to plan an attack against our enemies. I have also gotten rid of my car and, as of tomorrow, will drive a different car. The car will be under another name and registered in a different address. This is another step in separating us from one another. This does not mean that I will not come to the office to work from time to time as I will, but I will always make certain that I am disguised enough not to be recognized. Of course, once again I hope I do not have to come to your office often, Marty, as it will prove to be counterproductive. Once again, if anyone is watching the office, they will not recognize me as anyone they are looking for. When a movie is being shot, I will do my job on the set and will be in disguise, so the actors will not know who I really am.

"I want to operate in complete anonymity—the less everyone knows the better it is. I will always be diligent and aware, and if I detect any abnormality or know that we are being watched, I will take care of the situation in a proper and final manner. The less you all know of what steps are taken to insure your safety, the better it is for all of you. We must trust one another, and always say what you mean. The easy way to fail is to have anyone in our group feel discontent or left out. We must always speak frankly and honestly to one another, no matter how bad we may feel it could hurt one's feelings. The people out there will try every way possible to penetrate us—you must never weaken. They will try to convince you that one of us has told them things that they should not have done. These tricks are old and should always be ignored as none of us would say or do anything that would jeopardize us. So no matter what rumor or so-called fact is presented, remember we are family and always will be. Please never weaken, and we will win. I say all this because the best plans usually go astray when there is a weak link in the chain. We cannot afford that, and above all, we must realize that the Mob will kill all of you once they find out that we are a family. They have no loyalty to you, and if you turn on us, they will love you for only an instant and then get rid of you. A clean slate is what they want, and anyone of us will only cloud that. Thus we all have to go. As a team, they cannot beat us, so keep that in mind at all times." I poured another glass of wine and continued, "I want us to have the largest and best adult company in the world. I want us to succeed in every way we can, so please keep the entire facts of our operations between us at all times.

"I don't want any bragging to anyone. I don't want any loose tongues at any time. Be very careful when drinking, and keep away from drugs. If you are going to party, then do so, and take on some other persona. No facts about us no matter what. If you are unhappy about something or someone, then speak up directly to us and no one else. Be ready to act as mature and strong adults that have sworn an oath of fidelity and secrecy to death. Love and respect for one another trumps anything that can happen or anything anyone can say. We will triumph as a team and will share the spoils of our hard work and our brilliant ideas as a team. We can handle anything that is thrown at us as long as we do it as a team. Okay, guys, let's hear your side of it," I said.

"Let me speak, please," Marty said. "I don't like to live this way, but I agree with Ron that if we are to survive we must take some drastic steps. I like the plan and am one hundred percent in favor of it. I would like to add that I feel we must act as if we are at war, and we must use strategy and brains to defeat the enemy. I know we can win and endorse Ron's plan."

"I am in and will always be with you guys no matter what. I trust you both and pledge my life to this," Mary Lou said.

"I am also pledging my life and loyalty to us and to this plan. I will not be coerced nor will I ever let anyone of you down no matter what anyone will do under the threat of death," Natalia said.

"Let's lift our glasses and swear the oath that can never be broken. Put your hands together and repeat after me, I will always be true to our triumvirate and will protect my fellow member of the family at all times. I shall be true and loyal and will never reveal any information no matter what is promised to me or under the threat of torture or death. I shall maintain this oath for as long as I shall live. This I promise and will never alter this, so help me God." Everyone present repeated the oath and clasped our hands together to seal the secret act of loyalty. We all took this very seriously and felt very proud of the things we agreed to tonight.

"Let's get drunk and have a little fun. It's a new day and a new beginning, and I feel so blessed to have friends like you, thanks guys," I said with a big smile on my face. We were very proud of ourselves as we had finally set an agenda and now felt very much as a real family—true and loyal to each other no matter what. The girls were so deeply affected by this that they cried for joy as they now felt they were part of a real family. Tomorrow we would begin our new quest, to rid ourselves of the enemies that threaten our very existence.

Tuesday, November 12, 1957

I woke early and went for a ten mile run to get my juices all worked up for the day ahead. It was around nine thirty when I finished my shower and dressed for the day. I said good-bye to the girls and went off to see Don and pick up my new car. I wanted to get rid of my old wheels as soon as possible, I was not comfortable driving around in them as it was a link to the past and could possibly be recognized, although I doubted it. I arrived at Don's a little before ten.

"How are you today, my good man?" I said to Don.

"Good morning, Ron. I'm fine. How are you doing?" he said, "Your new car is ready, and it is a beauty. I changed a few little things like the oil and spark plugs. Checked the car out from top to bottom, and it's in perfect shape. In case you didn't realize it Ron, the car is still under GM's new car warranty. You've got yourself a real deal. Enjoy."

"Thanks, man. I can hardly wait to get this baby on the road and see what it can do. You've been great, Don, and I appreciate it a lot. I owe you man, yes I do!" I said. I left my old car with Don with instructions to remove the plates and place it on his lot and sell it for whatever he could get. I told him I'd give him a very nice bonus for his help with the car. It never hurts to grease the palms of those who help you and can be very useful to you in the future.

I drove over to the office to see what was going on. I entered through the special side door that opened directly to Marty's office. I saw Marty sitting behind his new big desk and sort of lost in this large environment.

"Hi there, pal. How do you like your new digs?" I said to Marty.

"I'll grow into it. I'm sure of it. Right now, it's a little lonely being the only one here and no phone calls. Don't get me wrong, Ron. In a few days, this place will be a beehive of industry. I expect I'll be getting phone calls later today when the afternoon paper comes out. I wanted to talk to you about an office for you. I don't think you should be seen here at anytime. The reason we constructed the side door was to give you access, if need be, and that no one will ever see you," he said.

"I agree with you, Marty. As a matter of fact I came over to talk to you about that. I was thinking about my visits here and feel they would be out of place. I have to stay far away from this scene and will stay away. Having an office would defeat that purpose. I will hire someone to take care of the paperwork on all shoots and then report back to me. I want to protect you and this operation, and this is the only way. We can get together at night, and go over any details we have to. I'll also be very busy getting the theaters going. I'll feel a lot better knowing that you feel the same way as I do," I said.

"Thanks, Ron. It makes it easier for both of us to always be straight. You were right about never bullshitting each other," he said.

I left Marty's office and headed to my new apartment to wait for the phone company. Much to my surprise, the phone guy was there waiting for me. It took him less than thirty minutes to install my phone and additional phone jacks. He was gone and would not have anything to really remember about me or the apartment. The place was empty, and I didn't overtip. I also looked like someone else if he would ever be contacted. I sported a mustache and colored my eyebrows thicker. I wore glasses that made me look different even though they were nothing more than plain glasses. I had on a fedora that helped hide my features even more and spoke with a touch of a French accent. I went back to the office to see if Marty would recognize me. I walked into the empty office and heard Marty's voice on the phone.

"Jeb, I need to get set with some people for a shoot in two weeks. Should I stop in at your casting call this Thursday, or is too soon?" Marty was saying as he noticed me walking around the front office.

"Excuse me, Jeb." Marty put his hand over the mouthpiece and said, "Can I help you?"

"Jeb, let me call you back in a few minutes. Someone just walked into my office, thanks, man," he said as he hung up the phone. "Can I help you? I am Marty Robbins, and who are you?"

"A pleasure to meet you, Mr. Robbins. My name is Marcel Lamond, and I make blue films in France. I just was passing by as I was looking for office space when I saw your sign outside," I said.

"What sign?" Marty said.

"The one that said 'space for rent,'" I said.

Marty got up from behind his desk and went outside for a minute.

"Well, Mr. Lamond, I didn't even realize that the sign was still there. I just rented this space a few weeks ago, and I guess the real estate company forgot to remove their sign. I am sorry, but the space is not available."

"Well, I am sorry for disturbing you, Mr. Robbins. I will be on my way. By the way, do you know of any spaces available in this area?" I said.

"I'm afraid I don't, but if you like, I'll give you the name of our real estate agent and perhaps he can help you," Marty said.

"That is very kind of you. I'd appreciate that a lot, and when I am set up, I'll contact you, and maybe we can work together!" I said. "What a dumb shit you are, Marty," I said as I switched over to regular English.

"It's me, Ron. I just wanted to see if my disguise passed mustard, and it did." Marty looked like he was hit in the face with a pie,

"Ron, your looks sure as hell fooled me. What a great job! You look different, and your accent was so good. Wow! I can't believe it. What a super job. You certainly had me fooled."

I left Marty and returned to our home and was just organizing the rest of my day when the phone rang. It was Marty.

"I hired a warehouse manager who will handle everything. He was recommended by Jeb and used to work for one of our competitors. His name is Keith, and I'm very impressed with him. I think it will work out real fine. He is married and has two kids. He lives in Simi Valley and seems like a real down-to-earth guy. I agree with your rule, so please don't stop by as Ron. Of course, if you want to stop by as Marcel that would be fine," Marty said.

An hour later Marty called back and sounded very excited,

"Ron, it's me. I just hired this great secretary. Her name is Cathy. Cathy will be our receptionist and Gal Friday and Keith our warehouse man. We do not require any other personnel at this time or at least until we really get started and get the show on the road." I was very pleased to hear the excitement in Marty's voice. It was like he was a new man and now had some real goals to reach. I knew in my heart that Marty would be very successful and would make the very best films possible. Most importantly, he would be happy, and a happy Marty was good for us all.

I spent the rest of the day organizing the file procedures on how I wanted each film catalogued and how the actors should be filed and cross-referenced. All copies of identification must be attached to each file for that actor as well as any person who may work on the set of an adult film. No one under the age of eighteen can work for us in any capacity at all no matter what. It was a good day, and things were getting done so that we might be able to proceed with proper record keeping and, most importantly, keeping it straight all the time. With things being the way they were, there was no use in us getting busted for a Mickey Mouse violation like bad record keeping, hiring underage personnel, or some other shit. There were enough things we could get busted for, and we certainly didn't want to be stupid.

My real estate agent called me to see a property he'd just found on Sherman Way. He explained that this street was a main artery running north and south. Traffic was heavy, and it would give the theater a lot of exposure. I drove over to the building and met the agent. He opened the building, and I was hit with a terrible odor.

"What is the smell? Is there something dead in there?" I asked the agent.

"No, not at all. The place has not been occupied for a few years, and I guess there is some mold. All it needs is some fresh air and a little paint."

Deep down this place was perfect, but it was hard to imagine how a theater would look in the middle of this block.

The minute I got back, I called Marty, "Guess what, Marty, I found a perfect spot on Sherman Way and Independence for our first theater," I said. "It's a great location, and we can have it for one K a month—no questions asked. We will have to build it out to suit our needs, but it can be done. We will need a projection room and add the seats as well as a lounge, a shop, and a few other things. With the purchase of the projection cameras, the seats, carpets, as well as the labor, signs, and other stuff, I estimate we will need about thirty-five K. A small investment for the profits we will reap. I plan on starting work tomorrow, and maybe we can open before Christmas."

"Sounds great, Marcel. Let's get the show on the road. What do you need from me?" Marty said.

"You don't have to call me, Marcel. I was just kidding with that disguise. When we are alone, I am Ron and hope I'll always be, please. Kidding aside, I need a feature film for the opening as well as a preview trailer. I want to make sure that everyone who sees the first show is enticed to come back, so make the preview better than the film. I need to put the marquee up first so that people will see that this is the new Pussy Willow theater. Always showing first-run adult features.

"I want the reputation of the theaters to be that all Pussy Willow Cinemas show first run, never seen before features. If we can establish a reputation that we only show first run and the latest releases, we will always be number one. If you can't give me a new shoot in time, how about the last one you shot in New York? We need something colossal to bring them back over and over again," I said.

"Good idea, Ron," Marty said. "I have the film. It was for Carmine, but fuck him. Let's use it in the new theater. I'll give it a title tomorrow, and you will be able to put the name on your marquee. I'm so excited, Ron. I just love the idea. This is going to be great. I can just feel it," Marty said with a great big smile in his voice.

"Don't worry about Carmine. You can give the film another title for him, and he will be the first to show it in New York. Let's make as much money as we can with the film!" I said and hung up.

I got in touch with our new attorney, Stanley Schwartz, who was recommended to Marty by Jeb Johnson. I spoke with Stanley regarding my new business and obtaining the business permit for the theater on Sherman Way.

Of course, as all attorneys, he asked me to come to his office on Ventura Boulevard and see him personally. The real reason was to get some bucks from me. I spent an hour with him and went through the entire plan and asked him to represent each theater on an individual basis, because each one will be leased under a different name. He agreed with my plan and added a few touches so that we would always be protected and then had me sign a retainer agreement and leave him a thousand dollars as a retainer fee against any work I may request of him. We covered every area and discussed client/attorney privilege because I wanted to be clear to him that anything I may say is protected under that rule; even though it was the rule and attorneys cannot reveal what their clients have told them in confidence. The problem is that we also run into attorneys who just talk too much. I wanted Stanley to know that loose tongues would not be tolerated. We discussed community standards and how they applied in Los Angeles at this time. The obscenity laws were based on community standards which really meant there was no cut-and-dried formula as to what really constituted obscenity. It was a gray area that suited the feds just right; nevertheless it was what we had to work with, and Stanley was considered the foremost expert on this.

I left Stanley's office and called Sally at the bank, "Hi, Sally, how are you?" I asked.

"Just fine, Ron. What's up?" she said.

"I will have five or six new accounts that I'd like to introduce to you. Each one will bring a lot of business to the bank and some very substantial deposits. I am sure this will be a feather in your cap. I would like to meet you for lunch tomorrow and discuss this as I want to set up a meeting with the companies and principals. Once I have the meeting set up, I will want you there so that I can introduce you to everyone. Can we discuss it over lunch tomorrow?" I asked.

"Ron, I'll have to cancel a not-so-important lunch meeting to meet with you, but I'll be happy to do so. How about twelve thirty at the Red Rooster? You know where that is?" she said.

"I think so, but, just in case, please remind me," I said.

"It's on Ventura and Corbin on the North East corner. You can't miss it. There is a large rooster at the corner, and they have a great bar," she said.

"See you tomorrow, Sally. Have a great day." I hung up.

I called Marty to see if there was anything he wanted me to do. He didn't have anything special for me, and there were no messages. Of course, how could there be? Who would call me? I didn't give my number to anyone. I went on to the Red Rooster just to familiarize myself with the place and to make sure I knew the best way to get there. I always like to check out any place I am to have a meeting in, in advance. I don't like surprises, and I don't like to be late. It's bad manners and not good for business. I then went to Sears and bought a bed, a dresser, and a small but nice dining room table and chairs. I needed a fridge as the apartment didn't come with one, and Sears was the place to get a nice one. I arranged to have everything delivered to my new apartment on Friday. The rest of the furnishing and other things I needed, I would leave to Natalia. It will keep her involved, and I knew how much she loved to shop.

It was near seven thirty when I left Sears and called Natalia to see what was up. She didn't have dinner yet but wanted me to know that she has been in the kitchen with Mary Lou cooking a special dinner for Marty and me. This was a big surprise to me; I always thought she could not cook at all. The day was a long one, and I felt good as I had accomplished a lot. I went over to the house to see what was going on and to enjoy a few hours of fun with the girls and Marty and taste the wonderful cooking of the ladies.

Wednesday, November 13, 1957

I got up early as usual and began my preparations to maintain my Marcel Lamond look. It would make me very happy if the Willets would see me leave the house in my new identity. That way, he could easily get used to the fact that one of the girls had a boyfriend that came by every now and then and drove an Oldsmobile. I spent an hour in the bathroom coloring my hair and eyebrows and adding a mustache and a goatee. I had also bought a pair of elevator shoes that would increase my height by about three inches. All this added to the fact that I would wear a fedora with a wide brim and always wear a suit and tie when in this disguise. This should easily convince anyone that I am who I claimed to be—Marcel Lamond. I made sure that I could always duplicate the Marcel Lamond look all the time.

Everyone was still asleep when I emerged from the bathroom, so I was able to continue my makeup session leisurely. I had just finished dressing and adjusting my tie, when I heard, "Ron! Is that you?" Natalia said. "What time is it?"

"It's about nine, honey," I responded with my back to her. I wanted to give her a moment to awake fully and see if the disguise worked. I finally turned around and all I could hear was a shout,

"Who the hell are you? What the fuck are you doing in my bedroom?" Natalia shouted. At that same moment the door burst open, and Marty jumped on me from my rear and knocked me to the ground.

"Stop it," I yelled. "It's me, Ron! Relax I'm just checking to see if my disguise works. I guess it did. What a relief!"

"What the hell are you doing, Ron? You scared the shit out of me, you prick," Natalia said.

"Do you know you could have gotten hurt or even killed, you asshole," Marty said. "I usually do damage first and ask questions later. Please don't do this again. If you really want an honest opinion on how you look just ask us, and we'll give it to you. No more bullshit like this, Ron. Just tell us you are going to change your appearance. I know what Marcel looks like," Marty said as he came over and hugged me to show his true feelings.

"Okay, guys, I'm sorry, but I needed some confirmation that the disguise works and you were all asleep. I also wanted to make certain that our neighbors, the Willets, saw me. If they see me often enough, they will always associate that person as the one who drives the Oldsmobile. Familiarity makes one believe in the existence of the other persona. I have a lunch date with Sally and wanted to appear as I will at the meeting. By seeing her in this disguise, I will clue her in, and she'll keep it all very confidential, thus adding to the believability that Marcel Lamond is real. It is very important that we maintain this position at all times, because we will have to face the Mob sooner or later. Better they don't know who the hell they are up against. After all, we are in the movie business and can create any scenario we want. Let's do it so that it confuses the enemy," I said.

"Well, what do you think? Come on, and tell me honestly. Do I look good?"

"Come now, Marcel. It is you in every way. I guarantee it," Natalia said as she ran over and embraced me.

"You'd better remember how I look, because I'm going to need you to help reproduce this look many times over and over," I said as I kissed her gently on the lips.

"No problem, my master. I'll be your very special makeup artist. Never you fear, Natalia is here," she said with a good-natured laugh.

"I have a very busy day today. I have to meet Sally as I said and then I have to stop by the Pussy Willow to get things going. I hired a guy yesterday who is a high quality building contractor. He will handle the complete job of putting the place together. I promised him a full-time job constructing similar locations if he does this one on time and within the budget. I want to get him started on building the theater and then I have to meet with a sign guy at eleven to design and get the marquee ready. At one, I have a meeting with Sally to go over the plan and the schedule for the meeting I'm going to set up with the other adult companies. After I am through with Sally, I have to meet with a guy at the Valley Film and Camera Supply to arrange the purchase of the projection equipment we will need for our theater and future theaters. They are located on Ventura Boulevard near Van Nuys Boulevard. Stanley Schwartz recommended them as he has done some legal work for them and vouched for their integrity.

"It's going to be a long day, so I don't know what time I'll get through, but I'll call you later, and we can arrange dinner. It's very hard when you are getting started, but you just have to take people's word for it when they recommend someone. I will always be in this disguise when I meet with the folks today for safety's sake. I will always conduct business as Marcel Lamond whenever theater affairs are concerned. None of the suppliers, contractors, and other personnel will ever see me as Ron. By the way, the contractor is Mike Hanley. Seems like a very nice guy, and he was recommended by Jeb. We'll see what kind of guy we got in a few days, won't we?" I said.

"Hey, Ron, I see Irv leaving his front door. If you want him to see you, now is the time to leave as well, and let him get a good look at you," Mary Lou said. I grabbed my briefcase and went out the door and walked toward my car.

"Good morning, looks like another beautiful day in paradise," I said with a trace of a French accent. "Sure is. I'm Irv Willets and you are?" he said.

"I'm Marcel Lamond. A pleasure to meet you, Mr. Willets," I said.

"Please call me Irv. Have a nice day," he said as he climbed into his car. "You too, Irv," I said as I opened my car door. Once I saw that Irv's car turned the corner, I got out of my car and went back into the house.

"I'm certain he did not recognize me at all. It worked," I said. "Okay, I got to get going and get things done. By the way, Natalia, I need you to do the decorating and buying of the stuff for my new apartment. We'll go over there this evening or tomorrow so that you can see the layout and get a feel of what you want it to look like. I trust in your taste, and of course, you will be spending a lot of time there. You go buy whatever you think is right. Mary Lou can help you if you want her too and I'd certainly appreciate it an awful lot," I said.

I headed out and drove directly to the theater site to meet Mike.

"Hi Mike. I'm Marcel Lamond. Please call me Marcel. This is the building that I have just leased as you can see. It doesn't look like much now, but I can see a theater rising out of it even if you can't. We must convert this into a regular theater with a ticket booth out front, and we will need seats, a large screen, and speakers, and we will need a projection room. I want at least two hundred seats, and don't forget we must have two proper bathrooms—one for men and one for women. Let's check out the place, and we'll see what can be done," I said as we entered the building and began our walk through.

Mike took a pad and began sketching, measuring, and muttering things while he wrote things down on his pad.

"Okay, Marcel, we can do this job pretty quick. What you need is an easy formula to convert a warehouse into a theater very quickly and as inexpensively as possible. If you want me to handle the entire job, I can do it easily except for certain equipment that you will have to buy, and I will gladly make space for it. You will have to order the seats and make certain to get the specifications for them so that I can make sure the floor is ready to receive them. You will need to buy the projection equipment as well as the screen and the sound system you want. I will coordinate the installation of it all with your supplier.

"Once the first theater is completed, I will be able to handle all future installations from start to finish including signs and equipment. I am your man, and you can count on me. I'll prove it you with a top-notch job on this facility. I hope I can count on you, Mr. Lamond. I'm putting my entire future in your hands," Mike said as he continued, "You want to be open for Christmas! That will be tough, but we can give it a try. I realize you want me to pull permits and that will delay the job. I don't know how much of a delay, but it will cause some. We will start construction at once and operate on a renovation basis so that nothing structurally will have been altered. So if the city should come by, they will not have any reasons to hold up the job or the permit process. I will also do everything to code so that there won't be problems should they insist on an inspection. You will have to get a permit in any case to finally get a certificate of occupancy, because we are going to be open to the public. Think about it, Mr. Lamond, wouldn't it be better to get the permits right from the word go? This way, we are legitimate all the way and can't be closed on any technicality. The hell with the Christmas deadline. If we make it, great. If we don't, who cares? It will open a few days later," Mike said.

"I guess you are right, Mike. Let's not screw around with the first one. Okay, let's do it your way. What do you need, and when can you start?" I said.

"I need five K to buy material, and we'll start today by cleaning up the place. I'll have men on the job this afternoon, and I'll be at the Building and Safety office first thing in the morning with a set of plans to get the permit process on the road," Mike said.

"Great, Mike, and if you have any trouble with the city, please let me know, and I will call someone who can help fast-track the process," I said. "This job will give you the formula for the next one and all future theaters. Let's get to work, I'm excited. Oh, by the way, Mike, please let's not be formal, and call me Marcel from now on." I left Mike with a set of keys and told him to do what he had to do and keep me informed.

I was now off to the Red Rooster to meet Sally, it was a little after twelve when I arrived. I called Marty to see what, if anything, was happening.

"Things are getting along. The contractor will be out of here in a couple of hours, and we will finally be fully operational. I have just spent a few hours working with a new editor on the film we shot in New York. It will be ready in about two weeks. I will be ready for you. I just haven't given it a title yet. I'm trying to come up with a catchy one that will drive people into the theater. If you have any ideas, please let me know," Marty said.

"Okay, I will. Right now I am waiting for Sally to get here and will set things up with her. Did you hear from Irv?" I asked.

"No news yet from his end. I hope he does call soon. I want to get this show on the road," Marty said.

"I'll call you later and bring you up-to-date. Have a great day," I said.

I entered the restaurant and found Sally sitting at a table. She must have arrived a moment before while I was on the phone with Marty. I went over to the table directly, "Hi, do you mind if I join you?" I said.

"I'm sorry, but I am expecting someone," Sally answered.

"It's me, Sally, Ron. I am wearing a disguise as you can obviously see. I'm sorry if I made you wait," I said, as I leaned over and gave her a kiss on the cheek.

"Don't be silly, Ron. I just got here. The funny thing is that I passed you when I came in but did not recognize you. What's with the change of looks?" she said.

"Let me explain the situation to you as it is very important you fully understand the entire scene. I do not want the people I bring to the bank to recognize me as Ron because of my connection with Marty. I have no hidden agenda, but I feel that if I am incognito, the reception will be better all the way around. Not all the people who are in the adult business have any business experience. By keeping this type of information separate, I won't be giving them any reason to feel they are being fooled or that I am getting something I should not. I need your cooperation as I do not want you to address me as Ron whenever we are in the company of new accounts. I'll alert you as to what name I am using in each case. For example, with the group I am bringing to you I will be known as Marcel Lamond. I really don't anticipate using any other names, but if I should, I'll let you know. Of course, Sally, I will always be Ron to you. Will you go along with me on this?" I asked.

"No problem, Marcel," she said with a big smirk on her face. I ordered drinks for us and continued, "Let me ask you this, Sally. Will you be upset if I offer you a little piece of the action?" I said in a lower voice.

"Listen, Ron, excuse me, Marcel, I love my job and have a lot of respect for my boss. I'd never do anything to compromise the bank. With that in mind, what is your deal?" she asked.

Greed is always a factor, and Sally was no different. She had a price and a level of trust that would allow her to forget her morals and accept my offer. It was my task to discover that threshold and use it for my benefit.

"I too will never compromise you or the bank. Anything that I do is legal and always profitable. I will always keep your integrity as my most important concern, this I promise. I plan on opening a chain of adult theaters. This will give me a very large cash flow, and most importantly, I will have in place an agreement that will give my theaters first choice on all top run films. This will be a big plus to me and will make us the number one adult theater in the country. Of course, there will be lots of money as the cash flow will be enormous, and your bank will handle it all—what a feather in your cap, Sally. I want to make sure you get a bonus or something like that. After all, Sally, without you and your cooperation, I could not swing these deals. All bonus money will be in cash, and perhaps you will be able to enjoy life a little better. No one need be involved in this other than you and me. I can agree to a fixed amount each week, or would you like to wait and see what the action will be. The choice is yours and yours alone. Tell me you are on board, and we can get started," I said.

"Well, Ron, I trust you a great deal and am honored that you trust me so much that you could talk this way to me. Even though you feel you owe me something, you really don't. You could have easily done this deal without offering me a thing. There is no reason that I should be sitting here listening to this, but you trusted me and cared. I am grateful and agree with you on the following conditions. I will accept a payment of one hundred per week as my bonus for the work I am doing and will continue to do. You will be the only one to pay me, no one else ever, and only you and I can ever know of this arrangement. If I am ever confronted about this, I will deny I ever accepted one penny from you. I hope that is clear. I will not tell my husband nor anyone else, and I understand that you will do likewise. Do we have a deal?" she said as she signaled the waiter.

We ordered another round of drinks to seal the deal.

"Yes, you have my word, and we'll start the process now. Here is five hundred dollars to cover the next five weeks. We will meet again close to Christmas time, and I'll make the next payments," I said as I handed her a roll of bills. We finished our drinks and left the Red Rooster, mission accomplished. I felt very satisfied about this as it would prove to be an important step in the ladder of success. I knew that Sally was going to get her own branch within the next few weeks. Once this happened, I would move my accounts to her branch and would have the new companies open them there as well. She would have the power I need, and we would use it together.

By the time I got home after meeting with the film supply people, it was a little after six, and I was tired. I still wanted to show Natalia my new apartment and get her started on the decorating of the space. We went over and she made a sketch of the place and took some measurements and with a great big smile told me that she would have the time of her life doing this job for me. She also said that it would be a labor of love, because she wanted me to know that she was head over heels in love with me. I was thrilled with this, because I was also very much in love with her.

Thursday, November 14, 1957

I called Marty at the office after my morning run and met up with him at a little breakfast joint on Topanga Canyon Boulevard.

"Things are great and moving along as planned. The theater is being built as we speak. The Bank has been taken care of, and Sally is one hundred percent on our team. Did you hear from Irv regarding the meeting?" I asked.

"Not yet, but I suppose I will hear today. I know these guys need a way to operate like real businesses, and this is their chance to achieve that. The only stumbling block will be the first dibs on all their new releases. I think, even though no one has talked to me about it, they would be worried about the Mob. These guys have power and can easily whack anyone of these guys just to set an example," Marty said.

"Well, why don't you call Irv and ask him if he can call a meeting of the guys before we set up the bank meeting so that we can discuss this offer and its inherent risks," I said.

"I could do that, but I think it will be best if I speak to some of them tonight at the casting call at Jeb's. This way it will be off Irv's back and give me more credibility," Marty said.

"That sound good to me, and I agree with you about establishing credibility. I think the closer you get to these guys by acting as if you are one of them, the easier it will be for you to gain their confidence. There is nothing they have to concern themselves with, but human nature makes one suspicious when being offered something that sounds too good. As a fellow adult filmmaker, you have concerns just as they do, and between all of you a solution can be found, and you will create a bond with these people. Our plan is sound and will benefit everyone right from the start and, of course, us in the long term. I don't see any downside to this deal for them or us.

"Now, between us, I have a solution to any future risks that may be out there. Why not hire our own security guys? Let's take a page out of Mob's own book and create our own organization. The Mob operates on fear and has the muscle to carry it out. Why not hire a few guys, and they will be our enforcers. Of course, we are not creating this army to attack people or to force our way with anyone. In our case it is for protection only and will be a defensive group. Our muscle is only to protect all those in our family, and if the Mob or anyone else starts trouble, they will get a lot more than they bargained for. I know it sounds like we are going to create a war, but if we fight fire with fire, we'll surely win. After all, we have brains and they do not. We are only interested in protecting our operations and our people, while the Mob wants to take over territories and eliminate competition. We do not and will not operate like that, ever!" I said to Marty as he sat there and looked at me like I was crazy.

"Are you nuts? We have enough trouble as it is, and now you want to start more! This is crazy and will only result in big problems," he said.

"Listen to me, Marty. In the first instance, we are not out of the woods just yet when it comes to Carmine and the Mob. You are starting to forget why we came out here to Los Angeles, and this could prove to be very costly. Remember, we agreed on always being very vigilant, and you are starting to let comfort rule. It will kill you in the end, please believe me. I heard from Moe. It was an emergency call. Yesterday, the feds raided a house in Apalachin New York and rounded up about sixty Mob guys. A lot more of the higher echelons ran away and are now in hiding. It seems there was a high level meeting of all the big guys, and the cops seemed to know all about it. It was at the home of Joseph "The Barber" Barbara.

"The shit has hit the fan. Maybe they'll forget about getting after me, and Carmine will run the other way—maybe or maybe not. We'll have to stay alert and be aware of all the details. Now let's look at this the right way and then make sure we are protected. The Mob is so busy right now trying to make sure their asses are not exposed and getting others out of jail that we are not top priority at present. Now is the time to create and form our own defense mechanism while the enemy sleeps.

"If the meeting with the adult guys goes the way I believe it will, they will need some sort of guarantee that they will be protected from the wrath of Los Angeles Mob, and this idea I have will satisfy that for all of them.

"If we get the adult companies to agree to this, we get a very small, but effective, army on our side to protect us. We will propose a fee that each company will pay for this service. Once they see the profits coming in, they will realize that the small fee they are paying for this army is a pittance. The difference between us and the Mob is that we are not interested in muscling anyone. We are not looking to take over any territory or whack anybody. Our army is for self-defense only—a cost of doing business. There is no doubt in my mind that Carmine will figure it out that Marty Loomis is that ratbag Larry Robbins of OTF Films, and in his mind you owe him. It doesn't matter if he is right or wrong. All he believes is that you fucked him, so he'll try to get to you any way he can. Maybe he will back off for a little while because of the Apalachin raid. How long do you think it will take the New York families to send special hit men out here to whack me? Not very long, I can assure you. So why bullshit ourselves, and let's take steps that help us all. Marty, we have the opportunity to take care of many problems. We must make sure we do and do it now! Once the theaters are open, I will be under attack from both the feds and the Mob. All that money we will make will do us no good in boot hill, so wise up and let's take the right steps, now!" I said angrily."

I left Marty and went over to the theater to see if the work had started. It seemed there were people working, so I decided to move on to my next stop. I stopped in at Valley Film to make certain that all the equipment was indeed ordered and would be here within the few weeks as promised. I called Natalia to remind her that the outfitting of my apartment was very important, and whether she needed me to take her over to the apartment before she left on her shopping spree. She said no, because she had made a complete plan of the place, and she also took my key when I was at the house last night. She might stop by with Mary Lou and then be ready for the biggest surprise of my life. She was so excited about her decorating job that she could hardly wait to get started and spend the five K I left her. I hope I didn't make a mistake with this, but deep down, I trusted her with my life.

I then went to Topanga Gun Range to practice shooting. I liked this particular range because it was out in the country, and I could spend an hour or two making sure I was still a good shot. I didn't want to get complacent and let my guard down.

My gut was telling me that the battle was soon to come. I then went back to the house to spend a few hours relaxing and getting my thoughts together. I must always be sharp and could not let anything change that, not until all threats were eliminated.

I must have fallen asleep on the sofa, because when I woke up, it was a little after seven, and no one was home. I knew Marty was at the casting call and probably wouldn't be home until the wee hours. I knew he wanted to play poker with the guys after the session was over. The girls were out shopping, so it was clear to me that they were having a blast and probably would not be home until the stores closed. I guess I'll wait until morning to discuss things with Marty.

Friday, November 15, 1957

I spoke with Natalia when she got home last night, and she informed me that she had spent the entire five K I gave her on some great stuff. It would be delivered today, and she would be there with Mary Lou to receive it and place it where she thought it should be. When I get home tonight, my apartment would be ready for me. She was beaming with pride as she told me about her day shopping and how proud she was with her ability to buy carefully and make my place a palace. It was great to see the look on her face; she was happy that she could please me.

I went for my morning run, showered, and dressed, and decided to call Moe in New York and find out what was going on.

"Hey there, Moe, how are you?" I asked when he got on the phone.

"I'm great, and how are you doing?"

"I'm doing real fine and getting things in order over here. I just wanted to hear your voice and to know that you are well, my friend. I miss you a lot," I said.

"Give me your number, and I'll call you back in a few minutes. I have someone in the office. I'll be through in fifteen minutes and will call you then," he said. I gave him the number and waited for his call.

As usual, Moe was right on time. "Hi, I couldn't speak before, Harry. I had someone in the office. Tell me all about Los Angeles. I couldn't ask too much when I spoke to you earlier, and yesterday I could not say anymore than I did. I'm sure you can understand what was going on with that raid. Enough of that for now, Harry. Is Los Angeles really as much fun as they say? Does the sun shine all the time? Come on, Harry, give me the skinny!" he said.

"Yes to everything. It is a great place, and I'm really very comfortable. What news have you got besides the news you gave me yesterday? I heard it all on the radio, and it was also on TV. This must have fucked up the entire Mob?" I said.

"The talk around here is that the Mob is still looking for you, and the hit remains in force. The feds have dropped their desire to get you because what information you may have is now too old and will not be of any use to them. They also have plenty of snitches now that the raid was so fruitful. There are a lot of Mob guys who are singing like canaries now that they are in custody, and the bosses seem to be running for cover. There has been a lot of pressure on your ex-father-in-law as these assholes have gone as far as accusing him of hiding you. There is also talk that you hooked up with a guy named Larry Robbins from the adult business.

"He is considered a loser, and they think he moved to Los Angeles. They are looking for him as well as it seems he owes a lower level Mob guy some money. I heard that he will get his legs broken when they find him, and when he gets out of the hospital, he will go back to work for this guy and make adult films for him just to pay back the money he owes. It is amazing how they think they can control everything and everyone," Moe said. "Of course, Harry, with this bust a lot of things will change. We just have to wait and see. Please don't let your guard down at any time."

"Don't worry about a thing, Moe. If they want to come to Los Angeles, they will find they have a fight on their hands. It won't be so easy for them like it is in New York. If I have to, I will go to war with these people once and for all. If I don't put a stop to this, I will not be able to accomplish anything and needless to say live much longer as well. I don't need any money at this time. If I do, I'll call you, but I will keep you informed on the progress of things. Stay well, Moe, and give the family my best. It was great hearing your voice." I hung up.

I was a little upset about the information Moe just gave me, but what the hell, I didn't expect any better. I couldn't fool myself any longer; the time was getting nearer when a showdown would be inevitable. Either I let these assholes know who they are fooling with, or I give up and die, and that I wouldn't let happen.

I would keep myself sharp and make sure I am a crack shot. If they want me, they'll have to get guys that are better trained than me! No way, the Mob has no idea what they are into; leave Harry Miller alone or you will die.

I got the girls out of bed early because they had to be at my place to receive the deliveries for my apartment. They made arrangements to have everything delivered today and someone needed to be there.

"Girls, it's time you got over to the apartment," I said as I pulled the sheet off Natalia.

"Please, let me sleep a little longer, please," Natalia said as she pulled the sheets back over herself.

"Okay, here's what I am going to do. I'll go over to the apartment and wait for you to arrive so that you can get another hour of sleep, but please get your beautiful ass out of bed and get over to the apartment as fast as possible as I have things to do," I said as I gently kissed her on the forehead and quietly closed the bedroom door.

Marty had left for the office, and there was no use in disturbing Mary Lou; Natalia would handle that when she got up. I left the house and went to the apartment to wait. It was near ten thirty when the doorbell rang; it was Sears with the fridge and the few things I had ordered. They were in and out in thirty minutes and were very happy with the ten dollar tip I gave them. I still had no idea when and what would arrive as the girls did all the arranging and knew the schedule. I could have called the house and find out when I should expect them, but I felt that could aggravate them and set them off into a bad mood and, of course, it would be me that would suffer their wrath. After all, it was my apartment and not theirs, so how could they get too upset? No, I will just let it ride and wait until they get here.

It was around eleven when I left the apartment. The girls had arrived looking like they were going out on a date. They were dressed to the nines and looked just great. I called Marty at his office.

"Hey, Marty, what's up? How was last night?" I said. "It was great. I got to meet most of the major players in this business. Irv was there, and he felt like a big shot as he introduced me, his new found friend, to the guys. The casting call was super. Some real cute chicks were there. I found one that I think will be our next superstar. I told Jeb that I want her at my office today at one. I will put her in the next movie that I have just finished writing. She is an absolute doll and innocent looking. She'll be a big hit. Her name is Suzie Wright, but I think I will have her use a different name. She looks like an angel. "Angel," what do you think? A great name for a star in porn flicks," Marty said with a big smile in his voice.

"It sounds great to me. I would love to be there when she comes in, but I really can't take the chance of hanging around your office," I said.

"Marcel, you are Marcel today, aren't you?" Marty said.

"Of course, I don't go anywhere looking like Ron," I said. "Then drop by and take a peek. It can't hurt." I hung up and went over to Marty's office through the front door and was shown in by Kathy.

"Hey there, Marty, how are you? I was just in the area and stopped by to say hello," I said.

"Okay, let's get back to what we were talking about," Marty said as he closed his office door and made sure we were private.

"Aside from her, you were absolutely right with the other guys. By my being there and talking with them, I became one of the boys, and it was easy to discuss anything on the same level. You are not part of the equation, so no one knows you at all, and we must keep it that way. Irv brought up the subject about banking, and it was easy from there. I said I have a friend who has an in with a legitimate bank and can get us all in without any deceit. They are completely aware that I am in adult operation. I have it easy now as no checks are ever returned, and they work with me like they would with any legitimate business. The guys were all ears and only wanted to know when they could become part of that deal. I mentioned that I spoke with Irv, and it would be best if we set up a meeting with the bank manager and the guy who is arranging it all. It is important for everyone to meet the guy who has the clout with the bank before we meet the bank manager. I think we should first have a meeting between ourselves and discuss what is involved, and if it suits everyone, then we will arrange a meeting with the bank. All I need is a date and a place where we can easily get together. Let me know, guys," Marty said as he related last night's events to me.

"That sounds great. It looks like we'll have a meeting very soon. I like that especially since Sally is going to have her own branch on Erwin & Canoga. She'll let me know when the branch will open. She hopes the branch will be ready in a few days as the final touches are being completed. This is going to be the greatest operation ever. You just wait and see, Marty, we are on the road to riches. Let's not fuck this up or let anyone else do it.

"Now I wanted to discuss another thing with you, about us and our safety. I think it is wise to hire a few bodyguards like I discussed with you. This is the best course of action for us so that we will at least have the power to fight fire with fire. Who would ever believe that I could be this cold? Honestly, Marty, that is not my nature, but these fucking Mob guys have made me into a ruthless bastard. I spoke with my man in New York, and here is the latest. The council still has a hit out on me, although it is not a priority because of the big bust in Appalachia. Carmine has told people that he believes you ran to Los Angeles and that you owe him a bundle of money. He has bragged that he will break your legs, and when you get out of the hospital, you will beg to work for him. No matter what we think, the trail will lead here eventually, and we'd better be ready. I don't know what I must do to convince these guys that I am no threat to them. They are making me a much bigger threat than I really am. I will kill every one of those bastards until they quit or run out of people. I think we need our own army and show some balls—they will run the other way. The Mob is not as strong in Los Angeles for many reasons. One is because of the Mexican Mob; they don't want a war with them as the Mexican's are more ruthless than they are. This is Mexican turf and they know it. Their strength is still back East and Vegas, and the Vegas guys don't really want to get involved in any war in Los Angeles when they got casinos and hookers to run in Vegas bringing in big bucks. What do you think, partner?" I said very clearly and with conviction.

"I guess you are right, Ron. I just didn't want to believe it. I love the life we have here, and it all seems to be going so smoothly. I know we will have heat with the theaters, and I know Carmine. Even though he is a low-level fuck, he has had his pride hurt and wants to set some example. I know all this, yet I don't want to believe it. I am all for taking whatever action we need to be ready. I just want you to know one very important thing, Ron. I am not afraid of dying or being beaten up. I am your partner, and you have given me a new lease on life. I'll never forget that, never. I am at your side and will kill anyone who gets in our way. Never underestimate my loyalty and willingness to stand at your side. I will always be there, Ron, and now that we are going to be rich, let's get some soldiers recruited in our army. I will sleep better when you have it all under control," Marty said.

"Thanks for that confirmation. I never doubted you and never will. Try to get that meeting set up as soon as you can," I said to Marty as his intercom rang.

It was Kathy letting him know that Suzie Wright had arrived. Marty instructed Kathy to show her in at once. The door opened and in walked a beautiful young woman with red hair and big blues eyes. She was around five feet five inches and probably weighed one hundred and ten pounds at the most with a pair of tits that probably took up half the weight. She didn't look older than sixteen, but those tits could have let her pass for twenty-one. She was everything Marty said and more.

"Hello there, Suzie. Welcome, it is nice to see you. By the way, this is Marcel, a friend of mine," Marty said with a big glow in his eyes that said "I told you so!"

I left Marty alone with his new star and could imagine what was going through his mind. I sure hope he does business with his head and not his heart or his other head. I passed by the theater to check up on what progress was being made and spoke with Mike. He was so proud of the fact that he obtained a permit without any fuss. I was happy as well and very excited that soon we will be in the movie theater business and taking in a lot of money daily.

I left Mike to continue his work and drove to Van Nuys to see an acquaintance I had met when in New York. His name was Jorge` Martinez, and when I met him in New York, he was down on his luck. He wouldn't recognize me as Marcel, but once I explain who I am, he will remember me and the kindness I showed him in New York. I knew I would get his cooperation, of this I had no doubts. I stopped and called the number I had for him, "Hey Jorge`, my name is Marcel. I was given your name and number from a dear friend of mine and yours, Dan All right. He told me if I needed anything when I am in Los Angeles., I should call my friend Jorge`, so here I am, man. Can I see you? I'm in Van Nuys now?" I said.

"Any friend of Dan's is a friend of mine. How can I help you?" Jorge` said.

"I'd prefer to discuss this person to person if it's okay with you?" I said.

"Sure, man, where are you?" he said. "I'm at Howard Johnson on the corner of Sepulveda and Moorpark in the coffee shop. I'll wait here for you," I said.

"Okay, man, give me ten minutes, and I'll be there. What are you wearing?" he said.

"I've got a blue blazer jacket and am wearing a black fedora. I'll be at the counter having a coffee." I hung up.

Ten minutes later, a guy walked in that had to be Jorge` as I remembered him from back East. "Marcel? I'm Jorge`. Nice to meet you. Let's take a booth where we can discuss things in private," he said.

I took my coffee and went to the booth and asked, "Would you like something Jorge`?"

"Sure thing, I'll have a coke and some fries," he said. With the order placed, I started the conversation.

"I am new here in Los Angeles and plan to start a few businesses here and need some people who I can trust to work for me. I need people who aren't afraid and will do their jobs well. I need bodyguards full-time, and the going could get rough. Can you do anything for me?" I said.

"Well, Marcel, I can set this up, but first I need to know what we are going to be doing? Who is the enemy? Are you talking about guns and heavy stuff? Please give me details. You can trust me one hundred percent, so anything you say to me will never go anywhere else. If I refuse you, then I'll forget what I heard. If I accept, I'll need to know everything," Jorge` said.

"Okay Jorge`, here is the deal. My partner and I are in the adult business and there are people who may want to muscle in. These people are Mob people, and even though I don't know who they are, I do know they will try to get at my partner and me. We can handle ourselves, but we don't have eyes in the back of our heads. I plan on opening an adult theater on Sherman Way and Independence in Canoga Park. How long do you think it will take for these Mob bastards to try to muscle in? Not long I figure, but if we have our own enforcement group, we can kick their asses and anyone else who wants to fuck with us. I need a reliable and loyal headman. It will be his job to recruit the rest." I stopped speaking so that it could all sink in with Jorge`.

"I understand your need, my friend, but this job is dangerous and will take a very loyal person. It will also be expensive. Can you afford it? We are looking at some serious dollars," Jorge` said.

"Money is not the problem. Loyal and trustworthy people are the most important. If you take this job, then we can set up a proper budget and adjust as we go along and get the feel of the situation," I said.

"I am your man, my friend. I will hire and control the men. They will do as I tell them, and only you and I will talk about things. I hope I can be worthy of the trust you will put in me, but I will promise you loyalty and honesty at all times. Most important is the way we relate to each other and the budget. I can't tell you just now what it will cost. Give me a day or two. Give me your phone number, and I'll call you. If you agree, we can then sit down and you can give me all the information, and I'll handle it," Jorge` said as he looked at me with piercing eyes that were as cold as ice.

I gave him my number and thanked him as he left. I waited a few minutes and then left as well. I wanted to make sure no one would follow me. Jorge`, true to my instinct, was long gone.

I made my way back to the apartment to see what had happened with all the deliveries. I walked in and couldn't believe my eyes; the place was beautiful. I loved it.

"Wow! This is unbelievable. What a place! What a great job, girls. I'm speechless.

"I'm so happy you like it. We worked real hard to make sure everything was right and that it would be a place you'd be very comfortable in as well as secure," Natalia said.

"Hey there, brother, isn't this great? I love it better than our house, and now I know for sure you'll never come to visit us," Mary Lou said.

"I doubt that, but this is great. Thanks girls. You did a wonderful job, and I'll always be grateful. Thanks," I said as I fell into the soft, luxurious sofa and just sat there in heavenly bliss.

The girls had chilled a bottle of champagne and now poured a toast to the new place. "May you always have happy times and good health in this great apartment. I will be happy to spend the night here in the extra bedroom. We bought enough linens and stuff to completely make this place your dream place," Mary Lou said as she picked up her flute of champagne.

The phone rang. It was Marty. "How does the place look?" he asked. "I really can't tell you, partner, but if you need your place decorated, I have two of the best interior designers in the world right here. Why don't you get in your car and get your ass over here and see the place right now, old buddy," I said.

"I'll be there in a few minutes. Hold the drinks for me!" Marty said and hung up. We spent the rest of the evening celebrating with a couple more bottles of champagne. We called Alfredos and ordered a full Italian dinner to be delivered we were eating in and staying home tonight with some real good friends in my super great apartment.

Saturday, November 16, 1957

I woke up with a head as big as a soccer ball. I lost track of what happened last night just after we finished the fourth bottle of champagne. Natalia was out like a light next to me; I sure hope we had some fun last night. I went into the kitchen and noticed a mess that wasn't there last night, not that I remember what happened. I looked into the next bedroom and there was Marty and Mary Lou fast asleep. I guess no one went home last night. I took a shower and dressed for my run. I did this very quietly as I certainly did not want to wake anyone up. I had to make my run as usual except that this was the first time I would be running this new route from my new apartment. I felt good exploring the neighborhood for the first time. It was nice and early, and I could see what the area really looked like when it was quiet. This area was a lot different than Woodland Hills. This was a heavily populated area of English—and Spanish-speaking people. It was a real working class area, although clean and neat. Not many of the cars that were parked were new or even close. When cars are this old, it speaks out loud about the neighborhood. I enjoyed my run a lot, because after running about ten miles, I still had a lot of energy left and could have run a lot more. I figured that was because I was so busy exploring the new area that I didn't give my run any thought.

Why couldn't I do that all the time? I returned to the apartment and found everyone still asleep. I decided to run by the theater and see if Mike had his crew working on a Saturday. I left them all to their dreams and went on to the theater. Sure enough, they were working and AAA Signs was there measuring and discussing with Mike what was required to make the marquee just right to handle the sign. I walked in right in the middle of their conversation.

"I will make the frame come out ten feet as indicated on my plans I submitted to the city when I applied for the permit. That will give you plenty of space to hang your signs on both sides. The maximum I can come out is the ten feet as I agreed with the Inspector. I don't want to rock the boat. This should make it easy for you," Mike said.

"Hi guys, how's it going?" I asked.

"Great, we are just coordinating the sign. I will bring the frame out ten feet on a triangle so that both sides of the sign will be seen from Sherman Way, no matter what direction you are coming from. I will wire the frame to take the lighting and will bring it back to your projection room so that the sign can be controlled from there. I will construct the ticket booth under the marquee so that the entrance of the theater will look like any other theater," Mike said.

"This is good enough for me," the sign man said. "When will you be ready with the frame?"

"I think we can have it done and ready for next Friday. Check with me on Wednesday to confirm," Mike said. I went inside and looked around. It was starting to take shape. Mike was doing a good job.

I left the theater and returned to the apartment to find everybody up and getting ready to face the weekend.

"A little too much champagne, huh guys!" I said.

"I love the stuff, but it does give me a headache the next morning," Mary Lou said with a big smile and a tired look.

"Well, guys, what are your plans for today?" I asked. "I'm sure you got something you all want to do. I'm all ears," I said.

"First, we have to spend an hour or two cleaning up this place, then we have to get back to our place and get it in order. That will kill most the day. I leave the festivities of the night to you. Any suggestions?" Natalia said.

"Well, I heard of this club on Sunset that opened last week. It's supposed to be the place, and I heard it has great food. It's called Chez Paris and has a show that is supposed to be super. What do you think? Want to give it a try? What time and I'll call for reservations if I can get them," I said.

"What about eight? That should be good for us," Marty said. I called and spoke with the Maître d', Henri, and lucky for us, we got a table. I told Henri that I didn't want any attention brought upon us while at the club. I explained that I was with a famous movie director and would have two of the latest movie stars with us. I further told Henri that I would take good care of him when I arrived there tonight. Once I said all that, it seemed that Henri could not find enough words to assure me that everything would be in order.

I explained to Natalia and Mary Lou that although I said I would not go out in public with them, I had tested my new look, and even people who knew Dan All right or Ron didn't put it all together and recognized Marcel like he was always Marcel, so I felt it was safe. I told Marty that he should pick me up here at about seven to make sure we would be there on time. I spent the rest of the day shopping for food and picking up odds and ends that I needed for my apartment.

At six fifty, Marty rang the bell as I put on my jacket and joined them for the ride to Chez Paris. We arrived at seven forty-five and saw a crowd of people lined up to get in. We gave the car to the valet and told the doorman our name and reservation time. We had to wait only a minute before we were ushered into the restaurant proper. The place was decorated in a French motif with stone floors and a large stage at one end of the room. There were a lot of tables as the place was far bigger than one would think when looking from the outside. I slipped the head waiter a twenty, and we were taken to our table. Once we were seated, I asked the waiter if he could send Henri over to our table. The drinks waiter came over to our table and got our drink order while a bus boy placed hot rolls and butter on the table. Each table had two candles on it that were unlit. While waiting for the drinks, a man approached the table,

"Hello, I am Henri. It is a pleasure to meet you," he said.

"It is my pleasure, Henri. I am Marcel Lamond, and this is Marty Robbins," I said as I shook hands with him and palmed him a fifty.

"May I introduce you to Natalia and Mary Lou?" I said.

"A pleasure to meet such beautiful girls. You are always welcome here. Just ask for me, and I'll take care of everything, "Henri said as he took each one their hands and kissed them gently.

After our drinks were served, the waiter came over to our table and lit the candles and said, "Welcome to Chez Paris. You will have a wonderful time tonight. The food is the best in Los Angeles and perhaps in the entire country. The show is first-class, and I hope you will find my service is to your satisfaction! My name is Gaston, and I will make sure you're every need is taken care of," Gaston said.

"Merci, Gaston. I'm Marcel. These are my friends, Mary Lou, Natalia, and Marty. We are thrilled to be here and hope that we will see you often. My French is limited, but at least I can speak a little," I said.

"Well, I hate to disappoint you all, but I don't speak one word of French. I am sorry, but my name is really Gaston as my mother was French," he said.

"No worries, Gaston, we will still be your best customers even if you don't speak French. Let's see what the food is like. Perhaps you can recommend something that you may think will demonstrate the specialty of the house?" I said.

The food was very good, and the service was the best we had experienced in Los Angeles. In the meantime, we were sent complimentary drinks from many people including a few Hollywood stars. The girls, as usual, made people look twice and wonder who they actually were. They were beautiful and the clothes they wore, or should I say almost didn't wear, made both men and women take a second look. If they had come in bedsheets, I think they would have started a new run on bedsheets. They were showstoppers, and we were the envy of the entire male audience. We watched the floor show that was spectacular in every way possible. We were sitting around after the show, and Gaston came to the table, "I would like to get you some after-dinner drinks, folks. These drinks are the compliments of Mr. Ralph Gidney. He is the owner of this club and has considerable other holdings in this city. What will you have?"

We ordered XO cognac and asked Gaston to please thank Mr. Gidney.

"Of course, Gaston, if Mr. Gidney is inclined, we would be honored if he would join us. Please convey that to him," I said.

"Hello, I'm Ralph Gidney. Please call me Ralph. It is a pleasure to meet you, and I hope you have enjoyed the entire evening here at Chez Paris?" he said. He was a good looking man about six foot three inches with dark black hair slicked back. He was lean and strong looking and had a very disarming smile. He was all class and quite articulate, yet I could detect a slight Brooklyn accent in his speech.

"I'm Marcel Lamond. This is Marty Loomis, Mary Lou, and Natalia. It is a pleasure to meet you, and thanks for the round of drinks. Can we buy you another, Ralph?" I asked.

"No thanks. I still have a long evening ahead of me. We don't close until two. One more floor show and then we can call it quits. I hope you will come back often. Please mention my name, and you will always have a table regardless of how crowded this place may be," he said.

"Thanks, Ralph. That will be great," I said.

"By the way, haven't I seen you in a film?" Ralph said to Mary Lou. "That is possible. I have only been in a few movies but plan on being in a lot more now that I am living here in Los Angeles," she said.

"I'll look forward to seeing you on the screen and in my club. You are too beautiful not to be in every movie," he said.

"Why, thank you, Ralph. That is so kind of you. I hope we will see a lot more of you. I love to hear nice things as often as I can. Marty is so busy writing and directing that he forgets to tell me what a wonderful actress I am," Mary Lou said to Ralph.

"What genre of films do you make, Marty?" Ralph asked as he pulled up a chair from the next table.

"I don't like to talk about business when I am out for an evening of fun. It's not good luck. I'll direct any kind of film I feel is good and can be a hit. I like films that deliver all the way through. If a film is not done right even with a great story line, the whole project will fail. The public is far too savvy to try to make them like a dud. I will direct a porn movie if the entire project is handled professionally and the story line has substance, not just sex alone," Marty said.

"Marcel, are you also in this movie business?" Ralph asked.

"No, I am not in the business like Marty. I run a chain of theaters and am opening a few here in Los Angeles. I'll be glad to have you as my guest on opening night," I said with pride.

"The girls are both beautiful and very talented as they are great actresses, singers, and dancers as well. Besides all that, they are the world's best interior decorators I have ever seen. Between you and me, Ralph, these girls are the best thing that has happened to Hollywood in a long time. They are going to be well-known all over the world very, very soon. Some people are taught how to act—these two girls have natural talent they haven't used yet. Keep an eye out. They will be up there very soon. This I can guarantee!" I said.

"Well, folks, I have to run and make sure the club operates up to the highest standards. Don't forget. Use my name and we'll get along real well. A pleasure to meet you all," he said as he walked away.

"Boy, that was a bit smaltzy, don't you think?" Marty said.

"No way, guys. There is no doubt that he is very interested in you girls. He's got it bad and wants to get to know us better. He may be very helpful in the future if we play our cards right. If we need to know what is going on in the industry, he will be our source. This I can guarantee you," I said.

"Okay, I agree with you, but you didn't have to tell them we were such great dancers, actresses, and singers. That's going a little too far, don't you think?" Mary Lou said.

"No! I don't think I went overboard. I know how good you guys are, and I've seen you act and dance and even heard you sing. So don't start with me. You are the next best thing that has happened to Hollywood and that is it," I said as I leaned over and kissed Mary Lou right on the tip of her nose.

"Okay, let's get the check and get out of here. I'm really tired after last night and do need some rest," Marty said.

We signaled Gaston to bring the check and finished our drinks. A minute later, Gaston arrived with another round of drinks,

"We didn't order those, Gaston. We meant we wanted the check, please," I said.

"I'm very sorry, Mr. Marcel, but these were sent by Mr. Gidney, a nightcap. As far as the check is concerned, I cannot find it anywhere. It seems that the check has already been paid. Please forgive me. I just work here and do what I am told," he said.

I took out a fifty and slipped it into his hand and said, "Thanks, Gaston, you have been just great."

"Mr. Marcel, I cannot accept this, please understand," he said. "If Mr. Gidney found out I took anything, he would fire me. When someone is his guest, he does it all the way, first class. I'm sure you understand!" he said as he handed the money back to me. "By the way, Mr. Marcel, please do not tip the valet either. Mr. Gidney has advised everyone that your party is very special and must be treated that way. He always takes good care of us, please understand!" We got up and said goodnight to everyone and left. We were amazed by the generosity of Ralph and wondered when he would be back for payment. No use worrying about it now.

Sunday, November 17, 1957

I took my usual run this morning from my new location and then made ready for the day. I wanted to hear from Jorge`. I was getting a little antsy but didn't want to show him any weakness and call him. He'll get in touch, I knew that; I just wished it was today. I waited until eleven to call Marty and see what was up for the day. Natalia stayed over with me and slept in until after eleven. I made arrangements to meet Marty at the Cantina in Calabasas for brunch at one. I told Natalia I was taking her for brunch and to get herself ready, because we had to be at the Cantina by one.

We proceeded to the Cantina and arrived at just before one. The parking lot was full and cars were in line waiting to park. There were plenty of motorcycles as well. The place was busy with a lot of people coming and going. The sun was shining in a cloudless sky with a temperature of seventy-two. It was very different than anything I had seen back East; I guess this was really the land of the stars. We finally found a parking spot and went into the Cantina and spotted Marty and Mary Lou sitting at a table on the patio. We walked through the Cantina over a sawdust-covered floor and tables running lengthwise and again widthwise filled with food of every description. It was very crowded as we made our way to Marty's table.

"Hey there, guys, sorry we are a bit late. This place is unbelievable. What a crowd!" I said.

"The deal is simple. Just stand in any line you wish and fill your plates with food and then return to the table and eat and then repeat the exercise. Pretty simple, isn't it?" Marty said. "By the way, there is a shot bar over there. Would you like to do a few shooters? Let's do them. It ought to be fun. Come on girls, join us and get a little wasted."

"Sure, I'm ready for anything. Let's do it," I said.

Off we went to the end table where they had a big bowl of oysters and bottles of Smirnoff's vodka.

"You take the oyster and place it in a shot glass and then they fill the glass with vodka and you shoot in down. If you can't handle it like that, they have some lemon wedges over in a bowl. Just squeeze a little lemon into the shot glass! One gulp and the oyster and vodka are gone, and if you have the courage you have another," Marty said.

Well, we had the courage and had another and another until finally we decided to eat and put the shooters on hold. Finally, we were sitting down and eating when a waitress came along and filled our glasses with champagne or mimosas, our choice. We spent three hours eating and drinking and just having a good time. We did not discuss business at all. It was just great to give our brains a rest. There was plenty of time for discussions tomorrow. When we finally did leave, we didn't feel like doing anything other than going home and taking a nap. Marty and Mary Lou went to their Woodland Hills house, and Natalia and I went to my apartment.

Monday, November 18, 1957

After yesterday's eating orgy, we slept like logs, and of course, Natalia was still asleep when I got up bright and early. If I ever needed a morning run, it was this morning as I needed to burn off all those excess calories. I ran with extra vigor as my legs carried me over the streets of Canoga Park. By the time I returned to the apartment, I was ready to face the day.

I showered and shaved and dressed ready to face another week and get things done. Irv had called Marty last night saying that he would like to set up a meeting with the boys at the Essence Films Studio for Tuesday at 2:00 p.m. Essence was located on Osborne Avenue in Canoga Park in the heart of the adult industry. I told Marty that it would be fine with me and to confirm this today. It was now ten thirty, and I had to get going as my morning was fast disappearing. As I was just about to go out the door, the phone rang. I thought about just letting it ring, but my sense of curiosity wouldn't let me,

"Hey Jorge`, how are you? What's up, man?" I said.

"I decided to come to work for you. We need to sit down and talk about how it will all work and just exactly what you expect from me. As long as you want only what is possible, I am your man. When do you have time?" he said.

"How about this afternoon? I can meet you around two. Just tell me where, or would you prefer to come to my place where we can be alone?" I said.

"That would be great," Jorge` said. I gave him the address and hung up. I looked up, and there was Natalia standing there wrapped in a towel. She had just come out of the shower and said, "What was that about?"

"I have a meeting today at two here at the apartment. You will have to make yourself scarce. Where do you want to go?" I said.

"Drop me off at the house. I need to pick up my car and call me there when you are done. I'll spend the afternoon with Mary Lou, and when you are finished we can have dinner together," she said.

"Sounds good to me. Get ready quickly as I have to stop at the theater and see what is going on."

She went into the bedroom to get dressed as I called Marty.

"Just checking with you on the progress of the new film?" I said.

"I got everything set and will star Angel in this one. I won't use the girls in this film. Let me tell them, Ron. I'm sure they will understand. I will discuss it with them tonight. I could use one of them but not both and just don't want any jealousy. Leave it to me. I'll handle it, Ron, and I'll handle it right. I'll let you know what is what as soon as I know," Marty said. "By the way, what's on your plate?"

"I am meeting with Jorge` at two today to resolve the security issue. I'm going to the theater to see what is going on and make certain things are on schedule. I'll call you later," I said.

Natalia and I went over to the theater and met Mike. "How are things going, Mike?" I asked.

As far as the construction is concerned, things are moving along just fine. Here, take a look!" Mike said. "It's starting to take shape. Another week and it will look like a theater," Mike said with a sad look on his face.

"Why so glum, Mike?" I asked. "I could tell that something is wrong. Let it out and we'll solve it."

"I was working this morning when this guy comes along and asks me who the owner is. I told him I don't really know. I just work here. He asked me for the number of the head office. I told him to give me his name and number, and I will have my boss call him when he gets here. He looked at me and said that if I want to be able to go on working, I'd better stop being a hard ass and cooperate with him. He'll stop this job if he doesn't get a phone call from the boss today. I asked him who the hell he was, and he laughed and said I really don't want to know. Mind your own business, or you will be out of business for good. He left me his name and number and said he'd expect a call today or else," Mike said.

"Well, don't you worry about it, Mike. I'll take care of it and no one will bother you again." I took the piece of paper from Mike and went back to the car and left.

"What is the problem, honey?" Natalia said to me as she put her hand on my leg.

"It's just a little matter of business. I'll handle it, please don't worry," I said as we drove to the house. It was noon already, and Mary Lou was walking around muttering how unhappy she was. "What is the problem, Mary Lou?" I asked.

"I'm not happy sitting here doing nothing. I want to get back to work, please Ron. I'm bored to death. Ron, I need you to talk to Marty about it, please," she said.

"Don't worry. I will speak to him and things will get busier. It just takes time to settle ourselves in a new place, and that is exactly what we are doing. Be patient, and it will all work out. You are far too beautiful and talented to stay at home. This is for sure. I wouldn't want your fans to miss out on seeing you back on screen. Don't worry, we will get you back to work real soon. I promise," I said.

She immediately smiled and her mood changed completely.

"Thanks, Ron. I needed that," she said.

"Okay, girls, I have to run and take care of business. I'll call you later, Nat. Be good and keep Mary Lou in a good mood. Love you," I said and left. I drove back to the apartment to wait for Jorge`.

It was a little after one, and I was anxious to call this guy back. I looked at the paper Mike had given me and saw that the name he wrote down was Joseph, no last name, and his phone number. It was an 818 number, so the guy or at least the telephone was in the Valley. I decided not to call until I concluded business with Jorge`. At least, I'll have a better chance to evaluate the situation then. With Jorge` at my side, it might be a lot easier. Without him, I'll have to seek additional help fast.

At exactly two, the doorbell rang. I let Jorge` in and offered him a drink. He wanted a tequila straight up, so I joined him as we sat down at the dining room table.

"Well, my friend, let me tell you the story. It is impossible for you to make a final decision until you know everything," I said as we threw the shot of tequila down.

"Based on our previous meeting, I will do the following. I will organize a group of people to handle your security needs. I will need information from you, as much as you can tell me, so that we know what we are up against at all times. I will give you my loyalty and will place my life on the line for you. Here is what we need, if this is to work properly. I need a place that will be my office where I can meet and instruct the boys. It can be an office space or a house—I really don't care. I prefer a building in a commercial area because a house puts a lot of people in harm's way. There are nosey neighbors, and with people coming and going all the time, questions will be asked. If a neighbor thinks there is something dangerous going on, they could call the cops, or if there are others involved, these folks can talk, and we could have a serious problem. If we take a building in a commercial area, no one will care or say anything. I think we can get a space under seven hundred dollars a month. I know of a few places, so if you want to leave that up to me, I can handle it. I will need a front to cover this operation, so we'll have to set up a company. I don't know shit on how to do that, but you do. So can we get that done as soon as possible? Maybe you will call it Valley Trading Company or something like that. We will need a phone under the company name and, of course, the lights turned on. I will need a payroll of two hundred per man each week. I will need two men who will work half the day and another two who will work the other half. That will make four men and then I need an additional four men to cover when these men are off. Our staff will be eight men who will be tough and will make sure you are safe all the time. That makes a payroll of sixteen hundred a week. Plus I need expense money, at least five hundred dollars a week. The expense money is to cover gas, food, and stuff like that. The guys must always be loyal to me and do what I say. I do not want any instructions coming from you. You understand in case there is ever a legal problem you will always be safe and far away from being involved. Your name can never appear anywhere, and if possible, let's keep you as far away from things as possible. Once a month, I'll need a few extra bucks to give the guys a little bonus when they do well. This can be decided each month, and believe me, it will go a long way in maintaining good morale and loyalty with the guys. Now, let's get down to me. So far the costs do not include me in any way at all, so how do we settle that? I'll not ask you for anything. I hate making demands of that nature, so I leave it up to you to take care of me. You were kind to me in New York and have shown me how generous you are, so I leave it in your hands," he said.

"Wow! That is a lot of bread, but I am sure it has to be done. It doesn't sound like you have added anything additional to that budget. Here is what I have in mind," I said. "As you know, we are opening a theater on Sherman Way and Independence. This is the first one of many that we plan. I want you to run that operation, and I'll give you two percent of the operation. The theaters are calculated to take in about twenty-five K per week. After rent and paying for projectionist as well as a manager and a couple of other odds and ends, we should have a net of twenty-two K. You will take your share of the deal off the top, and the balance will come back to me and my partners. I realize this is not a ton of money, but it will get a lot bigger as we open more theaters across Los Angeles. Once this is operating smoothly here, we will move on to the rest of California. As you can easily see, Jorge`, you can make more money than you ever imagined, and if we need more men, we will get them and pay for them from the proceeds of the theaters. I know it all sounds too good to be true, but you must take into account that we could have major battles on our hands. The Mob controls the theaters now and will not easily allow anyone to just walk in and open new ones without a real fight. I think once they realize they will have a battle on their hands and because they have so many other operations going, they will realize they don't have the time to fight about one small phase and will leave well enough alone."

"It's my turn to say 'wow!'" Jorge` said with a big smile on his face. "This is my big opportunity, Marcel. Thanks for giving me that chance. I promise I'll never let you down, never!"

"I appreciate that Jorge` and trust you will be my trusted associate. We begin at once, my friend," I said.

"We already have a problem and have to resolve this one first. I have here a name and phone number of guy who came by the theater today and in a roundabout way threatened my guys on the construction site. I want you to call him and see what he wants, and let's see if we can stop a war before it begins," I said.

"Okay, boss, let's call him," Jorge` said.

"Jorge`, please don't call me boss any longer. If I am to remain in the background just call me Marcel when we are alone, and avoid calling me anything when we are with other people, got it?" I said.

Jorge` called this guy Joseph while I listened on the extension in the other room.

"Can I speak to Joseph? This is Miguel calling," Jorge said.

"Yeah, this is Joseph. What can I do for you?" he said.

"You stopped by my place today and told my workers to stop working? What is your problem, man?" Jorge` said.

"Is that your place on Sherman Way?" Joseph said.

"Sure is. What business is it to you? And who are you to be asking me all this?" Jorge` said.

"Listen here, Miguel, my boss is in the movie business, and he don't want anyone opening up any X-rated joints. You get the message, don't you, man?" Joseph said.

"Well, that's great, man," Jorge` said. "But I do what I want, and I don't care what your boss said. I don't bother him, and he better not bother me. He can open as many places as he wants and so can I. I don't want to fight about it, but if you threaten my men or me again, I'll make sure it is the last threat you'll ever make, understand?" Jorge said.

"Look, man, you really don't want to go that route," Joseph said. "It could make things ugly for you, and I'm sure you really don't want that."

"Look, Mr. Joseph, if you want to meet me, that will be fine. How about setting up a meeting between your boss and me and we'll resolve this?" Jorge` said.

"I'm the guy you have to resolve this with. Now stop building or you'll be out of business by tomorrow," Joseph said half shouting.

"Fuck you, man. You want war, then you got it. You want peace, then have your boss call me. Here is my number." Jorge` gave him a number to call and hung up.

"No one's going to take my business away from me, no one," Jorge said` with a bad look in his eyes.

"Okay, partner, what do you want to do now?" I asked.

"You get going and establish our company, and I'll get the building we need. I also need to go to the theater today so that I can have men there tomorrow in case some shit may come down. I don't think these people will do anything that fast, but better be ready and take no chances," Jorge` said.

I took out five hundred K and gave it to him and said, "This is the start of it, my friend. Use whatever you need, and I'll get you more cash in a day or two. Let's get the show on the road. You can always reach me at that number you have—it is our only contact. I have yours, and soon we'll have an office number as well, let's go!" I said.

"First, let me call someone and let them know if someone should call for Miguel to handle it. I also want a few guys to stay at the theater tonight in case these fucks decide to start the war early," Jorge said as he picked up the phone and spoke with someone in Spanish. I did catch the name Miguel and Puta, but anything else I didn't quite understand. They speak so damn fast I wonder how they understand each other.

We left and went over to the theater where I introduced Jorge` as Miguel to Mike and explained that Miguel was the boss as he represents me at all times. I left them to discuss things and get the operation organized. I was very confident that we would now be able to defend ourselves and have an army that would be a force to be reckoned with. I did explain to Mike that Miguel will handle security, so he didn't have to worry about being in harm's way.

I also told Jorge to stay in touch with me at all times and keep me informed. I informed Jorge that I needed him to be my driver tomorrow as I have a meeting in Canoga Park at two P.M. I told him to dress the part, because from now on, I wanted him with me wherever I go.

"No one needs to know that we are partners, Jorge`. You stay close and you'll understand everything I do. So if something happens to me, you can easily take over. We are going to make a lot of money in this business, and I'll always take care of you. I'll introduce you to my other partners when the time is right. So get yourself a new suit and let's get the ball rolling," I said to him before I left the theater.

I called Marty at the office to explain what was going on. I told him about the threat Mike got at the theater and what Miguel did. I told him that I felt very confident with Miguel on our team. I explained how we were setting things up and how they were going to work from now on.

"We now have an army and will be able to operate without fear. I'll introduce you to Miguel tomorrow at the meeting as he will be with me. He is a big guy, but most important is that he is loyal and will protect us with his own life and can be trusted one hundred percent. I feel a lot better even though it will cost us a lot of money. It's just another cost of doing business. I know we will make plenty of money from the theaters, so the cost of "operation protect," although it will be steep at the very beginning, will be offset easily. I also feel that after the meeting tomorrow we will also get a small contribution from each company just to make certain that everyone is on the same page and fully protected. I really think I did well, Marty," I said.

Marty took a momentary pause and said, "Now don't go off feeling that you are invincible, and please, let's not bite off more than we can chew. I just don't want to get caught up in our own bullshit and then get whacked when we lose sight of the real picture. This is not a movie, Ron. It's the real thing, so let's be vigilant at all times. Okay, now that I've chewed you out let me tell you that I am with you one hundred percent as I always am and excited as well. We are now real," Marty shouted into the phone.

"Let's have a drink to our success tonight," I said. "I also wanted to talk to you about Mary Lou. She is very unhappy sitting at home. I told her I would talk to you about it. I explained that the resettlement takes time, but she didn't buy that. She needs to work, even if it is in a minor part. She won't be upset if she is not top billing. At least I don't think so," I said."

"I'll talk to her tonight, Ron. I promise," Marty said.

I called Stanley Schwartz and asked him to incorporate a company for me. I gave him a few names, and he said he would have to see if they were available. He would choose one of the names I gave him and use his office address temporarily for the company. He would also name his people as directors until such time we could elect proper people. He would get back to me tomorrow. He told me that it would cost about one K to get this done. I told him not to worry and to please do it as fast as he could. I then called Jorge` to see if things were on schedule and if he did receive a call from Joseph.

"Marcel, how are you doing? Yes, I heard from Joseph, and he wants to meet with me and his boss tomorrow at five thirty. I agreed. We'll meet in a very neutral place, and I think I can resolve this. In the meantime, we don't have to worry about anyone attacking the job tomorrow. Is there anything new on your end?" he asked.

"I'd like you to join me tonight. I want to introduce you to some people that are very important to me and, of course, very important to you as well. Meet me at my place around six, if that is okay with you," I said.

"No problem. I'll see you then, and I'll have the address of our new building as well. See you later," he said and hung up.

I spent another hour in my apartment where I brought the books from Marty's Company once a week to make certain that Kathy was doing her job properly. Marty was not a very good administrator, so I checked the books just to make certain things were right. I was not happy doing that job as I really didn't have the time for it and made a promise to find a proper accountant to take care of this stuff. It seemed like everything was going very nicely, and there was no need for me to hang around the apartment any longer. I went off to the gun range to spend a little time hitting some targets and making sure I was still sharp. I then went back home and called Natalia to let her know I would be at the house at about six thirty and would have a guest with me. I asked her to please make sure we had a few drinks and then we would go out for dinner. "We will go to Monty's Steak House and have a good time," I said.

Jorge` arrived at a little before six and looked great. He was wearing a black suit with a white shirt and a very nice tie. He looked the part in every way especially that he was a very handsome man. He was tall and looked like every muscle was taut and very well-toned. He was a very good example of a superman, and he was protecting me. I loved it and felt so comfortable with him. I was thrilled with my choice of people and that he was so responsible. This would work out real well for us all. We left my place and drove to Marty's house and arrived at six thirty.

"Hi, honey," I said to Natalia as she opened the door.

"This is Miguel. Miguel, this is Natalia, my sweetheart and love of my life."

"Pleased to meet you, Miguel. Please come in and make yourself comfortable. Mary Lou will be out in a minute, and Marty isn't home yet but should be here very soon," Natalia said.

I could see that Miguel was taken by Natalia's beauty and was doing his best to restrain himself when Mary Lou walked into the room dressed to kill. She was back on stage again and loved it.

"Hi, I'm Mary Lou and you are?" she said.

"Miguel," was all he could say; he was so taken with her.

"I would like to wait for Marty to arrive so that I can tell you all at once. Let's relax and have a drink and enjoy. It would be nice if we all got to know one another. We have a little time," I said.

A half hour later, Marty arrived. I introduced him to Miguel and suggested we all sit down and have a drink, and I would explain the entire plan to them.

"Okay, folks," I said. "I wanted to introduce you all to Miguel who is now the head of security for all of us and our operations. Your safety is his priority and will always be. There are some important rules that we must follow, and we must understand that we are taking this step because we have enemies who would like to do us harm. We are in a business that is very profitable. Because of this some unsavory characters would like to keep us out. We are in danger, and Miguel is here to make certain we are protected. Aside from this, there is the fact that we left some unfinished business back East, and it may come back to haunt us. It does not matter where the danger comes from. Miguel is here to eliminate that danger. I feel that we must fight fire with fire, and so I have taken it upon myself to engage Miguel, who will be the final word on all matters pertaining to security. I have tried to make sure that everyone involved is always protected including Miguel. I have not used his real name, because I feel it is better for his safety, and once again, it is to protect him and ourselves. We cannot keep anything secret from Miguel as he cannot effectively do his job if he doesn't know all the facts. All this is not to make you nervous but to help you understand the situation and ease the transition into a life that will require some getting used to. At no time is it Miguel's desire to screw with your freedom or your lives. It his job to serve you and protect you always. Please work with him. Okay, Miguel, the floor is yours."

Miguel stood at the end of the living room sofa, with both hands on the back of the couch. He made a very good impression because of his size and good looks and soft-spoken voice.

"It is a pleasure to meet you all and to try to get this program going with the least amount of inconvenience to anyone. Just try to evaluate how much your life is worth! A little cooperation will go a long way in helping to make sure that your lives are extended into old age. The way I see it, we have a number of problems that require remedies at once. The girls are movie stars, so they should not have any problems having security around them. From now on, there will be one bodyguard on duty whenever you go out. If you both go out in different directions, then please let me or your bodyguard know, and we'll put another one on duty for that period. I don't think you girls will have any problems, but we'll still keep a close eye on you both.

"No matter where you go now, you will be escorted and driven so that anyone who sees you will understand that you are both big stars. Security will not be something suspicious. It will be a part of success. Any questions so far?" Miguel said.

"I like the idea," Mary Lou said with a big smile. "I am now a really big star. Do I make up my schedule for each day with you Miguel or with Mr. Bodyguard?"

"I'll sit down with you girls a little later, and we'll work out the entire method of operation. Now for you, Marty. I think it would be best if you have a driver who will also serve as your bodyguard. This will give you the protection we are looking for and the appearance of success," Miguel said. "Of course, you will have your privacy, and if you should want to be with someone, just tell your driver, and it will all happen. You can drink to your heart's content now because you will never have to drive home. There is always a good side to everything," Miguel said with a little laughter. "You coordinate your schedule with your man daily. Let me know if you find something out of place or want to discuss anything privately. One precaution to all of you—you must be very careful what you discuss in front of anyone, even the people who are charged with your safety. You never know when one will turn against us for any reason whatsoever. Money is one of them. I'll vouch for all my men, but there can always be a turncoat. Of course, I certainly hope not, but being careful is a good precaution."

"If there is nothing more, please excuse Marty and me as we have to discuss some details with Miguel. Girls, please mix drinks for us. We are going to sit in the den," I said.

We went into the den and sat down with our drinks.

"Okay, Miguel, what happened with Joseph today?" I asked.

"Here is the story. I met him as he requested, and he claimed he works for Frank De Simone. You know who Frank is? If not, let me bring up to speed. He is the head honcho here in Los Angeles. He is the godfather of the Mob in Los Angeles and has absolute power. He is very strong and very smart and needs to protect his business assets but doesn't want any trouble. The last thing he wants is a war with the Mexican Mob. Frank wasn't there, but his right hand man, Jake Williams, was. They told me that they didn't want me to open any theaters in Los Angeles and would get very upset if I did not cooperate with them. They proposed an agreement that would settle the situation and allow us to proceed and avoid any type of battle. They will not open any theaters in the Valley, and we do not go into Los Angeles. I think this is a good deal, and it allows you to open as many as you want in the Valley and any other places in California. We won't have to fight a war, and things should move along very smoothly.

"Of course, they let me know that I will have to buy all the films from them because they have control over that end of the business. They will work with me because they are assuming I am attached to the Mexican Mob and they don't want trouble. I let them think whatever they want to and told them I would get back to them tomorrow. What do you guys think we should do?" Miguel said.

"I think you made a good deal, Miguel," Marty said.

"I like the deal," I said. "Let's go ahead with it, and we'll cross the film bridge when that comes to light. It will be hard to avoid some type of confrontation, but let's do so for as long as possible. Tomorrow I have a meeting with the film producers. Let's wait and see what happens there and then we can move forward."

"Okay, but how do we coordinate everything with Miguel? I want our lives to be as normal as possible, but agree that we have to have security," Marty said.

"First, let me add one more thing," I said. "I promised Miguel two percent of the theater operation. As long as you are loyal and remain true to us, you will always be a partner. If you decide one day to get up and leave or go to work for the Mob or anyone else that is a direct competitor of ours, then you will not get your two percent any longer and probably will get killed instead."

"Guys, listen to me," Miguel said. "Let's get serious about things. I want to organize this in the best way possible and make sure that we are always true to each other as a team and a family. It's my job to protect you all, and I will need your trust and complete confidence in my ability. I may be a Mexican, and you might have some negative opinion of Mexicans, but if you do, you have made a grievous error with me," Miguel said.

"Hey, guy, wait a minute, man. We don't and never have thought Mexicans are any different than anyone else, so get off that route. I came to you and gave you my word and my confidence. I stood at your side when you needed a little help. I didn't care if you were Mexican or anything else, and I still don't. I sure hope that is enough proof to show our unbiased feelings about you or anyone else!" I said angrily. "Now let's get down to business, and enough of this ethnic bullshit."

"Okay, sorry about that. I just felt I'd clear the air," Miguel said with a little smirk. "All right, I will organize the men and get things rolling. As of tomorrow morning, everyone will be assigned their bodyguard, and we'll work out the kinks from there. All my guys will be carrying at all times. You never know when they'll need it. They are all professional and will do everything to be respectful and take good care of you. Please leave everything in my hands, and everything will be all right," Miguel said as he headed for the door. "I'll see you tomorrow.

"We have to coordinate tomorrow's schedule. I do not want anyone of you going anywhere without your bodyguards. Is that clear? To make the first day a lot easier, we will meet you all here at eight P.M. After that we will expect you to make sure your daily schedule is organized each day. Marcel, I'll see you at the same time. Have a good night and be careful. By the way, if anyone feels uncomfortable with me or with anything I have said, then speak up now. If anyone feels threatened for any reason at all no matter what time it may be or how trivial you think it might be, please call the number on the card, and I'll be here with my men within fifteen minutes. I am your brother, your friend, and your protector, and I take my responsibility very seriously. So please make sure you do the same. I'm here for you," Miguel said as he left.

This has been a very exhausting day with the meeting of Miguel and the arrangements for our security. The meetings and the preparations required brought back to our minds how much danger we were all in. In a way it was good as it acted as a reminder that we must be true to each other and not forget even for one moment that danger was always nearby. I was certain tomorrow would not be any easier, but with the addition of Miguel and his crew, I feel a lot more secure and confident that our chances of success are getting better all the time. Taking this route sure beats being chased, and I'm much happier doing the chasing. I know I am going to have a good night's sleep tonight!

Tuesday, November 19, 1957

My doorbell rang at eight P.M. It was Miguel, right on time and ready for his first day on the job. I felt energized and at ease.

"Good morning, boss. Ready for a great day?" Miguel asked. Miguel nodded and raised his hand and six large, very well-dressed guys stepped out of two vehicles and walked toward the apartment front door.

"I would like to introduce you to everyone, but I won't at this time. You'll forget their names, and it isn't really important. What I want you to see are the little pins with the red head on. That pin will be worn on their right corner of their collar as you can see. I have had these made especially for us so that identification will be easy. If you see someone who does not have a pin, they don't belong with us and danger is upon us. The red dot on top of the pin is made of lead that is colored. No one is aware of how the head is constructed, so if you ever feel concerned, just take your fingers and gently press the red dot and you will feel it give. Lead is soft, and if anyone is copying our pin, they will not know that the head is constructed that way. If that happens, don't do anything to tip the phony off. Just let me know as fast as possible, and we'll eliminate the infiltrator. I did not tell anyone of my men how the pin is made. So if they try to duplicate it, they will most likely do it by copying it as it looks and not using the lead. It's just a precaution, and of course, I hope it works and keeps us all safe. My men, as you can see, are waiting outside for my instructions so they cannot hear anything about the pins. Please keep this information very private as your security is at stake.

"All I ask is that you cooperate with me and you will always be safe. My people are here to protect you, so please do not try to change their job instructions in any way at all," Miguel was telling me as Marty and the girls arrived. I immediately saw the reaction of the guards when they took a look at the girls. I imagined that they all wanted to be assigned the task of taking care of them; their eyes gave them away. Miguel spent the next half hour explaining the rules to everyone and the procedures of the task force. It seemed that everyone was pleased with the arrangement as smiles appeared on everyone's faces. The atmosphere was a very relaxed one, and I knew I had hit a home run!

"Are we all done, man? Let's go for a run and then we can get started," I said with a big smile on my face.

Miguel looked at me with a weird smirk and said, "You run, I drive. Let's go."

I didn't think Miguel would run dressed as he was in a black suit with a white shirt and a nice conservative tie. His shoes were so well shined you could see yourself in them; he really went all out to be the best, and I appreciated it a lot. I ran twelve miles and enjoyed every mile more and more as Miguel drove a little behind me. I felt very comfortable and safe. I showered and shaved and dressed in a nice suit, ready for the day.

"Hey, boss, I want to explain something to you about the pin. If you look at the pin, you will see that it shines like it has a battery. Well, it doesn't have any battery but has a special paint on it that makes it shine. If you do not know this, you would never see the illumination, but now that you are aware, can you see it?" Miguel said.

"Now that you have told me, I can see it clearly. It's amazing I didn't see it before. Wow! That is really something, Miguel. Did you tell the others about this?" I said. "No, I didn't, and I won't because I don't want to scare them. I will count on you to explain it to them when you are alone with them. Here, take one and keep it as your demonstrator. Give it back to me after you have told everyone. Okay, Mr. Marcel, let's get the day started," Miguel said as we headed for the door.

Our first stop was the theater where we checked on Mike's progress.

"How are things going, Mike?" I asked. "You have met Miguel. He will be my driver. You will be seeing a lot of him. If Miguel tells you to do something, please consider it as if it was coming directly from me. You do it—no questions asked. We have taken care of the problem with Joseph, so there won't be any further things to worry about. When do you think we will be ready? I want to look at another location and set up the deal with a target date. A little help from you won't hurt in setting a schedule."

"Well, I can't really say. Give me another day or two, and I'll give you a date. We are working as hard and as fast as we can. This I can assure you," Mike said.

"When I look at a new location, I want you along with me. If you say no to the spot based on construction difficulties, then I pass on the location. I also want a time frame for each theater. For example, Mike, each theater will take five weeks from start to finish, so I need to know if this is realistic or not. Of course, that is just an example. You get the idea, don't you?" I said. I want to open twelve new theaters this coming year. Can we do it?"

"Okay, Marcel. I understand what you want. Just give me a couple of days and you will have all the answers," Mike said.

"Okay, Mike, see you later. We got a few meetings to attend today. Hey, Mike, you're doing a great job. Thanks," I said as we walked out of the theater to our car.

As we drove away, Miguel said, "Marcel, please don't act any different when I tell you this, but I think there is a car that is following us. I noticed a black Caddie that was behind us when we arrived at the theater, and now it's still there. Don't look back, please. I don't want them to know we have spotted them. I'll make a few turns and see if they stick with us, then I'll know for sure. I hate to be paranoid, so just sit back. You're in good hands with me, so don't worry about a thing."

We drove along for a little while when Miguel made a wide turn off Sherman Way onto Corbin and proceeded north until we came to Nordhoff and then he took a turn left and proceeded to De Soto and pulled into a parking spot next to Parthenia. All along, the Caddie stayed with us; there was no doubt that we were being watched. I say watched because they did not take any precautions to keep out of sight.

"It looks like they want us to know, Miguel. It does not smell like a hit at all. I think someone just wants to know what we do and where we live. What do you think we ought to do?" I said.

"I think I should walk over and ask them who they are and what the fuck they want. Let me do that now so that we get rid of this vermin on our back before we go to the meeting," Miguel said.

"Okay, Miguel, let's do it!" I said.

Miguel got out of the car and walked directly to the black caddie and knocked on the driver's window. In a few minutes, he returned to the car and said, "These are Ralph's guys. They are just making sure we keep our end of the deal by keeping an eye on us. They'll back off now that I have assured them we are sticking with the deal. I told them if they want a war, we'll give to them or just back off, now! They made a phone call and told me they were leaving and it wouldn't happen again."

"What a line of shit, but I am glad they are gone. We'll have to stay very sharp and keep our wits about us and watch to see if anyone else is following us. Remember we have a meeting at Essence Films today. It's on Osborne Street. I gave you the exact address, didn't I?" I said.

"I know Marcel. We'll be there on time. We are only a few blocks away. Relax!" Miguel said as he drove on to Essence Films. Miguel parked the car in their parking lot adjacent to their offices.

"Let me walk you in and announce that Marcel Lamond is here to see Mr. Calvin Powers," Miguel said.

"Okay, let's play this to the hilt, old buddy. You are to be with me at all times, even in the meeting. You will stand in the background and just listen. This should send a message that I am not someone to be fucked with," I said as I got out of the car.

We walked into the lobby and could not believe the opulent scene that greeted us. The lobby was filled with miniature palm trees; each one perfectly maintained. There were two sofas that looked as comfortable as your own bed along with a table in the center filled with magazines and sheets that announce coming attractions. On the wall were framed photos of some of their stars. Each one had a light positioned on it to make the star look almost real. In the center of the lobby was a fountain that erupted every forty-five seconds with a display of colored lights that made the water action spectacular. At the far end of the lobby, there was a desk with the most gorgeous woman sitting there in very revealing clothes. She was very beautiful and knew it.

"Can I help you," she said.

"Mr. Marcel Lamond to see Mr. Calvin Powers. He is expecting us," Miguel said in a most polite way. She pressed a button on the telephone and then looked up and said, "Please have a seat. Mr. Powers will be right with you."

We waited a minute or two when the door to the left opened and out walked Calvin Powers. We both stood as we stared at Calvin; he was about 6' tall and was easily two hundred and twenty pounds with blond hair and big blue eyes.

"Welcome to Essence. It's a pleasure to meet you. I'm Calvin Powers," he said as he extended his hand. I took his hand in mine, and it felt like I was a little pea in a very big pod.

"I'm Marcel Lamond. A pleasure to meet you. This is Miguel, my assistant," I said as I extracted my tiny little hand from Calvin's grip. Miguel extended his hand and at least was equal with Calvin.

"Follow me, gentlemen. Most of the people are already here."

We followed him along a long corridor until the very end where he opened the door into a large room with a very long table and chairs. There were a lot of folks sitting around the table when we walked in, and they all got up and waited while Calvin went to the head of the table and said, "I would like to introduce you to Marcel Lamond and his assistant, Miguel. Gentlemen, please introduce yourselves one at a time," Calvin said.

One by one, they introduced themselves and their companies.

"A pleasure to meet you. I'm Frank Judd of Backdoor Productions. Welcome to this meeting. I'm looking forward to hearing from you."

"Hi, I'm Perry Stanford of Cherry Babes Features. A pleasure to meet you."

"Hi there, Marcel. I'm Luke Remo of Stairway to Sluts Films."

"A pleasure, Marcel. I'm Marty Loomis, CEO and owner of OTF. Let's get the meeting started."

"Hold on a moment, guys. We have to wait for Irv and Steve to arrive. They should be here any second." Just as Calvin said that the door opened and in walked Irv and his partner, Steven Paul.

"Sorry, we are late," Irv said.

"I'm Irving Willets, and this is my partner, Steven Paul, from Pumped-Up Films. Let's get started."

He sat down, and so did everyone else, including myself, as Calvin finally stood up and announced, "This meeting was called in response to Irv Willet's request that it is time the adult industry turned the corner into the legitimate business market. The adult industry generates millions of dollars in revenue each year and is growing faster than any other business in today's marketplace. We need to come out of shadows and declare ourselves a legitimate industry and that is where Marcel Lamond comes into the picture, so to speak," he said as he continued. "We want to hear what Marcel has to offer in the way of some sound business moves that will help put the industry on the map. Up to now, we have had to do what the Mob wants, and we are given a fraction of what our films are worth. There is a new medium that is growing bigger and bigger each day, television, and we are shut out because we have to operate underground. We have to worry about the Mob on one side and feds on the other. It is hard to defend an industry when you are dodging attacks from all sides. This meeting will enlighten us about coming out of the dark and being what we can be—proud producers of adult films in every aspect.

"We have to set standards that will be adhered to and a governing body that will police the industry making us legitimate. Mr. Marcel Lamond is here to address the beginning of that procedure and a possible start toward that goal. It is my pleasure to present to you our guest speaker, Mr. Marcel Lamond."

"Thank you, gentlemen, for inviting me to speak with you today and allowing me to outline a plan that I believe has merits toward your ultimate goals. It is my pleasure to propose a few things that will indeed help put this industry on the map once and for all. Of course, all changes from the status quo will require some sacrifice, hard work, and a lot of brain power. Most importantly, you must work together and trust one another even though you are all competitors. It is natural that each one of you wants to be number one in this field, and that is acceptable as it exists in every industry, but to establish the legitimate aura that is needed your cooperation will be required. If you can put any animosity aside and respect each one's position to be number one, then we can achieve the results required to be up there as one of the top industries in the United States.

"If you study the history of the legitimate film companies, you will see that although they competed tooth and nail, they also innovated and made their industry more profitable. There is so much business out there that the pie can easily be sliced in everyone's favor. The profits are very big, and with mutual trust and cooperation you will all become very wealthy as long as you remain united. If you decide to fight among yourselves, then you will all be losers in the end. The Mob is a perfect example as they always fight each other for a bigger piece of the pie, and in the end they spend their assets on this war, and their business gets more difficult to control each day. One day, their final time will come, and they will have nothing but jail time or death. The Mob doesn't use long-term planning—this is a major mistake for them. We must not use the same logic, and success will be ours. In time, this industry will grow to a billion dollar a year or more in sales.

"We can and will rule this market by sharing and working as a team to make the adult industry strong and, most importantly, accepted. My business plan is very simple and can be implemented only if you all cooperate and work toward that goal. We have to set standards that will be followed in order to make this industry acceptable to the general population. These standards can be agreed to by establishing a committee that will help set them up.

"In the first instance, you will need a bank that will allow you to operate openly and do business like any other enterprise. Right now the only way you can use a bank is to lie about your operation and this is unacceptable. I can offer you this as I will take you to a bank that will do just that. You will be able to receive and give out funds as well as borrow like any other company. You will be able to justify your very existence, because you will be legitimate. Even the feds will not be able to screw with you about illegal business practices, and because you will have paid your taxes as any other business does now, you can keep real records.

"This I do for you not because I am a philanthropist but because I, like you, am a businessman. I am not greedy, but I am astute enough to understand that there is a price for everything. When I establish my method of operation, you will find that my reward is fair and with a long-term result. Therefore, I propose the following in repayment for my arranging the most important steps to success for all of you. I want you to give me first right of refusal on all your new releases for a period of three years. I will give you a fair market value for each release, or you may share in the revenue derived from showing the film in my movie theater chain. I am not in the movie making business. I am in the movie showing business and need the best first run new releases to keep my audience, your meal tickets, coming into my theaters. If you choose to be part of the movie chain, you will receive forty percent of all income derived from the box office. If you indeed made a good film and the stars are of the quality that will keep the viewers coming back to theater, then your share could easily be many hundreds of thousands of dollars for each release. The share of the revenue is very simple-forty percent of the take from each showing of your film. If you are concerned that the theater receipts will be doctored, then you are all fools. As the owner of the theaters, I haven't any time or any desire to scheme to change the receipts and lose out in the long run. When running a chain of theaters, it would be foolhardy to attempt such a scheme as each theater is run by a manager who is concerned with being honest.

"Gentleman, the odds are all in your favor and will bring you more money for each release than you have ever seen. It will also eliminate the paltry sum you now receive under your distribution deal in place. Of course, you can still sell your new release to your old sources but only four weeks later. And in four weeks you are still in the marketplace and getting additional revenue along with the rest of the world distribution. The choice is yours, gentlemen! Why you may ask do I ask for a three-year term. Let me explain that as well. At the present time, I have but one theater and that one is only under construction. It is located on Sherman Way and Independence Avenue and should be open by January first. I plan on opening twelve new theaters this coming year, across the entire country and look forward to having over one hundred theaters working within four years.

"I can try to open more but cannot guarantee that the locations and permits will come quick enough. I plan on opening adult stores complete with peep shows across the country and will be one of your best customers. I plan on implementing a revenue-sharing plan for all my peep shows as well. All I can say is that the profits are far beyond anyone's imagination. To show my good faith, I will set you all up with the bank at once and will keep you informed on my progress with the theaters. Of course, you can still sell your films to the Mob or anyone else, but only four weeks after I have shown them in my theaters. You will now be able to get maximum dollars from the Mob for your films as you will not need any funding from them. I suggest you start a schedule to have regular monthly meetings to discuss your progress and to air out any complaints you may have with one another. I will not attend your meetings unless you invite me to do so, because you have a definite problem that concerns me.

"I estimate that the box office on a good film should be in the neighborhood of taking in ten K per week, thus a four K return per week for a good film. Even if my figures are wrong and you can only bring in half that amount, you will be earning far more per film than ever before. Of course, this number will increase as more theaters open. The earnings I have stated are for one theater only. I realize that the earnings are not too high when one theater is involved, but as I said earlier, you must look at the long term. If you : receive only two K per week on your film, you will have easily received in excess of ten K after five weeks. Now in the long-term all you need to do is multiply this by the amount of the theaters now open. I leave the math to you, and I know it far exceeds any amount you are now getting. If any of the companies that are represented here today decide not to participate, that will be acceptable to me, but I will point out that at no time in the future when the theater chain grows will those who opt out will be able to have your films shown in my theaters. Please understand that this is not a threat. It is a fact of life and good business practice. If my plan is not good enough for you today, then I'm afraid it will never be good for you and will demonstrate your shortsightedness.

"This is about it for now. Please let me know how you feel about this and if you are in or not. By the way, I am prepared to place ten K in every company's bank account who agrees to these terms and conditions. This will be an advance payment for your first film. If you do not think this is a show of good faith, gentlemen, then I think you should turn down my offer.

"I also want to be candid and aboveboard at all times. There is a risk that the Mob might try to use some muscle. They will not be very happy losing a market that they control. Right now, they take in millions on your films, and you are lucky to get ten K for each one. I have taken steps to protect myself from their strong-arm methods. I have recruited my own force and now travel in safety and with confidence that anything they may throw at me I can handle. Miguel is my security chief and gentlemen. You are welcome to use our force if you so desire. The costs involved in maintaining a force of this sort is not cheap at all. It gets a lot cheaper if we all participate in funding this security force. I urge you to think about it as there is no use in being the richest man in the graveyard. Please direct any security concerns you may have to Miguel, and I'm sure he can take care of them. That is it for today. I will await your answers. Please try to be objective and quick.

"I am moving ahead and would like to be part of this industry with you, but rest assured, I will move forward without you if I have to. It is a lot easier to make a deal with all the film companies now while the industry is still small, but I can assure you I will negotiate with individual companies if I must. I'll be happy to answer any questions you may have. Thank you for your time," I sat down.

The first one to address the proposition was Luke Remo. "Tell me, Marcel, why are you so generous to us all? Isn't there a hidden motive here? How are you different than the Mob? I would like to know just where the catch is.? All this is too good to be true, and when I think something is too good, I worry," he said.

"A very good set of questions. I sure hope I can answer them all for you and everyone else here! In the first instance, I don't think you can term it as generosity. This is, as far as I'm concerned, a good straightforward business deal. I'm taking advantage of a situation that has affected me as it has you. I have not told you this, but I was threatened by the Mob about the theater business. A man named Frank De Simone sent out some people to warn me and my workers that there will be trouble if I open a theater. After setting up my security force and meeting with the Mob guys, it was agreed that I will not open any theaters in Los Angeles and they won't open any in the Valley. They also let me know that all adult films are controlled by them, so I will be dealing with them like it or not. This is not what I like and will not be threatened by anyone especially scum like Frank De Simone. I met Irv Willets and asked him if he wanted to become legitimate, and he said yes and here I am. If you don't trust me, then forget the deal. There is nothing done yet that would compromise anyone. I have not revealed which bank and who my sources are, so if you do not like the deal, you can walk out on it now. I feel insulted that you would try to put me and my business plan on the same level as the Mob. In the first instance, I never threatened anyone and have never used force or ever will to make a competitor yield to my wishes. I will use force when force is used against me, and I do so with regret. I don't use any strong-arm methods as demonstrated in my plans and there never will be any. It is inconceivable that I should be compared to the Mob at any time. I am smart enough to know I need you guys as much as you need me. It's not too good to believe as you say. It is a great fit, and only you guys can queer the deal. Let me emphasize it once again. I don't guarantee that there won't be danger, but nothing comes easy. I don't guarantee that my theaters will all be successful, but I am going to open them and give it a try. I am not out to screw you. I am out to make you and me rich," I said.

Marty stood up and said, "Marcel, when can you arrange the bank? I also want to point out that I was muscled by the Mob when I said I won't be making any movies for a little while. I'll leave the names out, but I was threatened to have my legs broken if I didn't work with them. This is my way out and I'm in. I'll sit down with Miguel and arrange security for my company and I'm doing it now."

"Guys, if you haven't been threatened yet, you will be, and only through a combined effort can we kick their ass. I urge you to get it together," I said.

"Thanks for everything, Marcel. We'll get back to you shortly. Thanks for coming. It was a pleasure to meet you. I look forward to a profitable relationship," Calvin said.

Miguel and I took the cue and got up to leave. We shook hands with everyone, and Miguel left his number in case anyone wanted to get in touch.

We left and drove off to my place.

"I think that went well, Miguel. Don't you think so?" I said as we drove along.

"Yes, sir, Marcel. I believe they will all come around. They can't afford not to. There will be a war soon, and we'll earn every penny. It won't be pretty, I promise you that," Miguel said.

Wednesday, November 20, 1957

When I woke up at six thirty, Miguel was in my apartment ready for a new day.

"Good morning, Marcel. Hope you are well. I think we will hear from the boys today about the security arrangements. I will be ready for them if they call. I think a payment of one K per month for each company will do. I feel that this amount is really very reasonable as it guarantees each company the security they need in the event they are attacked in any way at all. I will make certain to give them a real strong and loyal group of guys that will be available at all times. If anyone wants full-time bodyguards they can advise me, and I will make them a special price. The plan I am offering them will assure them protection if anyone fucks with them. The owners of the companies will not have to deal with any of the Mob or anyone else who presents a security risk. The owners will direct them to deal with us," Miguel said.

"I think that you should only ask for five hundred a month. Once they get used to paying for protection in the same manner they pay for insurance, you can always increase the price based on additional costs and dangers present. If you ask too much at the very start, they will run the other way and might feel we are as bad as the Mob," I said as I put on my shorts and laced up my running shoes and headed for the door.

"Let's run a little and see if we can work off the pounds I seem to put on after eating all the crap I do each day. I want to stop at the theater and see how Mike is doing and then over to see Marty. Okay, we're off!"

I finished my run and showered and dressed for the day. I took out my gun and made sure it was loaded and placed it in a holster that I wore when I left the house. Miguel was also armed, but I just could not risk not being ready for anything. Today I had a feeling that something was going to happen even though I was not a psychic!

We went over to the theater to see Mike. "How are things today, Mike?" I said.

Mike seemed a little distracted today, and his look was not the usual happy-guy look.

"I'm very concerned about trouble, Marcel. I have a wife and kids and don't want anything to happen to them. If I was by myself, I wouldn't care. I can kick their asses. It's troubling me, and I really want this gig with you because it would guarantee my living for the next few years. What shall I do, please tell me!" Mike said.

"Listen, Mike, and listen to me well. You have nothing to worry about. This I can assure you with all my heart. Miguel will take care of things, and all you have to do is do your work. If anyone bothers you, refer them to Miguel, and then forget it. I don't want you to refuse to cooperate with anyone. Just refer them to Miguel and then forget about it. If you follow this line, you will never have trouble with anyone ever, I promise you!" I said.

I asked Mike why his concern was so strong today. I asked him if something happened that we are not aware of.

"No, Marcel, nothing happened today, but you know what happened the other day. I know how the Mob works, and if they can't get to me, they will use whatever means they can to get what they want. This leaves my wife and kids very vulnerable if trouble was to take place. I was just worrying about it and wanted to let you know," Mike said.

We inspected the work done to date. The place was starting to look like a theater. Soon it would be ready and money would start to flow in our direction. We then went to see Marty as I wanted to get his feedback as to what happened at the meeting after Miguel and I left. We now entered Marty's office through a private entrance directly from the street. No one would know that we were visiting Marty, and no one would know when we came or left.

"Hi, Marcel, how are doing today? That was a great presentation yesterday. I'm certain they will all jump on the bandwagon especially after the meeting we had after you left. They were impressed with your offer of $10K in their accounts and the fact that you were willing to put your words in writing and back it all up. They are very concerned about a Mob war as they don't know what to expect. You understand these guys are really legit and have never faced any adversity. Of course, they are in the porn business and expect problems both legal and illegal. In regard to the Mob, they only know what they have seen in movies and read in the newspapers. I explained to them that these assholes are human like anyone else except for one difference—we are fighting for our survival and they are just worker bees. The big bosses never get their hands dirty, so the guys who are out there will run the other way after a few of their guys get blown away. I told them that I will have to go out of business if I don't get help from someone like Marcel. I can't continue to make movies and get next to nothing for them from a bunch of greedy pricks like the Mob. The same thing applies to each one of them. If I go along with Marcel, I will take the sixty/forty deal and take in a lot of money—a lot more than I get now and, most importantly, I will be free to do what I want. I will be able to expand my market to Canada and Europe and make more bucks. Having a bank that will work with me will open the whole world to my company, and in a year from now, I'll be a very solid operation with nothing but money. This industry is changing, and soon we will be in markets, we have not dreamed about. There will be new equipment that will make making movies easier as well as ways of marketing them.

"Money will flow from every corner of the land if we act now. If we don't, the Mob will reap all the benefits, and without doubt, they will put us out of business very soon. The Mob is so greedy that they always screw things up, and in the end, they choke the very life out of the people that feed them. We will work with the feds to make the industry legitimate. Just think about the mail order business. What a gold mine, and we need the feds to trust us if we are to succeed. I believe they understand the whole concept and are ready to move forward. I expect that you will get many phone calls today, Miguel, to get the security end started. I think Irv will call me to arrange a meeting with the bank and to sign an agreement. I'm so excited, Marcel. I think we are on the way to success. Oh, one thing they asked me, Marcel. How do I know we can trust you when it comes to an accurate count on the split? I answered as follows: I trust Marcel one hundred percent as he has no reason to screw anyone of us. Our films will keep his theaters in the forefront and our pockets filled. Let's say he skims some off the top, and instead of receiving the full forty percent, we only get thirty percent and that amounts to thousands of dollars. Isn't that more than we get now? Yet I don't think it is in his interests to alter the records nor does he have the time. The more theaters he opens, the better his record keeping must be so that he doesn't get screwed by his own employees. No, I don't think he would shortchange us in any way. If his word is not of the highest quality, then we should not make any deal with him. He is the only one that has opened the door to us and has given us the opportunity to make or break our own destiny. The Mob only wants to fill their pockets, and they don't give shit what happens to us. Look at Bijou Films. We know it's their operation, and what do they produce? Shit and more shit and half the porn stars won't work for them, because their pay is never as agreed. You can't take the gangster mentality out of those folks. Marcel has no desire to own our companies. He only wants you to succeed! I'm in as of right now!" Marty said.

"Wow! That was some selling job. Thanks, old buddy. But you know, Marty, you are right in everything you say. I sure hope these guys are not blinded by their own egos," I said.

Miguel had just walked back into the room and said, "I received two calls, one from Perry Stanford and the other from Luke Remo. They want to get together as soon as possible and get the security situation set up. I made an appointment to meet at Luke's studio at three o'clock this afternoon. I'll have my assistant stay with you Marcel while I'm away."

"I told you they'd call Marcel. Yes, sir, I think they all will, and we will be in business very soon," Marty said with a big smile and the I-told-you-so look on his face!

"I guess you were right, Marty. I'm getting out of here now before your ego inflates anymore. I'll call you later. How's the new film coming along?" I said.

We left Marty to his script writing and went over to my apartment. When we arrived, Natalia was there waiting for me.

"Hi, darling, how's your day going?" she asked. "So far so good. How are you doing?" I asked as I kissed her on the lips. Before she could speak, Miguel jumped in and said, "Excuse me, sweetheart. I have a few things I have to discuss with Marcel before I leave. You can stay. I have no secrets from you. Marcel, I think we should be serious about car bombs. We have to get some equipment that will detect any explosive device on the car. I don't want to see you or anyone in the organization getting into a car without them being swept clean, daily! I also want each day carefully scheduled so that I can make arrangements to have security on hand at all times. No sudden trips. These are just precautions, but they are very important to us all," Miguel said as he headed for the door. "My man, Hector, will be outside your door until I get back. Please do not leave the apartment until I return," Miguel said as he left. Natalia and I spent the rest of the afternoon making love and enjoying the quiet of the afternoon.

It was after six when Miguel returned, "So how did it go, my friend?" I said.

"Really well better than I expected. While I was at Luke's place, Calvin called as well as Irv, so I invited them over. I thought it would be easier to do it all at once. They all agreed to the five hundred per month without any complaint. They wanted to know what I thought of you, and, of course, I told them that I had never met a finer person than Marcel Lamond. Everything he has promised he has delivered. Gentlemen, you could not have made a better agreement. You all have my phone number. Please call me with any concerns and security questions no matter what time of the day or night. It does not matter how small your question may be. We are dealing with security and must always be vigilant. Call me always. I want to remind you that the war has not yet begun, but it will, and we must be ready, and as long as we are, we will win," Miguel said.

We went for dinner at the Whitehorse Inn on Roscoe Boulevard in Northridge. All though it was more of bar than a really good restaurant, it was known for its roast beef. Miguel joined us for dinner as we wanted to enjoy our successes. We drank and ate and celebrated the fruits of today. We got home at ten thirty and called it a night.

Thursday, November 21, 1957

I was up as usual and got ready for my run. I was thinking that my exercise routine was far too predictable if someone was looking to whack me. I figured I'd better discuss it with Miguel as it would be foolish to allow anyone to get me so easily. Miguel arrived at seven just as I was about to leave the apartment for my run.

"Good morning, Marcel. Don't you think you should wait for me to arrive before you start running?" he said.

"I was just thinking about that. I think we should alter the schedule in case anyone is watching and keep them guessing. We must always look at how the Mob operates: Vincent Gigante tried to get Frank Costello in the lobby of his apartment building in Manhattan; on June seventeenth, Frank Scalise was gunned down by Vincent Squilante; and then on October twenty-five, two masked gunmen shot and killed Anastasia in the Park Sheraton Hotel Barber shop. You know what these hits have in common, Miguel?" I asked. "No, I don't, except they were all Mob bosses and probably did something the other bosses didn't like," he said.

"That might be the reason they killed them, but the one common thread here is that they were killed so easily because they followed a routine. Costello escaped with a head wound because Gigante was a lousy shot—the others weren't so lucky. They all made it easy to be picked off, because they did the same thing day in and day out. We must learn by this and make sure that our schedule is a mystery to anyone who is watching. We must also make sure that no one but you and I know the schedule, because you never know who within your own organization will try to betray you one day. Another thing, Miguel, we can never be on time for another appointment just to be on the safe side. We'll either be late or early but never on time. If this sounds like I am overly paranoid, you bet I am, Miguel. You bet I am," I said. "No run today, maybe later but not now. Let's go to the gun range and fire a few rounds so that we both stay sharp. We'll plan the rest of the day later. Let's go."

"Okay, boss, I agree with you one hundred percent, but don't you think you should change into something else?" he said.

"I didn't realize I was still wearing my shorts," I said as I laughed at myself. "I guess I was so wrapped up in this that I forgot, sorry. I'll just be a few minutes, and we can get on our way. Thanks, Miguel, for understanding," I said as I went into my room to change.

We spent the next two hours at the firing range and honing our skills. If those assholes wanted me, they will have to fire better shots than me. I'll bet most of those guys don't train like we do. "Where are we off to now, Marcel?" Miguel asked.

"I want to check on the theater, but I have been doing so every morning, so let's stop by later in the afternoon. Let's take a ride to Santa Barbara. I want to scope the place out for a theater. It really is the perfect place to open, and it's not in Los Angeles, so we are keeping our word," I said. I want to open across the state as well as a few more in the Valley. Tomorrow we can look around the Valley for some more locations."

We took a drive to Santa Barbara and looked around. The area was just beautiful and filled with sites that were breathtaking. It is a high-priced place for the rich to play in. It is also a big college town with a lot of very well-to-do students. I decided to stop in Carpentaria and liked this town a lot.

It wasn't a big place, but it was discreet enough to accommodate an adult theater and give folks the entertainment they need. People would fill the theater here, because it is not too far from Santa Barbara and will not offend anyone. I decided to make some calls in the next few days and see if there were any locations available. There were plenty of other locations including Sacramento, Bakersfield, and truck stops along route 5 that would stay filled with patrons. Yes, sir, the theater business was going to be a very lucrative and successful operation.

We headed back to Los Angeles and stopped by Oxnard to check out the area. I liked the place a lot and told Miguel that we should actively find a location here and get it open as soon as possible.

We left Oxnard and passed by the theater.

"Hey, Mike, what's up?" I asked.

"Nothing much, but we are moving along real well. Take a look at the place. It will be ready for the seats by Monday, and I think you can start bringing in the projection equipment by the end of next week. We will start painting tomorrow and then the place will look different in a few days. We better make sure our security is tight. You don't want to bring in equipment and leave the place open to thieves. How about getting an alarm company to install a system?" Mike said.

"That is your job, Mike. You should organize this with Miguel and get the best deal you can with the best of protection."

"Oh, by the way," Mike said. "Marty called and told me to tell you to call him when you get here."

"Listen, Mike, anytime Miguel or Marty call, you make sure you tell me right away. Don't wait or forget. You understand me?" I said.

"I'm sorry, Marcel," Mike said. "I'll make sure that they are always priority."

I called Marty at once, "Sorry, Marty, Mike didn't tell me you called when I first came in. What's up, pal?" I said.

"I need to see you and Miguel at once. I'll meet you at The Shed in ten minutes," Marty said and hung up.

"Okay, Miguel, we have to go. Mike, Miguel will take care of the alarm, and I'll see you tomorrow," I said as I left the building.

"There is something wrong with Marty. He doesn't usually get stirred up, but I could tell in his voice that he is worried about something. Let's go, Miguel. We're meeting him at The Shed," I said as I wondered what it was. It could be that Carmine had reared his ugly head. It could be a lot of things, but I decided to wait the few minutes and hear it from Marty. While we were driving, I told Miguel that security was his job and that included whatever we needed at the theaters. I told him to handle it and do whatever he thought was necessary to protect our investments. We arrived in less than ten minutes and went right into The Shed. We spied Marty sitting in a booth at the rear of the place; he looked nervous and agitated. "Hey, Marty, what's up?" Miguel said. The waitress came over and we ordered drinks.

"Okay, Marty, what is the problem? Come on, out with it. Let's hear it," I said.

"Carmine has sent two hit men here to get me," Marty said.

"How do you know this?" I said.

"I got a call from Irv Willets asking me if I had ever heard of Larry Robbins. I asked him why, and he said his Mob man, Alfredo, called and asked him. When he asked Alfredo what it was all about, he was told that this guy owes some people in New York a lot of money and these guys are out here to collect. He then asked Irv if there had been any new companies that opened up in the last month or so. Irv claims he said he didn't know of any new adult company that opened in the last month, but he is scared. He thinks they will stop in at every place and put two and two together. Between us, Marcel, once they see the girls, they'll know it's me. What shall we do?" he asked with a very frightened look in his eyes.

"Don't worry about a thing," Miguel said. "I'll place a man with you at all times until we get rid of these two guys. You may be in a little danger right now, but I have your back. Killing these two guys will send a clear message to your friend, Carmine. Now let's get the logistics straight, and from now on you are protected twenty-four hours a day anywhere you may go." Miguel got up and went to the pay phone to make a call. He returned in a few minutes and said, "A man is on his way. He'll be here in less than ten minutes, and he will be with you until he is relieved. Rest easy, my friend. Everything will work out, I promise you!" We ordered another round of drinks and waited about fifteen minutes. The door to the bar opened and in walked this giant of man. He was dressed in black and had a white shirt with a tie neatly done. His hair was slicked back and held in a pony tail at the back of his neck. He wore a big black overcoat that he left unbuttoned as it hung loosely at his sides. He had a chiseled face that was next to perfect with big brown eyes that looked right through you. He was hell warmed up, and I would bet no one would want to fuck with him. Miguel got up from the booth and approached him as he walked toward our table. They said something to each other and then came back to the booth. Miguel said, "I'd like you to meet, Roger. He will be your guide for a little while. The only person who can bring a replacement is me or my brother, Dante, no one else. Is that clear?"

"Yes, it's clear to me," Roger said and Marty nodded in agreement.

"Okay, from now on, do not tell anyone where you are going. Only Roger and I must always be in the know. Do not follow a set schedule, but go to work as usual and get your movies done. No one will be able to visit with you unless it is cleared by Roger. Do not use your car for a little while. Roger will drive you wherever you need to go. I should have the bomb detectors by tomorrow. Until then, be careful at all times. Order in tonight, have a few drinks, and relax. Roger has it all under control. Okay, let's go!" Miguel said as we all moved out of the booth and left.

Marty went back to the office in Roger's car while Miguel took his car and drove it back to Marty's house in Woodland hills and parked it in his garage. I followed in Miguel's car and then we drove back to the apartment.

When we arrived, Natalia was there watching television.

"Hi guys, did you have a nice day?" she asked.

"It was great and filled with excitement. I'll tell you all about it later. What are we doing for dinner," I asked.

"Gee, I don't know, honey. I didn't think about it much," Natalia said.

"How would like some Chinese food tonight?" I asked.

"Okay with me. How about you, Miguel? Will you join us? Let's go the Lemon Tree on Ventura Boulevard. It's supposed to have outstanding food," Natalia said as she mixed us a drink.

"Okay, let's go now so that we can get home early. I don't want to baby sit you guys all night, and if we go early, we'll miss anyone who may be looking for us," Miguel said.

We had dinner at the Lemon Tree. It lived up to its reputation; the food was great and the service was just as good. It was a little after eight fifteen when we arrived at the apartment. Miguel came in for a nightcap as we discussed tomorrow's schedule.

"The shit is going to hit the fan very soon, Marcel," Miguel said. "I think we should make sure our battle plans are set. I have enough men and can set up a complete undercover network that will have you and Marty under surveillance at all times. I also think we have to get rid of the two guys from out of town. The message will be heard by the Mob, and they will tread very lightly when coming to Los Angeles. They'll also learn that the adult industry will not be threatened by anyone. It must be done, Marcel. We have no other choice," Miguel said with a great deal of conviction.

"I know you are right, Miguel, but that could start an all-out war, and they have a lot more men and money than we do! Of course, once our strength is demonstrated I think they'll back off. They certainly have enough problems with this Apalachin thing and the upheavals that have taken place in their organization this year. I think they will put this on the back burner once they see some action. They are used to getting their way through fear. Once they see that it does not work, they will abandon their attack. I believe this and hope my intuition is right! Okay, Miguel, get your crew on the job. Let's clear the battlefield," I said.

Miguel finished his drink and assured me that the crew would be at work tonight and would continue until the threat was over.

Friday, November 22, 1957

I woke up early as usual and decided that a run today would be okay as I had plenty of surveillance. I left the apartment at six forty-five; it was still dark but daylight was on the way. I didn't see anyone on the street or in any car nearby. Nonetheless I started my run and didn't worry. Having a lead car and knowing that Miguel had people scattered all over the place gave me the confidence to forget everything I had been preaching about being alert at all times.

I continued my run, and I didn't pay any attention to another runner who turned the corner directly behind me. He must have been no more than fifty yards back and was gaining. Still I paid no attention as I was deep in thought and in my rhythm when I turned the corner and started on the straightaway. As I continued the run, I started to feel the presence of another runner and looked back. As I looked back, I saw the runner pull closer to me and the gap between us slowly closing. I tried to run faster, but my legs just didn't cooperate as he was closing in faster now. I looked back again, and he was no more than twenty yards behind me and closing in fast. My adrenalin kicked in when I noticed a knife in his left hand; a large knife that made me run as fast as I could. I started to panic because I was not prepared at all I didn't bring my gun with me and had no weapons to use as a defense. The lead car seemed oblivious to what was happening; I wondered if the driver was blind. Didn't he use his rearview mirror? He would certainly see that I was being followed by someone who wasn't there when we started if he bothered to look! The runner was now only ten yards away; I could hear the footsteps directly behind me and could almost hear and feel his breath as he now brandished his knife quite openly getting ready for the strike. He was now only two or three feet away. I could clearly hear his breathing. He would strike out at me any second. I tried to think what the best defense would be when I heard a popping noise and then a thud. I turned back and saw my attacker lying on the pavement with a hole in the back of his head. He wasn't moving any longer and still had the knife clutched in his hand when one of Miguel's guys came running up. "That was too close for me," I said. "What took you so long to act?" I asked.

"Never mind that now. Let's just get your ass out here and get this stiff off the street. I'm sorry, Mr. Marcel, you better get the hell out of here and go straight home. No more running," he said. I ran all the way home and locked the door as soon as I entered the apartment. An hour or so later, Miguel walked in with a sour look on his face.

"What the hell do you think you're doing?" He was pissed. "I can't protect you when you won't help. You could have been killed out there. If the guy had used a gun, you wouldn't be here now. I can't be responsible for your safety if you won't follow simple rules."

"Miguel, I'm sorry. It will never happen again. I promise you! I thought I was fully covered because I had a lead car. I thought I had a full contingent of guards on this run and just didn't worry about it," I said. "What happened to the guy?" I asked.

"It's not your business, but we have gotten rid of the body. When they find him, they'll never know where he was killed and who he was. He had no identification on him, so we could not figure out anything as well. We know we have never seen him here before, but how did he know about you? Or was he sent by Ralph? Now that he is gone, I can't get any answers, thanks to you," Miguel said.

"I know how you feel, and I'm sorry. It won't happen again. Now let's move on please," I said.

"I can't help but be pissed. You could have been killed, and that would have been the end of my job and my reputation. Never, you hear me, never do this again." Miguel poured us each a shot of tequila and sat down and wiped his brow.

"I thought we agreed that we would not follow a schedule? I thought we agreed we would establish a schedule together and we would make it very different? No running or anything unless it is approved by me. No more. You understand me, Marcel?"

"What a day! We are lucky, but luck won't be with us all the time. What happened to caution, my darling, caution? I'm shaking. I'm so upset. You could have been killed, Miguel could have been killed. What were you thinking? I need you, please, honey. Never again, please," Natalia said as she held me close.

I knew that I fucked up, and I was very shook-up about it. There was nothing I could do about it now except to make sure it never happened again. Miguel called Marty to check up on him, "Everything all right with you?"

"Yes, everything is fine over here. Are you guys having some trouble?" Marty asked. I can hear it in your voice, Miguel. Is everything okay?"

"We had a little trouble, but it's been handled, I just thought that you better be a little more careful. Tell Roger to call me as soon as he can, and Marty, stay alert, please!" Miguel said.

A few minutes had passed when our phone rang. Natalia answered, "Hello, sure thing, hold on a minute," she said. "It's Roger, and he wants you, Miguel," she handed the phone to him.

"Roger, take a little extra care. We have had an attack. It's all taken care of, but this could be the start of something. Call in some additional guys, and keep everyone at your end protected. Call me on my mobile if you need me, thanks, man." He hung up.

We spent another hour drinking a few tequilas and just plain relaxing. Miguel thought it would be best if I stayed home for the rest of the day. He was going to discuss hiring someone who would impersonate me when we required such a tactic. My double would not meet with anyone but would get in and out of the car and would act as if he was me. This was just in case someone was watching so that they could get the message that I was all right and it was business as usual. We had to keep up appearances at all times and make them believe that we were not intimidated in any way.

"I want to bring in a double who will take your place when I need to fuck up the enemy. I need your okay, Marcel, to cover the added expense. I'll stop in at the theater and see Mike and make sure things are on schedule. I'll make a couple of other stops like visiting Marty at the office and then I'll make sure we are not followed when we drive back here. In the meantime, I'll have crew here checking out the apartment. I want to make sure there aren't any bugs anywhere, so don't make any calls. Just wait for my return. You will be protected at all times. Just lay low for today, okay?" Miguel said.

Miguel finally left, and Natalia and I spent the day watching television in each other's arms. It was easy to duplicate my appearance; all we needed was someone who was my height and build, the rest was up to makeup. Miguel's guys did a thorough search of the apartment checking for listening devices and found none. They checked the phones once again to make sure there weren't any bugs planted in them.

Around three thirty, I received a call from Marty. "Hey, how are you doing?" he asked. "I heard you had a little excitement today."

"Just a little, partner," I said. "Well, the guys checked out the apartment and said it's clean. I think they are going to your office to check it out and then to the house."

"They've already been here and this place is clean. I wouldn't call you if it wasn't. I figured that by now they are at the house. They are also checking the cars and the theater. I'm sure they are all clean as well. By the way, I got a call from Irv. The boys are ready to sign your agreement and want a meeting with the bank. How about early next week? Can you set it up?" Marty said.

"That is good news. We certainly can use some today, don't you think?" I said. "I'll set it up and call you back," I said as I hung up. I called Sally and arranged the meeting for Tuesday at one P.M. at the Red Rooster.

I called Marty back. "Hey there, the meeting is set for Tuesday at one P.M. at the Red Rooster. Please don't tell them the location until Tuesday at twelve. Let them know that I'll have Miguel drop off a copy of the agreement on Monday at each one of their offices and will expect it to be signed and returned to Miguel at the meeting place before the meeting starts with the bank. This will give anyone plenty of time to call Miguel with any objections, if they have any," I said to Marty. "I'll speak to you later." I hung up. This was the best news I could have had in an otherwise dismal and sad day.

I spent the evening relaxing with Natalia and watching the news to see if anything regarding the dead guy would appear. Nothing came up, so we decided to watch a movie. Natalia and I had a talk about the dangers of staying on with me. I gave her the full picture of the Mob from New York and the Mob from Los Angeles and who knows who else may want to get rid of me. I laid it on as thick as I could, because I didn't want her to be misled in any way at all. The dangers were real, and she really did not have to be a part of it. I wanted her to make a choice with full knowledge of what was possibly waiting for her. I wasn't surprised when she said that no matter what the dangers were she was staying with me. She said she loved me and love doesn't just count when things are going right. Most importantly, she said, "I don't want to go on living if you are not in my life any longer. I want to stay and will be with you no matter what. I told you that before, Ron, and I still mean it. I love you, and when I say that I do love you, it is for always." That was plain and simple. I could not have gotten the message any clearer. I held her in my arms and kissed her and thanked her for being so wonderful. Miguel called saying that he would see me in the morning. "Don't worry about a thing. You are fully protected." I thanked him and went to bed.

Saturday, November 23, 1957

It was seven thirty in the morning when Miguel arrived. He was looking very chipper.

"I guess you had a good night's sleep?" I said.

"Well, don't you think it is about time I was able to sleep undisturbed?" Miguel said.

"Well, what have we got in store today?" I said.

"I want to go see Marty. I told him we would meet him at Norm's Diner on Lincoln and Olympic for breakfast. I think it is very important we make this meeting, so please get dressed, and let's get going. Please don't worry about Natalia. She will be fine. There is somebody here watching over her at all times. Now please hurry, Marcel," he said.

I put on a pair of jeans and a sweater and my jacket. "Ready, let's get going," I yelled out to Miguel. We took Sepulveda all the way to Santa Monica and then took Olympic Boulevard to Lincoln and pulled into the parking lot at eight forty-five. We went into the diner and found Marty and Roger sitting at a table in the back of the place.

"Good morning, guys. Hope you had a good night. Please sit down," Marty said. The waitress came by and filled our coffee cups and asked if we were ready to order. We placed our breakfast order and waited until she was gone before we began to talk.

"I want you guys to understand how serious this stuff is," Miguel said. "Yesterday, we had an incident with an assassin trying to eliminate Marcel, and only because we were diligent did we manage to eliminate the threat. Later that day, closer to six P.M., two men arrived at Marty's office. The only people at the office at that time were Marty and Roger. They flashed badges, a little too quickly as they put them away before we could examine them. They obviously did not expect to see Roger at the office and were a little shaken by his appearance," Miguel said. "I'd like Roger to continue with what happened next. Roger, please."

The waitress arrived with our food, so Roger remained mute until she left.

"I asked them to let me see their badges once again. I said I'd like to call their office to verify that they were supposed to be there at that hour to see Marty Loomis. I saw the look in their eyes when I made this request and was ready for action. The lead guy put his hand in pocket as if he was taking out his badge back out. One problem though—he had put the badge in his left jacket pocket, and he was putting his hand in his right pocket. I pulled my gun and they froze. I told them that I would kill them if they moved a muscle and instructed them to slowly remove their hands from their pockets and hold them in the air where I could clearly see them. I instructed Marty to reach into their pockets and remove any weapons they may have. I then had Marty remove their handcuffs, but guess what, they didn't have any. I instructed them to sit on the floor and sent Marty outside to fetch Abel Sanchez, our other man, who was waiting outside. Once Abel was in the room with us, I instructed him to get some rope or tape and bind those guys up very tight. I gagged them so that they would feel more threatened and get the message. After we had secured them, I removed the gag from their mouths and went to work. I asked them who they really were and told them that it would be a lot easier if they told me the truth right away. If they decided to lie, I would cut off one finger at a time, and after the fingers were gone, I would cut off each toe, one at a time. If they cooperated, I would let them go, and they could tell their bosses that if anyone came back they would be killed, no ifs, ands, or buts. They looked at Abel who over six foot five inches and was about three hundred pounds and on a good day looks like he could kill half the world. I'm sure they felt intimidated by this crazy-looking guy. They started to bullshit me with the very first question when I asked who they work for, so I cut off one finger of the lead guy. He screamed, so I put the gag back on and spoke with the second guy. I told him if he wanted to save his life as well as his friend's, he had to answer all questions truthfully. He told us they were working for Carmine and were told to rough up Marty and bring back an ear. I asked them how they knew Marty was Larry, and they said they put two and two together after Calvin Powers told them that a new guy just opened a studio here in the Valley. I asked him if they spoke to Carmine yet and he said no!

"They decided it would be best to go see Marty and rough him up a little until he admitted who he really was. They said that they came directly here and waited until everyone went home. They didn't know I was here. They also didn't spot Abel because he was inside the car that was parked a little way down the street. We parked the car that way in case anyone did stake the place out, they wouldn't associate the car with this place. As you can see, it worked out well and helped in this situation. I suggest that we always park our vehicles a little distance from the exact address we are watching. It gives us a lot more scope and will confuse anyone who is trying to calculate our firepower. Sorry, I got off the track.

I continued to interrogate these guys and found out that Carmine is not really liked here in Los Angeles, so these guys flew in to Long Beach and then drove here. They didn't contact anyone from the Los Angeles Mob as that would have been a lot of trouble for them and Carmine."

Roger stopped his recount of yesterday's events and took a moment to eat his breakfast. He continued, "These guys were just soldiers, but they were ready to hurt Marty, even kill him if need be. I had no conscience on hurting these guys at all. My thought was only to eliminate any threat to Marty and anyone else. Abel and I took care of those guys last night. I don't think they will be back real soon, and no one needs to worry about them."

"Well, that is quite an adventure and very informative. We now know the war has begun, and we must be very careful at all times. I really don't want to know what happened to these guys. I imagine you sent them on their way back to New York. That should be the last we'll see of them," I said and let it go at that.

"All right, let me bring up a few things that I feel are very important," Miguel said. "I don't want anyone feeling any remorse about any casualties that may happen. We are at war, and they would do us terrible harm if allowed to do so."

"You're right," Marty said. "We have to be aware and stay on top of this always. Fuck those bastards. Let's give it to them. I am concerned in one area where I think we are weak. When I shoot a movie, we are most vulnerable and can easily be duped into a lull of complacency. We need to step up our security to make sure that everyone who is there should be there and that an attack will not screw up the film shoot or kill one or all of us. The costs of these security measures are high, but I'm sure we can add the costs to the film, and we'll pass it along to the buyer. Let's keep on this now so that we don't lose a beat. I'm planning on starting a shoot next Tuesday, so let's be prepared."

Miguel spoke up with a grin on his face, "Most of my guys want to work on the set when you are doing a shoot. I'm sure they would love to work on the set without pay. I don't have a problem getting staff for this, but I do have a problem with making sure their attention is on the job of security and not on the porn stars. This is a very difficult job as there will be so many people, and how do we separate the low—and high-risk people? This assignment is tougher than watching the President of the United States and should demand a higher wage scale due to inherent risks. I guess when my boys see the first female porn star, they will forget hazardous pay." He laughed.

"Kidding aside, we'll have a full crew on the site. We'll have a couple of our people hanging around as if they are part of the acting crew. I'm sending over a very good-looking female operative who will be on the set during the shoot. Don't underestimate her. She probably could take any guy apart. Of course, Roger and Abel will also be on hand, so please don't worry, Marty. We will have it covered. I will need to meet with you and go over a complete list of actors and actresses and other personnel who will be here. I cannot have anyone on the set unless they have been pre-approved and that means you have to be one hundred percent certain about each and every person. There cannot be any last-minute arrivals, and no one can use your name to get in. If they are not on the list and do not have proper identification, then they don't enter. Please understand that we are dealing with your life and cannot take any unnecessary risks and cannot make any exceptions even if it is the main star. There is one other area we have to cover, and that is someone who is on the list but has been compromised. There is no way to predict that, so we just have to be extra diligent especially you, Marty, as you will undoubtedly be the target. Marcel will not be on the set, so we do not need to worry about him. Thank goodness for one less problem," Miguel said as we paid the bill and left in our cars.

We went to the theater to check up on Mike while Marty went back to his office to continue getting ready for the shoot on Tuesday. It was amazing how fast the theater was coming along; it now looked as if a theater was always there. The marquee was up, and the ticket booth was now installed.

"I'll make sure the marquee is well-lit by next week, and the sign will say, "Coming Soon." I'll have to get the exact title from Marty," I said. It was so exciting; even Miguel liked it. We then went back to the apartment where Natalia was waiting. She wanted to go shopping and could not until Miguel gave her the okay. I decided it would be best for me to stay home for the rest of the day while Natalia was out. I would relax a bit, watch television, and even take a nap. I also wanted to review the agreement for the boys before I sent it to them on Monday—just double-checking that there were no errors and it was as I requested. It was better to sure. Tonight, we are supposed to be going to the Willets for dinner. I wasn't too crazy about it, but I had to go just to keep up appearances and had to change back to my Ron look. This was crazy, but it had to be done if I was to continue this charade.

Natalia came waltzing in loaded with bags followed by Miguel carrying more bags. She must have bought everything in the store; nothing unusual for women. Miguel came in, and I fixed a couple drinks for us as we sat down and relaxed.

"What a day," Miguel said. "She really knows how to shop, doesn't she?"

"I'm certain she holds a degree in shopping. She is quite an expert at it as she does it so well," I said with a big smile on my face. As we sat down to enjoy our drinks Natalia came into the room and placed a package on my lap. Being as generous as she is she also laid one on Miguel's lap.

"These are for you, guys. I hope you like them," she said.

"Wow! What a beautiful shirt. This is what I always wanted," I said enthusiastically to Natalia. "And you got my size right. Thanks a lot, sweetheart. I really needed this."

"Thanks a lot, Natalia," Miguel said as he held a beautiful sports jacket in his hands. "If it doesn't fit, Miguel, you can bring it back and exchange it. I have the receipt," Natalia said.

She was so happy that we liked our gifts. She really had a good heart. It was so visible in her expressions. I was certain that she had the most satisfaction just watching Miguel and me open and love our gifts. She was the greatest.

We spent the evening at the Willets enjoying some great steaks done just right on the BBQ. I made sure we didn't discuss any business as wanted to keep it a night of fun and good eating. We shot the shit and came home at ten thirty and hit the sack. This was a very stressful week that brought the ever-present dangers closer to home and woke me up from the lackadaisical attitude I was falling into. Let's hope next week would be a lot quieter. Sleeping over at Natalia's was also a little difficult because of the security detail, but it wasn't too bad at all.

Sunday, November 24, 1957

I woke up early as usual but left the house at once to go to my apartment where I spent another half hour working on becoming Marcel again. I then read the Sunday paper while I waited for someone to arrive before I went on my run. It was close to eight thirty when Abel arrived and told me that his instructions were that I could not run this morning.

"What the hell is wrong now?" I asked as I was now annoyed. "Miguel has had some information that a hit is out on you and could be imminent. He wants to make sure you are not an easy target. You are my meal ticket, Mr. Marcel. I certainly wouldn't want anything to happen to you. Please relax and wait for Miguel to call or come by. It shouldn't be long until we hear from him," Abel said.

"Sorry, Abel, I got upset. I shouldn't have. I realize you are doing your job and, if I might add, quite well, and I thank you for your concern. You are right. We'll just relax and wait for Miguel. I enjoy living and just want a little peace once and for all. Let's have something to eat. I have a lot of food in the kitchen. It's about time we ate some of it," I said as I walked into the kitchen.

I scrambled a few eggs and made some great coffee and toast. Abel and I ate our breakfast and talked about football. We were back to a good mood and a mutual respect for each other. Natalia had arrived and used the excuse that she had to help make me up for the day, so she jumped out of bed at Mary Lou's and came right here. I waited for her to change and after a few minutes went into the bedroom to see what was holding her up. I found her back in bed fast asleep. This was incredible to me, but I loved her, and she was so beautiful. I didn't make her any eggs because she was back sleeping but kept the coffee hot. An hour later, Miguel called and said he would be by in an hour to talk to me. Until then I should stay in the apartment. Natalia finally woke up and looked beautiful as ever as she walked around the apartment in her pajamas. I made her eggs and had coffee with her while I settled back to wait for Miguel. She went to work on me, adding a few touches here and there as if to justify her returning home to help make Marcel look good. The early football game was on, and even though I had not been following it closely, this year I decided to watch the Rams who were playing somewhere in the East.

My mind was not into the game at all as I could only keep thinking about the situation I was in. In the last ten months, I had been married twice and traveled back and forth across the country. I had dodged bullets, knives, and other assorted mayhem. I had gone through a few cars and a home built and lost in less than two months. To say the least, my life had not been dull at all. As I sat there watching the football game, I started to think about Rachel and how she might be doing with our daughter. I don't know why this came into my mind, but it did. I promised myself that I would look her up when things settled down and find out all the details about my child.

Finally Miguel arrived and sent Abel out to maintain his vigil from another vantage point on the street while we talked.

"I heard from a friend of mine that there is a hit out on a guy named Harry Miller. The New York Families have issued a two hundred and fifty K hit on this guy, and somehow they are thinking that you may be that guy. I don't know how they figure you are the guy. You don't look like him at all," Miguel said.

"How in the hell do you know what this guy looks like? Do you know this guy from New York?" I asked.

"Not really, but I did get a picture of what he looks like. I got it from a friend who said he knew the guy and got me a picture from the year book at NYU. He electronically sent it to me, and this guy doesn't look the same. It seems that the fact that you and that guy seem quite different didn't change their minds, so I do expect someone will be coming this way, and I want to be prepared," Miguel said.

"You are taking this seriously! I can't see how they can just say I'm the same guy," I said.

"Let me tell you what I have discovered and then we can decide what we are going to do. I've learned, through some very good sources, that Calvin Powers, who is a real asshole, called a friend who is connected to the Mob and told them that two new guys appeared on the scene here in Los Angeles in the last few weeks, and one of them has opened a film studio and the other is opening theaters. It seems he believes that by doing these guys some special favors, like passing information along, he will be rewarded with favors as well as a piece of the price the Mob placed on this guy's head. He really doesn't know the Mob real well, but it seems he is enthralled by them and would like to be one of them. In view of the meeting you had with the other adult filmmakers, he is dangerous and something must be done. He doesn't belong in this business. He thinks that the Mob will treat him as an equal and not muscle him. He really doesn't know how wrong he is. Once they have him in their grips, they will own him. He can't be allowed to remain in this business and be a part of our meetings and our strategy that should remain private. The guy is a rat, and rats should be caught and eliminated. After offering him the best of the best and allowing him to pay into the security group, we have left ourselves open to attack by the Mob. They have an informer in our group, and he must be wiped out. All I want Marcel is the truth from you. I am putting my life on the line for you, and we agreed that we will always be truthful with each other. I need you to be that way now!" he said.

"You are right, Miguel. You have demonstrated loyalty and integrity, and I will always be truthful as agreed," I said.

I spent the next hour telling Miguel everything. I left out minor details; however, I covered all the pertinent details. I felt I had no other choice and must place my trust and safety in his hands.

"Well, that is some year you have had so far. No one could make up a story like that. Truth is stranger than fiction, and your adventure is proof of that, and it doesn't look like it will end real soon! Thanks for believing in me and telling me the truth. I can assure you that no one will ever know what you just told me. We will continue to carry on as we have, and only the two of us will know the truth," he said.

"Well, that is not quite true, Miguel. Marty knows as well, and the girls know a little. As a matter of fact, you and I met in New York when you were in trouble, and I helped you out. I was Dan All right back then. I guess my change of looks was pretty good that even you didn't recognize me," I said.

"You have my undying loyalty and trust. Now let's see what steps we can take to protect ourselves," Miguel said.

"I also want to make something clear, Miguel. In regard to Calvin, I do not want to deal with him, but I also don't want to become like the Mob and hurt someone. It's true he is a rat, and we must conduct our business without him, but we can't just go around killing people, no matter what they seem to do. We will have to come up with a plan that will eliminate him from our group, but, Miguel, no killings," I pleaded.

This was a very emotional meeting with Miguel that drained my spirits. Miguel made me promise that I would run the business and not mix into the security end of things. I must leave that to Miguel at all times. I will carry my gun with me wherever I go, just in case, but it is best I don't know anything further about the safety aspect of our operation. I gave Miguel the agreements to be dropped off at each adult company tomorrow in advance of the meeting on Tuesday. I told him that I did not want any agreement left with Calvin Powers.

"If anyone asks about Essence Films, just advise them that we cannot include this company in our deal." I also told Miguel to talk to each owner and explain to them that confidentiality was very important and that Calvin and his Company Essence Films had violated that confidence.

"If any of the companies object, they too can join Calvin, and don't leave them a copy of the agreement. You can explain that Calvin would prefer to spend a lot of time with the Mob and is, without doubt, in their pockets," I said to Miguel.

I felt that I had delivered the message to Miguel once again that I was against causing him any bodily harm. I spent the rest of the day at home with Natalia watching football and just relaxing as best I could. I was still shaken by all the revelations I'd heard from Miguel and needed a little time to calm myself. Natalia ordered Chinese takeout and then sent one of our security team to pick up the food. We ordered enough to feed the security boys as well as ourselves. We stayed at home for the remainder of the night.

Monday, November 25, 1957

Miguel arrived early looking like he was ready for a new week.

"Good morning, Marcel. I hope you feel better today," he said.

"I'm still a bit shaken but I'm getting over it. After all the things that I have gone through in the past year, I guess this is not the most frightening. I must admit that I'm glad you were able to uncover this rat before too much damage was done," I said.

"I wanted to talk to you about this situation. Let's go for a drive," Miguel said.

I grabbed my coat and we went to the car and began driving nowhere. Miguel sat in the rear with me while Abel drove at a moderate speed toward Mulholland Drive.

"It's about the meeting tomorrow. It must be changed. You cannot have it at the Red Rooster especially after all the things we know about Calvin. I want it changed, and I want to do it as follows. I will decide where we meet, and I'll advise all the people involved. Calvin will not be at the meeting and he will no longer be part of the group. We can't just ignore him, because he will talk with the other owners and could influence them or try to influence them in some way. He will without doubt try to hurt us, because the Mob will put him up to it, and as you know, once involved with them always involved. We can't tell the other owners what we discovered about Calvin as that would blow your identity and could get you killed. We are in a box and must take offensive action. This I will do. You need not be involved or aware of what must be done. You just have to proceed with your plans and remain alert, and things will work out," Miguel said.

"I still think you can and should tell the other owners who Calvin is. I think the best course of action is to label him a turncoat, and let the Mob take care of him. It's got to be easy to send out the message that he is a double agent and has been giving information to us as well as to the Mob. Let the Mob take care of him in whatever way they want. He is not useful to them any longer, and he certainly will not be welcome with us. I don't think it will cause me any additional problems, at least not anymore than the ones we have now! In regard to his blowing the whistle on me, I don't think they really know where Harry Miller is. If they did, my source in New York would have called me and warned me. They have been guessing for almost a year, and so far they have not been lucky at all. I think they have put two and two together with the help of Calvin and their policy is not to take chances. If they are wrong about me, then why would they care about another dead guy? It isn't going to enhance their reputation in any way at all. They are just trying to be certain and will evaluate the situation when the guys they sent turn up. Calvin, without doubt, stirred up a lot of interest, and Marty sure as hell looks like Larry Robbins because he is not changing his looks. Once they felt Harry was tied up with Larry, but now they may not be so sure, but it may be a lead. In any case, I still feel it best that we exclude Calvin from the deal and tell him that he is not welcome. I feel we should explain to the group that Calvin has chosen to work with the Mob and because of that there is no room for him in our union. We plan on becoming legitimate by taking this industry to the public and proving that we do not have ties with organized crime. Right now the feds think the entire adult industry is controlled by the Mob and that it's only a cash cow for them.

"We must show the authorities that this is not true and that we are only interested in making this genre of the film industry free of any Mob ties whatsoever. If we do this, it will do much more harm to Calvin and his dream of being a part of the Mob. Most likely he will be ostracized from the Mob and of course, from the adult industry as well and it will leave him out in nowhere land. It will also be a feather in our cap that will demonstrate our loyalty to the group and add confidence. One last message these actions will deliver to them all—the fact that they cannot betray a confidence and get away with it. The consequences are too severe," I said.

Things certainly had gotten out of hand since I began running to save my life. My goal was to be left alone and begin a new life, not to hurt anyone. Now it seems I was as bad as the Mob and that was never my intent. Each day, I seemed to get in deeper and deeper and had to do things in the name of self-survival that I never imagined I would ever do! How did I get into this bind? How did I become so cold and calculating? I asked myself. I finally decided that it was too late to lament over deeds that had been forced upon me, and I couldn't worry about things that would happen, so I'd better be careful in the present. I was convinced that I was a good man and only did what was necessary. Of course, some would say that this was rationalization just to make myself feel better. I certainly hoped that that was not the case, because I had never hurt an innocent person and hoped and prayed that I never would. I was not a monster and never wanted to be one, and I was sure of that. Killing a Mob assassin did not make me a bad person; it simply was self-preservation.

We drove by the theater. Miguel and I went in and checked out the place. It was looking great and would be an awesome place in a few more days. Mike was so busy at work he didn't see us come in and didn't pay any attention to us. Miguel's security man came over to us and said to Miguel, "Can I talk with you for a moment? It's important."

"Excuse me, Marcel. I'll be right back," Miguel said. I walked around inspecting the stage area and then went to the projection room to scope out the place. I then went to the office where the proceeds of each day's receipts would be tallied. As I was getting ready to leave the office area, Miguel came in and said, "We have a small problem. Some guy came by today looking for you. He looked very much like a Mob guy and said he would be back. My man gave him my number to call if he wanted to talk to the owner. We'll see what happens, but be prepared."

We left the theater and drove back to the apartment. No one was home because Natalia was working on the shoot today and wouldn't get home until nine or ten. Miguel left me at home with my security detail and went off to do whatever he does. I was relaxing on the sofa watching the news and half dozing when a news flash came on. It seemed the police had found a body today in the trunk of car that was parked in Simi Valley next to fire hydrant.

It was a male around thirty-five years old and had no identification. He was shot twice through the head and then stuffed into the trunk of the car. A spokesman for the sheriff's office said it looked like a gangland slaying. The reporter said they would have further details as they come in. I didn't give it too much attention; another murder in Los Angeles I thought and went back to my dozing.

Tuesday, November 26, 1957

I woke up early as usual and picked up the *Los Angeles Times* and saw a picture of the man that was found shot to death yesterday. It shook me up, because I recognized him; it was Calvin Powers. I guess Miguel was right, he wouldn't be at the meeting today. I wonder why he got killed. Did he screw around with the wrong people?

I never thought for a moment that we could have had anything to do with it. Miguel finally arrived, and I said to him when he arrived, "Did you see the news?"

"No, not yet. What happened?" he said.

"Our little rat seems to have screwed with the wrong people. He is no longer a threat to us or anyone else for that matter," I said as I showed Miguel the *Los Angeles Times* article.

"Hey, that's great now. We don't have to worry about him," Miguel said.

"Anything else new today, my good friend?" I asked.

"Not much. I didn't get any calls from anyone, so I guess the guy who visited the theater didn't want to talk about anything," Miguel said.

"What about the meeting? Where is to be held and what time?" I asked. "We'll meet at one today. Everyone will be informed of the change of venue at about noon, and you don't need to know because we are driving you there. Pretty neat, isn't it?" he said with a smirk.

I called Moe in New York, because I was very concerned about this Calvin thing and also I wanted to see if he did hear anything about Harry.

"I want you to know, Harry, that things seem to be very quiet over here. I have not heard any news about you lately and must feel they have placed you in second place in regard to priority," he said.

"I read in the Los Angeles paper that a guy named Calvin Powers was found shot to death a few days ago. I met the guy last week under my new identity and just wanted to know, if you can find out, who offed him and why," I said. "Okay, my good friend, I will make some discreet inquiries. Call me back in two hours," Moe said and hung up.

We left the apartment at twelve fifteen and drove along Ventura Boulevard to Tarzana and finally parked our car in the rear of the Country Club Bar & Grill. We were met at the side door by one of Miguel's men and escorted into the place and into a private room. The place was set up with some tables and one big table in the center with ten chairs. This would be our own private area where everyone could relax and discuss anything they wanted without fear. The place was pronounced "clean" by Miguel's men who went through the place with a fine tooth comb. It was twelve fifty, and no one was there but us. We ordered a few drinks and some Calamari appetizers. A few minutes later, Frank Judd arrived and just behind him Perry Stanford walked in with his very sexy and beautiful redheaded secretary. Next to arrive was Marty Loomis and his superstar, Mary Lou, an outstanding beauty that made the room stand still. She was dressed to the nines and looked perfect. We all sat and waited a few more minutes when Irv Willets and his partner Steven Paul walked in and right behind was Luke Remo dressed like the finest pimp you ever did see, wearing a white suit with a black shirt and white tie and white shoes and a pink hankie in his suit breast pocket. He wore a great big black fedora and looked like he'd just stepped out of a leading men's magazine. The players were all here, and we were ready to proceed.

I stood and said, "I welcome you all here today. I appreciate the fact that you were able to find this place. Our banker will be here at one thirty to go over the details. I would like to take a minute to express my sincerest regrets and condolences to the family and friends of Calvin Powers. I am referring to the untimely death of Calvin Powers.

"I didn't know Calvin other than the first meeting we had. If I may take a moment of your time in regard to Calvin, I realize we are here to get the business deal going, but in view of his sudden demise, I think I'd best inform you what I found out. When I saw this in the paper I made a quick investigation and found, through sources, that Calvin was involved with the Mob. I could not discover what he did that would cause his death, but it must have been something unsavory. I mention this because I cannot stress it too strongly that we must keep all our dealings very confidential at all times."

"Marcel," Luke Remo said, "If I may speak about Calvin for a moment. I have it from very reliable sources that he was in deep with a bookie and did not pay his debt after many promises. I heard he was in for over $50K and lost last weekend once again. It is rumored that the bookie had sent out a message that if you play, then you must pay. I just thought I'd share that with everyone. I am sorry for his death, but he was a habitual gambler."

"I would like to urge you to please order some food. After all, we are here to conclude a business deal and do require a little nourishment every now and then," I said as the entire gathering laughed at this remark and the ice was broken.

I felt a lot better when I heard what Luke Remo said about Calvin. For a little while, I'd thought Miguel had done this and was very conflicted about it. I now felt so much better and much more relaxed.

Miguel collected the signed agreements and placed them in a briefcase and left the room. A few minutes later, Sally came in carrying her briefcase and looking bright and cheery as usual. She came over to me directly and kissed me on the cheek and whispered in my ear, "Thanks, Ron, oops, Marcel."

I got up and knocked my fork on a glass to get everyone's attention, "I'd like to take this opportunity to introduce you to Sally Thornton. She is your bank executive who will take care of your every need. Sally, the floor is yours," I said.

"Hi everyone. It's a real pleasure to meet all of you. I don't know your names yet, but before the day ends, I will know all of you. I want to extend a big and warm welcome to you all from the Bank of the Valley and to tell you that the days of hiding what you do for a living are now over. After lunch, you will be able to operate in the open, write checks, and deposit money without concern. Bank of the Valley welcomes your business, and we'll work with you in every way possible," she said.

Sally sat down and picked up her drink and looked at me and said once again, "Thanks, Marcel. I'll make you proud."

I left the boys with Sally as they set up their business. Miguel and I went back to the apartment.

"It went well, don't you think?" I said to Miguel.

"I think they are all happy and it seems that Calvin got what he deserved and is long forgotten. I wonder who will take over his company or will it just close up. They really don't have a large library to sell, and I don't think he had any new films in the can. All they really have is fancy aquariums and nice plants. Perhaps they can get a few bucks for that, but I'll bet not too much. It's not our affair. I'm just happy that he is gone. It saves us a lot of trouble and the bother of getting rid of him," Miguel said with a very wide grin on his face.

I called Moe and he told me that this guy Calvin Powers owed over one hundred K and had not been paid his bookie in weeks. The final straw was last weekend when he bet ten K on some horserace and promised to stop by and pay the bookie fifty K on account. He never showed up, and the rest is history. In regard to Harry, he'd found out nothing and pointed out once again that they would always be looking but now they were overly concerned with the big bust that took place in Appalachia. "They put Harry on the back burner, but don't ever drop your guard."

I hung up and waited for Natalia to get home and then went to bed. She really isn't any fun when she works on a film all day. She must have had a real hard day, no pun intended.

Wednesday, November 27, 1957

With Thanksgiving Day coming up tomorrow, this day would be a rather boring one. It seemed that everyone starts their holiday early especially when it falls on a Thursday. Miguel came over and off we went to see Mike and make sure everything was in order for the long weekend. No one would work on Thanksgiving Day, and being a nice guy as I was, I would give Mike and his crew the weekend off.

We arrived at the theater and met with Mike. He was thrilled to take a few days off and spend some time with his wife and kids. I gave him the payroll he needed and threw in a bonus of two hundred dollars and told him to have a nice weekend. We then went over to see Marty and take a gander on how the shoot was going. We entered through Marty's secret entrance directly into his office. We could see the entire scene and what was going on through a one-way glass that was installed in his office. I was happy that we had done all this as I did not want to be seen by anyone. The less people who saw me near Marty, the better it was for us all. The place was filled with people moving in every direction, moving lights around others, putting on makeup, and others just reading their script.

"Hi, Marty, how's the shoot going?" I asked as he entered his office. "Another day of hell, but I love it. We'll start shooting about two today and hope to wrap it up around eleven tonight," Marty said as he shouted some details to someone who unfortunately could not hear him.

"Hey, Marty, relax a little. No one can hear from in here," I said. The food tables were being set up with lots of sandwiches and other assorted foods and drinks. It seemed that food was one of the most important items on the set. This was the first time I saw Angel on a movie set; she was truly very beautiful and had the face of a very young-looking schoolgirl. Innocence seemed to ooze out of her. She was great to look at. I sure hoped she would be Marty's future star. With Marty, love was found and lost on a weekly basis; he fell in love every week with a new porn actress. My only concern was about Mary Lou. I didn't want any ill feelings between her and Marty or anyone else for that matter. I would talk to Natalia about it and see if we could keep a lid on it all. Miguel and I hung around for another hour and then returned to the apartment.

I had a lot of cooking to do for Thanksgiving; we were having Miguel and his brother, Dante, as well as Roger, Abel, and a couple of his boys over for the holiday. We also invited the Willets and Don, our car dealer friend. He could hardly contain himself as he went crazy with gratitude. All he kept asking if there would be any porn stars joining us.

Marty had invited Angel to spend Thanksgiving with him, so we were a crowd. We were going to eat at Marty's house, because it was so much larger, and it was easier to handle a large group of people. I had to make sure I had my Marcel disguise in order at all times during the festivities.

"Miguel, we have to stop at Gelson's and pick up my turkey and the sides I ordered. I told the store I would pick them up at eleven tomorrow morning. The store closes at two, so please put it on your schedule. We'll also need some soft drinks and more wine. Do you think we should get that today, or can we pick it all up tomorrow?"

"I really don't know about that stuff. Why don't you get Natalia and Mary Lou to help?" Miguel said.

"Of course, they are going to help, but I don't expect them to lug around wine and things," I said.

"Okay, Marcel, let's stop at Luigi's wine shop and get the wine. If we give him a nice order, we will get a discount, and he could be a useful friend in the future. The other stuff we can pick up at Gelson's when we pick up the turkey," Miguel said.

"Great stuff, Miguel, that's why I have you taking care of these things," I said as we drove toward the apartment.

"One more thing I want to discuss with you," I said. "It's about the theater. Because we stand the risk of being busted by the feds, I must have a stooge who we can use to put the lease under. If we get busted, all the feds can do is fine this guy, because it is only a misdemeanor even though they know he is not the real boss behind this. Because it is only a misdemeanor, the whole thing won't be much. If a guy gets busted more than once, the offense becomes a felony, and there is mandatory jail time. In order to avoid this, we need a simple guy to front the place until we do get busted, then we will put another guy in. We take care of all the fines that the first offense incurred and give this guy a bonus, thank him for job well done, and send him on his way. Can you take care of this detail and make sure you always have someone who will be the front man?" I asked.

"No problem, boss, I got it covered. When do you want this guy to start?" Miguel asked. "Monday will be soon enough," I said as we arrived at the apartment. We went in and decided to have a few drinks. Natalia was not home yet as she was still on the shoot and probably wouldn't be home until late. Miguel left and promised me that he would handle the pick-ups. I decided to just relax and get ready for tomorrow, Thanksgiving Day!

Thursday, November 28, 1957

I got up early as usual and looked outside to check on the weather. I didn't trust weather forecasters as they were usually wrong. It was, as usual, going to be a very sunny day that California was known for. It seems to me that Thanksgiving Day always seems to be a very quiet and sort of lazy day. Most stores are closed, and all restaurants except Chinese are closed.

It is a day reserved for family get-togethers where everyone seems to eat at three o'clock in the afternoon. Traffic was light, and there were virtually no people walking the streets. This was not a day for a hit man to whack someone. Seeing that traffic was so light, he would be detected a mile away. Nevertheless, we weren't going to be lax just because it was a holiday! I remembered that Valentine's Day was also a holiday of sorts, and look what happened when one rival gang whacked out so many mobsters in Chicago.

We had to pick up the turkey and stuffing as well as the sweet potatoes and sweet carrots. I had to get to Marty's to make salad and get things ready while Miguel was picking up the stuff at Gelson's. Abel knocked on my door and asked if I was ready to go to Marty's. I told him I'd have to wake Natalia up, and he suggested I go over now and get started, and he would come back and get her when she woke up. I agreed and left with him to Marty's place. As we drove, I was aware how quiet and deserted the streets were. No doubt this was a major holiday and the lack of activity was a testament to the importance of this day to most people. Even though I felt this was not a good day to rub someone out as we drove along, I changed my opinion. The quiet streets would make getting away a lot easier, and the odds were in the favor of the perpetrator because the cops would also be at half staff. The downside was that the light traffic and lack of people would make identifying the killers easier. I was just in dreamland while we drove to Marty's house. I arrived at Marty's and found that Mary Lou and Angel were still asleep. Marty was walking around the house in his bathrobe and a cup of coffee in his hand.

"Good morning, Happy Thanksgiving Day to you, my good friend," he said.

"The same to you, buddy. How are things going with both women in the house?" I asked.

"Not bad at all. It seems that Mary Lou understands and is taking it well. I reminded her that we had agreed at the very beginning that we would be close and remain dear friends always, but I was very clear that I must have my freedom. I reminded her that we understood that we could not allow our relationship to create enemies especially between us. She only wants to be a superstar and make certain our friendship will always be intact. She is not jealous and will not cause any problems. It's a great relationship with a healthy respect for one another."

"I sure hope so, Marty," I said. "I don't know how you would react if she brought some guy home for a few days. I sure hope that healthy respect holds true both ways."

"Enough of this. How about a drink? I have some super single malt scotch. Let's have one to give thanks for all the good things we have been blessed with. I love you, my friend. You are my brother and always will be, and I know the feeling is mutual," Marty said as he poured two snifters of scotch. "This is sipping stuff, my good man. Enjoy L'Chaim!" and we drank our first sip together.

I worked the rest of the morning and part of the afternoon preparing the salad and my special salad dressing. Natalia arrived along with Miguel and boxes of food he'd picked up. Natalia set the table along with help from Mary Lou and Angel while I placed the turkey in the oven to keep it warm along with the stuffing and other stuff. The fridge was filled with drinks and deserts as well as a few bottles of champagne.

This was going to be one of the best Thanksgiving Day celebrations ever. We had to maintain our security at all times even though I was convinced no one would try anything today.

We finished our sumptuous meal and after-dinner drinks at about six thirty. Darkness had already fallen, and we were all very satisfied and ready for a relaxing evening. The Willets left around seven thirty, and Miguel's guys started to talk about going home in a few minutes. It must have been closer to eight when Abel said, "I have to leave and get some sleep. The food was great. Everything was perfect. Thanks to you all, I enjoyed this Thanksgiving best of all."

He walked to the door when Roger spied a car coming real fast down the street directly toward the house. "Get down, everyone, get away from the door. Trouble is on the way," he yelled.

Miguel already had his gun out, and Abel ran to the side of the house while the rest of us ran back to the kitchen and hit the floor. The car sped by the house, and from the passenger's side of the car out of both windows, bullets were being fired directly at the house. They had to be using submachine guns Chicago style just like the Capone days. It all happened so quick no one had time to think; all we could do was react. Miguel and his men began firing back from their different vantage points. The guys in the car didn't expect any return fire and started to panic. One of the bullets from our side went through the front windshield and hit the driver in the neck. The car swerved recklessly and continued a short distance back on to the main street and crashed right into a telephone pole. The guys who were firing the submachine guns must have run away, because when the police arrived, there was only one guy, and he was dead. Once we saw the car leave our street and heard the car crash, we began cleaning up the place the best we could.

The story we will give the cops was simple: We were having Thanksgiving Dinner and had just finished and while cleaning the table we heard the screech of a car that was speeding around the corner and fired some shots at the house for no reason at all. We then heard another car that must have been chasing the first car. It was very noisy, because all we heard was *pop*, *pop*, and then another *pop* and *pop* again and the car's wheel screeching, and by the time we got to the door they were both turning the corner then we heard a loud crash. We were too scared to run out and see what happened; we just stayed in the house. That was the story we were going to follow. Mary Lou was going to be the spokesperson when the cops do come by and start to ask questions. Her first task was to call the police and act frightened, tell them that someone just fired a gun at her house, and she was alone and very scared. If asked about other guests, Mary Lou will say that they left before this happened. We certainly had to remain as ignorant as possible as we wanted to limit the police investigation. Our security detail would remain at their posts but would stay well back of the police. They would try to remain out of the way when the police came by. The girls were very upset and tried to remain calm. I told Mary Lou to act like she was very nervous and upset. Mary Lou would act in complete ignorance, expressing her reaction that she couldn't understand why anyone would do this. This would be her shining hour as an actress. Before leaving, I asked Marty, "Marty, I need to ask you a very serious question. Let's go in the back. The cops will be here very soon. Are you sure Angel has the proper identification? We don't need any problems, so please handle this."

"Don't worry, Ron. She'll be fine. I know she looks young, but her papers say she is nineteen, so don't worry about it. It's covered," Marty said with far too much bravado.

I was worried about it and said, "Why don't you and Angel take a ride or go to a movie so that when the cops get here you won't be here?"

"Good idea. We'll leave right now and call you a little later to make sure the coast is clear," he said. He yelled out to Angel to grab a jacket and follow him. They left, and I felt a lot more comfortable and suggested that I return to my apartment. If the cops wanted to talk to me, they could call me.

I signaled my driver, and Natalia and I went home. What a night! I'll never believe that things wouldn't happen because of a holiday any longer. Natalia called Mary Lou to check up on her. We both felt it was very lousy of us to leave her all alone to face the music, but she understood and wanted to prove how capable she was. Much to our surprise, the cops came to the door and inspected the house. They questioned Mary Lou and asked her to give them the names of all the guests.

They pressed the issue of whether she was aware of anyone having an argument with anyone who was at the house that night. Mary Lou put it on very thick as she cried during the entire interview and expressed her concern that she did not understand why her home was fired upon. The investigation went well, and after a couple of hours, the police left.

It was beyond belief that they would not check out the entire area, but who were we to tell the local police department how to operate? Natalia and I were expecting a telephone call or a visit from the police, but no one came by or called. We finally went to bed, made love, and went to sleep.

Friday, November 29, 1957

Miguel arrived at the apartment real early because, as he said, "We have to talk."

"Okay," I said. "Let's talk I'm listening."

"What happened yesterday caught us by surprise. It won't happen again, this I promise, Marcel," Miguel said.

"There is no need for you to feel so guilty. It wasn't your fault. Now let's not hear about it again. We have other things we must do," I said.

"No, Marcel, I can't just forget about it. I didn't sleep well last night if at all. It is my job to protect you, and I did not take enough precautions. It will not happen again, this I promise. I am beefing up our security detail, and there will be no more going places without my approval. I will need time to set up a perfect protection plan whenever we travel and visit anyone at all. Mary Lou, Natalia, you, and Marty could have all been killed because I wasn't careful. No more letting our guard down at any time. This cannot and will not happen again. This I can guarantee, my friend. No drinking on the job for anyone. We cannot lose our edge ever! Please follow my instructions always from now on, please!" Miguel pleaded.

"Okay, Miguel, you got the reins. Use them the best way you see fit. Now let's get the hell out of here. I got to go see the camera shop and make sure the equipment is ready for delivery to our first theater. I also want to stop by the bank and see Sally and check with her as to what is going on with the new customers. Do you have those agreements? I need to put them away when I am at the bank so that they will be safe. Let's get going. We'll leave Natalia here. She's still asleep anyways," I said as I put on my jacket.

We left and went directly to the Valley film and supply to inquire about the projection equipment. They were very proud to take me into the back area of their showroom and show me the boxes of equipment that had arrived and would be shipped to the theater on Monday. Installation would begin on Tuesday, and training would begin on Thursday. I introduced Miguel to the manager and asked him to please coordinate everything with him and left the two of them alone while I walked around the showroom.

When Miguel announced that he was finished with the manager, we left and proceeded to the bank. Miguel said as we drove, "I will have one of my men handle the projection equipment and learn all about it. This guy will teach each new guy how to use the stuff. I don't want anyone being able to identify you at any time if it ever comes down to it. You will not ever show your face at this theater or any other one in the future. We have to be very careful and make sure you are always clean. Now just sit back and let me handle it. By the way, Marcel, you met my brother, Dante, at the house during the Thanksgiving dinner. I want you to know that he is my second in command, and if anything should happen to me, he will take over at once. I have been grooming him for a while, and he is fully aware of everything that goes on. Up until now I have never included him in our payroll as he took no funds from us. I want to include him from now on if it's all right with you."

"Of course, Miguel, you can do whatever you want, and you don't need my approval on something like this. I am so happy your brother will be a part of our operation. I'd like to get to know him better and hope this can happen real soon. Bring him around a little more often so that we can get to know one another. After all, Miguel, you are like a brother to me, and it would be nice to get to know my other brother. You have my blessings as you always do!" I said.

"As far as the additional costs that will be required for the added security, we will find the money somewhere. This I promise, Miguel. After all, I'm not going to just lay back and get killed."

"No way, boss, just come up with more ways to make more money, and we'll take of it all. You are a smart and good man, so please use that brain, and let's move forward. Now that we have a finished one theater, you will not need to visit anymore sites. We can build them from your prototype, and that will help keep you out of the limelight," Miguel said.

We arrived at the bank and had to wait a few minutes to see Sally. She was so excited with the new customers that she just couldn't stop smiling.

"Ron, how can I thank you? With these new accounts, my branch will be number one this month, and hopefully we'll be number one again next month. It means a lot to me, Ron, thanks," she said.

"I need a safety deposit box. Can you arrange this for me?" I asked. "No problem. I'll fill out the forms, and you will be in business," she said as she ran off to get some papers and returned to her desk. I completed my stuff at the bank, and off we went to the theater to see if Mike did work today or not. We found the place closed, so we surmised that Mike and his crew took the Thanksgiving weekend off as we had suggested.

We returned to the apartment and found Natalia all spiffed up. She looked great. "Hi, babe, where are you going?" I asked.

"Nowhere. I just wanted to look good for you," she said with a big smile. I thought that you and I could go out for dinner, all alone, just the two of us. I miss being with you without all the other people hanging around. What do you say about that?" she said as she threw her arms around my neck and kissed me like it was the first time.

"You're right. Let's do it and get a little drunk and have some fun," I said as I looked at Miguel.

He smiled and said, "What time, boss?"

"How about thirty minutes? I just want to change and freshen up. How about choosing a quiet place that is romantic and with a great food to boot? Surprise us, Miguel. You'd know what we like and what is safe," I said.

"Okay, you got it. I'll set it up for one hour from now. Go, get ready, and I'll take care of it," Miguel said as he picked up the phone.

Natalia and I were ready in less than thirty minutes, and Miguel was ready for us. We left the apartment and drove along Valley Circle Road until we reached the 101 Freeway and then took it north and exited at Los Vergennes Road and took that through the mountains until we came to a road and made a left turn and moved higher up the mountain. Within a minute or two, we reached the very top of the mountain and there was sign that said, "Valley Inn, the only restaurant in Los Angeles that serves fresh caught steaks and chops, seafood, and mountain-fresh vegetables." We'd never heard of this place, but it looked great. It was built out of stone and logs with a rustic look that made it so inviting. When you walked up the steps to the restaurant, the view of the Valley on one side and the ocean on the other was breathtaking. Natalia could not believe her eyes and held my arm tight. The inside was filled with stuffed heads of deer, moose, bear, and other animals. It looked like a hunter's lodge in the middle of the forest. The dining area was filled with tables all with checkered tablecloths of different colors all with a very plain candle in the middle. The atmosphere was truly rustic and very friendly. We ordered drinks and read the menu for half an hour; more out of curiosity than what to order. Natalia ordered wild boar, and I had venison with some type of mushroom and a fresh salad. We drank and ate and listened to the music of a very quiet and romantic band. The piano player sang every once in a while, and if you cared to, there was a small dance area where you could hold your sweetheart close.

We had a great time and were able to forget the things that had happened, at least for a little while. We finally called it a night and went home; it was nearly midnight.

Saturday, November 30, 1957

This day was supposed to be an easy one as it was a Saturday on a Thanksgiving Day weekend, so nothing would be happening. I told Miguel that Natalia and I wanted to go to the shooting range and practice for a while. We had to stay sharp and be prepared. I also wanted to meet with Marty later today to discuss what we should do next week and get his opinion on opening a few new theaters fast. I think Bakersfield, Sacramento, and Barstow could easily handle about six new places, maybe more. I think Sacramento alone should be good for at least four theaters. We waited until Natalia was awake and then went to the range and spent two hours there. It was now close to two, and Natalia wanted to be dropped off at Mary Lou's place because they were going shopping. A new indoor mall was opening on Ventura Boulevard and Sepulveda, and of course, the girls had to check it out. We took Natalia to Mary Lou's and then went over to the office to see Marty.

What got me was how conspicuous we were when we traveled. I told Miguel a few times, "Do you really think we are being low-key?" I said. "Every time we go anywhere, it is like a funeral procession—a car in front of our car and a car behind our car. If someone was looking for us, all they have to do is to wait until they see this auto procession. It's so silly."

"Well, Marcel, have you got a better idea on how we should do it?" Miguel asked.

"Certainly, I do," I said. "First, we should travel in a car that no one would suspect. If I have to go somewhere, I think we should use an old car with only a driver and the passengers. The second car should be a low-key one as well and act as if it is just another car. We should have a couple of those so that we don't always use the same car. We will blend in on the road, and I don't believe anyone will be able to spot us. The problem with the Mob is that they always seem to use the same type of cars, the same color, and model. You can see a Mob car a mile away, and they still haven't figured out why people know they are coming. Of course, I think the Mob has adopted that strategy because the presence of those cars makes one shudder at the thought that the Mob is coming after them. I still think we should still use the funeral procession method, but I should never ride in it and neither should you. If they decide to attack it, they'll find that there isn't anyone in those cars worth dying for. It's a simple way to hide in plain sight and stay safe. Maybe it is a little costlier but it is a lot safer, and that is our main concern at all times. Think about it, Miguel. I think it is genius in its simplicity," I said.

"I like the idea, and I think you are right it is safer," Miguel said. "Let me work out the logistics, and we'll start using this new plan. Could you please call your friend in the car business, and see if we can pick up a couple of used cars from him for very little?"

"I will call Don later today and see what we can arrange. I'm sure this will be an easy solution, and it won't be too costly at all," I said.

We arrived at Marty's at three fifteen and sat down to discuss the theater business.

We spent another two and one half hours on the subject and came away with the plan that we would open at least six new theaters and would make full use of the new releases that the other studios would provide under our agreement. The whole thing would prove to be the driver of a steady cash flow and would grow and grow into a million-dollar-or-more-a-month operation. We would not be hurting anyone, and we would be building a real strong organization. Miguel would be a very rich man as his small percentage would be worth a lot. We were very happy with the results of our meeting and returned to the apartment to relax and wait for Natalia. No going out tonight; we would just relax at home and make love.

Sunday, December 1, 1957

I woke early as usual and went for run with two cars watching over me as well as an additional runner who would run besides me. Miguel assigned a lead car that would stay a little ahead and a car that would follow behind. He felt that would stop any attempted attack while running.

I had just come out of the shower when the phone rang. Miguel answered and motioned that it was for me. I took the phone from Miguel and listened, "Harry, this Moe. How the hell are you?" he asked.

"I'm fine, Moe, and you?" I said.

"I'm great and the family is wonderful. Enough of this small talk, Harry. I have to talk to you about a few things. My phone is clean. Is yours?" he said.

"My phone is clean as well. We can talk forever, so don't worry. What's up?" I said.

"I was asked to attend a meeting yesterday," Moe started to say when I interrupted him and asked,

"Can I put this on the speaker, Moe? My trusted assistant, Miguel, is here, and it will save me time in retelling what you said."

"Sure Harry. You are certain your place is secure?" Moe asked.

"One hundred percent, Moe. Please don't worry," I said.

I pressed the speaker button and said, "Moe, this is Miguel who is now listening in on our conversation."

"Hi, Moe, it is a pleasure to hear your voice," Miguel said.

"As I said, I was asked to attend a meeting yesterday, and of course, I did. I could not maintain the trust everyone had placed in me by refusing to attend this meeting. I met with Larry Casparizzi and a representative of each of the five families. Carmine Valone was there as well a few other lieutenants with a mandate to settle this feud. We met at six yesterday afternoon, and I made notes so that when I tell all this to you I can be as precise as possible and avoid any misunderstandings. Remember, Harry, you're not dealing with people who always operate logically. In the first case, Carmine claims he is upset, because when he sent people out to talk to your friend, Larry Robbins. His people disappeared off the face of this earth. There have been many soldiers that have gone after you because of the two hundred and fifty K being offered for your head, and they have disappeared as well. This is strange as people don't usually disappear just like that. Larry is under a lot of pressure because he was your father-in-law and brought you into the business.

"Carmine is under pressure because the families can't understand why he sent anyone to rough up a filmmaker that has supplied him so well over the years and had paid his debt in full. They also could not understand why Carmine would jeopardize the relationship between this filmmaker and all our theaters, why he would screw up the delivery of good films that only make them all money, including him, and why he has relentlessly chased Larry Robbins. So a lot of shit has come down within the families without too many answers, and the big boys want some answers now. They have enough trouble with this Appalachia deal and the couple of changes of leadership with the assassination of Albert Anastasia. Of course, you know that Frank Costello has stepped down from the leadership of the Genovese family after he came very close to being killed in an assassination attempt and is now retired. So when you put it all in perspective, you're just another pain in the ass that they can live without. As far as the feds are concerned and from what I've heard as well, you are no longer a person of interest. Since Appalachia, the feds and locals have their hands full, and you are on the back burner. If you came around today, of course, they would grab you and hold you until the end of time. Right now, you're not important enough as they have so much on their plate that they don't need you and don't want you mucking up the works, and that gives you plenty of freedom, at least from them. Now, let's get back to the meeting as it is important. Carmine claims that his guy Larry threatened to stop selling him movies. That may be true because Carmine is not known for keeping his word and paying his debts as agreed. The fact that Carmine never pays for the movies and is trying to extort money and movies from this guy Larry is causing a lot of trouble for nothing and making the families unhappy. The message sent to Carmine from the families is that you pay for what you get as long as you are making a profit. Don't make waves within the family. They have enough shit to handle that they don't need another war. Carmine also feels that Larry is being assisted by Harry and that is why he has bolted from Carmine. An order from the top families has been issued to Carmine to leave Larry alone and to buy his films from the families' own company.

"They told Carmine that if he wants to buy a film from this guy Larry, then buy it and pay for it, and no more of this strong-arm stuff. They don't want anymore heat especially from two coasts—there is enough shit going on. They want a peace pact with you, Harry, one that will end this war once and for all. As a peace gesture, they are offering you half a million and forget about the past. If you fail to accept this they will pull out all the stops and make certain you are stopped. They are calling for a peace conference and want you to attend," Moe said.

"Look, Moe, I'm not attending any peace conference. These guys are crazy," I said.

"My take on this is not to trust anything they say," Moe said. "Remember, we had a conference a few months ago to cancel the hit and what happened? The next day, the hit was on and people were still trying to kill you. No, Harry, I'd be very careful with these guys. I think they are still going to try to kill you no matter what. The only thing they respect is brute force, and if you are stronger than they are, they will walk very carefully. Larry, your ex-father-in-law is nothing more than a junior and does what he is told. He runs a very large segment of their numbers racket and is their largest loan shark operator as well as the fact that he is Italian.

"He makes them a lot of money and is very loyal. He is on the hot seat because you are a threat to the entire Mob as Larry's operation was so involved with the Genovese and Colombo operations. They don't know how much you know, and no matter how hard you try to deny any great deal of knowledge, they will still want you dead. Larry fucked up as he allowed you free rein in his operation. What Larry has done and has been aware of in regard to the money lending business and where the bodies are buried is very important and cannot ever be revealed. Therefore, you can never be allowed to live. The New York families can't afford the risk that you will not reveal the names, places, and dates of hits long forgotten. You are toast even if you don't know all that stuff. They do not take chances when it's their operation. The Mob has lived by "Omertà" for a long time and cannot afford to have it broken. Larry makes a lot of money for them, but if they had to, they would get rid of him immediately. A meeting will only bring you out in the open and make you an easy target, so forget it," Moe said again as Miguel agreed and shook his head to signify his feelings.

"Well, Moe, thanks for the heads-up. I really appreciate it. I want to apologize for getting you involved so deeply in this shit. I feel like hell, really I do!" I said.

"Forget it. I really don't mind in the least. I do a lot of work for these guys on the civil side, and they trust my integrity and want me to be their liaison. I don't want to screw up that relationship as the money is very good. If they ever ask me, I'll tell them that I have not heard from you and do not know where to contact you. I'll tell them that I'll deliver the proposition to you when I hear from you. There won't be any problem, so please don't worry at all," Moe said.

"Thanks, Moe, you are a good friend, and I know you are in my corner. You are a mench!" I said. "Do you need any money?" Moe said.

"No, I'm fine for now. What I need is peace. I can make money easily without worrying about all this shit," I said.

"Well, it would be impossible to operate in New York. You did make the right decision in moving the operation. Okay, I got to go now, Harry. Please do not worry about anything. I'll handle it at this end and keep you advised as always. Keep your head up. and always be on guard. Love you. my friend," Moe said and hung up.

"Whew! That was a heavy call, don't you think? "Miguel said.

"At least we are being kept in the know, and that always helps us a lot."

"Sure thing, but at least we know there is a war going on between them, and we are hurting them. I think all we have to do is maintain our security as we have been doing," I said.

"We must be careful, and we must always be alert. Well, Miguel, we will have to work a little harder if we want to make it, but we will make it. This I can assure you." I smiled as I slapped him on the back.

"What is your plan for the rest of today?" Miguel asked.

"I guess I'll stay at home. I don't have any special place to go today. Why don't you take the rest of the day off?" I said.

"Okay, Marcel, I'll see you tomorrow morning," Miguel said.

"Let's meet on Monday and review our security plans and decide what the formats will be for the future. This will all end very soon as long as we maintain a strong force and stay at the ready. Have a great day, and stay healthy. See you tomorrow," I said.

Monday, December 2, 1957

I spoke with Mike, and he advised me that the theater was coming along real well, and we could start putting on the finishing touches by Friday. He recommends that we have the projection stuff tested and do a few dry runs next week. The ticket booth will be ready to be installed next Monday, and the seats will all be in by Friday. The snack bar and souvenir shop will be ready on Wednesday. He will have the health department inspect it as well as the bathroom facilities next week. All permits will be inspected no later than the end of the second week of December, and if you want a date to open the place, it will be ready by December twentieth at the latest. This was great news. Now we could stop sending money out and start taking money in.

Each day will get rough from now on as the Mob and the feds will do whatever they can to shut us down, this is guaranteed. I believe, as I told Miguel, that the feds are the most dangerous ones of all in this scenario. We must always be very careful and be prepared for a bust at all times. Money has to be removed from the premises a few times a day to avoid them from seizing the receipts. When they make a bust, they seize all funds taken in that day and hold it as evidence. Your chances of ever getting the money back is about nil.

I waited for Miguel as we needed to discuss and set our strategies in place for as smooth an operation as possible. I would stay away from the theater as it would now be run by one of Miguel's men who would take the fall if there is a bust. Of course, the fine would be paid by me as that was the arrangement, and a new owner would be installed within twenty-four hours of the bust. As long as there was only one conviction against the owner, it remained a misdemeanor. From now on, all meetings with Marty would take place at a secret location as I would no longer go to the studio regardless of the secret entrance.

Miguel arrived at the apartment, and we sat down to discuss the future.

"I want to be very clear, Miguel. I am putting a lot of responsibility in your hands. We have an agreement of two percent of the gross take from the theater operations, and I will keep that at all times. I don't want any ill will at any time, and if you should have a problem, I want to know at once what it is, and we will solve it together. There cannot be any secrets between us, my friend, ever, please!" I said.

"Marcel, I am happy to be your partner and your friend. If not for you, I would not ever have had this opportunity to make a lot of money and to bring my life upto a standard I never dreamt I could ever reach. True, I have taken care of security, and you could have easily kept me as the head security chief forever, but you didn't. You gave me the opportunity, and you'll never regret it no matter what risks I have to take. I would give my life to protect you, and I would kill anyone who threatens your very existence. You never have to think about my loyalty. It is yours for all time," Miguel said.

"Thanks, Miguel. I needed to hear it from you. I was starting to feel that I am taking advantage of you. I now know that we must work together at all times and face any problem that may arise. It is our empire, and we have to make it grow bigger and bigger. I appreciate your honesty and know we can beat these assholes," I said.

Miguel and I went to the theater and were amazed with the transformation; it looked like a real movie theater, and in a few days it would look like it was always a theater. We loved it and left after spending an hour inspecting and suggesting things here and there.

"This will be my last time here as you will now take over," I said to Miguel. "You are the man who will run the entire operation. I want you to find someone who I can trust with my life that will replace you as head of security. You are now upper management, my friend, and even though you now are a big shot, you can still contribute to our safety with suggestions and orders if you like."

"Thanks, boss," Miguel said. "As I told you earlier, my brother Dante will take over as head of security, and I would like to start including him in every meeting we have if it's all right with you."

"Of course, I told you before that your brother is always welcome, and I shall consider him as loyal and true as you. Let's move on and get things established. Do you want to bring Dante along on our trip this afternoon?" I asked.

We left the apartment and drove to Oxnard to see a possible new location that was an old burlesque theater in a previous life. We picked up Dante and had him ride with us, which allowed me time to get to know him a little better. I liked him a lot as he was warm and very respectful. He was as big as Miguel but had a different look about him. We arrived around three in the afternoon, and I could see the disappointment on Miguel's face. The place was run-down and really needed a complete renovation, but it had a marquee, a ticket booth, and seats for the audience, although Miguel thought the seats should be replaced as they looked very raunchy. The most important thing was that the theater was zoned as property so that getting a permit would be easy. In a small town like Oxnard, getting a permit could be a big problem, but this location made that problem go away. I loved the place as I closed my eyes and could see beyond the dirt and run-down condition. I saw a magnificent theater rising out of the rubble and a magnificent looking and modern theater standing right in this very spot. I just loved every inch of the place. Miguel negotiated a very good lease and advised the owners that he was acting on behalf of the actual lessee who would sign the lease when he arrived in town early next week. The landlord could not care who signed the lease when he saw Miguel pull out a roll of cash; the fact that the place has been vacant for over four years was enough motivation. Miguel gave the landlord a $2K deposit to secure the deal. Once Miguel received a signed receipt stating that the theater was now leased for a period of five years, off we went. My name was never mentioned, and I never spoke a single word. No one could associate me with this operation, and having Dante with us added to the charade. I was excited because we could get this one open very fast. It would be the second one in the chain, and now I finally started to feel that we were on the road to success, and it looked like it was going along very smoothly. I was very excited with the progress we were making. Soon our dreams would come true, and perhaps we would be rid of the Mob and the feds and proceed to have a normal life.

We arrived back at the apartment at close to six. I called Marty and suggested we meet for dinner somewhere that was out of the way, and we could go over the developments.

He was just wrapping up the shoot for the day and could use something to eat and said he would love to hear what had happened today.

We decided to meet at Montes Steak House on Topanga Canyon Boulevard and Ventura at seven. Miguel agreed to the location and had Dante make all the arrangements for our security at dinner tonight. I spent a little time with Natalia who happened to be home because her part in the new movie ended earlier today, and she didn't want to hang around. She was going to meet Mary Lou at six and go shopping; they would have a bite while shopping, and she would see me when I got home.

We arrived at Montes at six forty and were taken immediately to a table in the far end of the place. We had our backs to the wall, and we could easily see the entire restaurant. This was the only way Dante would allow me to sit at a table in any public place. I should always make sure that any point of attack would always come at me straight on. When his people were making the arrangements, the table or booth would always favor me. Too many Mob hits were done on people who did not take these precautions, and once they realized they were being attacked, it was too late. We had rules: no sitting by windows and never in the middle of any restaurant, always stay with your back to the wall and make sure it is a wall that cannot be penetrated from the rear of the building, and we stuck to them for survival at all times. I always said that history was our teacher, and if we refused to be responsible pupils, we would lose out in the end. In my case, losing would be the last thing I would ever do. Therefore, I would follow the rules and, no matter what, would always stick to them. If for some reason the restaurant or meeting place could not accommodate our requests, we would pass on using that location.

Drinks were already on the table as Marty had arrived a couple of minutes before I did and made sure our pleasures would be satisfied.

"How are you doing, Marty? Thanks for the drink. Good thinking," I said as I picked up my drink. "A toast to your good health, my dear and my loyal partner, and to our continued success," Marty said as we clicked glasses together.

"Well, old buddy, I have a lot of stuff to tell you. It's been a very busy day. We've found another location in Oxnard, an old burlesque theater that hasn't been used in at least five years. It needs work, but who cares. The foundation is there and the place is already zoned for a theater. I think we can get this one open in a few weeks and start to take in some money. Won't that be nice for a change?" I said as I finished my drink and signaled the waiter for another round.

"We have given the landlord a deposit, and we'll begin construction the moment Mike finishes the first one. Exciting, isn't it, Marty? Yesterday, I spoke with Moe about the situation in New York. The Mob called a meeting and asked him to be there. They wanted to discuss both you and me but primarily me! Carmine was at the meeting and got his ass kicked by the families as they feel he was being a real asshole about you. They told him to stay away and not to make waves and to buy his films from their own studios. Of course, that presents a problem for Carmine, because he will have to pay for the films or his legs will become a little shorter.

"They wanted me to come to a meeting with them so that we can finally end this battle. They offered five hundred K if I would agree to call it quits, and we can all do our own thing without hassling each other. I told Moe that I would not attend any meeting as they are liars and cannot be trusted.

"The last time I went to a meeting about this, they agreed to remove the hit, and an hour after I left the meeting, they were looking for me. I know we are hurting them, not in the pocket book, but we are fucking up their reputation, and they can't let that be. We must remain alert and keep our wits about us at all times. Is your security situation up to your standards?" I asked.

"Marcel, please trust me. I don't like to be beaten either, so I'm very careful. Yes, I think Miguel is doing a great job, and I listen to whatever he or Roger says always," Marty said.

"For your information, Miguel is being bumped up to our theater operations and will run that no matter how many locations we may open. I feel confident that he will do a great job for us and will always be like a brother to us. His position of head of security will be taken over by his brother, Dante, who has sworn his loyalty to us and will always be there. Of course, you know Dante as you met at the house on Thanksgiving Day when we had that fine meal. He is in charge as of today even though Miguel will be working closely with him for the next few months until he gets his feet wet," I said. "Let's order, man. I'm starved."

We ordered our steaks and another round of drinks. "How did the shoot come out?" I asked.

"This was the best movie I have ever made. It will be a big hit, and we'll make a lot of money with it. Angel came across like a child in heat, and Mary Lou and Natalia both added the beauty and class of a great flick. I'm naming it *What Gets Me Hot,* and it will keep the theaters full. I should have it edited by Friday, and it will be ready for viewing next week. This is the hit we have been waiting for, I promise you that, Marcel," Marty said. I could see the gleam in his eyes; he was very excited about this film and couldn't contain his enthusiasm.

"Can I start putting the title on the marquee?" I asked. "Of course, and I want you to also put up *"Introducing Angel"* Hot! Hot! Hot! Let's see how the crowds react. I believe we will sell out every performance, and Angel's fan club will be huge!" Marty said.

"As long as you believe in all this and are ready for the fight of your life, we can't lose," I said.

Marty signaled the waiter for another round of drinks and said, "Right on, pal. We are on a roll." We finished our food and had enough drinks. Marty was feeling no pain, and I was getting pretty light-headed. This was not good because we lose our ability to be sharp. Dante approached us and said quietly, "You have had enough for tonight. No more drinks, please. Let me take care of the check and get you both out of here," he said as he signaled the waiter and then asked him for the check. He then signaled one of his guys to come and help Marty out to the car. He told his man to order the car now and then put Marty in the backseat and take him home. He called the manager over and told him to get my car and signal him when it was by the front door. He slipped him a large bill, and the manager took his task a lot more seriously. We left, and Miguel and Dante made sure I was taken directly home and safely in the apartment. Natalia was not home when I got in, and feeling as I did, I went directly to the bedroom and fell asleep.

Tuesday, December 3, 1957

I must have had a lot more to drink than I realized. I awoke with Natalia asleep at my side. I was undressed and under the covers and had no recollection of ever doing this. When one doesn't remember what happened, it was not good. I must not let that happen again.

How many times have I said that? I bet I have promised not to drink again at least one hundred times. Thank goodness I don't smoke, or I would be giving that up as many times as well. I will apologize to Miguel and Dante as soon as I see them. I'll start using a lot more discipline from now on.

Miguel and Dante arrived just as I returned from a good and hard run. My security detail was getting healthier each day as we run although I am not certain they do appreciate it. In the last week, we had decided that it would be best to have a security guard run with me. We felt it would be safer and would dissuade a would-be assassin.

"How are you feeling, my man?" he asked.

"I'm feeling great but want to apologize to you about last night. I know I drank too much and that should not happen. I have to keep my wits about me, and that is not the way to do it. I'm sorry. It won't happen again," I said.

"All I asked was if you were all right, and what do I get? No need to feel guilty. That's why I am here—to watch your back. Certainly it's not good to do this too often, but once in a while everyone has to let off some steam," Miguel said.

"What is the schedule for today, Miguel?" I said.

"I think we best get the theater stuff ready. Remember we are back in business and have to have everything in perfect order. Remember, boss, I'm part of this operation. Now tell me what I must do, and let's get it done," Miguel said.

I went over the operation from beginning to end as far as the theater was concerned—how it was to be run and what movies were going to be shown.

We went over the schedule I had picked in regard to the films. I explained to Miguel what to do with the marquee, the exact wording that would attract the viewer, and where to place the names of the stars. He was going to take instructions from the camera supply people on how to run and maintain the projection equipment so that he would be able to train each new manager and operator. It was also important for him to understand the way things worked in case he had to run the show in the event of an emergency. He also decided that he needed a backup plan in the event of an emergency, so he decided to train Dante on the workings of the projection equipment and how the theater was to run. We were finally in business and on the way to fame and fortune, and in order to make sure we did succeed, every last detail had to be addressed over and over until they became second nature to Miguel and Dante.

As of this day, I would handle all business operations from home. I would no longer go out to the theaters or Marty's studio. It was the only way we could reduce the risk of a fatal attack. I didn't like this way of life, but there was no other option. When I wanted to leave the house and socialize, I would disguise myself as a different person, thus leaving anyone who was watching wondering who the hell I was.

I worked all day making phone calls and speaking with real estate agents regarding additional locations for our future theaters. I never realized how exhausting it was to work from home and make sure you were not distracted by the television or other things like a very sexy girlfriend. I also found out how easy it was to forget about time. I also found myself making many trips a day to the refrigerator to find something to munch on. This working from home was a challenge, and I was determined to conquer it.

Natalia and I decided to go out for a quiet meal and then return home for an evening of serious lovemaking. Another day without trouble; I just loved it!

Wednesday, December 4, 1957

This morning, Miguel and Dante came over to the apartment long after my run was over. He said he wanted to discuss our situation, because he thought he found how to solve many things.

"Okay, Miguel, I'm all ears," I said.

"Well, boss, I was thinking about all the things we have going on and that we will have a lot more stuff to contend with as time goes by and we get bigger and bigger. Our security resources will become strained very quickly, because we have so much to cover that we will become much more vulnerable. I think I have the solution and want to act on it right away. The biggest problem I have is money. I don't want you to think that I am a greedy person and that I don't realize how much it costs to run security. I am very willing to cut my two percent down to one percent and allocate the difference for security only.

"Please understand, boss, without you we won't have an operation, and two percent of nothing will leave me with nothing. Giving up 1 percent for our security will pay off in spades, so please consider these proposals and then let's agree.

"First, you must get an office space where you can conduct business each day. I suggest a large warehouse type of building that allows you plenty of room to do the things you must do, things like a complete gym so that you may exercise whenever you want in privacy. You will be able to run whenever you want because it is indoors and your own private area. You will need a kitchen facility so that you can eat healthy and have it prepared like you want. You need an office where you can meet people whenever you wish along with a secretary and other personnel you may need. It will be easy to design a very secure entry and exit system so that no one can get in unless they are trusted and carefully screened. You can make decisions in private and conduct whatever business you wish undisturbed. We will make the office look like a trading company, import and export of goods from Asia. Or we could easily make it look like an investment firm with very little signage and very little information available to the public. We can buy a building under a real estate corporation or a holding company that will not show your name ever. The building will be your fortress and will always have superstrong security and give you peace of mind. The building will be yours and in years to come will return a good profit on your investment.

"Step two is that you move out of this place to a new one that will be kept very private. No one will know where you live other than the people that are very close to you and, of course, your family.

"Cost is not a problem because the theaters will be operating and money will be flowing in faster than you can spend it. Marty's film business will begin to grow and more money will flow in. You're planning on opening a mail order operation and that I can assure you will bring in more money than you can imagine. Porn sells and always will. This I can assure you. All the expenses that will be incurred will be considered very small considering the big picture. If we don't take steps like these, you may not live long enough to enjoy the fruits of your labor. Please don't laugh at these suggestions or consider putting them off. We can't afford to do that especially that our first theater will open in a few days. This new office, sanctuary, gym, or whatever you want to call it, is essential, please!" Miguel said.

"I am in agreement with you and was going to talk to you about this. This apartment was supposed to be a private place known only to a very few. Now it seems everyone knows where I live. Let's make the move, and let's do it fast. When we do find a new place to live and the new office, let's move things in with our own men and keep everything very quiet. We will buy the building as well as the house and keep the title under a holding company. Natalia will be one of the directors under her real name—a name that only the two of us know! Let's keep this place for a while even though I won't be living here, but no one will know that. We will arrange to cancel the lease after we are fully settled in all our new places. I like this direction we are taking. Let's get to work, Miguel, *now!*" I said.

"To do things right, I want you to find a real estate agent and get him working on the building today, and we'll look into the house in the next few days. Tell the agent you have been hired by a South American company that is looking for a commercial space of approximately twenty thousand square feet. You will give the agent the complete details of the company once a building is found. Until then tell the agent to find a place here in the Valley and to do it fast. Dante, I would like you to act the part of the representative of the company from South America. You can speak Spanish, can't you?" I said,

"Yes, sir, I speak fluent Spanish as well as French and would be happy to do whatever is needed," Dante said.

"I will speak with Natalia to work with you as she will be my eyes when it comes to selecting a building. I will inspect the building with her while I will be wearing one of the disguises. I will set up a meeting with Marty as soon as possible!"

"Okay, boss, I'll get on it right away, and Marcel, thanks for moving so fast and accepting my suggestions. I really feel I am a part of your life and the operation." Miguel said as he left the apartment.

When Natalia woke and completed her daily exercise routine, I mentioned that I wanted to talk with her. We sat down with coffee as I explained exactly what I was doing and that she was to be an integral part of everything I did.

"I trust you with my life and am doing so because I love you and feel you're part of me. Would you feel better if we were married because I certainly want to marry you?" I asked.

"Ron, I love you too and would be very happy to spend the rest of my life with you as your wife or your girlfriend or whatever you want from me. Sure, I'd love to marry you, and if you want to do that, then let's do it. We don't have to tell anyone we can fly to Vegas and return the next day as man and wife. I'm yours forever, my darling, no matter what direction you take. I understand what kind of life we have and what dangers exist. I know it all as you know, my darling, but I'm still here. I'm willing to accept it all, and I shall love you until I die," she said as she put her arms around my neck and kissed me.

"Okay, Mrs. Miller, let's fly to Vegas tomorrow and get married. I'll clear it with Miguel, and we can become man and wife forever."

I called Miguel and told him that I needed to speak with him when he had time. He said he would be by the place in a few hours, and we could discuss whatever it was.

Natalia was excited beyond my wildest imagination. I asked her why she didn't tell me how much she wanted to get married, and she said she understood what I was going through and felt it would be best not to bother me with such things. She didn't want to put any pressure on me in any way. She was so good and so right for me, I felt happy that this was my woman and how lucky I was. She was beautiful; the envy of every man who saw her. She was smart, very smart, and understanding in every way possible. She was unselfish and very loving and was going be a true partner for all time. I was so happy with all this.

Miguel arrived late in the afternoon with some very exciting news. He found the ideal building on Nordhoff near Corbin. It was twenty-one thousand square feet, and the owner was very motivated in getting rid of the building.

"After a complete inspection, we found a lot things wrong with the place, but to us that is a plus as we are going to renovate the building from top to bottom. Basically the place is a mess and in today's market will not fetch a big price. He was asking ninety-eight K for the place and we agreed on sixty-five K in "as is" condition. We can close on the building in less than thirty days, and it is perfect. Believe me, boss, it's just right for us," Miguel said. I could see the excitement in his eyes and hear it in his voice. Miguel was a super person. I couldn't be more fortunate to have him at my side.

"Okay with me. I'll arrange for the money to buy the place. When can I see it?" I said.

"How does tomorrow sound?" Miguel said.

"Oh, that's what I wanted to talk to you about, Miguel," I said. "Natalia and I have decided to get married tomorrow. We want to fly to Vegas get married and come back. What do you think?" I said.

"I think it's great, except, why can't we do it this weekend? We will fly to Vegas Saturday morning. You can get married, and we can return Saturday night or Sunday. What do you think, boss?" Miguel said. I called Natalia over as she was making drinks for us and asked her if it was okay with her to do it all on Saturday. She agreed, and we decided to drive to Vegas and invite Marty and Mary Lou as well. Done deal!

I called Marty and asked him to stop by on his way home so that we could discuss some important issues. Marty arrived at seven. Natalia made us drinks, and we sat down in the living room and began our meeting. I instructed Natalia to get us something to eat because we would be busy for at least a couple of hours. I explained to Marty all the details regarding the building, the apartment, and the house. I also told Marty that I wanted to marry Natalia and plan to do so on Saturday in Vegas and sure as hell wanted him there as my best man. "I will be your best man, that's for sure. How can you even doubt that for a minute? You are my partner, my closest friend, and whatever makes you happy, makes me happy as well," Marty said as he poured himself another drink.

"As for as the rest of it, I can't agree with you more about the building. We need a place where we can discuss things and where we can organize our business operations. A place that is private and known only to us and those who really matter. I agree with the holding company being the owner and keeping all the shareholders and owners private. I am a little worried about putting all this power in Natalia's name. I know you are going to marry her, but you know that doesn't protect you and me," Marty said.

"Of course it does, Marty, because I will have Natalia sign her resignation at once and leave it undated. If there should ever be a divorce or some other thing that may happen, all we have to do is backdate the resignation. I will have her sign and endorse the shares now so that if we need to use them in the future they are ours, and we do not have to ask Natalia's permission. We will keep these items locked up safely in a safety deposit box known only to you and me. I think that we will have covered our asses in every way possible. It is also agreed that Miguel gets two percent of the take from the theater receipts. Although I would never change our agreement with him, Miguel has requested we change it to one percent for him and the difference go toward the costs of the security expenses. I was really touched by his suggestion and will honor it, but remember, Marty, it always must be lived up to no matter what. Remember, I gave my word, and he is an important part of keeping us alive. I also care a great deal about him and would never ever hurt him. He is like a brother, and I do not ever cheat a family member or anyone else for that matter. My biggest worry is that I am getting to be an evil person with some of the things I have done in the name of survival. Please know that I am not really a bad person. Please don't ever lose sight of that, and never go back on your word. If you should give your word, Marty, I will honor it no matter what, and I am sure you will do the same for me. I am sure we agree on all of this, Marty?" I said.

"No problem, Ron. No matter whatever happens to either one of us, the one remaining will make sure it will always be taken care of," Marty said.

"The most important thing is that we move on this stuff now because the Mob will be making their move very soon. They don't like to be turned down when they make offers. You should know that the meeting

Moe was asked to attend was nothing more than a sham to get us to come out in the open. They wanted a reaction so that they could take a very positive action, like killing us! Once we don't bite, they'll send the troops in and try to blow us apart, so we best act fast," I said.

"Okay, let's look at the building tomorrow, and if it is suitable, we buy and get things rolling," Marty said, "By the way, Ron, how do we work the ownership of the building?"

"You and I will own the building as partners, as we do with everything. Whatever money I spend out of my pocket must be paid back to me to keep our partnership straight. I will arrange the financing, and I'm sure things will go very smoothly," I said.

"As far as your house goes, I want you to choose a really private and very safe place with lots of land so that we can have security at all times. The house is yours and should be owned by you only. Let's get the show on the road. By the way, Ron, *What Gets Me Hot* will be ready next Monday. We will have a private showing on Tuesday and then it's ready for public viewing," Marty said.

"Great, we'll have the premier on December 13—Friday the thirteenth. That should be quite a day, and we'll set box office records. I can hardly wait," I said.

"I also wanted you to know that the movie we shot in New York is also ready, and I've taken some of the scenes and made a trailer to show at the theater. Coming attractions will be great but will not be ready for the opening."

We wrapped up the meeting around ten. Marty left, and Natalia and I relaxed for the night. Things had gone well. Let's hope they always go this well.

Thursday, December 5, 1957

I had Miguel call the other film producers to inquire as to when we can expect their first new release films.

"Boss, we got to go see the new building at eleven thirty. The real estate agent will meet us there," Miguel said.

"I'll be ready, but first I have to make a phone call and make sure things are in place. Please excuse me while I take care of this," I said as I headed to the bedroom where I could make my call in privacy.

I called Moe in New York and told him all about our plan to buy a building and explained the reasons. He agreed with my plan as well as the house.

"So you see, Moe, I will need some very good mortgage rates for these properties. What I want is for you to loan the purchase price to our holding company and hold the mortgage as collateral under your name or some corporation that you choose. The reason for this is to make it even harder for anyone to know who owns the building and who the tenant is. You can use my money if you like and just put the funds back into my account with every payment. I do not want anyone to know where the funds came from except that a mortgage company loaned the funds to the company. It will be a dead end at this point and will give me a lot more protection. Will you take care of this, please?" I said.

"Of course, Harry, don't I always handle these things for you! I'll call you tomorrow with the name of the mortgage company and their address. You can give this information to the escrow company, and it will be handled from there. My pleasure to help in any way I can. I see that you are moving in the right direction. Let's hope you will finally settle down and, with a little help, get your life on the proper path. Your brother, Morty, sends his love and hopes he will be able to see you soon. He is doing well and so are your folks. They send you love and kisses," Moe said as I hung up.

I then had Natalia do a transformation on my looks as she placed a gray wig on my head and applied makeup that made me look at least twenty years older. I now had bushy eyebrows and some wrinkles I didn't know I should have. Nevertheless, she did a great job as I looked like an old man looking at a building. In this way, the real estate agent as well as the owner would only see this guy once.

"Okay, Miguel, I'm ready, let's go!" I said as we grabbed our jackets and headed for the door. Miguel told me that Marty would meet us at the building, so off we went to check it out. We inspected the building, and although there were many obvious faults, it served our purpose. We told the agent that we were prepared to make a written offer even though the price was already agreed upon. The paperwork was completed in less than an hour, and we left and allowed the agent to do his job. Around four in the afternoon, we received a phone call from the agent that the owner has countered. We decided that we would refuse to consider any counter offer and advised the agent.

We further told the agent that if we did not get an approval today we would look at other buildings; we did not have any time to waste on back-and-forth negotiations. At six, we received a call from the agent advising us that we had a deal and would close escrow in thirty days. We agreed and felt great about this deal. It was a good one and would be the start of the empire we wanted to build. We were on the way, and there was no looking back.

Friday, December 6, 1957

I called Moe and gave him the information regarding the new building, and he in turn gave me the name of the corporation that he would be using as the mortgage holder. With all that out of the way, I went for a run and thought as I ran how nice it would be if I could exercise whenever I wanted to inside my own building. No worries about someone trying to kill me or waiting for my security detail. Miguel and Dante arrived while I was still out running and waited patiently as they sat and drank coffee with Natalia.

"Sorry, I didn't know you guys were here. I would have hurried a little more. So what is new?" I asked.

"The guys I spoke with confirmed that their new releases will be ready in a couple of weeks. Irv said his latest films are in the can as we speak but still need titling and a few corrections and will be ready in a week or so. The others all gave me the same response that they are almost ready and will have some stuff ready for you before Christmas. I don't know what you are going to do with all these films. We only have one theater and maybe a second in a few weeks. We really need a lot more if we are to absorb this many films. Your agreement prevents them from offering the films to anyone anywhere for a period of sixty days from the date of your release. They will start to object if your release dates take too long. I anticipate some problems there, what do you think?" Miguel said.

"I don't anticipate any problems at all. Once we have enough theaters, we will be the best source of distribution they ever had, remember, Miguel, they get forty percent of the gross take. That could amount to a great deal of money, and that flow will continue as long as that film is playing. If they make lousy films, we will not show the films more than a few days, and they will lose big time, so it is in their interest to always produce top-notch productions. No, Miguel, there will not be any problem as we are the cash cow!" I said and went to take a shower.

It was our job to begin the house search as soon as possible. We decided to get an agent and tell him what we were looking for and that we would not settle for anything less. The agent would be instructed not to bother us with anything that did not meet the criteria we had laid down. Needless to say, we did not tell the agent that what we really wanted was a fortress, but that is what we needed and what we were going to find. Of course, I stayed away as we did not want the agent to ever know of my involvement or who the real owner was. Loose lips sink ships, and we were going to make sure that this did not happen.

Miguel had one of his men dress up in a very expensive suit and look very distinguished to act as the buyer. All interactions would take place with this guy, and the agent would never know differently.

We finally found a wonderful house that was located on Coldwater Canyon Drive, high up on the mountain that overlooked the Valley as well as Beverly Hills. The only access was a road straight up the mountain. There was no way one could gain access from the other side as it was a sheer drop of over one thousand feet. The house was a little under ten thousand square feet but was in very poor condition. It seemed that the previous owner could not afford the place and let it run down. We finally reached an agreeable price, and I bought the place for less than our original budget. We now had a lot of work to do to get all these projects moving along. Miguel suggested we hire an outside contractor to do the house and make sure I never appeared there while any workers were present. Our first priority was to hire an architect to help get the house back in shape and to add the security systems that normal homes would use.

I then called Al Fogel, my security man from Pennsylvania. I promised to send him a set of blueprints of the house and then fly him out to Los Angeles. Once here, he could obtain everything he needed and do his construction using the labor we had or bring in his own people.

We agreed on a price for his services plus material. We left it to Al to do whatever it took and to make sure the confidentiality of the system would always be secret. No one would be able to get any information on the security system as they would not know what it consisted of and who designed it and how and where it was installed. I felt we were taking the right step to protect us.

The next step was a meeting with Mike to see if he could hire additional people and get the second theater up and running fast. The building that would contain my office and the running track would be done by an outside contractor that would deal with another one of Miguel's crew. Therefore, we would not be known to anyone.

Mike met us at a diner on the corner of Nordhoff and De Soto.

"Hi, Mike, how are you doing?" I asked.

"I'm tired but doing fine. There is a lot of work, but the place will be ready next week," Mike said.

"Thanks for coming. I know you really don't have time to bullshit over some lunch, so I'll get to the point. We need another theater done up yesterday, this one is in Oxnard and should be a lot easier as it was an old burlesque showplace. It hasn't been used in a few years, but the floor is slanted, there is a stage where the screen will go, and the rows are set, and the seats are there. We may have to change the seats, but that work will be done by the company we buy them from, so it will not interfere with the other things you have to do. I know it is a rush job, but we need it done," I said to Mike.

"Listen, I am so thankful you gave me this opportunity to work full-time, so you just tell me what you need and I'll get it done, I promise you," Mike said.

"Thanks, Mike, we appreciate it a lot and will make it worth your while. How about Sacramento, Barstow, Bakersfield, and places north?" Miguel asked.

"Hey, guys, I'm your guy, whatever, wherever you need me, I will take care of it. Just tell me what you need and when you need it, and as long as it's possible, it's done! Just keep me busy all year long, that's all I ask," Mike said. When we work out of town, I will be the coordinator of the project and will hire a company or men from that locality. I will need your okay to drive or fly home every weekend to be with my family. Other than that, I am your man and will always be at the helm for you."

"No problem with that, Mike. This way we can be certain that every theater will be to our standards no matter where it is located. I love it, really I do," I said.

We left Mike and promised him a schedule by tomorrow so that he could get his stuff together and take care of things. The theater in Canoga Park would be ready to open in a week. Mike would have two of his guys make sure that the finishing touches were all done by the time we opened. Miguel and Dante would be training the staff, and Marty was putting the final touches on the new film and getting the posters ready. The posters had to be plain and could not reveal any parts of the female anatomy that may be considered lewd. The posters had to be displayed outside the theater, and therefore we could not prevent any person under the age of eighteen from looking at them. The cops would love to bust us on obscenity charges, and the posters were a very easy way to do that. Of course, we did make them as sexy as the law allowed.

We made our way toward the apartment when Miguel cautioned me that he detected a suspicious car following us. The car looked like a typical Mob vehicle, big and black, windows tinted very dark, menacing in every way. It was possible they were not interested in us, but we could not take any chances, so Miguel ordered the driver to lose them while he called another one of his men on the mobile car phone to dispatch another car to our location. He gave them instructions as to where to join us and what to look out for. Our attempts to shake the other car proved to be useless and confirmed that they were indeed interested in us. It was useless to continue to take evasive action, so we proceeded along Roscoe Boulevard to Valley Circle road and then took that through the mountain and past the Rocketdyne plant. The car was still there, but now our other car had joined us and was behind them. Miguel instructed the driver to pull up ahead where the road was deserted and narrowed considerably and stop the car and park it so that it would block the road. By doing this, we would make it impossible to pass. He told the car behind us via his phone to box them in. There would be no place for the Mob car to go; they would be forced to stop and it would now be caught in the middle of a perfect roadblock.

The cars followed Miguel's instruction, and within a few minutes, the Mob car was hemmed in with nowhere to go. Miguel and Dante got out of our car and walked over to the Mob car while two of our men exited the rear car and stood back a little way with guns drawn while Miguel signaled the guys to get out.

"Why are you following me?" Miguel asked the driver as he rolled down his window.

This guy was big and looked very menacing as he said, "We aren't following you. It just so happens we are going the same way. Now get the fuck out of our way before I crush you to death," he said in loud voice with a definite Brooklyn accent.

"I don't think you are going to crush anyone to death. Please get out of the car now as you can see we have you surrounded, and my men will fill you full of lead if you should attempt anything fancy," Miguel said in a very relaxed and even tone.

The men got out of the car and stood there wondering what to do next. They obviously knew they were outnumbered and outgunned. Miguel walked over to the guy who was standing near the driver's side of the car, and Dante went directly to the other. Each guy was searched and relieved of their guns.

"Just relax and tell me why you are following me and who sent you. If you want to play rough, we'll blow you away and forget the fact that we are giving you a chance to get out of here alive. Now answer the questions and answer them honestly. No more bullshit, I'm waiting, man, and my patience is very short," Miguel said.

"Hey, man, we don't mean any harm to anyone, so fuck off and let us pass, and we'll be on our way," he said.

At that moment, Miguel moved his hand in a side motion touching his ear and then the tip of his nose, no doubt a signal just like a baseball coach to his hitter. At that moment Dante slapped the other guy across the face with his gun. It looked like he broke this guy's nose as blood began to gush everywhere.

"Hey, what the hell are you doing?" the giant yelled as he reached into his jacket. "Pull that hand out, and it better be empty or it'll be the last time you breathe. Now take your hand out slowly and you better not have anything it. I thought I searched you properly, but if I did leave you a weapon, you'd better use it fast. Do it now, or I'll blow your brains out! Do it now, shitface!" Miguel yelled as three other guns were now pointed at these guys.

"Now I am going to ask you one more time, who sent you and why? You have one minute to answer, or it's over. No more fucking around," Miguel said.

"Listen, man," the guy with the broken nose said. "We are here from New York. We were told to find you and follow you and let them know what is going on. No one asked us to hurt you in any way at all. Let us go, and we'll tell them we couldn't find you, I swear."

"Okay, as long as you tell me who sent you and then you can go. If I find you anywhere in Los Angeles again, I promise you I will kill you both on sight. Now who sent you?" Miguel said.

"We work for Larry Casparizzi. He gave us the order. We were told it came from the council, and we were to handle this for them. It would give us a chance to move up in the organization. That's the truth, I swear!" the nose-bleed guy said.

Miguel signaled his guys, and they instantly shot both these guys right through their heads. The guys then picked them up and put them into their car. One of our guys got in and drove their car away while the backup car followed. Dante left with the backup car as Miguel got back into the car and we drove off; that was the last I ever saw of those people. They just disappeared off the face of the earth, car and all. I wondered how long it would be before I would hear something. I really didn't care about these assholes and wondered why Larry would send anyone unless he wanted to make a showing to his bosses that he was as interested in finding Harry as they were. All I could think of was self-preservation and nothing else.

We went back to the apartment where Natalia was waiting. "How did it go, guys?" she said. "Pretty good. The theater will open next week, and we are starting work on the new one. Things are moving along quite nicely. How was your day?" I asked.

"I didn't do anything except sit around and wait for you. I missed you, honey!" she said as she threw her arms around me and kissed me.

"Are you ready for the big day?" I asked as I held her in my arms and kissed her gently.

"Are you crazy? Of course, I'm ready. Why not drive to Vegas tonight and spend the night in a special pre-wedding room and be all set for tomorrow. Did we set a time for the wedding?" Natalia said.

"No, not yet. Hey, Miguel, what do you think about this plan?" I said.

"You are two of my favorite people, so whatever you want to do we will do. If you want to drive tonight, then let's get going. Marty, Mary Lou, and Angel will meet us in Vegas tomorrow. Dante will drive them early in the morning. I could call them and see if they want to go tonight as well, and we could all drive there in a limo. I have a friend who has a great one, and I'm sure we can get it at a very good price. Let me call him and arrange it while you call Marty and see if he can be ready," Miguel said.

Everything went well as Marty and Mary Lou loved the idea of going today and confirmed that they would be ready within the hour. Miguel left us and picked up the limo and assigned Roger to do the driving. Miguel and Dante were going to have a ball this weekend as they said, "We are off duty." Miguel called ahead and made arrangements at the Dunes so that our rooms were reserved. He had also made arrangements for the chapel and the wedding ceremony including all the necessary things we needed. There was nothing left out of this small but very loving wedding. Everyone was very excited, especially Mary Lou and Angel. One thing for sure when we walk into the Dunes—I guarantee all eyes will be looking at the girls. Here we had three of the most beautiful women you could imagine, and they were dressed to tempt everyone. It was going to be fun and exciting.

Saturday, December 7, 1957

What a good time we had last night. When we arrived, we were shown to our rooms, which were luxurious and filled with champagne, fruits, and cheeses.

Natalia, Mary Lou, and Angel decided that this would be Natalia's last night as a single woman, so they should party by themselves in the casino. There wasn't a chance in hell that we could say no. So Marty, Miguel, Dante, Roger, and I went to the bar and drank for a little while until Marty decided to play blackjack. Miguel and Roger decided to play craps while I watched Marty won over sixteen K in the next four hours. I then went back to my room and went to sleep. Natalia was beside me this morning, and that was all that was important to me.

Our wedding was scheduled for three this afternoon with a special dinner in a private room following the wedding. The Dunes was going all the way to show us a good time. I suspected they wanted their sixteen K back from Marty, but who cared as long as we were having fun. Natalia didn't want a wedding dress. She only wanted a special outfit that she could wear on other occasions. She bought her dream outfit at one of the boutique shops in the Dunes at a cost of a thousand dollars and looked outstanding. She was beautiful with or without this outfit, but today she looked radiant. She had a massage and her hair and nails done and looked like a doll.

The wedding went off on schedule as the music played, and the Chaplin dressed in a beautiful grey suit waited at the altar. Marty was the best man and Miguel along with Roger were the witnesses. The whole thing took about thirty minutes, and we were man and wife. We used the names of Ron Majestic and Natalia Petrov in order to make certain no one would see the name of Harry Miller anywhere when registering the marriage in the Las Vegas City Hall. To both Natalia and me, it didn't matter what names we used as long as were together. We then went off to the private room and opened our first bottle of champagne as man and wife. The party went on until we could hardly stand and had our fill of food and wine. Natalia and I went off to the casino just to walk around and work off some of the food while the boys went to the craps table and the girls decided to play blackjack with Marty. We were so very happy and thrilled just to hold hands and walk around and watch people stop and stare at the newlyweds. What could spoil a night like this, filled with love and joy?

I was aware that the Dunes was run by the Mob, and they always had their spotters, as all casinos do, watching for people who cheated or who won too much. They also watched for people who were addicted gamblers or those who usually owed money to their operations. The Mob is the Mob and is affiliated with those out of New York and New Jersey. These guys had on their list a guy out of New York named Harry Miller and his description. Even though I did not look like Harry, they also had a note that this guy Harry might be travelling with an entourage of beautiful women. While walking through the Casino with Natalia at my side, I was approached by one of the Dune's personnel. "Excuse me, sir. I was wondering if I may have a word with you," he said.

"Certainly, how can I help you?" I responded.

"I suggest we go back to the office for a little privacy, if you would please follow me!" he said.

"I'm sorry sir, but I think not. You see we were just married here in the hotel tonight, and I would like to spend the next few hours with my bride alone. If there is something I may do for you, please tell me now because we are headed to our room," I said with a smile.

"My name is Tony and you are?" he said.

"I'm Ron. A pleasure to meet you, Tony. Can we get on with this as I do want to spend some time with my bride? You understand, Tony?" I said.

"I thought I recognized you, Ron. You look like a friend. I know his name is Harry, Harry Miller, and he's out of New York," he said.

"Well, I'm not this Harry, and I'm from Los Angeles. Please excuse me. It is obvious you have made an error. It was a pleasure meeting you, Tony," I said as I turned back to Natalia and said," Let's go, honey."

As we made our way toward the room we stopped by the craps table so that I could confer with Miguel. He came away from the table and put his hand out for a handshake. This was done in case Tony was watching.

"I think they are suspicious and are trying to shake me down. What do you think we should do? Should we pack up and get out tonight or wait until tomorrow?" I said.

"No, you go back to your room and act normally. I'll make sure Roger is watching your room, and Dante will cover your back. They will stay on duty all night and make sure you are not disturbed. After all it is your wedding night. We will leave tomorrow like we planned. Don't worry about a thing. I'll handle it," Miguel said.

"Okay, buddy, see you later. Have a good night and win lots of money," I said as Natalia and I walked away arm in arm.

We entered the room and knew immediately that someone had been in there looking through our stuff. It was easy to see what was disturbed and that they were not looking to steal anything as nothing was missing. They were looking for some way to identify who I was. Of course, there was nothing in the room that would suggest anything close to Harry Miller. There were a few papers that said Ron Majestic but other than that nothing at all. Natalia and I decided that it would be best not to say a word and just go on with our lives. We both understood that the room was most likely bugged, so our conversation would be controlled to supply as much misinformation as we could.

"I love you, my dear wife. This is the happiest day of my life. I promise I will make you so very happy always. I'm so happy, and I know we are going to be very happy for a long, long time," I said as I kissed Natalia.

"I'm sorry that guy Tony stopped us. He sure did mistake you for someone else, didn't he? Nothing can change the way I feel about you and how happy I am to get out of this beautiful dress and make love with you," she said.

"Give me a minute, Ron, and I'll be there. I love you too and always will. Too bad we have to go back to work on Monday."

"I know. Isn't it a shame? But at least we can now start planning the honeymoon. I love you with all my heart." We spent the rest of the night making love and having fun as newlyweds should.

Sunday, December 8, 1957

We were awoken by a telephone call from Miguel, "Good morning, folks, hope you are well rested after a night of frolicking? Please pack up as we must get going as we have to get home and get ready for work tomorrow. The room has been taken care of, so there is no need for you to check out. The limo will be waiting for you out front, so please hurry. I know you won't believe this, but Marty and the rest of the gang are all ready and waiting. Roger is outside your door. He will take your bags. Please follow him out of the hotel."

We grabbed our bags and opened the door, and sure enough, Roger was right there waiting. We followed him through the lobby and out the front door. We jumped into the limo and off we went.

"I'm glad we are on our way," Miguel said. "If I had remembered that most of these casinos are Mob-run, I would have suggested we have this wedding elsewhere. We aren't out of the woods yet. I think they may try to intercept us along the way. Many a body is buried out there in the desert, so I think we should make haste before they realize we are gone. No stopping until we reach Barstow. Keep your eyes peeled, and be ready for some action if we should need it. I called for backup last night before going to sleep. Our boys should be meeting us about thirty miles out Vegas, so let's get the lead out and move," Miguel said.

"Well, Marty, how did you do in the end?" I said hoping to lighten up the atmosphere a little.

"I gave back most of the sixteen K but had a great time. Drank for free, ate for free, and played for free and left with two K, so I can't really complain. Now I only hope I can stay alive long enough to spend the money," Marty said with a chuckle.

We were riding along route 15 about twenty-five miles out of Vegas when Dante yelled out that a car was coming up fast behind us and should be on top of us in about five minutes at the most. Miguel started to yell out instructions at once, "Everyone pay attention and follow my orders. They are most important and could be the very action that saves your life. Stay down as close to the floor as possible. Do not look up to see what is going on as that could prove fatal. Our boys should be able to intercept the Mob's car, so there will not be any danger to us but, just in case, stay down."

A couple of minutes later Miguel shouted, "Our boys are here just as planned. They know exactly what to do, so just sit back and let the battle proceed. We'll be home on time and all the danger will pass. Roger, keep this bus on the road, and keep going toward home. Dante, keep your gun ready and pay attention to the Mob car and report," he said.

As soon as the car following us drew closer, an intercept car came out of nowhere and was now between the Mob car and us. Every time the Mob car tried to pass our intercept car, they would drift out so that the car could not execute the passing maneuver. Another car pulled out onto the highway and remained behind the Mob car at all times. Now we had the Mob car boxed in while the limo could floor it and move on. It was a neat operation, and there was no need for any bloodshed at this time. We moved fast, and soon we were well out of sight of the three cars. We all breathed easier as we drove on toward our home turf.

We arrived home at about twelve thirty at the apartment and decided to relax the rest of the day. Sunday football would keep me entertained while Natalia putters about putting away her souvenirs from Vegas and our wedding. We now shared some history as December 7, was a very solemn day in American history. Pearl Harbor was struck on that day in 1941, and we were married on that day as well. We would always remember Pearl Harbor as we would always remember our wedding day.

Miguel called to thank us for a wonderful weekend and to congratulate us once again. He said he hoped to meet some nice woman real soon and settle down as well. He was a swell guy and took good care of us all the time. He was a very good friend. We spent the rest of the day enjoying being married and taking good care of each other,

Monday, December 9, 1957

I awoke feeling very good and ready to tackle a new week. The Bijou would open this week, and with a little luck, Mike would start on the Oxnard location. We would close escrow on our new building this week, and construction could begin as early as next week. Our new home up on Coldwater Canyon should be on a fasttrack-closing process.

A lot of stuff was taking place this week, and a lot of new doors were opening for us. I was stoked, filled with an excitement I hadn't felt in a long time. Finally, money would start to come into our pockets instead of it all going out. Up to this point, I had put out a lot of money and certainly would like it if some came back.

Miguel arrived at ten, and even though I wanted to go the see the theater, he wouldn't let me go there as we had agreed. He said, "Marcel I don't think it is wise for you to leave your apartment at this time. There is far too much danger out there, and it's stupid to give your enemies any opportunity to get at you. Don't you trust me?"

"Of course, I trust you with my life, but Miguel I just can't sit at home and do nothing," I said.

"You are full of shit, Marcel," Miguel said. "When you stay at home, you create and direct the entire operation. We could not move forward without you, don't you realize that? If you are killed, your dreams will die with you because no one in this organization has the leadership qualities that you have. No one else can take us to the top as you can! We need you safe and sound always, and if staying put makes you safe, then that's what you must do. I don't care how boring you may think it is as the end result will justify this period of additional caution. So please get off the ego trip and do what you must do—lead us to the top of the mountain. We are taking steps that will insure our part of the future. We will be a very big operation in another year or two. Don't fuck it up because you want to see what the theater looks like or what anything looks like. Be patient and lead us as you must, and let us take care of the battles and make sure you and your name does not ever surface. Please, Marcel, listen to me. It's very important, and it's from the heart," Miguel said.

"I'm sorry, Miguel, you are right. Please take a look at the theater and see that everything is okay. I just have to learn to have faith and trust the people who do the work for us. I'll work from home until the building is ready, and I'll be sending you all over the place to do my errands. I will remain the unknown man behind the scenes until we are certain that the danger has passed. I'll do as you say. I'll stay home. By the way, Miguel, I know I don't have to say this, but I will. Please take care of Natalia always. She will not remain in isolation and will want to do things, many things, and will need your help," I said.

"You got it, sir," Miguel said. "I'll make sure she is always safe and that she can enjoy whatever she wants. I love you, Marcel, and I will love Natalia as well. You are both my family, always!"

Miguel arrived back at the apartment an hour later.

When he walked in I said, "What a short day! I guess you couldn't stay away from me too long, could you? How was the theater?"

"It looks great and will be ready for opening day. We are set to go, Marcel. I just wanted to let you know. Mike did a super job. Everything is very professional and first class. He is on his way to Oxnard to get the next theater open and will start work tomorrow."

I worked the rest of the day discussing with Miguel the various ways the marquee was used and what it meant to the passing traffic.

The movie would make everyone come back over and over again, but the marquee would bring them into the theater. The message we put on that marquee was the teaser that made them all want to see the movie. It was also important that we remove the stigma that only perverts go to adult theaters by making sure everything was always first class. We had to make sure that the seats were all in perfect order, and the adult shop located in the lobby was all stocked up with gels, rubber goods, and other goodies that would sell very well to the patrons. "First Time On The Big Screen: '*What Gets Me Hot*' Starring: *Angel*." That was one of the shining moments, when the marquee lights up for the first time that I would miss. No matter, Miguel is right. If I am to remain alive, I must put things in proper perspective and stay away from the limelight. There will be plenty of time to enjoy the fruits of my labor.

The day went by slowly but, productively, as I made all my requests through my assistant, Dante. Miguel assigned Dante as my personal assistant and secretary. Anything I needed done, Dante was there to do it. He was my new confidant and, as assured by Miguel, the most trustworthy person you would ever want at your side. I never really knew Dante before except seeing him either driving a car or handling some message for Miguel. He was at the Thanksgiving Day dinner and has been with us since then but has rarely said a great deal. Finally he was assigned to be my personal assistant, and I liked him a lot. He was a handsome young man, who stood around six foot tall—all muscle packed into his one hundred and ninety pound frame. He was soft-spoken but filled with confidence and gave off an aura of strength. I felt very comfortable with him and trusted him completely. If Miguel vouched for his brother Dante, then that was good enough for me; no questions asked.

Tuesday, December 10, 1957

I wanted desperately to exercise as working out of my apartment left me a little short in that department. I started doing sit-ups and running in place to get my heart beating as fast as possible. I needed more than sex to get the required heart exercise. I just finished my routine when Dante entered the apartment.

"Good morning, sir, how are you today?" he asked.

"Just great, Dante. How are things with you?" I asked cordially.

"Ready for a new day, sir. Is there anything you need done at this time? I am at your disposal, and may I add, I just love this job. I'll always be in debt to Miguel for giving me this opportunity. Working for you is so exciting and interesting. I want you to know that I will be your trusted friend for as long as you will have me. I will never reveal to anyone what we discuss or anything that goes on between us or anything with others. I know you don't know me very well, sir, but I'd like you to trust me. Please, I'll never let you down," Dante said very sincerely. I believed him and felt that this guy could be trusted with sensitive information. Dante was Miguel's younger brother and was as respectful and likeable as Miguel. I just felt good about him and would place my trust with him. Sometimes you can feel the connection between yourself and another person, and you take it from there. In this case, I felt Dante was true and would be honorable, no matter what. Some people would think I'm nuts. Natalia didn't think so as she felt as I did about him.

If I'm wrong, God help us, but if I am right, we have found a son!

"Dante, I believe you, and only time will tell if you are what you say, but be assured, I feel the way you do, and as long as you feel this close to us and continue to demonstrate this loyalty and honor, we'll be like father and son," I said very seriously.

Miguel came by and reported that the theater was ready and could open any day we wanted. "What is a lucky day to start a new venture?" I asked.

"I think we should open on Friday. Friday is a good luck day, and that would make this venture a big success," Dante said.

"I think Thursday is a very lucky day, and the theater should open then," Miguel said.

"I think you are both right on the money. All new movies start in the theaters on a Friday. I'm not sure if that is good luck or not, because there are plenty of films that are failures and open on a Friday. Yet I've also heard that Thursday is a lucky day when opening a shopping mall or a new retail location, so there is a simple way we can solve this dilemma. Let's open on Thursday and call it a sneak preview and then have the grand opening on Friday. What do you think of that?" I asked.

"I like that idea. Let's do it that way," Miguel said. "What about ticket prices? What do you want to charge, and do you want a different price for different times?"

"I think we should charge five dollars no matter what time of day. We will be able to show each film eight times a day by opening at eight A.M. and closing at midnight. I don't think we can stay open after midnight, and even if we could, I don't think we should, because we will be accused of bringing bad elements to the neighborhood. By staying open until midnight, we will create a following that will spread the word to others about the shows we have. Once we are established and the authorities see that there has been no trouble and the word is out that our shows are great and we have multiple locations, we will be able to be the first twenty-four-hour-movie theaters in California.

"Most locations that will be outside of Los Angeles will service truckers and highway travelers, and being open twenty-four hours a day will be a very important part of being very profitable. Los Angeles itself may not be profitable, but it will be offset by the other locations. What is our capacity in the new theater?" I asked Miguel.

"We have five hundred and fifty seats but probably won't run at capacity. I think if we count on two hundred per showing, we will be close to the correct amount," he said.

"Okay, I'll go along with you even though I think we will see a little more than that per showing. But at two hundred viewers per show, that will give us eight K per day revenue. That would give us fifty-six K per week not counting sales from the shop-and-snack stand. I think we will do very well even if we don't reach those numbers. The opening though will bring in a lot more as it might run at capacity a couple of times," I said with a big smile.

"Okay, boss, I'll get things ready for the show," Miguel said.

"By the way, Miguel, I want you to introduce Dante to the owners of the adult companies so that they can deal with him if the need arises," I said.

"I don't think that's a good idea. I can deal with them for now. I think if they see Dante, they will eventually connect you to each other. I think the longer Dante stays unknown to folks, the better it is for all of us."

"Okay, Miguel, I'll go along with your view on this," I said as we wrapped up the meeting.

Natalia sat in the living room reading her magazine, but she was listening a lot more than reading. When I sat down next to her I said, "What did you make of all that crap we talked about?"

"You know I am not one for business, but it is so interesting to hear it all go down. It's not easy to run a business successfully. It takes discipline and most of all you have to understand economics. I just love to watch you because you are so confident and make so much sense. I hope to be able to help you one day when I understand what business is all about. I love you so much, sweetheart," she said as she laid her head on my shoulder.

"Anytime you want to go back to school and get a degree in business, please let me know, and we'll get you enrolled. You would make a great executive, and I'm sure you know I love you very much," I said as I kissed her passionately.

Wednesday, December 11, 1957

Moe called me to let me know that the Mob had removed me from their hit list. The two hundred and fifty K was off the table, so no one would be looking for me. "Good news, huh, don't you think?" Moe said.

"Not if it is just bullshit. We still can't take any chances," I said.

"That is why I called you to warn you against lowering your guard. I think what they are going to do is send out a special hit team to find and whack you. They think it will be easier when you are under the impression they don't care about you any longer. Please don't lose your vigilant attitude, please, Harry, not for one moment as that could be the one wrong move you can make, and before you know it's over. You know why they kill people so easily? It's because those people don't suspect they will send someone to kill them. You be careful and watch out for everything. By the way, I took care of the money for the building and the house. Good luck, Harry," and he hung up.

I spent the rest of the day attending to small details about the opening of the Bijou tomorrow. Not only did I expect a strong turnout, I was also anticipating a little hassle from the Mob as well as the feds. It wouldn't be easy but nothing really worthwhile was easy.

I worked out a battle plan for the next few days. Miguel and Dante would handle the details after I laid them out. I spent a lot of time where each of our men should be stationed in the event of trouble. If all went smooth, then the boys would enjoy a great porn flick a few times a day. The manager was well schooled on his job and what to say if there should be any raid by the feds. Miguel also instructed him as to what to do if the Mob sends over some heavies to disrupt the show. I did not feel there would be any violence as that would only prove futile to those who chose that route.

"I haven't come this far to be fucked over by a few Guinea bastards," I told Dante. "Make sure that these plans we have discussed are followed to the letter, and make sure you are aware of all that is going on for next two days."

"Sure thing, sir, you can rely upon me. I'll make sure Miguel gets his copies and they are clear," Dante said as he rushed over to the phone to call Miguel.

Natalia and I ate a simple dinner at home and had a glass of wine and went to bed. Tomorrow was a big day, and although I would not be there physically, my mind would be. The preview showing would be at two P.M. and again at eight P.M. Advance ticket sales had been brisk as we sold two hundred and twelve tickets for the two P.M. show and four hundred and thirty-two for the eight P.M. show. That was more than I expected as we did not advertise this anywhere at all. We relied upon passing traffic and our notice on the marquee. I didn't tell anyone that I had not yet figured out how to advertise as an XXX rated theater.

The papers would not take our ads as they claimed it was against their policy to advertise adult films. We couldn't send out flyers because we would violate the law if someone under eighteen read the flyer. It was a dilemma, and the only solution was to advertise on our marquee. We placed the title of the film, the name of the star, and a warning that no one under the age of eighteen would be permitted entry. If someone looked young, they had to show identification at the ticket booth.

Thursday, December 12, 1957

This was the day—the day we would see how many view this film and that would be the base we start from. Of course, that was only the records concerning how many people viewed the film at any given showing and then there was a one-day total and so many other variables. And most important to me was to see what challenges the local cops and the feds would throw in front of us. We were challenging authority each day we showed a film. Then there was the Mob. Would they take some sort of offensive action or not? How would it all unfold? I certainly didn't know but held my breath and hoped with all my might that this day should go by smoothly and no one should get hurt. On one hand, we had the feds to worry about as they would very much like to bust us on obscenity charges, but they had one small problem. The film we were showing was made in Los Angeles; therefore it did not cross state lines and could not fall under the Fed's authority. The city of Los Angeles may or may not try a bust but would lose in court as community standards would prevail as Los Angeles was filled with strip clubs and other revenue-bearing operations that were sexually orientated and open to the public and, of course, considered risqué. As far as we were concerned, we had clear sailing with the authorities, but did we have the same with the Mob? Miguel felt that it was imperative we place our men near and inside the theater. Better be prepared than get caught with our guard down. We agreed and he organized a full-battle plan predicated on defense. We were not going to initiate any aggressive action but would be ready if anyone, no matter who, tried anything at all.

It seemed like a million years until the first showing started at two, but it did finally start to a sold-out house. Most of the patrons were men; I believe there were only nine women in the audience. The receipts were beyond our expectations as the souvenir shop did a brisk business. There weren't any incidents by the Mob or the feds and anyone else for that matter. The viewers were very orderly even though we did discover some stains on our new seats.

All in all, it was a resounding success in all respects. Financially, we took in more than we imagined and had no problems at all. The night showing was almost as full but not quite like the afternoon showing. We were not disappointed because we had anticipated a drop in attendance as many people were married and could not attend an evening show. We still had eighty percent capacity, and all in all we were very pleased. Money was flowing in, and it felt damn good. It was real nice to see the flow of money into our bank account rather that going out. This day was great for us all, and we anticipated that tomorrow would be even better.

Friday, December 13, 1957

It was a great day, and I was stoked. Dante was as thrilled as I was with the results of the theater. Miguel arrived at the apartment in a very good mood; I could tell by the way he walked.

"Well, boss, everything went real well. The show was a success. We'll follow the same plan today and will continue to do so until Monday. I spoke with Mike, and he is already working on the next one in Oxnard. He said it will be ready to open in about two weeks. He's working hard on it and has put on a couple of extra men. I think we should give him a nice bonus to show our appreciation and keep him working very hard and fast. We'll have to get him to Sacramento as soon as we can as I want to open there before the end of January," Miguel said with a big smile.

"I like your enthusiasm, Miguel. Could it be the smell of making a lot of money? Only kidding, my friend. I'm so happy that things have gone well, and we can start to see some daylight. Have you arranged a schedule and a system for the pickup of the box office receipts? Remember, Miguel, we cannot leave any money at the locations longer than ten minutes after the box office is closed. If there should be a raid, they will seize everything, and money especially has a bad habit of disappearing," I said.

"No worries, boss, the money from the box office was removed less than one minute after the box office closed, and the money from the shops was removed just as quickly as it came in. I would like to see a system that has a runner who takes the money to a designated spot where it is picked up by one of our messengers and taken to our counting room. There are only three people who will know where the counting room is, and you are not one of them. I'm one of them, and Roger is another, and the third is Natalia, in case of any emergency. The messenger doesn't know a thing, because he leaves it at a vacant storefront and then goes on his way. Roger picks it up from there. Roger and I are the only ones who do the counting and bring you the sheets on a daily basis. The money is deposited in our bank on a daily basis except on the weekend. The tally sheet lists how the money came in, for example how much from box office, adult shop, and concession stand. All tickets are accounted for, so the manager cannot skim anything off the top. We will, from time to time, make a head count to make sure the ticket sales match the receipts. I think we have it covered from head to toe. I will have to duplicate this system in every location especially the ones that are farther away with some revisions. I believe we are on the way to being very rich and for this, boss, I thank you," Miguel said humbly.

"I know how excited you are, Miguel, and I do appreciate your diligence. I trust you will handle all these affairs properly, but I do recommend you find another second in charge in case you may be ill or, for some unknown reason, not able to perform. Roger is fine but I don't think he is strong enough to handle all that responsibility. I will also speak to Sally about weekend deposits. There must be a way we can just drop money into the bank. It would be safer that way, don't you think so?" I said to Miguel.

I further suggested to Miguel that I felt Dante was the perfect person to be the second in command, if need be. Showing him the methods and where the counting was and how to run the show should be number one on his agenda. Of course, I told Miguel that it was only a suggestion, and I would go along with anyone he may choose.

So far the receipts had yielded a little over twenty-five K for the first two days. I did not believe that the cash flow would remain the same once the theater was established, but if we took in half that amount, we would do very well multiplied by as many theaters we might have. This was going to be a very successful operation and the beginning of a very lucrative industry. Friday the thirteenth was going to be a great day.

Natalia was very pleased with the results and only wanted to celebrate. We decided to open a bottle of Tattinger and drink to a future filled with success and hopefully one with peace and quiet.

Saturday, December 14, 1957

The last two days were euphoric as the theaters went about their business without any problems. Today would be our first day of normal business with five showings per day. I was now ready to concentrate on the building of the warehouse as construction was moving along very nicely. Miguel had found a friend of a friend who was a very good building contractor. He put him to work at once and worked very closely with my architect. The builder spent a lot of time working with him going over the blueprints and making sure each detail was clearly understood and followed.

My security man, Al Fogel, was handling the security at both the house and the building. I was very pleased to have Al aboard as he was, as far as I was concerned, the world's best security expert I had ever known. He did my place in Pennsylvania and thwarted an attack that would have easily cost me my life if it was not so ironclad perfect. Now he would make sure that our protection was equal or better than anyone else could have done. When the government needs super good security for someone, they call Al. Now it would be impossible for anyone to penetrate our buildings without our knowledge. Feeling safe and secure, as I knew I would be, was what it was all about. I was so grateful that Al agreed to fly out here to Los Angeles that I offered him my room at the apartment for as long as he had to stay.

Al was here incognito and that was also very important to me and demonstrated how loyal and efficient his was. I would make sure he got a nice bonus when his work was done even though he did not expect it.

Marty came over to relax a bit and go over what was taking place at his end of the operation.

"I had drinks with Irv last night, and he was wondering what happened to you as we don't see you anymore. I was a little amused, but pleased that there was a separation between us. I told him that you went in your direction with the theaters and have been very busy with that. I also let him know that the first theater was now open and the second one would be open in a few weeks. I mentioned that the sooner his movies get to you, the sooner he will be making money. He liked that a lot," Marty said.

"Well, I'm glad he was happy because what you said was right on the mark. We had a great opening weekend, and it looks like we will take in over one hundred K for the period. This is more than I expected, but the best thing of all is that we're not hassled by the cops or the Mob, at least not yet! It cost us a few bucks for additional security, but it was worth every penny. The film was great and will continue to bring in big bucks for a quite a while. I think you should offer the film to the Eastern guys and demand your price, to be paid in advance, of course," I said.

"Don't forget to send a check for your rental of the film. The picture costs us over fifty K to make. And your check of forty K will go a long way in repaying the cost. I will ask twenty K for the Eastern guys for a showing of two months and ten K per month for the next six months and five K per month after that. I think those are reasonable numbers, especially after its spectacular showing in Los Angeles. I also wanted to run this by you. Claude from Belgium has asked me if I will give him European rights to the film. He is willing to pay us fifty K, and he will take all the risks of shipping the master from here to Belgium. What do you think?" Marty said.

"In the first place, we have to offer the film to the local Mob so that they can show the film in their theaters. We want to avoid any confrontation with these guys, and I know we can by offering it to them, and we will remove any problem. I think the terms should be the same as the terms being offered to the Eastern boys. In regard to this film, I'll let it run until attendance drops to a very low level and then I'll bring on a new release. What I need is a few trailers, and I need them now. The other companies are not making trailers, and that is very silly as they are not promoting their next releases. I figure the reason they are not doing that is because they don't have any money to shoot more than one film at a time. You, on the other hand, must be one step ahead of your competition and make sure you have two or more films in production at all times. This is the only way to grow faster than the others, so don't let any grass grow under your feet," I said.

"You are right. What a fool I have been," Marty said. "Why didn't I think of that instead of sitting on my ass and waiting for funds to trickle in? What an asshole I've been, Ron. I just can't believe I didn't think of this. Wow! Enough of that crap, old man, just get the creative juices flowing and get another film or two in the can. As a matter of fact, once you have your script, bring in some of the main characters and shoot the previews only. This could cost a couple of thousand, but who cares? It will be edited into the complete film. If you are using the girls in the next film, they are available right now.

"Forgive me, Marty, I wasn't trying to tell you how to run the film business. I know you know best, but get it done as soon as you can. I need to show the audience some trailers as soon as possible. Each day, I don't have trailers to show. I lose potential viewers and you lose income. You are in the skin flick business and understand what drives people to the next showing. These people are stuck on sex and want new stuff all the time, and the results of good productions will be an overflowing bank account," I said with a great deal of enthusiasm.

"I honestly don't know what went through my head. I know the business better than anyone else and never gave it a thought. Sorry, Ron, it won't happen again. This you can be sure of," Marty said.

"You know, Marty, being a partner in your business motivates me to see bigger profits," I said with a big smile. "But please don't ever stop being careful. The Mob is after us, the feds are looking for every angle to stick it to us, and our competition is looking to sign every super-looking broad as their exclusive star. Just be careful and always be alert. I want you as my partner and friend for a long time to come," I said as we walked toward the door.

Marty left with a check in hand for forty K, and I went back to my thoughts of the day. All I wanted was to build a solid organization that would prosper and be good for everyone. I didn't want any trouble from anyone but clearly understood that I had very little control over my enemies. I knew that if I built a safe organization and took extreme care in all we did, the dream would be achieved, but it would not be easy.

Sunday, December 15, 1957

Miguel came over to thank me for the very nice check he received and to discuss the work on the building. Natalia was still asleep, so we stayed in the kitchen and talked over coffee.

"I wanted to thank you for the check. I didn't expect it so soon, but I will keep it. Thanks, boss," Miguel said.

"I hope I have to write you a check every week for even more. One thing we do have to discuss Miguel is the tax ramifications. There is no use in making a lot of money and then losing most of it to Uncle Sam. I suggest you use our accountant and arrange to pay your taxes each time you get paid. Of course, we can deduct your taxes, but that would remove your status as an independent contractor.

"We pay your company for the security services you provide and then you take care of all appropriate taxes, and I think you should do the same with the check for your share of the revenue to date. As a matter of fact, I suggest you discuss this with your accountant, and let me know if you would like your checks made out in your name or the company's name. I just don't want any IRS problems ever. It's the road to ruin. Please let me know, and I'll rewrite the check if need be," I said.

"Okay, boss, I'll let you know. I wanted to discuss the building with you. I got the builder working on the place, and I'd like to clear up the running track with you. I have instructed him to make the track a quarter mile and setting it up in the rear of warehouse. In the middle of the track area, we are building a sauna, a handball court, and a complete gymnasium.

"This will give you plenty of exercise anytime you feel the urge to do so. Next to the track on the left will be the shower area as well as the kitchen so that you can juice your vegetables each day as often as you want. The rear door will be completely secure as well as all the entry points in the building. Your friend, Al Fogel, is busy doing his job, so I am sure the place will be as secure as Fort Knox. He sure knows his job, and he doesn't allow anyone to see how he is wiring the windows and doors. He is very careful about the information being available to anyone—he's just overkill. The offices are almost done, and the building itself looks so different except for the exterior. We thought if we just give it a coat of paint, it will suffice. The inside is to die for as it is now a very modern and sleek looking place with room for everything and everybody. Your office will be isolated from the main traffic area, and you will have a private entrance so that you can come and go whenever you want without being seen. No one will ever know when you are in or out except your security detail. I suspect you will want to handpick your own staff and put an office manager in place. We'll cross that bridge when you move in. I estimate that should be in by January. I don't want you in until everything is perfect.

"As far as the house is concerned, I am working with Natalia to get the place decorated and set up the way we want it. Of course, we have to wait for Al to complete his security job and then we can start the moving process. Until all this is ready, you must remain out of sight so that we can maximize the protection we give you. I'm working real hard and only care about your safety. After all, boss, you sign my paycheck," Miguel said with a big laugh.

"Thanks, Miguel, I appreciate your honesty and loyalty and will follow your instructions at all times. I want you to know that I will choose a new personal assistant to take care of a lot of things for me. I will do this early next year and hope that you will be able to supply me with a few candidates and help me chose wisely? I would like Dante to be your second in command, and I would like you to start using him as soon as you find me a replacement. I need this because there is far too much to do, and I cannot expect you to handle everything, and I don't want Dante to be doing this any longer. I know you are capable, and so is Dante, but there is a limit to how many directions both of you can be stretched out. I know you understand what I'm saying," I said as I hugged Miguel in a show of sincerity.

"I understand, boss, really I do. I know how important I am to you, and I know you love me as if I were your son, so anything you decide is fine with me. No one has ever given me the chances you have, and I will always be appreciative and loyal no matter what. I owe you my life—that is for sure. I know you can't understand how one can feel this way, but I really do. I was headed for a nowhere life. Maybe this Mexican," Miguel said as he thumbed his chest, "could have become the head of some factory or a warehouse manager, but could this guy ever become wealthy? Could I ever feel like I am part of this society and could contribute? The answer is no until you came along, and for this I owe you my life. I know that some people would say that the road to success has been strewn with some pretty horrible things I have done, and maybe they would be right, but I never hurt any innocent people in my life. I realize this is not a rational argument to profess that my hands are clean, but to me it stands strong. I killed those who would have killed me, those who made their living killing people, and who were mean and hurtful to anyone who got in their way.

"I am no different than a soldier who kills his enemies, because they are trying to kill him. Yet when the soldier returns home, he is a hero whose hands are considered clean. Well, boss, I didn't do any different when I killed those killers who would have murdered both of us without hesitation. No, sir, I don't feel guilty at all. I repeat, once again, I am so thankful for the opportunity you have given me, and I believe I am dealing with clean hands."

"I agree with you, Miguel," I said. "I can assure you and anyone else that if we were to live our lives to the fullest from this moment on, we would do so without ever hurting anyone physically and mentally. No way do I feel we have committed any sins, and we will continue to protect ourselves as long as we have to. Now let's get back to work and keep our heads up at all times, and Miguel, thanks for everything."

Miguel left, and Natalia and I spent the rest of the day relaxing and watching football on television. Miguel called to let me know that the Bijou was maintaining a sixty percent capacity at every showing. Not bad at all, and this was only the beginning.

Monday, December 16, 1957

Miguel called early, quite unusual as he just drops by the apartment, to let me know that he was meeting with Mike in Oxnard to check out the progress on the new theater. This one should be ready pretty quickly because it was a burlesque theater in another life and would only take a minimum amount of work. He said he would report back later to let me know what was what. No sooner did I disconnect from Miguel when the phone rang again; this time it was Moe calling from New York.

"How are you, Harry?" he asked.

"I'm just fine after a very nice weekend of great results from our first theater. How are you doing?" I asked.

"I'm just fine except for the news I have for you. I heard through very reliable sources that the families have sent out a hit team of six to put you away. They feel you are a liability and want you out of the way, and this group of six was commissioned to do the job. They will be getting paid a very handsome sum upon completion of the job. They are convinced that you are in the Los Angeles area and suspect that you will be found with Marty. They have no idea who you are and where you live but feel they will be able to find you through some very careful surveillance of Marty. Please be very careful as there is no information on these guys, and no one knows who they are, so I can't help you with any descriptions. They may have been recruited from out of town and would not be known in New York or California. Be wary of any new people you may meet, and advise your people to be extra vigilant. Although they are not out to whack Marty, it would be best if you do not meet with him for a few weeks in case they are very good and are undetected. We have to minimize the danger to both of you. Stay away from meeting with Marty in any public place, and keep the girls far apart from both of you. The thing is, Harry, the Mob feels it must conclude this in order to keep their reputation intact even if they are mistaken.

"They cannot afford to have their reputation tarnished in any way at all. Fear and muscle is their example of supremacy, and they cannot afford anyone thinking that they were weak. They cannot have any talk of people fighting back and succeeding. In any case, please be very careful as they are very fed up with this situation," Moe said.

"Thanks, my friend, I'll be very careful and I'll report to you on a weekly basis," I said.

"I won't be around for two weeks. I'm taking the family to Florida for some sunshine and a little rest. I'll call into the office for messages from time to time, so just leave word that all is well in the city by the bay. I'll understand its meaning," Moe said.

"Have a great vacation and kiss everyone for me and send lots of love," I said and hung up.

Miguel called me and let me know that the Bijou in Oxnard should be ready to open for business by January one. Things were moving along faster than expected as Mike was doing a super job with his construction crew. I asked Miguel to pass by the apartment as something very important had come up. He said he would be here as fast as he could with traffic. He pointed out that Oxnard was not around the corner.

It took Miguel a little less than an hour to make the trip from Oxnard to Canoga Park. He walked into the apartment, looked at me, and recognized the deep concern on my face. "What's up, boss?" he said.

I went over the call from Moe and expressed my concern that this time we didn't know who these people were and if they are going to act as a team or individually.

"I am not concerned at all, boss. It is impossible to get at you in your present situation. As long as you remain in this apartment, no one will be able to penetrate the security we have in place. Marty is another story as he is always on the move, and everyone knows where his film studio is. We have him very well protected, but we don't know their attack plan. I believe they do not want to kill Marty, but they will beat the shit out of him, if they have to, just to locate you. I will take steps to cover his ass. You needn't worry about it. Leave it to me. I think I know how to cover this situation so that Marty will be protected no matter what. You remain here at all times. No going out at all for the next few weeks or until we get rid of these people. I'll keep busy with the opening of the new theater, and if you need anything at all, I will get it for you. This includes Natalia. She can't go out either as she is a direct lead to you. I know Marty wants her for one of his shoots, so we'll have to figure it out when we do take her there, but other than that, she will have to stay home," Miguel said.

"Okay, man, I leave it all up to you as always," I said.

I spoke with Natalia and explained the situation. She understood and promised me that she would not do anything stupid and would remain at home with me. She really paid me a wonderful compliment when she said, "What could be so bad? After all I am struck in the house with the man I love." We spent the rest of the day and evening at home enjoying some television and a little personal fun. I did all my work by phone, and Natalia rehearsed her lines for her role in her upcoming movie.

Tuesday, December 17, 1957

I was thrilled with the results from the Bijou; the crowds were still coming and enjoying the shows. So far we hadn't had any trouble from anyone, but I knew the good times would be short-lived. I just had that feeling.

Miguel arrived a little before noon and had another guy with him. I was a little shocked, because we were not supposed to let anyone know where I was.

"Hello, boss, this is Michael, my very dear friend and stepbrother," he said as Michael extended his hand to me.

"A pleasure to meet you, Michael," I said as I shook his hand. I think Michael, who was built like the weight lifting champion of the world, was a handsome man and stood tall with a great deal of confidence. He stood at six foot five inches tall and was a large powerfully built man. His features were without a blemish; he was very handsome and very imposing.

"Boss, this is the plan from now on. Michael will be your personal assistant. He will always be here to protect you from danger and to make sure you are always safe. He will sacrifice his life for yours, if need be. Of this you can be certain. Please consider him as your brother, because from this moment on, he will be yours. He will be living with you from now on, and by the way, he is also a great cook. Natalia will now have a personal assistant, and that will be Roger. He will be with her anytime she needs to leave home, and he will not leave her side no matter what. I am taking him away from Marty and placing Ramon Sanchez in his stead as his personal assistant and bodyguard. These moves will help me keep my security plan in tip-top shape and give all of you maximum security at all times. I don't want any arguments from you or anyone. Just trust me and all will work out, I promise you, boss!" Miguel said.

"I have survived all attacks up to now with your help and guidance. There is no reason to doubt your ability now. I'll follow whatever plan you lay out. I just wish this crap would end, and we could just go on and enjoy life as we should. I just feel so lousy that I have brought all this mess upon everyone I came into contact with. Sorry guys, really I am!" I said as I left the room and headed for my bedroom. I was bummed out by all this and just wanted to be alone.

Marty called late this afternoon and started to complain about losing Roger.

"Listen, Marty, so far you have been safe. Miguel and his men have taken good care of all of us, so cut out you're complaining and let's move on," I told him.

"I know you are right, my friend, but I get a little frustrated every now and then. Money isn't the only criteria for a happy life. I can still remember when I was down and out, I would have agreed to any deal. Life looked so bleak back then, but now we are back up on top thanks to you; yet I still forget to be humble. Sorry, my dear friend, I'll try not to let this happen anymore," Marty said.

"No worries, Marty, I felt the same way. I think we all get upset when danger is near and change comes about. I remember when I was five years old and my folks told me we we're moving to New Jersey from Queens. I went ballistic as I thought my life would end. I'd lose all my friends, and I'd never ever be able to be happy again. Six months later, I couldn't remember my life in Queens and would not have been very unhappy if we moved away from New Jersey. It all works out as my mother always said, 'It was meant to be' and life would move on!" I said.

"So what else is new?" Marty asked.

"I was curious how the trailers were coming along. You know, we will be able to open Oxnard next week, and I'll show the same film that we are showing in Canoga Park. I need more material, and I need it soon. Please get it done," I said and hung up.

Wednesday, December 18, 1957

Miguel arrived at the apartment nice and early. He said he wanted to discuss the security plan he had in mind. We sat down with a cup of coffee and began our conference privately.

"I believe," Miguel said, "that we have to be one step ahead of the Mob. These guys have money and patience and will wait until we make a mistake to complete their mission, which is to get rid of you! To always stay one step ahead of them, I want to hire someone who will act as your double as we did a little while ago. When we leave the protection of your home or building, we will need to create a little magical act. Presidents use them, so why can't we do the same? If they are going to whack you, and as sure as I am here in this room they will continue to try until they are successful, we want to make sure they never are, so we need to have an ace in the hole. Using a double will give us the heads-up we need. Of course, we will protect the double no differently than how we protect you. By doing this, we can act as if there is nothing unusual in our routine, and we can also learn when an attack is imminent and take steps to avoid it. Right now, we have some hit men on their way here to Los Angeles to whack you, yet we don't know who they are and if they have arrived in Los Angeles or not. Using the double system will tip us off on both counts. Don't worry about the double as he will be guarded carefully and with a little luck will not get hurt. I want to move forward with this program without delay, and I need your approval and complete trust. No one can know about this, absolutely no one!"

I picked up the coffee mug and brought it over to the sink and said, "Miguel, you have my approval and my full trust. You always have my approval when it comes to taking care of our security. Move forward with this program, and let's get the show on the road. I am so sick and tired of this type of life, but it does beat the alternative. I hope this will soon be over. If not, I will have to take the initiative and attack the Mob on their own turf. My silence is no longer the issue as it has gone way out of orbit. These nuts want to whack me to keep up appearances even though I have never said a word to anyone. They know that I have not spoken with anyone, but they cannot act any other way."

"Well, I don't think they think as you do, Marcel," Miguel said as he laughed. "I'll get this project underway at once. I have a feeling the Mob guys are here already. I just wish I knew who they were!" Miguel said as headed out the door.

Natalia came into the kitchen and sat down at the table, "Honey, I love you and want you to be happy. I'm ready to go anywhere with you. Movies, glamour, and money mean nothing to me without you. I love you and want you near me always. I sure hope we can solve this dilemma real soon. I want a couple of kids, and I promise you I will be a good mother, and I know you will be a wonderful father. Tell me what you want me to do, and I will do it," she said as she threw her arms around me and kissed me.

"You are my world, and I'll always protect you no matter what." I held her in my arms and kissed her gently.

"I promise you I'll always be very careful, and no matter what comes down, I will not let anyone harm either of us. I love you and only want a life of peace and happy times. Please don't worry about a thing as Miguel, Dante, and I are taking care of everything, I promise. Now what would you like to do today? Name it, and we'll do it together even if Miguel doesn't like it," I said as I held her close.

"I just want to be with you. I don't care if it is at home or out and about. I'm not kidding you. I really don't want material things. I want only you," she said.

Miguel called to say he wanted to stop by and introduce my double to me. I gave him the okay and settled back waiting for him to arrive. An hour later, Miguel walked in with, get this, me at his side. I could not believe my eyes. I was looking at myself. This guy was the spitting image of me down to the very last detail. The only two things that were different were his voice and his ears, which were larger.

"I'd like you to meet Victor Corsky," he said.

"A pleasure to meet you, sir," Victor said. I could detect a slight accent that sounded Russian.

"Well, Victor, you certainly do look a lot like me. Do you think you can carry this out when we need you?" I said. Miguel jumped right in and said, "Boss, he doesn't speak English too well. We don't need him to speak, only to walk and act like you. It is good thing you are made up as this made it easier to duplicate your looks. All we needed was someone who was your height and build. I don't think anyone could tell if he is you or not from a distance of twenty feet or more. The only thing we want is for someone to try to take him out nothing more! Victor will do. I'm sure of it."

"Okay with me, but how do we reach him? How do we tell him what we want?" I asked.

"I'll handle all that. All you have to do is follow my instructions, and everything will be fine. Please, boss, relax. I have it all under control," Miguel answered me.

Thursday, December 19, 1957

Miguel decided today that it was time I left the apartment and took a look at the new building. The plan was simple: he was taking my double, Victor, out for a drive around the Valley. This would give our security detail a heads-up if anyone is following. It will also give us an indication of whether the apartment was under surveillance. They left at nine thirty and did not return until twelve forty-five.

Miguel reported no suspicious activity and could not detect anyone watching the apartment or the neighborhood. He sent men around the area to check out any activity and could not detect any anyone watching.

It was now my turn to leave the apartment and proceed to the new building. Miguel had Victor stand downstairs and carry on a conversation with one of the guards while I was to dress differently wearing a hat that would hide my features. On the way out, I made as if I had a conversation with Victor and then shook his hand as I left and got into the car with a strange driver. Off we went alone in the single car and waited around the block to see if anyone was following us. The plan worked perfectly as no one seemed interested in our old car or the people in it. I arrived at the new building at two and went in through the side door. Miguel was there already and was beaming because his plan had proved successful, and he could relax a little. It was also very evident how proud he was by the transformation of the building. The front offices were just magnificent with a large waiting area faced by a receptionist station that prevented anyone from going any further. To enter the office area one must pass through a set of doors that appeared to be wood but were constructed of steel plate and covered in a sheet of wood and then painted. The doors were programmed to remain locked and could only be opened one at a time. No one could pass through the second door unless the first door was securely locked. This was a safety feature that could not be overridden at any time unless you had a special key, and no one was permitted to have that key other than Miguel and myself. I wondered why I would ever need the key, but I would place it in a safe place. On the other side of the doors, another receptionist area existed with a large waiting area containing a large sofa as well as a few very comfortable armchairs for visitors. In this area, Miguel had placed a large aquarium filled with tropical fish. A long corridor led to many offices including a large conference room. At the very end of the corridor another door existed that once again was steel plate disguised to look like a plain wooden door. Once you entered that door, you were now in the main warehouse facility that contained a very beautiful kitchen complete with the most up-to-date appliances. From the kitchen, another door led back to the conference room in order to serve food and drinks. At the other end of the building, a large running track appeared full circle of the warehouse. In the center of the warehouse, there was a full complement of free weights and benches where one could exercise to one's heart's content. On the right hand side, there were steel shelves that seemed to rise up to the very top of the building. It was an awesome sight to see in the middle of this building. Everything one would need to stay fit and live here was built into the warehouse proper. Miguel was proud of his work and so was I. Al Fogel was also on hand to demonstrate his security systems that he had installed.

"State of the art, that's what you have here. Fort Knox couldn't have more security than this place. You have an early detection system that will alert you at the slightest breach. If someone is trying to cut through the roof or tamper with any devices, the system will let you know even if the electricity is cut. The system has its own generator that will cut in within four seconds of a power break. This system makes your security system active at all times. Any breach will trigger the system and a signal will immediately be sent to Miguel and his team as well as your security team. The bunker is equally protected, so never fear. If there is an atomic bomb attack, you are safe," he said.

"What bunker?" I said. Al and Miguel walked to very back of the building and pointed to a rubber mat on the floor near the back wall.

"Just press this button on this wall and see what happens," Miguel said.

I pressed the button and the mat automatically rolled up and a door in the floor opened. A staircase appeared in the floor and it was all lit up and Miguel said, "Let's walk down and see what we find." They were having a hell of a time showing off their handiwork. I went down the stairs with everyone close behind me, and was overwhelmed by what I saw. I entered the bunker that could have easily been my apartment complete with a living room, kitchen, bathroom, and three bedrooms. I checked the fridge, and it was full of provisions, and the pantry had enough supplies to feed a lot of people for a long time. In the back area was a generator, so electricity would not be a problem, and buried somewhere underground were storage tanks containing enough gasoline and water for at least five years. In the rear of the bunker there was a complete hospital with five beds and every type of medical equipment one would need if they were going to receive treatment in an emergency. I was flabbergasted at what I saw and thrilled that these people cared that much to make sure that my family and I would be safe. Miguel told me that four people could live here for five years without ever leaving. Even the President didn't have such an elaborate safe haven, or at least not that we knew about. This was by far the most secure and best hidden place I had ever seen. No one would ever realize that anyone was living in this building. This place was safe beyond my wildest imagination. I felt protected against all evil that may happen. People love to brag especially when they work in a place like this. It was almost as if Miguel could read my thoughts, "The guy who built the bunker was from out of town and was brought in to build it by Al. He has no idea where the building is and does not know any details as he was kept in the dark the entire time he was here along with his workers," Miguel said.

"This really floors me, guys. You've done a magnificent job with this place, thanks!" I said. "When can we move in? I'm anxious to start working in a different environment than the apartment. I really need to get out of there as it's too confining."

"Well, I think we can start making arrangements for your move as of tomorrow. I'll need to make security arrangements for you and Natalia. I really think it would be best if we waited for the house to be completed so that we can make a game plan that will keep us under the radar. The house should be ready in about a week and then we have to furnish it. I'll coordinate that with Natalia as you really don't count when it comes to that. We'll start using the building tomorrow and see that everything is in order. Your man, Al, really knows his security stuff. He is the best, boss, glad to know him," Miguel said.

We went back to the apartment where Natalia was waiting. I sat down with her to describe my experience with the new building. My excitement was so contagious that Natalia was caught up in it instantly. I found her sitting at the edge of her chair as she listened to each word. I could imagine her mind making sense of my descriptions and putting them in the right perspective. The more I described the building, the more excited I got. It was a masterpiece finally finished. "When can we go there and see it?" she said.

"Tomorrow, Miguel is devising a transfer method so that we can easily go there daily. What a way to live, sweetheart, isn't it?" I said.

I called Dante and Miguel because I wanted to discuss the function of the building. I went over the details as to what the building should be used for, and we came up with the following scenario. All employees will be hired on a basis that they must receive full security clearance in order to be accepted. Their jobs, although different, the ultimate goal will always be the same, the security of this country. No person can ever discuss what they do or hear or see with anyone ever. This place is top secret, and if we have to let them believe that they will be prosecuted criminally, then we must do so. We agreed to discuss it further tomorrow and get a proper game plan down!

Friday, December 20, 1957

Natalia and I were ready bright and early as we wanted to get to the new building. I wanted to show off everything I saw yesterday, and Natalia could not wait to see what her mind created from my detailed description. The entire day began with excitement and joy as we were anticipating seeing this building.

Miguel arrived with his crew, and we were off to the new building. The first car left with Victor in it a little earlier, in case there was any danger. It was our plan to use Victor as the double and see if there was anyone out there. If the coast was clear, Natalia and I would take the next car and proceed to the new building. A few minutes after the first car left, we got a call from Roger that a car was following them. Miguel told them where to go and what route to take. He then dispatched another car to catch up to the pursuers. His plan was to box the car in as we did before and then take them out. At no time were they to know that the real quarry was not in the car ahead. In the meantime, we took another car and made our way to the new building.

Natalia was blown away when she entered the new building.

"It's awesome," she declared. "This place is just how you described it. Wow! It's wonderful. Let me see the special safe house, please!" she said. We went through the entire warehouse and gym section and finally reached the back of the building and stopped. "This is it, sweetheart," I said.

"Are you kidding, Marcel? There is nothing here unless it's outside in the back." I opened the panel on the wall and pressed the button, and the floor opened up revealing the staircase. The lights went on adding to the wonderment of what was down below. She went down the stairs and could not really hold back her emotions any longer as she said in an excited voice, "Honey, this is unbelievable. We could move in today. Everything is here including a baby's crib. This is fabulous and so wonderful. Thanks to everyone who helped make this come true. I love it!" She was filled with emotions as tears welled up in her eyes. She was as touched as I was by the care taken for details regardless of how trivial it was. "It certainly is a work of love and care. I know you appreciate the efforts of our friends as I do! It's too much for words, really it is!" I said as we walked through the emergency safe house.

We spent the rest of the day organizing our offices and setting up the place the way we wanted. I was certain that I could easily guide my empire from this command center. The building was all I could ask for, and now all I could hope for was the end of this war with the Mob.

Around three that afternoon, Miguel received a call from one of his men regarding the confrontation with the guys following Victor earlier this morning. I was sitting in my office behind my big mahogany desk when Miguel knocked on the door, "Can I come in, boss?" he said.

"Of course, Miguel, please come right in and sit," I said.

"I just spoke with one of my guys and wanted to report what happened this morning. We found a car following Victor's car and dispatched another car to box them in. We finally got the car boxed in on Valley Circle Road and forced it over. We found a driver and one passenger in the car. The passenger was not one of the hit men from New York. He was from Los Angeles, and his claim was that he was told to follow Marcel and report back to his boss. He had no gun, and there was none in the car as we searched it thoroughly. He did have a notepad that contained detailed entries about the comings and goings of Marcel as well as how many security guards were on duty. It seems he has been watching the apartment for a few days. I am very upset over that because I thought I had everything covered, yet he was able to see what was going on without being detected. He finally told us that he was way up the block and used high-powered binoculars to maintain his vigil.

"I sent Victor's car on ahead as we detained him and his driver. I didn't think I should harm them as it would not do any good at all and may cause a terrible problem with Frank. I confiscated the notes and the binoculars and told them to report back to their boss that if they want to know more about our security or what we are doing all they need do is give us a call and we will make an appointment. We are only interested in full cooperation at all times and will work toward that goal. I told them to leave Marcel alone and that they will be left alone. No one wants a war, and no one wants to bring attention upon one another, so if they insist on continuing this type of underhanded surveillance, they will find themselves in a serious battle where there cannot be any winners. We are ready to attack the Los Angeles Mob was the message, and if they want a war with the Latinos, then all they need to do is continue the surveillance. I know they got the message and were very relieved to be released unharmed. The one thing we did learn was that they didn't know Victor wasn't you. The deception worked real fine. There was no suspicion at all of any switch, so we did accomplish what we set out to do. Victor was last seen going into the apartment where they think he is now. I think we will move you and Natalia into the new house and have Victor come and go from your old apartment for a few weeks and see what happens. I'm certain that the hit men will concentrate on the apartment, thus revealing who they are. I think we are on the right track, boss," Miguel said.

"I am a little disappointed that we didn't detect this guy earlier. From now on, we have to expand our perimeter so that we don't get caught with our guard down. I don't want Victor to get hurt at any time. Just because he is impersonating me, he should not be fair game for anyone. He's an innocent person, and even though he is getting paid to accept the risk, please make sure he is protected at all times. I'm not a killer, Miguel, and never will be, so please take extra care with Victor's safety," I said in a very firm but calm tone.

"Will do, boss," Miguel said. "One more thing, boss. A little while ago I received a call from Frank's right hand man, Salvatore, that he appreciates the respect we showed by releasing his man and wanted to assure me that they will communicate from now on and will not do that again. Our truce and agreement to respect each other's territories must be adhered to, and they apologize for the error made by one of their men. It will not happen again. I thought it was a great call, and our plan of leaving their man alone worked to our advantage," Miguel said. Okay, Marcel, let's get down to something a lot lighter. How was your first day in your new offices?"

"Pretty neat, Miguel. I loved the way time went by. I enjoy working in this environment, and I love the staff you have chosen. I am not questioning your ability to get the right people, not in the least, as you have shown me in the past that everyone you have employed has been just right and has always proved to be loyal. One question, Miguel, do they all know how to maintain secrecy here and at home?" I asked.

"Listen, boss, everyone who works here thinks they are working for the CIA or some such government agency. Each one thinks they have gone through an extensive background check and had to sign the official secrecy agreement we concocted. They have all been told that the penalty for revealing any information would be to be arrested and charged with treason under the Secrecy Act. They could face life in prison or the death penalty if convicted. Not even spouses, relatives, friends, or anyone at all may know anything of what takes place in this building. They have all been through a full week of training on the cover story about this building should the postman or anyone ask what goes on here. There is a full cafeteria here in the building, so they can have their lunches here if they choose and avoid personal contact with outside people. Our cover is an import export company with head offices in Asia. The company specializes in highly sensitive parts used in the space program. No further information is available, and if anyone insists on speaking with someone, they will eventually be directed to me, and I will get rid of them. The safe house is top secret and is known only to you and very few others. The staff does not know anything about it and will not ever be apprised of its existence. Dante knows about it, as he is your personal secretary and my second in command and must be aware of everything at all times. I have not even told Michael about the safe house and will not do so unless you decide you want to. No one will enter your office unless they have been cleared by Dante and he alone will allow them to pass. All information that is sent your way will pass through Dante and me. The proceeds from the theaters will go directly to the bank through the courier system we have set up and will remain that way. You will be supplied with daily reports regarding the operations of all businesses we are in. All the affairs of Marty's film company will be reviewed on a daily basis, and reports will be placed on your desk.

"I have cleared this with Marty, and he agrees that this is the best way to handle all the business affairs. We will have a full-time accountant on staff doing nothing but the books for the theaters and Marty's film operation. We will have a full-time office manager who will oversee all internal operations and will make sure that every job the staff is assigned shall be in the form that would appear exactly as we have presented to them, as an import-export firm. One more thing, Marcel, we have not started our mail order business at this time, but once we do in the next few months, we will have a lot of work to do to sort and prepare the orders for shipment. That will take a lot of thought and, of course, a system that will be secure for all of us. I think I have covered most everything and hope that we have kept most of the doors closed that would compromise your safety," Miguel said.

"Contact the other adult film companies in the next few days and find out where the hell are our movies. I want the film operations to run smoothly as we have our hands full handling all the other problems that exist. If you think for one minute that things will always be peaceful, you are sadly mistaken. The feds will try to bust us real soon especially as we grow. The Mob will be more dangerous than ever and will do everything in their power to whack me for two reasons. They will not be so pleased with our success and will want to get their piece of the action, or we can expect some action. The other reason may be that they suspect Marcel is Harry, and if so, they will be even more motivated to whack me. So let's not ever let our guard down and constantly keep watch on all people who work for us. If anyone should start using drugs or alcohol, you must fire them at once. No waiting, Miguel, substance abuse is a sign of weakness, so take action at the very first sign. I hope the agreement they all signed covered substance abuse? I want to make sure everything runs like clockwork and make sure everyone does their job. I can't emphasize this enough, Miguel, we will need strength and brains to win this battle. Please keep it organized and make sure it runs smooth as silk," I said.

Saturday, December 21, 1957

Miguel called to tell me that the work on the house was well under way, and we would be able to move in early January. He was very pleased with the progress and wanted to share it with me. Dante was waiting for me in the kitchen where he had made coffee and asked, "What would you like for breakfast? I can make almost anything and would like to make something you would enjoy. Is Natalia awake? I'm doing the cooking today, because Michael has the day off. It is my hobby and can cook with the best of them. Let me make something special for you and Natalia."

"She is busy putting on her face and getting ready to face the world once again. She'll be out in a minute. Why not make some pancakes? I'm sure she'll enjoy that a lot," I said.

"What is your plan for today, boss?" Dante asked.

"I would like to take a ride to Oxnard and pass by the theater. I also want to know what is going on with the deal in Bakersfield and Fresno. See if you can find some answers for me, please," I said as I got up from the table and went to greet Natalia. She looked radiant as usual even though I hadn't told her about the trip I'd like to take later today. She would welcome the break in our routine.

"Good morning, sweetheart, how are you feeling? You look great as usual," I said as I kissed her on the cheek.

"Would you like some coffee?" Dante said. "I'm making pancakes. They will be ready in less than ten minutes. I know you will enjoy them a lot." We had breakfast and got ready for our trip to Oxnard. In the meantime, Dante let me know that the negotiations for Bakersfield, Fresno, and Sacramento locations were well into the final stages and should be concluded within the week. The receipts from Oxnard were starting to come in and were very gratifying. Things were going well, and with a little luck, things will be okay.

Dante took care of all the details for our trip and set it up for Victor to leave the area first in another car along with Miguel and a couple of other guys. We waited for the "all clear" and then departed for Oxnard. As we entered the 101 freeway, Dante's car phone signaled a call. It was from one of the men in Victor's car. I watched Dante's expression as he listened and said almost nothing. "Is he all right? Is everybody okay? Come on, man, give me the full report. Are you taking him to a hospital as we speak? I want answers now!" Dante screamed into the phone.

"What the hell is going on?" I said to Dante.

He didn't respond until he finally set the phone down.

"There was an attack. Evidently they thought Victor was you. They used an additional car to join the chase as we usually do and cut off our car. They opened fire and hit Miguel. Victor is okay! Our second car that was trailing came from behind and killed two of the attackers, the third and the fourth attackers got away. Miguel is pretty badly hurt and is on the way to the hospital. I don't know how they missed the guys who were following them. It just doesn't make any sense at all. We take such care to scan the area when we leave, and we are always watching front and rear. How in hell did we miss this? They'll call us back in a few minutes to let us know which hospital they are taking Miguel to!" Dante said in a very concerned tone. I'll call them back and tell them to take him to Holy Cross Hospital on Sepulveda and Rinaldi in Mission Hills. I will call ahead and speak to the hospital administrator, who is personal friend of mine. There won't be as many questions asked, and he will get the best treatment possible."

Dante called and instructed them to proceed to Holy Cross and then he called his friend at home. After a short conversation, Dante replaced the phone and said, "He'll get VIP treatment. Things are being made ready as we speak. I think we can cancel the trip to Oxnard and proceed directly to the hospital, agreed?" Dante said.

"Without any doubt, Dante, please step on it. I love that man and just can't understand what went wrong. Please get us there fast, please," I said.

We arrived at the hospital within fifteen minutes and went right in through the emergency entrance. We were told that Miguel was taken to surgery and was in very serious condition. We could do nothing until the surgery was over and just had to wait it out. Dante called his friend and was told that he wasn't in, but he had left a message for him.

"Everything that can be done for your brother is being done."

There was nothing left for us to do except wait and not cause any trouble.

"Dante," I said, "set plan two into motion at once. Make sure the hospital is covered and that no one gets in here, in case they try to get at me again tonight. So be vigilant."

"No worries, boss, we got it covered, and no one will get within a hundred yards of you. This I promise," he said.

Sunday, December 22, 1957

We waited all night at the hospital while Dante made sure our security was intact. I called Marty and let him know the news. He was shocked and very saddened. Mary Lou and him arrived around ten last night and sat with us all night. It was near five thirty in the morning when a doctor came into the waiting room. His look was not encouraging at all as he looked exhausted.

"I'm sorry. We did everything we could, but the wounds were too severe. We lost Mr. Martinez a few minutes ago," he said to Dante. "I will have to call the Police and file a report of a death by gunshot. I'm so sorry, we did all we could."

We were all in a state of shock as the news hit us like a ton of bricks. We never gave death a thought, especially to one of us. It hit home now and it hit hard.

Dante addressed us all, "I lost a brother today. I do not intend to lose anyone else. I want you to follow my instructions to the letter and we'll be fine. I'll handle the Police, so all of you get the hell out of here. We will meet at the office at two P.M. this afternoon. Until then, get some sleep and stay alert whenever you move about. Security will be tighter, and we will make certain that we cover all bases. I'll handle the funeral arrangements for Miguel as per his request. We discussed what should be done in the event either one of us would be killed. He has no family except for Michael and me. So please don't worry about anything. I am terribly saddened by my brother's death, but that is the risk we take when we are in this business. There were no illusions as to the dangers involved, and Miguel understood that very well. The opportunity you gave him, Marcel, was all he ever talked about, and he would want that whatever the plan for the future was we should not change it. He would want us to move forward and to remember him as someone we all loved. He didn't want us to mourn him at all. We can't help our emotions especially when we get attached to those we work with and love them so dearly. Miguel loved you all and was so happy to be part of a family, and although his time was short, it was a good time for him. I feel the same way, and I will take care of my family always. Now get the hell out of here!"

This was a eulogy for Miguel delivered from the heart. There was no bullshit in Dante's words, and we all knew that there would not be any funeral for Miguel, our deeply loved brother. This was good-bye to our dearest friend who always put us first. We all left before the Police arrived. We were silent all the way home. I guess all that needed saying was already said. This was a great loss to us all, and I felt like I had indeed lost a part of me. I was very saddened by the events of last night. I swore I'd get even with whoever shot my best pal. Most importantly, Miguel taught me that vengeance was best tasted cold. This lesson I would always remember and use it well.

We met at the office, Dante, Michael, Marty, Roger, and me. Business had to be done, and we could not allow ourselves the luxury to let Miguel down and let security fall apart.

We also all knew that if the situation was reversed and Miguel was heading this meeting, he would proceed with business at once and so we did. Dante spent the next half hour outlining our defenses and setting up new methods to accommodate our lives. Victor was a problem as he was now scared out of his mind and really didn't want any part of this job any longer. The problem here was that when he looked like me he could easily be mistaken thus placing his life in grave danger. Removing his makeup and allowing him to revert back to his normal self did nothing to allay his fears. Dante suggested we send him to another country for a year or two. We would pay his expenses and take care of him during that time. The biggest problem was our security breach that allowed this situation to take place. There was a mole in our midst even though Miguel was convinced that all his men were loyal to him and would take a bullet for him if need be. All except one and who could than one be? We ran through our security protocols over and over again until we were able to isolate the problem to three men. We decided to set up a fake run by implementing a plan that would have us take one of Dante's men on a ride that would appear to be a normal meeting. We would announce the trip at the last moment as we did with all trips and leave at five today. The car would have two men in the trunk equipped with machine guns and two cars would follow a mile behind while another two cars would always be coming toward us. Each car would have a full complement of four men fully armed and ready for action. The cars would remain in touch through our mobile phone system that would remain on at all times in conference-call mode. Our telephone supplier, AT &T was experimenting with a more versatile mobile system and were more than pleased to test it out for them. The Multiple Conference Call System as they called it seemed to work quite well. The only people who knew all the details about this trip were our group of four, no one else. The plan was to load all the cars and place them in their positions fifteen minutes before we even announced our trip to the three men we suspected. Once the men were advised about the trip, each one was to be watched carefully from a distance, so that we could see who, if any, may try to signal their coconspirators.

We let the three know that Marcel was making a trip in the next fifteen minutes and everyone should make ready. Miguel's death was due to the fact that no one paid any attention to a group of assassins that followed us easily, because one of our trusted guards did not pick them up on purpose. As we got closer to departure, things got more intense as we prepared for the announcement. At precisely four forty-five, Dante called the three suspects into the apartment and announced the trip in detail.

He told them that an emergency trip was required and that we would be leaving in fifteen minutes. While we checked out the area as we would if it was a real move, we kept a close watch on our three suspects. As we suspected, one of the men, a man named Alfonso, left the area for a moment and signaled using a red handkerchief toward an apartment building across the street from ours. It only took a few seconds, but a signal was given, and there was no doubt he was our man. Dante's plan was to proceed with the plan and get these guys as well as our mole.

We proceeded along our route as planned when we spotted the car following us and watched it as it began to close the gap. Our front-runners spotted the other car they used coming toward us. Now we had two cars with killers on board ready to pounce upon us and kill us all. This proved what we saw earlier, and now it was time to put our plan into action. Dante instructed the cars that were a mile behind to come up fast and cut the attack car off. He further told the cars coming toward us to close of the trap. The plan was to instruct the car and its occupants to follow the lead car. We would all proceed along a road just off Valley Circle that led into the mountains. Once we would be high and isolated enough, we would remove the assailants and proceed to question them. Our plan worked to perfection as the cars were taken by surprise because they were boxed in. Our two other cars came up to the scene, and all our men jumped out and surrounded the cars and instructed the people inside to throw out their weapons. They could see that they were outnumbered and had no chance to fight it out. The guys all got out of the car and removed their weapons. Dante then had one of our men search them for any additional weapons and then instructed them to get back into the car and follow them. We proceeded up the mountain until we reached a dirt road that seemed to lead to nowhere. Dante signaled for the entourage to stop. Our men got out of the cars they were riding and surrounded the attacker's car. Dante signaled them to get out and had them stand in a circle, each one facing a man with a machine gun aimed at him.

Dante spoke to them as a group, "I will give you one opportunity to save your lives. I'll ask a question and expect a truthful answer. If you do answer and it's a lie, I will have you killed at once. There are no second chances. If no one answers, I'll kill one of you and ask the question again. If you cooperate with me, I'll release you. I know you don't believe me, well, that is your problem because you don't have any other choice. I urge you to cooperate and live. Even though we know who your contact is in our organization, I want one of you to point him out! *Now* do it!"

He yelled and waited patiently while one of our men was directly behind Alfonso in case he tried anything at all. None of the men said anything. Dante stepped forward and said, "I won't ask again. You have ten seconds." He stared at the men and then lifted his gun and shot one of the men in the leg. "The next one will go right through your head," he said as he lifted the gun once again.

"It's Alfonso. He's standing right there behind you," he said as he pointed toward Alfonso.

"You, crazy man, I would never betray my friend, never. Please, boss, he's lying," he said.

Dante turned around and looked directly at Alfonso as he spoke, "We knew it was you all the time. We only wanted a confirmation, and we now have it. You are a murderer and the lowest of the lowest scum. You don't deserve any mercy at all." Dante pulled the trigger and Alfonso went down in heap. The bullet went through his head and left a small hole with just a trickle of blood. "I was a lot kinder to this piece of shit than he was to Miguel. Now let's get on with this," he said as he turned and looked at the four men.

"Answers to my questions or silence forever—the choice is yours. I don't have anymore time to waste. Who are you working for?"

"We really don't know. We work for Frank and were told to follow this guy, Marcel. We were told that there is an informer who will let us know when you are on the move. We were supposed to hit this guy Marcel if we can. If not we have to report his movements as there are hit men from New York here to take care of it. There was a ten K bonus to anyone who got him," one of the guys said.

"Then why did you shoot one of our guys on Saturday?" Dante asked in a calm voice.

Another one of the guys said, "It wasn't us. It was the hit men. I swear, we had nothing to do with Saturday's attack," he said.

"Okay, then what do these hit men look like? What are their names?" Dante asked in a menacing voice.

"These guys are tough. One guy's name is Vinnie "the Horse" Lambusco and the other is Slavatore "Animal" Tomassino. They are good at what they do, and they want to make the money that they will get when they find a way to eliminate this guy, Marcel. They'll probably kill us for telling you," one of the guys said.

Dante looked him in the face and fired one shot through his head and said, "He doesn't have to worry about them killing him, does he? Now what are we going to do with you guys?" Roger came over to Dante and whispered in his ear. Dante looked at the three guys that were still standing.

"I gave you my word about saving your lives, and I will keep that word. If I see you ever again, I'll kill you without warning. If I hear from you again, I'll make sure that your boss knows you cooperated. What I am going to do is to have you load these dead guys into your car. Then I'll shoot some holes in your car so that it will look like you were in a gunfight. Get rid of the bodies and move on and never look back. Got that straight?" Dante said. They all nodded and got to work moving the bodies into their car. Dante then ordered his men to fire a couple of rounds into the car. He then emptied their guns and gave them back to the guys.

"Now get the hell out of here, and don't ever forget what I said," Dante said as we all piled back into our cars and headed home.

Monday, December 23, 1957

Marty and I met at my office to discuss what had happened and where we had to go from here. It was close to Christmas, but we weren't in the holiday spirit. Miguel's spirit was all over us, and he was imploring us to carry on and fulfill the dreams he held so dear. It was hard to adjust after having him around day after day making decisions that were so important to all of us. He was instrumental in maintaining our safety. We all missed him a lot, and I missed his showing up early in the morning and greeting me. I know Miguel dreamt of a peaceful future; one where he could relax and perhaps marry and raise a family.

"Marty, come on in, please," I said as Marty came into the office and sat down. "I was just sitting here thinking about Miguel and how much he meant to us."

"I know how you feel. I'll miss him a lot. He was a great person and made life a lot easier for us. He was like a brother. I loved him, Ron. I loved him a lot," Marty said.

"You can say that again. I loved him a lot and miss him more and more each day. There are so many things that happen each day that remind me of Miguel's wisdom and the love he gave us all," I said.

"I think it's time we started taking this war a lot more seriously and see if there is a way to clear the air or wipe these people out. We can't continue to live like this, but until we resolve this, we have very little choice," Marty said.

"I agree with you, but Marty, you and I both know that we cannot defeat the Mob. There are too many of them. I want to get Dante in here in a few minutes and see if we can come up with some kind of strategy that will accord us a lot more peace of mind. In the meantime, we need more films from you and trailers. Is the New York film ready? You certainly have had enough time to have it edited and titled by now, and I could use it as a new feature," I said to Marty.

"It's all ready, Ron. I'll deliver it to the theater tomorrow, and you can show it whenever you want," Marty said with a smile.

"I know the others are going to deliver their movies, so we'll have enough variety for the theaters, but soon we will need more than they can produce as we will have at least twenty-five new movie houses this coming year. We are doing unbelievable business in both locations and will open in Sacramento and Bakersfield in late January. I'm certain we are going to get busted real soon as the feds can't just sit back and let us operate freely. It would be against all they stand for, and if you have been listening to the US Attorney General, William Rogers, he has made it clear that he will not tolerate pornography. Pat Brown, California's Attorney General, doesn't quite feel the same way but wants to please Washington as much as he can, so we'd better get our shit together and always be as prepared as possible. I spoke with Stan, and he has laid a plan that will insure our continued operation no matter how many times they bust us. Of course, we are following the guidelines of using the maintenance man as the owner/manager. I am not concerned about the state or the feds bothering us. It's the fucking Mob I have on my mind at all times, and I think we have to take some decisive action so that they get the message once and for all," I said. "Let's get Dante in here and see what he has to say."

Dante came into my office and asked, "How can I help you, boss?"

"We need some answers and perhaps a good plan will emerge to keep us all safe," I said. "Before we get started on that, did everything get taken care of for Miguel's final resting place?"

"Yes, I took care of everything, and I followed Miguel's wishes to the letter. He is fine, boss and will always be watching over you. He loved you very much. What did you want to discuss, boss?" Dante said with a snicker as I understood his play on words.

"I am moving to my new house and am very confident that with all the systems Al put in place and the people we have on staff we will be safe. The office building carries the same security safety net as the house. The big problem is anywhere we travel and most importantly Marty's complete safety as well. He can't shoot films in a vacuum. It just would not work. He has to meet people, and he has to be able to run his movie set properly. This means he will come into contact with a lot people who come and go all day long when he is in a shoot. You can see the problems when it comes to him, can't you?" I said.

"Without doubt, boss, but it can be overcome. Stop and think about it for a moment. The President operates everyday and everyone knows there are a lot of people who would like to kill him, yet he carries on. We have the same problem, so we have to approach it the same way the Secret Service does.

"All of Marty's areas must be secure at all times. No one gets in unless they are cleared and that will include all actors, makeup people, cameramen, the caterer, and anyone else who is authorized to be on the set. Of course, Marty, you will have to give me a list of all personnel who will be involved on this film and when they will be expected to be on the set.

"I realize that not everything runs on schedule, but we do need to be as accurate as possible, or we can't do our jobs. I will also post a couple of sharpshooters in strategic places to keep an eye on things. There is always the possibility of a breach, but very unlikely with all these precautions in place. Also please do not share schedules with anyone. Pass them by me first, and I will then go over the schedule with those who must be in the know and make sure they are advised. I don't think we can make this any tighter, and I don't think we have to worry about the office and the set. How do we take care of your home, Marty?" Dante said.

"We can have Al put in some very sophisticated security devices. Other than that I do not know what we can do!" Marty said.

"Well, my dear friend, we have to also concern ourselves with Mary Lou and other females you may want to bring home from time to time. That is quite a normal action for a single guy, but it leaves a hole in the security blanket. What if they send in a beautiful-looking young girl and you take her home and she either let's their assassin in to kill you or she does it herself? What if, there can be a list as long as your arm with what ifs. We will have to rely upon your good sense. The hard truth is we have to protect you no matter what the conditions dictate. I recommend that we establish a cover story that goes something like this. If anyone asks why all this security the response is that you are working on a special government film project and are not at liberty to reveal any details. You are obliged to follow certain government regulations and security procedures, no matter who it may affect. This will keep all your friends and coworkers feeling a lot better about being subjected to search and other security procedures. Most importantly, we have to keep chatter to a minimum as people like to talk, and this might arouse suspicion. The rest is up to me and my guys who will keep you safe at all times. I don't think we can do anything more than this to keep you safe as long as you keep me informed about everything, always!" Dante said.

"What can we do when we have to travel? This is one of the weakest areas in our armor," I asked.

"I think we have that pretty well covered. I will tighten up our system so that we can eliminate any future sabotage like what took place when we lost Miguel. There will be some redundant functions put into place so that no one person will be able to be coerced to sell out our operation. I will also let everyone know that if one is ever discovered to be disloyal, the penalty will be death. No trials, no reprieves, just fast action and death. I'm certain that fear will stop anyone, no matter how many dollars they are offered. Trust me, please, it will never happen again. This I promise!" Dante said.

We concluded our meeting with hugs and kisses as we all knew how we felt about our loss. We wished with all our hearts that Miguel could be here with us to share our good fortune and celebrate the holiday season. He would be in our hearts forever. This I knew for certain.

Tuesday, December 24, 1957

Today was the day before Christmas as well as moving day, so there would not be much work done although I still wanted to make the trip to the theater in Oxnard. I don't know why I was so interested in making the trip especially when Miguel and I had agreed that I would not make anymore trips to the theaters. The receipts were really great, and there was no sign of business slowing down. Money was flowing in from the two theaters as well as the film business. Marty was moving his stuff and getting paid as well. Carmine was not a factor as far as we could tell at this point. Of course, he was only a lower worker bee in the Mob hierarchy but was a thorn in Marty's side and controlled the adult business out of New York. Things were going very well, and in the big scheme of things we had a great year except for the tragic loss of Miguel. Dante had organized the entire move to the new house. He rented a large truck even though it was overkill as we did not have any furniture to move. We had a few of our own men load the truck while he had a group of men patrol the area around the apartment to make certain there wasn't anyone watching. He had another crew maintain a safe distance from the apartment to spot any cars that may attempt to follow the truck. He covered every base to make certain that the new place would remain unknown to anyone who wished us harm. Natalia and I were taken by car to our new home. We did not need any furniture as the new place was completely furnished; only our personal stuff was required. The apartment was to be kept for at least three months as a drop and to keep the Mob off guard. Dante would make use of it and would eventually shut it down as if it never existed.

The best news of the day was Natalia's news. "Sweetheart, I love our new home. I know I've seen it before and bought all the furniture, but this is special. This is the first day of our home together. Our home! What a nice thing to hear and guess what, sweetheart, it will soon be home to one more. Yes, I'm pregnant! Isn't it great Harry? I sure hope it's a boy, but regardless, we'll love it with all of our hearts and forever," she said with a smile as wide as could be.

"Wow! That is terrific. I hope this move is not too much excitement for you. Sit down and relax. This is great. I love you so much," I said as I held her in my arms and kissed her gently. "I guess this ends your film career until you give birth. When is the due date?" I said.

"The doctor estimates August. He said he will be able to be more accurate in another month or so. I have an appointment in three weeks and will know more then. We have plenty of room, and now I have to start decorating a room for a boy or a girl. I think I'll wait a little longer before I commit to the color. I just love you, Harry. Please be careful always, please. Our new baby needs a daddy to love and enjoy, and I need a husband at my side. I love you so much," she said.

What a day! The move, the news—it was all overwhelming and so wonderful. I was so very happy and felt different about life.

I couldn't explain what it felt like, but something came over me now that I was to be a father. Of course, I was already a father with Rachel having a baby girl, but we had separated, and the thrill of it all was not the same. I still had not seen my daughter and didn't even know her name. I guess it was better that way, because I would not have liked to see her and her mother in any danger, ever. If I stayed away, she would grow up without fear and danger would not be a problem. With all this I kept thinking about myself and the life I have had thrust upon me. Not that I wasn't a good person before, but now I had to be a better person, and above all I had to get rid of this curse, the Mob. I knew at that moment that I would not be at peace until this situation was resolved, one way or another. What an easy task! This year's New Year resolutions would not be too hard to make this coming year. Would I be able to keep them? I sure as hell was going to try for us all!

Wednesday, December 25, 1957

Christmas Day! If you walk outside, you can just about hear a pin drop. The world seemed to stop this morning in order to welcome this day for everyone. I made sure that everyone who worked for me received a very nice bonus for their great and dedicated service. Loyalty deserved rewards, and the only way I knew how to take care of everyone was with cash. I hoped it showed them all how much I appreciated their part in my world and how much trust I placed in them.

The doorbell rang at nine thirty, and Dante appeared at the door. I asked him why he just didn't come in. After all he had a key and did not ever have to ring.

"I know, boss, but today being Christmas Day, I wanted to be a little formal. I wanted to wish you and Natalia a Merry Christmas. I wanted to thank you so much for that very generous gift you left for me. I also wanted to assure you that my loyalty to you goes far beyond anything you could imagine. I am yours until death do us apart. I love you, boss, and thank you for the opportunity you gave Miguel, Michael, and me. You'll never regret your decision to keep me around. Let's make 1958 a year to remember and remove any threats that may be out there. I wanted to let you know that I took care of Mike as well, and he is so appreciative. He said that Sacramento would be ready January 12 for operation and Bakersfield on January 23. He also wanted me to remind you to please find a couple of new locations. He needs the work," Dante said as we all laughed.

"Thanks, Dante, I appreciate your kind words. I too care a lot about you and will always consider you as my son. I want to break the news to you first. Natalia is pregnant and soon we'll have a new addition to the family. You're going to have a brother or a sister and you will there to help. I am so excited about it, and of course, I want to make sure this world will be the best place for my child. I want to talk to you about something that I did not have time to bring up earlier. As you know, I had an arrangement with Miguel regarding a piece of the action, and each time the receipts would come in, he would get his share as promised. Of course, due to the fact that Miguel is no longer with us, the arrangement ceases to be in effect. I want you to accept a similar arrangement as you are my right hand, and as I said, I treat you as my son. Please tell me what you would like to see, and let's see if we can get it agreed upon and move on," I said.

"Wow, boss! I didn't expect anything like that at all. I am at your side and would be if you did or did not give me any piece of the action. Miguel did not ever tell me what the deal was between you except that whatever it was you kept to your word to the last penny. He did tell me he never had a written agreement with you and would never need one. Your word was true and would always be stronger than a written contract. I really don't know what would be right but how about a two percent bonus on all income that comes into the operation. I don't care where it comes from, and there is no need for me to check the figures—it is what it is. I know you have a real bookkeeper, and you don't fool around with stuff like that. Miguel told me once that you do not fuck with the IRS as that would be the downfall of the empire. We're all on the books, and we all pay taxes. No cash deals on the side. All income is reported and deposited in the bank, always! This two percent deal is fine with me and will make me happy at all times," he said. "Okay with me, Dante. As of this moment you are a two percent owner of the operations. I will advise the bookkeeper tomorrow, and your payments will begin at once. I suggest you open an account at the bank, and we will deposit your funds directly. And thanks for being fair and for your pledge of trust and loyalty. I truly appreciate it," I said.

We spent the rest of the day relaxing and getting the house in order. It was nice to be alone for a change. I asked Natalia what her opinion was on a subject that was a concern to me. "Honey, I wanted to ask your opinion regarding Michael. He is Dante's half brother and is a part of the family. He is now our personal assistant and looks like a real find and, as far as I am concerned, very trustworthy. I want to make sure he never feels that he is left out. Do you think I should give him a share of the action or just leave it alone?"

"I think you should discuss it with Dante and, if need be, talk directly to Michael. They are both very nice and good people, and I would like you to treat them as you would family and not think about leaning one way or the other. They are men and understand the situation and will always be faithful no matter what the pay is," she said. Boy, she was smart and quite right. I'm sure I would have to speak to them both and will do so right after the holiday.

Thursday, December 26, 1957

Although Christmas was now over, it seemed like the world was quiet and everything seemed so still as if we were waiting for something to happen. The news broadcasts seemed to be filled with news that was old and even the newscasters seemed very laidback on this day. Everything was quiet in our neighborhood as well, so it seemed that Los Angeles was just treading water as the world was restarting.

Dante arrived early in the morning with a couple of people in tow.

"Good morning, boss. Happy Holidays to you and the Missus. I hope all is well? I would like to give you the few special surprise gifts I have for you. I want you to meet Robert Gagne who will be your full-time cook. Robert has been cleared by the secret service and will live off the premises. I suggest you and Natalia and Michael get together with Robert and organize your likes and dislikes as well as the schedule so that things will work out as planned. All shopping will be done by Robert with one of our men, who will accompany Robert to the market as he doesn't have a car," Dante said.

I shook hands with Robert and welcomed him to our home. I introduced myself as Marcel Lamond and Natalia as Mrs. Natalia Lamond. I left Natalia and Robert to handle the kitchen affairs and turned my attention back to Dante.

"Hey, boss, we're not done yet. I'd like you to meet Mary Gaite. She will be your full-time housekeeper. Mary, Marcel," he said as I shook hands with Mary. She was a very nice-looking young woman that stood around five feet tall and had very dark hair with big brown eyes. She had a rounded face with a slight slant in her eyes. Her smile was warm, and her voice was soft and caring. She was nice-looking and would make a welcome addition to our home.

"It is a pleasure to meet you, Mary. I'm sure you will be happy here. I'm really the wrong person to discuss things about the house as my wife, Natalia, is the one who knows what is expected of you. Welcome to our home and family, and please treat this place as if it was your own," I said.

Dante took Mary with him and left the room to find Natalia. The place was starting to look and feel like a home with a family to fill the many rooms. I liked it a lot and felt good; maybe this New Year would be good to us all. We needed some noise around the house as well as the human interaction. Natalia and I did not like spending the days at home and not being able to have some connection to others, even if the only people were those who worked for us. This was a wonderful day, and I could not say enough to Dante about these great Christmas gifts he bestowed upon Natalia and me. The rest of the day was spent relaxing around the house and greeting a few friends for drinks and holiday wishes. Before leaving, Dante came in to see me and had Michael with him.

"We wanted to talk to you about a few things, if we may?" Dante said.

"Sure thing, guys. Let's go into the study and have a drink while we talk," I said.

"We want to clear the air in regard to Michael and myself," Dante said.

"First, we want to understand that we are brothers and have always been very close. When Miguel was alive, we shared everything and always covered each other's backs. We didn't know how much money Miguel made, because it was not important to us. Miguel always made sure we never went without, and he always kept to that rule.

"We considered ourselves very lucky to be brothers and agreed to always take care of each other. You must remember, Marcel, before you came along, we were three guys who did everything in our power to stay away from gangs and keep on the straight and narrow. The leader was Miguel as he was the oldest, and he always tried to guide us in the right direction. We were suffering a lot when you came along as we did not have jobs and didn't have any money to continue with our education. Food was a luxury, and I can tell you, Marcel, there were days when we did not eat one meal at all. When you made your call to Miguel, it was a call from heaven as we were in dire straits. Miguel was a proud man and would never have let you know that things were bad. Your offer of job was the very thing that he wanted desperately to say yes right there and then but felt that he had to show strength and wait. When you and Miguel agreed to go to work together, you gave him an advance that he was able to use to pay our back rent and buy some food for us. Miguel was an honest, hard working person, who had integrity and a great deal of pride. You saved all our lives. Even if you don't realize it, that was what happened. We are just repaying you for the wonderful things you have done for us and will always be grateful and, of course, loyal! This still holds true with Michael and me, so it doesn't matter what deal you make with me or Michael as we share everything anyways. We have no secrets, and we both love you, so please never worry about us. We know that you don't play favorites, so don't sweat it, please! In regard to our jobs, I take care of the theaters just as you had Miguel doing and Michael will be taking care of all security details. He will confer with me, and we will both make the final decisions. Your safety and that of your family is job one and will always be for us. All in all, I want to reiterate our loyalty and love for you and promise you one hundred percent dedication and the loyalty that we can only demonstrate on a daily basis. We are your team, Marcel, and always will be!" Dante said as he walked over and hugged me.

"Thanks, guys. This makes me feel great and a lot more comfortable. Thanks again. I love you both," I said.

Friday, December 27, 1957

I spent most of the morning exercising and doing target practice. Aside from the gym and the great running track, Miguel installed a shooting gallery. It was a work of genius as he built a room at the rear of the building and made sure it was soundproof as well as lined with some sort of material that absorbed the bullets. Once the back sheet is filled with spent bullets, the sheets are removed and new sheets are installed. The entire operation takes about ten minutes. He also made sure that a target system was installed via a system of pulleys that dropped a target at intervals of fifty feet upto a maximum of one hundred feet. It was upto the shooter to decide what distance they wanted. An electronic logic board then sent the target along shooting lanes one or two as requested. Miguel had this super room built as a surprise for me and was planning to unveil it to me. Dante was sworn to secrecy, and he kept his word until now.

The firing range room was disguised to look like a storage room where records are kept and blended into the warehouse so that when walking through the building it appeared to be just another area that I would probably never visit. When Dante explained the room to me and Miguel's Christmas present, I was very emotional and could hardly contain my feelings. The memory of Miguel, his thoughtfulness, and simple way of showing me his love was very touching. Once I had contained myself, I had Dante go into the firing room and shoot a few while I remained outside. I wanted to see if I could hear the reports from the guns or anything at all. I also wanted to smell the cordite from the spent weapons. I was convinced that Miguel would never have this built if he didn't take everything into consideration. That was Miguel's way for all projects, except for a turncoat that had betrayed him and cost him his life. I was pleased that there wasn't any noise or smell at all. We could have guests in the building using the gym, and they would never know about the firing range. I was grateful to Miguel that even in death he was taking care of me. He made sure I'd have better shooting skills than the assassins who would do me mortal harm.

Dante opened the door and smiled, "Did it go as you thought it would?" he asked.

"It certainly did, with flying colors. Tell me how the smell of all this shooting disappears?" I asked.

"Simple, boss, we installed exhaust fans that suck out the odor double-quick. The fans blow out to the backyard. Miguel insisted that the fans should be insulated and empty into a large exhaust pipe which would then run under the floor and exit in the rear of the building to avoid any noise and questions that may be asked by the curious. He was a stickler about being careful and covering all bases. When the exhaust fan is operating a deodorizing pellet dissolves in order to mask the cordite smell. When the exhaust finally reached the back area, the odor is one of lilacs. He loved you with all of his heart and above all wanted to protect you. Boss, your life is as precious to Michael and me as it was to Miguel. Please don't ever forget it now. Let's get a few shots in. I'm sure you need the practice, and we certainly want to be prepared. I think we are going to see an attack very soon and must always be ready," Dante said.

I was so excited about the firing range that I spent almost two hours shooting my gun at different targets. I also couldn't wait to tell Natalia about this and to continue assuring her that all would be well especially now that we were having a baby.

Tonight would be the first night that we would be dining in our new home and having our own cook to boot. I was going to love it, and I would be able to just relax and enjoy some wine and good food. I also couldn't wait to tell Natalia about the firing range and the emotions I felt about Miguel and the feelings I had about Michael and Dante. We were so lucky to have found two sons that genuinely loved us and would be at our side no matter what. This night was going to be the start of an exciting life filled with love for my wonderful wife and unborn baby.

All I could say about the entire night was that it was as wonderful as I had expected. Natalia loved being served, and the food was outstanding. This was what the good life was all about, and I liked it a lot.

Saturday, December 28, 1957

Dante and I decided to have lunch at Luigi's Restorante, an Italian restaurant that we found in Thousand Oaks when Miguel and I went to Oxnard to look for theaters a while back. I was not able to eat there too often due to the fact that I had been confined because of the threats against me. We invited Marty to join us as well as Irv Willets, as I wanted to discuss the situation with him as the spokesperson for the other manufacturers of adult films. We were very careful to make certain that no one was following us and made sure no one knew where we were going until we were on the way. I, as usual, carried my gun with me as a precaution. All the guards carried guns at all times while on duty. Marty and Irv drove out to Luigi's together, and we had a lead car as well as one that followed. We didn't want any surprises nor did we want to let our guard down. Even though Irv didn't know it, he was very carefully protected when he drove with Marty.

Our meeting went quite well as Irv enjoyed his food and the conversation.

"So far, Irv, you have not supplied one single film for me. The others have not delivered any as well, and I am a little disappointed, not to mention the great deal of money you are missing out on. I took the liberty of bringing you a copy of the checks sent to Marty's company. As you can see, his company has received over fifty K in a few short weeks, and there is more on the way. When was the last time you received over fifty K for one of your films?" I asked.

"Marcel, you are absolutely right. It is shame that we are so slow in producing films, but we are working on it and will have plenty of material ready for you by mid-January. We have been under some severe pressure from our old customers for new films. It's not easy jerking them off as they are getting a little frustrated. Thank goodness, it is holiday time, or I think they would be on our asses very heavily. January will be a tough month for us all if we don't deliver something. To be honest with you, Marcel, we are a little short of funds. That is why we are behind," Irv said.

"We are opening two more theaters in January and will be able to absorb more films. By April, we plan to have at least four more locations up and running and at least twelve by the year's end. We will need a steady supply by February, and it must be quality. Please talk to your associates about this, and make sure they understand how lucrative their operations will become. Don't miss the boat. It would be a shame," I said as I got up and excused myself.

I left Luigi's and proceeded to the theater in Oxnard. I had always wanted to make an inspection of each theater. It was a stupid desire as I had people who took care of the places, and there was no need for me to place myself in jeopardy at any time or show my face. Dante had begged me to stop this obsession, and although he was right, I still wanted to visit them. Any other sane person would have agreed with Dante and not taken the risk. We arrived at the Bijou in Oxnard at about 2:00 p.m. Dante asked me to please wait in the car as he checked everything out and made sure the way was clear. He didn't want any of the staff to see me as it was not good business to allow anyone to identify me as the owner or anything to do with the theater. I made a complete inspection of the place and came to the conclusion that my people had done a great job and there was no further need for me to frequent any of these locations. We got out of there and drove back to the house after satisfying my urge to see the place.

"I promise, Dante, I won't be inspecting any theaters anymore. I am very satisfied that they are all well and good and will bring back a tidy profit without my inspections," I said.

"Listen, boss, we don't need to make my job harder by you exposing yourself to danger when it is not at all necessary. I promise you that we will always maintain the high standards you always want for these places. If you trust me with your life, please trust me with the operations of the theaters. You know the cops are going to raid one of these places any day even if they don't have anything that will stick. They want you to close and go away, and they will harass you until you give up. The last thing we need is you being present when they make the raid. Our system doesn't give them any opportunity to connect you to these operations, and we don't want to give them any. They are trying to prove racketeering as a system of earning money, and if they do, they will pass a law that will be able to take away all the money you have. By staying away, we eliminate their ability to connect you to these operations. Please, boss, relax and trust!" he said.

"I agree with you and apologize for my silly attitude. I'll make sure that I will not take any unnecessary risks, especially no-brainer ones, I promise!" I said.

We arrived at the house close to six. "How about joining us for dinner?" I asked Dante.

"Thanks, boss, I'd love to," Dante said.

"It's been a long day, and we might as well relax. Have a couple of drinks and enjoy the cooking mastery of Robert. Last night's meal was great, so why not try for two in a row?" I said.

Dante agreed and joined Natalia and I for a great meal prepared by Robert, our master chef.

After a very old and good cognac, I said to Dante, "I need to do things that will be stimulating. I can't sit around here forever, so I thought I could take up golf. What do you think, Dante?"

"Well, boss, that would be a great idea except golf takes a lot of time, and security will be very difficult especially being out in the open for that length of time. Anyone who finds out about your golf could easily find a weak spot, and you could be in serious danger. We can't possibly guard against an attack on such a wide perimeter. I don't like it at all, but I will look into it and see if it is possible at all," he said.

"I thought a private club might be the ticket. Please inquire and don't bother with the Los Angeles Golf and Country Club as they do not welcome Jews at all. Or perhaps you can look into a club here in the Valley that will offer me the camaraderie and enjoyment I need. I know you will be discreet, and you will make certain we are as safe as possible.

I know we can't go on indefinitely living like hermits even though it is essential under these circumstances. I just need a break from all this. Please, Dante, see what is out there!" I said.

"No problem, boss. I'll do the best I can," he said.

Sunday, December 29, 1957

Natalia and I had great breakfast together on this really beautiful day. It was so nice I decided to sit outside near the pool and read the

Sunday *Los Angeles Times*. I was expecting Dante and Marty at noon, so this was a good time to relax and catch up on any news I may have missed. It was nearly noon when the phone rang. It was Dante.

"Boss, I am going to be late. Sorry about it, but the Bijou was raided a few minutes ago by the LAPD Vice Squad. I've already called Stanley, and he is on the way there. I wouldn't worry about a thing as we expected this to happen. The manager has it all under control as he has told them he is the owner. They want to seize the film as they claim it is evidence in charging the manager with showing obscene material and is in violation of some law, except no one knows which one. We will be back in operation and up and running within an hour. Stanley will handle bail, if there is any, but most likely, they will just issue a ticket to appear in court. It's a misdemeanor, so it's no big deal. Just a pain in the ass and a little distraction. I'll call you back as soon as I have an update," he said as hung up.

Well, finally it had happened, and I felt relieved as I wanted to see the system tested and see what we are faced with. It was simple when your attorney told you there was nothing to worry about, but everyone, especially me, needed to find out on their own if this was so. We had a great deal of money invested in these theaters, and we needed to be aware of all possible problems at all times and stay on top of it. The only regret was the timing as we were at war with the Mob and couldn't handle too many distractions. Marty should be along very soon, and it would be very interesting to see his reaction to the bust.

Marty arrived a little after noon and was shocked to hear about the bust. Of course, he wasn't really upset because he too wanted to find out how strong our theories were. We were opening a lot of new theaters this coming year and must always make sure we have all our ducks in a row. Too much money hung in the balance, and the effect of anything that threatened the operation would hurt many people, especially the film producers who had entered into an agreement with us!

"Well, we knew this was going to happen, so let's see what Stanley has in mind and how we resolve this. I, for one, welcome this bust. Once and for all, let's get this shit out of the way and move on. Would you like a drink?" Marty said.

"I spoke with Dante. He will get here as soon as he can," I said as I ordered two cognacs for us.

It was close to three when Dante arrived.

"Sit right down, my friend, and tell us all about it. Would you like a nice smooth cognac?" I said.

"That sounds great, boss. I sure can use it," he said. "Well, it went as Stanley predicted. They ordered the manager to appear in court on Tuesday, and they took the film with them as evidence. We have another copy, so we are back in business as the two o'clock showing was delayed an hour but it is now showing.

"The new manager is already at the theater. It is most important that the old manager does not engage in the showing of adult films in Los Angeles any longer. He will be able to manage the Oxnard location, if we want him to, as that is not in Los Angeles county as no deal was made concerning Ventura County. I do not think he should be running any theater any longer just in case there is a law we don't know about that could come back to bite us. In the meantime, he will be happy just to retire and take his severance pay. Stanley was smooth and very professional. It went as he said it would. I don't think we have anything to worry about as Stan pointed out. All we will have to come up with is a fine of about five hundred dollars or a little more. The penalties change depending on how many convictions. By using the method set out for us by Stan, we will never have the same person take the fall, so every bust will be a first-time offence and will keep the fines to a minimum. So far, things look pretty good. It's just another cost of doing business," Dante said.

We ate a late lunch and an early dinner combined as we discussed the events of the day. It was around six thirty when Stan called and spoke with Dante. We waited in anticipation as Dante didn't say much except for "Okay, I understand, sure thing," stuff like that. Finally he got off the phone and smiled, "Order another round of drinks please, and we will go over Stan's call," Dante said.

"Okay, man, out with it. What did he say?" I said as I asked Mary to bring another round of drinks for us. Mary brought the drinks and placed them in front of us. "Mary, please bring the bottle and leave it here. There is no sense in running back and forth every time we want another drink. Thanks!" I said.

"Stan said that he spoke with the head of the vice squad about the bust. He was told that pressure was put on the squad to take down the theater from above. There are other theaters operating in Los Angeles, and they have not had any pressure to bust them, just this one. He did what he had to do but assures us that a fine will do, and you can go back work whenever you want. It'll cost us about five hundred dollars in fines, and we will not get the film back. That is the end of it for now, and we can go back to work. Most likely, the Mob put pressure on their contacts to push the vice squad for action. I don't think we will have anymore trouble for a long while. The problems will come from the feds, and that will only happen when we have theaters in other states than California. In the meantime, we have a lot of places to open in this state and can look into ways to cover our asses when we do open in other states," Dante said.

"Well, that's a big relief. I'm glad it went according to plan. Now, let's get things ready to neutralize the Mob and make some money," I said.

Monday, December 30, 1957

Everything was back to normal on this day as we all waited for the year to end and bring on a new year that we all hoped would be filled with good things. I knew I would be a father once again, and that was very exciting in itself. Natalia was busy getting the house all ready for our New Year's Eve celebration.

We were having a small party for our close friends, because Natalia felt that we didn't see enough of them and should spend time together especially this time of year. She felt very guilty about not seeing Mary Lou as often as they used to. She was her best friend, and now they seemed so far apart. Heads turned when the two of them used to walk into a room, and the girls missed that ego-boosting time.

We also agreed that the Willets were new found friends but nonetheless were our friends and should help us bring in the New Year. Needless to say, we had to have Dante and Roger as well as Don Coleman and a few others we were close with. In order to allow everyone to party to their heart's content and to remove the fear of being stopped for drunk driving, each guest would be picked up and taken to the house. Whenever they wished, they would be driven home without question and without worry. It served two purposes for us as we would be able to keep the location of the house pretty secret as we were located off Coldwater Canyon in the hills where the streets look alike and the cliffs make every house seem the same especially at night. In order to keep our location as secret as possible, we would blindfold each guest using the ruse that we wanted to surprise them when they removed the blindfold and see our new home. The drivers were instructed to make sure the passengers would not be able to identify the exact address of the house by taking a route that would confuse them. The other factor was that no one would be stopped by the cops as the driver would be sober. We didn't want anything to spoil this party. Natalia wanted it to be perfect and that was going to be a real fun time for everyone.

Dante called and asked me if I was up to a meet with Frank De Simone, the head honcho of the Los Angeles Mob. He said he wanted a meet between the two of us to see if we could start the New Year on a good footing.

"He feels that this fighting will not help either one of us. He wants to meet this afternoon around two, just the two of you! What do you say, boss?"

"Where does he want to meet? Will it be the two of us only? What do you think, Dante?" I said.

"I will have the meeting place checked out thoroughly, and if I think it's clean, I suggest you have the meet. Boss, it would be best if we can work together and both of us make some real money!" Dante said.

"I agree with you, Dante, but do you think the New York families are aware of this proposed alliance and will allow us to operate? I don't think so, but I'm willing to listen. Check it out, and I'll be there!" I said.

"Okay, boss, shall do and call you back!" Dante said.

Dante called back and said, "It's on, boss. I will pick you up in half an hour, and we can get this thing over with."

Dante arrived and said, "We are going to a place in the mountains just off Santa Susana Pass. It is the place they make western movies. He likes that place because no one will bother us, and it is isolated in the Simi Valley area and should be very secure. Also, it is easy to see if you are being followed or set up in any way. I will be close by watching that no one will disturb you. Trust me, boss, I'll take good care of you."

We took Santa Susana Pass off Topanga Canyon Boulevard and rode another fifteen minutes until we came to a town that looked like any Roy Rogers or Tom Mix western town.

It was amazing to see the main street and, of course, the saloon, general store, and the other buildings one would see in the movies. It was very exciting, and as Dante said from this vantage point, it was very easy to spot trouble. We seemed to arrive a little before Frank. A minute later we saw the black Cadillac coming down the road and pulling up to the main street of the western movie town. I remained in the car as Dante went over to meet Frank and to make sure all was in order.

Dante returned to the car and said, "Okay, he's ready for the meet. We will drop you off at the saloon, and they will do the same. Your meeting will take place in there while we make sure no one disturbs you."

Dante dropped me off and I went into the saloon. I felt like I was in a western as the saloon was deserted, but the vibrations I had made me feel that any second a gunslinger would walk in and demand a whisky.

Frank came in alone and said, "Frank De Simone. A pleasure to meet you, Marcel Lamond," he said as he put his hand out to me.

I shook his hand and said, "My pleasure, Frank. I am pleased that we finally meet and talk."

We sat at one of the tables and Frank said, "I asked you to meet with me because I don't think it's very productive for either of us to fight when there is plenty to go around. I was in the theater business long before you came along, and I really don't like anyone coming along and trying to take over my business. So far you have kept our agreement by keeping out of Los Angeles, but who knows when you will become greedy and want to take over? I must warn you, Marcel, that I will not tolerate that kind of action. If I wanted to, I could easily put you out of business but it does not suit my purpose to do that. We both know that the feds are trying to put us out of business, and it would be best if we worked with each other to make sure they do not succeed. I don't only run theaters as I have other enterprises that I must tend to and don't need any distractions. I would like to offer you the opportunity to come and work for me. I think we can make a lot of money as a team, and you will have the protection you need as an independent."

"Let me tell you something, Frank," I said while looking straight into his droopy eye. He was known as "One Eye," because one of his eyes always seemed to droop down, but I didn't think it was wise to mention that. "I don't scare easily, and I don't want to work for you. I have no intentions of getting involved in any of your businesses no matter what they are. I am in the theater business and have no desire to get into anything else. I'll continue growing and opening new locations, and I will honor our agreement about the Los Angeles location. The rest of the country is fair game. I don't want a war with you, as it would be better to live and let live. As long as we continue to work together, we will grow as we have agreed without any encroachment on my behalf.

If you decide you don't want me to continue growing, I will be forced to fight you if I have to. You run whatever your businesses are, and I promise you I will not interfere as I have no interest in any of them. I just want to be left alone and run my theaters and only theaters. Porn is fun, and I like the action, and that is all I want. If this doesn't meet with your approval, then I am sorry, and we shall have a fight on our hands. I will not work for you, and I will not be threatened by you," I said.

"Well, Marcel, you are pretty cocky, aren't you?" he said. "I am not a man who threatens anyone. If you and I cannot agree, we will be at odds and that could prove to be very unhealthy for you. I have considerable connections that could cause you a great deal of harm. I could fuck you up every which way and Sunday. I am trying to remain peaceful, but you are not cooperating with me. I am a man of my word and am very determined. Don't push me too far, Marcel. It wouldn't be very wise."

"Listen to me, Frank, and listen well," I said. "I have no wish to fight you, but I will if you make me. I am a college graduate just like you, and I want to own and run theaters across the country and will do so. If you don't want me in business, then send your army in to fuck me up. Just remember that I can also screw with you. I will honor my agreement as my word is my bond, but don't fuck with me, and don't make threats. I have not ever made threats to you and will not do business that way. The world is big enough for you and me to operate our own businesses and not fuck with each other. Look, Frank, I know you had a problem with the Appalachia bust last month and that it will bring some heat on you. I honestly believe that you are making a big mistake in considering me as your enemy. We can fight the cops and feds as a team by working together and sharing information and by not wrecking each other's operations. The days of muscle are over, Frank, and with our brains, we can easily be winners. I will not screw you over, Frank. This I can assure you and feel that if we cooperate with each other, we can easily establish theaters across the nation using friendly competition to control this market. Think about it, Frank, think about how we can easily control the adult business in almost every aspect and make millions of dollars. Let's not fight, because there will never be winners only foolish people who didn't have the vision to see the future. Here are the numbers, Frank, for every day one of my theaters is out of operation two of yours will also be down. For every one killed, I will kill ten, and for every dollar lost, I will make sure you lose one hundred times as much. You don't want to fuck with me, Frank, really you don't, and I don't want to fuck with you. Let's be smart and agree to help each other and not steal from one another. I know it's not the Mafia way, but who has to know? No one, Frank, just us and being business people as we are, we can easily have the tiger by the tail," I said as I got up to leave.

"Wait one second, Marcel, maybe we got off on the wrong foot. Please sit down," Frank said. I was a little wary of the change in his attitude, but who knows, maybe my little speech made sense? "I like your attitude, and I agree with you, Marcel. How can we organize our two operations? Please help me work it out and then let's move forward."

"Give me your private number, and I'll give you mine. Let's get together right after the January 1 and set some parameters up. In the meantime, if anything comes down, I'll call you and you do the same. I do not expect anything to happen until after New Year, but just in case," he said.

"I like it this way, Frank. It is a lot easier on us when we are friends and have the same goals in mind. By the way, I want to assure you one thing, Frank, I'll never mix into your other business, and I'll never open another theater again without first informing you where I am planning to open and when. If at any time my theater would interfere with you, all you have to do is tell me, and I won't open it. It is easier to change locations than to spend all those bucks and then have a war to tear it apart. Good business is to use common sense and to work with your competition, whenever you can. I think that sums it all up, including my intentions.

"I do wish you and your family a very Happy New Year. It was a pleasure meeting you, and I hope this is the start of a new relationship that will prove to be rewarding to both of us. By the way, Frank, I am opening a theater in Bakersfield and also in Sacramento. These should be open no later than February. I do hope it is okay with you?" I said as I stood and extended my hand to him.

He took my hand in his and with a firm grip said, "Happy New Year to you and your family as well, and Marcel, those two theaters are fine. As a matter of fact, the farther away from Los Angeles you are, the better I like it."

We exchanged telephone numbers and left the saloon together laughing and feeling very satisfied with this meeting. I felt that we had accomplished a great deal and avoided a very nasty war. Of course, only time would tell if we were truly going to be at peace or not, but at least, we would have some period of trust, even if it was only for a short time.

Dante was waiting for me and looked quite nervous. "How did it go, boss?" he asked.

"Very well, Dante, better than I expected, and I hope we will have an extended period of relative peace and mutual cooperation. Now, let's worry about the Eastern front as attacks from the New York families are still in the air. I just have that gut feeling that they haven't quit just yet. Let's go home and relax. I'll buy you a drink, and we can get ready to bring in the New Year," I said with a big smile and a sigh of relief.

Frank wasn't so bad. As a matter of fact, he was quite gentle and articulate. I knew I could work with him, and he would find out that he could certainly work with me.

Rumor was that the Los Angeles Mafia was a "The Little Mafia" and that it in no way was it anything like Chicago or New York. Frank, who graduated in 1933 from USC law school, was considered the lawyer of the Mob in Los Angeles and was handed the leadership through a supposedly rigged election and because his father was the don before him. We also learned that Jimmy Fratianno and Johnny Roselli, both underbosses in the Los Angeles Mob, quit after the election and went to work for the Chicago Mob.

Tuesday, December 31, 1957

The last day of a very difficult year. A year that changed my life and put me on the run forever. A year that has caused me to do things I never dreamed I would ever do or even had the stomach to. Who knows what the New Year would bring but whatever it shall toss on my plate I would be there fighting for survival. Last year, I thought I was in heaven, married to a beautiful woman, had a job that paid far more than I ever expected. My plans were simple, and all I wanted was to enjoy my life and have some kids to get old with. I dreamt of giving my parents a few grandchildren to enjoy and build a family. All this came to a crashing end when I discovered I had stepped into a viper's pit—the Mob! Well, there was no use in looking back. All I could do is look forward and build a decent life with the cards dealt to me. I was versatile and could survive because of my brain and the love I had found with Natalia.

I was on the way to building a family and had a caring and loving wife to stand at my side. All I had to do was live long enough to share and enjoy the time on this planet. Today, we would kick out the old and bring in the new, and let's hope that this coming year would bring us peace and happiness. This year's celebration would not be the same without Miguel. He would be missed but never forgotten as he gave his life to protect me. Be well, Miguel, wherever you are on your journey.

Everything was ready for our guests as our chef made some wonderful treats and Natalia added a few touches to make this New Year's Eve celebration one of the best ever and one that would not soon be forgotten. I was proud of her as she took over and did her thing as a super wife and great partner. The guests arrived at nine thirty, each one bringing a gift to welcome the New Year and have something for the gift exchange we planned on having a little after midnight. It was early, but the fun started even though everyone had not arrived. It was great to spend the last day of the year and welcome the first day of the New Year with those we loved and shared your success with. This is what sharing one's life was all about and we were a part of it. What surprises would the New Year bring us? Who knows? But we would be ready for it, and best of all, we would welcome a new addition into our lives.

Wednesday, January 1, 1958

A new year and a new day were upon us. Natalia and I sat up talking until five A.M. We wanted to clear the air on how we felt and how we were going to face the new challenges this coming year. We both agreed that it was a lot simpler when there was only the two of us, but now we had a new addition to our family and we really had to make sure that our child would have security, love, and happiness along with good health. Natalia expressed her feelings about our lives and the battle with the Mob. It was a war that just couldn't be ended by negotiations as the aggressor had no scruples and would not adhere to any agreement. The only solution was annihilation by one side or the other. We both agreed that we had taken every precaution possible and now could only wait and see what the future would bring. One thing we both felt was that if we left the country and went to live in another part of the world, we would probably see an end to this vendetta. The problem with that was that we did not have enough money, and why should our child or children be deprived of a super education and the opportunity to be whatever they wanted to be in the United Sates? If we went to England or Australia, we would not be able to live in peace as the Mob worked there as well. It would only be a matter of time until the Mob zeroed in on us and either killed us or forced us to run again. Sicily was sort of the head office of the Mob and from there they could easily find us if we were to live in Europe. We could go live in a third world country, but then our lives will be without an opportunity to provide the best for all of us.

No, we decided we could not run forever, and we couldn't find any other place farther away. This is where we would remain, and if we had to make a stand here we would. It was up to me to fight the battle and protect those I loved. My New Year's resolution to Natalia was to love and protect her and our offspring with all of my might. No harm would come to them while I was alive. I sure as hell believed that I could and would protect them always.

Bring on the New Year, and I will face it head-on.

Thursday, January 2, 1958

We were now settled in our new house, and I wanted Natalia to feel relaxed at all times. While the house was being redone, I had the construction people build a secret passageway beneath the house. The passage was an escape route that led to the cliffs nearby. No one knew it existed except Natalia and me. The underground passage had a storage room attached that was filled with canned food, water, and a supply of guns and ammunition. This was an emergency room and was to be used as an exit only in the event of our home being attacked or in danger of being bombed or some such catastrophe. Although we lived in an earthquake country, I opted to build this secret tunnel/passageway. There are no records on any set of plans indicating this—no permits were ever applied for—and the crew that built this was brought in from West Virginia and paid very well. Once the project was completed, they returned to West Virginia.

They never saw me or heard my name and had no idea who lived in this house. They were given forms to sign that stated that their work was highly sensitive and in the interest of national security. If any of them revealed the nature of their work, the location, and when it was done, they would be prosecuted to the fullest extent of the law. This was presented as a highly sensitive project along with the caveat of severe punishment if they were to reveal any information regarding the project. Their loyalty to their country was rewarded with the additional bonus they received. They were all told that their country appreciated their contribution to a very important project. There was no way in hell that anyone of these workmen would ever speak about this special project. I felt very secure that this passageway would remain unknown to anyone except Natalia and me as well as Dante who I hadn't told yet.

Natalia and I were very happy together as we took in the thrill of being expectant parents. Although the child was still in her body, we both could feel the baby kicking and made us feel that our baby was now a part of our lives forever. It was a real joy to us to make plans for a wonderful life for the new addition to our family.

It was very hard to describe the feeling I had now that brought our new child closer to us each day. Here I was living in a war zone, so to speak, with the Mob looking to wipe me out, and I was still planning a normal life for my new child. It was mind-boggling, to say the least.

Natalia was so happy with our new home and could hardly wait for the big day. In the meantime, life had to go on. Dante called to say that he would pass by a little later today to go over the receipts for the last week. Business was good, thus justifying our plans of opening additional theaters.

Dante arrived late in the afternoon. "Hi, boss," he said as he sat down on the sofa. "I got all the figures with me, and they are good. The new theaters are on schedule and things are going well, even better than expected. So what more can I tell you, boss?"

"I love news like that, and I'm so glad that things are so good. That's the way to bring in the New Year, my good friend. Would you like a drink?" I said as I signaled Robert.

"Mix up a batch of great martinis, Robert, if you don't mind, and please join us," I said.

"I also wanted to talk to you about our security," Dante said. "You know they are not going to stop trying to get you. I suggest you hire a full-time makeup artist. We can make sure your appearance remains uniform by having a full-time makeup artist. Anytime you go out of the house, you will look like Marcel Lamond. This should get them off your back and convince them that the person living here is not the guy they are after. Of course, they will have to first find this place, and the way we have things organized, that should never happen. It will also give you the chance to visit Marty and anyone else you would like. Of course, any time you want to change your appearance you can, and that would confuse everyone as well. You will have to go to the hospital when

Natalia gives birth. Let's remove the chances they will associate you with Marcel when you change your appearance. I think it's worth the chance. Think about it, boss, please do it," Dante said.

"You are right, Dante, my dear friend. I have to think differently now that I am to be a father," I said. "It's a New Year, and money is not the most important thing any longer. I'm going to be a dad. I need some stability and safety for everyone. Let's work on it. Please help me."

Dante left through the secret passage in order to avoid anyone seeing him come and go. He was upset that I didn't let him know about this passage sooner, but he quickly got over it. He was the only one who knew about the passageway aside from Natalia and me. We had agreed that from now on he would visit me via that route only. If the Mob was near the house and had it under surveillance, they would never see him come and go. He was known as one of the important people in my operation. It was further agreed that we would have a moving van appear in the next few days and go through the motions of a new family moving in. This we hoped would throw them off if they were still watching. Of course, we did not know with any certainty if they were watching the house or not. The odds of anyone even knowing about this place was almost a million to one. Watching the new house was almost impossible as we had taken every step possible to keep this place a secret.

Except for the New Year's Eve party, we did not allow anyone to know where it was. The care we took to bring the guests here on New Year's Eve helped solidify that precaution. Dante took care of the various other details regarding the house. All bills like utility and taxes etc. were being billed to a Martin Smithern at the same address. It was Dante's belief that if we used another name, it would help in establishing the new guy at the house. We were starting the New Year with a very positive outlook even though we were cautiously watching things around us. I knew I could not visit the theaters, but that didn't bother me as long as I had a strong infrastructure, and this I believed I had.

Friday, January 3, 1958

Marty and I met at the office to bring things up-to-date on all projects including the progress with the other adult companies. He made sure he was not followed and was dropped off two blocks before the office and switched cars for the rest of the way. His entire drive was monitored by our security team as they looked for anyone who would be following him or taking any extra notice. This day was a very quiet day as it fell on a Friday, and it was a holiday weekend. Traffic was very light, and it was felt by Dante that because of the long weekend and the holiday the precautions taken were very necessary. No staff was on duty today as the offices were closed because of the holiday and the generosity of the manager that gave the staff off until Monday. Most other companies reopened for business on the Friday after the New Year celebration. The drive over only took a few additional minutes as the route Marty took was carefully laid out by our security crew. It was planned to make sure that no one could use binoculars or any other device to follow Marty to his final destination. Even then, Marty was let out of the car a few buildings before our actual address.

"Hi Marcel, Happy New Year, how the hell are you?" Marty said. "I haven't seen you in a few days, since the party."

"I'm fine, and so is Natalia. We are in very good hands, so please don't worry about us. I'm really concerned about you, my dear friend. You are forgetting that you are a target as well and must be careful at all times. We are so busy taking care of me, we are forgetting about you. I want to set up a meeting with Dante, you and I, and see if we can come up with a plan to protect you even more so than we do now! We can't wait any longer, Marty, please believe me. You are playing with fire," I said as I picked up the phone and called Dante.

Dante said he would be over in about one hour. In the meantime, Marty and I discussed the situation regarding the adult companies and their releases.

Dante and Michael arrived, and we went into my office to discuss the situation. "Marty and I have been talking, and we feel we have not taken the situation about his security very seriously. It is obvious to me that the Mob will connect Marty with me, and, of course, me with him. We must put a program into place so that Marty can operate without fear, although I must say I don't believe Marty is afraid of anything," I said to both Marty and Dante.

"No shit, Sherlock," Marty said with a big smile on his face, "I'm scared out of my mind but have to continue to operate. I have plenty of muscle around me, and I'm keeping Mary Lou well protected as well. I don't know what we can do to tighten this up. I don't think there is a hit out on me, but you are right. I'm a lead to Marcel. I still have a business to run, but security is very tight at the studio. No matter what we do, we have to hire actors and we have to shoot movies. There will always be a security problem because of the many people we need on the set and the freedom of movement when shooting. It is a big problem, and it would be nice to resolve it now."

"I agree with Marty but don't have an answer to this problem," I said.

"Well, I do," Dante said. "First we have established who you are, and I believe the Mob bought into that. If the Mob does not believe Marty is who he claims to be, they still do not want to whack him. They only want to know where Harry is. Of course, they will cut off fingers and toes if they have to, but that is way out of whack, and I don't think we need to worry about that. This places the security problem in a different light, and it is in this direction that we must find a suitable solution. In the first instance, I believe we have Marty well covered in his home. In regard to the studio, we can only do so much if you are to run a proper movie operation. I think we should double the security detail when a movie is being shot.

"We will have some of the security people act as grips and other duties while keeping an eye on Marty. In this way, we will also learn anything that may be going on as our undercover guys will be one of the crew and may hear any news that might affect security. More than this, we cannot do other than to shut down the studio itself. All security measures must not appear as anything more than normal procedures. In this way, no one can report anything unusual taking place. Marty is not really a danger to the Mob, so he is not in the same line of fire as you are, boss. The fact that they might find you through him does make him a target. The only asshole who feels screwed is Carmine, and I don't think he is going to do anything right now. I honestly don't believe they will whack Marty at any time, but they might try to find out what happened to Harry Miller through him. I wish them luck!"

"Well, I don't agree with any of it and think you should take the following procedures. I am trying to use common sense, and I think the Mob will use theirs as well. Let's stop for one moment and think as any normal person would and how everyone else in the adult business operates. Not one single owner has a security detail! Not one of the people involved in the industry has any type of security working for them. What does that tell you? A very simple deduction, my friends. If you don't have anything to hide, you don't need any security detail, simple as that. It is my belief that if we leave Marty alone and let him go about his life as any other person, we would eliminate the spotlight we have placed on him. I agree with the added personnel while shooting a film, but that is security that will not be detected as our men will be invisible during that time. Have the security guys do the actual film work so that they fit right in and no suspicion can ever be established. Let Marty live his life normally. Let him go to a bar and pick up a woman if that is what he wants. Let him do whatever he wants, and I guarantee you he will not be bothered, and he will be accepted as Marty and no other person.

"This is the way to do it, and I'm sure the problem of Marty will disappear. The problem with Mary Lou is also not a real concern. The Mob is not concerning itself with her as they do not need to, so her security should be minimal except when she is with Natalia, and at that time she should be fully protected because Natalia is. This is my formula that we should start using in this New Year and cut some costs, and let those who are not in danger live their lives without fear. I welcome your opinions, guys. This is the time to set the policy for 1958," I said.

"Well, boss," Dante said. "I never thought of it that way, but it does make a lot of sense. Now that I think about it, I think Marty will be happier, and I think safer. He doesn't need any security detail, and by doing this, I agree that the suspicion he is under will disappear."

"I'm not certain," Michael chimed in, "but it does make a lot of sense. If you are who you claim you are, why in hell do you need security? And if you don't have obvious security, then you must be that person. The logic is there and I like it, but that does not mean I am one hundred percent sold on it. Let's try it out for a few weeks as we send out a real strong guy who can keep an eye on Marty from a distance and remain undetected. If things go the way I think they will, then you are right, Marcel, and we will stop all security. I'll feel better if we take that step now. I want to see this New Year be a peaceful one and really don't want to see anyone living like a prisoner. What do you think, guys?"

"Let's do it as of today, and we'll see where the chips lay," Marty said.

"Happy New Year, guys. Let's hope we will all have peace and good health this year. Happy New Year, Miguel. We miss you, man. We certainly do and will never ever forget you!" I said as I walked everyone to the door!

TO THE READER: It should be noted that this manuscript was copied from the journals that Harry Miller wrote and in order to maintain authenticity we have left the errors that he may have written intact: